LUNA RISING

FIFTH ANNIVERSARY

SARA SNOW

Cover design: Bold Books Cover Design

Alpha Rising

Luna Rising

Prequel

CHAPTER ONE
AXEL

I listened to the sound of my feet on the stairs as I made my way to the first floor. With my heightened hearing, it sounded like a hammer pounding right by my ear. I stopped focusing on it after a moment as I brushed my hand down my black shirt.

Finally, I nodded to a man and woman on the first floor as they walked by me. I could hear their conversation easily, even after I could no longer see them. I raised a brow at something the woman said and then shook my head as the man replied. The slap he received echoed in my ear.

I entered the kitchen to find my father sitting around the island. He looked up at me before looking back down at the files before him.

"Where are you headed?" he asked. He itched at his dark curly hair, much like mine, but longer.

I ran my hands down the faded sides of my hair and ruffled the curly top with a grin. "Out."

He looked up at me and closed the file before him as he inhaled deeply. "Are you sure that's a good idea? You do know what..."

"Yes," I interjected as I walked to the fridge. "I know it's a full moon tonight. I'm fully aware I won't be able to shift, Dad. I forgot one time, *one time* when I was fourteen." I removed a bottle of water and closed the fridge's door before turning to him. "Dad, I'm twenty years old now, and soon I'll be taking over as Alpha from you. I am more than capable of keeping track of the lunar cycle and remembering when there is a full moon at this point." I took a sip of my water.

Dad crossed his arms. "You have a long way to go before you become Alpha, son. I hope you recognize that."

Of course, I knew that. Being an alpha was a lot of responsibility, but it was a role I'd been groomed for. It was a position I was *still* being groomed for. I definitely rejected the obligations of being Alpha when I was younger. I wanted to be my own person, free from the duty of running a pack. Unfortunately for me, I had to accept it's my burden by birthright.

"Yeah, I know. I'm going to make you proud, Dad. Stop worrying so much! I'll be careful tonight and avoid any supernaturals if I see any," I reassured him. I frowned as I noted the distant look on his face.

A deep frown appeared on his face.

I swallowed as my heart skipped a beat. I placed my bottle of water slowly onto the counter.

"Dad?" I said softly.

"I'm fine," he replied quickly. With the color now drained from his face, he still looked deeply troubled. He swallowed hard.

I slid my water across the island to him. Each time I saw him in pain like this, it broke my heart.

My father had been holding on for years after losing my mother, his Luna, but it was very difficult for him. For werewolves, losing a mate meant more than just grieving the death of a partner. Your mate was your other half, the beginning and end of your world. The death of a werewolf mate meant losing a part of yourself as well. You lost your mind, and many werewolves even lost their lives.

The suffering overwhelmed Dad sometimes, causing him to become angry and confused. An angry and confused werewolf could lose control of his or her wolf, becoming a danger to themselves and those around them.

Werewolves males always grow to be over 6ft in stature, and werewolf females were at least 5'6". Our bodies needed to be bigger for us to handle shifting into an animal. Despite my father's towering 6'4" frame, I could see how his previously massive, muscular form had wasted away since my mother's passing. Though he's still a force to be reckoned with in a fight, he barely ate or slept now. One couldn't even properly qualify what he was doing as "living". At this point, he was just existing.

I knew as a werewolf, and particularly an alpha-to-be, one day I would meet my own mate. She would be like the sun and moon to me, and she would become Luna for our pack. Let's just say I hoped I didn't find her anytime soon.

I watched as he finished the bottle of water and color began to return to his face. He gave me a sad smile. "I'm good. So..." he crushed the bottle in his hand. "Where are you going?"

I inhaled deeply and exhaled as I rubbed the back of my neck. "Um, Dmitri and I are going to a club. We won't be out late."

"Okay," he replied softly.

He opened the file before him once more, and his shoulders rose and fell as he sighed. He licked the tip of his fingers and turned a page. "So, will you be attending the mating ritual this year?"

Hell fucking no.

That's what I wanted to say to him, but then I thought better of it. Like I said, he could still kick my ass for cursing around him if he wanted to. I'd never seen another man so easily triggered by expletives.

"I think I'm going to sit this one out, Dad."

His jaws clenched before he looked over toward me with a scoff. "The ritual only happens every three years, Axel." He sat up straighter, a determined look in his eyes. "If you're to be Alpha, one day you will need a luna. Wolves from thousands of packs all over the world will be there in hopes of finding a mate."

This isn't a conversation I want to have right now.

I walked over to him and placed my hand on his shoulder. "I know, Dad. I will meet my mate—someday. I'm a long way from being Alpha right now, and I don't need to find my mate just yet." I patted his shoulder with a grin as he shook his head. "You'll get your grandpups soon enough."

I walked out of the kitchen, my face falling once my back was turned. I made it outside to my car without any further delays. Once inside my car, I pulled my phone out as it started to ring. A smile returned to my face as I answered and the most beautiful voice echoed from the other end of the line.

"Where are you? Dmitri is already here. You better be on your way."

I started the car. "No worries, baby. I'm on my way."

CHAPTER TWO
AXEL

The bouncer at the door to the club watched as I walked past the people waiting in line. As I drew closer to him, he opened the door for me. He nodded his greeting without saying a word.

To everyone around us, it looked like a gesture of acknowledgment and respect between two typical male acquaintances. While the acknowledgment and respect part was true enough, the "typical" bit wasn't. The werewolf bouncer was actually signaling deference for his alpha-to-be. Werewolves were scattered all around the world, in every country, in every profession. Along with the thousands of other supernatural beings, we'd blended in seamlessly with the humans.

I think that's the real reason humans would lose their shit if they ever find out about the supernatural community. They'd feel like fools that such beings, such power, had existed right under their noses the whole time.

The pounding music in the club had my heartbeat racing to match its tempo. It didn't take me long to locate her among the crowd. With the club's blacklights illuminating white, her hair was the only one glowing.

The corner of my lips arched with a smile. I stood and watched as Lilith, my girlfriend, held her head back and laughed. Her platinum blonde hair, almost white, hung as far as her bottom. It dipped even lower before she held her head up once more.

Both women and men around her couldn't stop staring. It felt good to know that gorgeous angel was all mine. I snuck up behind her, her friend Margaret and my best friend Dmitri smiling knowingly.

The moment I was about to grab her, Lilith spun around and threw her hands around my neck.

"Never sneak up on a witch," she whispered in my ear. Her light blue eyes flashed violet for just a moment. She pressed her soft lips to mine, and I picked her up off the ground.

I didn't care if anyone was staring. I could almost smell the jealousy rolling off the humans around us. So far, there were no other supernaturals other than Dmitri, Lilith, and myself. No other supernaturals that I could smell anyways, and that was the way I liked it. We didn't go clubbing much, but when we did, we only went to clubs other supernaturals avoided.

In the supernatural world, very few of us mixed socially with other supernatural species. It was considered even more taboo for werewolves. Because we all had pre-determined mates waiting for us to find them via the mating bond, we avoided socializing with other supernaturals and humans.

"Happy anniversary, babe," I whispered to her as I placed her back onto her feet.

She turned back to the table, grabbed a beer, and handed it to me. "It's going to be. Now drink up!"

I threw my hand over her shoulder as I bumped fists with Dmitri. I turned to Margaret, who I'd noticed had been looking at Dmitri every few minutes.

"Margaret, how are you?" I asked.

She smiled wide as she looked at Dmitri and then at me.

"Pretty good. Not gonna lie," she replied. "I needed this night out."

I nodded and kissed Lilith's temple. "University life isn't as fun as you thought, I guess?"

She pouted. "It sucks ass."

"It's not so bad," Lilith chimed in, her voice a soft melody in my ear compared to the pounding music around us. "You just procrastinate too much."

"Well, we can't all be perfect, now can we?" Margaret replied with a laugh as Lilith flipped her off.

Lilith turned to face me after a while. "So, will you go to that big event this year?"

I shook my head, knowing she was speaking of the mating ritual. "No, I don't have a reason to."

Margaret looked at us, curious to know what we were talking about. Dmitri quickly changed the subject with Margaret to distract her. Margaret knew about Lilith being a witch, but she didn't know Dmitri and I were werewolves. It had to be that way for her own safety. Humans who found out about werewolves were killed, no exceptions. When it came to this rule, the Werewolf Council meant business.

Many werewolves couldn't stand humans and avoided them at all costs. I wasn't one of them. Some of the humans I'd met were rather nice, much like Margaret. I love that she loved my Lilith since they'd been friends since high school. Margaret had earned Lilith's trust enough for Lilith to share the truth about who she really was. Instead of being scared or upset about her friend being a witch, Margaret had welcomed the news and shown incredible acceptance of Lilith's Wiccan ways. I almost envied how open Lilith could be with Margaret about her supernatural status. Sometimes it sucked to have to lie to everyone about who you really were.

When I was out shopping the other day, I noticed an aquamarine ring that matched Lilith's eyes perfectly. I knew it would make the ideal anniversary gift. Now was the perfect time to give it to her. I leaned over and gave her the ring.

"Hey," I whispered into Lilith's ear. "This ring reminded me of your beautiful eyes. Happy Anniversary!"

"Oh, Axel, it's gorgeous! Thank you so much!" She gushed effusively. She followed with a passionate kiss that had me wishing we were the only two people in the club.

We were startled out of our intimate moment when Dmitri knocked his knuckles on the tiny table we were standing around. "Hey! I'm gonna go get us some more drinks."

I sighed inwardly, cursing his terrible timing. "I'm going to help Dmitri carry the drinks, okay?" I said to her.

She nodded at me.

When we had walked away, I said to Dmitri, "I think Margaret's into you."

"Yeah, she's cute, but human. I'll just avoid that catastrophe, thank you. What if I hook up with her and find my mate tomorrow? Hard pass," he replied as he combed a hand through his dusty blonde hair. "I still don't know what you're going to tell your dad when he finds out about Lilith. She's not human, but still..."

A man looked at Dmitri strangely, having heard what he had said about Lilith not being human. Dmitri gave him a "none-of-your-damn-business" look, and the man turned away quickly.

I patted his shoulder as we stopped just before the bar. "Well, good luck with finding the one woman the goddess created just for you. For all we know, she lives at the North Pole. If I were you, I would not want to wait so long for companionship."

He brushed my hand off his shoulder.

"Hey, I didn't say sleeping with a human was against the rules —just dating them."

———

Lilith

I watched Axel walk away and smiled before looking down at the aquamarine ring on my finger. I sighed, my heart swelling with love. I never thought I'd love someone this much. Our love was forbidden, more so by his people than mine, but I didn't care. How could something that felt so right, possibly be wrong?

I loved him with everything I had, and it was a great feeling to know he felt the same. In the beginning, it had been hard. While it still was, the pressure and fear of being caught weren't so stifling. There was no law that we couldn't be friends. To everyone other than Dmitri and Margaret, that's all we were.

At first, I had spent countless nights worrying about the day our relationship would come to an end. I was no fool. He was going to become the alpha for his pack. One day he would meet his mate, his luna, and I would be the girl he once loved.

Some might say it was crazy or a waste of time being together if we knew it would end, but I'd accepted that inevitability. I'd decided I wouldn't give up Axel until I had no other choice. It'd hurt when that day came, but I'd find comfort in knowing we truly loved each other. After all, he would be with someone who would love him as I did. He'd have happiness, and so would I—after a while.

One day, I'd be the leader for my coven. So, much like him, my life had been planned out for me since birth. There were expectations for me, high expectations. I knew I would rise to the occasion, just as he must.

"It's gorgeous, Lilith," Margaret said admiringly.

I looked up from the ring. I stopped twisting it from side to side and smiled at her, "Thanks. It is, isn't it?"

"It looks expensive too," she commented as she walked around the table to stand before me. She squinted and leaned down to take a closer look at it. "He's got taste. Surprising, especially coming from someone who only owns tight black t-shirts."

She laughed as she stood upright again.

I chuckled and looked towards Axel's direction, waiting patiently for him to return to the table. He really did wear no other color than black, but it really worked for him. I took a deep breath and exhaled heavily. "I feel bad that I didn't get him anything. He told me he didn't want anything," I replied loudly. Axel could hear me speak easily, even with the pounding music around us, but Margaret, not so much.

Despite the fact she was human, we'd been best friends for years. I was closer to her than anyone else in the world. We're like night and day in appearance and personality, but I loved it. She was the *yin* to my *yang*—we balanced each other perfectly.

Margaret was outspoken and a natural badass, while I was reserved and soft-spoken. That's not to say I was a coward—I could throw punches with the best of them if I had to. I just preferred to avoid fights if I could, while she didn't mind starting them. Despite our obvious differences, there was just something about Margaret that had drawn me to her in high school, much like how I was drawn to Axel later.

After many years of deep friendship between us, I decided I could not hide my true self from Margaret anymore. When I confessed I was actually a witch, she took it so well. She was so open, so curious about what it was like to be a witch. I loved being able to share the supernatural side of myself with her, as much of it as I possibly could anyways.

Margaret dyed her shoulder-length hair ink-black and sported more piercings on her ears than I wanted to count. I preferred to keep my platinum blonde locks *au naturel*, though people often assumed my hair must be bleached in order to be as blonde as it was. I glanced over at her to look at her many piercings and frowned. I didn't even have my lobes pierced.

It might seem strange for me to detest piercings since being a witch required me to cut myself for certain spells. Tattoos I was okay with, but there was just something creepy about removing a piercing and seeing a hole left behind.

"Stop looking at them," she said without looking my way. I suppose she saw me staring in her peripheral vision—she knew how much I detested piercings. "Plus, I get why he doesn't want a gift. He has you, after all."

I rolled my eyes despite blushing. "Whatever. I have him, too."

"Look at you," she said with a wide grin.

I frowned. "What?"

"You're turning red, like bright red. You really love him, huh?"

I took a sip of my drink. "I do."

She sipped her drink as well and licked her red painted lips. "Well, I'm no longer mad about you snatching him up. I guess I believe you when you say you didn't know about my crush." My face fell when she said that, and she laughed. "Don't do that. Seeing you two together, I can tell you guys are perfect for each other." She grinned as she looked away. "Plus, I have my eye on someone else now."

Margaret was staring at Dmitri returning with our drinks. No doubt he had heard what she said. Based on the look on his face, Axel heard it as well since he was trying to hide his laughter at the nervous look on Dmitri's face.

Margaret could be very forward, and Dmitri had suffered through her not-so-subtle advances all night. Too bad I couldn't tell her she was wasting her time. Not many wolves were willing to break the rules like Axel and date someone from another species. Despite her "tough girl" exterior, Margaret was really a sweetheart on the inside.

"What did we miss?" Axel asked with a knowing smile as he threw his hand over my shoulder.

"Oh, just girl talk," I replied. I threw a look Dmitri's way as he handed a beer to Margaret.

She purposefully touched his fingers with hers.

Dmitri smiled at her and I squinted my eyes in confusion. He hadn't been mean to her so far, but it had been clear he wasn't interested to begin with. He threw his hand over her shoulder, and they both started singing along to the song playing.

I threw a puzzled look Axel's way, and he shook his head. "I'm not getting involved," he whispered to me. He turned me to him as he wrapped his hands around my waist. "Have I told you I love you tonight?"

I shook my head. "Nope, and I don't know how I feel about that."

He kissed my forehead, then my cheek, followed by my neck. "I love you," he whispered to me.

I suddenly felt lighter. "I love you too," I replied.

Not unlike Margaret, Axel had a tough exterior persona when he was around others. Yet with me, Axel was the most loving man on this planet. I loved knowing I was one of the few people to see this side of him.

I knew it was selfish, but I hoped he wouldn't meet his mate for years to come. He wouldn't be Alpha for a little while, anyway. For now, he was all mine, and I'd love him with everything I had while I had the chance.

"Guys, come on, you can get down and dirty with each other later! Now, let's get drunk!" Margaret screamed.

Lilith

I wasn't drunk, but I was definitely tipsy as Axel and I danced together. I closed my eyes and held my head back as I soaked in the music.

Axel's hands on my waist slid around me to rest just above my ass, and my eyes opened. He kissed me suddenly as the music's tempo increased. His lips on mine felt so soft. I pressed myself against his muscular chest to sink into the passionate kiss.

I pulled back, aware of his hungry eyes on me. I stepped away from him as I continued to sway to the music. It was not often we got to be like this, so carefree and happy. In moments like these, what I was and what he was didn't matter. All that mattered at this moment was our feelings of love and affection.

I kept my eyes on him as he stopped to watch me dance. When other men began to stop dancing to watch me, Axel took my arm and led me to the bar to sit down.

I chuckled. "Jealous much?"

He pointedly ignored me and asked the bartender for a glass of water as I kept my eye on Margaret and Dmitri on the dance floor. I frowned, my smile fading as I started to feel a little ill. I fervently prayed I wouldn't vomit. When Axel gave me the glass of water, I gladly took it.

Like I said, I didn't get to do this often. "Alright, no more drinking for me," I whispered to myself.

"I agree," Axel said as he sat down beside me. "You look a little pale. Are you okay?"

I nodded. "Yeah, I think I just need some air."

He stood up. "Okay let's go outside."

"Axel!" Dmitri called.

We looked in Dmitri's direction to see both Margaret and him waving at us. Dmitri pointed to Margaret's phone. "Come check this out!"

"Go," I told him. "I won't be long. I'll be fine."

"Are you sure?" He asked as he gently moved my hair behind my ears.

I sighed and tilted my head to rest my cheek in his palm. "I'm sure. It's just getting stuffy in here."

Indeed, the club was becoming more packed. I made it outside after what felt like ten minutes of forcing my way through the packed crowd. Upon stepping through the club's doors to the outside, I instantly felt a thousand times better. I inhaled the fresh air as the chilly wind seeped into my skin.

I moved to the side to allow three girls to enter the club, their voices loud as they hung onto each other to prevent falling. I nodded to the bouncer as I wrapped my hands around my waist and turned left. I walked slowly past the short line of people waiting to get into the club until the music echoing through the walls of the club was faint.

Other than the distant sound of music emanating from the club, the world was asleep. I loved the quiet.

Unexpectedly, the hair behind my neck stood on end, and I frowned. Being the daughter of a coven leader, I'd gone through years of training in not only magic, but martial arts as well. When my instincts told me to pay attention, I listened.

Without warning, I spun around and landed a massive punch on the man standing behind me. As he staggered away from me, I noticed his red eyes.

A demon?

"What do you want?" I asked. I called to my magic and held my hands up defensively. Looking around quickly, I nervously realized there was no one else in sight. While I would be protected from humans accidentally seeing me use my magic if I needed to, it also meant Axel was too far away to hear me if I called for help. "Speak, Demon! What do you want?"

He smiled at me, exposing his multiple pointy teeth. It reminded me of a shark's mouth. "You, little witch. I want you."

———

Axel

Fifteen minutes passed and still, Lilith hadn't come back into the club. I tried not to be the overprotective werewolf boyfriend, but sometimes I couldn't help it. As a witch, she was more than capable of taking care of herself, but I felt like she shouldn't have to when I was around.

"You've been staring at the entrance of the club since Lilith left," Margaret slurred, "I'm the one that drinks, not her. She's just not used to it."

I turned to look at her.

"Maybe we should have done something else to celebrate our anniversary," I replied.

When I chose this club venue to celebrate, I wasn't exactly thinking about how easily the girls could be affected by the alcohol. I would regret it if the night ended with Lilith getting sick, and Margaret was already well on her way to being totally wasted. In contrast, Dmitri and I were perfectly fine. It took a lot to get a werewolf drunk.

Dmitri supportively patted my shoulder.

"She'll be okay, bro," he said, trying to reassure me.

Margaret narrowed her eyes at him. "Why aren't you drunk? You drank more than me," She pointed a finger at his chest and then at mine, "What's wrong with the two of you?"

Someone bumped into her, and she turned around with an off-balance swing. "Hey!"

Dmitri grabbed Margaret's hand in time to stop her from punching the girl.

"Alright, I'm going out to check on her," I announced.

I pushed my way through the crowd as a bad feeling settling on my chest. I was not the clingy type—never had been—but something felt off. The feeling grew worse as I approached the exit.

I swung the door open and came face to face with the bouncer from my pack. I held my head backward to sniff the air, and I recognized the scent instantly.

A demon—here? But why?

The bouncer looked just as perplexed as I did. There was one thing we both knew—whenever a demon showed up around humans, it almost always ended badly.

"I'll check it out," I said to him. "I'll let you know if I need you and Dmitri."

"Are you sure, Axel? We don't know how many of them there are," he replied uncertainly. "Don't forget, it's a full moon tonight."

A bright flash of light appeared to our right behind the crowd of people. With the volume of the music wafting out from the club and more than half of them clearly wasted already, most didn't seem to notice.

"Lilith," I said under my breath and started running.

My legs just started moving without my conscious thought. The feeling in my chest was growing worse as I pumped my legs as fast as I could. Another flash of light appeared. As I got closer, I could hear Lilith's heavy breathing and that of a demon.

I gritted my teeth and clenched my fists. Of all the nights for this to happen, why did it have to happen the only night of the month when I couldn't shift?

Maybe it was for the best. I couldn't exactly wolf out in the open, anyways. Thankfully, there were only drunk humans out and about now, so sporting just my claws and fangs wouldn't be particularly noticeable.

I unclenched my fists. My nails lengthened into claws, and my sharp canines appeared. I couldn't shift, so just my claws, fangs, and the extra strength I was born with would have to do.

I wasn't foolish enough to think I could fight a demon in this state and win, but I had to try.

"Lilith!" I roared.

I found them in an alley. The demon held my precious Lilith up against the wall by her throat. As soon as he sensed my approach, the demon growled. He swiftly ripped her off the wall to press her back to his front, his long black claws drawing blood from her neck.

"Come any closer, and she dies," he said, his voice baritone and hoarse. I noticed a wound on his other hand and one on his head, no doubt from Lilith's attempts to defend herself.

"Listen, whatever you want, I'll get it for you. Just let her go," I offered, trying desperately to reason with him. I had no choice but to play this calmly until the other guys arrived. My heart hammered loudly in my chest as I glimpsed the terror in Lilith's eyes. "Just let her go."

The demon smiled widely. In the blink of an eye, he ripped her throat open.

My world utterly shattered in an instant. I rushed forward, calling on the Change, but nothing happened. The demon began to fade into smoke as Lilith fell to the ground.

I caught her before her head could smack against the pavement. I placed my hand over her throat, trying desperately to stop the blood from gushing.

"Lilith, Lilith, stay with me, okay! Just-Just stay with me!"

Her eyes were wide and glossy.

My eyes began to sting with tears as she began to gasp.

"I-I I'm-dying," she whispered.

I started shaking my head. My entire body was shaking as I heard running feet behind me and knew Dmitri had arrived.

"Get help!" I yelled over my shoulder. "Get help now!"

A warm hand touched my face. I looked back down at Lilith as she cupped my cheek. Her hand slid away from my cheek to hold my hand that was pressed against her throat.

"I lov-love y-you," she said weakly. "D-don't ha-harden your h-heart, Axel."

Tears began to roll down my cheeks.

She began to cough, causing blood to splatter onto my hand and shirt.

I looked over my shoulder to see Dmitri still standing there, his eyes wide. "What the fuck are you doing! Go! Get help!"

"Axel," he replied, his eyes now glossy.

When I looked back down, Lilith's eyes were closed. Her body appeared still and lifeless.

"No!" I scooped her up into my arms and held her to my chest. "No, no, no. Please don't do this to me!"

I held my head back and let out a mournful howl. I howled as loud as I could, as long as I could, until my body grew weak. I collapsed beside her lifeless body.

She was gone.

My precious angel was gone.

CHAPTER THREE

AXEL

My arms hung limply at my sides as I stared bleakly down at Lilith's grave. The stench of death was strong within the graveyard, and in the distance, thunder rumbled. The wind picked up around me, sending leaves flying all around. The gloomy weather matched my mood perfectly.

I bent down to place the white roses in my hand onto her tombstone. The white of the roses reminded me of the pale color of Lilith's fair hair. Oh, how I had loved to run my fingers through her gorgeous platinum blonde locks. As I thought about how bleak my life was without her, I looked down to see I had crushed the roses.

Two months had passed with no leads on the demon that killed her. My anger grew every moment I thought about how that demon bastard was still out there, running free, while my angel was no longer by my side. I wanted to crush him to pieces with my bare hands, just like those flowers.

Since Dmitri was the only one out of my pack who knew the true nature of our relationship, it appeared to everyone else as if I'd suddenly changed without reason. I knew I'd become cold, distant, and quiet. While I'd never been much of a jokester, whatever sense of humor I did possess had disappeared, taking my smile with it. No one, not even Dmitri, understood how much I was suffering. How could I laugh and smile—how could I even pretend to be happy—when the source of all my happiness was lying dead beneath my feet?

I hadn't even been able to attend her funeral. While her coven knew about our relationship and had somewhat accepted me, there would be too many questions if a werewolf showed up at a young witch's funeral.

Lilith had been everything to me. She had broken down my walls, never giving up when I tried to push her away. In the beginning, I hadn't wanted to break the rule of never dating another species. It didn't take long for me to fall hopelessly under her spell, and I couldn't resist any longer. She was too perfect, too angelic to ignore.

Now I wish I hadn't wasted all that time rejecting her.

I wiped at the tear that escaped from my eyes as I opened my other hand. A new wave of anger slammed into me as I stared at the aquamarine ring I had given to her, the one that matched her eyes. I swallowed hard as I closed my fingers around it and placed it back into my pocket. I'd have to find somewhere to keep it safe. I knew I'd never be able to look at it again. Yet, for some reason, I couldn't part with it.

I heard footsteps approaching me and sighed as Lilith's mother appeared by my side. I turned to look at her and met her light brown eyes. Despite the difference in eye color, I found it hard to look at her without being reminded of Lilith. They had the same long blonde hair.

"I saw you by the trees the day we buried her," she commented as she turned to stare at the grave.

"I had to come, Ms. Clayton. I couldn't stay away," I said by way of explanation as I sighed again.

She nodded. "Please, call me Cassandra. And I know." She turned to face me. "I know you loved my daughter, Axel, truly loved her. It is why we allowed her to be with you, even knowing it could never last. But, now she's gone and..." she hung her head and pinched the bridge of her nose. She held her head up after a moment, her eyes glossy with tears she was trying to hold back. "Anyways, we've tried every spell we can think of to find the demon that had killed her, but nothing has worked. We...I didn't want to do this, but I have no choice."

My brows pulled together with confusion. "All my attempts to track down the demon failed as well. What choice are you talking about?"

"Black magic," she answered solemnly.

I rubbed at the wrinkles between my knitted brows. "Are you sure you want to do that, Ms. Clayton...I mean, Cassandra? I mean, you're the witch, obviously you know the risks. Black magic is unpredictable. The price of a black magic spell might be more than you are willing to give."

"I lost everything when I lost my daughter, Axel. There is no price too high to pay. I need to know who killed her," she replied in a snippy tone.

"Okay. I understand," I said softly as I looked down at Lilith's grave. "Can I be there?" I looked her way once more. "I'll do anything to find that demon—to know why he killed her."

"That's good to hear. Typically we don't allow outsiders to attend our rituals. Under the circumstances, we'll make an exception for you." She shoved her hands into the pockets of her jacket as she stooped down to Lilith's grave.

"We'll find the demon that did this to you," she vowed, as her voice cracked. "I won't stop until he's dead."

———

Axel

I stood to the back of the room and kept my mouth shut, despite my discomfort. In order to do the ritual, Lilith's blood was needed. There was a reason most supernaturals avoided black magic. There was almost always a price to be paid for tapping into dark magic, and many times it backfired unless the person truly knew what they were doing.

It was a risk, and it felt like using Lilith's blood like this was defiling her memory. Still, I just crossed my arms over my chest and remained quiet. I needed to find that demon. Since every other option had already been exhausted, this was the only thing left to try.

If using black magic meant we found the fucking piece of shit that killed Lilith, then so be it. I didn't have to like the process.

I observed closely as the black magic user, a heavily wrinkled Caucasian woman with grey hair to her waist, poured Lilith's blood into a large bowl. I noticed her eyes were a pale blue—nothing close to as beautiful as Lilith's, though.

Lilith's mother and two other witches stood within a circle on the floor created by the old woman. I'd met the two other witches once before when I came to meet Ms. Clayton—Cassandra—for the first time with Lilith. They'd been introduced to me as Fiona and Cordelia, Cassandra's two closest friends in the coven. They'd known Lilith all her life, and I could tell even then they'd loved Lilith as if she were their own. It didn't surprise me that they chose to be by Cassandra's side today.

Cassandra, Fiona, and Cordelia watched silently along with me as the old woman opened a cage with a white mouse. She laid it on the table and killed it mercifully with a quick slice from her knife. Then she skillfully removed the heart.

She dropped the heart into the bowl and called Lilith's mother forward. As she began to mumble under her breath, she made a small cut on Cassandra's finger and allowed her blood to drip into the bowl.

The volume of her voice grew louder and began to echo in the room like a thousand voices speaking at once in a language I couldn't understand. Cassandra groaned as she placed her hand on her stomach and hunched forward.

I frowned as the old woman stopped chanting, and Cassandra stood up straight once more. "The price has been paid," the old woman declared, her eyes as black as tar. "Let's begin."

Cassandra returned to the circle, and I narrowed my eyes at her. I wondered what price she'd been forced to pay, though I knew it was really none of my business. My eyes drifted towards the old woman as she stepped into the circle as well. She glanced at me for a moment before looking down at the bowl in her hand. She waved her palm over it, muttering inaudible words before dipping her hand into the bowl and covering both her eyes with its contents.

I watched as the blood began to roll down her cheeks like tears.

Then, as if it had a life of its own, the blood began to move against the force of gravity back up the old woman's face. As the women chanted louder and louder, some of the blood began to seep into the old woman's eyes, making them appear red instead of black.

The old woman began shaking until she fell to a knee. The three witches kept chanting as the old woman began to groan in pain. She looked in my direction, the veins in her neck bulging under her skin as if she was straining, while her eyes darted rapidly back and forth. Abruptly, she vomited blood.

The women stopped chanting. Cassandra gave her hand to the old woman to help her stand and another gave her a towel to wipe the blood away.

When she removed the towel from her face, I sent Cassandra a look of utter shock. The old woman no longer appeared old, while Cassandra now had a white streak of hair.

So that was Cassandra's price—she gave away some of her life energy. This would cut Cassandra's life shorter, though exactly how many years the black magic user had taken, I couldn't tell.

The now vibrant, blue-eyed woman sighed as she closed her eyes and inhaled deeply. "I can open a portal to the demon's exact location." She opened her eyes once more and looked my way. "I saw her death. I saw you there, and I could tell you loved her. Wolves don't usually associate with witches."

"I'm not like other wolves," I replied, and she gave me a smile before turning away.

"Be ready. I won't be able to hold the portal for long," she warned us over her shoulder.

"We're ready," Cassandra said confidently.

The other two women nodded as they removed silver daggers from under their shirts.

"I'm coming," I declared, stepping forward.

"It's best if you stay out of this," Fiona told me.

Cassandra placed her hand on the woman's shoulder.

"He deserves to be there," she told both Fiona and Cordelia. Her eyes shifted from brown to bright violet as she turned back to look me in the eye. "I kill it. Do you understand?"

I gritted my teeth but nodded. There were many other things I could do to inflict serious pain without actually killing the demon. Tonight I wasn't hampered by a full moon, and I had no intention of holding back.

Axel

I stepped into that portal with the confidence of someone who did it every day.

Unfortunately, it wasn't something I had ever done before, and I wasn't prepared. It was as if I was walking against a strong wind. At either side of me was a white, smoke-like substance. It was thick, like paint, and from time to time an image of a location would appear. I felt like my mind and body were being pulled in all directions.

"Ignore the pockets that keep opening up!" Cassandra shouted from ahead of me. "Focus on your breathing. Don't resist the portal, or you'll be sent somewhere else. Let it take you." She pointed ahead at an image that wasn't fading like the others.

"I'm trying!" I replied through clenched teeth.

I called on my wolf for extra strength, causing my fangs and nails to elongate. I kept pushing forward as our exit came closer and closer...until Cassandra stepped out of the portal. I followed quickly behind her.

The two other witches emerged after me, and I looked behind us only to see that there was nothing visible in the space we had just emerged from. I had expected to see some kind of spiraling swirl, but it looked like we had stepped right out of thin air.

"This can't be right," I heard Cassandra say.

I turned back around.

She was staring up at a house that looked oddly familiar to me. My eyes widened as I realized whose house it was.

"This is where Margaret lives," I said with confusion. "Do you think the demon is going after her next? Or did your black magic user send us to the wrong place."

Cassandra nodded. "It is her house. There is only one way to find out why we were brought here," she replied. We crossed the street to Margaret's home, which was shrouded in total darkness.

"I hear Margaret's heartbeat inside, and it's pumping a slow, steady rhythm. That means she's probably sleeping," I whispered as we walked around the side of the house.

"Her parents?" One of the witches asked.

I listened closer, but I could only hear Margaret's heartbeat.

"She's alone," I replied as we made it to the back door.

Something felt wrong about this whole situation. The demon shouldn't be anywhere near Margaret.

It's not that demons never murdered humans—they certainly did on occasion. Still, I'd never heard of a demon hunting down a witch and then targeting her human best friend. That was odd, indeed.

It had to be one of two things. Either the demon had a personal vendetta against Lilith, which I found hard to believe. After all, what issues could she have had with a demon that I didn't know about? Or, someone hired the demon to kill Lilith for them and now Margaret as well.

Either way, I intended to get some answers tonight, once and for all.

Cassandra waved her hand over the door's handle, and the door unlocked. The utter darkness of the house wasn't an issue for me with my heightened senses, so I led the way as we cautiously entered. After a few minutes inside, I held my hand out as I stopped walking. The witches stopped to look at me.

"What is it?" One of them whispered.

I looked in the direction of the staircase.

"She's not sleeping," I replied quietly. "Her heartbeat's changed." My nostrils flared as I picked up the demon's scent and made a dash for the staircase. "It's here!"

I rushed to the second floor with the witches in hot pursuit behind me as I followed my nose to Margaret's room. The closer I got to her door, the stronger the demon's scent became. By the time I reached her door, I was concerned that we might not make it in time to save Margaret from whatever the demon had planned for her. Images of losing her the way we lost Lilith were playing through my mind, and I prayed we were not too late. But nothing could have prepared me for what I saw when I kicked the door in.

In the open doorway, I froze in shock and utter horror as I watched the demon slowly enter Margaret's body. The witches almost ran into the back of me as they came flying through the doorway behind me just in time to see the demon fully enter

Margaret. As the Margaret-demon looked our way, her lips stretched into an impish grin.

"You guys took your sweet time getting here."

CHAPTER FOUR
AXEL

After watching Margaret absorb the demon into herself, I immediately looked to Cassandra. Her jaws were so tightly clenched, I wondered if her gums were hurting.

I looked back at Margaret as she bent her neck from side to side before inhaling and exhaling deeply. She sighed as she opened her arms wide, a look of relief and contentment on her face.

"That felt amazing," she gushed, her voice a blend of hers and the demon's.

"You...you killed Lilith?" Cassandra stammered as she stepped forward, and Margaret just smiled, black veins now appearing all over her face. "How could you kill your best friend?"

Margaret snorted. "Best friend, you say? Lilith wasn't my best friend, and she hasn't been since the day she told me what she really was. I accepted her, you know. I loved her even more for it, but she refused to teach me. She still kept secrets. She didn't tell me her little boyfriend was a werewolf!" She laughed. "A freaking werewolf! She didn't want to tell me all about the supernatural world. I'm sure you were all laughing at me behind my back—'Look at the poor, pitiful human who knows nothing and has no special abilities.' Lilith wanted me to just settle for whatever tiny scraps of info she was willing to throw my way. She didn't want to share her power!"

I clenched my fists. "That's because knowing the identities of other supernaturals as a human could get you killed. She was trying to protect you. Did you kill Lilith for that? You took her life, Margaret."

"And I would do it again!" She shouted.

I stared at Margaret with disgust and growing rage. She had fooled us all, Lilith included, and look where it led. This was why humans should never know about the supernatural world. They were fragile, weak, greedy beings. A witch, a daughter, a friend, and the love of my life was dead because this human bitch was jealous of what she couldn't have.

"But I guess I got the last laugh after all, didn't I? I found a way anyways," she walked away. She began pacing. "I didn't find the demon, though. He found me. He offered me real power of my own."

"And what was the price, Margaret?" Cassandra asked.

Margaret puckered her mouth thoughtfully before shrugging casually. "I never liked my parents anyways."

"You murdered your parents, too?" Cassandra asked in astonishment.

Margaret shrugged yet again. There was no guilt or remorse evident at all in her face. It was clear that this girl no longer had a soul.

Talking to her would get us nowhere. That demon saw her moral weakness and targeted her. He knew exactly what he was doing, and it was clear he'd been very successful with this possession.

"Yes, I did kill them." A wicked smile grew on her lips. "It was a small price to pay for this..."

Cassandra and I reacted quickly when Margaret suddenly turned to smoke and dove directly at us in a mad dash for the door. Fiona popped out from where she had been standing to the side outside the door just in time to slash at Margaret with her dagger.

I expected the dagger to pass through the smoke and leave Margaret uninjured. I was surprised to see Margaret abruptly return to her solid form, sporting a large gash where Fiona's dagger had sliced her.

She screamed as she backtracked into the room. Her right hand held the left one as she looked at the cut on her lower arm, now oozing black blood.

"You fucking bitch!" She screamed as Fiona and Cordelia fully entered the room behind Cassandra, blocking the door.

I watched as the wound on her hand began to heal slowly.

Margaret hissed at us, enraged.

Without warning, she changed into smoke again and sank into the floor, leaving us alone in the room. We looked at each other, and Fiona spun around to head back downstairs.

"We can't let her get away!" She yelled. She stepped through the doorway.

Immediately, Margaret swung the knife in her hand toward the witch.

Fiona reacted quickly, dodging a mortal blow by mere inches. She yelped and jumped back, the blade slicing her across her chest. Margaret followed her knife work with a kick to the witch's chest, sending her flying across the room to slam into the window.

Fiona's unconscious body fell to the ground along with the shards of glass. Cordelia began to chant, her eyes shining a bright violet.

Margaret dropped the knife and held her head as she hunched forward in pain. I called on my wolf, using Margaret's temporary distraction as a chance to shift. My claws elongated as did my fangs. I charged at her, slamming her into the wall, and I heard a bone snap. As I went to stab her in the gut with my claw, she vanished into the wall, only to appear within the room seconds later.

Cordelia continued to chant, and Margaret decided to take her out first this time. She threw a knife directly at Cordelia's head, but the knife stood suspended in the air right before it reached the witch's face. Everyone turned to Cassandra, whose hand was up. She flicked her hand, and the knife fell uselessly to the ground.

"That's enough," Cassandra said in a low voice as she stepped forward. "We came here to protect you. We were worried you were being targeted next, but it turns out you're the evil creature that took my daughter from me. You will die tonight, Margaret. I promise you that."

Margaret snorted with a smirk. "We'll see, won't we? I'm not scared of you, any of you. Not anymore. I'm just as strong as you, maybe even more so." She pointed at Cassandra. "I don't fear death, so why should I fear you?"

"There are worse things than dying, child. You know nothing," Cassandra replied before whispering under her breath. I could hear her clearly, but it was a language I didn't understand. She began chanting louder, and Margaret was lifted into the air.

"Stop!" Margaret screamed as Cassandra walked forward slowly. Margaret screamed as her hand snapped behind her, breaking in an odd position. Her ankle bent as well, the sound of the bone-breaking echoing through the room, mingling with her screams.

Black smoke began to appear from within Margaret's body as if it was being pulled out. She began twisting and turning in the air, animalistic growls coming from her.

"What are you doing?" I asked.

Cassandra ignored me as she continued to chant.

"She's trying to pull the demon out," Cordelia explained.

"Stop!" Margaret screamed again. This time it was only Margaret's voice and not that of the demon. Her eyes became teary as she looked around the room, the black veins on her face vanishing. "What's going on? Please, Ms. Clayton, help me!"

Cassandra stopped chanting but kept Margaret suspended in

the air. "Your games won't work on me, Demon. Release the girl, now!"

Margaret smiled but spoke in the voice that was the blend of hers and the demon's again. "She doesn't want to be released, Witch Bitch." She began to shake, her eyes rolling back until all that could be seen was white. "The child and I are now one. She's a perfect host." I could no longer hear Margaret's voice at all—it was only the demon speaking. I realized her teeth had morphed into pointy little fangs.

A wave of black smoke emitted from Margaret, hitting Cassandra and me and sending us flying into the wall. I went through the wall and fell into the hallway outside the room, my head smacking onto a chunk of the wall on the ground. I growled as I got to my feet and turned to face Margaret, who was smiling at me sinisterly through the massive hole in the wall.

Out of respect for Cassandra and her wishes, I'd been holding back and staying out of the way. She wanted to kill the demon that had taken her daughter's life, but I'd had enough of standing on the sidelines. Cassandra was on the floor, her hand covered in blood where she held the back of her head. Fiona was still unconscious, and Cordelia was shaking her head as if disoriented.

Now, it was my turn. I snapped my dislocated shoulder back into place.

"Oh, is the little guard dog angry now?" Margaret taunted. "You want to hurt me, don't you?"

I said nothing as I began to call on my wolf. He'd been begging to be released, begging to be allowed to enact his revenge. My knee snapped backward and I fell to the ground as I began to shift.

Margaret charged at me. Before she could reach me, a bolt of lightning struck her, sending her flying through the outside wall to the ground below.

I looked Cassandra's way as she coughed, her hand falling to her side as she lifted the other to hold her head. I knew she had been holding back because of Margaret and the history she had with Lilith. Maybe Margaret was led astray by the demon, or maybe she'd always been a hateful little bitch. I didn't care which was true. She'd murdered Lilith without the slightest bit of remorse, therefore I had no reason to hold back. I wasn't going to leave here without seeing her dead.

Blood for blood.

If it was the last thing I did, I would sink my claws into her.

My shirt ripped off my body, and I fell forward onto my hands. I watched as my hands shifted into paws, as tufts of long jet-black fur grew out of my skin. Though it was painful, I smiled as I felt my bones breaking and reforming. I knew my wolf was all too ready to come out and play with our murderous little Margaret. He'd see to it that she lived to regret the second she decided to harm one hair on my Lilith's head.

"You can't shift, Axel. Not here. There are too many humans," Cassandra warned.

I looked her way. She was holding her hand behind her head, a glowing light emitting from her hand. She was healing herself, but if I waited for her to finish, we'd lose Margaret.

"I'll be fine," I said through clenched teeth, my voice deep and contorted. I winced as the skin on my back began to rip open.

Mid-shift, I ran forward and jumped through the window, completing the rest of my shift in mid-air. I landed on the ground as a massive wolf. Regrettably, I knew I had to remain in my first form, the one where I just looked like a large version of the typical wolf. While I would have loved to shift all the way to my final form, the one where I had wolf features but walked on two legs, it was just too risky with humans in the vicinity.

Since it was rather late at night, I hoped all the humans were heavy sleepers and didn't hear the commotion within the house. If they bothered to look outside, I figured the darkness should sufficiently obscure their vision.

I picked up Margaret's scent mingled with that of the demon

quickly. It made me wonder why I'd never smelled it on her before. I'd have to ask my dad more about it when I got home.

I followed the scent to the nearby forest. Pushing myself forward at wolf speed, I caught up to her quickly. I immediately noticed blood dripping from a wound on her leg.

She spun around to face me, and I realized there was a large cut on her forehead. Her eyes looked unfocused as she glared at me. In addition to the bleeding wound on her leg and her forehead, Cassandra had managed to break Margaret's hand and her ankle in her effort to get the demon out.

She looked beaten and broken.

Without the demon within her blocking her pain, she wouldn't have been able to make it this far. Black smoke rose from her body like steam as she held her broken hand.

I shifted into my human form once more and stood bare before her. Being naked around others was a hazard of being a werewolf, so I was far more comfortable with nudity than most human males would be. That being said, I felt the overwhelming urge to shower as I saw her staring at me. I tried to push the disgust I felt out of my mind. I needed to speak with her.

"She loved you," I said, shaking my head in utter dismay that both Lilith and I failed to detect the greed and moral depravity under Margaret's facade.

Margaret shook her head. "Loved me? She loved me? Lilith was selfish, and that's all she was. She loved no one but herself and *you*." She looked me up and down. "She knew I liked you. There was no way she didn't know."

I frowned. "What?"

Margaret nodded her head, her entire face now covered in black veins. "Yeah, I liked you. *I* liked you first, not her. But she just couldn't stand for me to get something I wanted. She swore she didn't know, but I know she was lying. She had everything—beauty, power, a loving family, everything. The one thing I wanted, she had to take that too." She bared her fangs as she hissed. "Before she even met you, I begged her to teach me magic. I begged and begged for years. I asked her to help me when my dad used to..."

My frown deepened as her words trailed off.

I narrowed my eyes at her. What had her father done to her? I shook my head. I didn't care. She lost any claim to my sympathy the minute she laid a hand on Lilith.

"Well, she didn't want to help me. She could have killed him. She could have killed him easily."

"Things don't work like that, Margaret, even for witches," I replied.

"Fuck that! I'm glad she's dead!" She yelled. Within the blink of an eye, she was slamming into me full force before I could react. When she had me on my back, she held her hand up threateningly above my head.

I watched her human nails grow and elongate into grotesque, black, demon-like claws. As she tried in vain to slash her new claws across my face, I swung into action and kicked her off of me.

I began to shift again, this time into my second, final form. In my first form, I'd be vulnerable to many of her attacks. Standing on two feet as a blend of human and wolf would give me the advantage I sought.

It was clear to me she could no longer change her body into smoke, or she would have done it already. Her body must've sustained too many injuries. Demons needed to possess a healthy body in order to have full access to their abilities.

I realized what I needed to do to end this.

I watched her panting on the forest floor before getting up slowly. She spat black blood on the ground, and the flower she spat on sizzled and burned as if had been dipped in acid. Her head snapped my direction as I stepped forward, the thud of my footsteps pulling her attention.

While it was quicker to shift into my second form, giving my human and wolf equal space within my body required more of my energy. I hunched forward, my eyes on her as I bared my teeth.

She scrambled towards me on her hands and legs like something from a horror movie, and I dashed forward to meet her. We collided in a burst of claws, fangs, and ripping flesh. I howled as she bit into my arm. I grabbed her hair and pulled, causing her teeth to tear through my flesh as I threw her towards a tree.

As her body slid down the tree, I picked her up and threw her again. My anger, sadness, and pain consumed me. I howled to the sky as a memory of Lilith smiling appeared within my mind.

I looked at Margaret crawling on her hands and felt nothing but a thirst for her blood—to see it spilled on the forest floor the way Lilith's blood had been in that dirty alleyway. Because of her petty jealousy, I would never again see Lilith's smile. I'd never hear her laughter or feel her touch.

The demon left Margaret's body, a cloud of smoke floating up to the sky. It came rushing at me, the smoke turning into the solid form of a man mid-air. I jumped up to meet him, our bodies colliding.

His loud shriek of pain met my ears as we slammed back down to the forest floor.

I got off him. As I did so, I removed my hand from where it was buried in his chest, ripping his heart out swiftly. It pulsed in my hand, black blood rolling down my arm to my elbow. He watched, alive still, until I crushed it in my palm.

I dropped the heart onto the ground. It immediately disintegrated, along with what remained of the demon's body.

I felt an immediate sense of relief and peace. The weight of the burden I carried to find justice for Lilith had finally lifted.

Without warning, I felt something sharp pierced into my back. I howled in pain and spun around to find Margaret standing behind me, her head held back as she stared up at me defiantly.

I reached around me and pulled the knife from my back before snarling at her.

She smiled, her body swaying.

I made no attempt to catch her as she fell to the ground, now completely unconscious.

———

Axel

I placed Margaret onto her bed and stepped back. Cassandra, Fiona, and Cordelia, now completely healed, stepped forward to look at her. Cassandra's face twisted with hate.

"The demon is dead, but Margaret is all yours," I said to her.

She turned to face me and reached a hand out to me. I hesitated with surprise before holding my hand out to meet hers, grabbing her forearm as she grabbed mine.

"Thank you, Axel," she said softly, tears in her eyes. "Lilith truly loved you, I know that. Now I can see why. We—the coven and I—are forever in your debt. Whenever you need us, we'll be there."

I nodded, speechless, and she released my hand.

I frowned as Cordelia and Fiona began healing Margaret.

"What are you doing?"

Cassandra looked over her shoulder as Margaret's eyes began to flutter. "We need her alive," she explained. She turned to stare at Margaret again. "There are fates much worse than death."

Margaret's eyes popped open.

The sheets on the bed magically wrapped around Margaret's body, encasing her as if she was a mummy. Her head remained bare.

With my enhanced hearing, I listened to her beg for her life as I made my way down the stairs and outside the front door.

Before, I hadn't been able to enjoy the cool night's air. Now I took a deep breath outside and exhaled, finally feeling a sense of freedom now that Lilith's killer had been dealt with. My heart still ached for Lilith, but killing that demon had given me at least a small measure of peace. At last, Lilith had justice, and no one would ever have to worry about that evil demon again.

I heard Margaret's scream echo through the night in the house behind me. A bright light flashed, shining briefly through all the windows on the first and second floor.

I inhaled and turned to walk away as the house returned to darkness. I could no longer detect the heartbeats of the witches or Margaret.

"Axel," a voice whispered to me.

I froze, a chill going down my spine. Then I frantically looked around, my eyes wide, for I knew that voice all too well.

"Lilith?" I called softly.

"Hey, Handsome."

I spun around, my chest tightening as I looked Lilith up and down. She appeared just as I always pictured her in my mind, though perhaps a bit paler. She was wearing a sky blue gossamer gown that grazed her ankles. The color of the gown accentuated the blonde of her hair, and I ached to wrap my fingers around even just one small strand as I used to do when I held her. She smiled at me, and I swallowed hard. I rushed to her, desperate to feel her in my arms, but she held a hand out to stop me before I could reach her.

I couldn't believe it...I couldn't believe I was actually seeing her.

"Lilith?" I asked again.

She nodded. "It's me, but you won't be able to touch me." She held her hand out and reached for mine.

I tried to hold her hand, but my hand just passed straight through hers. My heart dropped. Irrational as it was, a part of me had hoped that she was real and alive—that her death had been just just a horrible nightmare.

"I can't stay long," she whispered.

I shook my head, and all the words I had longed to say to her came pouring out. "Are you okay? Where are you? I'm so sorry that it took so long for me to find your killer. It was Margaret—she did all of this out of greed and jealousy. I'll never forgive myself for not realizing what a snake she was and not protecting you from her. I've missed you so much I can barely stand it."

My soul was filled with a bittersweet feeling as I watched her luminescent smile grow wider. I had always been willing to do just about anything to put a smile like that on her beautiful face.

"I've missed you too, Axel, more than I can ever tell you. But I've been sent here with a message. You must do everything you can to keep your father's book safe."

My face dropped as I stared at her in confusion. "What book?"

"*The History of the Damned*, Axel," she replied. "Keep it safe."

"That book? Why? It's just a book of myths and legends," I answered, genuinely puzzled. I started to panic as she began to fade. "Wait, wait, please don't..."

"I'm sorry," she interjected. "I have to go. Just do as I say, Axel, please. And remember what I told you—don't harden your heart."

She reached out as if to touch my face.

I stepped forward. A chill ran through me as her finger disappeared into my cheek. I closed my eyes, longing to feel even one second of her soft skin touching mine.

"Not all humans are to be hated."

When I opened my eyes, she was gone. Tears ran down in rivulets from my eyes as I looked around me. The world suddenly seemed so much emptier.

"I love you," I whispered to the night.

"I love you too. I always will," Lilith's voice echoed softly in my mind. As her voice faded, all the love within my heart faded with it.

Alpha Rising

Book One

CHAPTER ONE

RUBY

Life is finally about to stop kicking me in the ass, and the world is going to know my name. Everything is about to change.

I repeated my morning affirmation three more times as I exited the cab and looked around at my new school. I am in college. I, Ruby Saunders, have made it to college. I'll still have to work my ass off to maintain my grades and qualify for my full ride, of course, but nothing is going to deter me from my path. I've worked too long and too hard to get where I am now, so all distractions can go to hell. I'm not saying I won't attend the occasional party, but I know the opportunity I've been given will be gone forever if I lose it. I can't pay for college on my own; I can barely pay for lunch.

"Damn babe, nice ass."

My eyes narrowed as I stopped walking. I sighed as I turned around while pulling my hands out of the pockets of my leather jacket. The distractions were starting earlier than I had expected, and I wasn't in the mood. Five minutes. Only five minutes had passed on my first day, and I already had this to deal with.

Sure enough, there was a boy behind me eyeing me up and

down, his bright blue eyes twinkling with lust. I tilted my head to the side and smiled, and his face lit up even further. He wasn't bad looking, but he was a distraction and I wasn't about to be his next victim.

"What did you just say to me, you little bitch?" I said. His eyes widened as I raised a finger to his face. "Shut the fuck up."

"Ahh, I..."

I turned away before he could spit out whatever it was he was trying to say while behind him, his friends started laughing. I know what you're thinking, I didn't have to be that mean. But if you knew the life I've lived, you'd understand my determination to stay focused, which meant no boys.

For most of my life – almost all of it actually – I've been alone. I've been looking after myself for as long as I can remember, and that's how it will continue to be. People like me don't get offered help. Nor do we need it. I can take care of myself.

After leaving the admissions office a little earlier than I had expected, I decided to do a tour of the school. My first class wouldn't be starting for another hour, so I had some time to kill.

There was a dark academy aesthetic about this place that I knew I'd never grow tired of. From the moment I had seen this place online, I knew this was where I was meant to be. So, after receiving my scholarship, I packed up what little I had (which fit into one suitcase), pocketed my last three hundred bucks, and came here.

I inhaled deeply as the wind picked up and whipped my hair around me, the red strands tangling around my face. The buildings were all of a gothic design with vines going up the walls. People mostly spoke in hushed voices, and with the sky being overcast, the campus was shrouded in darkness.

I was at home.

Sometimes in life, you'll get a feeling in your gut, a feeling that pushes you to do or say something, and more often than not you end up living with regret if you ignore it. So far, I'm happy I took the risk of coming here.

The library is hands down my favorite place here. The quiet that greets you along with the slightly musty air gives you the feeling you've stepped into another world. As soon as I stepped inside I was inundated with the smell of old books, and my heart rate sped up. Victorian style lamps lining the walls and a giant chandelier hanging from the ceiling provided soft lighting that left shadows all over the library.

I made my way through the shelves, taking deep breaths as I glided my fingers along the spines of the books.

Oh yes, I'd be spending a lot of time here, a lot of time indeed.

Ever since childhood, books have been my way out, my escape from the shitty reality I live in. One day something I've written will offer someone a means of escape. Yeah, I know, weird idea since I'm a law major.

I had exited the shelves upon shelves of books to take a seat when, a few tables away from me, a guy got to his feet.

It was like watching a giant who had been crouching down stand tall. The man before me was at least six foot four with raven black hair, a square sharp jawline, and perfectly shaped thick brows. He was looking around the library and, if his knitted brows were anything to go by, he was angry.

Maybe he had been waiting on someone and they had stood him up. But who would stand up a guy like that? He was clearly a gym junkie, with one of his arms as big as my two arms combined.

As the man began to walk away, I heard a voice behind me. "He's hot, isn't he?"

I looked over my shoulder to see a girl bent down to my ear level, her blue eyes glistening with amusement. "Don't waste your time, honey. Every woman on this campus wants a piece of him, and he gives none of them the time of day."

Who was this girl and why was she talking to me? She had

caught me checking that guy out, whoever he was. So what? Was she a jealous ex or something?

"Um, okay. Don't worry, I'm not interested."

Her eyes widened as if I had said the world was flat before a grin pulled at her lips, and she sat down. "Hmm, how interesting. I get the vibe you don't run with the crowd. That's good." She stuck her hand out to me. "I'm Natalie."

I shook her hand because, why not? She seemed nice. "Ruby."

"Fitting name, Ruby, with your red hair and all." She squinted and leaned closer. "A natural redhead at that. Nice!"

Now I wouldn't say I'm the most beautiful woman to walk the earth, but my hair has always drawn attention to me, both its color and the fact that it reaches below my ass. And the bangs that stop just above my eyebrows make my small oval face appear smaller. I'm five foot five, have decent C-cup boobs, and I have some curvy hips. Hence, the comment I had gotten from that poor guy earlier.

Natalie, however, was a model. I've never been the type to be jealous of another woman's looks, but Natalie was tall, five foot seven at least, with legs like a gazelle and platinum blonde hair. Her ice-blue eyes were the icing on the cake.

"Yup. So who was that guy then?"

She smirked. "Oh, so you *are* interested?"

"I'm curious," I corrected her. "Only curious."

And that was the truth, because he *was* hot. Gorgeous even. He was tall and muscular, and while he was extremely handsome, there was an aura of seriousness about him that I liked.

She exhaled and looked in the direction he had gone. "He's Xavier Blackwood, son of Mathieu Blackwood." She looked over at me and smiled. "Xavier is part of the rich-kids crowd, although he rolls alone. That actually makes girls want him more. I'm not sure if it's a trick or not, but there you have it. You can try your luck, sis."

"I'll pass, *sis*."

She shrugged, not in the least bothered by my snappy response, and I found myself liking her. Looking at her, you'd think she'd be a materialistic "oh my god I, like, so need a skinny latte" type, but she seemed rather chill.

I can't stand a calorie-watching bitch. Eat food!

I checked my watch, and my eyes widened. I couldn't believe my hour was almost up. I got up and picked up my bag. "Hey, sorry, but I have class. I can't miss my first class."

She got up with me. "Sure, what building are you going to?"

"Law."

She grinned. "Nice, so am I. Let's go. You can tell me how you've managed to get an ass like that."

I laughed, and she winked at me as we left.

Yeah, I like her. That makes my first day a success because I usually can't stand people in general.

The day I had arrived in town I started job hunting. Mind you, by then I was down to two hundred bucks and still needed to find a place to stay. But my determination has always gotten me through, and finally, the fourth diner I visited needed someone immediately. For my job interview, all I had to do was serve customers for an hour. With my years of experience waiting tables (since it's the only job I've ever been able to keep), I landed the job easily.

My supervisor knew someone who knew someone who had just moved out of their broom closet apartment, and I was more than happy to take it. Now, two weeks later and with school started, I felt like my life was slowly coming together.

I'd even made a friend.

"Thanks, Ruby," a regular said to me. The old man tipped me twenty bucks. "This place needed a pretty face like yours."

"I heard that Mr. Jackson, and I take offense."

Mr. Jackson flipped Brittany off. She's my coworker and the only other employee besides my supervisor. She laughed and went back to cleaning the tables. She's Goth, with a million piercings in each ear. And even though our supervisor Rosette keeps telling her to stop wearing black lipstick, Brittany would wear it anyway and say it's not lipstick, it's her natural lip color.

Everything was going great until Natalie walked in, and I nearly had a stroke when I saw who was walking in behind her.

Xavier Blackwood strutted into the diner like he owned the place and took a seat. With him was a girl who was giving everyone the stink eye, her brown hair in a slick high ponytail, and a guy with curly blonde hair who looked extremely bored.

"Hey, gorgeous," Natalie called to me as she glided over to the counter I was leaning on. She plucked a cookie out of the jar beside me and winked at Brittany, who to my surprise started blushing.

Strange.

"Don't 'hey gorgeous' me! Explain. You're part of that crowd?"

Natalie glanced over at her shoulder. "Oh. Well, that crowd is my family. Xavier's my cousin."

What the fuck did she just say?

"Excuse me? You called him hot."

"Yeah, I know."

"He's your cousin, Natalie. No one calls their cousin hot."

She ate the last of the cookie and grinned. "I was only voicing what you were thinking. Anyway, what time do you get off?"

"First of all, I wasn't thinking that. And I'm doing a double shift tonight."

She pouted, but it only lasted a second. "Fine, I just wanted the guys to try the burgers here. If it wasn't for you, I wouldn't have known they were so good."

She kissed my cheek and pranced over to Xavier and friends. I stood there, rooted to my spot. I wasn't bothered by her kissing my cheek. I've only known her for two days, but it feels like I've known her for decades. Her cheery personality is hard to dislike.

What had me rooted to the spot was Xavier's eyes. They were

like black pits and they were trained on me. Why was he staring at me, and why did he look upset?

His brows were so tightly knit I figured he was going to get a headache soon. The girl he had come in with didn't like his attention being elsewhere. She threw her hand over his shoulder and began whispering to him, but her eyes were on me.

Oh honey, if only you knew how much I *don't* want Xavier Blackwood.

My brows pulled together as I turned away and placed my hand over my heart. My heart rate had spiked, and a horrible feeling was rolling up my chest. I coughed, but that had been a mistake.

"Um, Brittany, I'm taking a break."

My chest was burning, and I felt light-headed. I could feel the vomit making its way up my throat. What the hell is happening? I don't get sick, ever. I've caught the flu probably only twice since I was a child.

I turned and headed for the door, passing Natalie's table.

"Ruby?"

"I'm taking my break, Natalie. Someone else will take your order."

She got to her feet as if to follow me outside, a look of worry plastered on her face, but the other guy, the one who looked bored, grabbed her arm. I didn't care because the world around me was starting to tilt. As I ran outside, I held onto the wall and threw up until I fell to my knees.

———

Rosette gave me an hour break, instead of fifteen minutes. I stared up at the ceiling in the office where I'd been lying down for that hour. I've never thrown up so much in my life, but the feeling was almost gone. With my stomach now empty, I felt drained of all my energy.

I tried to remember what I had eaten that could have made me sick, but all I've had since this morning was a sandwich and then a muffin when I got to work. Maybe what I needed was a proper meal.

I grimaced. The thought of food was making me feel sick again, and I decided with the feeling passing I'd better get back to work. Rosette had argued with me for ten minutes that I should go home, but I need the money. My scholarship covers my school expenses, but I still have to eat.

I made my way back into the diner to take over from Brittany when my eyes landed on Xavier.

What was he still doing here?

He was alone but sitting in the exact spot he had been before. He looked up as I was putting my apron on and his eyes lowered into slits. My hands froze from tying my apron as his face morphed from relaxed to angry.

What in God's name did I do to this man?

I've only seen him once before, that day in the library. And considering that I'm friends with Natalie, what reason does he have for looking at me as if I'm a plague beast? Did Natalie tell him what I had said, that I wasn't interested in him, and he's somehow upset about it? That was the only thing I could think of, but I wasn't going to stand around and have this creep watch me my whole shift.

"Can I help you with something? Why do you keep staring at me?"

Xavier looked up at me and my heart lodged itself in my throat when he abruptly got to his feet, his nostrils flaring. I backed up, my eyes widening as his narrowed even further. My head was tilted back because of how he was towering over me, and just like that, I was hit with another wave of nausea.

My face twisted in pain, and he recoiled from me.

Was that it? Was he repulsed by me being sick or something? Jesus, what is with this guy? But God, was he even more perfect up close. I still didn't like him. Why is he acting like this? For a second there, I thought he was going to hit me.

He turned and stormed out of the diner, everyone having frozen to watch the scene.

"Do you know Xavier Blackwood?"

I looked over at Brittany and inhaled a breath. Throwing up even once more would surely kill me. "No. I don't know what his problem is."

She threw me a look I couldn't decipher before turning away to clock out for the day. From what I understood, Xavier's father was Mathieu Blackwood, the business mogul and millionaire. They were among the elite, and considering I was new in town, there was no reason for this man to hate me.

By the time the last customer left, I was again on the verge of fainting. I had munched on a few cookies throughout the night, but what I needed was rest. With tomorrow being Sunday and since my Monday assignments were already completed, I could sleep in.

I closed up the diner and zipped my jacket as the chilly air nipped at my skin. In the distance, I could hear music, no doubt from a bar or club or frat house nearby. Since my apartment was close by, many nights I walked home instead of calling an Uber. It's the only exercise I get since I've never seen the inside of a gym.

Xavier's face flashed in my mind, and I rolled my eyes. Something was seriously wrong with that guy, and you could bet on Monday I'd confront him for it. His father could be the president, I didn't care. You don't get to do stuff like that and walk.

My eyes narrowed and my steps slowed when before me, a man in a hoodie pushed himself off a wall and turned in my direction. He just stood there staring at me, his face cloaked in darkness with his hoodie pulled over his head.

Shit.

I turned around, but a chill ran down my spine when behind me was another man.

Oh, Jesus.

I turned and walked briskly down an alleyway, my hand rummaging through my handbag. I closed my eyes and cursed inwardly, my heart pounding in my head as I realized I'd left my pepper spray at home.

Behind me, I heard a whistle and another man appeared before me. No, no, this was not happening right now. This wasn't happening! Two weeks, I've been here for two weeks! My life was turning around! I got a scholarship!

The most gruesome thoughts started going through my head. I turned to run, but my way out of the alleyway was blocked by the first two men. They charged at me, grabbing both my arms and holding them apart.

"Hey, babe," the man who had appeared in the alleyway whispered, his voice low and gravelly. My skin started to crawl as he reached a finger out and ran it down my cheek. "Why are you walking home alone, princess?"

"I like to stretch my legs." I kicked him in the gut, sending him staggering backward. At the same time, I yanked on my arms, but only one came free. Before I knew it, the two men had grabbed me again. This time, one of them held my face, squeezing my cheeks.

The man before me started laughing and removed his hood, revealing a deep scar running down the side of his face. His skin was pale and his breath reeked of alcohol. I wanted to cry. My eyes were stinging, and I knew what was coming next when he smiled at me.

"I love 'em feisty."

My world started crumbling when he started grabbing at me, his cold fingers prying at my body until I felt them, like ice cubes, dip into my top and grab my breast. I screamed. I screamed for my life, for someone to save me, when suddenly the man to my left was yanked away.

I slapped my attacker in the face and pushed the other away

but it proved unnecessary. They had already forgotten about me because, behind us, their friend was suspended in the air.

His neck snapped to the side with a sickening sound that echoed in the darkness around us. I couldn't believe what I was seeing. What man has the strength to hold another off the ground like that?

The body was thrown to the side, and I got my answer as Xavier stepped forward.

CHAPTER TWO

I think I've fallen into some alternate reality where a man who looks exactly like Xavier can hold a grown man off the ground like he's a doll.

"What the fuck did you just do?" the man to my right yelled, but he made no move towards his friend lying on the ground, his eyes open but lifeless.

I swallowed and backed up as my attacker, the sick piece of shit who had had his hand down my top, whipped out a knife. "You're going to pay for that! You're a dead fucking man!"

"Do you really think so?" Xavier asked. It was the first I'd ever heard his voice. It tickled my skin like a feather's stroke, but it also made me feel faint. I narrowed my eyes, for his voice was also softer than I had expected. He sounded so calm, so collected, for a man who had just committed murder. "Leave."

The man to my right pulled his hoodie down, revealing a bald head, and he too whipped out a knife. "We're not leaving, but you are. You're going to the fucking afterlife for what you just did, freak!"

Xavier's head tilted to the side. "I wasn't speaking to you." His eyes drifted to me, and my body went rigid. "Leave," he repeated.

My eyes widened as his dark brown irises, almost black, began to bleed into the whites of his eyes. His eyeballs turned entirely black, and a chill went down my spine that had nothing to do with the cold air. I started to sweat because he suddenly seemed taller and more muscular. But I wasn't going to let him order me to leave.

"What the…"

"Go!" he barked at me, and my body jumped as I stepped back. His teeth had elongated so much that his canines were touching the bottom of his lower lip.

The men on either side of me started backing up as well, their eyes wide with fear, as Xavier took a step forward. I swallowed, suddenly feeling the urge to piss myself, as his fingers began to twitch before black nails pierced through his cuticles. On second thought, maybe I would follow that order.

"What the fuck are you?" the man to my right said, his voice shaking, and Xavier raised his head, his nostrils flaring.

"The man who's going to make you wish you had picked another woman to fuck with."

This wasn't Xavier. I'd really stepped into an alternate universe or a fucking horror show! The man before me was a demon, a creature, a beast! He wasn't human, he wasn't Xavier!

I screamed as Xavier rushed forward, a deep growl vibrating up from his chest. I pressed my back against the wall. I watched in horror as he held onto the man's arm, the one that was holding the knife and the hand that had been down my shirt, and ripped it from his body.

I gagged, my nearly empty stomach wanting me to vomit the two cookies I had managed to keep down, as I watched Xavier throw the man's arm to the side, blood flying everywhere. He opened his mouth and sank his fangs into the man's throat, and my legs started moving.

I could hear the man's horrible screams as I ran from the alleyway. I closed my eyes for just a second as I heard the other man start to scream as well. I could hear the sound of breaking bones. I don't want to sound ungrateful for being saved, but I think I would have preferred being raped and left alone because now I'm about to be eaten alive!

What the hell kind of town did I move to?

I wanted to cry, scream, and curl up into a ball. I wanted an explanation for what I had just witnessed because, as terrified as I was, that was still the coolest thing I've ever seen in my life.

No, not the killing. That was surely going to scar me for life. But Xavier, what the hell is he?

The screaming abruptly stopped, but I kept pumping my legs, the mouth of the alleyway just before me. But I didn't get far, oh how I didn't get far, because the moment I screamed to hail a passing cab, a hand made its way around my mouth. I was out cold in the next second.

———

Ruby

I rolled onto my side and frowned, surprised I wasn't greeted with a view of the sky. I got out of bed sluggishly and pulled my curtain back, the way I always keep it. I wasn't a morning person. To get myself out of bed, all I need is to see the sky.

I sighed and rubbed at my eyes before looking down at the street below, my eyes following a couple as they strolled by hand in hand.

Cute couple, I thought to myself as my stomach began to growl loudly, like an animal was in there. I wasn't hungry, I was *starving*. I dragged myself to the bathroom to brush my teeth and tame my hair before making my way to the kitchen. I wasn't sure why I felt so tired or so hungry, but the sooner I had food in my system the better. I already felt like shit and didn't want to risk getting a headache.

"Oh my God!" I clutched at my chest as I walked in on Natalie sitting at my tiny island. "What the hell are you doing in my kitchen? How did you even get in?"

Natalie raised a brow. "Your door was open. I've been calling you all day. You missed class."

"What?" I looked away and frowned. "What do you mean I missed class? It's Sunday."

Her eyes narrowed at me. "Ruby, it's Monday. I've been calling you since yesterday, which was Sunday, and then all day today. I was worried about you, and your ass has been sleeping all this time."

What the hell was she saying? There was no way I'd been sleeping for two days. I held my head and sat down and she slid her mug, rather my mug, toward me.

"Have some coffee. You look like shit. What happened to you?"

I sipped the coffee and sighed. I wish I had an answer for her, but I was busy trying to understand how I had slept for two days. Why was I still so tired then? I pressed my fingers to my temples and peeped at her from under my lashes.

"Sorry I missed your calls. I must have been more tired than I thought after work on Saturday." My eyes widened. "Speaking of Saturday, your creepy ass cousin attacked me."

Natalie blinked slowly. "Xavier attacked you? Attacked you how?"

"In the diner. And he didn't literally attack me. He was staring at me, so I asked him what his problem was, and he, I don't know, reacted. I thought he was going to hit me."

Natalie looked away, her brows furrowed in thought. "He would never do that. Do you remember anything else? What else did he do?"

I gripped my cup with both hands and took another sip of my

coffee, already feeling my energy returning. "Nothing else. He left, and I got back to work."

That's odd. Something tugged at my memory as I looked at my left wrist. Slowly I placed my cup down to swipe a finger across my wrist. It was smooth, with blue-colored veins showing beneath my skin.

"What's wrong?" Natalie asked. I looked up at her and then down at my wrist again. Something was wrong here; something was *really wrong*. First, my curtain was drawn at my window; my curtain is always open. And now my scar was gone. A thought occurred to me and I looked over at Natalie once more.

"How did you know where I live?"

She shrugged and puckered her lips. "I went to the admissions office. I told you, I was worried about you."

I didn't believe her.

My eyes widened as she faded, becoming almost transparent right before my eyes, and I got up, almost falling off my stool.

"Who the hell are you?" I reached behind me and grabbed a knife. "Who are you? What do you want from me?"

She tilted her head to the side and dared to look concerned when I was the one looking through her body. "Ruby, you need to calm down."

The wall to my right cracked and I lost it. "Are you fucking kidding me? Tell me who you are right now! What have you done with Natalie? Where is she? What the hell is going on here?"

The knife dropped out of my hand as more walls began to crack and Natalie started to flash in and out of existence. I hadn't taken any drugs, I was sure of it. I've never even done drugs, not even once, so why was I tripping? I must be tripping, because none of this was possible.

My hand fell to my side as I looked into Natalie's eyes. "This isn't real."

I sat up in bed with a start, my breathing shallow as I clutched at my chest. I was under sheets that weren't my own, black silk sheets at that. And when I looked to my left, I backed up so much I almost fell off the bed.

Natalie was sitting in a chair by my bed. No, not my bed. I wasn't even in my room. She was holding her head, her face twisted in pain, with Xavier by her side. His hands were on her shoulders as he begged her to speak to him.

What the hell is going on?

I tried to get out of bed and away from them, but my focus was going in and out, my eyes blurry. Before my very eyes what I was seeing changed from the room with Xavier and Natalie to just Natalie and me in my kitchen.

"What the hell are the two of you doing to me?" My head felt like it was going to explode. There was a weight on my chest so heavy it was like something was sitting on me. "What's going on!?"

Xavier looked my way, his jaws clenched tightly, and Natalie held her hand out to me, her face red. "Sleep."

I wasn't given the chance to fight it. I was hit with a wave of drowsiness that was so strong I was out cold before my head smacked against the cold hard floor.

———

Ruby

The third time I woke up, I felt like myself. I felt rested, but I was still in a room that wasn't my own. I laid there unmoving, but my sleepy eyes were on the black ceiling. The rest of the room was shrouded in darkness, only illuminated by one lamp that was standing by the door. I waited patiently until I felt truly awake before untangling my hand from the sheet to wipe at the corners of my eyes.

I replayed the events that had led me to be in a bed that wasn't my own and fisted my hands. *How many days have even passed*, I wondered?

I wasn't dead, so that was something, but how long would that last? What had happened in that alleyway hadn't been a dream. Xavier had transformed before my eyes and killed three men. Natalie had created some kind of alternate reality inside my head, and then she magically put me back to sleep after I woke up from it.

I closed my eyes and inhaled deeply before exhaling and then repeated the act once more. I could easily imagine that everything that had happened was impossible, but I would be foolish to do that when I had seen it all with my own eyes. Maybe what had happened with Xavier was a dream.

I rolled onto my side and my heart skipped a beat as I looked into Xavier's eyes. He was sitting in a chair at the far end of the room with one leg crossed over the other. I could only tell it was him when he leaned forward into the light. He was wearing a white T-shirt and washed-out jeans, and even in the light, his face was unreadable as he stared back at me.

He placed his elbows on his knees before interlocking his fingers before him. All I could see as I looked at him was the creature I had seen the previous night, but I was surprised at myself for not feeling fear.

I should be screaming and banging on the door. I should be doing something other than staring at him.

"How are you feeling?"

I sat up and looked down at the white nightgown I was wearing. "You didn't change my clothes, did you?"

"Don't flatter yourself."

"I assure you there is nothing flat on my body except for my stomach."

He combed his hand through his hair, and I watched as the silky strands jumped back into place. "How are you feeling?" he repeated.

"As good as anyone who's been abducted."

He reclined in the chair, and his face was once again hidden. "Abducted?"

I sighed. I wasn't in the mood to play around with Xavier. I was already calmer than I should be. If he was going to kill me, he would have already, right?

"What happened?"

"You already know. You saw something you shouldn't have."

Well, that confirmed that I wasn't dreaming, and I wished it wasn't so because now I had questions. A lot of them. "I don't remember what I saw."

Maybe if I pretended I hadn't seen anything, he'd let me go. I had a bad feeling about where this conversation was going, and considering that I knew he could rip me to shreds, I shouldn't say anything to upset him. I shouldn't even be thinking certain thoughts. What if he was reading my mind?

He got to his feet and walked over to the bed, his hands buried in his pockets, and my body went stiff. But what really got me was when he stepped into the light and his eyes were as black as they had been that night.

I swallowed hard and threw the covers off me. I stood and looked up at him, into his obsidian eyes, and slapped him across the face.

"You knocked me out."

He reached up and touched his cheek, his head turned to the side. The side of his mouth twitched, and my eyes widened, shocked at what I had just done, but I stood my ground, my legs shaking. If I was going to die, I'd rather die bravely anyway.

"That's what you're worried about?" His head turned back to me. "When you know I could have done so much worse?"

"Are you going to kill me?"

He stepped closer, and my heart started to hammer in my chest. He looked me up and down, as if he was sizing me up, and I clenched my fists so much my nails began to dig into my flesh. Was he checking if he could swallow me whole?

I crossed my arms over my chest and, to my surprise, a smirk found its way onto his lips. It was small, but it was there.

"You're hiding your fear very well, but I can smell it." I lifted my hand again to slap the smug prick, and he caught my wrist. "Hit me again, Ruby, and I will hurt you."

"Where am I? I want to go home, Xavier. I don't care what you are. I'll keep my mouth shut, just let me go home."

He threw my hand down, and I stepped back as I held onto my wrist. He hadn't squeezed me, but if he had so much as a muscle spasm, he would probably shatter the bone in my arm. I had slapped a werewolf. Me, Ruby Saunders.

The black in his eyes disappeared, and he crossed his arms over his chest, causing his shirt to stretch taut over his bulging biceps. I turned away, my eyes scanning the room. "Just let me go."

"I can't do that, and you know it."

I spun on my heels, my temper getting the better of me. "I don't know shit! I don't know shit! I don't even know what you are! What I know is that three men died, and I got knocked out. And now I'm here. And what the hell did you and Natalie do to me? You know what? I don't want to know. I want to forget all of this, and that means you, her, and this entire mess. Now let me go!"

"Any human who learns about werewolves has to die."

My heart stopped beating. I hated how calmly he had just said that. Did I even hear him correctly? I couldn't have.

"What?" I raised a shaky finger to his face as I forced all the bravado I had to the surface. "You've got to be kidding. You're joking, right? How does that make sense, Xavier? That was something you were aware of? And now you're saying something like that so casually, as if you weren't the one who chose to reveal yourself to me?"

We stood in silence for a moment, my angry eyes piercing into his. I watched his face shift from relaxed to furious within seconds. When he took a step toward me, I stepped back, tripped, and fell onto the bed.

"You humans are all the same." His mouth was barely opening as he spoke, but his voice was projecting throughout the room. He was pissed, livid, and my fear pinned me to the bed as he leaned over me. "You humans are all ungrateful. You're ungrateful. I saved you from being raped and murdered, but yes, that was my mistake."

He stood up and stormed from the room and my body jerked as he slammed the door. I swallowed, despite how dry my mouth was, as tears began to roll down my cheeks. I wasn't ungrateful. He had saved me from a horrible attack. But now I was going to be killed by werewolves?

CHAPTER THREE

XAVIER

Never before have I hated my exceptional hearing until now.

No, that wasn't true. Every day of my life, having to live alongside humans has been a headache. They are loud, messy, and my only place of peace has been my home. Until now.

I rested my elbow on the marble island and pinched the bridge of my nose as Ruby continued to pound on her door on the fourth floor.

Is she going to get tired at any point? She's been at it for an hour.

My hand slid to my cheek as I sat there, still shocked that she had slapped me. She's brave, I'll give her that. Or maybe she isn't as smart as she looks. What human slaps a werewolf when they are fully aware that a werewolf could rip them to shreds?

Images from the night I had killed those men flashed in my mind, and my face morphed into a deep scowl. I took a deep breath, which was what I should have done that night, instead of losing my cool. It was too late now anyway, what was done was done, and now there were consequences to accept.

I didn't feel bad for those men; they got what they deserved. If their victim hadn't been Ruby, it would have been someone else who wouldn't have had someone like me to protect them.

I shook my head. I hadn't actually saved Ruby at all. Because of me, she jumped out of the frying pan and into the fire. By law, werewolf law, she would now have to die. Humans can never be trusted with the truth that the monsters from their Hollywood movies are real. Even though those movies are so inaccurate.

History has proven time and time again that humans can't handle knowing that they are almost at the bottom of the food chain.

"Xavier, fix your face. You look like shit."

I looked over at Natalie as she walked into the kitchen and made a beeline for the fridge.

"She's giving me a headache. She won't stop screaming."

She threw a bottle of water across the room, and I caught it easily as she took a seat at the island. "What do you expect? She just needs time to process things."

"How do you process being told you're going to be killed? Or that werewolves are real?"

She puckered her mouth, looking thoughtful for a moment before shrugging. "You may have a point." She then pointed at me. "She's handling things much better than I expected, though. If I was in her position, I'd die from a heart attack. I think the entire house heard that slap." She chuckled, then sipped her water as I narrowed my eyes. "She's got balls, I'll give her that."

"She's not brave, she's stupid."

Natalie rolled her eyes. "Oh please. Just like how you *should have* walked away and not gotten involved the other night?"

"You know I couldn't," I said through clenched teeth. Her brows furrowed for a moment, and I looked away from the emotions in her eyes. I didn't need her pity for the shit I've landed myself, and ultimately the pack, in with this situation.

Ruby was a problem, a loud fucking problem. It's been years since a human was condemned to death because they've learned of our secret. My father isn't going to be pleased that his son, a pure-blood and alpha-to-be for our pack, lost his cool. Now a smart-mouthed human girl who was just in the wrong place at the wrong time would have to die.

My mind took me back to Ruby's room when she had slapped me and made a face. What I should have done was rip her arm off. That's what any other werewolf would have done. I was the son of the alpha, damn it. And here I was, being slapped around by a human as if I was a little pup.

Why didn't I just walk away? I'm a Blackwood. I should have fought my urges and kept moving because a smart wolf would have seen past his anger and known that once she saw the truth she'd have to die anyway.

But her screams had been deafening, her fear so thick that the scent was overpowering.

A loud crash echoed through the house, and I winced as I clenched my fists. She was going to draw more attention to herself. Only a handful of people knew about her presence on the pack grounds, and it needed to remain that way, for now anyway.

I combed my hair back, my ears twitching now that she finally had stopped screaming for help. "You know this is a delicate situation, Natalie." Her eyes grew serious and I crossed my arms on the island as I leaned forward, "No one can know what's really going on here. What's really going on with..."

"Thank Jesus, she finally stopped screaming." I swallowed my words as Anna walked into the kitchen, her brown hair up in its usual high ponytail. "Someone needs to kill that human bitch already. Why is she here and not in one of the cells? I knew she looked like trouble from the day I saw her at that diner."

My fist came down hard on the counter as I growled. Anna gasped and drew back, her eyes wide with shock. I pinned her with a stare that had her scurrying out of the kitchen, and it only annoyed me further when Natalie started laughing.

"I think that's the first time I've seen you get upset at Anna.

She's like an itch under your feet when you're wearing sneakers. She seriously needs to get over her obsession with you."

"Natalie, be nice."

She snorted. "Oh, like you just were? I still don't know how you managed to date her for a year."

Natalie and I looked to the door as my father walked in. Just like that, the headache that had finally eased returned with a vengeance.

"Natalie, what did you find out?"

"Alpha Mathieu, you're back. Um, I'm sorry, but I did not learn much. She saw through the illusion I created in her mind. I wasn't able to get anything from her, but I can tell you she's not a threat." Natalie bit down on her lip. "There's some kind of block in her mind. It's like a wall, but a strong one. I couldn't get through. The more I pushed the more painful it was for me."

Mathieu Blackwood, alpha to the Blackmoon Pack and my father, had a look on his face that I didn't like. This was a problem our pack did not need, especially right now. At forty-eight years old, he didn't look a day over thirty. He's six foot seven with a thick black beard and black eyes, just like mine. Just looking at him was intimidating, never mind the intensity that seemed to roll off him in waves. There was a time when I had feared him just like everyone else does, but not anymore. I'm to take his place soon. A strong alpha fears no one.

"Xavier." I looked up from the salt shaker that had been holding my attention. I knew what was coming. "This shouldn't have happened. You, out of all the wolves here, should not have lost control like that. And for a human! Alphas *must* have control, Xavier. Explain yourself."

Natalie's brows touched her hairline as she made a sound in the back of her throat. I threw her a look, and so did Mathieu. "What is it, Natalie?"

"You're not going to like what he has to say." She bowed to my father with respect before glancing up at him from under her lashes. "With all due respect, Alpha, Xavier didn't have a choice in the matter. They were going to rape her."

Mathieu frowned as his dark eyes darted from Natalie to me and then back. "So, what is it then? Someone needs to explain exactly what happened before this has to be reported to the Council. They won't give a shit about a human girl being raped."

"That's because the Council is made up of sick old bastards who only care about themselves."

Mathieu exhaled heavily with exasperation. "Natalie!"

"Sorry."

"The Council is there to protect us. You two might not have been around back when we were at war before, but another war, in this day and age, would lead to our extinction. We stay hidden in order to stay alive." He looked my way. "So all humans who find out about us *have* to die."

Over my dead body was Ruby going to die for my fuckup. This wasn't her fault.

"We'll have to talk in your office, Dad."

He frowned.

Living with wolves means privacy is limited because everyone has supernatural hearing. He knew that suggesting we talk in his office, which was soundproof, meant something was wrong.

He nodded and walked away. Natalie folded her lips inward, an apologetic look on her face, as I followed my father to the fourth floor.

I was about to pull the pin from a grenade by explaining to Dad why I had saved Ruby.

———

Natalie

I balanced the tray in my left hand as I knocked and opened Ruby's door. I frowned at the shattered lamp by the door before poking my head inside.

"Ruby? It's Natalie." I closed the door behind me when I found her sitting on the floor at the back of the room, her head against the wall. "I brought something for you to eat. You must be hungry."

She opened her eyes slowly, her cold stare making me rethink approaching her. I placed the tray on the coffee table before the sofa and sighed. Her eyes and nose were red from crying and her hair was wild and tangled. She looked a mess, and my heart went out to her. The hatred in her eyes cut me deeply, but I deserved it as much as Xavier.

She had witnessed three men being ripped to shreds, and now she was locked away in a room awaiting her own death. I'd want to rip some fucking limbs off myself if I was her.

Sighing, I pulled a chair closer to her but stayed at a polite distance so she wouldn't feel crowded. "I know you must be confused right now, and scared. I'll answer any questions you have."

Ruby only stared at me, her eyes dull and emotionless. This change was odd considering she had been screaming at the top of her voice less than an hour ago. The brave girl I had heard slap Xavier now looked broken and defeated, or was she just tired from screaming?

She looked toward the window at the swaying trees outside. I did the same thing, allowing her to speak on her own terms. I wasn't confident she would speak at all. Maybe our approach had been the wrong one, trying to pry into her mind instead of speaking to her. She had witnessed something previously unimaginable to her, and then I went in and stirred up her brain with my power. Too much was happening to her with little to no explanation or preparation.

Xavier certainly hadn't made the situation better by telling her she was going to be killed.

"What were you doing to me?" I looked in her direction, but she was still staring out the window. She looked so broken, so confused. "You were inside my head."

"I'm sorry, my alpha ordered me to." She finally looked my way and I sighed. "Okay. Some of the things you've seen in the movies about werewolves are true, and some are bullshit. We do live in packs. We do have an alpha. However, we don't change only during the full moon, and silver doesn't hurt us. We don't communicate telepathically, and we don't look the way you'd expect."

Ruby released the knees she had been holding to her chest and stretched her legs out. I took that as a sign of her slowly relaxing and starting to process what had happened.

"I'm not like Xavier and the others, though. I'm an Enchanted, a female wolf (or she-wolf if you will) who cannot and will never be able to transform. I still have exceptional hearing, speed, sight, and strength, but nothing compared to, say, Xavier. However, I have different powers of my own that no one else in the pack shares. All packs have an Enchanted, some more powerful than others. That's how I was inside your mind. I wasn't trying to hurt you, Ruby. I was trying to see if you're a threat to my people."

She scoffed at that and looked away. "I'm in a house filled with werewolves, and I'm the threat?"

I smiled; she had a point. "That's true, but humans are powerful in their own way. Humans are a danger to the supernatural world. That's why all supernatural creatures have their own way of dealing with humans who learn of their existence."

"What others are there? You said all supernatural creatures."

She was curious, and I was happy to tell her anything she wanted to know. At least it took her mind off the inevitable. Seeing auras was one of my gifts, and I had been drawn to hers from the moment I saw her. Pure white auras like Ruby's were rare. Very rare.

"There are witches, golems, demons, angels, gods, the whole works. They're all real. Some live alongside humans just like us wolves, and some live in other dimensions."

"When?"

I frowned. "When what?"

"When are *your people* going to kill me?"

I inhaled deeply. Even though I expected the question, it still caught me off guard. She didn't look sad or upset, she looked defeated. Somehow that was worse. "I don't know." She released a breath she seemed to have been holding in, and I could hear her heart rate spike. "Listen, Xavier is doing what he can right now to save you, okay?"

She arched a brow. "Xavier? He's trying to save me?" She laughed, but it held no humor. I frowned, not sure what she was laughing at. Was she losing her mind? "Xavier trying to save me is exactly what got me into this mess. Honestly, I don't like him, and it's clear he doesn't like me either." She leaned forward. "Let me go, please. I won't tell anyone. Use your powers and wipe my memory if you must. Why can't you do that?"

"I wish it was that easy." I got up and walked toward her, but her body tensed and her heartbeat increased to a frantic pace. She was scared of me. "You don't have to be scared of me, Ruby."

She got to her feet shakily and I listened as her stomach growled. She braced herself on the wall for a moment, then pushed forward and approached me. Her aura turned so white it was almost blinding, forcing me to avoid looking directly at her.

Where her eyes had been dull a moment ago, they now filled with a mix of anger and sadness. She stopped just before me. "I don't want to die."

"You're not going to. Listen to me Ruby, take it easy on Xavier. This has never happened before. It's new to him."

She threw her hands in the air, her brows knitting as she grew frustrated. She turned away, pacing to the window and then back toward me. "And I'm new to being abducted! I'm new to this, new to all of this! What exactly is new to him, Natalie? What? Help me to understand what he's used to, because I'm the one trapped inside this room waiting to find out if I'm going to live to see another day."

Silence fell between us. Our conversation wasn't going the way I had wanted it to, and I realized I had been foolish to think it would be any different. At this point, the less she knew the better. I couldn't explain to her why she could never be harmed in our pack. That was Xavier's story to tell.

She walked over to the bed and sat down, but I remained standing. Only a few days ago I had thought I had made a friend, the first human I'd ever found myself drawn to. It would have been best if I had kept my distance. The moment I sat down beside her at that table in the library, I had set the wheels of this disaster in motion.

This wasn't Xavier's fault. It was mine.

She tilted her head. "If it's your law to kill all humans who learn about your existence, then why try and save me?"

Shit.

Seeing the look on my face, she shook her head. "Forget it."

"You'll get explanations soon enough. You just have to trust me, okay?"

She arched a brow. "Trust you? *Trust you?* I don't know what to make of any of this. I'm still trying to figure out if this is all some sick prank. Werewolves and supernaturals are real, and I'm going to die because I know about it? I can't believe any of it. Trust is a two-way street, Natalie. Just leave me alone, okay?"

I understood her irritation, but I was only trying to be her friend. I'm still a wolf, with a temper just like any other wolf, and she was starting to piss me off.

"Fine. You're not going to die, Ruby, but I can't guarantee you'll ever be able to leave this pack. A human hasn't knowingly come into contact with a werewolf in a long time, and never from our pack. There's so much you don't know. If you want to live, I suggest when the alpha comes to see you, you should try to be chill and not snappy. Your emotions are all over the place, and understandably so, but it's certainly not in your best interest to piss him off."

I turned and left, leaving her as she had asked me to. No matter how annoyed I was, I knew her attitude and anger were warranted.

As an Enchanted, I'm allowed to be around humans more than Xavier or any other wolf. As long as I have control over my powers, that is. Even so, I'd never been interested in having a human friend until I met Ruby. Although, in truth, I mistook her for a supernatural until I smelled her. Her incredible aura had tricked me into thinking she was supernatural that day in the library. I had wanted to find out which type, but she just smelled human. Her personality had done the rest. I didn't want any harm to come to her. I really didn't want to lose my friend.

I came to a stop at the stairs and watched Xavier remove his shirt and jump off one of the balconies.

CHAPTER FOUR

Y*ou're not going to die, Ruby, but I can't guarantee you'll ever be able to leave this pack.*

Natalie's words ran through my mind in an endless loop. With each refrain, I felt another piece of my life crack up and slowly disintegrate. What had she meant? I can't stay here with a bunch of werewolves! Where even is "here"?

She had come to me to shed some light on my situation, and I had given her the cold shoulder. It was killing me. She didn't have to come to see me. She didn't have to offer any explanation, but she had. She'd even brought food for me, and I still pushed her away, the only friend I might have here.

But she's still one of them. It makes no difference that she's an "Enchanted" or whatever she called herself. She's still one of them. If Xavier's attempt to spare my life doesn't work, she'll have to stand by and watch me be killed.

Xavier Blackwood.

I rolled onto my back as that name echoed in my mind. I definitely thought he was strange, even before I learned he has fangs. Now, thanks to him, I'm not even sure whether I'm going to live or die. It's because of him I'm in this mess, but there's something about him that keeps pulling my thoughts back to him.

From the moment I'd seen him in that library, I had gotten the sense that he wasn't really happy. It seemed like he was just going through the motions in life and trying to make the best of it, kind of like I was.

I held my hand up and over my face before curling my fingers into a fist and resting it against my chest. I had looked into the eyes of a monster and had felt no fear. I had slapped him. Hard. I still couldn't believe I'd done it. Why was he trying to save me? It was obvious he didn't like me, so why go out of his way to save me to begin with, especially knowing I'd then have to be killed? Why go against your own law to spare a human's life, my life?

Was it guilt?

I had too many questions, and no one to ask for answers. Werewolves, witches, gods...they're all real. All the things that go bump in the night are real, and now I'm a part of that world. Or I will be for however long I'm permitted to live anyway. No, I don't want this. I rolled onto my other side to face the window and yawned, having not slept a wink the night before. Outside the moon's light was exceptionally bright, causing the trees to cast their shadows inside my room.

I could hear the wind howling outside...or was that a wolf?

I closed my eyes, all out of tears to shed, and fell into a deep sleep.

Do you prefer to die than to live? I woke up with a start to those words in my head.

The voice inside my head had asked a good question. I looked around the room and realized it was morning. It felt like I had only just closed my eyes to sleep.

However, being trapped here as a prisoner forever among people who hate my species isn't what I call living. Dying didn't sound fun, either. I should be thinking of ways to escape, but I'd be a moron to think I could get out without a house full of werewolves noticing. There was no way I could outrun a werewolf, let alone a pack of them.

Time to face facts: life as I knew it was over.

Two days. I enjoyed life at college for two whole days before this shit show began. I'd long since lost track of time. I was not sure how many days had passed since I was brought here, but I knew I could kiss that scholarship goodbye.

I shook my head and turned my back to the window. There was only one explanation – I was cursed. I think I've always known. It's time to stop pretending. What are the odds of almost being raped, only to be saved by a werewolf, who then tells you it's their law to kill any human who sees them?

Am I the only one who sees how ridiculous this s? I'm at risk of being killed for being saved. If cursed doesn't explain it, I don't know what does.

Unable to lie in bed any longer, I got up and took a quick shower. Thank God there was a bathroom and a room with a bed at least. I'd thought they'd throw humans into dark dank cells. I pulled on the jeans and top that I had woken up to find on the sofa across the room. There was a comb, toothbrush, deodorant, and other necessities in the bathroom as well. In addition to being given all these things to be comfortable, I was being fed twice a day. It seemed I would escape the "immediate death" option.

A quick glance in the mirror showed me I was starting to look pale from being inside for so long. If I'm forced to deal with another week or even a month of this, I'll become practically transparent. I couldn't help noticing how good my skin looked otherwise, though. There seemed to be a glow to my skin and a brightness to my eyes that had never been there before. I also felt a strength within my muscles that I'd never felt before. Maybe it was all the sleep I was getting?

I shook my head and threw the hairbrush down in disgust. I wasn't at a spa retreat, for God's sake. I was trapped in a house filled with monsters.

Do they hunt and eat people? How long will I survive living here before someone decides I look like a tasty snack?

I was making my way across the room to sit by the window when a knock came at the door, and it opened. My body grew tense and my heart pounded like a drum in my ears as the largest man I'd ever seen in my life walked into the room.

His body almost filled the doorway, and I swallowed hard as he bent his head to walk under the door frame.

He was tall, six foot seven, maybe? His eyes were black pools, and his beard was thick. It took me only a moment to realize he must be Mathieu Blackwood, Xavier's father and alpha of this pack. When I first heard Natalie mention him, I might have looked him up online. Just out of curiosity, of course. I hadn't been able to find any pictures of him, despite him being a millionaire.

Were all wolves this large?

He looked me up and down, his eyes and face revealing nothing of what he might be thinking. Like the good human I am, one who doesn't want to be eaten, I stayed quiet and rooted in place.

"Come."

He turned and walked away, leaving the door open for me to follow him. He didn't spare a glance behind him to make sure I was following. He knew I wasn't going to defy him.

I walked behind him quietly, my eyes trying to absorb as much of my surroundings as possible. I had imagined the house to be dark and mysterious, semi-lit, with antique furniture and creepy halls. As we descended a large double staircase, and then another and another before going outside, I was pleasantly surprised at how beautiful the house was. The décor was simple but elegant, with gold-handled doors and marble floors. Mathieu Blackwood wasn't just a werewolf; he was a wealthy man. Why would he not be living comfortably?

Yes, I'm curious about him, as well as Xavier and Natalie. I want to know what they are, what it means to be what they are. I want to know their history and their plans for their future. If I'm now linked to these people, I want to know everything about them. And not just werewolves for that matter.

I've always been a fan of the supernatural, and now I was a prisoner in their world. I might as well gain a better understanding of my new reality.

Once we were outside, I paused to stare up at the house, my hand on my forehead to shield my eyes from the morning sun.

I closed my eyes for a moment as I inhaled the scent of fresh air, and with my head tilted up to the sky, I smiled as I felt the sun warming my skin. My body relaxed for the first time in days as I felt the cool breeze brush over me. The view from my room had shown nothing but trees upon trees, so I had known we were in the woods. But actually being outside, smelling the fresh air, was so soothing.

"When I was younger, I used to do the same."

Just like that, my euphoric haze crashed back into reality. Since I had stopped walking and had fallen behind, distracted by the world around me, I hadn't realized he had returned to my side. Mathieu's deep baritone voice caused the air to vibrate with each word he spoke, pulling me from my daydream.

"I'd stand and inhale the air. The air in the city is stuffy, tainted." He looked down at me, and although he wasn't smiling, he wasn't looking at me with hatred either. "Do you like the house?"

Was this man really asking me about his house right now?

"I do. It's not what I was expecting."

He scoffed at that. "I know." He looked up at the house. "This house has been in my family for generations, with a few renovations here and there, of course. This is my home and the home for many wolves." He looked down at me. "A human being here puts them all, us all, in great jeopardy."

I swallowed. "Sir, I find it hard to open a jar of jam sometimes. I'm no danger to any werewolf, let alone a pack of them."

His brow arched. "Are you scared?"

"I'm scared of being killed. I don't want to die."

"Are you scared of the monsters that are surrounding you right now?"

I looked back as a man walked through the door we had just exited. He was shirtless, with both his arms covered in tattoos. I watched as he paused, sniffed the air, and then looked my way.

He stood there, his eyes piercing mine before he suddenly took off at a run. My eyes widened as within seconds he disappeared into the woods. Though my heart was hammering in my chest, I realized it wasn't from fear but excitement, and from curiosity about how he was able to do that. No, I wasn't scared of werewolves. They were people, just not the kind I was used to. It's not like I have a great love for humans anyway. Most people annoy me to no end.

"I'm not scared of werewolves unless one decides to attack me. What I am is curious. I want to know more. Humans, I know all about, and sometimes I wish I didn't. Werewolves are all new."

After a few seconds had passed without a response from Mathieu, I looked his way and found him staring down at me.

Shit, had I said something wrong?

"I um..."

"I'll release you," he said as he cut me off, and my mouth dropped open. "I'll release you to attend school and to work. I understand you work at a diner in the city. But you will be living here from now on. You may come and go as you please, but you will remain under my watch, my care. Say nothing about what we are to anyone, and I'll have no reason to harm you."

His threat didn't go unnoticed by me. I wasn't being given freedom exactly, I was just getting a long leash. My mouth opened and closed, and he tilted his head to the side as he watched me. I didn't have to ask. I knew my options were to take this deal or die.

"Okay," I replied, my voice a mere whisper. "But why? It's your law to kill any human who finds out about werewolves. It's already clear to me that humans are hated, that I'm hated. Why spare me and invite me to live with you?"

He turned his back to the house as he buried his hands in his pockets, his crisp white shirt stretching somewhat. We stood in silence, both of us listening to the sounds of the forest, but I knew he was hearing so much more than I was.

"My son spoke to me, as did Natalie. They've both convinced me to let you stay. There will be a time when humans and werewolves will have to come together again. And if you tell anyone I said that I'll rip your throat out." My eyes widened but I kept my eyes forward. "Times are changing, and we need to change with them. My wolves need to be comfortable around a human. We'll learn from you, and you'll learn from us. That seems fair, doesn't it?"

"Yes."

In my peripheral vision, I saw him nod his head and remove his large hands from his pockets. I was all too aware that those would be the hands to strangle me if I ever stepped out of line. Would the alpha do such a messy job, or would he get some sort of enforcer to do the deed? Would it be Xavier?

"The human saying is, 'keep your friends close and your enemies closer'." He looked down at me. In my mind, I heard jail cells slamming closed. "You will be moved to a different room, and someone will bring your things from your apartment. I'm afraid I must go, but it was nice talking to you, Ruby. I see what Natalie saw in you."

———

Ruby

Another sleepless night had me restless, my thoughts keeping me awake despite my tired eyes.

My new room would be ready tomorrow, the start of a new life as a guinea pig to werewolves. Mathieu had said his wolves would learn from me, but what was I supposed to teach them? Don't they all live alongside humans anyway? What had he meant when he said one day humans and werewolves would have to come together? He had also said *again*. Did that mean humans used to live alongside werewolves?

"I see what Natalie saw in you."

What had she seen? I still couldn't believe she had taken a deep dive into my mind. Maybe if I hadn't told her to leave me alone, I could've found her and asked her to put me to sleep the way she had before. In the daytime, I can force myself to think of other things, but night causes my doubts and fears to come alive and plague me.

I wasn't even sure if I was handling this all correctly. What's the correct way to deal with something like this anyways? First I'm to be killed, and now I'm a part of the family? Something else was going on here.

"Too many questions," I groaned as I pressed my thumbs against my temples.

Well, if I couldn't sleep, I might as well try to find something to eat. Since this was now my new home, I doubted anyone would hurt me if I took a walk to the kitchen, wherever that was.

It's easy to get an anxiety attack when you know you're sneaking around a house that's filled with people who can hear a pin drop from a mile away. The house was deathly quiet as I made my way to the first floor. I'd left my slippers in my room, figuring I'd be quieter in my bare feet, but it probably didn't matter. They'd hear me anyway.

I reached the first floor and heard a noise. I decided to check it out. Hopefully, whoever else was wandering around the house would be friendly enough to point me in the direction of the kitchen. I hadn't eaten anything all day, my appetite having been wiped away by the bomb Mathieu had dropped.

"Bingo!" I said under my breath as I spotted the kitchen. But as I entered it, I found Natalie staring right at me.

"You heard me coming?"

She smiled shyly and nodded. "Are you hungry?"

I nodded as well and walked further into the kitchen. My brow rose at her neon pink night set. "Yeah, I have a headache."

She got up from the island and walked over to the fridge. "So, I guess Mathieu spoke to you, then. It's not so bad here, once you get used to it."

She pulled out some rotisserie chicken and shoved it into the microwave before pouring us both some orange juice. I narrowed my eyes at her as she took her seat once more, the microwave rumbling behind her. She didn't seem upset with me, though not exactly her perky self either.

"I'm sorry for how I behaved before," I said.

She smiled again, although this time wider. "It's okay. I can't even imagine how confused and upset you've been."

I made a face as I took a sip of the juice, my eyes taking in everything in the kitchen. "Oh no, this has all been so much fun."

She chuckled, catching on to my sarcasm, and I smiled back, feeling like we were back where we were a few days ago. Before I had been attacked by disgusting men and kidnapped by a pissed-off wolf.

"I want to know more," I told her as she grabbed the chicken and split it in half. "About you, all of you. Why do you all hate humans so much that if one finds out about your existence, you kill them?"

Her hand paused in handing me my plate and a shadow flashed over her blue eyes for a moment. I took the plate from her, and she retreated to her side of the island.

"It's not that we hate humans." She puckered her lips. "Well, some wolves do, but I don't. Wolves and humans just have a bad history, a history that led to a lot of deaths on both sides." She inhaled after swallowing a piece of her chicken. "Decades upon decades ago humans and wolves lived together in peace, along with witches and other supernatural beings. Now those times were as dangerous as you might imagine because there's good and bad in all species. I don't remember the whole story, so I'll summarize what I remember; I haven't heard it since I was a child."

I nodded as I washed my chicken down and folded my arms on the cold marble island. From the look on her face, I could tell I wasn't going to like this story. Since wolves now hate humans and humans don't know of their existence, something horrible must have happened.

She looked broken, however, and I had a feeling she remembered the story a lot better than she was letting on.

"Werewolves aren't predators. We've always been protectors. We have the strength to hunt other supernatural creatures that plague the world. So back then there was a wolf pack living close to a human city. Both species found a balance. The wolves guarded the city and protected the humans, the king's castle, and their own pack as well. Things got complicated when a human girl fell for a wolf. However, there was a human boy who liked her as well." Natalie swiped her tongue across her top lip. "The human boy could not accept that a wolf had 'stolen' his girl, but obviously a human can't fight a wolf. The fight is lost before it even begins."

"The human boy did something stupid, didn't he? I feel like that's where this story is going. This stuff is always about love and jealousy."

She pointed her fork at me. "Listen. Eventually, the wolf found his mate and his relationship with the human girl ended. She was devastated and angry, so she ran right into the arms of the human boy who had loved her all along. On her wedding day, she and her new husband invited her old love, and they arranged for the wolf to be poisoned."

My eyes widened. "What?" After a few seconds of her saying nothing else, I leaned forward. "And what happened after that?"

"That's it. The human girl was the king's daughter, and the wolf was the alpha's son. You can imagine how that all played out, and here we are now, divided. Wolves turned themselves into myths to keep away from humans."

I sat back and sighed. "I can definitely agree that the princess was a total bitch for doing that. I can even understand why you all retreated to the shadows. But why release me, yet keep me here? I'm not going to tell anyone, and who would believe me?"

She ate another piece of chicken and waved the bone at me. "Someone will, trust me. That's all it'll take to start another war. Humans are more dangerous now than they were back then. Humans from this century are even more jealous, greedy, and power-hungry than before. And on top of that, now there are bombs, guns, and scientists that would..."

She trailed off, her anger was bubbling to the surface and her face twisting, and I couldn't say I didn't understand why. It's never been difficult for me to put myself in another's shoes, and right now I could see the pain in Natalie's eyes. No one wants to imagine themselves cut open on a cold table while doctors run experiments on them.

"You're right," I replied softly, and she looked over at me. "A war now would be bad, but why can't I just..."

"Give it a rest, Ruby." Natalie and I watched as Xavier walked over to the fridge and removed a bottle of water. I hadn't seen him since the day I had slapped him, and my fist tightened around my glass as he pinned me with a stare that could freeze water. I sent one back his way.

"Give it a rest? Are you serious? I'm being forced to stay here, with people who hate me just because I don't have fangs. Send someone to tail me, since you don't trust me not to talk. You've ruined my life, Xavier. I don't belong here!"

He slammed the bottled water down onto the counter and I

jumped. Even Natalie flinched as the bottle burst. "I've ruined your life? You're so selfish and self-centered. Even after hearing what Natalie had just told you, you still really don't get it? You don't want to be here, but there are people here who don't want you here either. Our pack doesn't kill humans. We've never had to. So you can't leave here, ever. You're lucky your life was even spared, but now I realize I should have left you in that alleyway to be raped!"

"Xavier, that's enough!" Natalie yelled, but it was too late.

"No," I said softly as I got up from the island. "He's right."

Natalie stood up as well. "Ruby, he didn't…"

"I'm going to bed. Goodnight."

I turned away and left the kitchen quickly before either of them could see the tear that fell from my eye.

CHAPTER FIVE

I stared at my laptop screen, but I wasn't seeing the coursework I had to do. It had been a week since I'd been sentenced to my new life, but instead of physically going to school I decided to take online classes. I still had my job at the diner, but morning shifts only.

Taking online classes meant I'd have to leave my room less, and I figured that would be best for everyone. I'd now settled into the routine of waiting until everyone's turned in for the night before making myself dinner.

I was accustomed to being alone, but living under these circumstances had me slowly losing my mind. How much of this would I have to endure? Weeks? Months?

Years?

I closed my laptop screen and reclined in the chair by my window as the sun began to set. The splash of colors above the green trees looked like picture-perfect computer wallpaper, and this has been my spot to sit and relax over the last couple of days.

Saying my new room was large was an understatement. I had my own living room, for crying out loud. And a bathroom that was larger than my old apartment. I hated to say it, but I was living comfortably for the most part, other than the isolation.

I hadn't seen Natalie or Xavier since our chat in the kitchen, and I didn't want to see either of them. Sure, Natalie hadn't done anything, but I wasn't sure I'd be able to handle the pity in her eyes. As for Xavier, I wouldn't mind never seeing him again.

Ever!

With leaving for work early in the morning and getting break-fast at the diner, I'd only run into a few wolves at a distance. However, the looks that I'd gotten would make anyone want to dig a hole and crawl into it. Getting home in the evening after work was even more daunting since there were even more evil stares and whispers to endure.

I got up and stripped, ready to take my shower before bed. I wasn't hungry tonight. My appetite disappeared after I got home and ran into two female wolves standing by the door. I hadn't been scared when one of them flashed her fangs. I didn't even flinch, which impressed even me. But you can only take so much hatred being aimed at you every day.

I stood under the warm water and allowed it to roll down my body. I switched the shower off and roughly dried my hair with a towel.

The only good I was seeing in this situation so far was that I didn't have to pay for rent or food. All I have to do is take my classes and go to work. So many people would kill for this, but would they be able to handle the price that comes with it?

The moment my head touched my pillow, Xavier's face appeared within my mind. His hurtful words to me began to ring in my ears. I've never felt so ashamed, hurt, and humiliated in all my life. There isn't any love lost between Xavier and me. I can't stand being around the guy without feeling nauseous, and it has nothing to do with his good looks. Yes, I have invaded his home, but to say something like that just wasn't right.

I rolled onto my back, my arms spread wide on my king-sized

bed, annoyed at myself because I could see how I'd come off as ungrateful. But my life has changed so much in such a short time! I've been given a lot to process and a lot to accept. I was given the choice to pick death or the only other available option. That wasn't a choice in my eyes.

I was studying law, so the significance wasn't lost on me that Mathieu was breaking werewolf law by keeping me alive and a secret. Now when, not if, my existence is discovered, what will happen to me? What will happen to him and his pack?

I can see it now – I'll be blamed for that as well.

"I should have left you in that alleyway to be raped!"

I rolled onto my side and pulled the sheet up to my chin, a stinging within my eyes forcing me to squeeze them shut as tears began to soak my pillow.

I'm not ungrateful. What I am is trapped and dying slowly.

———

Ruby

A nearby sound penetrated my sleep, but only enough for an eye to crack open and then immediately close again. I was exhausted after spending hours crying.

It was the first time I've cried, a true cry, since the start of the downward spiral my life has taken. There is a time for everyone when a cry that's started by one thing becomes a cry about everything, things from your past and present. You let all your emotions out and leave yourself bare, but afterward, you feel so numb, so light, the only thing left to do is sleep, a dead sleep.

The next time the sound came, however, it was enough to wake me completely. I sat straight up, my eyes darting around my room frantically.

Why did that howl sound so loud? So close?

I gripped the sheets at my sides as I listened. The night had returned to silence, but shortly after, another howl rang out. A horrible feeling settled in the pit of my stomach. Throughout my time here I hadn't seen a single wolf in wolf form. I hadn't even heard so much as a growl until now.

I had been expecting to see shirtless men walking around, and multiple brawls, or at least being forced to buy earplugs to drown out the howling at night. In reality, I've never slept so well in my entire life. Whenever my thoughts allowed me to fall asleep, that is.

Another howl penetrated the walls, but this one wasn't as loud. It sounded more like a wounded animal, and I swung my legs over the side of my bed and got up.

Yes, going snooping right now was a bad idea, but was I still going to do it?

Damn skippy.

I peeped out my door and looked up and down the corridor before slipping out and closing my door as softly as possible. Outside my room, I could now hear more howls. Quieter ones, but they were there. The further I walked from my room, the louder they got, but I was certain they were coming from outside.

No, I wasn't going to go outside. I'm not that stupid. But I was peering through every window I passed to see if I could catch a glimpse of anything outside.

Maybe a party is going on, I thought to myself. But with each window I passed, I saw nothing. If a party was going on, I'd hear music. I'd see people.

I paused and puckered my lips. Why do I never see more than ten people around, including Natalie and Xavier? There must be others. So are there other houses within the woods that I haven't seen? It would make sense if that was the case since this was the alpha's house. It should be separate from the pack, the community.

My brow arched as I realized there might be an entire little town here in the forest.

A piercing howl cut through my thoughts, and my steps faltered. The sound reverberated into the house through a window just up ahead. I walked over slowly, my heart in my throat, wondering what I'd see. Oh boy, was I not prepared!

Forget what you've seen in the movies of men turning into actual wolves on four legs. It's bullshit.

In the backyard were two wolves... creatures... beasts... restraining a man with chains. And Xavier was there, too. I couldn't hear what was being said – they were too far away – but my eyes were glued to the two beasts.

There were tiki torches all around them, as if a ritual was being held, the flames from the fires at their tips illuminating the darkness. The wolves were standing on two legs, their bodies covered in thick fur, their mouths no longer mouths but snouts, although shorter than a normal wolf. Their ears were large, long, and pointy, but I was surprised at how much their physique still looked human. Their abs and bulging muscles were still visible through their smooth fur. They looked to be at least seven feet tall, maybe more, with their backs slightly hunched. As I watched, their long tails agitatedly swiped back and forth.

Jesus, they're really real.

I swallowed the lump that had formed in my throat and moved to the side of the window, peeking around the frame. The last thing I wanted was to be caught snooping on something that was clearly private.

Was that man before Xavier human?

My eyes drifted back to the wolves as a sudden urge to be close to them, to touch their fur and feel the strength in their arms, overtook me. Yes, they were scary, but they were truly majestic beings as well. One of them shifted his weight from one leg to the other and the clear power as his muscles rippled had a smile forming on my lips. I bit down on my nail. I felt like I was going into shock the longer I stared at them. My breath caught as the man in chains lashed out at Xavier. Odd that my heart would skip a beat for

Xavier's safety, but he didn't even flinch. I couldn't see his face clearly, just his profile cloaked in shadows.

I couldn't tell if he was speaking, but the man in chains was becoming more furious, pulling and twisting until he fell to the ground. The wolves quickly yanked him back to his feet. Suddenly, a tail swiped at Xavier, the tail belonging to the man in chains. I guess he was a wolf after all, though he wasn't fully transformed. Xavier leaned back and avoided the blow, and my hand flew to my mouth as I gasped at what happened next. Xavier reached forward, and his entire hand vanished inside the man's chest.

My body started shaking as he stepped toward the man and then yanked his hand out. I gagged, and although I wanted to step away from the window, I couldn't look away as he dropped the heart that was in his hand while the wolves caught the lifeless body.

What did I just watch?

My heart was pounding so loud it was drowning out the growls from the wolves. I'd just watched Xavier take a life! I was in shock, no doubt, but what had I just watched? That man was a wolf, one of his kind, so why kill him like that?

The two wolves walked away with the body and Xavier watched them leave. Then his head lifted as if smelling the air. Before I could step away from the window, his eyes pierced into mine. The next thing I knew, my legs were taking me back to my room as if I was being chased.

Ruby

Falling asleep again had been hard. I had lain in bed on my back with my sheets up to my chin, but my eyes were trained on my door, wondering if at any moment Xavier would burst in to confront me for snooping around last night. I had seen something I shouldn't have, that was very clear.

My brain kept replaying him reaching into that man's chest as easily as if it was butter and his hand was a knife. He had seemed indifferent, almost as if he was doing a mundane task like buttering his bread, not taking a life.

I realized that while I'd been so busy isolating myself, I'd also been wasting the chance I'd been given to learn about the people I'd be spending an unknown amount of time with. Hiding away in my room was not the way to survive in this new life.

I rolled onto my side and scratched at my cheek as the morning sun began to warm my skin. I was thankful to have a window close to my bed, to be able to wake up to the feel of the sun. Much as I wasn't into the mood to get out of bed, I decided it was time to get out of this room and explore the house I was living in. Natalie seemed to be the only person willing to talk to me, so I'd start by hunting her down and getting answers to all my questions.

I opened my eyes and had to bite down on my lip to stop the scream from escaping. Xavier's black eyes calmly watched as I rolled to the other side of my bed and away from him.

"What the hell are you doing here?" I asked as I pulled the sheet up to cover my chest. How long had he been sitting by my bed and watching me sleep?

"Are you scared of me?"

I frowned. My irritation began to fade as I took in his appearance. He was wearing a black T-shirt and sat with his arms crossed over his broad chest, his massive size making me wonder if the chair would collapse.

He arched a brow and I looked away, blinking rapidly to rid myself of the image of him killing that man. The man sitting beside my bed didn't look like a killer.

"He had lost his mate," he said, and I looked over at him. "All werewolves have a mate, a partner. At their first meeting, they instinctively know they're meant for each other. The legends say the bond ensures each wolf meets another who complements them perfectly in order to strengthen their bloodlines. Not all mates end up together, however. But a wolf rejecting another is rare." His jaws clenched tightly and he looked away. "When you meet your mate, it feels like a part of your life that you didn't know was broken off glues itself back together." He inhaled and unfolded his arms, both hands combing his hair back. The side of his mouth arched. "So when you lose that person, the pain is unbearable."

He pinned me with his eyes, and I couldn't look away. Why did he look so broken?

"He was a good man, but after losing his mate he made several attempts to take his own life."

My eyes widened as my brows knit tightly and my mouth turned downward. I've never been in love before, but to love someone so much that if they die, you wish to be dead as well seemed unreal to me. I looked away as my feelings of horror from watching that man die turned into pity. I remembered the way he had been lashing out at Xavier, the way he had been crying. And to know it was all because he had lost his mate made the situation so much worse. Xavier hadn't murdered another person; he had saved a person from unimaginable emotional pain.

"Instead of allowing him to die like that, I gave him an honorable death." He leaned forward and I glanced at him from the corner of my eye. "So, do you think we're monsters? That I'm a monster?"

"No." The word had escaped my mouth too quickly. "I mean, having seen what you guys really look like, you don't look like angels but, no, you're not monsters. You've explained what that was last night, and now I know that was an act of mercy."

"What if it hadn't been?"

She sighed. "Then I don't know, Xavier. What I know is that I was permitted to live, and you have saved my life twice. You're not a monster for that. Even so, am I living, Xavier? I don't mean to seem ungrateful about you saving me that night, but what is the purpose of me being here? Really? How long do you think this will last? It feels like my death is being drawn out and that just makes me feel worse. Get it over with."

He didn't look away, but he didn't respond either. I hadn't meant to say so much, but once I started talking, I couldn't stop. Why should I stop anyway?

"And what you said that night in the kitchen was a real dick move. I'm going to punch you in the nuts for it one day."

His brow arched, and to my surprise, he began to smirk. It wasn't helping that he was freaking gorgeous right now, sitting there looking all cool and mysterious. Why was his smile growing?

He reclined, a full-blown smile on his face, but I made a face as that smile vanished as quickly as it had appeared.

"You're bipolar, aren't you?" I said. What had that smile meant?

"I'm sorry for what I said. I shouldn't have said that to you. No one, werewolf or human, deserves what almost happened to you. Get dressed."

I looked over at him as he got up and started walking towards the door. "What? Why?"

He opened the door before looking back at me and he sighed. "For once, Ruby, do as you're told and get dressed. Be ready in the next hour. I'm leaving, with or without you."

He slammed the door behind him as he left.

CHAPTER SIX

RUBY

Now I understood how dogs felt when their owners decide to take them outside. I was out of the house! I was out of the house, and it wasn't for work. And while I didn't know where I was going, *I was excited*. I had gotten dressed as Xavier had demanded and had found him outside just as he was getting into his car.

The asshole really was going to leave without me.

I could feel eyes on me as I got into the car, but there was no one outside that I could see. For a moment my excitement faltered, my imagination painting a picture of wolves hidden in the trees watching me with vengeful eyes.

I sat back as Xavier pulled out, his matte black Audi speeding toward the large iron gates that led to my freedom. No matter how temporary it would be. I knew I would have to return to this place at the end of the day, but I sighed and pushed that thought away. I decided to just be in the moment.

During the long drive to the gate, I stared ahead at the towering trees that lined both sides of the driveway. I watched as the limbs swayed and a smile made its way onto my lips. I'd been trying to deny it, but being surrounded by nature is peaceful. I awaken every morning to a breathtaking view and the sound of birds. With the fast pace of the city left behind, I'm starting to appreciate nature's beauty a lot more.

"How many werewolves are in your pack? So far I've seen less than ten people."

"Fifty-two."

My eyes widened as I looked over at him. "Seriously? Wow. Where are they? Are there other houses here in the woods like yours?"

He held the steering wheel with one hand and my breath hitched as he reached over to me, his arm brushing against me. He grabbed my seatbelt and strapped me in without taking his eyes off the road.

I frowned, a churning in my gut. He smelled amazing.

"There are a few houses here in the woods, yes, but some wolves live in the city. Only a few though."

"Oh."

He pressed a button on his keychain and the gate swung open. We drove in silence for a couple of minutes before I was unable to hold it in any longer. "What's it like? Changing into a wolf?"

He didn't answer right away, and I held my breath waiting to see if he would. Mathieu had said I would learn from them, so I was going to ask every question that came to mind. I had originally planned to find Natalie, but for whatever reason, Xavier was being nice to me right now. I was going to take advantage of it.

"The first change is painful. It happens from a young age, between ten years old and thirteen. As we grow older, it becomes easier. You don't notice the pain anymore. Being a werewolf is like when you're sitting in an uncomfortable position and your leg falls asleep. You can feel your leg, but at the same time, you can't really feel it. I can feel that side of me there, under my skin."

I turned in my seat to face him, my interest piqued. "And when it comes out?"

"It feels like I'm truly myself. My leg isn't sleeping anymore, and I can feel it, truly feel it." His mouth twisted into a smile. "We already have heightened senses, but in wolf form, it becomes so much stronger. Everything becomes better."

"That sounds amazing."

His brow arched and he threw a look my way. "Does it?"

"Isn't it?" I countered. "To have such power and strength, it has to feel amazing."

He slowed the car for a stoplight and turned to look at me. "It's not always so. Some wolves hate being wolves because they have to keep so many secrets. We go to work and school and live alongside humans, but we have to hide so much, hide who we are. Living in a world like this with the abilities we have is hard. One slip-up and that's it, we go viral on YouTube." The light turned green and he drove off. "Yes, being a wolf is amazing, but it has its downsides."

He didn't say anything after that, and neither did I. I hadn't thought about the pressure wolves must feel trying to be normal, pretending to be something they're not just to remain safe. My mind took me back to last night, and I couldn't remove the image of the transformed wolves from my mind.

They were scary, but they were beautiful. But I knew not everyone would see that beauty.

He continued to drive quickly but confidently, and I sank into my seat, my mind taking me back to the story Natalie had told me. Yes, my heart would be shattered if I fell in love with a wolf, only to have him leave me for someone else. My heart would be shattered if a human left me for someone else, but I would never in a million years do what the princess in that story had done.

She could never have really loved that wolf if she played a part in killing him. Her love wasn't real. The man Xavier killed out of mercy had known love. I would probably never know what a mate bond felt like. What I know, however, is that for a bond like that to exist, even if it's meant to strengthen bloodlines, the unconditional love it creates between two wolves must be amazing.

Well, I'd think more about that later. For now, I still had more questions. "So, you guys don't need the full moon to transform, do you?"

Xavier shook his head as he turned into a parking lot. I hadn't even realized we were in the heart of the city. "No, we don't. We can change at will." He looked over at me and for a second his eyes were completely black, and my heart skipped a beat. "During a full moon, however, we can't transform."

"Wait, really? That's the complete opposite of what books and movies say."

He chuckled. "I know. My ancestors created that lie. During the full moon, we can't transform, and that's when our pregnant women give birth. A pup born outside of the three days surrounding a full moon can kill the mother. We're born in human form under the full moon, but outside of a full moon a pup is born as a real pup, a transformed wolf."

"Jesus," I said under my breath as I imagined a woman being ripped open by a baby wolf. "Have you ever seen that happen?"

He turned the car off. "No. I think that's more myth than fact. A child has never been born outside of a full moon, that I know of, anyway."

We got out of the car and made our way toward a restaurant I'd never seen before. It looked like a tavern you would find in the 1900s, and I was instantly intrigued. Its walls were made of wood with a large wooden sign hanging just above the door, "The Witches Brew" written on it in red paint.

"Wow." Since I hadn't even been in town a month yet, there were so many places in the city I had yet to see. Over a week ago, the thought of maybe never getting to see the city again would have made me angry, but I've fallen in love with the woods. Which I wasn't going to admit to anyone. However, I missed the sounds of the city, too. "I love this. Is this owned by a wolf?"

Xavier stepped ahead of me and pulled the door open. The way he looked down at me with a sly grin had my stomach doing backflips.

Damn, what is happening right now?

"I thought you might, and a witch actually; hence the name," he answered.

I paused, one foot inside the tavern. "Huh? A real witch?"

He nodded, and we stepped inside. As the door closed behind us, a bell rang above our heads. I felt like I'd been transported into the past. Just picture an old tavern from any movie you've watched, and you'd be spot on. The tables and chairs, the bar and shelves, were all solid handcrafted wood. The tavern was cloaked in semi-darkness, with only a single window above the door and a few dim lamps on each table. It was oddly cool inside as well.

There was a surprisingly large number of people inside. Xavier led me to the bar, and I hopped onto one of the wooden stools. I spotted a boy with a hoodie over his head in the corner of the room, his fingers dancing quickly over his laptop's keyboard. "Is there Wi-Fi in here?"

"Of course. We're not barbarians." My head whipped around to find a woman standing behind the counter with a towel thrown over her shoulder. "Well, not anymore."

She swiped at a strand of black hair that had come loose from her high bun. "The usual?" she asked Xavier, and he nodded. "And you, lass?"

I arched a brow. Who was she calling lass? Was she the witch who owned this tavern? She looked young, late 20s young, with sun-kissed skin and freckles over her nose.

"Whiskey."

She gave me a little smirk. "Whiskey at 11 a.m.–you're my kind of woman." She nodded and turned away.

I watched as she walked away, noticing that her left arm was completely covered in tattoos. They were all some form of writing in a language I did not recognize. "So, is she the witch?"

"Yeah, her name's Willow. She's been running this tavern since it opened in the 1600s."

Wow, I thought to myself. I wasn't too surprised, however.

Since I now knew for sure that werewolves were real, I guess all other supernatural beings were probably real, too. I spun slowly around on my stool, my eyes darting over everyone sitting inside the tavern. I couldn't help wondering if they were humans or supernatural; maybe there was a blend of both.

The boy in the corner looked my way, and I stopped breathing. He had red pupils with vertical irises like a cat's.

"What is he?" I leaned in and whispered to Xavier. He merely glanced at the boy, and then looked away.

"He's a demon. I wouldn't keep staring if I were you. He's a dream demon. You don't want him latching onto you. They plague humans in their dreams, feeding off their fears."

I looked away instantly, but I could still feel those red eyes on me. "Everyone in here is supernatural?"

Xavier shook his head as Willow appeared with our drinks. "No lass," she said. There are humans here too, but they are none the wiser about the supernatural beings around them." She pointed at the boy with the red eyes. "He's a demon, a young one." She then pointed to the other end of the room where a girl with green hair was sipping on her drink and tapping at her phone. "That's a fae."

I arched a brow as the girl's eyes darted our way before she sniffed and looked back down at her phone.

"Hmm, rude," I said under my breath, and Willow chuckled.

"Yeah, fae aren't very friendly." She tilted her head to look at Xavier, and I saw a flash of violet in her brown eyes. "I'm curious to know why a wolf is hanging with a human, Xavier. Things have been boring around here lately. Why don't you give me the details so I can have a good gossip?"

I watched their interaction silently as Xavier took a sip of his drink before answering. "You'll find out one way or another. I'm not going to make things easy for your nosy ass."

She tossed her head back and laughed. "Fine." She looked my way, her eyes still violet, and I couldn't help leaning in closer, intrigued by the odd color. "You're a strange one, though." She looked me up and down. "A strange one."

What the hell did she mean by that? I mean, I've never been one to blend in with a crowd. I've always stood out because of my flaming red hair. But I could feel in my bones that she meant something other than my looks.

"What do you mean?"

She shrugged and turned away. "Holler when you're ready to pay the bill. I have an appointment in the back with a woman who says her dead husband is still trying to have sex with her."

————

Ruby

Xavier looked up and down the street before crossing, and I followed close by his side. After leaving The Witches Brew, we hadn't gotten back into his car. We left the parking lot, turned left, and had now been walking for ten minutes.

We hadn't really talked to each other during our walk, but it wasn't an uneasy silence. It felt comfortable. I felt protected. Was it because I knew about the power within him? I hadn't expected to be getting along with him so well. Why did he offer to do this? Why be nice to me now? Was it all just because of his guilt over what he had said to me?

"So, supernatural creatures are all friendly with each other?"

"No, Ruby, they aren't all friendly with each other. Just like not all humans get along with each other." He tapped my shoulder for me to follow him and turned left. Ahead of us appeared a large fountain.

"Wow," I said under my breath. "I only just moved here for school. I didn't get the time to explore the city." When we finally stopped at the fountain, I dipped a finger and then my hand into the water. "Why did you do this? Why take me to that tavern and here? Why are you being kind to me now?"

I turned around to face him but was forced to take a step back. I hadn't realized he was so close to me. I frowned at the warmth that spread throughout my body. He took a step forward and I stepped back, but the back of my leg bumped the edge of the fountain.

I was trapped, but despite the intensity in his eyes, I didn't feel threatened. We were in public anyway, what did I think would happen? He'd wolf out right here in the open?

I crossed my arms over my chest, and he just smiled. "Do you mind?" I asked. "I can see your pores with how close you're standing."

"Do I make you nervous?"

I kept my face straight, but my nails were digging into my arms. "Do I look nervous to you? You're just invading my space, Blackwood."

He bent at the waist. "I can smell it," he whispered. He stood up straight as I started grinding my teeth, an impish smile on his face. "Don't worry, you smell good."

He was playing with me. That's what this had to be about. I watched him closely as he stepped around me to stand at the fountain's edge as well, the air alive with the splashing water.

"Despite what you might have thought, I don't hate you, Ruby." He dipped his hand into the water and scooped some of it up. "My life was calm until I met you." He slapped the water. "Now my life is like this, disrupted."

"If you were trying to say something nice, it's not going in that direction. I didn't mean to uproot your life, but my life has changed, too."

He turned to me and stepped closer, forcing me to look up into his eyes. "Is it so bad living at my house?"

Was he being serious?

"Um..." I exhaled and looked away at the clear glistening water, before looking up at a slowly drifting cloud. "No, it's not so bad. But it would be better if I wasn't living there and being kept on a short leash."

His hand brushed against mine, and a bolt of electricity shot up my arm, forcing me to step back. When I did, he grabbed my arm. I gasped and looked up at him, but the irritation on his face was only serving to confuse me. What was that feeling when he had touched me?

He reached out, and my body went stiff as he reached around me and grabbed my ponytail. I swallowed as he loosened my hair and pocketed my scrunchie. "I told you to let your hair down, didn't I? You're not on a short leash Ruby. You can come to the city. You can start going back to your classes. You can live a normal life."

"I can't take the constant stares..."

He frowned, and his hand fell away from my arm. The spot he had been holding was no longer warm, and I wanted to tell him to hold me again.

Okay no, no. Slow down, Sonic the Hedgehog, you're moving way too fast right now.

I shook my head. "The few wolves I've seen look at me like they want to claw my eyes out. A girl flashed her fangs at me."

"What?" Xavier yelled, catching the eyes of two men walking by. He didn't spare them a glance, however; his anger was aimed at me, and I wasn't sure why he was so angry. After all, he was one of the people who were mean to me. "Who did that?"

"I don't know her name," I replied with irritation. "I do want to know more about you guys, and demons and witches and stuff. I want to know everything since I'm a part of this world now. However, it'll take some time to get used to living with people who hate me because I wasn't born special."

He inhaled deeply and rubbed a hand across his forehead. "Okay, look, when we get back, I'll give you a proper tour of the house and grounds and introduce you to a few people. Everyone just needs to get used to the idea of you being around and trust that you won't betray us."

"Do you trust that I won't betray you, Xavier?"

The world around us seemed to vanish as our eyes locked. Heaviness began to settle on my chest and my palms grew sweaty when he took a step closer to me. I felt faint suddenly, but I was unable to break eye contact. Since the moment we'd met, his eyes had been unreadable. Until now, and what I saw within them was frightening.

Raw, uncensored, desperate need.

He reached out and wrapped a strand of my hair around his finger. "I trust that you won't, Ruby."

I hadn't seen it coming, and I wasn't sure if he had seen it coming either, but when his lips pressed to mine I felt like a volcano erupted inside me. I leaned into his chest and the heat coming off him was staggering. Why was he so hot?

My fingers curled into his shirt as he pulled my bottom lip into his mouth and I caved into him, literally. He wrapped his arms around me and pulled me up and off the ground. Somewhere in my mind, a voice was yelling for me to push him away, but I couldn't. I felt drawn to him suddenly, more than I ever had. All thoughts of anything but here and now flew out of my head. Nothing was going to stop me from exploring this kiss. His lips tasted so good, his arms were so strong, and his body was so warm.

I pulled away first, the fog in my mind clearing, and he released me immediately. "I'm sorry," he said, his voice low, but he didn't sound apologetic.

"It's okay. Um, why did you do that?"

I wasn't complaining. *Oh no, most definitely not!* I'd never been kissed like that in my entire life. But why had it happened, why had it felt so good? Like an acid flashback, I remembered Natalie's story about the tragic end of a werewolf and human relationship and I took a step away from him.

Oh no.

"Um, actually, that just now, it never happened. Okay?" I turned and walked away, my legs like jelly. "We should head back to the house. I want that tour."

What the fuck did I just let happen?

———

Ruby

The drive back to the house was a quiet one, and this time the radio blasted to cover the awkward silence. Xavier had kissed me, and I had let him. I wasn't sure how I'd face him after this. I couldn't even handle turning my head to look in his direction. Why had he done that?

I thought he'd never dated a human, from what Natalie had said that day in the library. I had been convinced he wasn't even attracted to *my kind.* So why, out of all the women throwing themselves at him, did he decide to stick his tongue down my throat?

My day had been going so well. He had been on the brink of making me think this could all work out, and then he had to ruin it. My life before this hadn't been perfect. My life has never even been close to perfect. My financial worries had disappeared since being forced to live here. Despite how nerve-wracking this had all been, I was slowly falling in love with the woods, but now I'd give it up in a heartbeat with no second thought. *Xavier had kissed me. This could end badly!*

I'm no longer the human girl being allowed to live, but the human girl Xavier kissed. If that's not a can of worms, I don't know what is.

I bit down on my lip as the gates leading to the house opened.

No, I was lying to myself. Sure, werewolves exist, and so do demons; but I was one of the few, perhaps the only, human in a position to know about this hidden world. Sure, it would take some time to get settled, but I was going to make the best of this. A kiss wouldn't ruin that.

I groaned inwardly.

An already awkward situation was just made ten times worse.

We pulled up to the entrance of the house and Xavier got out before I did. As I opened my door a loud crash could be heard inside the house. I glanced over at Xavier. With his heightened senses, it seemed he could hear what was going on, and his face was turning red with rage.

What's going on?

The front door flew open and a man's booming angry voice met my ears. My body tensed when I could finally make out the words he yelled.

"Where the FUCK is she?!"

Faster than my eyes could track, something bolted out of the front door and slammed into Xavier. Within the next second, Natalie appeared by my side, but my eyes were glued to Xavier and the man who attacked him.

The men pulled apart, both rolling in opposite directions before getting to their feet. Xavier's claws were elongated, his eyes black pits of rage, but when I looked at his attacker my face twisted as a wave of nausea slammed into me. Hazel eyes were piercing into my green ones, and my body started to feel hot.

Natalie grabbed my arm as I staggered backward, my hand slowly rising to clutch at my chest. I felt like the world was caving in on me. I groaned and doubled over as the hazel-eyed man growled and his eyes turned black.

He attacked Xavier, the sound of them fighting only making me feel worse. Why was I getting sick right now?

"Stop them!" I yelled as Mathieu appeared on my other side.

"What's going on?" The man swiped at Xavier and his claws dug into Xavier's side. "Stop!"

No one was listening to me. No one was even trying to stop the fight as Xavier grabbed the man by the throat and threw him down. More people were appearing around us, no doubt hearing the fight, but no one was doing anything.

The man got to his feet, and my skin started to burn as he looked my way. A surge of pain racked my body, and Natalie's hold on my arm grew tighter. I looked down at my open palms as they began to shake violently before looking at the newcomer again, Xavier's blood dripping from his claws.

My body suddenly felt numb, my legs growing weak.

"You have no right to keep her! Release her to me!" The man yelled as he looked Xavier's way, his body shaking with rage as he spoke.

Who was he talking about? Was he talking about *me*? I don't even know this man. Was he a part of the Council? Had they found out Mathieu was keeping a human pet? What the fuck is going on?

"I have every right to keep Ruby, and she's on my land." Xavier growled back, "You have no claim to her!"

Xavier seemed to have said the wrong words because the man fell to the ground and I watched as the back of his shirt began to rip. He was changing, right before my eyes. His skin was tearing and opening, blood pouring from his body as his nails dug into the ground. I've never seen a wolf transform and seeing it now was making my stomach turn. Why had no one told me it's as if the wolf is literally bursting from their body?

Vomit was rising to my throat quickly, my chest feeling heavy with it, but it stopped, along with the rest of the world, when the stranger spoke once more, his voice deep and contorted.

"I have all rights because she's my mate! Release her!"

A chorus of gasps could be heard around us and Mathieu stepped forward, finally showing some concern. At first, he hadn't seemed concerned that his son was battling, possibly to the death, with this clearly deranged man. But what the fuck had he just said?

I'm his mate?

No, no, this has to be a joke. He's a werewolf, I'm a human. Who is this man?

Mathieu stepped before me, his large body blocking me, and to my surprise, they both growled at him.

"Ruby can't be released to you. She's not just your mate, she's Xavier's as well."

Oh no, the fuck I'm not!

Pain blossomed within my gut, and I hugged myself as I leaned forward. "You're all crazy," I said. But before I could properly finish the sentence I vomited, my body shaking violently as I fell to the ground.

The world around me blurred as the two men rushed my way, but I was consumed by darkness before they could get to me.

CHAPTER SEVEN

I could hear muffled voices through the darkness around me, but I was comfortable. I didn't want to give in and wake up. I wanted to remain asleep, swaddled in the warmth around me.

I wanted to tell the voices to be quiet, but my eyes cracked open regardless. The talking around me stopped. I groaned as I swallowed. My tongue felt like sandpaper against the roof of my mouth, and I sat up, rubbing at my temples.

"You're awake."

No shit, can I go back to sleep?

That's what I wanted to say to Xavier, but I remained quiet. The moment I had opened my eyes, I remembered some of what had happened. I just wasn't sure if everything I remembered was from reality or a dream. I inhaled deeply and swung my legs off the sofa to curl my toes on the cool marble floor, my eyes wandering from Xavier to Mathieu. Xavier was standing beside the chair Mathieu was sitting in. Mathieu crossed his legs, his steady eyes watching my every move.

I preferred sleeping forever over facing what I'm about to.

"What did your father mean when he said I'm your mate, Xavier?"

My eyes flicked to him, and he shifted uncomfortably "I told you about mates. That is what we are. What you are to me. That's why you weren't killed."

I started laughing. I wasn't sure why, but the laughter bubbled to the surface, and I could not hold it in. He was joking. There was no way I was his mate. But they didn't look amused.

I sobered up, and a feeling of foreboding settled on my shoulders.

"You're serious? You can't be serious!"

"A mate can't be harmed," Mathieu said calmly. I sat back, sinking into the sofa's cushions. "Under any circumstances. There has just never been a human mate before. We needed to handle this delicately."

"Delicately? Delicately as in keeping me here by telling me some crap about learning from each other. I knew that didn't make any sense. Why did no one tell me about this?" I looked at Xavier, my rage growing greater by the minute. "How long did the two of you plan on keeping this a secret? This affects my life too." I leaned forward and covered my face with my hands. "This can't be real."

"That's enough, Ruby. It's real, and you need to accept it."

I looked up slowly. I didn't care if Mathieu could kill me with little effort, he was pissing me off. "With all due respect, Mr. Blackwood, don't tell me I need to accept this. I'm not from this world. I just fell into this world! Now I'm his mate? Can you give me a minute to catch up?" I pointed at Xavier and shook my head as I stood up. "You're both lying." My hand fell to my side limply. "You're lying," I said more softly. Xavier took a step toward me but stopped himself from taking another.

He crossed his arms over his chest. Despite the sternness on his face, I could see regret within his eyes. "It's why you got sick the first time we were close to each other. You felt our bond."

His jaws clenched, and my shoulders slumped as I lost what little strength I had to argue with him. Of course, he must be affected by this as well, but why keep a secret like this from me? Sooner or later it would be revealed. So why wait? This was all becoming too much for me.

My face smoothed out, the crease between my brows vanishing. That's why he had kissed me. That's why he had lost his cool that night and saved me. It all made sense now.

He inhaled, and the sudden irritation on his face caused my fading anger to return. If anyone had the right to be irritated right now, it was me. "So you've been planning this since then? That's what you're saying?"

"No. What happened that night wasn't supposed to happen, Ruby. Things were set into motion too quickly. We knew this would be too much for you to handle right now, with you just getting settled here. I figured, maybe if you learned to be comfortable here, telling you that you and I were mates wouldn't be such a devastating blow.

"I couldn't have you leaving the pack. If this were to get to the Council's ears before we had more information, you'd be unprotected out there. None of this was planned. The day you met Natalie in the library, I picked up your scent on her. That's how I found you. But I didn't say anything to her until I visited the diner with her. Your scent seemed off when I had smelled it on her, but I hadn't given it much thought until I saw you and you turned out to be human. That's why you got sick when I saw you. A mate bond being discovered is different for wolves, though. They feel it more. They feel a deep connection or pull between them and their partner, but it doesn't make them sick."

He exhaled as if he had been holding his breath, and my headache grew worse. No wonder he had looked so pissed that day.

Natalie has known all this time as well, and she said nothing!

"This has to be a trick. This has to be a witch's doing."

I spun around to find the stranger who had attacked Xavier leaning on the wall by the door. My sanity was hanging on by a thread here. He was real, the fight was real. So does that mean... No, I can't be his mate, too!

I looked around at Xavier, at the way he was staring daggers at the man, and I finally noticed his ripped shirt and the dried blood on it. I clenched my fists as I looked at the stranger once more.

He was wearing a black leather jacket with his arms crossed over his chest like Xavier. He was taller, however, and more muscular, with a brown complexion and long curly hair tied back in a low ponytail. Where Xavier was refined and polished, he was rougher and more roguish, and he had a leaf earring dangling from his ear.

With everything now calm, I could really stare at him. The dislike that I had for Xavier in the beginning was nothing compared to the disgust in this guy's eyes as he looked at me.

He looked older, mid-twenties maybe. But was that right? Mathieu looked to be in his mid-thirties and I was sure he was older. Was Xavier even twenty-two years old?

"This girl can't be real." He looked me up and down, and I made a face. "A wolf can't have a human mate, let alone the same mate as another wolf. Not even wolves can have two mates. She's a witch." His hazel eyes narrowed at me, and I looked back at him with the same intensity.

"I'm standing right in front of you, so I'm as real as your attitude, and I'm not a witch. Don't worry, I share your disgust, but don't speak as if I'm not standing right here."

He growled at me. In response, I raised a brow and placed my hands on my hips. This guy didn't scare me. Okay, who was I kidding? I was terrified. But he didn't need to know that. He pushed himself off the wall, not satisfied that I hadn't cowered in fear at his little growl. I held my ground as he came closer.

Behind me, Xavier growled, and the stranger stopped in his tracks. "Axel, that's close enough."

Axel.

I narrowed my eyes at him and held my head up. He sneered and unfolded his arms. "I don't have time for this. The mouthy little secret is out now..." I frowned. Who was he calling mouthy? "And the Council is going to hear about it."

Did this fucker just call me "it"?!

He looked Mathieu's way, and his spine straightened as he did so. I was only human, but even I could feel the waves of dominance that radiated off him. Like Mathieu. Was this man an alpha?

"You're fools to think they don't have people placed in your pack solely to watch and report. I don't want any part of this." He looked me up and down again. This time he smiled, but it looked more like an evil sneer to me. "But I think this problem will solve itself. If she isn't claimed by time the Council finds out, we'll both be forced to reject her, and then she'll die anyway."

Natalie

I closed my eyes as I listened to Ruby's soft sobs.

I could tell she was trying to be quiet since she knew she could easily be heard. If I hadn't come to her door, I wouldn't have heard her crying. Instead of knocking, I pulled the door open slowly and entered the room.

With the evening sun lighting the room I easily found her. She was face down on her bed with her face pressed into one pillow and another pillow over her head. I sighed as I approached her bed and sat down. Despite her heart skipping a beat from her fright, she didn't physically jump. She fell silent, and I waited for her to sit up. When she didn't, I tapped her leg.

"Ruby, it's only me." She sat up then, the pillow on her head falling to the floor, and I could see her swollen and bloodshot eyes. "I'm so sorry."

"You could have told me," she said weakly, and I shook my head.

"I couldn't, babe. Alpha's orders. But I wish I could have." I reached out to smooth down her hair, but she suddenly swatted at my hand. I quickly pulled it away.

"You've known all this time, Natalie. You've known I'm Xavier's mate all this time. You all made me think one day I might die, instead of simply telling me I'm Xavier's mate and can't be touched." She chuckled and hung her head. "But even that won't save me. Axel said I'll die when they both reject me. Is Axel really my mate as well?"

I nodded. It had been a shock to everyone when he had arrived for a meeting with Mathieu only to go ballistic after smelling Ruby. Mathieu had tried to calm him, but it had been no use because Xavier returned with her at that very moment.

"He is,"

She slid down to the edge of the bed and sat beside me. When we had first met, there had been this spunk to her, a refreshing attitude. Now it was gone. "Every time my life seems to be making a change for the better, something goes wrong. Maybe both men should reject me, let me die because at this point I don't want to know what's going to happen next."

I picked her hand up and squeezed it gently. "Over my dead body. He only said that because rejection is pretty harmful to a wolf, and if you get sick from just the mate bond being discovered," I made a face, "we think you might die from rejection. Everyone is as confused as you are, honestly; there has never been a human mate. Imagine a piece of string getting knotted. You try to unknot it, but you can't, so the string snaps. That's what rejection is like for a wolf, a bond gets ripped apart. That won't just be hurtful to you, but to the guys, too. The rejected feels it more than the rejecter."

Her voice was low and shaking as she said, "That does sound horrible. I saw Xavier kill that man who had lost his mate. It seems to me with wolves there is just too much that can hurt them." A sad smile appeared on her lips as she moved her hair to one shoulder. "I must be crazy for feeling sorry for Xavier and Axel if either one of them has to go through that. Well, Xavier more than Axel. I don't even know the guy, or like him."

"You just met him, and you didn't like Xavier at first either."

She arched a brow and turned to face me. "Why do you sound like you're on Axel's side, or sympathizing with him or something?"

"Trust me, I'm not. But at the end of the day, he *is* your mate, Ruby. If you don't feel anything for him now, you will. And no matter how much of a dick he might be, he doesn't hate you."

I think.

I have yet to find my mate, and honestly, it's not something I'm excited about. I've never been good with romantic relationships.

She just grunted and fell backward. "Yeah, you didn't see the way he looked at me." Her head lolled to the side, and I leaned down and propped my head on my hand. "Tell me about him, who is he?" she asked.

"He's Axel Grimmwolf. Like Xavier, he's next in line to be alpha. His pack and ours have been rivals for a while. His pack split from ours decades ago. I don't know why, but there has been bad blood for years." I took a deep breath and lay down beside her. No one was going to walk away from this unscathed. I could feel in my bones that a storm was coming. "He was here for a meeting with Mathieu. But while things have been peaceful enough, I think this may have just changed everything. Axel and his pack aren't like ours. They despise humans and are ruthless. To be honest, I can't be sure he won't try to hurt you."

"Now more than ever I won't be able to leave the house, huh?"

I nodded. "Xavier won't want you out of his sight. He might become overbearing, but try to understand why he's protective of you. You're not feeling the pull from the bond like he is. Axel said there might be a spy in our pack for the Council, but that spy was found a long time ago. The Council won't hear about you from us, but now we have Axel to worry about. It's more likely that Axel will reject you than Xavier will, and we don't know what that'll do to you yet. So for now," I gave her the sternest expression I could, "don't leave the grounds unaccompanied."

She rolled onto her stomach, and I did the same, watching her as she pressed her face into the pillow. We stayed like that in silence for a moment and I heard a wolf howling in the distance. It was too far for Ruby to hear it, but I knew it was Xavier.

I couldn't imagine the stress and worry he was now walking around with. He's the son of an alpha, and he'll soon be the alpha, which would make Ruby the pack's luna. No doubt he was worried about the impact that would have; a human as a luna is ludicrous.

"I should have seen something like this coming." Ruby's words were muffled before she turned her head to lie on her cheek. I could see the fresh tears she was desperately trying to hold back. "Things are only going to get worse from here on in. I just know it."

Colorful leaves floated down around me as I walked through the woods. I figured with the pack now knowing that I'm Xavier's mate, I could walk around more freely without thinking someone might kill me.

I was sure the moment I ran into any wolves I'd still get cold stares, but honestly, I wasn't so bothered anymore. I had more important things to think about, like Axel jumping out from behind a tree to reject me.

I needed fresh air. I couldn't handle being trapped in the house another second with my chaotic thoughts, not after what had happened yesterday.

So here I was, out of the house, following a path I had noticed a few days ago. The woods around me were filled with the melodic calls of birds and the wind whistling in the trees above me. I needed this. I needed a moment alone to collect my thoughts and try to piece everything together.

I'm Xavier's mate.

I smiled as I bent down to pick a flower and secure it behind my ear. I then ran a finger over my lips as I remembered the way his lips had felt against mine, the way I had fit so perfectly in his arms.

I now understood why I had given in to that kiss so easily, why my body had seemed to crave more and more of his touch the longer we had been pressed together.

Ever since Natalie and I talked yesterday I haven't been able to stop wondering what it's like for him to have found me. For me, all I had felt was nausea. But what had gone through his mind the moment he had smelled me on Natalie and had known that, whoever this person was, she was his soulmate?

Natalie had said wolves are territorial, so no wonder he had lost his mind and killed those men who attacked me in the alleyway. He had only just found his mate and had to deal with seeing her in danger of being raped.

Voices on the wind made me stop in my tracks, but there was no one in sight. I looked behind me. I couldn't see Xavier's house anymore.

Shit.

I took a deep breath and strained my ears, wishing I had a were-wolf's super-hearing to tell me if I should be running for my life. Instead, I heard laughter and decided to leave the path to see what was happening. It didn't take five minutes before an opening appeared ahead of me.

There was a two-story house and in front of it were seven men and three women, all training. Some were lifting weights, others were stretching. My heart skipped a beat as I saw the rest of the group circling Xavier as he sparred with another man.

He was shirtless, his body glistening in the sun with the sweat covering his body. His hair was damp and sticking to his neck and forehead. I drew closer and took a seat as he and the other man charged at each other and began fighting.

He caught the man in a headlock and then released him. I watched as he explained the move to the onlookers, all of them nodding with understanding, their eyes glued to Xavier.

"So, you're the redhead I've been hearing about."

I looked over my shoulder to find a man with similar red hair to mine grinning down at me. His hair was curly and covered his ears and forehead. He wasn't as bulky as the other men I'd seen around. However, he was smiling at me, and that was a pleasant surprise.

"That's me," I replied, and he walked closer to sit next to me on the log I had claimed for my seat.

He stuck his hand out to me. "The name's Randoll. I'm the beta for this pack." I shook his hand while looking at him skeptically and he chuckled. "Don't worry, I don't bite. It's nice you're getting out of the house."

"Is it?" I asked as I turned my attention back to Xavier, who was now fighting with someone else, a girl with a blonde bob.

"It is," Randoll replied. "Wouldn't you prefer to show who you really are yourself, or would you prefer to have them make up their own stories about you instead? So far, you're just the human at the alpha's house. Well, now we know you're not just a human." He made a sound and I glanced over at him to see his freckle-covered nose scrunched up. "Then again, that has only caused more whispers about you."

This guy was a talker, but that was good. He looked like he'd be happy to tell me anything.

"Is that so? Like what?"

He shrugged. "That you're a witch. That you were created by a witch. Just a lot of witch rumors, honestly."

"I met a witch, Willow. She seemed nice, but I'm starting to get the idea that werewolves and witches aren't friends."

He drummed his hands against his thighs and nodded. "Have you heard about the Salem witch trials? Werewolves helped humans with that massacre. Of course, that was years ago. But hatred and grudges like that are passed down through generations, you know."

"I see." I watched Xavier step away from the group to check on the other wolves who were exercising, and I smiled as he showed one guy the right way to do push-ups. Everyone's eyes were glued to him, and I could understand why. He was obviously skilled, and his movements were fluid.

"So, is it true you're mated to Axel as well? I wasn't there yesterday to see the fight, but news travels fast around here. These morons don't know what it means to capture something as epic as that on video."

I looked over at him and found him already staring at me intently. "Yes," I said as I narrowed my eyes, and to my surprise, he started grinning. "Why are you laughing?"

"That's insane. That's never happened before! Not even to a wolf, and now two wolves have a human mate. The same mate! So, tell me, what was your reaction when you found out about us, that werewolves are real?"

"I was freaked out, yes, but I was also curious to know more, you know? There is a world around humans that we can't see, even though it's right before our eyes."

"So, you didn't get the urge to hunt us with silver knives or anything like that?"

I couldn't help smiling at his face-splitting grin. What was with this guy?

"No, of course not. Why would I do that? You're not monsters to be hunted." His grin flattened for a moment, and I looked down at my hands. "You're people, just like me. You all belong on this earth, just like me. Why discriminate against you all just because you're stronger and faster. That's just jealousy."

"Something humans have in abundance."

I laughed. I liked this guy. He was like the male version of Natalie, although he seemed a little more animated. "Yeah, I know."

I looked up and found a few wolves looking our way, but Xavier's back was turned as he spoke to another wolf. I had forgotten that they could all hear me clearly, and surely now they could hear by my heartbeat that I was panicking because of their sudden attention.

Randoll placed his hand over mine, and my head whipped his way. "You're not what I expected, Ruby." I smiled at him gratefully.

In the distance, a loud growl could be heard. Randoll rolled his eyes and didn't even look. I started looking around frantically only to find Xavier staring daggers at Randoll. His shoulders were moving up and down with his heavy breathing, and a few wolves stepped away from him.

What's his problem?

"So," I drawled as I tore my eyes away from Xavier. "This Council I keep hearing about, what's up with that?"

"Hmm. Humans have a government and wolves have a Council. There are three Council members, so the world is split into three. One governs all of Asia and so on. You get the gist."

I removed the flower that was behind my ear and let it fall to the ground. "Yeah, so fat old men who think they're the shit."

Randoll almost rolled off the log as he busted out laughing. The collar of his shirt shifted to the side, and I squinted my eyes at a faint scar there. Were those teeth marks?

"I really like you, Ruby."

We both looked toward the wolves who were training as a loud crash echoed through the forest. Thick silence followed Xavier dropping two dumbbells, and my eyes widened at seeing they were broken. The wolves around him all looked between him, Randoll, and me.

Seriously, what's his deal?

"That's my cue," Randoll mumbled beside me, and he got up the moment Xavier started heading our way.

"Wait, where are you going?" I yelled to him, but he only waved goodbye over his shoulder.

"I like my life, ma'am. I'll see you around, he's all yours."

When I looked around Xavier was already standing in front of me, his eyes narrowed and his bare chest rising and falling rapidly. He was upset, I could tell, but I wasn't sure why. Was he mad that I was talking to Randoll? I scoffed inwardly. He couldn't be.

Sure, he's my mate, but we aren't together. My eyes slid to the side with that thought, and it suddenly hit me that actually we were. We might not have verbally committed to each other, but if I'm his mate, we're in a relationship, right?

What about Axel?

He threw his shirt over his shoulder, but before he could sit beside me I reached up and grabbed his wrist. He looked at my hand around his wrist as if it was burning his flesh, his eyes growing dark, and I quickly released him.

"Um, can we talk?" I peeped behind him at the wolves who had all gone back to training, "In private?"

He held his hand out to me, and without hesitation, I slid my hand into his. "Come."

He pulled me up, and I regretfully let go of him. He looked down at me for a moment, his breathing much slower, but I couldn't meet his eyes. I couldn't handle his naked chest, slicked with sweat, being in my face. The corner of his mouth twitched as if he knew what I was thinking, and then he turned away.

Weirdo.

We walked into the trees, but I kept silent by his side until we came upon a rocky cliff. I stopped walking when we got close to the edge, but he walked a few more steps before realizing I had stopped.

"What's wrong?"

"I'd rather not get too close to the edge."

He returned to my side. "I thought you feared nothing," he said as he laid his shirt on the ground and pointed at it. "Sit."

I sat down and crossed my legs lotus style. He sat down beside me, long legs stretched out as he leaned back on his hands.

"What made you think that?

He dropped his head back and closed his eyes. "You slapped a werewolf. I'd think only a person without fear would do that."

I jabbed a finger into his side, and he yelped and covered the spot with a hand. "Be quiet." He smiled and his eyes cracked open. "So, are you okay?" I asked.

He closed his eyes once more. "I am."

"Yeah, I don't think the dumbbells you just killed would agree." He didn't say anything or even move, and I turned my body to face him. "Come on Xavier, you're my mate." His eyes cracked open. "You can't be okay with knowing that I also apparently belong to someone else."

He sat up then, and I was struck once more by his beauty. He reached out and tugged on the bun in my hair and watched as my hair tumbled down and over my shoulders. My body grew tense, my heartbeat hammering in my ears, as he inhaled deeply. I knew he was inhaling my scent.

"You're mine, Ruby, no one else's. Remember that."

Now if any other guy had said that to me, I would have punched him in the face. That sounded too much like I was an object to be owned. And while I felt the urge to tell Xavier he was dead wrong about that, I also liked the sound of it.

"I don't care that you're human. The goddess made you my mate, and she doesn't make mistakes. I trust my goddess, but I do have to wonder what the hell she's thinking making you Axel's mate as well." He finger-combed his damp hair backward.

"So, there is someone I can blame for this mess then? What goddess are you talking about?"

He smiled as he looked up at the sky, his eyes following the darkening clouds. "You'll learn about her soon enough. I used to come here every day at sunset and stay until the moon came up. The moon from this spot always looks like it's in reach." He grew serious and his jaws clenched tightly. "I won't let anything happen to you, Ruby. I hope you know that. That's why I've been thinking about taking you to an old Enchanted. She's like Natalie, although way more powerful."

I liked the sound of that. "When can we go?"

"Soon, and hopefully she'll be able to tell us how a human is mated to two wolves. I'll need to let her know we're coming because if the Council finds out about you they'll try to kill you. I have a bad feeling, Ruby, especially about Axel, and my feelings are never wrong."

"Natalie told me his pack hates humans."

He said nothing, but he didn't have to. I could see it on his face. I pulled my knees up to my chest and watched as the grass and flowers around us swayed in the light wind. "Yeah. I'm sorry about all of this," I said.

He cupped my cheek and turned my head toward him. I stopped breathing as his thumb began to move over my cheek. A feeling of belonging blossomed inside me and my eyes fluttered closed as I relaxed into his touch. His thumb glided over my lips and my eyes opened to see him leaning forward, his voice so husky the hairs on my arms stood on end. "Don't be sorry. You have nothing to be sorry about."

He kissed me gently, his lips barely touching mine, but the electricity that surged through my body could power a small city. He had kissed me chastely, but I could feel his emotions in that simple touch.

"I want to see you in your wolf form," I whispered against his lips, and he pulled away but kept his hand on my cheek. "I want to see the real you."

He leaned forward and pressed his lips to my forehead as thunder rumbled in the distance. "You will, but not today. It's going to start raining soon." He stood up and held his hand out to me. "We need to head back."

"So, are you going to carry me on your back or what?"

———

Ruby

My fingers glided along the railing of the staircase as I made my way downstairs. Amid the chaos that is my life, I've found a reason to smile.

I wasn't entirely sure what was between Xavier and me, but after the day I had with him, I was eager to find out. I was petrified of Axel and the Council and the future in general, but in the here and now I had a reason to be happy.

For the first time in a long time, I wasn't being swept away by sadness or thoughts of dying, but from the memory of Xavier's lips on mine. Where my appetite had been off for a while, it had decided to return at 1 a.m. this morning.

I finished my sandwich, did the dishes, and was having a glass of water when a girl walked into the kitchen and took a seat at the island. I recognized her as the girl who had accompanied Xavier the day at the diner.

Why is she wearing a full face of makeup at 1 a.m.?

"You're not his mate."

I inhaled and placed my glass into the sink. I knew sooner or later someone would no longer hide behind their stares and whispers and speak up. "Oh really?"

"Yes, really. You're a weak human, that's all you are. You're not special, and you're not Xavier's mate. You will never be luna."

I smiled and I rested my elbows on the island. "What's your name again? Anna, right? Tell me something, Anna. What did you think was going to happen? You do realize if I'm not Xavier's mate, it still won't be you? Right?"

I walked away and she hopped off the stool to block my way out of the kitchen. Her eyes changed to black as she took a step closer to me, mere inches between us.

"I don't trust you, bitch." She growled. "I'll be right here when Xavier rejects you."

Who did this bitch think she was talking to? I might be human, but I wasn't going to give her the satisfaction of scaring me. She might be a werewolf, but I've met her kind before.

"It's funny how you're not getting it through your thick skull that no matter what happens, you will *never* be luna. I'm not going to fight you for something that I don't even want. Unlike you, I hold no delusions. If I don't become luna, it's not the end of my world. But whether I do or not, it'll be the end of yours. I might not know what being a luna really means, but I can tell right away you're not it. You're being a bitch about a title and a man who will never be yours, honey. Have some self-respect." I flipped my hair over my shoulder and stepped to the side so we were shoulder to shoulder. "Put your fangs away before you hurt yourself."

I walked away and didn't spare a glance backward as I made my way to my room, my bare feet absorbing the cold from the tile. Girls like her exist in all species, I was certain of it. I refrained from stomping my way up the stairs, pissed that she had ruined my good vibes. When I got to the landing of the second floor and glanced out the window, I spotted a man outside.

I looked more carefully, and my eyes widened as he removed his shirt and I realized it was Xavier. I arched a brow as he bent his head from side to side and then rolled his shoulders.

"What the hell are you doing?"

I looked down at my bare feet and then back through the window as he vanished into the dark forest.

"Damn it."

I ran back downstairs and headed outside, the cold air instantly nipping at my exposed legs. I didn't have the time to run to the third floor to get shoes or I'd lose sight of him completely.

The damp cold grass felt nasty between my toes, but I kept walking slowly through the trees, my eyes squinting, nothing but the moon's light keeping me from tripping and falling onto my face.

This was a bad idea. Xavier can navigate the darkness and he's more likely to be the predator out here than the prey. I was the prey.

What sounded like a large branch breaking startled me and a

twig grabbed at my arm as I spun around. I hissed and held my hand up to see a small scratch when I heard another branch break.

Xavier is out here, so if anything jumps out of the bushes at me, I'll scream and he'll save me.

I sank my teeth into my lip as I went in the direction of the snapping branches and soon I could hear groaning. My heartbeat sped up, wondering if it was Xavier and if he could be hurt or wounded. I started walking faster, swatting at the bushes and branches that seemed to be reaching out to me, when suddenly something stumbled into my path.

I jumped back, a scream on my lips, but I swallowed it as I realized it was Xavier. Or at least I thought it was. The werewolf before me was bigger than the ones I had seen, eight feet tall maybe. I stepped back and the creature's head tilted to the side.

I froze, my chest rising and falling rapidly. Seeing those werewolves through a window at a distance was nothing compared to what I was seeing now. The creature tilted its head to the other side and my breath hitched.

"Xavier?" He made a sound like a snort and my need to piss myself vanished. "Gods, you scared me!"

He took a step closer and this time I didn't step back. He made another sound and raised his head to sniff the air before looking down at me once more.

"I saw you from inside the house. I just wanted to see what you were up to."

He suddenly fell onto all fours, and I jumped, a small yelp leaving my lips. He walked forward until I could feel his hot breath on me. Even on all fours, he still towered over me. I took my time admiring him. His fur was light brown with white running from under his chin to his chest.

His tail began to swish behind him, and I moved to the side, my eyes darting from his obsidian ones to his tail. I circled him until I reached his other side, and I held my breath as I reached a hand out.

His tail smacked my thigh, and he snorted through his nose as he quickly moved away.

Is he playing with me right now?

"Be nice or you won't get to kiss me ever again," I said. He growled and I pointed a finger at him. "Don't growl at me."

He shook his head and began sniffing as he came closer once more. I lifted my hand, and he pressed his forehead to it. I closed my eyes as he pushed forward, like a dog begging to be petted, and I shoved my hand into his fur. It was soft and smooth. My body stiffened as he pressed his snout to my chest and inhaled.

"Hey!" I said as sternly as I could muster, but I didn't mind. If anything, I liked it.

I was standing under the half-moon with a werewolf, with my mate, and any onlooker would yell at me to run for my life. But I've never felt safer, barefoot in the woods and all.

He circled me and laid on the ground, his eyes on me almost expectantly. I barely hesitated before sitting beside him and nestling myself into his side. His body was radiating so much heat I soon began to feel drowsy. I must have fallen asleep for a minute because I was jolted awake to find Xavier shifting back into human form.

First, his shoulder snapped, and then his neck. I blinked rapidly, my eyes wide until he was fully human again. He smiled and combed my hair back from my face. I was trying hard not to look at his naked torso.

I started to blush, and his smile widened into a devilish one.

"Stay here with me for a while. I'll be right back. My clothes are in those bushes." He leaned forward and rubbed his nose against my shoulder, and I swear my body started to melt. "I'll keep you warm."

CHAPTER NINE

The more the night had progressed the darker it had gotten, but I knew that wasn't a problem for Xavier. He could see and hear things I couldn't, and he had made a show of having me stand directly in front of him as his eyes transformed to his wolf's eyes, black like the darkness around us. Since I had run out of the house barefoot, I finally got that piggyback ride from him as we made our way back to the house.

I pressed my cold cheek to his warm shoulder as my body swayed with each step he took.

With my eyes closed, I could see him within my mind, the real him. I smiled as I remembered the feeling of his fur between my fingers and his warm body at my back when I had lain beside him. The sudden onslaught of feelings confused me. Were they real, or was my bond to him creating them? If there was no bond between us, would I still find him attractive? Because if the answer to that is no, my feelings couldn't be real.

Who was I kidding? I had found him attractive from the moment I had laid eyes on him in that library. Sure, at the time I only thought he was hot, just not my type, as I had judged his personality without even knowing him.

I wrapped my hands a little tighter around his neck. "What was it like? When you smelled me on Natalie. What happened to you?"

He stepped over a broken branch. "Usually in human form, you can't feel your wolf," he began. "You know it's there, just under your skin, but you can't feel it the way you do when you call it forward to transform. When I smelled you, my wolf awakened on its own. The hairs on my body stood on end, and I felt as though if I didn't find you I'd rip the world apart."

"In the diner, when you got angry, it's because you saw that I was human. I'm human, and no matter the bond we have, I can never be luna. That puts you in a complicated position." I swallowed. "You'll have to reject me."

"A luna is the woman who stands by her alpha's side and offers him strength. A luna has always been a wolf, but there is nothing in our laws that says a luna can't be from another species."

I scoffed at that. "I think that's because it's a given that it can only be a wolf."

"Ruby, I won't reject you and I won't step away from one day being the alpha of this pack. You don't have to take on the duties of being the luna. My dad has been running the pack on his own for years. My mom's passing took a toll on him, but being the alpha, he *had* to pull through."

I frowned. "He didn't end up like the man you killed?"

I could hear the pain in his voice as he replied. "Almost. Something like that takes a toll on a wolf, but some more than others." He cleared his throat and I made a mental note to ask him about his mother another time. I had noticed Mathieu's wedding ring but the lack of a mate. "The point is, a luna is important, but not mandatory for a pack's survival."

"So, it's like cereal tasting better with milk, but you can still eat it without."

He chuckled and nodded his head. "Yes, exactly, but you don't have to worry about any of that right now. One step at a time. That means contacting the Enchanted as soon as possible."

I knew the thought of losing me was painful to Xavier; I could hear it in his voice whenever the topic of losing a mate arose. I was just as scared of dying as I had been when I first came here, but now I simply couldn't stand the thought of what might happen to him if I... No, no, I won't think like that.

No one knows the future, but I had to believe I wouldn't die this young. However, I hadn't been able to get what Axel had said out of my mind. What if I really was created by a witch? But to do what, exactly? In a world of the impossible being possible, a weak human mating a werewolf was the impossible made possible. I'm surrounded by werewolves, a species that shouldn't exist, yet still, I'm the puzzle among them.

Xavier stopped walking, his head turning to the left and then right, and I lifted my cheek off his shoulder. As I felt his body growing tense, I grew nervous. What would make a werewolf nervous at night, in the middle of his own woods?

"Xavier?"

"Shh."

Oh god!

He tapped my thigh, and I untangled my legs from around his waist so he could place me gently onto the ground. My eyes were wide as they looked around, but whatever Xavier was seeing or hearing, I couldn't.

"Ruby, I want you to go back to the house." He stepped away from me. "Now." He began removing his shirt and instead of backing away, I approached him. He stopped me with just a look. "Run!"

I jerked my hand away as he yelled. His voice was contorted and deeper as his shoulders hunched forward. Before I could ask what was going on, I got my answer. A werewolf barreled out of the bushes and Xavier stepped protectively in front of me, punching the wolf in the face and sending him flying backward.

Xavier began to shift, his skin tearing and ripping, his body growing in size. With it, his pants began to rip until there was nothing but shredded clothes on the ground. My body was shaking with terror, my eyes wide, and my hand clutching at my heart. My brain was telling my legs to get the hell out of here, but I couldn't.

The wolf Xavier had hit reappeared, and my legs finally started to comply with the commands coming from my brain when a second wolf appeared, its eyes on me. I stepped back and the new werewolf stepped in my direction, only to be blocked by Xavier.

Xavier howled, and I winced and covered my ears as the sound rolled up to the sky like a peal of thunder. It was like nothing I'd ever heard before, and my body shook with its force. His howl was met with two others, and I turned and ran.

I pumped my legs hard as I ran through the forest. Branches tugged at my clothes and scratched at my skin, but with the battle I could hear behind me, the animalistic growls and snapping branches, I was more worried about Xavier. He was more capable than I was, clearly, but why weren't there wolves out patrolling or something? Were those two wolves from this pack?

Tears began rolling down my cheeks as I heard one of the wolves cry out behind me. The sound was horrific, and I prayed to any god that could hear me that Xavier would be safe.

My legs were aching and no doubt bleeding, but I couldn't stop running. I had to get back to the house and let everyone know what was happening. What the hell was even happening? Who were those wolves?

Lights from the house appeared ahead, and I began screaming. Someone must have heard Xavier. There had to be someone already outside and heading to the woods. Someone had to hear me!

"Help! Help me!"

The lights from the house grew brighter the closer I got and I swatted at the tears that were blurring my vision. This can't be happening, not now! At every turn, whenever I have a moment of joy and peace, it's immediately taken away from me. I'm sick of it!

"Help me!"

I saw the wolf a second too late.

I saw its fangs and claws just as I was slammed into a tree, as pain blossomed throughout my body. I crumpled to the ground, groaning and hugging my midsection, and a massive clawed paw was the last thing I saw before I was consumed by darkness.

———

Xavier

My fists came down hard on the island, breaking a chunk of the marble off and leaving the rest cracked. Everyone who had been speaking fell quiet as my growl rumbled through the house. My wolf was losing its mind, and I was quickly losing control.

She's gone. Ruby's gone!

"We'll find her," Natalie said, but her soft voice wasn't offering me comfort.

I started pacing back and forth, my eyes closed, as I clenched and unclenched my fists. Ruby's smile kept flashing within the darkness in my mind. I kept seeing the fascination that had been on her face only a few hours ago when she had seen my true form.

I had been worried about scaring her, but she hadn't been scared at all, not in the least. I felt like a fool for thinking she would run for the hills.

Ruby's strong, she's brave, and whoever had taken her was going to die a million deaths by my hand.

I had heard her screaming for help when suddenly the two wolves I had been fighting turned and ran. They had been nothing but a distraction. They had done their job of keeping me busy while someone else went for Ruby. I never should have told her to run back to the house without me.

"Fuck!" My fist went through the fridge, and my dad walked up to me and placed his hand on my shoulder. "We tracked the wolves far east before their scents just vanished, Dad. Her scent as well. Those wolves aren't from any pack I know, so who the fuck were they?"

He squeezed my shoulder and I held his stare as he spoke. "We have wolves out right now looking for her, so the second someone finds something, anything, we'll know. I also sent Anna to get Willow. Maybe she'll be able to do a location spell to find Ruby. We'll find her, Xavier."

I ran my hand down my face, pulling the skin taut as I looked at Natalie and Randoll, both of them sporting angry expressions. "I want her back," I told them, and Natalie nodded.

"We'll find her," Natalie replied. I could see that she too was trying to control her rage. I knew she blamed herself for everything that had happened because if it was not for her, I wouldn't have found Ruby at all.

But I could never blame her for bringing my mate into my life.

"Do you think it's the Council?" Randoll asked as he looked between my father and me. My dad shook his head.

"I don't think so," he replied, his eyes on the broken island. "This isn't the way the Council does things, but we also can't overlook them. I can reach out to my contact, but doing that means they'll learn about Ruby if they weren't the ones who took her."

I placed my elbows onto the island and began rocking back and forth. "No. We can't risk that. We'll find out who did this *when* we find Ruby."

The feeling of panic and rage I had experienced the night Ruby had almost been raped was returning with a vengeance. That night I had been there. I had been able to act swiftly. But now I had no idea what danger she was in. I had no idea what was being done to her while we all stood around chatting.

"Maybe it's rogue wolves," Randoll suggested, and I nodded in agreement. Rogue wolves are rare but real. Most of them become mercenaries for anyone who will purchase their services, so it's possible rogues were hired to take Ruby. "My question is this, how would rogue wolves even know about her unless someone in this pack broke Dad's command to not speak of her to outsiders?"

"I'll call a meeting. I'll find out if someone here betrayed us." My dad left the kitchen and Natalie and Randoll shared a look. Disobeying my father is rare because everyone knows he can be as cruel as he can be kind.

"How are Jackson and Raven?" I asked Randoll. They were the wolves assigned patrol duty tonight. He sighed heavily. That was a bad sign.

"They're in pretty bad shape, but alive."

Natalie turned away. "I'll go to her room and find something that her energy is tied to strongly. Willow will need it."

My dad walked back into the room as he pocketed his phone and Natalie stopped in her tracks. The look on his face gave me pause, a sick feeling settling in my gut.

"They picked up her scent. Her blood was found, but there's no way to track it. Her scent started and ended where they found the blood."

I began taking deep breaths as my urge to shift grew stronger. In times of heightened emotions an accidental shift can happen, and losing my shit right now wouldn't help anyone. It wouldn't help Ruby.

They had found her blood. Those fuckers were dead men walking! I went to walk past my dad when he grabbed my arm. He looked at me, his eyes narrowed before he looked at Randoll and Natalie as well. "Something's coming and Ruby's going to have a big part to play. We need to find her. The goddess doesn't make mistakes."

———

Ruby

·   ·   ·

My bones ached as if they had all been broken and then reset and were on their way to healing. I was at a loss for why my body felt so fucked up, but I remained still until my throbbing headache eased.

I inhaled and my nose crinkled from a horrible stench.

What the hell is that?

I cracked one eye open, but surprise soon had my other eye popping open as well. Why was there a stone ceiling above me?

I bolted upright as I realized I was in a dimly lit dank cell and not my room at Xavier's house. An odd heaviness on my left leg pulled my attention and my heart started pounding harder at the sight of a chain attached to my ankle.

What the fuck is going on?

My headache returned in an unpleasant wave, and I hunched over and held my head. Images began flashing within my mind, of me running into the forest, of Xavier's wolf hitting me with his tail, of a strange werewolf attacking me and sending me flying through the air.

"Fuck," I said under my breath as all my memories returned to me, and my mouth went dry as I took a closer look at the cell I was in. There was the bed I was sitting on and an old, disgusting toilet but nothing else. With only a single window high above the bed, I was sitting on, very little light was coming into the room.

It was enough, however, for me to suddenly see someone standing in the shadows outside my cell. I swung my legs off the bed, the chain on my leg slowing me down, but I got to my feet and dragged myself forward.

"Who are you? What am I doing here?" The person didn't move or speak, and my nostrils flared. "Hey, dipshit! What the fuck am I doing here? What do you want?" The chain stopped me before I could reach the bars separating me from the creep who was watching me.

"Answer me! Let me out of this nasty-ass cell right now!"

"So, you're the human mate." My mouth slammed shut at the deep booming voice of my watcher. "I was expecting more. Even for a human, you look so fragile."

"Yeah, how about you unchain me, and you'll see what this fragile human can do, huh?"

The man chuckled, and a chill went down my spine that had nothing to do with how cold it was. My breathing became labored, and I suddenly felt overwhelming fatigue. How the hell was I going to get out of this?

Being a bitch won't help you.

I gritted my teeth at the voice in my head and did my best to straighten my spine. "Look, you've got the wrong girl okay? I have nothing, literally nothing, that anyone wants. Let me out of here, please."

"Oh, you're the right girl."

My shoulders slumped and my head fell back. "What do you want? Tell me what it is you want then."

"Oh, you'll find out soon enough. What are you?"

I frowned at that. Did I smell like a wolf or something? Because that was the only reason this person could be asking me such a stupid question. I bit my tongue to hold back my sarcastic response and tilted my head to the side.

"What do you mean? Can't you tell that I'm human?"

The man tsked. "No, you're not. No human can be mated to a wolf, and you're mated to two. You're not human, and I'm going to figure out what you are."

"Look, buddy, all of this is a shock to me as well, okay? I'm human. Just unlucky enough to be the first to be mated to a wolf... or wolves."

The shadow moved as if the person had planned on stepping into the light, but they froze. "If it was up to me, I'd kill you." I clenched my fists at my sides and I bit the side of my cheek. If this guy's plan was to scare me shitless, it was working. I couldn't believe it. At first, I had thought I was in hell being at Xavier's house, but that was a palace compared to where I found myself now. "But it's not up to me, not yet. News of a human being mated to a wolf can never get out. Weak wolves like Alpha Mathieu who think they can live peacefully with humans will never hear of this. They'll never think it's possible to bond with humans."

The man turned to leave, and the words tumbled from my lips before I could stop them. "He's going to find me you know!" He paused but didn't turn around. "Xavier is going to find me, and when he does, whoever the hell you are, you're going to be sorry! You hear me! Sorry!"

He continued walking and a door opened, blinding me. "Help! Help me!"

The door slammed shut, leaving me alone in the empty cell as I continued to scream.

Please find me, Xavier, please.

CHAPTER TEN
NATALIE

Willow hadn't been able to locate Ruby, and it had only enraged Xavier further. However, using the scratch that Xavier got on his arm from brawling with one of the strange wolves, she had been able to locate that wolf.

Xavier hadn't waited a second before he was out the door with Randoll and six others.

I was left behind to help Mathieu with creating a mental link with the entire pack to see who had gone against his command and told someone about Ruby. Creating a mind link is allowed only under specific circumstances. Alphas demand total obedience, and once an order is given it's almost impossible to disobey. But some wolves are strong enough to overpower the will of their alpha. In circumstances like this, a mind link through an Enchanted may be done.

It's taxing on an Enchanted, however, having all the thoughts and memories from the pack flowing through their minds to then be sent to the alpha. No one was guilty of talking about Ruby, though, and it left us with more questions than answers.

There was a time when the Enchanted were shunned, beaten, or killed for not being able to transform. Different is rarely accepted in the werewolf community. A she-wolf who can't trans-form, but can delve into the minds of others, who can see the past and get glimpses of the future, was a little too different for most werewolves.

I'm happy to have been born in a time when I don't have to live in hiding from humans *and* wolves. Would a time come when I wouldn't have to live in hiding from humans as well? Was Ruby's existence the start of a new world?

I've heard that some Enchanteds get so powerful they are almost like witches. If only I had those powers, I'd be able to find Ruby. I'd be able to break through that wall in her mind and see what lies behind it. I'm still young and my powers are still develop-ing, so there's only so much I can do, but there is someone else who is able to do much more. So before Xavier had left, he had asked me to find the only Enchanted he knew of who could help.

Raindrops pummeled my body as I walked briskly through the street, people running in all directions to get out of the sudden downpour. I spotted my destination on the other side of the street and dashed across as lightning flashed overhead.

I pushed the door of the shop open and stepped inside, water dripping off my body and onto the wooden floor.

The shop was dark, lit by only a few candles, and the air was thick with the smell of incense. I looked around at the shelves that lined the walls, all stacked with books, jars of liquids and powders, and other mysterious objects.

"You're three minutes late," a woman said as she entered the shop through a curtain of beads at the back of the room. "At least I was right about the rain," she mumbled under her breath as she approached me and handed me a towel.

Her eyes were white, completely white, and so was her hair, which was in messy dreads and piled high on top of her head. She was shorter than me, five foot four maybe, with bracelets covering both her arms and crow's feet at the corners of her eerie eyes.

"How did you know I was coming?" I asked.

She dismissed my question with a wave of the hand and turned away. "Child, don't insult me. One day you'll be able to do the same." She pointed a finger at me over her shoulder. "You're a strong one. I can sense it. You'll possess greater powers than I." She stopped at the curtain of beads and looked back at me. "Are you coming, or do you plan on standing at my door the whole day?"

I dried my hair as much as I could as I followed her through the curtain and stepped into a very modern-looking living room. What a contrast from the dark gloomy shop! It was brightly lit and aesthetically furnished in black and white. There was even an electric fireplace.

"Um, you're Adolfa right?"

The woman nodded and took a seat before waving her hand to the sofa. "Sit. Xavier sent you, and we need to get this over with quickly." She folded her wrinkled hands together in her lap as I sat down. "Times are quickly changing, and I'll be leaving soon."

I narrowed my eyes at her. She has to be blind. There is no way her eyes look like that and she's not blind. I waved my hand. "I'm sorry, but are you blind?"

"In one sense of the term, but my inner eyes show me everything I need to see. Stop waving your hand."

My hand fell onto my lap. "Sorry. So, where are you going? You said you'll be leaving soon," I asked her, and she laughed and reclined in her chair.

"Do you know how people like us were created?"

I shook my head and then remembered she couldn't see me. "No."

"Many wolves worship our goddess, but they don't believe she really exists. Yet they've all met her through an Enchanted. Did you know that the first Enchanted was the goddess's half-human child? To meet an Enchanted is to meet the goddess. So, if we're being honest, all Enchanted are royalty. They all have divine blood."

She has to be joking right? Why had no one told me this before?

I looked down at my hands as if I could find confirmation

there that what she was saying was true. I'm a descendant of the goddess? Why isn't this widely known? Enchanted are still looked down upon even now in some parts of the world. Some accept us, but others are just polite and skilled at hiding their disgust.

"I didn't know that. Why isn't this widely known? Enchanteds are teased and bullied, called witches when in reality we're demigods."

She raised her hands and shook her head. "Now, now, while we do have the goddess's blood, we only have a little of it. As centuries have gone by, we've lost our power. Its potency has been diluted as our bloodline was mixed with those of normal wolves. We aren't demigods, Natalie, and werewolves have forgotten a lot. Maybe too much. And they're going to pay for their negligence. I'm not one to support the Council, but they do their best to preserve our history and our origins."

"And Ruby? You knew I was coming, so you must know about her."

A smile began to grow on her lips, an answer without words. She knew whom I was talking about. I had known it. Deep down I had known Ruby was special from the moment I had seen her. I was, however, also an expert at knowing that in this world there is no one more hated than a supernatural that is different than other supernaturals. I might not be able to see Ruby's future, but I know she'll be facing a lot of backlash for merely existing. No human I've met has ever had such a pure white aura.

"Mm, yes." Adolfa interlocked her hands under her chin, her nails long and pointed, their tips black, and I watched closely as she closed her eyes. "Young Ruby...she has her father's hair."

Her father?

I sat forward, my heart skipping a beat. Was she seeing her?

With being so caught up with everything that had been happening, I never thought to ask Ruby about her life before she had moved here. It was clear it hadn't been a life filled with rainbows and unicorns, but where had she come from?

Mathieu would have done a background check on her, surely. But as her friend, I should have asked, and for that, I felt horrible.

"Why did the goddess allow her to be mated to two wolves, and two future alphas at that? Nothing good can come from this. A human being mated to one wolf would have been bad enough. But two? This is a problem, for everyone."

"Indeed it is my child, indeed it is. But the goddess doesn't make mistakes."

I sighed with exasperation and rubbed at my forehead. "Yes, I keep hearing that, like there is something I'm missing like there is something I should know. I'm here to find out what that thing is. She was taken, Adolfa. Someone abducted her."

She nodded. "I know." She opened her eyes once more and I frowned as they began to dart frantically from left to right. "Ruby isn't the problem, Natalie." She stood up and walked over to me as she reached out and cupped my cheek.

"Then what is she?"

Her wrinkled face brightened with an almost sinister grin, and before I knew what was happening she shoved one of her fingernails into my forehead. My body went as stiff as a board and then jerked as she pressed her nail deeper.

My body grew cold, and I breathed out through my mouth, unable to move as I stared at the fog my breath created. The world around me began to fall away. She began speaking under her breath, and my eyes rolled back. My mouth slowly gaped open, and a scream was torn from my chest.

Xavier

As it was daytime, transforming wasn't an option. Our senses would be heightened, but the risk was too great, so we stayed in human form as we surrounded the warehouse.

The warehouse was less than a mile away from where Ruby's blood had been found and her scent didn't go past this warehouse. Even though I was right outside, I still could not smell the unknown wolves. A wolf has never been able to block their scent so completely.

With each passing second of not having Ruby in my arms, I grew more and more aggravated. I had only just found her; we were just getting close, and now she's gone.

She's not gone forever!

I clenched my fists before looking to my left and nodding to Randoll, his signal to move forward. He nodded in response and whistled, and the wolves who had surrounded the warehouse charged in.

Yells, growls, and loud crashes could be heard as they stormed inside. While we were unable to smell these wolves, I was certain they could smell us and had been preparing for our attack. But were they as pissed off as we were? They came onto my land, our land, and took one of ours.

"Maim, not kill! Not until I have answers!" I reminded my pack.

I had to hold myself back from joining the fight, for I wouldn't be able to stop myself from killing, and we needed information. My wolf was scratching beneath my skin to be released. He was begging to take over so he could go on a rampage to find his mate.

Doing that would get me nowhere; dead men don't speak.

"We'll find her." I said under my breath, my gums tingling with the need to sink my teeth into something. "Calm down."

I entered the warehouse and inhaled the pungent smell of old iron and waste. My nose crinkled in disgust. The place was run down, but it was clear these wolves had been using it as a home, or maybe just a meeting place.

Two wolves were battling it out with four of my men, but they stood no chance. I inhaled deeply, trying to find Ruby's scent through the onslaught of smells around me, but I couldn't smell anything. She wasn't here.

"Xavier!" Randoll yelled. But I was on guard and ready for a fight. I spun around and landed an uppercut on the man who had been trying to sneak up on me.

He staggered away from me and wiped at the corner of his mouth as blood instantly bubbled to the surface. I narrowed my eyes at a deep cut on his neck and my fangs elongated. "You. You were there last night."

He smiled at me and my wolf howled so loud within my head my vision blurred. My thirst for blood had me ripping my shirt off. "Where is she?" He began removing his shirt as well and I widened my stance as he hunched forward, his nails piercing the tips of his fingers like needles. "I'll only ask once more, where is she?"

"Not here." The man growled.

He charged at me, but a gunshot echoed in the space around us. The man was thrown to the side, blood spraying as he fell to the ground.

Scanning the warehouse, I saw Randoll lower his gun. I turned back to the dying wolf, black lines spreading from the wound.

I stepped over to him. His eyes glared at me with hatred, and I sighed and folded my arms over my chest. "I don't have time to fight with you. Tell me where she is, and I'll give you a quick death." The lines were spreading quickly, and he began to wheeze. "There is wolfsbane in that bullet. The poison will keep spreading. Speak up, and I'll help you. Who hired you to take her? Where is she?"

He started laughing and the neutral, impassive look on my face disappeared. I reached down, my hand shifting as I did so, and my claws wrapped around his throat. I picked him up, lifting the six-foot-two man off the ground as if he weighed less than Ruby before slamming him back down, the floor cracking beneath him.

Blood bubbled to his lips and spilled from the sides of his mouth and his cry pierced the silence around us as the nails on my other hand sank into his thighs, cutting through flesh and bone.

"How are you able to hide your scent?"

Harming another wolf, enemy or not, was something I hated and never took joy in doing. But in this case, they fucked with the wrong girl, and they deserved what was coming to them.

"Where is she?" I yelled and the man grew still. He was still breathing shallowly, and I bared my teeth as he began to smile.

He stuck his tongue out, and my eyes widened at the small pill on the tip. I removed my hand from his thigh and grabbed at his face, but he had already swallowed the pill. The reaction was instant as he began to shake and foam at the mouth.

I released him as the other two wolves my men had secured started foaming at the mouth as well, their hands and legs twisting in odd directions as their eyes rolled back.

"The fuck?" Randoll said under his breath, a look of surprise passing between him and the other wolves.

I saw red.

I punched a pillar to my right, breaking it in half, and the roof of the warehouse groaned almost in pain. I howled so loudly an already cracked window shattered as I stormed outside.

"Burn it down!"

My phone began ringing and every fiber in my being was telling me to throw the thing into a wall. I need her! I need her back!

Natalie was the only hope left now, and I hoped she had gotten some information from the old Enchanted I had asked her to see. If not, we'd be officially lost, with no way of finding her from this point. The first few hours of a person going missing or being taken are the most crucial. We barely have anything to go on as it is.

"Yes, Dad?" I answered.

"Xavier, what did they say?"

I sighed and placed my hand on my forehead, my temples

throbbing. "Nothing. The fuckers just took some kind of pill and offed themselves. We got nothing!"

I heard something shatter in the background, and I clenched my teeth. "Then we have a serious problem."

"What is it?"

"Get back to the house."

My hold on the phone tightened, and I heard a crack as I switched it from one ear to the next. "Damn it, Dad, just say it. What is it?"

There was a long pause. The longer the silence stretched the more my body began to shake with panic. "Natalie is missing, and Adolfa is dead."

———

Ruby

I jerked awake and looked around. When I realized I was still in the dreary cell, I closed my eyes and turned onto my side. I had hoped that the man in the shadows and the chain around my ankle were just a bad dream.

But as usual, I never get what I want. The universe has been dishing out shit to me since the moment I was born.

Waking up and finding Xavier watching me while I slept was something I'd pick over this any day of the week. I missed him. I missed him so much, fresh tears sprang to my eyes and threatened to fall. I squeezed my eyes closed to stop them and tried to remember what it felt like to have his warm body close to mine.

Whoever abducted me might be watching me right now, might be listening, and I wouldn't give them the satisfaction of seeing or hearing me cry. I wanted to scream at the top of my lungs, but what would that change? My hair was tangled so badly my fingers could not run through it, and I didn't need heightened senses to know that I was starting to smell funky.

None of that would be changed by my screaming and losing my voice in the process.

I wasn't sure how much time had passed since I'd been here, but I'd seen two days and one night come to an end and now it was nighttime again. I'd been sleeping nonstop, and wouldn't be surprised if at some point I'd slept through an entire day.

Am I going to die here?

I missed Natalie as well, and her perky warmth and ability to make me feel better. I felt alone, utterly alone in this place, and I was starving! I was starting to feel weak, my body in need of sustenance. Only once since I'd been here had I woken up to find bread and water inside my cell, but since then I'd had nothing to eat or drink.

'What are you?'

The shadow man's question whispered in my mind, and I took a deep breath. What I am is cursed, that's what I am. All I had wanted was to get an education, to earn my degree and pray that it would be something to change my life for the better.

Two weeks in, and the shit had hit the fan.

My stomach growled and I turned onto my other side, now facing away from the window, and my heart stopped as yet again someone was standing in the shadows. This time I remained still, too weak to get up anyway.

I couldn't see the man's face, but I could feel his eyes on me. So I stared back, my eyes blinking slowly.

"Are you hungry?"

"No, I've been eating all day. I'm kind of full, thanks."

Dumbass, of course I'm hungry!

I realized this was a different voice. It wasn't as gravelly and painful to the ear, but still deep and husky, like the voice a man has when he just wakes. I placed my hand under my cheek and narrowed my eyes.

"You're not the man from before. Are you able to tell me why I'm here or will there be someone else coming to watch me in the dark after you?"

"Something really needs to be done about your smart mouth."

Who the hell is this guy?

"Sorry, there is no cure." I sat up but left my leg with the chain on the bed while the other hung over the edge. "So, who are you? It's creepy to watch someone while they sleep."

"It's not creepy if the person I'm watching is my mate."

I tasted blood in my mouth as I bit down on my tongue when Axel stepped out of the shadows. I clenched my fists and got off the bed, dragging myself closer to the iron bars. I eyed him up and down, and my stomach turned as a sickening smirk grew on his lips.

"What the hell are you doing, Axel? What's going on?"

He buried his hands into his jeans pockets and shrugged. "Isn't it obvious?"

"No, it's really fucking not. What's going on? How are you even doing this? I thought mates couldn't hurt each other."

I couldn't believe what I was seeing. Was the man before me really Axel? It looked like him, dark clothes, dark smirk and all. It was him. I saw his eyes look down at my ankle quickly before they met my angry stare once more.

"Who told you that?" He crossed his arms over his chest. "You'd have to be my mate for that to apply."

"You just said I am your mate!"

"Be quiet, child!"

Child?

I recoiled as his yell stung my eardrums and he walked forward until he was holding onto the bars. His eyes were burning with such hatred I looked away, confused at the tightness within my chest. How can he hate me so much? He doesn't even know me.

My voice was low when I spoke, almost unrecognizable to me. "I didn't ask for this. I didn't ask for any of this."

His hands fell away from the bars and I looked at him, his face now smooth but his eyes still intense. "Neither did I, but this happened anyway, and now it will be handled. I don't want you."

"Reject me then."

His eyes lowered into slits and I held his stare the way I had in the living room days before. Silence reigned around us as we stared at each other, and I crossed my arms over my chest. His eyes followed my every move, and I arched a brow to show that I was waiting for his response.

"Reject me."

"Well, aren't you brave? I don't know what rejecting you will do to me just yet. You're human. This is unknown territory. Maybe you were created for this, to have me reject you and I get hurt instead. I have a lot of enemies who want to see me fall."

"That's not surprising." He shook his head, and I shifted my weight from one leg to the other. "You know, one wouldn't peg you for a nut job just by looking at you. Do you even hear what you're saying? For the last time, I wasn't *created*. I'm a real person!"

I stepped forward, but the chain dug into my leg, making me wince. I saw the way his face twitched as his eyes looked down to my leg, and I felt a flicker of hope. No matter how much he pretended to hate me, he was still affected by our bond.

Maybe I could play on the bond's strength, get through to him by begging. "Please, Axel, don't do this. Let me out of here, please."

His head tilted to the side as he regarded me curiously. I felt like an animal at a zoo. His eyes roamed up and down my body, and I grew self-conscious.

"You really think that will work on me, don't you?"

I frowned.

"Do you think batting your lashes and flipping your hair will get you out of this?" He held onto the bars once more. "This is real life, Ruby. Charm won't get you out of this. Xavier's weak. It's not surprising he fell for you, but I won't. You're a *human*, a weakling. You're not fit to be my mate."

His words stung me more than I expected, and I bit my tongue again to stop the tears burning behind my eyes from breaking free. "Then what will get me out of this? Tell me! Tell me what I need to do or just reject me. Reject me and be free of me then, instead of telling me over and over again how much I disgust you. You can't stand the sight of me, and that is clear. I'm not your biggest fan, either. But don't keep me down here. This won't change the fact that I'm your mate. You don't want me, but Xavier does. Let me go back to him."

His jaws visibly clenched at the mention of Xavier's name and his low growl had me stepping back. I wasn't blind, I could see the killer within his eyes. I had seen it from the first time we met.

He and Xavier are like night and day. Xavier brought the sun to my world, but Axel was darkness personified.

"No." He replied, his voice low and almost inaudible. He turned his back to me, and I stared at him. I didn't need him to like me or love me, I just needed him to let me go. I hadn't asked to be his or Xavier's mate. Why punish me like this? There had to be more to this story.

"Why are you punishing me like this? Did a human do something to you?"

He spun around. "Are you serious? What are you doing? Do you think I'm going to open up to you?" He laughed, but it held no humor. "I'll reject you soon enough, so sit tight. Do you want to know why you're here? I've been trying for years to be rid of the Blackmoon Pack. They're weak, they aren't real wolves, and they're the ones sitting on prime land while my pack has to settle for scraps. Now you've presented the perfect chance for me to strike."

I stepped back until the back of my leg hit the bed. "W-what do you mean?"

"Aww, you thought this was about you and this mate bullshit? Sure, I can't stand the thought of you being my mate, but you, little Ruby, you just single-handedly brought down an entire pack." A sick feeling began to settle in my chest as he backed away until he was cloaked in darkness again. "You see, humans always bring destruction, and this will all be blamed on you. Let's see if Xavier loves you after that."

The door opened and he vanished through it.

I collapsed onto my bed as I hugged myself, my tears finally breaking free. My breathing started coming out in sharp gasps as I slid off the bed and onto the cold floor. No, no, what did he mean by saying I brought down the Blackmoon Pack?

I looked toward the door through the iron bars and started sobbing. Whatever he's planning, Xavier won't fall for it. He won't. I pulled my knees up and rested my forehead on them, and for the first time since being in this cell, I cried until I lost all the strength in my body and fell unconscious.

Luna Captured

Book Two

CHAPTER ONE

RUBY

Have you ever been so hungry that your stomach feels like it's caving in on itself? So thirsty you can barely pry your tongue from the roof of your mouth? Your mind focuses on nothing but food and drink, drink and food. How a stale piece of bread, a glass of water, or a single French fry might save your life.

If you've never felt that, you're lucky, and I hope you never do. I wasn't suffering from hunger only. My hair was matted to my skull, and I was getting sick of my own foul odor. I'd lost track of how long I'd been chained up in Axel's dungeon, and I was passing out more frequently due to hunger and dehydration.

My eyes cracked open as I listened to the dripping water coming from somewhere inside this dark dungeon. It was making this situation a hundred times worse. Every time I heard it, I thought about how even one tiny drop in my mouth might make this situation a little more bearable.

My tongue felt like sandpaper, and my back felt sore from lying down for so long. I, however, didn't have the strength to turn onto my side. My eyes started to sting with what should have been tears, and I lifted a shaky hand to brush them away. But no tears came. My body had none to spare....

My hand fell to my side as my body was wracked with sobs.

This is what my life has come to. Over the years I've endured my share of horrible hardship but this, this takes the cake. I had finally accomplished my dream of getting into college and now, less than two months later, I've been abducted by a werewolf with a vendetta. Yes, werewolves are real. I had the rotten luck of being mated to not just one, but two werewolves. One hates me, and the other was just starting to warm up to me before I was taken away from him.

Axel has locked me in a dungeon, while Xavier had convinced his father to let me live with him and his pack. Where Xavier is sweet, quiet, and calm, Axel is crude and cruel. They are polar opposites, as apparently are their dueling packs. Whoever their goddess is that has done this to me, I need to have a talk with her. I had wasted time thinking Axel would reject me because I'm not a wolf, never realizing he had other plans until it was too late.

I sighed and found the strength to roll unto my side. The chain on my ankle felt much heavier than it had earlier since my strength was quickly diminishing, and it took a few tries before I was able to move my leg.

Axel's threat that he was going to use me to get rid of Xavier's pack replayed in my mind yet again, and my dehydrated body managed to spare a tear. I had no idea how he planned on using me to accomplish that, but whatever his plan was, he would fail. I was pretty sure he would fail, anyways. Mathieu and Xavier's pack didn't seem like they would be easy to take down.

Why do I have to be the first human to be mated to a werewolf? And two at once? This is all new to me, and them as well. Even if Xavier were to find me and free me from Axel's chains, I would still have to worry about the fact that the Werewolf Council, their governing body, is after me as well.

There won't be an end to this unless I die. That's becoming clear.

My life has been nothing but a series of unfortunate events since I was a child. I'm tired of it all. Weeks ago I was a normal college girl trying to get through life with a bright future ahead of her, and now I am wasting away in a dungeon waiting to see how I will die (and at whose hands). That's just the kind of shit that would happen only to me.

The door to the dungeon opened. With my back turned, I didn't bother to look around. Whoever it was, they would leave eventually if I pretended to be asleep. My heartbeat accelerated when I heard keys jiggling in the lock to my cell and then, rusted hinges screeching.

Someone was coming into my cell, and whomever it was could most definitely hear my heartbeat. I remained still, now frozen with fear when I heard footsteps approach me. A warm hand grabbed me by my hair.

"Get off me!" I screamed.

I was yanked onto my feet, and then thrown back down onto the small bed. I looked up into Axel's hazel eyes as I sunk my teeth into my lips. Natalie, the only wolf that has been kind to me from the start, had told me mates can't hurt each other. Clearly, that had been bullshit.

He bent down and began to remove the chain from around my ankle before rising to his towering height again. My heart was pounding, my eyes wide as I watched him. He didn't speak. He didn't even look at me before throwing the chain to the side and grabbing my arm.

"You're hurting me! What are you doing?"

His tight hold on my arm would leave a bruise, but I was too scared to care. He was dragging me out of the cell and outside, my weak legs struggling to keep up with him. Fresh air filled my lungs, and my eyes closed for a second before I was yanked forward to keep up with him.

"Where are you taking me?" He didn't answer. "Axel, where are you taking me? Please, you're hurting me!"

I channeled what little strength I had left into pulling away from him. He released me, but within seconds he grabbed me by the hair. Fire blossomed at my scalp, my hair felt like it was going to be ripped out, and I clenched my teeth to stop myself from screaming. My eyes grew teary as I reached up to hold his hand, and I felt him loosen his hold. I could barely see his face, but his eyes were like headlights.

He continued walking, and I dug my heels into the ground to not move and started screaming. If he was going to kill me, I wasn't going to die quietly. Oh, hell, no! I didn't ask to be mated to him, and if I could change that, I would in a heartbeat. I've done nothing to deserve being treated like this.

He released my hair to grab my chin, his fingers digging into my cheeks, but not painfully so. It was as if he had forgotten just how strong he was at first, but was now being cautious. I knew if he wanted to, he only had to squeeze a little and my jaw would break.

His face dipped to mine. I was able to see him clear enough and quickly fell silent. The color in his eyes vanished, replaced by blackness as they transformed into that of his wolf.

"Be quiet, or I'm going to rip your tongue out."

I said nothing as I stared up at him. We stood in silence. No doubt he was waiting to see if I'd speak, and when I didn't, he released my face and grabbed my arm. He continued dragging me through the woods, twigs, and stones poking and piercing into my feet as I silently followed him.

I felt like I could no longer ask if he would hurt me or not. That wasn't a chance I wanted to take. Suddenly, I tripped and almost fell. His hold on my arm quickly tightened, and he pulled me up. He didn't stop and continued pulling me before I properly had my footing again.

The woods around us were thick, even thicker than where

Xavier lived, and I almost collided into him as he suddenly stopped. I was panting as if I had been running for a mile when a man appeared from behind a tree, his body cloaked in darkness. I squinted to see his face, but I could only make out an outline. Soon I gave up, deciding instead to focus on catching my breath.

"That's a human," the man said and I stopped breathing. "Why is there a human here?"

"That is none of your business. Continue with your patrol and tell no one about seeing her. Do I make myself clear?"

Axel walked away before the man could respond, and I kept my head down as my legs worked to keep by his side. I felt like gravity was pulling me down further and further as my body began to feel heavy. I was exhausted, my legs now putty.

Lights from a house appeared through the trees ahead and I swallowed, a million scenarios of what was about to happen running through my mind. I had assumed Axel's little dungeon had to be on his pack's land but now he was taking me to what looks like his house. I was terrified but I was too tired, too burned out to care. All I needed was a glass of water, nothing else.

I collapsed, my body shutting down finally, and Axel grabbed me before I could hit the ground. He shook me violently, and I was rattled awake.

"Don't you fucking fall asleep. I'm not carrying you."

"Water," I whispered, and he pulled me back onto my feet.

He wrapped his arm around my waist instead, and we made our way inside the house. I had no idea when we had even left the woods to approach the house, but here we were. Bright lights burned my eyes as we entered the house. I squinted my eyes as he continued dragging me, cool tile now beneath my feet.

If he was going to kill me, now was the best time. I was too tired to feel anything. But when he pulled open a door and we descended a flight of stairs into pitch-black darkness, I started to panic. Had he taken me from one cage to put me into another? No, no, I wasn't doing that again.

"Axel, no, let go!"

He threw me to the ground, and a light turned on. We were in a basement, but it looked like it had recently been cleaned out. There was a bed, a table and chair, and nothing else, but it was so much better than being locked up in that cold dark cell.

I got onto my knees as he turned to leave, and he casually pointed to a door I hadn't noticed. "Take a bath. You smell horrible."

He closed the door behind him and didn't spare a backward glance. I remained on my knees as my bottom lip began to tremble. Holding my hand out, I looked at the dirt that had built up on my skin and under my nails and fell to my side to lie on the ground. I began to shake, my hand flying to my mouth to silence my sobs.

"I fucking hate you," I said softly before inhaling deeply and sitting upright. "I hate you! You hear me!"

After mustering up what strength I had left, I got up off the ground and walked towards the door he had pointed to. Behind it was a tiny bathroom with clothes already folded onto the closed toilet seat along with a comb. That was all that was provided, and I was grateful for it. I stripped slowly and avoided looking into the small mirror above the sink. I didn't need to know what I looked like. Besides, I knew if I looked, I would end up more broken than I already was.

"Xavier, please come for me." I prayed as I climbed into the tiny shower and pulled the shower curtain. "Please come for me."

I turned the shower on, and ice-cold water shot out to pelt my body. I didn't care how cold it was, I was too happy to see water to complain about the temperature. I drank the water until I couldn't anymore, and as I lathered up my body and hair, I started to cry yet again. Only this time the tears came.

What is it about taking a shower while sad that makes all your emotions bubble to the surface? My tears were washed away with the water, but they kept coming. What was going to happen after this? Why had he moved me? Where is Xavier?

So many questions began to ricochet off the walls in my mind. What was Axel planning? He had said I had provided him with the perfect chance to be rid of the Blackmoon pack. How had I done that?

I watched the dirt and muck wash down the drain and kept scrubbing my body until the water was no longer colored. I shook my head and stepped out of the shower to grab the small towel that was under the clothes on the toilet and began patting my body dry. If I continued like this, I would only stress myself out more than I already was. There was simply no way for me to know what Axel's plan was, and I was only hurting myself further by imagining endless possible scenarios.

I got dressed in the jeans and small black t-shirt that had been provided for me before taking a look in the mirror.

My eyes and cheeks were a little sunken, my collar bones were more prominent, and I could pull the waist of the pants away from my body easily. My hair was still its normal vibrant red, maybe more so now because I was now a lot paler. In conclusion, I looked a mess.

There was a travel-size toothbrush and toothpaste, so of course, I brushed my teeth twice. I felt like I was a new person afterward, and made my way back into the room, my mind set on going to sleep. The cold shower had been enough to force a little energy back into my body. I felt rejuvenated, but yearned for a good night's sleep. Despite having plans to fall into bed and sleep for a decade, my stomach had its own plans as it growled loudly when my eyes fell on a large bowl of fruits on the table.

That hadn't been there before, I said to myself. I took a step towards it before stopping myself. My eyes then wandered to the stairs and door, and I went up the stairs instead.

I knew the odds of it being unlocked were low, but I tried nonetheless. It didn't budge, and even though I had been expecting as much, I still grew angry. Karma was going to take care of Axel for me. Whether I lived or died, such cruelty cannot go unpunished.

I looked down at my arm and sure enough, my skin was bruised from his dragging me through the woods, his fingerprints still visible.

"Let me out!" I screamed. Hoping he could hear me. "You fucking asshole let me out! You can't keep me locked away forever!" I started pounding on the door, anger filling me up with energy. "Let me out dammit! Axel! Reject me then! Coward!"

The door swung open and I staggered backward, almost falling down the stairs as a man filled up the frame of the door almost completely. A single arm was both my arms combined, and if his size wasn't scary enough, he pinned me with his black stare. My body froze as he flashed his fangs at me and growled, and although I tried, I wasn't able to conceal the way I jumped with fear.

He looked me up and down as if I was shit stuck to the bottom of his shoe before grabbing the handle of the door and slamming it shut. Then I heard the low click of the door locking once more, and my bravado and energy disappeared all at once.

"I hope you can hear me, Axel," I said as I went back down the stairs and towards the bed. "I fucking hate you."

I stared at the small window across the room that was too far up the wall for me to try and break through. Sure, I'd be able to reach it if I stood on the table, but what would happen after I got outside? I'd get chased by wolves that I could never outrun. Where would I even run to? I had no idea where I was to begin with. For all I knew, there was no one but wolves for a hundred miles in every direction.

It was morning, but I pulled the covers up to my chin and snuggled further into bed. The small old mattress that had passed for a bed inside my cell hadn't been much. While this wasn't great either, there was nothing for me to do, nowhere for me to go, so why not stay in bed a little longer?

I had eaten all the fruits and was still full, so I was fine for the most part. All I could do now was wait for Axel to make his next appearance.

I turned onto my side, but backed up with a scream on my lips as I came face to face with Natalie. She was lying beside me with her hand under her cheek, her blue eyes piercing into my green ones. I blinked rapidly, unable to believe what I was seeing, and she started to smile. She reached out and moved a strand of my hair out of my face, and happiness blossomed in my chest as her finger brushed against my face. She was really here!

"Hey babe," she said and my eyes widened.

"Natalie, is it you? Is it really you?"

It looked like her. Her icy blue eyes were the same, but her platinum hair was now snow-white, more silver than blonde. I frowned at that but said nothing. He nodded to answer my question, and I moved to hug her but froze. No, I needed to think. This can't be real. How did she get in here? I looked down at my wrist, and the scar that was there from my suicide attempt as a teen was gone.

"This isn't real," I said sadly, and the excitement I had been feeling vanished. "You're in my head again, aren't you?"

She gave me a sad smile, and I sighed before lying down again. "I figured. How are you doing this? Am I going to wake up and find you and Xavier in my room?"

"You're not. I'm sorry, but I know Axel is the one that has you."

"You lied to me, Natalie. You said mates can't hurt each other." I tried not to tear up, but I failed. "Get me out of here! You've told Xavier where I am, haven't you?"

She moved her hair behind her ears and pinched the bridge of her nose. She didn't say anything for a while, and I started to worry. I reached out to her and touched her hand, but she felt so cold that I quickly pulled away. I hadn't touched her the last time she had entered my mind like this. I wasn't sure if cold skin was normal, but I noticed she looked like she was in pain.

"Sorry." She said as she moved her hand away. "I've never done this from such a far distance. Finding you alone has been hard enough. I can't stay with you long, Ruby, but I want you to play along with Axel's game. He'll be coming for you soon to tell you he'll be taking you somewhere. Play along, okay? He's told the Council about you, about what's been happening, and now they'll be coming for Xavier."

"Shit."

She exhaled and began to fade and I sat up quickly. "Wait! You've told Xavier, right? Warn him about Axel and the Council. Axel said he was going to use me to finally get rid of the Black-moon pack."

"It won't get to that, but yes, I'm heading to Xavier now to warn him. Axel is a fool to think the Council won't turn on him, too. You're his mate as well, no matter how much he denies it. The Council wants total obedience and control, so anyone that steps outside of that always suffers. Mathieu and Xavier broke the law by not killing you. It won't matter to them that you are Xavier's mate. All they will care about is the fact that you are human."

So, in the end, it really will be my fault. I never should have moved here.

I felt like screaming, but she reached out and placed her hand on my cheek. Her hand was freezing, but I closed my eyes and allowed the cold to seep into my skin without moving away.

"I don't know if I'll get to Xavier in time, so I have to go."

By now, I was able to see through her as she faded more and more. Her hand fell away from my face. I didn't want her to go, I didn't want to be left alone, but I knew she had to leave. Xavier was now the one in danger.

"Axel won't hurt you, Ruby. He'll act like he can, but it hurts him even more."

I rolled my eyes.

Tell that to my arm that's still bruised.

"H-how is Xavier? Is he okay? Please tell me before you go. I-I..."

Could I say it? I wanted to tell her to tell him I miss him, but even though we had kissed and had been getting close, there was still so much left for us to say to each other.

"You'll see him soon. You can tell him everything yourself then."

She vanished, and I woke up with a start and took a large

intake of breath. I looked around the room frantically before plopping back down.

Yes, finally some good news.

I rolled onto my side to stare out the window again as I began to smile, a genuine one. It's been so long since I've felt a pinch of happiness or hope. But my smile died quickly because I was now worried for Xavier. With the way Natalie and everyone else has been speaking about this 'Council,' it was clear they were to be feared. Natalie seemed to be on top of it, but I just hoped she would get to him in time.

———

Anxiety had me pacing around the room, sitting on the floor, and climbing onto the table to see through the window, which revealed nothing but endless trees. Soon I settled for sitting around the table, my hunger returning. Compared to the torture I had endured up until last night, I could ignore the growls my stomach was making.

I've thought about going to sleep a few times in hopes of Natalie returning, but she had mentioned how hard it was to reach out to me. She needed her strength to get to Xavier, so I resisted my impulse to nap just for the sake of talking to her again.

My fingers drummed on the stained surface of the white table as I wondered if she had warned Xavier yet.

I recalled the night I had been abducted, the bliss that had come before the chaos that is, and a heavy sadness settled on my chest. Xavier and I had laid in the woods in each other's arms. I was starting to feel the bond between us, I think. Just when I began to feel drawn to him, I was ripped away. That night he had told me about their goddess, an entity that created the very first werewolf, who decides on each and every wolf's fate. One who had clearly decided on my fate as well.

As far as I could see, she wasn't doing a very good job, considering she managed to link three people together that could never possibly work out.

I heard the door open and looked to the stairs to see the giant man from last night leading a woman down the stairs. She was wearing combat boots and had red streaks in her black hair. She nodded to the man, and he turned away to head back upstairs. He left the door open, however, and I stared at the woman expectantly while she looked me up and down with disgust. At this point, I was starting to get immune to those stares. I watched as she crossed her hands over her large bosom and walked forward.

"You don't belong here," she said, and I crossed my arms on the table.

Had Axel sent this woman to scare me or something? He could do a much better job with only a glance. Was she here to remind me how much I don't belong here?

I narrowed my eyes at her, and it clicked. No, she knows exactly who I am, who I am to Axel, and it's clearly killing her.

So, I have another Anna on my hands. Lovely.

"We can both agree on that, at least."

A deep crease appeared between her brows as if she hadn't expected me to answer. "It speaks." She said with a smirk, and I blinked slowly at her, doing my best to force a look of indifference onto my face.

"Can I help you with something? As you can see, I'm quite busy."

She hadn't been expecting that response, either. It clearly struck a nerve, because, within the next second, her light brown eyes turned black.

"You have no idea who you're talking to, human."

"That's because we don't know each other. Trust me, you don't want to know me, either. I have enough shit to deal with right now, so whatever issue you have with me *despite* us having *never* met before will have to be resolved at a later date."

I sat back and crossed my arms as she uncrossed hers. She

hunched her shoulders a bit and her mouth opened to reveal that her fangs had come out to play. Her nails began to descend into claws, and I quickly got up from around the table.

I had nowhere to run, but I sure as hell would defend myself as much as possible. This girl wasn't like Anna–she was worse. Where Anna had been all bark and no bite, it was clear this girl was ready and willing to rip my throat out.

"A weak thing like you can never be a wolf's mate."

She charged at me. and my hand rose to protect my face. I was saved by Axel's thundering voice as it echoed through the room.

"Stop!"

I looked up to find the girl's claws frozen inches away from my face. There was a look of straining on her face, and she slowly lowered her hand and turned around.

Behind her, Axel was standing by the stairs with his hands clenched at his sides. His eyes were narrowed dangerously. His curly black hair, usually kept in a ponytail behind his back, was loose now, and it fell in waves over his shoulders. Even I couldn't deny that he was a handsome man, the kind with an aura of danger that draws women in.

"She doesn't belong here." The girl said through clenched teeth. "This weakling can't be your mate. A strong breeze can knock her over. She can't be your mate. She's not worth..."

Axel stepped forward, and the girl swallowed whatever else she was about to say. "Know your place, wolf. My business is not yours, so I'd suggest you leave before I kill you. You are not allowed in here."

She opened her mouth to speak, and Axel's eyes turned black. He growled at her, the sound filling the space around us, and she quickly bowed her head and backed away. She scurried from the room, and Axel's eyes slid to me when he heard the door close behind her.

He turned his body to face me, and his head tilted to the side. "I don't want you talking to anyone."

"You say that as if I get visitors often enough for me to even have the chance to speak to anyone. I wasn't talking to her. She came in here to throw a tantrum."

"So, you said nothing to her? Not one word?"

Why are we even talking about something so trivial? It's not like I had spilled secrets to her. What we needed to talk about was when the hell he'd be getting me out of here. Natalie had said he'd be taking me somewhere maybe that's why he was here now.

Good timing because a second later I would have been mincemeat.

"No," I responded, and he inhaled before walking forward.

I stood my ground despite my heart hammering, and I tilted my head back to look into his black eyes as they slowly changed back to hazel. His eyes roamed over my face, and I frowned. Being so close to him was definitely something I didn't need. He was a gorgeous man, but there was no way I'd never ever let a handsome face make me forget what an asshole he is.

I looked away, my face twisting as my heart began to race. I wasn't attracted to this prick, I couldn't be. Hell no!

"You need to step back," I said with my head still turned to the side. "There is no reason for you to stand this close to me," I added, and his hand shot out to grab my face.

He wasn't squeezing me tightly, but merely holding my face to turn it back towards him. I grabbed his wrist and tried to move away, but he casually slapped my hand away with his other hand.

"I don't like being lied to." He said the words slowly, his minty breath fanning my face. "Do not lie to me, Ruby. Ever, about anything. Now I don't want you to speak to anyone unless I say so. Do you understand me?" I kept my mouth shut, and let the hatred in my eyes speak for me. "Good girl. We'll be going somewhere soon, and I suggest you be on your best behavior."

I had a million things to say in response, but Natalie's words echoed in my mind. I reminded myself that it was my job to play along with Axel's plan. I settled for pulling my face away, and his hand fell to his side. He didn't move away, and neither did I. He didn't look away, and neither did I. I might be weak in strength, but I would not be cowed by any man, wolf or no wolf. Strength isn't only physical.

I frowned when the corner of his mouth began to lift into a smirk, and he shook his head and stepped back. What the hell was he smirking at? Was this fun for him? I narrowed my eyes at him and realized it was. The punk was messing with me.

"Your fire is cute, Ruby, but you will end up getting hurt because of it. Werewolves like obedience. Disrespect and disobedience aren't tolerated, so remember what I just told you. Speak to no one, and you'll continue breathing."

He turned to leave, and I stared daggers at his back, my nails digging into the palms of my hands. What he didn't know was that I hated being told what to do and being given orders, and it didn't matter who was doing the ordering. That wasn't going to change even if the orders were coming from someone who could rip me to shreds if I were a mere sheet of paper. Trust me, I'd had more than my fair share of consequences as a result of my inability to shut the hell up, even when it was probably in my best interest to do so.

Maybe one day my mouth will get me killed, but at least I'll die standing up for myself.

CHAPTER THREE

XAVIER

I could hear a bird chirping in a tree a few meters away, but it sounded like it was resting on my shoulder. My ears twitched as another bird answered the first one's call, and I tried my best to tune them out. I focused on the wind in the trees instead as I continued to walk along the path in the forest. I was heading to the cliff where Ruby and I had sat and talked so long ago.

No, it wasn't so long ago, I thought as I shook my head. Only a week has passed with her being missing. While it was only a week, it was far too long for comfort. It felt like an eternity.

Natalie has been missing for just as long, and I'm not sure how much longer I can survive not knowing what has happened to either of them. My hands clenched at my sides as my rage began to consume me yet again.

Being without Ruby and not knowing if she was hurt or not was taking its toll. My wolf has been clawing under my skin to the point that I've woken up with my sheets and clothes ripped by my claws and fangs out without my conscious command.

There have been no leads on finding Ruby, and no one has called for ransom or to make any demands. She is just gone, vanished into thin air.

Gone.

I turned off the path and headed into the thicker forest, but I didn't get far. I closed my eyes as the haunting sound of Ruby's scream entered my mind. She had screamed when that wolf had attacked her, and that was the moment when I had realized my mistake. They were after her and her alone. The attack on me was just a diversion carefully designed to separate us, and I had played right into their evil hands.

Now Ruby was God-Knows-Where experiencing God-Knows-What while I waited for some sign, any sign, of where I might find her. I growled low as I unclenched my right hand, and I winced a little as my hand began to shift. My bones broke and shifted, and my fingers elongated while my claws extended. I gritted my teeth as I swung around and swiped my claws at a nearby tree.

The mangled tree tilted to the side as if to fall, but stopped, the trunk in shreds. I closed my eyes as I started to lose control of my shift. My fangs began to elongate and graze against my bottom lip, and I clenched my left fist that hadn't shifted and hunched forward. I exposed my right arm and it began to return to normal, my fingers bending in odd directions as my bones broke and reset.

I opened my eyes as I stood upright once more, and I looked down at my hand before clenching and unclenching my fist. My nails were itching to tear through the flesh of whoever had taken Ruby.

"Send her back to me," I said to the forest, but I was hoping the goddess was listening.

I paused for a moment, a familiar scent licking at my nostrils, and as the scent registered, I spun on my heels to find Natalie standing behind me. I blinked rapidly and took a step towards her before stopping.

Something was different about her.

Her eyes were still ice blue, but her hair was white—snow white. She was just standing there staring at me, but there was rigidness about her as if she was frozen to the spot. There was a distant look in her eyes as if she was seeing through me, and I became on edge. I looked her up and down, trying to see if this was somehow a trick. My stance widened to prepare myself for an attack. Her mouth curved with a smile, and I got a glimpse of the Natalie I had known.

What happened to her?

"Natalie?"

"Your wolf—with Ruby being gone you're losing control," she responded as she pointed a finger at me.

I nodded. "Yes, where have you..."

"I can help," she interjected as she began moving towards me. She had her hands raised to show she posed no threat, no doubt having noticed my defensive stance.

I allowed her to get close to me, but my eyes watched her every move. It felt odd for me to be so cautious with her. Her scent was the same, so I knew it was her, but she looked so different. Something was definitely wrong. Why had she vanished? To get her hair done? That's unlikely because Adolfa was found dead.

She raised her hand and pressed her thumb to my forehead. Instantly, warmth rose within me, and days of feeling on edge vanished as my wolf calmed. I sighed as she pulled away. I looked down at my hand, my claws no longer feeling as if they'd appear at any moment.

"How did you do that?" I asked her, but she merely shrugged and stepped back. "What happened to you, Natalie? What happened with Adolfa?"

At the mention of Adolfa's name, she grimaced. "She transferred all of her power to me."

She turned away, and my eyes widened. "How? I didn't know Enchanteds could do that."

Despite the fact that her back was turned to me, I could see her nod. "I didn't know either. There was a lot I didn't know." She turned to face me. "She showed me where Ruby is as well."

That had my wolf stirring yet again and hope blossomed inside me. "A-Are you serious?" She nodded. I laughed and turned away, my legs pumping as I began to run through the forest to head back to the house. "Where is she? We need to get back to the house."

I felt alive for the first time in days. I've been wandering around either on edge or dragging myself like a zombie, but just that quickly, my energy returned to me full force.

"Xavier, wait!"

I skid to a halt as Natalie's voice echoed through the forest. "What? If you know where she is, I need to tell dad. We have to go get her."

"No, we don't. We can't," she said as she walked towards me, and I frowned in confusion. "She's safe where she is for now. We have more immediate issues to take care of."

I stared at her as if I was looking at someone deranged. How could she expect me to not go searching for Ruby? What else could possibly be more important? I've been losing my mind for days wondering where Ruby is and if she's okay. Not to mention how worried I had been about Nathalie herself.

"Where is she?" I asked her, my face now twisted with anger. "There is nothing more important than finding her, Natalie, and you know that."

She stepped forward, her eyes narrowing, and I blinked in surprise at the dominance that was radiating off her. All wolves radiate some level of dominance, but it gets stronger depending on your bloodline and your rank in the pack. Enchanteds can't transform into actual wolves, so they don't radiate as much dominance as the rest of us do.

The stronger the Enchanted, the stronger their dominance level, but Natalie hadn't been this strong before. What else did Adolfa change?

"She is only safe for now, Xavier. The Council knows about her, so they are coming for you. You broke the law by sparing a human."

"She's my mate, I couldn't kill her!"

"They won't give a fuck! She's human. They won't care that she's your mate. You broke the law, and that is all the reason they need to step in. Then they will focus on how a human can be mated to a wolf. They might even try to bury the entire Bloodmoon Pack to hide this. You know they can! Ruby is safe for the time being, but that is all."

I knew she was right, but I needed to find Ruby. We were just getting close to each other, and having her ripped away from me so suddenly left a large hole in my chest. I felt weak without her, and I wondered if she felt the same. Being human, the mate bond didn't affect her the same way. Was she missing me?

"Who has her? Why did Adolfa even transfer her powers to you?"

Natalie pinched the bridge of her nose as she stepped past me, her white hair blowing in the wind. "Why she did it isn't important right now. What's important is getting back to the house and warning your dad. We have an hour before they arrive. Xavier, we don't have time to waste."

I pulled up at her side, and we walked briskly back to the house. There was a lot she wasn't saying, that was clear, but she was right. If the Council was on their way, then we did have a more pressing issue. However, I couldn't help asking one question. I wanted to know who had the balls to take my mate? Who even knew about her? How could she be safe when she had been attacked and taken?

"Who took her?" I asked her and her shoulders moved up and down as she sighed. "I need to know, Natalie. How do you know she's safe?"

"She's safe because she's with Axel. He's the one that took her from you, and he's the one that reported you to the Council."

I should have known that scumbag had something to do with her abduction! Axel's her mate, too. What he doesn't know is that by reporting her and our mate bond to the Council, he just got her killed, and maybe even himself, too.

CHAPTER FOUR
NATALIE

"Axel's a fool to think the Council won't try to dissect him as well for having a human mate. Whatever judgment falls onto our pack because one of us is mated to a human will happen to him, too" Xavier said.

I watched him as he paced back and forth, his hand on his chin. We were filling Mathieu in on what was happening, and word had been sent to the rest of the pack to stay indoors until their alpha said otherwise.

All that really needed to be said was that the Council would be visiting, and all wolves would scatter without being told to anyway. Everyone avoids contact with the Council as much as they can. No one wants their lives looked into, their privacy invaded and stripped down to nothing. That's what the Council likes to do. They feed on knowledge like rats feed on garbage.

"Axel thinks he's acting in the interest of his pack," I said and Mathieu, who was sitting with his elbows on his knees and his hand over his mouth, looked my way. "But he isn't seeing the bigger picture, so yes, there are multiple holes in his plans. He's one of the few wolves left that trusts the Council. Abducting Ruby might have been the only good thing in his plans."

Xavier gave me the same look as before as if I was crazy. I blinked slowly as I stared back at him to show I wasn't about to change what I had just said. When Adolfa transferred her powers to me, I saw more than I honestly wanted to. There was so much I couldn't say, so much I couldn't tell them.

"How was that the good part of his plan? I need Ruby here, with me. She has to leave with us." He turned to Mathieu, who had yet to speak. "Where can we go?"

"I'm not leaving, we're not leaving," Mathieu finally said as he reclined in his seat. He combed his raven hair backward and cracked his knuckles as he stared off into the distance. I knew, however, that the wheels in his mind were turning.

Mathieu didn't earn his place as one of the most respected alphas without being a patient and calculating man. He was a man of few words, but his actions always spoke volumes.

He looked at Xavier. "There is nowhere to go, Xavier. Wherever we go the Council will find us. If Ruby were here, you would leave with her, but that would still leave me, Natalie, and the rest of the pack to suffer. Not all of us can run." He looked my way. "I assume that's why Axel took her—to stop her from leaving with Xavier?"

I nodded and so did he, having already figured out a part of Axel's plan. I was sure he was close to figuring out the rest. He was right, however. There was nowhere any of us could go that the Council wouldn't find us, and Mathieu would never abandon his pack.

"If we run, Xavier, we incriminate ourselves even more," Mathieu added, his fingers now interlocked on his lap. He looked so calm, so collected in the face of danger, it was admirable but if only he knew the chaos that was coming. "We didn't commit a crime or break a law. One of our most fundamental laws is to protect our female mates, the ones that will carry our children to continue our bloodline. She's a human who's found out about us, yes, but she's also a human who's mated to a wolf. I would say that our law to protect her stands above the one to kill her."

Xavier turned away, his shoulders rising and falling with his deep breaths. "Let's hope the Council sees it that way and aren't blinded by their hatred for humans."

Since I had yet to find my mate, I hadn't understood the turmoil within Xavier for not having Ruby by his side. When I had touched him to calm his wolf, however, I had felt it all.

I had felt his fear, the gut-wrenching panic and anger he wrestled with since her abduction, and the blame he was placing on himself for not protecting her.

Finding one's mate is something many wolves look forward to. Supposedly it is like feeling whole for the first time in your life. But me? I wouldn't mind not finding mine right now. I am terrified of one day feeling the agony Xavier was now experiencing. I was young and had fledgling powers when Mathieu had lost his wife, our Luna, but I had a much higher respect for him since I'd felt Xavier's pain. And Ruby was only missing. Mathieu had survived losing his other half.

"I should kill him," Xavier said under his breath, and his words rang with truth and intention.

"Axel took Ruby to stop you from running off with her. The Council is coming because they want to see for themselves if this is all true if a human is truly mated to a wolf, and to two at that. We can use that to our advantage, Xavier. The Council will try to see if either of you is weakened by her." I crossed my hand over my chest and stepped forward. "They will see her as a weak human, someone that can't feel the bond, someone that shouldn't affect you and Axel. Prove that's not true."

"You talk about tricking the Council as if it's child's play, Natalie. They invented trickery."

"And students surpass their teachers every day," Mathieu added, and Xavier made a sound in the back of his throat as he turned to walk away. "Right you are that the Council can't be trusted or easily tricked, but we can't just sit on our hands. Running will solve even less than trying our luck at playing the Council's game and winning. They aren't Gods. They are wolves, just like you and me, Xavier."

Xavier said nothing in response, but I could understand his anxiety. He didn't know what was coming. What he also didn't know was that what was coming was much worse than he could imagine. I sighed and closed my eyes, wishing I could remove the burden on my shoulders. but Adolfa had trusted me to carry it.

"We don't have any more time to debate this," I mumbled as I opened my eyes. "They're here." Xavier spun around, and he tilted his head to listen to the car that was pulling into the driveway outside. "Whatever happens," I whispered, "neither you nor Axel can reject Ruby. She's weak in that sense. She'll die."

"I have no plans to reject her, Natalie," Xavier said, and I nodded and turned away.

We made our way outside in time to see the door of the SUV that had arrived open. A woman stepped out, and I instantly knew she was an Enchanted like me. It was more than just the fact that her hair was white like mine, plaited in a single braid down her back. I could sense her power.

She stepped back somewhat as a foot appeared out of the car, and then a man stepped out. While I refrained from expressing the frown I felt tugging at the corner of my lips, Xavier could not. Instead of the Council representative we all expected to see, before us stood one of the three actual Council members - Olcan Crescent, the Council member for North and South America. He had come in person, which even I hadn't foreseen, and it meant this would be harder than I thought. I should have known this would be a matter he'd want to handle himself.

Mathieu stepped forward to shake Olcan's hand. "Olcan, my brother, I hadn't expected your visit."

Olcan's eyes were deep blue at the outer rim, leading into a paler blue and then brown just around his pupils. He wasn't as bulky as Mathieu, but he was just as tall, with his head shaved clean. The Enchanted stood close behind him, but her chocolate eyes were on me. With her white hair and dark skin that was glowing from the early morning sun, she exuded an ethereal beauty.

"Is that so?" Olcan said as his eyes drifted to me, and he released Mathieu's hand.

"I find it hard to believe you weren't told about us coming," the Enchanted said, her eyes on me, and I refrained from arching a brow or narrowing my eyes. I could not tell if I was hearing hostility in her deep voice or not.

"This must be Natalie," Olcan said as he approached me to shake my hand, his eyes narrowed as he looked me up and down.

"It's a pleasure to meet you, Mr. Crescent."

I held his stare. He nodded, as if with approval, and released my hand. Why should I look away or act cowardly? Mathieu had been right. The Council is made up of wolves, not Gods. If only they knew what real Gods looked like...

He then turned to Xavier, who was standing beside me and took his hand. "And you must be Xavier."

Xavier shook his hand firmly. "Welcome to our pack, Mr. Crescent. I hope your flight was a smooth one."

"It was." The side of Olcan's mouth curved as he spoke. "It was. And if it wasn't, this was still a...*necessary* trip."

Olcan turned away to stand by the Enchanted's side, and Xavier narrowed his eyes at him, then her. He glanced over at me before looking her way once more. "You're an Enchanted, yes?"

She nodded. "I am–you can see that from my hair. However, not many Enchanteds have white hair, especially young ones." Her eyes drifted to me as she said that, and this time, I arched a brow in response.

From what I understood, the stronger the Enchanted, the more white in their hair. She could sense the strength of my power when I should be nothing but a fledgling, so that comment was a jab at me. She looked to be in her early thirties, so she was young to have white hair as well.

"Well!" Olcan said as he clapped his hands, calling attention to himself. "I'm famished. Mathieu, how about we have a meal and catch up until the human arrives?"

Xavier stepped forward, a growl leaving his lips as he pinned Olcan with a glare. I quickly grabbed his arm and squeezed. Xavier wasn't one for talking, much like his father. Xavier, however, did not have his father's self-control. The corner of Olcan's mouth curved even further as he stared at Xavier, unbothered by his disrespect. It was never smart to growl at a Council member.

However, it was all part of Olcan's plan. He could easily see just how on edge Xavier seemed and would try to play on that. He would provoke Xavier to say or do anything that might show just how emotional he is because of a mere human. I had warned him about this.

"Pardon my son, Mr. Crescent," Mathieu quickly added. "We won't beat around the bush. We know why you are here and, as you know, this is a sensitive matter for everyone involved, including the Council."

Olcan tilted his head to the side at that. "I assure you, while this is, indeed, a sensitive matter, it's different for everyone involved." He gestured towards the door. "Shall we?"

Mathieu stepped aside and allowed him to pass before glancing over at Xavier. A silent message was passed between them, a clear warning telegraphed in Mathieu's expression. Xavier turned and left with both men.

I sighed and began to make my way inside as well. Thankfully, the introductions had gone smoothly (or as smoothly as could be expected under the circumstances). I was exhausted, although I was sure I was hiding it well. Locating Ruby and then projecting myself into her mind from such a distance had been taxing. I had only just woken up and had immediately started on my hunt to find her. I had woken up in the middle of the woods miles outside of town and had to hitch a ride with a trunk driver.

I was certain the truck driver had been worried about my mental health since I had sat there, spine straight with my eyes closed. Getting control over my newfound strength had been hard, especially at first, but I had no choice but to push myself. Time was running out.

"Wait," the Enchanted said behind me, and I paused, pulled from my thoughts. I turned to face her, and she walked forward to stand a step away from me. "There is something off about you. I can sense it. How does an Enchanted so young have so much power? More than many seasoned Enchanteds I know." She looked at my hair. "Who are you?"

"You know who I am. I'm Natalie, and that's all. You know some of us are born with more power than others."

This was indeed true, but maybe not the whole truth. I didn't know this woman, and I didn't trust her to tell her what really happened to me. Not yet.

"I can sense your power as well," I said to her. "You know something is coming, don't you?"

She didn't respond, but she didn't look away either, her dark eyes piercing into mine. "Yes." She finally said under her breath. "I can feel something coming. I just don't know what it is as of yet." She stepped closer to me, our faces only inches apart. Her skin was flawless, her plump lips covered in a light tint of red. "However, I have a feeling you do."

My mouth stretched with a small smile as I turned and walked away. I didn't hear her following me as I entered the house and went up the stairs.

She might be a fellow Enchanted, but she worked for the Council. I wasn't going to trust her until she proved that I could. I stopped walking abruptly as I looked down the stairs, my fingers drumming on the railing. Maybe I was thinking about this the wrong way. Maybe I was the one that needed to prove to her that she could trust me–that she could trust us.

No doubt she would be the one conducting the mind link between Ruby, Axel, and Xavier to prove they are mated. Her word was valued by the Council, clearly. Looking at this situation from the outside, you have the anomaly of Xavier having a human mate, and now there is also me, an Enchanted that's much too strong for her age. If I were her, I'd be intrigued with the Bloodmoon Pack, and maybe not in a good way.

I continued up the stairs and ran into Xavier, his eyes black pits as he stared back at me.

I sighed and cocked my head to the side for him to follow me. "Where are they?"

"Dad is giving him a tour of the grounds and of our training area. There hasn't been a report of an out of control supernatural posing a threat to the humans, but Dad wants to show him that we are still training and staying alert."

I looked over my shoulder and even though his voice was low and controlled, his eyes were still black. He was pissed, and I didn't need him doing something stupid.

"Isn't it funny how so long ago all wolf packs worked to protect humans? We were their protectors from other supernaturals that wanted them for food or whatever else. Now only a handful of packs protect them." I opened the door to Mathieu's soundproof office and locked the door behind me after Xavier entered. "Now wolves hunt them, too."

Xavier immediately started pacing. I approached him slowly and held my hand out.

"I can help."

He glanced at me and looked away. "No. I can handle it. That fucker is on our land and is about to stir shit up. Yet Dad is acting like he's just a relative visiting or something."

"Xavier, they have known each other since childhood."

"I don't care!" He yelled back at me, and I sighed and walked away to sit down. "He's here to cause trouble, to send us all to jail or worse, to kill us and Ruby. This isn't a peaceful visit. I hate acting."

I shrugged as I crossed my legs. "You're bad at it, too."

He stopped pacing to give me a nasty look and shook his head. His eyes returned to their normal color as he finally sat down and ran his hands down his face as he exhaled heavily. We sat in silence, and my eyes soon closed as my body and mind started to fall asleep.

"Enchanteds can see into the future sometimes, right?" Xavier asked, and I cracked an eye open.

"Yes. Why?"

He leaned forward, and I dreaded the question he was going to ask next. My parents had passed when I was young, and so Xavier and I had grown up like brother and sister. He could always tell when I lie.

"Do you know what's going to happen with Ruby? You're different. Natalie. Stronger, I can see it. Can you see into the future? Because I have a feeling you can."

I closed my eye again and laid down on the sofa. "Enchanteds can, and I've tried. I can't see her future. Maybe it has something to do with the block in her mind."

"Maybe you can get through it now that you're stronger. Not being able to see her future.... maybe means she...does not have one?"

I nodded, and my voice was low with sleep as I said. "I don't think so Xavier, and I wouldn't suggest you think like that. This is new territory for us all. We don't know what's right from wrong with her and this mate-bond you three have. Let's focus on keeping her out of the Council's paws."

He grunted, and I listened as the chair he was sitting on made a creaking sound from his weight. "She's coming here, from what Olcan said. I think they already have her in their paws."

I fell silent. Even after five minutes turned to fifteen and Xavier left the room, I still was wide awake. My eyes opened and I clenched my fists, as a tear fell from my eye and onto the sofa. Of course, I had seen Ruby's future. I had seen everyone's future. Even though it was all only one *possible* future, it was still enough to have me curling into a ball and crying until sleep finally took me.

Axel woke me up while it was still dark outside and ordered me to take a bath. He gave me new clothes, told me to brush my hair, and then gave me toasted bread and an apple before dragging me outside.

The cold air nipped at my exposed arms and face as we walked briskly to a black SUV. My eyes danced from left to right but it was useless to try to see anything. It was too dark for me to make out anything other than the house we had just left.

He opened the door for me, which had been surprising. I had expected him to throw me into the backseat blindfolded and handcuffed with the way he's been treating me, yanking and throwing me around as if I'm a bag of potatoes. After two and a half hours after driving what seemed like endlessly, I realized where he was taking me.

The sun had finally come up, and the world around me was finally visible. We were heading back to the Blackmoon Pack. I could tell that's where we were going the second we drove past the Witches Brew Tavern Xavier had taken me to what seemed like so long ago. More and more things began to look familiar to me, and I felt like decades had passed since I'd seen this place.

I sighed and unclenched my hands. I glanced over at Axel, who had one hand on the steering wheel and the other on the door, a deep crease between his brows. Moving my mouth from side to side and I wondered if I should speak to him, but I didn't want him to pull over and throw me into the trunk.

Fuck it.

"Why are you doing this?" I asked, and I stared at his jaw as it visibly clenched.

"Have you forgotten what I said? I told you–no talking."

I made a face, my mouth turning downward. "You told me not to speak to anyone. I didn't realize that meant you as well."

"It did," he responded sharply, and I looked back at the road.

I started to hum when I got to the point where I felt like I would lose my mind if I had to suffer one more moment of awkward silence. In my peripheral vision, I saw him glance over at me. If looks could kill, I'd be a dead woman by now, so I folded my lips inwards and fell silent once more.

I was smiling on the inside, however. He deserved to be annoyed, the smug prick. I spent the first part of the ride in a panic, thinking he was taking me to the Council. Now that I knew he was taking me back to Xavier, I felt a burst of energy, of hope.

I turned to look out the window as a thought occurred to me. Natalie had said the Council was going after Xavier. Had they arrived yet? Had she gotten to him in time? Was that why Axel was taking me back? Was the Council at Xavier's house and waiting for us?

I swallowed and closed my eyes. Of course, he hadn't had a change of heart. He wasn't returning me. He was turning me in. I opened my eyes and glanced over at him again, a loose strand of curly hair brushing against the side of his face.

"Why are you doing this, Axel? Why do you hate me so much?" His grip on the steering wheel tightened, but I didn't look away. I kept staring at him to show him I wanted an answer. "Well?"

"Humans are all the same. They are all selfish and greedy, and they can't be trusted. You *have* done something to me, Ruby. You exist." His words hit a nerve, and I narrowed my eyes at him. "You're my mate, and that's a problem. That's THE problem."

I looked away as I shook my head. I couldn't believe this man was so ignorant and biased. "You see, the thing about what you just said is," I turned to him as he glanced my way, "if I had met you before Xavier, I would have said all werewolves were cruel, cold monsters. But you and Xavier are the perfect examples to show that not all werewolves are the same. You don't get to speak generally about humans being bad. The same way I can't about werewolves." I looked away. "All the things you just listed about humans are qualities you've shown me so far. You're selfish, greedy, and you can't be trusted."

I placed my elbow on the edge of the door by the window and sighed as my skin pressed onto the cool glass. The car was filled with silence once more, and this time I intended to stay quiet. I hadn't asked to be this man's mate, and I didn't want to be his mate. He abducted me, kept me locked away in a dungeon, starved me, and dragged me through the woods. All because I have wronged him by simply *existing*.

I didn't want to believe that everything he just said was what he truly believed. He could not possibly be that ignorant. Maybe he was trying to convince himself of all that?

"My pack is my priority," he suddenly said. "Protecting them is the singular purpose I have. Therefore, I can't strengthen my bloodline by being with you, a human." He spat the last word out like it was akin to being an incurable disease.

Since I'm sure strengthening a bloodline means having kids, I can assure you of one thing, buddy, I will have zero impact. There's no way I'm opening these legs for you.

That's what I wanted to say, but I kept quiet instead. For the first time, he was speaking to me as if he was talking to another person. He wasn't giving me orders or talking down to me, and I couldn't help looking at him.

His expression was still one that screamed 'talk to me and get punched,' but his voice didn't hold as much exasperation. However, I didn't respond. I couldn't fault him for looking out for his pack's interests, but I was certain there were other ways for us to handle this situation without resorting to abduction and involving the Council.

"Who was the man that came into my cell?" I asked after a while.

He looked over at me, a confused look on his face as he shook his head. "What man? I was the only one that visited you in your cell."

Had I been hallucinating or dreaming? No, someone else had visited me.

"There was someone else. I know that was real."

The car slowed at a stoplight, and his hand fell away from the steering wheel. "I remember you asking who else would be coming to see you and I found it odd. No one else was allowed inside the cell, Ruby. Whoever was there wasn't from my pack."

The light changed to green, and he drove off as the side of my mouth curved with a smile. "Maybe now you'll understand how it feels to have people sneak onto your land."

"The land the Blackmoon Pack is on *is* my land!"

I rolled my eyes. That was none of my business. I had bigger things to think about, like if I'm about to be killed thanks to him. The closer we got to the pack, the worse my anxiety grew. Not knowing what was about to happen with my own life wasn't a comfortable feeling. I had no idea what was going to happen in the next hour, and I knew if I asked Axel, he wouldn't tell me.

"What did the man look like?" He suddenly asked, and I frowned.

That's what he's still thinking about?

"I don't know, Axel. He remained in the shadows. I didn't see his face."

He didn't say anything else, and we drove in silence for the rest of the journey. I tried to hide my excitement as Axel drove up the long path to the house. My mind took me back to the first time I had gone out with Xavier, and a bittersweet feeling had my eyes stinging with tears. In the beginning, I had wanted to get away from this place, from Xavier, and now this was the only placeI wanted to be.

Axel parked the car in front of the house. I hurriedly got out and began making my way to the door. He remained at my heel, however, not allowing me to get too far away from him. The front door was thrown open the moment I reached out to grab the handle, and Natalie grabbed my arm and pulled me into a huge hug.

She cupped my cheeks and bent my head from side to side as if inspecting me, and I allowed her to. I was too stunned at how different she looked to do anything else anyways. Her eyes drifted to Axel standing close behind me, and I smiled as she narrowed her eyes at him.

I was sure Axel wasn't bothered by the hatred dripping off her, but I was happy to finally be with someone other than him and his nasty mood. Her hands fell away from my cheeks as she took my hand and began leading us inside and into the living room.

My heart felt heavy as my eyes wandered around a house that I hadn't been sure I'd ever see again. I was happy and scared all at once, and the mixture of feelings had me feeling sick. Those feelings vanished though, when we entered the living room, and my eyes found Xavier.

He was standing by Mathieu's side and, while I knew there were two other people present that I didn't know, I couldn't tear my eyes away from Xavier. It felt like I hadn't seen him in years, and my fingers began to twitch with my need to feel his warm skin.

My heart was beating so fast, it felt like it would beat its way out of my chest. I didn't care that everyone in the room could hear it.

You're okay.

"Xavier..." I whispered as I stepped forward, but Axel grabbed my elbow almost painfully and yanked me back to him.

"What did I tell you?" He whispered in my ear. "Speak to no one."

Xavier's growl rolled through the room like a clap of thunder. He moved forward and was halfway across the room in a flash, his eyes obsidian. Axel shoved me behind him as he widened his stance for Xavier's attack, his nails changing into claws.

The man I didn't know appeared between the two of them in the blink of an eye. Xavier stopped, his chest rising and falling rapidly, his eyes still on Axel.

"Now, now, now," the man said as he looked from Axel to Xavier, "there won't be any fighting. It is interesting, however, how two alphas-to-be are willing to rip each other apart for this," he looked at me with obvious disdain, "girl."

I made a face, not liking the way he had just said that, and he walked over to me. He looked me up and down, his nostrils flaring. I watched in confusion as he glanced over at the woman I didn't know.

She, too, was looking at me, her dark eyes piercing into my green ones.

Who are these people? Are they from the Council?

I narrowed my eyes at the man as he stepped back, the light from the bulb above us causing his bald head to glisten. *Of course, they are from the Council. They must be.*

I looked at Mathieu who was silently staring daggers at Xavier. "Xavier," he called and Xavier stood up straight, his eyes returning to their normal color.

"Axel has her in his possession, so he has the right to do what he wishes. She is his mate as well, is she not?"

"That's bullshit and you know it!" Xavier yelled.

"Xavier!" Mathieu said again, this time louder, as he got to his feet. "That's enough."

Xavier's jaws clenched as he bowed his head. "With all due respect, Father, Axel can't be making rules off the top of his head if this is something that has never happened before."

Mathieu approached his son and placed his hand on his shoulder. "This is new territory, so it's best to let the Council do what they think is necessary. She *is* his mate as well, Xavier." Xavier made a sound, and Mathieu squeezed his shoulder. I felt so useless, a lamb amongst wolves, and feared what would happen if I opened my mouth again. "He is. We all want this over and done with."

The bald man waved his hand, beckoning to the woman with white hair. She went to him obediently. *Are they mates, I wonder?*

"Indeed, we all want this over with. I've seen enough for today, Mathieu. My flight was long, and tomorrow is going to be an even longer day–for all of us. Thank you for giving me a tour of the grounds, but I think I'm going to get some rest before dinner."

He turned and left the room, and I didn't miss the way he glanced at me from the side. I didn't like this man. Each time he looked at me, I got a terrible feeling like snakes were crawling all over me. I looked toward Natalie, who had remained by my side throughout the whole ordeal, but she merely held my hand and squeezed it before turning away.

I moved to reach out to her, and Axel cleared his throat, causing my hand to freeze mid-air. I looked at him and forced as much distaste into my eyes and expression as possible. I was out of that cell and room he had kept me in, but somehow, he still had chains on me. My eyes found Xavier once more, and a feeling of warmth came over me as I looked into his eyes, the longing I could see there.

I hadn't realized just how much I had missed him until this very moment.

"Let's go," Axel said through clenched teeth, but I remained still. "Now."

Xavier's eyes shot down to my arm as Axel held onto me, and it felt like a knife was twisting in my chest as he then looked away. His demeanor changed instantly, and I could almost see a wall appear between us. I yanked my hand away from Axel, but Xavier was already walking out of the room.

A deafening silence filled the room as my heart fell and shattered. I looked behind me at Mathieu, a plea in my eyes, but he only shook his head.

"I'm sorry, child, but this will all be over soon."

CHAPTER SIX

XAVIER

As the night stretched on, I felt more and more awake. I rolled onto my back and stared up at the ceiling, but I was so lost in thought that I wasn't really seeing it.

Somewhere in the house was Ruby, so close, yet still so far out of my reach. *Is she asleep? Is she awake? Is she sleeping in the same bed as Axel?*

That last thought had me clenching and unclenching my fists as I rolled onto my stomach, causing my sheet to roll down to my waist. The cool night air blew into the room through the open window, and I inhaled deeply as it chilled my exposed back. When I had seen Ruby today, a part of my world that had been in ruins for a week instantly mended itself. That is until that asshole Axel had put his hands on her.

The rage I had felt on the night I had saved Ruby in that alleyway so many weeks ago returned in a crashing wave. I had wanted to rip Axel to shreds. My skin dotted with goosebumps the moment she entered the house and I could smell her. But when I saw her, I felt like killing someone.

Her skin was still smooth and unmarred and her hair still a vivid red, but she was thinner. Her collar bones and shoulder blades were so pronounced. She had lost so much I could barely believe she had only been gone a week.

I rolled out of bed, my temper getting the better of me the more I thought about what she might have gone through. I threw a shirt on and made my way downstairs and into the kitchen to grab a bottle of water. Sitting through dinner with my dad, Olcan, and his Enchanted, Rieka, had been painful. I had hoped Axel would join us along with Ruby, but they had remained in their room.

I still think it is rubbish that Olcan was allowing Axel to keep Ruby away from me. Yes, he's her mate, but so am I. I hated the way he had said "She's in Axel's possession," as if he was talking about a mere object and not a person. What's worse was that I had no idea what plans he had for Ruby, myself, and my dad. What I fear most is being forced to reject her.

Maybe that's what Natalie had meant when she had said the Council would try to see what effect she has on Axel and me. Right now, I was more worried about Ruby than myself.

Natalie didn't have to tell me Ruby wouldn't be able to take it. Then again, she might not feel anything, while I felt it all. When our bond was discovered, she got sick, but the almost paralyzing need that came after wasn't something she seemed to feel. Maybe if Axel or I rejected her, she'd merely feel sick again and then get over it.

I threw the empty water bottle in the recycle bin and began making my way through the house to go outside. It was a tranquil night with a clear sky and a calming breeze. I sorely needed something calming right now.

My plan to relax outside until I felt sleepy crumbled to the ground as I stepped out the door and saw Axel standing outside. I paused, my eyes lowering with annoyance, but I wasn't about to turn and go back inside. This was my house.

I pulled up by his side, but neither of us spoke. He dropped the cigarette he was smoking and crushed it under his boot before blowing out a cloud of smoke.

"Why did you do this?" I asked him. "Why did you tell the Council about Ruby? She's your mate as well, Axel. Do you really not have a soul to feel anything when you think about her getting hurt?"

He didn't respond, and we both kept staring dead ahead. An owl hooted in the distance as the trees swayed in the winds, and I finally looked over at him. He was older than me, but clearly not wiser if he thought this bullshit move was a good idea.

"All we needed was time to get some answers because you and I both know the Council won't show her mercy." He looked at me from the corner of his eyes. "You've fucked us all over, and for what?"

"How long would it have taken for us to get any answers? Huh?" He asked. "The Council will do that, and faster."

"The Council will search for a reason to kill her! She's a human that's mated to us both!"

He turned to face me, a deep crease between his brows as he pointed a finger at my face. We're about the same height, and while he might be older with more fighting experience, he wasn't as pissed off as I was.

"She's your mate, Blackwood, not mine. I'm sick of saying that. Do you want to know why I'm doing this?" He stepped closer to me, and my nose twitched at the smell of the cigarette on his breath. "You're weak, and she's making you weaker. You'll have to take over for your dad soon, and you are nowhere near ready. You're not built to be an alpha."

"You don't know shit about me," I said through clenched teeth, and he chuckled mockingly.

"I know more than you think. Alphas are supposed to put their pack before everything and everyone. A single human knowing about us can be detrimental, and just because she's your mate, you spared her. What, Xavier, are you going to make her Luna for the pack? Is she going to bear your pups? Can she even survive a werewolf pregnancy? You haven't thought about any of this, that much is clear. Doing this saves her, Xavier, or she's going to live a life of rejection and pain. When it comes right down to it, you can't make the tough decisions. Rejecting a mate is the hardest thing for any wolf to do, but an alpha must be prepared to do it. She won't just be your woman, she'll be your pack's Luna. It will be her job to birth the next alpha. Have you ever heard of a half human and half wolf child becoming an alpha?"

I said nothing, and he made a sound and turned away while shaking his head. I swallowed hard. Everything he had said was true, and of course, I've thought about those things. But like I'd said, we just needed time to know what we're dealing with. Maybe he's right, I'm not ready to be an alpha. One thing is for sure, I am not ready now, nor will I ever be ready to be the man that kills his mate.

"It'll kill her. You know rejecting her might kill her, don't you? But hey, you don't care. Tell me, Axel, what choice does she have in all of this? If you don't want her, fine, that's great news. But just leave us alone then. Don't preach to me about what I should want, or what's good for my pack. My people are different from yours, and always have been."

He crossed his hands over his chest. "Goddess, do you even hear yourself?" He shook his head and looked down at the crushed cigarettes on the ground. "You know what, you're not my problem. Olcan will handle it. Ruby is just a means to an end for my pack to return to these lands."

My head tilted to the side. This man was talking about me not being a true alpha when he was putting my pack, his pack, and an innocent girl's life at risk, all for some land?

"That's what this is about? Land? Are you serious, Axel? You can take your pack anywhere, *anywhere,* and you've brought the Council here because of greed?"

He spun around to face me, his eyes blazing with anger.

"Greed? This is my land! My pack's land! We deserve to live here! You have no idea how hard it is to relocate or even find suitable land to hide werewolves. My people have made their lives here. They live comfortably enough among the humans, but we have to live somewhere with trees, thick trees so we can be comfortable. So we don't have to fear shifting and being caught."

This time I stepped forward, my face inches away from his. I wasn't going to be challenged or disrespected on my land. His pack left ours years ago, the decisions made by people in the past were none of my business. Not right now.

"For years our packs have come to an agreement and have lived peacefully *away* from each other. Now you want to start a war over this, and you've included the Council that you think is only going to stick to one matter and not dig deeper into our lives. So that's it, you wanna use Ruby to give the Council a reason to say we are a weak pack, that we don't deserve this land? What about your pack, Axel? Do you think the Council doesn't know about your wild pack members that had attacked those humans?" I shook my head. This man was delusional. "You've fucked yourself, Axel, and your people, too. The Council might hate humans like you do, but they don't tolerate dumb shit like that."

His face twisted, and I realized I had hit a nerve. Of course, he didn't know that bit of information had gotten out. My lips curved into a sinister smile.

"The wolves that did that were taken care of." He said slowly.

"Do you think the Council will care? They'll just say you don't have a strong enough hold on your people for that to have *ever* happened to begin with. All you do is spew hatred for humans, so of course, your pack members will act wrongfully because of the bullshit you fed them. Where the fuck is your father? If I'm not ready to be alpha, then neither are you. Where is your father? You're not alpha yet, and a true alpha doesn't resort to trickery or go as far as to abduct another's mate."

"She's not only your mate, but she's also mine as well, remember?"

My gums began to ache as my need to rip his throat out grew stronger. This man didn't even know what he wanted. One minute he claimed she wasn't his mate and then the next minute he claimed she was. Ruby didn't deserve that, and he did not deserve her.

"She is, but she'll never choose you! She'll never choose you!" I looked him up and down, my face twisted with disgust. "You'll always be a savage, no matter what land you and your pack live on." I flicked my finger under my nose as his cigarette breath became unbearable. For werewolves, every sense is heightened. I have no idea how or why he smokes those things. "Where is Alpha Sirhan? He knows this isn't how wolves act. This isn't the way we handle things. Humans behave like this. They go behind each other's backs, so their wars never end. But wolves are *better*. We work things out civilly to keep the peace."

I stepped back and made a sound, one to show my repulsion, while he continued to stare at me, his lips in a thin line. I knew that, even in the current situation, his father, Alpha Sirhan, would never condone an action such as abducting someone's mate. It was an unthinkable act of hostility and aggression.

"You act like you know everything. You stand there and judge me as if you're better than me. What kind of alpha has Sirhan raised? You're acting more human than wolf. You're a fucking disappointment!"

I saw his fist coming, but he had moved so quickly I hadn't had the time to dodge it. His fist connected with my jaw, sending me staggering backward, but I caught my balance quickly. My hand shifted and swiped at his chest, cutting through his shirt and chest.

He howled in pain and dove for me, his shirt ripping off his body as he began to shift when Olcan appeared before him. Olcan slapped Axel across the face, sending him flying backward.

I stared in shock at Olcan's strength, while Axel skidded to a stop on the ground. He had backhanded Axel as easily as if he were swatting a fly.

He turned to face me; his eyes black. "You two are both disappointments." His voice was low, his expression neutral, but his words were dripping with rage. "I had hoped we could all stay under the same roof for one night. I wanted to see what hold that girl has on you both, on two promising alphas. Look at you!" He looked over his shoulder at Axel, who had finally gotten onto his feet, his chest already healing. "You were both ready to fight each other, to kill each other, for a human. You both failed my test miserably. Whom would she fight for either of you?"

"Olcan, I..."

"Silence!" He yelled at me as my father appeared outside as well. He pointed a stern finger at me. "I've had enough of your attitude. Do not speak unless spoken to, wolf! Know your place!"

I turned to look at my dad, and the weariness in his eyes had me swallowing what response I was about to give Olcan. I don't care about Olcan or Axel, but disappointing my father was the last thing I wanted to do. I'm his one and only son. His only heir to carry on the Blackwood name. I was making a fool of myself and of our pack.

Natalie had warned us that this would happen, that the Council would watch us closely to see what effect Ruby has on us. This wasn't Ruby's fault. This was Axel's fault and my own. Frankly, it was more his fault than mine. *He* was the one who invited the Council.

"Do you want to know what I've seen so far?" Olcan said to no one in particular as he walked away, his hand on his chin. "I see two men who aren't ready to be alphas."

"Olcan, this isn't..." Axel began to say but clamped his mouth shut as Olcan growled at him.

Olcan pointed a finger at Axel and then at me. "Neither of you is ready. You're both too emotional. Despite what issues are between your fathers, have they ever behaved like this? Sure, this is a little different, because you both have the same mate. But do you really?" I frowned at him, and he shrugged. "Is she really mated to you both? I would have liked a good night's sleep, but I guess that won't be happening." He turned to my father. "Wake her up. We're having the trial tonight."

Natalie

I watched Xavier make his way outside and knew disaster was about to strike. I remained by the window on the second floor, his and Axel's conversation floating up to me on the cool wind.

I listened as their conversation grew more heated and knew this was what Olcan wanted. Xavier had been ready to rip Axel to shreds today when he had arrived with Ruby, and Olcan had left Ruby under Axel's care for the sole purpose of seeing how Xavier would react. Would he remain cool and collected, or act on his instincts to be with his mate and not have another man touching her.

Of course, Axel wasn't just another man, and that would bother Xavier even more.

It was a setup. I knew I was right to think so as soon as Axel punched Xavier and Olcan made his appearance to lecture them both. I had expected Xavier to throw the first punch, but I had been wrong. However, I was just as curious as Xavier was about Axel's father. Axel was here alone when his father's presence as alpha was needed as well.

That was strange, but really none of my concern.

"She's a lucky girl," I heard Reika say behind me.

"How so?" I asked, and she appeared by the window to stare down at the men.

"She has two alphas fighting over her. A Council member making an appearance in person that we all know is dangerous for him and a powerful Enchanted as a friend." She looked over at me. "I'd say she's a lucky girl."

I turned to stare at her, and she gave me a teasing smile. "I'd say she's a girl that didn't pick any of this and wants it to end like everyone else."

"Well," she looked away, "I'll see for myself if that's true. Apparently sooner rather than later."

I looked back down at the men, and my ears perked up as Olcan announced that he'd be conducting the trial tonight. I sighed and swallowed hard.

"What will you do to her?"

Reika moved her hair behind her ears as she turned her back to the window. "A mind link. From what I've been told, you tried and learned nothing. For an Enchanted so strong, how was that possible?"

I wasn't about to answer that. "And if it doesn't work for you either, what then?"

She shrugged. "Olcan will decide. Take comfort in knowing that he actually likes Ruby."

I turned my back to the window as well. "Does he? Why? I'd think he'd despise her. She's creating chaos- although indirectly of course."

"Of course." She drawled before looking over at me. "Olcan has yet to find his mate and is quite the man whore. He thinks she's beautiful, *but* he's also very intrigued by this entire thing." She turned to face me, a new fire within her eyes. "Imagine what will happen if this gets out? A human mated to a wolf." She smiled. "There is no known record of hybrids. We have no idea what a child between a human and a wolf would be like. Axel thinks it will weaken a wolf's bloodline."

"Don't you think so?"

She inhaled deeply and turned around to look up at the night sky. "What I think doesn't matter." She murmured before looking down at me. "What I think, Natalie, is that if this isn't some kind of witch's trick, what Olcan has planned is going to really piss our goddess off."

"And what does he have planned?" I asked her, my eyes piercing into her, but she began walking away.

"Let's just say there might be a spike in hybrid children if they prove to be strong. That's if the human mothers can even handle the pregnancy. That, I will never stand for."

CHAPTER SEVEN

I had pretended to be sleeping when Axel called me. He could probably tell I wasn't sleeping, and so he only called me twice before giving up and leaving the room. I plopped over onto my back the moment the door closed and sighed with relief. I was finally alone.

Immediately after eating dinner (proper food might I add, and not just scraps like Axel had been feeding me), I had climbed into bed. Axel had given me the bed to myself while he slept on the couch in the room. *Maybe there's a working heart inside his chest after all.*

I had expected him to tell me to sleep on the floor.

No matter how comfortable the bed was, the hours ticked by, and I still couldn't drift off to sleep. I was too anxious and too scared of what was going to happen when the sun rose again.

Olcan, that's the name of the bald man I had met when I had arrived. He definitely gave me the creeps, and not just because of his strange eyes. It was the way he looked at me. I felt like he had been trying to see inside me, and I didn't like it. The Enchanted with him, however, she might actually be able to see inside my mind, the way Natalie had tried. Would she be able to break through whatever wall was there? Natalie hadn't been able to, and I'd be lying if I said I wasn't curious to know what was there. What had I placed under such a secure lock and key that not even I could remember?

Xavier's face flashed in my mind, and I called out to the image as it slipped away. His face reappeared, and I sank further into the bed. A heavy sadness rested in my heart. It had felt like the air had been sucked out of my chest when I had seen him. He had looked tired and weary until Axel had held onto me and pulled me back. Then he had changed into an animal, ready to rip anyone who stood between us to shreds.

He would do that for me, and a smile curved the corner of my lips. I wished I could get out of bed and go find him right now, but with Olcan and his Enchanted around, I didn't want to do anything to give them more reason to dislike me.

I got out of bed to get a glass of water from the bathroom, my feet pattering on the cold tile. I stared at myself in the mirror, dark circles under my eyes, and my sadness grew worse. Why had Xavier looked away like that earlier? He looked as if he had just given up and left me to Axel. I felt like a piece of meat being thrown around for everyone to take a bite.

In a few hours, Olcan would be taking his bite. I splashed water onto my face to try and wash away the horrible images being created in my mind. No, Xavier won't let that man kill me. I have to believe that.

I made my way back into the room to lay across the bed towards the open window. Resting my chin in the palm of my hand, I tried to remember the voice of the man that had visited me before Axel. If he wasn't one of Axel's men, who was he?

His dislike for me had been clear, but I suppose I can only add him to the growing list of people that want me gone. According to him, wolves never thought they could be mated to humans. Now I felt like agreeing. Look at the stress that has been dished out to me for something that neither I nor the wolves have any control over.

Yet still, I'm being treated as if this is all on me. You'd think I had stolen something from them, spilled their secrets, or had committed murder.

I was sick of the back and forth. One minute I felt like this life might not be so bad, and then right as I became comfortable enough to give this all a chance, the rug was pulled right out from under me yet again.

I pressed my face into the sheet and screamed as loud as I could. I didn't care if anyone could hear. I liked Xavier so much, but being with him, or the thought of being with him, was only causing heartache. I knew without a doubt if anything was to happen to him, Natalie, Mathieu, or the pack in general because of me, I'd never recover. If I had to choose between Xavier's pack and Axel's, Xavier deserved to be left alone, and he should be applauded for saving a life, especially since that life belonged to his mate. That's not how this world works, however.

No good deed goes unpunished. That saying isn't just for humans. It works that way for werewolves as well.

I sighed and turned onto my side; my knees pulled up to my chest. Whatever happens, happens. I just hope no one dies, including myself.

Two knocks came at the door, and my heart skipped two beats simultaneously with the knocks. I fisted my blouse at my chest as a sick feeling began to spread through my body. I climbed off the bed and made my way to the door, praying that beyond it stood Xavier. I flipped the switch to turn the lights on before ruffling my hair and pinching my cheeks for some color I knew I was lacking. However, when I swung the door open, my shoulders immediately dropped with disappointment.

"Well, you don't have to look that disappointed," Natalie said as she entered the room, her white hair blowing behind her like a curtain.

I closed the door and returned to bed. "I'm not."

"Oh, you and I both know who you wanted it to be standing

outside the door. Don't front, Ruby." She sat on the edge of the bed. "I didn't think you'd be awake."

"I can't sleep. Not when I know tomorrow Olcan might order someone to kill me."

"That won't happen."

I plopped down onto the bed and covered my face with my hands. "Still, I don't think anything good is going to come from that trial tomorrow. Well, today, when the sun is up. What time is it anyway?"

Natalie didn't respond and I peeked at her through my fingers. "It's two in the morning," she finally replied. She then got up off the bed, and I propped myself up on my elbows. "What did Axel do to you?"

I made a face. "I was in a dungeon for days before he dragged me to the basement of his house, where he finally had the decency to feed me scraps of food and give me some water. Something weird happened while I was in the dungeon, though. I was alone most of the time, except for a man that visited at one point. I couldn't see his face and didn't recognize his voice, but he knew about me and my mate-bond to Axel and Xavier.When I questioned Axel about it, he said no one else was allowed to see me at that time. I'm not sure what to make of that.. "

Her eyes narrowed, and she looked away. "No one else knows about this. Well, no one else *should,* unless someone's lips got a little loose."

"Do you think it's the Council?"

She shook her head and walked away, her fingers combing her hair backward. "No. Since Olcan came himself, this is serious to him. He doesn't want this getting out just yet."

"Yeah, so no one will know when I'm killed. A girl that no one knows can't be missed." Nathalie walked back over to the bed and sat down. She sighed heavily as she stared at me, and I frowned. Why did she suddenly look so gloomy? "What's wrong?"

"Axel and Xavier got into it just now. They had to be parted by Olcan.

That can't be good.

"Why were they fighting?"

She pinned me with a stare. "Do you really have to ask that?"

I smiled a little because I knew I didn't. I, however, found it hard to believe that Axel was fighting over me. Surely he was pissed about something else.

"Xavier might get angry over me, but Axel is upset about other things. I don't see how he and I are mated. I know I feel the bond differently from you guys, but it's like he feels nothing."

"Or he tries not to," she added, and I shook my head.

"Well, he has a future in acting. I can't imagine Xavier ever leaving me in a dungeon. With the way you have all said this mate thing works, I was surprised Axel could do something like that to me. Shouldn't I be feeling more?"

The side of her mouth arched upwards as she hunched her shoulders, "No one knows what you should or shouldn't be feeling. What do you feel when you're around them?"

I bit down on my lip, and a shy smile made its way onto my lips as I thought of Xavier. "I don't feel this instant overload of love, or whatever, but I feel warm and comfortable around Xavier. I know he'll do anything to protect me, he'll do anything to keep me safe." My smile fell away, and I covered my face. "Despite what Axel has done, and I do want to cut his dick off, I...I feel...protected around him. That's so fucked up considering what he's done, so maybe that's not the right word, but there is this thing about him... He's like a mean bodyguard, you know. We might argue and get on each other's nerves, but if it ever comes down to it, I know he'd protect me. That's what I feel. But then he yanks me around by my hair or leaves me without water for days, and I think he's just soulless. There's no way he can be feeling the bond."

"They both feel it, trust me. Think of it as Xavier just being more open-minded than Axel. Axel is older than Xavier, and he might have had terrible experiences with humans in the past. He's grown up in a pack that is still trying to stick to how things were immediately after the war between wolves and humans. Look at it this way - he's the alpha to be., It's a big role to fill to start with, then add in having a human Luna in a pack that hates humans, and you have a big problem. He must be stressed. If he doesn't reject you, his pack will force him to. He'll have to choose between you, or what he was born to be. That's a terrible choice for anyone to have to make."

When she explained it that way, I could understand the rock and a hard place he must be stuck between. His life had probably been going as planned for him to be the next alpha. All of a sudden, here I come, a human girl that he feels compelled to be with on a deep level, yet he can't because he has to stick to some twisted hatred passed down generation after generation.

"Yeah," I drawled. "I guess his mind must be a little effed-up right now, but that won't save him from my wrath. That bastard left me in a dungeon!"

Natalie raised her fist, and I bumped mine against it. "That's my girl. But I need you to come with me." I gave her a look, and my chest tightened as she stared back at me with regret. "He wants to do the trial tonight."

"Olcan? Why?"

I felt like the world around me froze. A chill danced down my spine as my eyes widened, and I began shaking my head. *No, no, I'm not ready. I thought I had one night to prepare myself and now this?*

"What's going to happen?" I asked. "What's the trial going to be like?"

"I wish I had time to explain, but they're waiting on us." She got up and held her hand out to me. I could only stare at it, and I knew she could hear my racing heart. "I need you to trust me. I'll be right there, Ruby, right beside you. I promise."

I had trusted Natalie from the moment I had met her. That

moment seemed so very long ago. While I was still curious to know what inspired her hair transformation, I knew hair wasn't the only thing that had changed about Nathalie in the time since I was abducted.,. From the time we first met, I had been drawn to Nathalie's spunkiness, her bubbly and chatty nature. I could consistently count on her to flash one of her charming Nathalie grins that practically touched her ears and made her eyes twinkle, and before I knew it, I'd be beaming right along with her. But now her smiles didn't even reach her eyes.

I took her hand, and she pulled me up. "Natalie, what happened?"

She blinked once, seemingly caught off guard by my question. "Nothing that didn't need to happen. I'm okay."

"Are you sure? I mean, your hair is the same as the Enchanted that came with Olcan, Reika, or whatever her name is. Coincidence?"

"Enchanteds of a certain power level have white hair."

I looked from left to right. So within the short time I had been gone, she became so much more powerful. *How?* No wonder she had been able to find me. Now wasn't the time for me to press her for answers though. Olcan was waiting, and I'd rather not piss him off before this trial even gets started. Knowing me, there would be more than enough time for that to happen later, whether I wanted to or not..

"Okay, we should go, but this conversation isn't over. I want to know what happened because I know something did."

We exited the room. I followed behind her slowly, my legs taking short steps. "I got a little help with seeing the world a bit clearer." She said almost inaudibly. "That's all. I know I'm not myself, but sometimes seeing more than you wanted or needed to see changes a person."

She stopped walking abruptly, and before I could react, she pulled me in for a hug. At first, I just stood there, shocked and mildly confused, before I wrapped my arms around her. I sank into the hug as she did, and we both sighed at the same time. While Natalie is only twenty years old to my nineteen, she has become someone that I look up to. She is an old soul, and I'm sure that was why so many people gravitated to her.

"No matter what happens tonight," she whispered. "I'm happy I met you." She pulled away but kept her hands firmly on my shoulders. "Us odd girls have to stick together."

I cupped her cheeks. "I'm ready."

———

Axel

I stood by the window with my hands buried in my pockets and my eyes glued to the starry sky. Natalie had told Mathieu she'd wake Ruby, but that was almost half an hour ago. The longer they took to come downstairs, the more irritated I grew at being forced to be in the same room as these people.

Xavier had no right to talk about my father. I'm here. I'm handling things, and that's just the way things are. How dare he act like I don't know what I'm doing? My eyes wandered from the sky to the towering trees and I clenched my jaw. This land, this entire fucking land, belongs to my people, too. We barely have enough space in the area where we've been forced to settle for years, whereas both packs could easily spread out on this land and never even come across each other in passing.

I glanced over at Xavier whispering to his father, low enough that not even I could hear. They looked at me at the same time before Xavier stood up straight and crossed his arms over his chest. I looked away, not bothered in the least by his attitude. Olcan and Reika were busy talking about a fundraiser, the two of them not bothered by Natalie and Ruby taking so long. I would have thought Olcan would have torn the house apart by now.

Was this the Council that everyone fears?

I wanted this over with. Everything had been going smoothly for me until I came to this damn house and picked up on Ruby's scent. I looked out the window before closing my eyes, my senses taking me back to that day. I had never before smelled something, someone, so mouth-watering. I had tried to picture her just by her scent, but nothing in my wildest dreams could have prepared me for those devastating green eyes, vividly red hair, and that heart-breakingly human heart.

Then I had smelt Xavier on her, and I completely lost it.

I couldn't believe my mate was human. But even more than that, I couldn't believe my mate, my other half, was also mated to another wolf. It didn't make sense to me then, and it doesn't make sense now. I never thought I'd even find my mate so soon. That has never been something I was eager about.

After meeting Ruby, however, I've felt more torn than I ever have before. I can feel her, smell her, and I constantly sense the pull of our bond. But I can't bring myself to trust her. I feel like this isn't real. A human mated to a wolf brings about so much tension, so many questions. How will a human survive a wolf pregnancy? When I do finally mate, I plan on staying that way for life. I won't become attached to someone that will just leave eventually. At this point, she's more Xavier's mate than mine anyway. She has made her choice.

That scent, that hypnotizing scent, drifted into the room, and I looked to the door as Ruby appeared with Natalie. She looked my way as she walked in. I could see the fear in her eyes, but otherwise, she appeared calm. That's something I could easily admit to admiring about her. Even in the face of danger, she puts on a brave face and tries to stand her ground.

"You ladies certainly took your time," Olcan said he took a seat and nodded to Reika. "I'm sure everyone wants this over this. So, how about we begin?"

Ruby said nothing as she held Olcan's gaze before looking at Reika, who stepped towards her. Her eyes darted to Xavier, and my hand twitched as their eyes locked. They stared at each other, an unspoken message passing between them before she looked at Reika once more.

I wasn't jealous.

Okay, I was. But at the same time, I don't want to be with her. We have zero possibility of a real future together. She is just a means to an end to get what I want. Mate or not, she's human. We'll never work out, and mate or not, Xavier broke the law to spare her.

"This will be simple and painless," Reika said as she held her hand out to Ruby. However, Ruby only looked at her hand before looking at me. I stared back at her, not sure why she was staring at me so intently. I nodded to her nonetheless. Reika shook her hand that was still outstretched, pulling Ruby's eyes away from me. "Take my hand. I'll create a mind link to see within you. That is all."

"That was already done," Xavier said. "Natalie did that, and it didn't work. There is some kind of block in her mind."

"We're here to find out who she is, Xavier, to start," Olcan replied. "That is what we will be doing."

Xavier shook his head, "Trying again might hurt her. You can't force through a block like that. It takes time, breaking it piece by piece. It should not be done by brute force."

I wasn't going to say it aloud, but I agreed with Xavier. Yes, I wanted to have this all figured out, but I didn't want Ruby to suffer unnecessarily. Wolves fear the Council so much, but they should remember that the Council is just wolves like us. They only want the best for all werewolves. The Council members over the years have remembered and held onto many of our old ways in order to secure our safety and protect our secrets. We must do so at all costs, even if it means that some lives are lost in the process.

Nevertheless, my deal with Olcan hadn't included hurting Ruby. I would reject her. Xavier would be given the choice to, though I knew rejecting her was something he'd never do. He didn't have the balls to make the tough calls for the pack. He, his father, and the entire Blackmoon pack would then be dealt with accordingly. That is what would happen here.

Though I had to admit, I was curious. How could a human girl, who was already responsible for bringing so much chaos, also be capable of sealing off her past so tightly that an Enchanted couldn't get through? What exactly had happened to her? What did she want so badly to forget?

"If something in her past was hiddenbehind such a strong block, then it must be important. Maybe it'll explain who she is, where she really came from. Maybe it'll explain why she can be mated to two wolves."

"I'm a normal girl, Axel. You keep talking about me as if I fell from the sky or something," she replied, and I shrugged.

"We'll find out soon enough, won't we?" I replied.

"Of course, you wouldn't care if she gets hurt or not," Xavier shot my way, and my brow knitted.

"I care about getting this thing over with. I don't care if..."

"Enough!" Ruby yelled, and all eyes turned to her. "Can both of you stop it?" She looked from me to Xavier. "I can handle it okay. I want to know what's locked away in my mind, hidden from even me. I can do this."

Olcan leaned forward. "Okay, that's enough. Xavier, your opinion is welcomed, but this will be done whether or not you or Ruby want it. *I* want to know who this girl is. *I* want to know if she can be trusted with our secrets. Mathieu, you've allowed a human to walk free amongst our people without knowing her true self. You should have broken through whatever wall was there before you made a decision like that. Whatever is concealed in her mind might hurt more than just your own pack. She could very well be dangerous to all wolves."

Mathieu remained reclined in his seat, his left leg crossed over the right. "She was spared because she is the mate to a wolf, human though she may be. Yes, our law is to protect our secrets at all costs.

However, I didn't think it was my place to break another even more important law in order to uphold that law. Harming another wolf's mate is punishable by death."

Xavier looked my way. I knew he was thinking - I could see it in his eyes. If only I weren't Ruby's other mate, he'd have been well within his rights to kill me with his own handsfor abducting her. If she wasn't my mate, I would have no reason to be here other than to watch the fall of the Blackmoon pack.

Olcan sat back, a cunning smirk on his lips. "Right you are, Mathieu. But," he lifted a finger, "that law is for female wolves, not humans."

No one spoke for a while as Olcan and Mathieu continued to stare at each other. Olcan was right about that, and Mathieu knew it. Olcan then looked at Reika and nodded, and she took both of Ruby's hands into hers.

"I'll help," Natalie suddenly announced as she walked up to Ruby to stand behind her. "Maybe with the two of us it won't be as much pressure on you or Ruby. We'll take this slow."

Reika stared at her for a moment before looking at Ruby, who nodded her consent. She was beginning to look more terrified, her bravado slipping, and I couldn't blame her. I'd hate to have anyone roaming around inside my head. Reika released Ruby's hands to press her fingers to Ruby's temples, while Natalie placed both hands on the sides of Ruby's head.

Natalie closed her eyes as Reika did, but Ruby's eyes remained open. I watched as she swallowed hard. I looked away, annoyed that I was starting to worry about her. This is what I hate, this connection to her that won't allow me to maintain my indifference like I want to.

Both Enchanteds began to speak under their breath, their chant growing steadily louder. Ruby's eyes fluttered close as her body grew stiff, and even Mathieu sat forward. I could not understand their words as their voices grew louder and louder, but I could feel the sudden burst of power within the room.

I stepped forward quickly but stopped myself just as Natalie and Reika stopped chanting. Then the heads of all three women fell back at the same time.

———

Ruby

I was on the verge of shitting myself as Reika and Natalie both held me. I had been doing my best to hide my fear, but I couldn't cover it fully any longer. These women were about to take a deep dive inside my head, and no one knew what was going to happen when they did.

I swallowed as I heard them begin to whisper words I didn't understand, and a chill went down my spine. It didn't take long for whatever they were doing to kick in because soon, my body started to feel weak and my eyes fluttered closed.

The moment my eyes closed, there was a burst of blinding light. I opened my eyes slowly as it began to die away, and I found myself standing in a white room. It was more like a box with no doors or windows, just white walls.

I looked down at my hands before touching my face and exhaling. I'll never get used to how real this all feels.

"Natalie?" I turned in a circle. "Reika?"

My echo was the only response. Within the next second, there was a loud boom, like a bomb going off, and I crunched down. The white world around me began to change. People started appearing around me, along with cars and buildings. Everything was hazy and hard to see, preventing me from making out faces or anything distinctive. All I could tell for certain was that the people running were all humans.

I was facing one way, and they were all running towards my direction, their cries and screams mingled together. They were running from something, but I couldn't tell from what. I started walking, moving out of the way to dodge them, although I knew they would just run through me in this fake reality.

What is this?

If this was a memory, when had this all happened? I stopped as a woman tripped and flipped onto her back. I couldn't tell what she was looking at, but she was crawling backward on her hands. A black shadow appeared before her, and my brows knitted. It was a shadow of another person, and as they jumped on top of her, I screamed.

As I reached out and screamed,a large crack appeared just between her and the shadow.

"Ruby!"

I spun around as Natalie called my name, and another crack appeared, followed by yet another. I looked back at the woman on the ground and the frozen shadow above her. I took a step forward, and as I did so, a sharp pain surged through my head. I hunched forward, my hand on my head, before glancing up at the shadow once more.

It was shaped like a human, but why was it black? I could tell the color of the clothes of all the humans and their complexion despite everything being hazy, so why was this human just a black shadow.

My eyes widened.

A supernatural?

"Ruby!"

This time it was Reika's voice, and then another sharp pain, worse than the first, had me falling to my knees. The hazy world around me began to speed up, the humans began to run faster, and more black shadows appeared. The screams got louder as the humans were attacked, and I grabbed my head and hunched forward until my forehead was touching the cold ground.

What is this?

"Ruby!"

That voice I didn't know. It was contorted, neither male nor female, but a mixture of many voices. It was the last thing I heard before I blacked out.

———

Axel

They had been standing there for ten minutes before I noticed they were moving. First, it was Reika, when a small crease appeared between her brows. Then it was Natalie, with the way her hand had begun to twitch.

"Something's wrong," I said as I narrowed my eyes.

"They're fine," Olcan replied as he got up from his seat. However, he didn't approach them, and as I did, he held his hand up to stop me. "Small movements are nothing to worry about. We don't know what they are seeing."

Natalie and Reika's heads suddenly flung forward and then backward, their eyes wide open and as white as clouds.

"Is that normal?" Xavier yelled as he stepped forward, and Mathieu stood up as well.

"No," he said to Xavier as he placed his hand on his shoulder, "something's wrong."

Both women began shaking, and my heart skipped a beat as Ruby began to shake as well. "No fucking shit something's wrong! How do we stop it?" I ran forward, not waiting for someone's response. Just as I reached out to grab Reika's arm to pull her away from Ruby, Olcan grabbed me and pulled me back.

I didn't have time to be impressed by just how quickly he had gotten to me. I was more worried about Ruby and the way her eyes were now fluttering.

I flashed him off me. "If something is wrong, we need to pull them apart."

"If we force them apart, we will do them more harm than good. We might kill them."

I made a face and turned back to the shaking women. This was all new for me. My pack doesn't have an Enchanted, and while I've educated myself about them, there was still a lot I didn't know. My father never saw the need for an Enchanted.

"Mind links can be complex," Olcan said as he began circling them, his hands clasped behind his back. "Sometimes it's not just a link between minds. Right now Reika and Natalie aren't just seeing what's inside Ruby's mind, they are *in* her mind. Force them apart and their either their minds break or," He looked at me, and I clenched my fist at the smile on his face. "they die."

"And you're smiling because?" Xavier asked.

Olcan shrugged, "It's fascinating."

"Fascinating! Something is wrong with her!" I yelled, and Olcan arched a brow, that annoying smile on his lips still.

"So, you're worried about the human after all?"

My lips formed a thin line. "If she dies, if all three of them die right now, won't that be a problem?" He returned to his seat and sat down. There was no trace of concern or care in his eyes, not even for Reika. *What kind of man is this?* I turned away with my fingers rubbing my temples when I heard gasps.

I spun around as Reika and Natalie suddenly pulled away from Ruby as if she was the sun's surface. They both hunched forward, their hands on their heads as they began groaning in pain.

Mathieu grabbed Reika as Xavier made a dash for Natalie who looked dangerously close to fainting. Ruby was no longer shaking, but she was just standing there. I hated that my heart was racing, that I wanted to know if she was okay. When she finally started moving, I rushed forward. It was as if time was moving in slow motion as she began to sway and then fall. I reached out to her, her red hair covering her face as she fell when Xavier appeared and grabbed her just before she plummeted to the ground.

I watched him move her hair out of her face. She was saved from falling, so why was I so pissed all of a sudden? Why did I want to rip him limb from limb as he gently held her cheek and began calling her name?

"I-I don't understand," Reika said to herself as she held her head.

"What did you see?" Olcan asked, and she turned to stare at him. She looked like she had seen a ghost as she then looked down at Ruby in Xavier's arms.

"What is it?" I urged her on, and she shook her head and winced.

"She- I- I saw Elder Lovette," she whispered, and my eyes widened along with Olcan's and Mathieu. Olcan got to his feet slowly, his eyes flashing black as he looked at Ruby and then at Reika.

"Are you certain that…"

"Yes," Natalie replied as she lowered herself to the ground. "She's telling the truth."

Reika staggered and was caught again by Mathieu, her eyes becoming teary. This was not good, not good at all. If this was true, my problems weren't about to end, they were just beginning! "Why does a human have a memory of an Enchanted, of our Grand Elder Lovette?"

All eyes fell on Ruby because no one had an answer. I could see it in Xavier's eyes, the spark of doubt that I've felt for Ruby this whole time, and I sighed and left the room.

CHAPTER EIGHT
XAVIER

Reika released my hand while Axel removed his hand from her shoulder. I watched as a thin glowing string unwrapped itself from around my arm and Axel's and Ruby's as well. It vanished into thin air as she gently laid Ruby's hand on her stomach, her eyes still closed as she slept soundlessly.

It's been half an hour since she had fallen unconscious, and as the time stretched on, I became more and more anxious. Reika and Natalie had to be given the time to eat and replenish their strength. The rest of us - Olcan, my dad, Axel, and myself–have had to sit and wait to find out what had happened.

I spent the time trying to understand what Reika had meant about Ruby knowing one of the most well-known and beloved Enchanteds. My mind was straying and creating insane theories. There was one question that I just couldn't get out of my head: *what if Ruby really wasn't sent by our goddess?* What then? Was she truly my mate, or was this all some kind of elaborate spell or evil trick?

"Well?" Olcan asked, and Reika got to her feet rather shakily. Performing the spell she just did so soon after what happened with the mind link had severely weakened her. I turned and walked away once she was on her feet because my heart was in my throat waiting for what she might say in response.

"It's real," she whispered. "I can feel their bond. It's not a spell."

I glanced at Axel and found him already looking at me. If Natalie had known how to do this, or if we had even known this could be done, we would have done it from the start. It might have eliminated any reason for Axel to send word to the Council.

I glanced over at Olcan, who was now looking at Ruby thoughtfully. I wondered why the spell wasn't completed before Reika tried to see into her mind. Wouldn't it make more sense to find out if our bond was real to begin with? Because if it had been fake, it would've given Olcan and Axel the ammunition they needed. I suppose trying to invade Ruby's privacy came first on the Council's list of priorities. I shook my head. I suppose I had no right to be judgemental when I had forced Natalie to do the same thing once before.

"When will she wake up?" I asked as I turned around, and Reika shrugged.

"I don't know. What happened was extremely taxing on Natalie's body and mine, so just imagine what it might have been like for her. Forcing her awake isn't a good idea, so we'll just let her sleep."

My eyes darted to Olcan and caught the way he narrowed his eyes at her. Reika failed to notice because she was busy staring down at Ruby on the sofa. Natalie was sitting across the room with a cup in her hand as she stared out the window, her legs crossed lotus style.

"And what exactly happened just now?"

Reika looked Olcan's way before turning away to sit down. My dad entered the room at that moment and gave her a cup of tea before sitting down as well, a solemn expression on his face.

"You said you saw Lovette," he said as Reika blew on her tea, his baritone voice filling the room. "What exactly did you see?"

Natalie looked away from the window as the darkness outside

started to be chased away by dawn, and Reika glanced her way for just a second. I frowned when I noticed how she held her forehead slightly to somewhat shield her eyes from Olcan while taking a sip of her tea. The look that passed between Nathalie and Reika was quick and all but imperceptible, but I was sure it meant something.

Despite my suspicions, I remained silent as she reclined in her chair and inhaled deeply. "Even with the two of us in there, we were only able to make a small crack. When you guys mentioned a wall in her mind, I had expected the normal defense mechanisms humans use to suppress memories. But there is an actual mental barrier within her mind. A strong one. And it was definitely made from magic." She closed her eyes and pinched the bridge of her nose. "I was only able to get a small glimpse of what is behind it and what I saw...who I saw, was Lovette." She opened her eyes and stared sternly at Olcan. "She was in tears, distraught about something, but that's all I saw before Ruby started to force us out."

Olcan made a sound of frustration. "How did she force you out? You're both strong Enchanteds. She's a frail human girl. So, we still know nothing and now have more questions than before. What will it take to break through?"

"A witch is needed for this, and a strong one. Powerful magic was used to create the block in her mind, and only powerful magic will be capable of bringing it down."

"I thought you Enchanteds were like witches," Axel said, and I had to stop myself from laughing. This is the future alpha of the Bluewater Pack? I had heard rumors that they didn't have an Enchanted among them, but I hadn't believed it. The Bluewater Pack has always been peculiar, right down to their practices and rituals. I could not deny that they've all been trained well, though, both from what I've heard and from fighting Axel myself.

"They are like witches, yes, but they have limits that witches do not," my father replied.

"I'll ask Willow to help," I said, but Olcan immediately shook his head. "No. The Council will find a witch," He got up and walked over to Ruby. He stood above her for a moment before walking away, his hands clasped behind his back. "How is it possible that she knew Lovette? It makes no sense."

Ruby groaned as her head turned from left to right. She raised a hand and held her forehead, and Natalie smoothly joined her on the sofa.

"Hey, take it easy," she said as she helped Ruby into a sitting position. "How do you feel?"

Ruby inhaled deeply, a deep crease between her brows as she looked around the room. "Like I was attacked by a wild animal," she said as she stared at Axel as if she suspected that he might have been that wild animal. He narrowed his eyes in response. "What's going on? What happened?"

"You forced Reika and me out of your mind, just like you did the first time I did a mind link with you."

"So, it didn't work then?" She asked weakly, and Natalie shook her head. She looked at Reika and frowned. "There is something, though, isn't there? What is it?" She looked my way. "What were you guys just talking about?"

"We saw something, yes," Reika replied, and Olcan crossed his arms over his chest.

If he was going to find a witch to break through the barrier in Ruby's mind, did it mean he was planning on staying here longer? Or would he force Ruby to leave with him? Neither of those options sat well with me, not with the way he kept staring at her as if he would happily open her skull himself to see what's inside. Ever since Reika had said what she had seen inside Ruby's mind, he'd become increasingly agitated.

My father cleared his throat and slid to the edge of his seat. "When I did my background check on you, Ruby, I found nothing about your parents and no record of where you actually came from. I just know that you were left at the hospital when you were born. If you know anything at all about where you're from, can you tell us now?"

"And no one thought that was odd and decided to press her for that information from the start?" Axel asked.

"That's not odd, Axel. Haven't you ever heard of an orphan? Believe it or not, I'm not the first human to grow up without their parents" Ruby snapped at him. "No, I don't know my parents or where I'm from. I was in and out of foster homes my entire life."

Olcan uncrossed his arms and buried his hands into his pockets. He tilted his head to the side like a curious dog. "Do you know a woman named Lovette?"

She looked thoughtful for a moment before shaking her head no. "I don't know anyone named Lovette. Why? Should I?"

"No. She's a Grand Elder for the Enchanteds. The same way wolves have a Council and Witches have High Priests and Priestesses, a Grand Elder is the most powerful of the Enchanteds. They often lead very sheltered lives because of this power." Ruby started to look confused, and my dad continued. "As I'm sure Natalie has told you, Enchanteds have lived with a lot of discrimination from other wolves for years due to the fact that they can never transform. However, there is something special about them that only a few outside of the Enchanted know - they are all descendants of our goddess."

"What?" Axel and I yelled in unison. I looked at Natalie and Reika for their reactions, but neither looked surprised at all. It's not like I doubted the existence of our goddess, but hearing something like this was blowing my mind. "Are you being serious right now?" I asked my father, and he nodded. "Why is something this important not widely known? So, you're telling me Natalie is related to our goddess?"

"Yes. The Council banned that information many years ago."

Axel hung his head and laughed. "Of course they did." He pinned Olcan with a glare, "If other wolves found out there were actual descendants of our goddess living among us, they would demand the Enchanteds have a seat on the Council. Maybe they'd *be* the Council. Why listen to other wolves when we can listen to the children of the goddess that created us?" He shook his head. "But the power you Council members have would then be nothing compared to," he looked at Ruby and I was surprised to see awe within his eyes, "a demigod. Wolves deserve to know this."

"They will never deserve a seat on the Council," Olcan said through clenched teeth, his face turning slightly red. "Even though Enchanteds are wolves, they aren't pure wolves. They are a different species. The Council is for pureblood wolves only. That's why the Enchanteds formed their own faction. Enchanteds play an *amazing* and *honorable* role in our society, despite the fact that they aren't pure wolves. The Council has worked hard over the decades to stop the discrimination. Keeping this a secret isn't for the purposes of oppressing anyone. It is for the Enchanteds' own safety. Demigods invariably end up being used, abused, hunted, or killed for their powers. Why do you think demigods from other cultures are kept a secret or hidden? It's a sad fact that we cannot count on people's better natures to keep our precious resources safe. "

"I'm sorry but what does all of this have to do with me?" Ruby asked, and Olcan turned to her, anger now in his eyes. I stepped closer to her.

Grand Elders worked closely with the Council, so I understood his anger and confusion. He had lost a friend when Lovette had disappeared. All wolves had grieved the loss.

"Lovette gave up her post as Grand Elder suddenly and vanished." His jaws clenched. "Her body was later found, and to this day, no one knows exactly what happened. All Enchanteds that show a strong connection to magic are appointed Grand Elder because they have the strongest connection to the Goddess. Because of this they don't...mingle, with anyone outside of the Council or even their own people. Even under those circumstances, contact is limited. How do you, a human girl, with no people and no past, have a memory of our revered Lovette?"

Ruby frowned and looked away. "I-I don't know. I don't know anyone named Lovette."

"Do not lie to me!" Olcan roared. Mathieu swiftly got to his feet and placed himself between Ruby and Olcan. Axel and I stepped forward in unison as Olcan's breathing became labored, his eyes now black.

"Olcan, control yourself. You know she knows even less than we do." My dad said to him. "Yelling at her won't miraculously help her to remember things that were sealed away from even her."

Olcan took a deep breath and straightened his spine. Everyone watched as he cleared his throat and ran a hand down his shirt as he calmed himself. "I apologize for my outburst." He looked at Mathieu and then me. "It's clear Ruby isn't just an ordinary human girl after all, in more ways than just the fact that she is a human mated to two wolves."

He sideglanced at Axel, whose jaws clenched in response. I didn't trust either man, but Olcan even less so than Axel (and that was saying something). I had a bad feeling about how things were going to turn out forRuby with the addition of yet another unexplainable mystery. One that I, too, wanted answers to. Her knowing Lovette didn't have to mean something bad, but in what capacity could she have possibly come to know her? And why had Lovette been crying in the memory?

"So, Ruby met Lovette presumably sometime after she stepped down. Even so, correlation is not causation. Just because they had a relationship does not mean Ruby is the cause, directly or indirectly, of Lovette's demise.." I pointed out. Who knew my college Research Methods class would ever come in handy while trying to save my mate's life? Olcan's face twitched from the anger he was trying to contain. I could feel his dominance rolling through the room and poking at my flesh like needles. "You have no idea what the Grand Elder did after she left. You don't know everywhere she went and all the people she met." He didn't seem pleased to hear that, but he said nothing. He knew I had a point.

"If we knew everyone she had come into contact with after she left, everyone would be a suspect in her death until proven otherwise," Olcan said through clenched teeth, and Ruby got up and turned her back to everyone.

She stood there for a moment before stepping away, her face in her hands. Her hair was a tangled red curtain around her, and my finger twitched, yearning to feel one silky strand. If it wasn't for Axel'sgreed and his stupidity for involving the Council, Ruby and I would be so much closer now. Instead, I have to watch her deal with all of this from a distance.

I looked in Axel's direction where he rooted himself close to the door. I frowned because his eyes were glued to Ruby. They didn't hold the same indifference I've come to expect from him when it comes to her, and a stab of jealousy gripped my heart. Despite everything he's said, I know he's feeling the need to take her into his arms and protect her, the same way I am.

I don't think I'll ever be comfortable knowing that some part of her belongs to him. I can't help it; I want all of her to myself.

"Look, I'm sorry to hear that this Lovette person died. She was clearly important to all of you, and I would freely share with you anything I knew about her. The fact is, I just don't know anything about her. " She shrugged as she turned to face us, her eyes droopy and bloodshot from exhaustion and unshed tears. "I mean, maybe I do, but I can't remember. There is one thing I do know for sure, and that is that I sure as hell did not kill anyone. You came here to see if I'm really Axel and Xavier's mate, and I am." She said to Olcan and Reika before looking at Axel. "Xavier broke a law by saving my life and revealing to me that werewolves are real. So, what's going to happen now in terms of that?"

She looked Olcan's way once more. His face was now an unreadable blank canvas. "Those are the things you're here to clear up. Let's clear one thing up at a time, please, and tell me what's going to happen next. What's going to happen to me? Will I be spared because I'm a mate, or will I be killed because I'm a human that knows too much?"

No one spoke as they waited for Olcan's response. I sighed and looked away before walking to the window. The sun was now out and the world outside was bright and alive.

"I came here myself because I hadn't wanted this to get to any of the other Council member's ears. I wanted this issue resolved and put to sleep quietly." He made a soft chuckle as he pinched the bridge of his nose. "A human mate is unheard of, but here we are. Neither Axel nor Xavier will be forced to reject you because we don't know what effect that will have on you, or them, for that matter. You will be spared, Ruby, but now I have no choice now but to involve the other Council members. This is much bigger than it originally appeared to be. You will be coming back with Reika and me to Romania."

I felt like a cold hand had wrapped around my heart and was squeezing the life out of it the moment those words left Olcan's mouth. I glared at Axel, and I wished he could see the images in my mind of me ripping his fucking tongue out. Now, look at what he did! There will be no end to this any time soon, and Ruby is still in danger.

"I'm sorry, what?" Ruby announced as she stepped back, her eyes wide. "I'm not going to Romania. Fuck that! If I go anywhere with you, I don't need anyone to tell me that means my life is over. Whatever needs to be done will be..."

"Shut up!" Olcan yelled, and Ruby clenched her fists. I bit down on my tongue to stop myself from speaking, to hold back the urge to bite this man's throat out for speaking to my mate like that. The tension within the room was starting to become stifling, and Olcan closed his eyes and held his head back. "Know your place, human. Be grateful even being given this chance to live and come with us." He said calmly. "You don't have a choice in this matter, and neither does Xavier or Axel. They will both be coming with us as well. " He said this as he opened his eyes to stare at my dad, daring him to object. Despite the anger evident on my father's face, he remained silent. I love my father and have a lot of respect for him, but I hate how easily he rolls over sometimes.

"A witch is needed to get through whatever wall is in your mind. Hopefully, we will find out who created the wall in the first place, and that will all be done in Romania. You might have vital information about Lovette, so I can no longer keep this a secret from the others. You *will* be coming, and we *will* be leaving tomorrow. *All of us.* You all have one day to get your affairs in order."

He turned and left the room, and Ruby's wide teary eyes jumped from me to Axel and then back before she too ran from the room. Natalie sighed and leaned forward to palm her face, while Reika got up and left wordlessly. Axel remained standing by the door, but now he looked close to exploding. None of this had been t the outcome he had wanted. I had to admit, even though things were now fucked for everyone, I was secretly happy the smug prick was caught up in it, too. He made his bed, and now he was going to have to lie in it. ***

Ruby

That bald fucking asshole wants to take me to Romania. Romania!

I kicked at a stone outside and watched as it bounced away from me. The only place I felt like I was alone was in the forest, although I knew, in reality, there were werewolves for miles around. I wasn't really alone, and it was clear I probably never would be again. Come to think of it, I still haven't received a tour to see any of the other houses. There was a whole community here, and all I'd seen so far was the main house and the training area. I guess that no longer matters. At this point, I'll be lucky to ever see this place again. I've been alone my whole life. There was always a part of me that had yearned for that to be different, but now with all this chaos and being constantly surrounded by people I wasn't sure if I could trust, I missed being alone. The fact was, I missed my old crappy life. As horrible as it had been, it was nothing close to this madness. Olcan had spared my life, but had he really? Dealing with one Council member had been bad enough. I just knew the moment I set foot into Romania, I'd have two other pompous asshole Council pricks gunning for me and whatever secrets I have hidden away in my mind. Once they find what they are looking for in my head, and once the story of Axel, Xavier and I start to spread, that'll become another whirlwind of problems. My impression of the Council is that anything that became too big of a problem to them tended to disappear conveniently. I was not excited to discover just how the Council intended to take care of me and all the problems I represented for them.

I sighed heavily and continued walking, the morning sun shining down through the gaps in the trees. As I hightailed it out of the house as fast as my legs could carry me, I had felt the intense urge to sob uncontrollably with all the anger and frustration that had built up over the course of the trial, but the moment I entered the woods I felt much calmer. Well, I wouldn't qualify it as calm exactly, but at least no longer on the verge of spontaneous combustion.

Birds and insects sang around me, but all I could hear were Olcan's words replaying in my mind.

I have no idea who this Lovette woman is...or was. And the more I thought about it, the more my head began to hurt. I stopped walking and held my head. My headache was becoming unbearable. It was at the point where I felt like it would be less painful to slam my head against a tree to just stop the overflow of thoughts, which continued to intensify the pain. *There are things from my past that I no longer know. There are people I've met; things I've said and done that I don't know. Am I who I even think I am?*

I felt like screaming.

The shadow of a bird above passed over the forest floor before me, its high-pitched cry echoing through the forest. I looked up in time to see brown wings before it vanished, and a tear finally slid down my cheek. I wish I could fly away from my life, from myself.

I have no idea who I am.

An image of what I had seen within my mind, of the running and screaming people, resurfaced, and more tears began to cascade down my cheeks. Was that a memory? It must have been, but what had happened? Who were those shadow people? Who took my memories from me?

"Fuck!" I screamed at the blue sky above, my body shaking. "Fuck!"

A twig snapped behind me, and I spun around and came face to face with a wolf, his black eyes narrowed with his massive tail swishing behind him. The last and only time I had seen Xavier in wolf form it had been night time, so now I could truly admire his size and beauty with the light of day. His paws were massive, his nails black and pointy. No one would mistake him for a normal wolf if they ever came across him. He was simply too massive.

He shook his body, and his fur ruffled somewhat. The jeans and shirt in his mouth swayed from side to side. He stepped forward, his paws digging into the ground as I dried my tears. I staggered back as he pushed his snout into my chest and dropped his clothes into my hand. His heavy breath fanned my face as he towered over me, and I giggled as he licked my cheek.

"Why do I need to carry them?"

He lowered his head for me to give him a head rub, and I closed my eyes as I gently pushed my fingers through his fur. He exhaled heavily before stepping away, and I opened my eyes as he started to circle me.

"What?" I asked and he stopped at my side and plopped down. His black eyes blinked at me, and I shrugged. "What?" He shook his head and licked his shoulder before growling. "Do you want me to get on your back or something?"

He shook his head again and looked away as he angled his body more towards me. I made a face as I stared at him for a moment. *So, I'm about to ride a werewolf. Well, okay then.* I sniffled before tucking his clothes under my blouse, and he turned his head to look at me. I swallowed as I grabbed his fur, worried I might yank on it too hard, but after two tries I finally made it onto his back.

He got up suddenly, and I screamed, clenched my legs, and pressed myself to him. I've never ridden anything in my life, so it was hard to get past feeling like I could fall off of him any second. And it wasn't exactly a short distance to the ground. "Hey, hey, you're not wearing a saddle, sir. Please be careful." He shook his head and leaned forward, causing me to slide down closer to his neck. The ground was so far down. All I had was his fur to hold onto, which I didn't want to yank on too much for fear he might throw me off. "This was a bad idea."

He moved off, slowly this time, and I swallowed the lump that had lodged itself in my throat. I could feel the power in his body with each step he took, and I soon relaxed and leaned forward until I was lying on the back of his head. I could feel his heartbeat, strong and fast, and soon I closed my eyes before I realized it.

"Thank you," I whispered as the vibration from his heartbeat calmed my thoughts. He growled in response, and I smiled, when suddenly he jumped. I grabbed onto his fur and sat up to see what was happening, but he had only jumped over a log.

He started to walk faster. I gripped his fur and lowered myself the way I've seen people do while riding a horse. He slowly began to pick up the pace until he set off on a run. At first, I panicked, scared that I would be thrown off him, but soon the wind in my hair, his heartbeat beneath me, and the freedom I felt had me laughing and urging him on.

We zoomed through the trees, leaving the house, the pack, and my mysterious past behind. If I could freeze time and create an endless loop, this would be the moment I would choose to repeat. I could be free forever with Xavier.

He slowed down until he was walking again, and I frowned as

the sound of water met my ears. I was panting as if I was the one that had been running as I looked around, and soon a waterfall came into view. My eyes widened and excitement set in as he crunched down and I slid off him. We walked together down a small hill down to the waterfall, and I placed his clothes on a rock as I walked forward to see the falls and pond surrounded by vibrant bright flowers and full bushes. It was like an oasis in the middle of the forest, This was what I needed.

I scratched him behind his ear, a face splitting smile on my face. "Thank you."

He made a sound and walked forward into the pond. I watched as he dove in,and I waited as seconds went by and he didn't resurface. I frowned and began removing my clothes.

"Xavier?" I called as I entered the pond. I closed my eyes for a moment as I bent down to scoop up the cool water. "Xavier? Stop messing around. You're a wolf, not a merman."

Something brushed against my leg and instead of screaming in surprise like I'm sure he had intended , I dived in to grab him. We resurfaced together, his arms around my waist.

"Well, look at you, trying to be a badass. I could have been a piranha or something. "

"Or something," I replied as I wrapped my hands around his neck. The smile on my face fell as I stared at the falls behind him. "Too bad you're showing me this now when we'll be leaving tomorrow."

He released me and moved a strand of hair that was stuck to my face before pushing off, "Don't think about any of that right now, Ruby. Right now, nothing else matters. After today, whenever you feel down, you will always have this memory to think back to. "

And I know I have a lot of sad days ahead. "On the upside, you'll be there with me."

"So will Axel," he added before he submerged himself and reappeared again. He combed his hair back and swam to me.

"Although I'd rather him not be there at all, he needs to be there for you."

I frowned. "Be there for me? You'll be there for me. He's the one responsible for bringing in the Council, to begin with, which is the only reason we have to go at all. Everything is going sideways thanks to him."

"When it comes to blaming Axel, I'm happy to be first in line, but I don't think we can lay this completely on him. I think this would have all happened eventually, to be honest. You have some kind of connection to a Grand Elder. I don't think that would have stayed buried forever. I think it has to mean something."

I sank lower into the water until my chin was covered. "You're right, let's not talk about any of this." I swam away from him towards the falls and took a deep breath as I dived under.

I came out on the other side of the falls where there was a dip in the rocks, almost like a little cave. I climbed onto the rock and sat down, and soon Xavier popped up out of the water.

He nestled his way between my legs, and I couldn't stop myself from combing his hair back, the wet strands gliding through my fingers. "Can I ask you something?"

He nodded lazily, "Sure, as long as you keep doing that."

"Are mermaids real?"

He pulled back, his lips curving into a smile. "Seriously?"

I shrugged as I laughed. 'What? I wanna know."

He nodded, and my eyes widened. "But they aren't gorgeous women with long hair and seashells for a bra." He reached up and moved my hand from his hair to kiss my palm, and the action sent a burst of electricity up my arm. "I'll take you to meet one someday."

"Angels?"

"Yes, they're real," He replied as he kissed my wrist.

"Demons?"

He nodded as he kissed the dip at my elbow, and my toes inadvertently curled under the waterline. My lips parted to ask him another question, but he pressed his lips to mine before I could. I swallowed my words and my eyes fluttered closed as I wrapped my legs and arms around him.

He gripped my waist and pulled me closer as his tongue explored my mouth, and I moaned into his. I had missed him so much. The sky could open up at this very moment to rain meteorites down on the earth, and I wouldn't let him go.

He pulled away and pressed his lips to my cheek and then my neck. "I missed you," he whispered. I sighed and pressed myself to him even more, his words music to my ears. "Even if Olcan hadn't *ordered* me to go to Romania as well, I'd still find my way there just to be with you." He pulled away to stare into my eyes, and I pouted as sadness set into my heart once more. "I'm not letting you out of my sight again, Ruby, and I don't care if you get tired of me."

I shook my head. "I'll never get tired of you. But Xavier, no one knows what's in my head, what's in my past. I don't..."

"Nothing from your past will ever change how I feel about you. We're in this together."

CHAPTER NINE

I could still feel Xavier's lips on me and his strong hands holding me, even hours later. Amid this chaos, he had made me forget everything so easily even if it had only lasted for a few hours. I had needed the distraction, a break to experience some form of normalcy. I know now that, if given the choice to go back and time make different choices that would allow me to live my life as I had been, I would still make the same choices again. That might be the selfish thing to do, but I'd still want to know Xavier, Natalie, and Mathieu. I'd still want to know about werewolves and witches.

I paused as I looked from left to right, my mouth twerked to the side in contemplation. I'm not sure I'd want to meet Axel. That prick has single-handedly ruined everything. Well, at least now he's been pulled into the madness against his will, which he deserves, of course. I don't get how he thought he could walk away from this unscathed. This is just further proof of what I've thought all along - karma's a bitch.

One thing I did fear was the idea that perhaps Xavier might come to resent me one day for all the trouble I have caused him and his pack. Yes, he wasn't feeling that way now and professed to be ready to leave his pack for good to be with me, but the trouble certainly wasn't over yet by any means. Axel has proved he's ready to reject me or pawn me away for his pack. Was it only a matter of time before Xavier came to feel the same?.

Will he eventually hate me because he picked me over being something he was born to be? Maybe he'll learn to hate me long before that because no one knows what's in my past. I shook my head to be rid of those thoughts and continued walking down the corridor.

I've been locked away in my room since returning to the house with Xavier, a different room than the one I had been sharing with Axel. I didn't want to see or speak to anyone, and the last person I wanted to run into was Olcan. I had only eaten when Natalie had turned up with dinner. She had finally filled me in on how an Enchanted named Adolfa had transferred all her power to her and the significance of her hair color change.

I was still blown away by the fact that she's a descendant of a goddess, a real goddess. It had been hard to follow everything that Olcan and the others were talking about this morning, but that bit of information had been mind-blowing. I hated the fact that I would be leaving her behind, but at the same time, I was happy she wouldn't have to be dragged to another country as well on account of me.

Considering it was already 10 pm and we all had a dreaded day ahead of us tomorrow, everyone had retired to their own spaces early. This was the perfect time for me to roam around or whip something up in the kitchen. It really wasn't hunger driving me to leave my room.I was just too anxious to stay in one place any longer, and I was eager to stretch my legs. I wanted to take one last long look at this place. Despite everything I've been through here, this was the best home I have ever lived in. I hoped my socks were allowing me to move around without being heard and that was proved to be accurate when I walked by a slightly cracked door and heard Axel talking.

"This isn't what we agreed on."

I frowned and pressed myself to the wall beside the door before peeping inside. Sure enough, Axel was standing with his back to the door, his hair loose around his shoulders. I couldn't see whom he was speaking to, but I had a strong suspicion about who it might be.

"Plans change," I heard Olcan respond in his usual indifferent tone, and I edged closer to the door.

"My father has been ill for a while, and I've already taken over as Alpha. You know that."

This was news to me and I had a feeling it would be news to Xavier as well. I pressed myself closer to the wall instead of looking into the room and risking being seen. Did they know I was standing here? Surely, they could smell me, or were they too engrossed in their conversation to notice?

"I can't leave my pack and go to Romania. Can you even say how long I'll have to stay there? No, you have no idea."

Olcan sighed. "This isn't up for debate, Axel. I think it's obvious that you can't be left behind. You are the girl's mate as well. Your presence will be needed."

"This *is* up for debate. This is not the deal we made. This is a bad time for me to leave my people," Axel growled.

"Deals change! A lot has changed! This was a bad time for me to drop everything to come here, but here I am. She is a problem, Axel, much more than you had portrayed, and more than any of us had thought."

"Because she knows Lovette? This is how she is treated because of that? You don't know what she knows."

"Exactly!" Olcan yelled. "No one knows what she knows! No one knows who she is!" My eyes fluttered as I looked down, his words cutting through me. "I need to know what she knows, everything that she knows." His voice grew deep and threatening, and I clenched my fists, my nails digging into my palms. "And I will learn it all, even if I have to cut it from her skull myself. I don't give a fuck about her being your mate or Xavier's. She's not one of us, and she never will be. You're both alphas-to-be. In fact, you're already an acting alpha, so act like it."

Was Olcan saying what I thought he was saying? Was he talking about killing me? He couldn't be. *No.* My heartbeat spiked as I continued to listen, but they were no longer speaking. As the silence stretched on, I started to panic that maybe they had finally realized I was eavesdropping right outside the door. I had just started to move away when Axel's voice met my ears, his voice as low as Olcan's.

"What are you saying, Olcan?"

"Don't tell me that now after all this you actually care about what happens to her, Axel. I'm here because you brought me here. Xavier is already too close to her and that will be taken care of, but don't you join him, Axel. You'll meet the same fate, and I don't want to lose yet another promising Alpha, especially one who understands the Council's vision. A human can't be mated to a wolf. Period. Imagine the chaos and uncertainty within the wolf community if something like this ever got out. We must understand how this happened and how to prevent it from happening again."

I turned away slowly on tiptoe until I felt like I was far enough away from the room. Then I started running. *I have to get out of here. I can't stay here. I can't!* I ran down the stairs to get to the second floor but as I rounded a corner, I heard whispering. I stopped running, my chest rising and falling rapidly as I listened, but the whispering had stopped.

I started walking down the dimly lit hall, the hairs on the back of my neck standing on end as the faint whispering started once more. I spun around in time to see a black shadow disappear inside the wall to my left. My eyes widened as I immediately turned and started running. Ghost or not, I wasn't sticking around to find out.

I pumped my legs as the feeling of being chased grew worse. I heard a scream, much like the ones I had heard during that vision inside my mind. I skidded to a halt as the world around me fell away, and I was once again at that place in my mind with all the humans running in fear.

I rubbed at my eyes, and when I opened them, I was in the hall once more.

What the hell is going on?

"Ruby?" The voice hadn't registered until I had spun around and my fist was caught inches away from crushing a nose. Xavier's head tilted to the side; his brows knitted as he lowered my fist. "What are you doing?" I threw myself at him and buried my face in his chest. "Ruby, you're freaking me out. Why were you running like that?"

"Something was..." I looked up at him. "We have to leave, Xavier."

He stared down at me sadly. "We have to go, Ruby. We don't have a choice."

I untangled myself from him as I shook my head. He had no idea what was about to happen. "They're going to kill me." His expression of pity didn't change, and I felt like punching him in the face for real. "I'm not being paranoid, Xavier. I heard Olcan say it aloud. He's going to kill me. I don't know exactly what he has planned for you, but I doubt it'll be pleasant."

His face slowly morphed into one of confusion and anger. "What are you talking about? You heard Olcan talking when? To whom?"

"Just now, on the third floor, he was talking to Axel. He wants to know what I know, and he's prepared to do anything to get that information. He said I'm not one of you and I never will be. , He doesn't care that I'm mated to you and Axel. All he wants to find out is how I'm mated to a wolf, to begin with, and how to stop it from happening again. He has no plans of ever letting any wolves get a whiff about our mate bond. He's going to kill me, Xavier. We have to leave now."

He stepped away from me, his face turning red with rage. With his black T-shirt and jeans and the semi-darkness around us, he blended into the shadows around us easily while pacing back and forth. "Axel's the Alpha now because his dad is sick," I said, and as I expected, he turned to me with confusion written on his face. Obviously that was news to him, too. "He's mad about being forced to leave his pack behind to come with us, but Olcan doesn't care about that either. He doesn't care about any of us."

"She's right."

Xavier looked over his shoulder to find Natalie standing in the shadows a few steps away from us. She walked forward and into the light, her hands buried in the pockets of her leather jacket.

"Olcan doesn't care about any of us, but especially not Ruby," she said as she came to a stop beside Xavier. "He cares about control, and this is quickly becoming something that's out of his control. You both need to leave."

"That's easier said than done, Natalie, and you know that. Today is a full moon, or had you forgotten? That means I can't shift if we run into trouble. We'll be sitting ducks if we're caught. " he replied. "When Olcan catches us, then we'll absolutely be screwed, and that might even extend to the whole pack."

"We can't stay here, either," I said to him, and he sighed and pressed a finger to his temple. "There has to be something we can do."

"There is," Natalie replied, and Xavier and I looked at her as she turned her back to us. "There is a way you can both leave without Olcan noticing. Just leave it up to me. I'll cover things here, but be packed and ready to leave in a few hours."

"Are you sure?" Xavier questioned, and she turned around to face us once more. Her eyes were glossy, and it tugged at my heart because it was clear this was all painful for her. She nodded before walking over to him and hugging him. "But you and dad..."

"Will be fine," she said to him as she stepped away. "You and

Ruby need to stay *together*, no matter what." She looked at us both sternly, and we nodded.

She pulled me in for a hug as well, and my eyes began to fill with impending tears. I felt like I was stuck in a nightmare that kept going from bad to worse instead of me waking up to find out it was all a bad dream. "Pack and be ready by midnight. Just meet each other outside and leave. I'll take care of everything. Always remember that I love you both. Trust no one, and try not to worry. I can always find you both at any time and do a mind link. We'll stay in touch."

She turned away and vanished into the shadows down the hall. "Where will we go?" I asked, and Xavier pulled me to him and kissed the top of my head. My heart was beating so fast I felt like I could faint any minute. "I- I..." I wanted to be strong for him, I wanted to be brave when I needed to be, but the reality was I terrified. I felt betrayed that Axel had conspired with Olcan in planning to kill me, but I'd never say it. I thought that he felt enough of the bond to keep him from wanting to end my life, but I guess I had given him more credit than he deserved. Apparently, he is just like Olcan - all he cares about is power. "I want this all to end."

He pulled back and kissed me gently on the lips. "It will, but first we need to do this."

"Will you tell your dad?"

Pain flashed within his eyes, and he shook his head. "I can't risk him trying to stop me and I'd rather that he have plausible deniability about being involved when Olcan realizes we've left. Get packed. I'll see you soon."

Natalie

I had to change my sheets after waking up. They were damp with my sweat, and even my hair was wet. I looked as if I had taken a dip in a pool. Like so many things in the supernatural world, astral projection was definitely not as easy as they made it seem in movies or on TV. After taking a shower, I went looking for Ruby. I didn't bother going to her room. I already knew she wasn't there.

Now that they both know what Olcan is up to and are ready to leave, everything is about to fall apart...as it must.

I felt like punching something as I made my way back to my room. Things were already set into motion, and there would be no going back.

I rounded the corner to get to my room and spotted Reika standing by the door. Her eyes remained on me until I stopped before her, my arms crossed over my chest.

"Did you tell them to go?" I heard her ask in my mind, and I nodded.

"Yes," I replied telepathically, and she stepped aside for me to open my room door. She followed me inside, and I crossed the room to sit by my window. "I told them to leave. They're getting ready now."

I previously had no idea Enchanteds could communicate telepathically, but now I had Reika to thank for bestowing that particular piece of useful knowledge. I stared up at the moon hanging low in the sky and a chill passed over my body as Reika pulled up beside me to stare up at the sky as well.

"Do you think Axel will follow them?" She asked me. Her voice in my mind sounded as clear as if she was physically speaking.

"He will," I replied. "No matter how much he tries to act indifferent towards Ruby, the connection he has with her is there. He won't be able to stay away. The more time he spends around her, the stronger the connection grows. So no matter how little he wants to, wherever they go, he'll follow. He might have started some of this all out of selfishness, but he was also trying to be a good alpha, to give his people better lives and a better home to run free. Wolves need space. Now he has learned the real truth about the Council." I shook my head. "They are all the same, selfish, power-hungry leeches." I looked over at her. "No offense."

She shrugged. "None taken, I merely work for Olcan in matters like this when an Enchanted is needed. At first, I, too, was blind to the Council's true nature. Yet, even after I figured it out, I stayed."

"Why? You could have left and joined a pack."

Her mouth turned downward. "I could have, but to be blunt, I didn't have the courage to. I turned a blind eye to their corruption like so many others do in order to ensure my own survival. Because I'm pretty sure my life would have been forfeit if I left. The Council doesn't hesitate to put a target on the back of anyone they consider to be a threat. I know too much. " I walked over to my bed and sat down while she remained at the window, her head still held back as she stared up at the sky. "I love the full moon. It is the only time the other wolves experience what it's like to be us." She said, and her chuckle echoed loudly in my mind. "I'd never trade what I am to be like them. All of what Olcan had said about Enchanteds playing an honorable role in our society was bullshit. We're used and looked down on not because we are "precious resources" to them, but because they are jealous and afraid of our power. So what if we can't change into hairy beasts? We are the goddess's children. Yet we still live under the thumb of their oppression.."

"Not for much longer," I replied, and she looked my way. I could see the questions within her eyes, and I quickly looked away. "Are you sure you'll be able to do what you need to do tonight? Without you putting Olcan and Mathieu into a deep sleep, Xavier and Ruby will be caught."

"I'll get it done, Natalie. Just trust me."

We didn't speak for a while, my mind taking me elsewhere until Reika crossed the room to sit on the bed beside me. The burning behind my eyes grew worse, and I looked away. Xavier has always been like a brother to me and I've grown close to Ruby. It killed me that there wasn't much more I could do to help them, to prepare them for what was to come.

"I wish there was something more I could do. Something I could tell them to warn them. I wish I could warn everyone, but I can't. Even if I wanted to, I couldn't. I'm bonded by oath. If I interfere with what's to happen, it'll only be worse."

"They'll be okay, Natalie," she whispered in my mind again as she took my hand and squeezed it gently. A tear fell from my eye, and I quickly swatted at it.

"If only you knew what I do."

"That's because you refuse to tell me everything," I said nothing in response and pinned her with a look. "But, *but*, I know you can't. You joining that mind link and showing me what had happened with Adolfa, what had happened to you...that was something. I'm just thankful you trusted me enough to show me. I've only ever heard rumors about power transfer. To suspect in theory that an Enchanted can pass on her gifts to another is one thing, but to have seen it done with my own eyes is something else. It must have been excruciating. , I suppose the Council is responsible for suppressing information about Enchanted power transfers as well."

Of course, they wouldn't want something like that to get out. Enchanteds would surely become too powerful if they found out they could take on the powers of another. A loved one that has become too old and was ready to die would pass on their skills to the younger generation. I could see where we would push the boundaries of mortality. I could see the many Enchanteds lives that could be lost if the practice was misused. Not all wolves are like the Council members, and not all Enchantedshave good intentions. It would be chaos. Despite my dislike for the Council, I actually couldn't fault them for keeping this a closely guarded secret. "It was excruciating, and a life was lost. Yet, for what's coming, it was completely necessary, and a small price to pay. We are all going to need as much strength as possible for what's to come."

"Who is Ruby?" The question caught me off guard, and I pulled my hand away from hers. She turned to face me. "Did she truly know Lovette?"

"She did. You saw that she did." I got up and walked away before turning to face her. "Reika, there are things that I don't know. In fact, there is a lot I don't' know. My job is to keep Xavier, Ruby, and Axel on the right path. That is all."

She didn't respond and got up. "I understand." Her voice echoed in my mind as she walked to the door. "It's time for me to do what I need to do."

She left, and I returned to my bed, this time plopping down face forward. Despite the full moon and the light, it was blessing the earth with tonight is the beginning of dark times. I'd be setting Xavier, Ruby, and Axel on their path tonight for better or worse, and my job would come to an end. Unfortunately, that will not erase what I know. and That burden I will have to carry with me to the end.

I got up and ran my hand down my clothes. There was one last thing for me to do while Reika performed the sleeping spell on Olcan and Mathieu.

I walked to the center of the room and closed my eyes, and when I reopened them, I knew they were no longer my typical shade of blue but instead, a milky white. I waved my hand, and what looked like a shimmering sheet of light began to crawl over the walls. Once the room was sealed, I walked over to my closet and removed a small rectangular box from under a pile of clothes.

I sighed as I stared down at the wooden box, strange writings engraved on it that only I could see. "I hate this part. I really hate this part."

I returned to the middle of the room and sat on the floor. I placed the box in front of me and exhaled as I closed my eyes, fear gripping me in a tight embrace. I knew what I had to do. I didn't have a choice. I listened to my breathing for a moment before opening my eyes and repeating the words written on the box.

As my chanting grew louder, the words began to glow, one letter at a time. Once all the letters were glowing, I opened the box to reveal a silver dagger. I swallowed as I picked it up and turned it over in my hand. If anyone was watching, they would think I had maybe removed a spell from the box. In fact, I actually summoned this dagger from somewhere else, another plane to be exact.

The double-bladed dagger was warm to the touch. I held its' crystal-encrusted handle with both hands and closed my eyes. I didn't give myself time to think before I plunged the dagger into my chest.

My body stiffened instantly and, my eyes grew wide from the pain that was burning through my chest. I felt my life force draining away, and my head fell back as I started to scream. Tears began to flow from my eyes, but instead of falling downward, they started to float above me. Suddenly, my head was thrown forward.

I could hear whispering voices, and a chill went through my body.

"Yes, I can hear you." I didn't recognize my own voice as it was deep and contorted. I sounded possessed. I tightened my hold on the blade handle, blood soaking through my blouse. "I did as you asked." The whispers echoed through the room, and my head bent to the side. "Yes, I know, but I had no choice." My head bent to the other side, and I sighed. "I understand." I listened to the whispers, to my new instructions, and my body jerked as I felt the feathery touches of a hand caress my cheek. "But there has to be some way to..." The whispers grew loud, and I winced, more tears leaving my eyes to hover above me. "Okay, I understand."

The dagger in my chest vanished, and my hands fell to my sides. I gasped as I fell forward and then started to cough as air filled my lungs. The pain in my chest was gone, as if stabbing myself had just been a bad dream, but my body was shaking uncontrollably. I pressed my cheek to the cold ground as the images before my eyes started to clear, and I knew my eyes had now returned to their normal color.

I laid there for a moment, my energy completely depleted. The pain I had felt as I thrusted that dagger into my chest was nothing compared to what I had just seen.

I'm not sure exactly when I dozed off, but when I woke up, I was lying on my back, dried tears on my cheeks making my skin feel stiff. I felt strong enough to get up, so I made my way to the bathroom. I removed my bloody top and touched a finger to my chest. There wasn't even a scar.

I'm glad that was the first and last time I'd have to do something like that. I felt like I had been hit by a bus. I soaped up my rag and began scrubbing at the dried blood on me. The water was scorching hot, but I barely felt it. I was too lost in my thoughts.

Had I really just killed myself?

"Natalie?"

My hand froze where I had been washing my legs, and I stood up straight.

"Yes? Did you do it?" I asked Reika through our mind link.

"I did. They're asleep, and neither will wake until the morning."

I turned the tap on full blast and stepped under it. "Good. Now all they need to do is survive."

CHAPTER TEN

RUBY

I packed immediately after getting to my room and stashed the backpack under my bed. I had a suitcase packed and placed by the door just in case Olcan decided to stop by and check up on me. He'd see that I was ready to leave. I just wouldn't be leaving with him.

All that was left to do was for me to wait until midnight to meet Xavier outside, but waiting was harder than I thought it would be. I spent the time pacing back and forth in my room until I got paranoid that someone might hear me moving around and wonder why I was so excessively active late at night.

I laid on my bed after that, twisting and turning until I settled on facing the window. With the moon's light shining down, it appeared unusually bright outside. While it looked beautiful, I was worried. Xavier wouldn't be able to shift tonight, which made both of us vulnerable. I know he would still be incredibly strong, but nowhere near his best.

Natalie said she would take care of everything, whatever that meant. I was trying to put my faith in her and not worry. That is really hard to do when you are used to something always going wrong. That was my childhood in a nutshell, and my young adulthood wasn't shaping up to be any better so far, that's for sure. I wasn't sure why it was still surprising to me that Olcan wanted me dead. I had no doubt going to Romania wouldn't have been a vacation but being killed wasn't in my plans. Considering that Reika had confirmed for him that the mate bond was real and mates are protected by law...but hey, who am I kidding? The Council were the ones making all the rules. They can change them, or even break them, as they see fit. Who would even know about it to challenge them on it?

Axel was the other person I wanted to castrate. Why wasn't he tearing Olcan a new one for talking about killing me! That's another thing I should stop being surprised about. Axel isn't Xavier, and he'll never be Xavier. I might be mated to him, but the connection is barely there. The only time I had even felt something towards him was during our drive here when he had opened up to me about wanting to be a good alpha. He was like a parent that would do anything to provide for his kids, and that at least I could understand. Conspiring with Olcan was something I couldn't, wouldn't forgive him for.

The hours went by agonizingly slow, but eventually, I was standing in front of my door with my backpack on. My hair was wrapped into a bun, and I pulled my hoody over my head while I zipped my sweater to my throat. Not for the first time tonight, I wished Xavier could shift. I'm sure we could cover more ground with me riding him.

I reached out and held the door handle, my hand shaking as I opened it slowly. I didn't make a sound, but I continued to move slowly, opening it just enough to slip through and taking my time to close it quietly once more.

Whatever Natalie planned to do, I hoped she had already done it. I wasn't about to go running through the house to test it out. I was sure it took twenty minutes at least to make it outside. When I finally did, my heart was pounding out of my chest. I gratefully inhaled the cool night air.

A shadow appeared from behind a tree at the forest line, and my heart skipped a beat until the shadow waved at me. I narrowed my eyes and when I realized it was Xavier, I dashed towards him. I threw myself into his arms, and he kissed the top of my head before taking my hand and leading me into the forest.

"We made it out," I whispered to him as he stared at the house. I bit my lip as the muscles in his jaws clenched. He threw his hood over his head and turned. "Are you okay?" I knew I was a stupid question to ask. He was about to run away from his home, his father, and his pack. I just didn't know what else to say.

"I will be, once we get far away from here."

He took my hand, and we started walking briskly. We stopped from time to time for him to listen to the forest. Even though his hearing was ten times better than mine would ever be, his heightened abilities weren't at their usual level because of the full moon. We were still in his pack's territory and running into another wolf wouldn't be good. With our backpacks on our backs, it was clear that we were running away and not just going out for a late-night stroll.

"I wonder what Natalie had to do to 'take care of things'," he said as he avoided walking in a pocket of moonlight beaming down through the canopy of trees above.

"Why?"

"We made it out and made it this far. Council members are like royalty, which means they are stronger than even alphas. Their senses are heightened to the max, so I'd expected old Olcan to be on high alert tonight. He'd be the first hear when someone so much as coughed in bed, much less when two people got up and left the house."

I moved a tree branch from before my face. "Natalie's different, stronger. Whatever she did, it worked." Despite how briskly we were walking, I knew he felt like we were moving too slowly. He was going at this pace just so I could keep up. "Have you ever met any of the other Council members?" I asked as I picked up the pace to show him that I could go faster. Yes, I was tired, but knowing what I was running from was motivation enough to keep me going.

"No. Olcan's the first Council member I've met. Council members don't usually make appearances like this. They send representatives."

I didn't respond, and we kept walking until Xavier suddenly stopped. "What?" I asked, and he pressed a finger to my lips.

He pointed his head to the sky and inhaled asI started looking around us. Despite the moonlight, the forest was still too dark for me to see much. I wanted to ask him what he was hearing or smelling in the air but kept my mouth shut. I had grabbed a knife on my way out of the house, and I removed it slowly from where it was tucked into my left sleeve as Xavier turned his back to me and positioned himself protectively in between whatever he sensed and me.

"Come out. I can smell you," he growled, and my heart fell to my feet.

Fuck, they caught us!

I remained behind Xavier when I heard leaves crunching under feet. *Hell, noo, I'm not going back, not without a fight!* I stepped out from behind him, my knife in hand.

"Axel?" I looked him up and down with my knife still raised, and he looked down at the blade reflecting the moon's light. His eyes flicked up to mine and the corner of his mouth arched a little before Xavier growled and it fell away. They stared at each other for a moment and Axel rubbed at his nostrils and shook his head.

So Olcan sent him after us. How theatrical.

"Did you really think I couldn't smell you standing outside the door?" He asked before his eyes slid to me once more, and I glared at him.

"So, you knew I could hear you talking to Olcan about killing me? Yeah, that makes me feel so much better. I get the message,

Axel, you care that little about me." I widened my stance. "I'm not going to Romania."

He shrugged. "Good. I'm glad. "

"What?" I asked, shocked at his response.

"Why are you following us?" Xavier added, and I finally noticed the backpack Axel was carrying.

"None of this was what I wanted," he said, and I scoffed.

"Yeah, you just wanted to get rid of the Blackmoon Pack," I snapped at him, and to my surprise, he nodded. *This man clearly has no shame.*

"Yes, I wanted to get rid of the Blackmoon Pack, but not like this. All I've wanted is to be allowed back onto this land. It's big enough for both packs to co-exist comfortably. All I've ever wanted is a better existence for my pack."

"Yeah, I heard you're Alpha now," Xavier replied, a growl in his voice. "What's wrong with your father?"

Axel's face morphed into one of anger. The last thing that needed to happen right was another fight between these two. "That's not important right now, is it? I'm not here to take you guys back, okay. I'm coming with you."

Xavier laughed, and I lowered my knife. Axel, however, remained serious as he waited for Xavier to realize he wasn't kidding. *He wants to come with us? Why? He started all of this because of his duty to his pack, and now he is ready all of a sudden to make himself a fugitive and leave them behind?* Yeah, I didn't believe him either.

"We don't need you to come with us, Axel. I think you've done enough. So, you want me to believe that you're suddenly willing to leave your pack to follow us? The Council will be coming after us and you."

"I don't blame either of you for not trusting me, but believe it or not, I'm on your side." I laughed. and he stepped forward. Xavier immediately held his hand out to block me. Axel stepped back, despite the growl that had left his lips. "I'm already on the

Council's radar now, and my pack will be as well if I return to them."

Neither Xavier nor I said anything, and he sighed and held his forehead. This was the most words I've ever heard from his lips. If he was acting, he deserved an Oscar.

"Trust me if you want to, or don't. but I'm on your side. No matter what you both think, I don't want to see you die, Ruby. None of the three of us asked for this, but this is apparently how it is going to be. Fighting it, and each other is only making all of our lives worse."

Xavier's hand dropped after blocking me to adjust the strap of his bag on his shoulder. I couldn't tell if he was buying what Axel was selling, but I was (despite my better judgment). Maybe I'm stupid, but why would Olcan send him and only him to take us back? Then again, it's not like he could send Reika or Mathieu. I felt torn. It bothered me that I was so easily trying to find reasons to give him the benefit of the doubt, considering that this entire mess was his fault. As I went over the conversation between Axel and Olcan in my mind again, I realized I never actually heard Axel agree to my death. In retrospect, I realized, if anything, he had sounded surprised that Olcan had said it.

"Look, Ruby, you are my mate. I'm not good at this kind of stuff. I still have my doubts because you know a Grand Elderand it changes a lot." He turned to Xavier. "Olcan wants what's inside her head and if he gets it, he's going to kill her and everyone that knew about her. We are wasting time standing here and debating this. Besides, the Council will be hunting you guys. If that's the case, the way I see it, you need all the help you can get."

"Okay," Xavier replied, and I frowned. I stared at him, surprised he was agreeing. Axel removed his bag from one shoulder and swung it around him to open it.

"What? Are you serious?" I whispered to Xavier, although I knew Axel could hear me just fine. "*Okay*? Just like that?'

"He's right. If the Council gets their hands on you, we're all dead—my dad, Natalie, everyone. With Axel with us, he'll be able to protect you as well. That doesn't mean I automatically trust him. Believe me, I will be watching him." He said that bit loudly, but Axel only kept searching through his bag.

"Here," Axel said as he approached us, three small vials of slightly brownish liquid in his hand. "I had these created by witches for my pack. It masks a wolf's scent. I was able to track you guys all too easily."

"I'm not drinking that. You said it is for wolves." I pointed out as I crossed my arms. This could be some kind of trick - maybe a sedative that would put Xavier and me to sleep.

"It masks anyone's scent. You were given it when you were taken." He took one of the vials, popped it open and drank it. "See? Make no mistake, by morning they'll be hunting us so our scents need to stop here."

I didn't feel comfortable doing this, but what other choice did I have? We had wasted too much time standing here chatting as it was. Xavier and I each took a vial and chugged it. Let me tell you, the taste was utterly repellent, but within seconds, Xavier pointed out that he could no longer smell me or Axel.

We walked on in uncomfortable silence, and I remained close to Xavier's side while Axel followed behind us. After an hour passed, exhaustion began to set in. My legs were dragging and I was slowing down, despite my initial resolve to keep up. Axel and Xavier were still maintaining at the same brisk pace they had set throughout the journey with no outward signs of fatigue that I could see.

"I'm exhausted," I said, and Xavier took my backpack. The weight off my shoulders was a relief, but my legs were still killing me.

"Where are we going anyway?" Axel asked as he removed a water bottle from his bag and handed it to me. I only stared at it before taking one from my bag. I wasn't ready to trust or forgive him that easily after what he had put me through. Not yet, anyway.

Animals and insects of the night sang around me, and I wished I could mute them all. I had to admit that I, too, was suddenly curious about where Xavier was taking us. I hadn't even bothered to ask before we left.

"I don't know. First things first. I'm getting us as far away from the pack as possible. We'll put a few cities between us and this place, and then find a town with no wolf packs and lay low."

Axel stepped around us, his hazel eyes shining oddly bright as he stared at the forest around us. "Okay. Well, I have a safe house, and no one else knows about it. It's about two days' drive from here, though. If we can make it there somehow, we can lay low more safely and take a little extra time to figure out our next move."

"Why do you have a safe house?" I asked as we started walking once more. Axel was now ahead of us and honestly, I didn't mind. I hadn't been comfortable with him walking behind me.

"All packs do. All *alphas* do. Wolves are very territorial, and not all packs are large. There has to be a place an alpha can go if he's challenged and he loses. That's if he survives the fight long enough to make it to their safe house. Don't you have one, too?"

I assumed that question was for Xavier, so I said nothing as I drank more water. This wasn't going to go well, I could tell. Nothing good could come from all three of us being together. They both hated each other.

"Yes, but all of those locations are known by at least two others. Olcan will no doubt have them checked out anyway."

"Well, fortunately, mine is completely off the grid. We'll need a car."

Axel

A wolf walking almost three hours on a full moon isn't smart. By the time we made it off Blackmoon territory and found a road and a gas station, we were all exhausted and irritable. Well, I wouldn't say Xavier and I were exhausted. We were tired and definitely hungry, but Ruby was on an absolute warpath.

Neither of us had been able to speak to her until she had eaten three bags of snacks and drank the two coffees that I got at the gas station. Yes, I said *got* them there, not *bought* them there, since it was three in the morning and I had to break in.

Even with limitations of the full moon, Xavier and I had been clearly able to hear her crying in the bathroom. She came out with her face dry and her sassy attitude back to being less than appealing as if she hadn't just spent five minutes bawling her eyes out. I admired her for it, though. Our situation was one that would drive anyone crazy, and she was keeping it together better than I had expected.

It had been funny to see her standing there with a knife in her hands. I had no doubt in my mind that she wouldn't have hesitated to use it. It amazed me that she was ready to run headfirst into a fight with a werewolf, despite the obvious futility of such an action. The full moon wouldn't be enough to keep a werewolf male from incapacitating her, and she knew it. She as brave like a wolf, so I guess it made sense that she ended up mated to one... well, with her attitude, I guess it made sense she was mated to two of us.

Neither Xavier nor Ruby trusted me right now, and I couldn't really fault either of them for that. I wouldn't trust me either after the additional problems I've caused. I will always regret ever trusting that bastard Olcan. I should have known he had his own agenda. Killing Ruby or Xavier was never what I wanted.

I hope my beta had received my message and had taken my father away from the pack. While Mathieu's pack will be fine for now, Olcan might feel the need to get revenge on me and mine for me betraying him.

It was almost morning and the potions we drank would be wearing off in a few hours. Olcan will realize we're missing soon, if he hasn't already, and then we'll have people keeping an eye out for us. Or worse, rogue wolves. The faster we get out of here, the better. I looked up at the moon and buried my hands in my jacket pockets. This was going to be a journey and then some because neither of them trusted me or wanted me around. I wasn't in the mood to go out of my way to prove myself, but I'd have to work to gain their trust eventually or this would be much harder it needed to be. We had wasted precious minutes back there standing and bickering.

Also, while Ruby had been in the bathroom, Xavier had taken the time to warn me.

"I'm only okay with you being here because she needs to be protected, and I can't do it on my own if the Council decides to treat us like rogues."

"I think that's exactly what we are now, Xavier. But it's big of you to admit you can't care for her the way I can."

Of course, I knew that's not what he meant, but I hadn't been able to stop myself from razzing him just a bit. I hated how she stared at him as if he was the sun or moon and her world revolved around him. I hated how much she hung on to him as if he was keeping her grounded to the earth while she looked at me like I might steal her panties. I've treated her badly from the start, so I know I don't deserve her kindness. But dammit, I'm not a monster.

"You have nothing to worry about," I had told him to head off the inevitable argument. "Your girlfriend is yours and yours alone."

I closed my eyes and inhaled deeply. Why was I bothered about all of that anyway? I said it myself - I don't want to be with her - so why am I wasting brainpower obsessing about the connection she has with someone else? They were made for each other, and I was just unlucky enough to get tied into their romance. Maybe the goddess was punishing me by giving me a mate I can't really have

They were standing a few steps away from me bickering, and I honestly had no interest in listening to their conversation. We needed to find a car. I could smell rotting garbage, gas, and nature, and I frowned as I forced my senses to do better, to stretch further After a moment, I caught onto the scent I was looking for.

"There are humans near here," I said, and they looked my way as I removed my bag and placed it on the ground. "Maybe it's the owners for this place, but either way, I'm going to check if they have a car."

I started walking off when Ruby spoke. "Don't kill them."

I froze. I'm not used to words being hurtful because I rarely give a fuck about what people think of me, but that had stung. *So that's what she thinks of me? That I'm a cold-blooded killer?* I may hate humans, but I have never and would never kill them without reason. I shook my head and kept walking. "Don't worry, Ruby, I'll only kill them if they see me."

———

Ruby

Axel had been gone for twenty minutes before he returned with an SUV. It was a relief to get off my legs, but the awkward silence in the car was driving me up a wall.

I was sitting in the back while both men were in the front. I don't think either of them was particularly excited about being in such close proximity to each other. I looked from one man to the next, my annoyance peaking since neither made a move to turn the radio on. Did neither of them know that playing the radio is the number one way to cover an awkward silence? We'd been driving for almost an hour and no one had spoken since we had left the gas station.

I knew we were on the run for our safety, but at this point, I think Olcan's company would be preferable to these two brooding men. Olcan might be evil, but at least he was chatty. I hated awkward silences.

It was getting closer to dawn, and I desperately needed sleep. It had been a long night. No, a long couple of days and nights. I scooted closer to the door to rest my head against the window and sighed as I closed my eyes. They soon popped open after I started seeing more of those disturbing images behind them, the very things I didn't want to see more of.

No matter how exhausted I was, however, no matter how my legs felt like they were going to fall off, I couldn't sleep. I was haunted by the events that have happened so far, each and every time I closed my eyes. I kept seeing Olcan staring at me ,and I kept hearing screaming. Falling asleep would offer me a few minutes or hours of escape from this world, but now I wasn't even being afforded that basic luxury.

I tried to bring a good image to mind, the one of Xavier and me at the hidden falls. I focused on remembering the sound of the crashing water. I focused on the feel of it on my skin and tried to remember exactly how relaxed I had felt. After a while, my eyes closed and I must have fallen asleep because whispering voices had me jumping up. Thankfully, it wasn't the voices I had heard in the halls of Xavier's house. It was just Xavier and Axel talking.

I closed my eyes once more but tried to listen to what they were talking about. I soon gave up and moved forward so I was between them.

"What are you two talking about?" I asked as I looked from one to the next.

"Private conversation," Axel replied, and I flipped him the bird.

"Once we get to Axel's safe house, our next move has to be finding a way to break through that wall in your mind," Xavier replied. Axel, who was driving, nodded. "We'll just need to find a witch, a strong one."

"One that won't tell the entire supernatural community

about us," Axel added. "Witches gossip too much, and it'll be hard to find one that'll want anything to do with wolves, to begin with."

"What about Willow?" I suggested. She was the only witch I've met so far, and Xavier seemed to trust her. "If she's not strong enough to do it, maybe she'll know someone that is."

He nodded. "We'll see. You didn't sleep very long. How do you feel?"

"Like shit. I swear I'm usually more fit than this."

"I'll believe it when I see it." Axel murmured under his breath, and I pinned him with a glare. I was just about to give him a piece of my mind when Xavier leaned forward.

He looked from left to right on either side of the road, and soon Axel started to do the same. *Is this a wolf thing?* I wondered as I watched them when Xavier suddenly pinched his nostrils.

"What the fuck is that?" Xavier asked, and Axel's face twisted with disgust. I didn't smell anything however and it must be fuel with the way they both looked.

I inhaled deeply, but still, I didn't smell anything. "What? I don't smell anything."

"I can't explain it," Xavier said as he started to look in the back of the car, but there was nothing to see but our bags and me. "It's like something is rotting or dead, but there is another underlying smell as well. I feel like my eyes are going to start tearing up. What the hell is that?" The car suddenly swayed, and I was thrown against the door. "Axel, what the fuck?!"

"Something just ran across the road!" Axel yelled back, and the car suddenly accelerated. "Something's wrong here. Something is outside. That's what we smell."

"I've never smelled anything like this. What is it?"

Axel didn't respond. I leaned forward again, my hand holding onto Xavier's seat while the other massaged my shoulder that had smacked into the door. "Is it a supernatural?"

"With the incredible speed it ran across the road with, it must be. No human is that fast," Axel replied and his grip tightened on the steering wheel.

I couldn't see his face since I was behind him, but I could see his jaw and the way it was clenching. I looked over at Xavier, and he, too, looked more disturbed than I'd ever seen him. Then I remembered they still couldn't shift. They were vulnerable with some unknown supernatural creature following us.

"Maybe it's the Council. Maybe they sent someone, or something, after us," I said as I sat back. Axel was hitting 160mph, and I knew if he suddenly stepped on the break, I'd be thrown through the windscreen.

Axel shook his head, "They would have had to track our scent. The potions haven't worn off yet. Do you have a gun?"

Xavier nodded, "Yes. Ruby?"

I had grabbed for his bag as soon as he had said yes. As the lone human here, I wasn't happy knowing that there was something unknown out there that was threatening enough to rattle two male werewolves. For once in my life, just once, I'd like the universe to give me a win. And by a win, I mean a fucking break.

My hand touched something cold. I pulled the gun from the bag, but as I handed it to Xavier, something slammed into the car. I was thrown back against the door, my head slamming against the dark glass. Axel was cursing profusely as he tried to regain control of the car.

I didn't have time to see if my head was bleeding because I had to grip Xavier's seat with all my strength until the car stopped spinning. We swerved back and forth as Xavier dived into the back of the car to grab the gun that had fallen out of my hand and onto the seat.

Something barrelled into the car on the left side where I was, and I was thrown to the other side of the car as we were sent off the road.

"Xavier!" I screamed, but as soon as his name left my lips, the car came to a stop as it slammed into a tree.

I groaned and held my head, my hazy eyes trying to focus on the roof of the car that was still spinning. Whatever was outside was definitely trying to kill us. I sat up slowly, my hand holding the back of my head. Although I couldn't see anything, I could feel the warm liquid and knew I was bleeding.

I swallowed and blinked slowly, my eyes finally focusing when Axel appeared in the space between the seats, blood running down his face from a cut above his right brow.

"Ruby? Are you okay?" He asked me as he reached out to me. I pointed to Xavier, my hand shaking because there was a large crack in the windscreen where his head had hit it. He wasn't moving.

Axel grabbed him and pulled him back so he was sitting back in his seat and not hunched over the dashboard. He started to regain consciousness as he groaned and raised his hand to hold his head.

Neither of them was healing as quickly as I knew they could. "Xavier?" I called, my voice weak and broken, "It's still outside the car."

I shouldn't have said that. I never should have opened my mouth because a second later, Axel's door was ripped off the car. A clawed hand reached in and pulled him out.

I screamed. I screamed like I've never screamed before in my life as Axel's deep cry pierced through the night, and Xavier instantly regained full consciousness. He opened his car door shakily, and I did the same. I stumbled out, and strong hands grabbed me before I could fall onto my face.

This can't be happening. We've come so far; we had almost gotten away! Xavier started pulling me, but I was looking behind me for Axel. *We can't leave him, we can't just leave him.* The night had fallen silent once more, and my heart felt heavy with dread.

He can't be dead! Please don't let him be dead!

"Xavier!"

"Ruby, I need you to…"

He didn't finish his sentence as he was yanked away from me. I fell backward as I watched a man cloaked in darkness climb onto him. Xavier's howl pierced through the night as he fought the shadowy figure.

"Run!" Xavier yelled. "Ruby, run!"

*I can't leave him! I can't*I got to my feet, nonetheless, and started running. My eyes were blinded with tears, my body aching with pain, and my heart-breaking as I listened to Xavier's howls and cries. I pumped my legs despite the burning, but I didn't get far.

Something grabbed me and threw me forward. The pain burned through my left shoulder as I skidded on the cold highway. I tried to get up, but I only fell forward once more. I could hear slow footsteps behind me, and I rolled onto my back.

It wasn't a shadow. It was a man, but it was like no man I've ever seen. He was pale, his eyes like two flashlights in the dark, but what chilled me to my bone was when he opened his mouth and revealed his massive fangs.

I began dragging myself backward, the pebbles on the road cutting into my arms, but I couldn't stop. He was advancing on me, his lips pulling away into a wide smile.

"Please," I begged, my hot tears cooling as soon as they fell from my eyes to slide down my cheeks.

He tsk-tsked at me, and the last thing I saw as he fell onto me were his glowing red eyes. The last thing I felt was the piercing pain of fangs ripping into my throat.

Luna Conflicted

Book Three

CHAPTER ONE

Have you ever been stabbed? Have you ever felt anything razor-sharp piercing into your body, tearing through skin and flesh? Do you have any idea how excruciating that is?

I could feel the man's pointed fangs slicing through my skin as if I was made of butter. I could feel his curved claws digging into my shoulders as he held me down to feed on me. I listened in abject horror as he slurped noisily on my blood.

So, this is how I die—being slurped on like a milkshake?

I screamed. My wide eyes that had been glued to the dark sky above in fright screwed tightly shut as I screamed for my life. I could feel my body growing weaker and weaker, the more he fed on me. My screams were muffled as he covered my mouth and forced my head to the side.

Xavier, Axel...are they dead?

Are they being fed on the way I am?

I could feel my tears sliding from my eyes. When I opened them, I could barely see the world around me now as blurry as an impressionist painting. I could still feel the pain in my neck, but it felt almost distant. I was dying.

That was when it appeared—a shadow above the vampire. He was too busy feeding on me to notice it.

My eyelids felt like they were being weighed down by an anchor and though I tried, I couldn't call out to the shadow for help. I couldn't even move.

The vampire pressed down on my face and the world around me finally faded away.

I bolted upright, my hand gripping my chest as I gasped for breath. I started looking around me frantically, my eyes wide and my body shivering.

I was in a room, a dark room. For a second, I thought maybe it had all been a dream until my hand flew to my neck. My shoulders slumped as I felt the bandage there. Unfortunately, it had not been a dream, but instead a real-life nightmare.

Xavier. Axel.

The names echoed in my mind and I looked around the semi-dark room once more as I got out of the bed.

Where am I?

My only hope was that whoever saved me also saved Xavier and Axel as well. I had too many questions and no one to answer them. I decided to look for someone.

The hallway was dark, but I could see light down the hall coming from a room. The tiles were cold under my feet, my steps slow as I walked on my toes to prevent any sound of my approach. Whoever it was in that room might not be friendly. I still didn't know why that person saved me, or what their intentions were.

I stopped walking as I held onto the oversized shirt I was wearing. *Maybe it's the Council. Maybe they caught up with us just in time to save my life.* But if it was the Council that saved me, then my survival was merely temporary. After they got what they wanted from me, my life would still come to an end, just at their hands instead. *I need to find the guys. I hope they are alive to be found.* My chest tightened at the thought and I clenched my fists.

What was that man that bit me? I thought to myself as I

continued walking. There had been just enough light for me to see his pale skin and crimson eyes. I still knew so little about the supernatural community, I could only guess that maybe he was a demon or a vampire. No, he couldn't have been. If Axel and Xavier couldn't tell what was hunting us by its scent, no way could he be a vampire. They would know what a demon or vampire smelled like, right?

From what I understood, werewolves used to act as protectors, assuming the role of watchdogs – no pun intended – for both the humans and the supernatural world alike. Now only some packs chose to function as guardians. Like Xavier's pack–they hunted down supernaturals who sought to create havoc or do harm. So wouldn't Xavier know any supernatural creature well enough by its scent?

Whispering voices met my ears as I drew closer to the door.

"We don't have a choice. We have to tell the others because they will be back. This will buy us time with the Council."

I felt a pang of relief as I made out Axel's voice, and then I frowned. Why was I so concerned for him? I rolled my eyes. I certainly was unhappy with his behavior towards me, but I didn't want anything serious to happen to him. Deep down, some part of me felt relieved he'd survived the attack.

"Once Ruby wakes up, we'll leave. Not before."

I closed my eyes and sighed as I heard Xavier speak. I walked into the room. Their gazes turned to me, but my eyes fell on a man standing to the left of the room.

His grey eyes found mine and he gave me a warm smile.

I returned it and looked away. "What's going on? What happened?"

Xavier walked over to me, his eyes glistening as he guided me to a chair. "Sit." He nodded almost imperceptibly at the grey-eyed man and then he backed away.

The stranger then moved to approach me, a strand of yellow blonde hair falling onto his forehead as he bent down.

I pulled away somewhat as the unknown man reached out to me.

He paused. "I'm only going to check your wound."

I looked at Xavier and then Axel, who had his arms crossed over his chest. I frowned because there was a thin pink line running from his left cheek down to his neck. No doubt, a wound he had suffered at the hands of the unknown supernatural that had already healed.

I exhaled and allowed the man to remove the bandage from my neck, wincing somewhat as the tape pulled at my skin.

He nodded as he stepped back. "All healed."

"Already?" Xavier asked, and Axel moved forward to see my neck. A look passed between them.

I reached up and touched the area. True enough, I was healed. The area felt completely smooth as if nothing had happened. I couldn't feel any evidence of the horrible trauma I endured, not even the raised skin of a telltale scar left behind. "Is there a mark?" I asked.

The man shook his head. "There is none," he replied as he glanced at Axel and then Xavier. He crossed the room to throw my bandage in a bin.

I watched him with narrowed eyes. *Who is he? Where the hell were we, anyway? How long had I been asleep in order for my wound to have healed completely? And how could I have healed without so much as a mark?* That man—creature had ripped into my throat.

I hadn't realized I had been slowly massaging the area until Xavier held my hand. It was as if I could still feel something there, despite being healed.

"How are you feeling?" he asked me, as he looked me up and down.

Suddenly aware that I was wearing nothing except a large T-shirt barely reaching my knees, my cheeks began to heat. "I feel fine." I pulled my hand away and interlocked my fingers on my lap.

"I feel fine, just kind of in shock, I guess. What attacked us? How long have I been sleeping?"

Xavier sat down across from me while Axel remained standing, his hazel eyes piercing into me.

I still couldn't understand why I was so panicked when he'd been yanked out of the car. I'd felt a stab of fear so strong, I could barely think. I don't want to care about him, but apparently, that isn't completely under my conscious control. Some part of me did care about Axel, whether I wanted to or not. When had this happened? Would I have ever known how much I cared about Axel if we hadn't been placed in a life or death situation? How could I have feelings for a man who once almost yanked my hair out from the root as he dragged me out of his dungeon?

Maybe because he showed you he wasn't a complete asshole by leaving with you and Xavier, thereby putting himself and his pack at risk.

"You've been asleep for a good while," Axel replied, his gravelly voice carried through the room. He then pinched the bridge of his nose and turned away. "We were attacked by vampires."

So, I was right after all.

I studied Xavier thoughtfully, taking in his beautiful face. As his eyes hadn't left me since I walked into this room. I thought I had lost him when I heard him screaming as he'd faced the vampire while the pain in my heart had damn near killed me. I sighed. "Why did neither of you know that it was vampires outside the car when you first smelled them?" My eyes drifted to Axel when he turned around to stare at me. "You two panicked."

"I didn't panic," Axel retorted.

I made a face. *Who is he kidding?* "Yes, you did. I was there...remember? Why don't you guys know what vampires smell like?" I stared at Xavier, whose lips formed a thin line, and I frowned. The room was filled with silence and my eyes found the blonde man who'd been listening to our conversation quietly.

He was holding his chin, a finger gliding back and forth over his lips.

No one seemed interested in answering me.

Axel dug his hands into his pockets.

Xavier's soothing voice licked at my ears, "This is the first time either of us has met a vampire."

Axel cleared his throat. "Vampires have been extinct for hundreds of years."

I frowned as I tilted my head to the side. "What?" The blonde man briefly drew my attention as he left the room, then I glanced back over at Axel. He'd certainly piqued my interest with that unexpected statement. *So, if vampires had been extinct for hundreds of years, how exactly had one just ripped into my throat?*

Axel sat down and crossed his legs.

I noticed for the first time just how exhausted both Xavier and he looked.

"What we know about vamps now comes from stories told to us over the years," Xavier said. "They were said to be bloodthirsty and animalistic, with no shred of thought other than the drive to quench their ravenous thirst."

Axel sat forward, his elbows on his knees. The strands of his hair loose from his bun slid forward to cover his cheeks. "Vampires were the parasites of the earth. Their only purpose was to exist, feed, and populate."

An image of the vampire that attacked me appeared in my mind as Axel spoke and a chill passed through my body.

"Their thirst for blood, any and every creature's blood, is insatiable," Axel went on. "As a result, they lived as outcasts. They belonged to no community, supernatural or otherwise, because they contaminated and killed everything they came into contact with. Years ago, werewolves, humans, and several other supernaturals banded together and waged war on them, wiping them out for good."

"Umm, I think they survived," I replied under my breath.

"Clearly." Axel nodded. "They were said to be pale, hideous creatures capable of turning any living being–human, werewolf, witch, anyone–into bloodsuckers like themselves. Their venom is so strong, it is capable of completely changing one's anatomy–completely erasing who and what you are. They were among the most dangerous supernatural beings in existence." He shook his head. "Still are, apparently."

I nodded.

Xavier ran his hand down his face, pulling his cheeks down. "I can't figure out how they've survived without anyone knowing. In all the stories I've heard, no one ever mentioned that their scent is so strong. How have they masked it for so many years?"

That vampire that attacked me had indeed been pale, but he hadn't been hideous. Maybe he hadn't shown his true self? He also hadn't seemed like a bloodthirsty, thoughtless creature. Well, bloodthirsty, maybe. But thoughtless? No, I'd gotten the feeling he'd been a lot closer to a human or werewolf in thoughts and motivations than Axel and Xavier's stories were depicting. "So, what are we going to do?" I asked as I looked at them both.

"We have no choice but to go back home," Xavier replied as he tapped a finger on the arm of the chair.

"No," I said as I shook my head. "I can't go back. The two of you know I can't. Vampires or not, the Council wants me dead. Have you both forgotten that?"

Axel huffed. "Forgotten it? It's the reason we left. It's the reason we were attacked by vampires. How can we forget, Ruby? You need to remember that they want Xavier and me dead as well now. This isn't only about you."

"Axel," Xavier said in a warning tone.

I bit my lip and looked away. Axel was right. My life wasn't the only one on the line here, but I was scared. Not only was I running from the all-powerful werewolf Council, but now there were vampires on the loose out there, ones that even intimidated two full-grown male werewolves.

These two men were alphas-to-be. In fact, Axel was an alpha in all but name. Yet, they had their asses handed to them when they'd faced off against that vamp. Sure, it had been a full moon, and they had been caught off guard. But still, I did feel terrified of anything that could strike fear into these two men. I didn't know about the guys, but I wasn't interested in becoming some vampire's lunch, or worse, getting turned into a vamp myself.

"Ruby?"

I looked Xavier's way as my name glided off his lips like honey.

"This new threat, it's very serious," he said. "If vampires are back and we know they are, this means trouble. We have to warn my dad and the Council. Other packs need to know this. I don't know much about vampires, but if the stories are true, then the entire world is in danger."

"The stories are true," Axel added. "Even if they have been altered over time, the danger vampires pose is real. They are savages, and because of their infectious bite, they multiply quickly. We don't know how many people were turned before we were attacked."

I wanted to ask him why we couldn't simply call Mathieu and warn him, but I knew that would be selfish. I'd been lucky to survive being bitten...I knew this. If vampires decided to attack now, how many more would die if they maintained their element of surprise? "Okay," I replied as I scratched at my brow and closed my eyes. I quickly reopened them when I started to get a flashback of the vampire as he attacked me, his glistening white fangs aimed directly at my throat. "Okay," I repeated, as I rolled my shoulders and sat up straight. "We do need to warn everyone."

Axel sat back and reclined in his seat, his eyes lowering into slits. "There's a book that has been in my family for generations. Supposedly, it holds the history of werewolves and other supernatural beings. I was never allowed to look inside it as a child. In fact, it's been so long since I've even seen it that I'd almost forgotten about it." He looked back and forth between the two of us, a contemplative look on his face. "It contains information on vampires, their weaknesses, and how to fight them. Any knowledge we can gain from it about vampires will be helpful since we know so little right now."

At this point, I was barely listening to him. My mind had taken me back to that highway, to the moment when I felt my blood gushing from my neck as that vampire consumed it. My shoulder twitched, something like a phantom feeling still present there.

"Ruby?" Xavier called to me.

My head snapped towards him.

He stared at me with concern.

I looked away, my eyes downcast to the floor. "I thought I was going to die," I said under my breath. "I thought you were both dead."

"We almost were," Axel replied.

I watched him from under my lashes.

He looked angry, and I could understand why. He wasn't someone that liked feeling out of control—this much I knew. He got his ass kicked and I could only imagine the level of his rage right now. The severity of the cut on his face underscored just how close of a call it had been.

"Who was he?" I asked. "The shadow. You know the person that saved us? Did either of you see him?" I lowered my voice. "Was it blondie?"

Axel frowned as he rose to stretch.

The action struck me as odd. It seemed too mundane coming from Axel. I supposed he must be tired. He certainly looked tired, anyways. Why did it seem as if neither Xavier nor he had rested the way I had? I glanced over at Xavier.

He'd been propping his head up with his hand, his eyes staring ahead. He appeared lost in thought.

I realized he'd barely spoken. "How long have we been here?"

His eyes shifted to me. "We've been here for two days."

"Blondie, as you called him," Axel interjected. "Wasn't the one that saved us. We're at my safe house right now, and he's the warlock I hired to watch the place. He keeps the place protected with warding. Whoever saved us and killed those vamps, got us here in a matter of hours."

I frowned as my eyes widened.

"He said there was a knock at the door and when he opened it, we were lying on the ground outside." Axel pointed at my neck. "Your wound was already almost healed and only bleeding a little. The same goes for us and our wounds. I, for one, feel drained. That fucker almost drained me."

I understood now, that's why they looked so beaten.

"On the other hand, you seem to have recovered rather quickly, especially for a human," Axel continued as he studied me suspiciously. "A little warlock magic was needed, but I would have expected your wounds to have healed slower. Your blood count would certainly take some additional time to replenish."

My eyes narrowed at his tone and the way he was staring at me. I shrugged, not sure what to say to him. How was I to answer that? "Considering this was my first time having my neck ripped open by a vampire, I don't know what to tell you. We can compare how fast I heal if it ever happens again."

And just like that, my anger at Axel returned.

"Whoever saved us must have done something to save Ruby first," Xavier said. "We were almost beyond the point of no return. It would have taken less effort to drain Ruby, I would assume, given her smaller size in comparison to us. Either way, I think it's clear that at least someone out there knows about these vamps and how to kill them. Were they just in the right place at the right time, or did they already know what was going to happen? And how did they know where to take us if this safe house is unknown to others, even Axel's pack?" He questioned, looking at Axel as he said it.

Then Xavier stood and ran his hand down his shirt. "There are a lot of questions about how we survived. All we really know is that we did. But right now, getting back to the pack has to be our priority." He turned to leave the room and paused. "Come on," he said to me. "You need to eat."

My stomach chose that moment to growl.

S ince we've been here for two days, that meant I'd been asleep for two days.

Xavier made me a sandwich. I immediately wolfed it down and asked for another. He finished his and vanished while I continued to munch on mine, eating much slower this time around.

He'd been quiet the whole time, and I could understand why. So much was happening. Too much was happening. At every turn so far, we collided with a wall. Every time a new solution presented itself, the walls started closing in. Before we knew it, we ended up trapped once more.

I looked down at the piece of sandwich left and pushed the plate away. I didn't see an end to this, especially now with this new vampire threat. I could feel it in my bones that things were about to get so much worse.

"Finally full, huh?"

I glanced over my shoulder at Axel, who stood leaning against the door.

His face lacked any expression as he stared at me.

I said nothing as I looked away. I closed my eyes and listened as he pulled the stool out beside me and sat down at the island with me.

When I opened my eyes, in my peripheral vision I could see him just staring at me. "What?" I asked as I tilted my head to look his way.

He didn't say anything and continued staring at me.

I held his stare with narrowed eyes. I didn't have time for this. Whatever game he was looking to play, I wasn't interested. I felt too tired and too worried to deal with his bullshit. "Seriously, Axel, what do you want? Am I sitting on your favorite stool or something?"

"How are you feeling?" he asked softly.

I stared at him. This wasn't what I was expecting, especially not from him. Was he being serious? Am I supposed to believe he actually cared? Less than an hour ago, he'd been looking at me suspiciously because I wasn't still in bed or battling for my life like he assumed a weak human should be. "I feel fine, Axel."

He tilted his head to the side. "The night we were attacked, I heard you. You didn't want to leave me behind. Why?"

Oh, for god's sake. I looked away and sighed. I picked up and ate the final piece of the sandwich, chewing slowly.

Axel rested his hand on the counter as his eyes continued to bore into me. "You were worried about me," he added.

I shook my head. "I wasn't."

"I know you're lying, Ruby." He leaned forward somewhat, his finger tapping against the counter. "I can tell because the octave in your voice changed, so you might as well tell me the truth. Why were you worried about me?"

He wasn't going to let this go...I could see that. I had no idea why he cared about this, but I didn't have an answer for him. I was too busy trying to figure it out myself. Why had I cared? He was the only reason we were running from the Council to begin with.

So what if he finally realized he'd fucked up and now wanted to be on Xavier's and my side? He could switch back on us at any time. He'd made it clear multiple times that his only priorities were his position as alpha and protecting his pack.

What if he was ever given an ultimatum: protect me or to remain an alpha? I wonder how that would turn out.

I smoothed my brows down as I turned to look at him. Thinking about all of that now would neither solve nor help our current situation in any way. If it ever came to that, we'd handle it then. I'd handle it then. "I don't know," I answered truthfully. "Just let it go, okay?"

"Okay," he replied easily as he leaned away from me.

I felt like I could finally breathe again. Actually, there had been something I wanted to ask him. "How are humans turned exactly? Do you know how long it takes before they start to change?"

He turned to face the island and replied, "You don't need to worry about that. I think you would have turned by now. That vampire was only feeding." He looked suddenly lost in thought.

"Are you scared?" I asked.

He looked over at me as if I'd spoken a language he didn't understand.

I could see it in his eyes the same way I could with Xavier. This was new territory for them both.

"No," he replied.

I rolled my eyes. "Yeah, I can tell when you're lying too."

His lips curved with a small smile. "So you think you know me now?"

I peered down at his arm, noticing yet another fading red line. Another wound he must have suffered while fighting the vampires. It started from just above his elbow and went all the way down to the middle of his forearm. I couldn't imagine how painful that must have been. "You know a lot about vampires,"

He turned his body to face me once more.

I scowled a bit because I hated it when he did this. The closer he got, the harder my heart pounded. It confused me even more and knowing he could hear it didn't help matters.

His brow rose. "I said I was *told* to never look inside the book. I never said I *listened*."

I couldn't help it...I laughed. It slipped out before I could stop it. "Of course you did. You listen to nothing and no one," I chided with a smirk as I shook my head. I should have expected something like that from him.

"That's right," he replied quickly and proudly.

I rolled my eyes yet again.

"My pack is one of few that still hold wolf history close," he explained. "As the years pass, things change and things are forgotten. That can't be helped, but we must have a place where history is kept and honored. No doubt, the Council has information on vampires stored away as well, but I won't be relying on them. Olcan showed me exactly how naive I have been when it comes to the Council and how they operate. My father might know more, so I'll consult him and the book. I had my beta move him to somewhere safe after we left. Olcan can't be trusted." His jaw clenched. "I know that now."

If only he had figured that out earlier, but it was in the past. When I eavesdropped on his conversation with Olcan, he'd revealed his father was ill. "What's wrong with your dad?"

He looked angry at this question.

I raised my hands. "You don't have to tell me if you don't want to. I was just curious."

"My mother died a few years ago during childbirth," he replied. "My baby sister died with her."

My eyes widened and I bit my lip, mentally slapping myself for being nosy.

"My dad hasn't been the same since. As an alpha, he carried on for a while as best he could. But unlike Xavier's father, he wasn't able to hold his broken pieces together." His eyes began to dance over my face.

Heat began to crawl up my skin. "Do you have any other siblings?"

He shook his head. "No. It's always been just me."

I could've been wrong, but I sensed so much loneliness in that response.

Axel must have realized it as well because his eyes darkened before he looked away. He got up and walked to the fridge to grab a bottle of water.

"I, um, I wonder what happened after we left, after Olcan realized we'd left." I wasn't very subtle about trying to change the subject. "Do you think he's still there?"

He finished half of the bottle in one swig. "I guess we'll find out soon enough."

"When are we leaving?"

He shrugged. "In a day or so maybe," he answered before finishing the rest of the water. "It's best if Xavier and I are back to full strength before we leave."

"I saw him, you know," I offered spontaneously.

Crossing his arms over his wide chest, he leaned on the sink.

"The man that saved us, I saw him just before I fell unconscious," I went on. "I wasn't able to see his face, but I want to know who it was. Why did they save us?"

Axel didn't meet my eyes as he uncrossed his arms to hold the edge of the sink. "I want the answers to those questions as well. I hadn't smelled anyone else, which is surprising since he must have been fairly close in order to have made it in time to save us. It wasn't another wolf."

Instinctively, my hand moved to my neck again.

Turning his head towards me, his eyes were glued to my hand as it covered the spot where my wound should have been. His grip on the counter grew tighter. "Vampires have become myths. In fact, some don't even believe they ever really existed. If they attack now, so many will die. How have they survived for so long without being found?"

I truly wished I knew the answer to that. "I didn't smell what you guys did, so maybe they've been hiding around humans. Maybe in places where there are no werewolf packs that could sniff them out?"

"Perhaps," he said thoughtfully. "They would have an endless supply of food and humans to turn. I wonder just how many of them there are now if they've been in hiding for all these years."

This was a troubling thought. There could be an army of them now, scattered all over the world. I would think a full-scale attack was only a matter of time at this point. But why would they show their faces now, and to us? A thought occurred to me and I sat up straight. "They attacked us on a full moon, but the potions we had drunk were still masking our scents. Maybe they thought they were attacking humans and not werewolves."

Nodding his head at this, he stepped forward. "You're right. That must—"

"You guys need to see this," Xavier suddenly announced from the doorway then turned and walked away.

Axel and I shared a look before following him.

What now?

We followed him into the living room.

I immediately took a seat, my attention drawn to the female reporter on the television.

She stood at the scene of a gruesome crime—an entire family killed. Every single victim had been drained of their blood.

My eyes widened as I realized what she was saying. I gazed over at Axel and Xavier in shock.

Xavier changed the channel.

This time a male reporter told of a similar killing in another city – a jogger murdered in a park. This victim, too, had been drained of his blood.

Maybe they hadn't only attacked us because they hadn't been able to tell that Axel and Xavier were werewolves. They attacked us because they were making their kills more public.

"They're slowly coming out of hiding," I said as I hugged myself.

"I'd say they are coming out of hiding rather quickly," Axel objected. "If they continue this, the humans will become aware of them. And guess who they'll be finding next?"

"Werewolves," I said under my breath.

Axel nodded. "Not just werewolves...the entire fucking supernatural community will be discovered," he growled through clenched teeth. "No offense to you, Ruby, but humans won't be able to handle this discovery. Vampires are starting a war and they don't even know it."

"Maybe they do," Xavier stated.

Axel and I looked his way.

His eyes were glued to the television as the reporter continued to speak. "It's like you said, Axel, they're making their kills known. For years, they've remained hidden. Now they are becoming sloppy with their kills, enough to make the news. Something is going on here. We have to head back to the pack now."

Axel stepped forward. "Yes, but we can't travel tonight."

Xavier nodded and turned the television off with a hard look on his face.

I didn't like the look he had. I wasn't sure what it meant because it was the first time I'd seen him like this.

Xavier threw the television remote down and combed his hair back from his face. "I know. We'll leave at dawn." He glanced at me as if to ask for my input.

I nodded slowly.

He sat down and so did Axel.

No one moved or spoke for a while until Axel got up to get us all drinks.

I've never been someone that drinks alcohol, even socially. Suddenly, I craved it in the dim hope that it would numb my senses, if only for a while. Why? Because tomorrow would be a new day and by now, I knew it would come with new problems.

This might be the last time I got to sit in comfortable silence with both Xavier and Axel for a long time to come.

This could be the last time I felt like I was out of danger and protected, especially since it was clear—a time was coming where no one would be safe.

I couldn't help wondering if somewhere out there in the darkness, someone was being violently attacked and drained.

I rested my forehead against the cool glass gingerly as I closed my eyes. Unfortunately, they popped open again within seconds when an image of frightening red eyes flashed through my mind.

"Fuck."

I swallowed, but my mouth was suddenly too dry to produce any saliva. What had really happened that night? Had I died? Did our mysterious savior bring me back to life? I remembered feeling like all the life was slowly draining out of me. I hated the fact that I could still feel the fangs in my throat.

Now wasn't the time to develop PTSD. From what Axel and Xavier had told me so far, I knew a war was coming. I fisted my hand and slammed it down against my thigh. That motherfucking vamp damn near killed me!

My lips formed a thin line as I stared into the darkness beyond the window. I was right to be afraid. Under these circumstances, it was nothing to be ashamed of. Nevertheless, I was determined to channel my fear into anger and anger into action. These creatures, these vampires, had suddenly crawled out of a hole and were on a path that would turn this world upside down. We had to find a way to stop them.

I sighed. *Who am I kidding?* No matter how angry I got, I'd never been a match for even the feeblest vampire. Though they might have been weaker than usual, if two full-grown male werewolves were almost killed, I was toast. *If I'm in this world now...I* shook my head. *No, I AM a part of this world now, and I need to be able to protect myself.*

Being mated to two werewolves would only shield me for so long. There was also no doubt in my mind that the Council, that bald prick Olcan specifically, still wanted my head–or my brain, to be more accurate. I personally wanted to know more about the woman they were talking about, their Grand Elder, myself.

If I knew her like the Enchanteds thought I did, then I wanted to understand how it could be possible that I had no conscious memory of her. Maybe she was just someone I'd encountered briefly along the way? For all I know, she could be just a customer I'd served in the diner one day.

I started chewing on my lip nervously. *Yeah, wishful thinking.* What were the chances of me knowing a Grand Elder and having a powerful supernatural barrier placed in my mind while also being a just a normal human girl who simply discovered the supernatural world by accident? Evidence of something greater going on kept stacking up, and I didn't like speculating what that could mean. There was still a slim chance this was all a strange coincidence, but I wasn't ready to bet the farm on it. In fact, it gave me a headache every time I thought about it.

I looked down at my open palm. Who was I before? Have I always been this person or was a part of me locked away? What would happen to me if I ever remembered my past?

Someone cleared their throat behind me.

I jumped around, a gasp on my lips. I blinked rapidly at Natalie.

She stood in the middle of the room, staring at me with a smile. "Hey, Redhead," she said.

I rushed to her. I hugged her tight and felt like my bones would crush with the way she hugged me back.

"Are you okay?" she asked.

"I have so much to tell you. You won't believe what happened, Natalie."

She released me and stepped back. "Try me."

"Vampires," I said. "They're real. I swear I'm not kidding..."

The smile on her face faltered. "I know."

I frowned. "How?"

Natalie turned away from me. "Olcan was called away after you guys left," she explained as she turned back around to face me.

I tried not to smile when I heard that Olcan was no longer there. Considering the fact that I'd be returning soon with the guys, Olcan was one more complication I'd just as soon avoid.

"A pack was attacked," she explained.

My brows dipped with a frown.

"They were all killed," she went on. "Women, children—every single pack member was brutally slaughtered."

I walked away from her this time, my hand over my mouth. "Jesus." I combed my hair back before my hand fell to my side. These vamps were certainly taking advantage of the element of surprise while they had it. The faster the news about their existence got out, the better people would be able to protect themselves. "We were attacked after we left the pack," I told her as I closed my eyes and pressed a finger to my temple. "One of them almost—"

Her hand came down on my shoulder as she stepped around me. She placed her hand at my neck, the spot where I'd been bitten. "I know that too," she replied sadly. "I'm so sorry."

I opened my eyes but avoided looking at her. I didn't want her to see me crying as I nodded. "You saw it?

"Yes."

"I-I can't even explain the pain. I—um," I swallowed, not

wanting to think about it. "We were saved by someone. None of us saw him. Well, I kind of did before I blacked out. All I could make out for sure was his shadow, but whoever he was, he saved us and got us here."

Natalie's gaze shifted away from me.

I narrowed my eyes at her. This wasn't the response I'd expected from her. Maybe she'd seen that as well. Either way, I let it go. Something else was more important. "Did you know about vampires being alive long before I was attacked? I assume you saw the attack the night we left?"

She nodded. "Yes." She gave me a tight-lipped smile.

Why couldn't she look at me?

"Yes, I got the vision the night you left," Natalie stated.

My eyes narrowed. She was lying, I could tell. And it had been confirmed by the awkward silence that followed. If she'd known and I think she did, why hadn't she warned Xavier and me? Why hadn't she stopped us from leaving? If I'd known it would be a choice between Olcan taking me to Romania or having my throat ripped out by a vampire, I think I'd have chosen Romania. "So, Mathieu already knows about the vampires and everything? We're leaving tomorrow to head back."

Moving away from me, she answered, "Yes, he knows. The Council is trying to keep what happened to that pack under wraps, but I spoke to Reika. She told me what happened."

I shook my head. "That doesn't make sense. If these vampires are out hunting, werewolves need to know about it. Xavier and Axel got their asses handed to them, Natalie. They had no idea what the scent had meant when they picked it up until it was too late. We were all almost killed! Xavier and Axel said most werewolves have forgotten how to fight vampires. That's why the wolves need to know what's happening, while they still have a chance to prepare. Not only that, but humans are being attacked as well."

She turned to face me, a vein popping in her forehead. "I know that, Ruby! I had a friend in that pack! I understand why the Council is trying to be cautious. They fear that wolves might start to panic. In fact, I hope they do panic. Then at least they will be on guard. Otherwise, they will be sitting ducks, ripe for the hunting," She sighed. "Whoever or whatever saved you had to be supernatural, and strong at that, to have killed the vamps that attacked you guys. If we're lucky, maybe they'll show themselves soon. "

"Yeah, Axel said the same."

The side of her mouth arched at this.

I frowned. "What?"

"So, on a brighter topic," she said. "What's it like being around the two of them?"

I wasn't sure why I started blushing. "It's—fine. Okay, I guess."

"Okay? That's all you have to give me, Ruby? Really?" Her smile broke out into a grin.

I rolled my eyes and lifted my shoulders in a shrug because I had no idea what she wanted me to say. Actually, I knew what she wanted to hear, and right now things weren't like that. "Things are fine for now. The guys are still tired and weakened. They lost a lot of blood. Xavier has been quiet, and Axel is...well, Axel."

"What did you feel for Axel when you thought he was dead?"

Oh, come on, her too? Why is that so important?

"I was worried. That's all. He left his pack to come with us. If he dies, who looks after them? Who will be their alpha?"

"For someone you hate, you certainly spare a lot of thought about his people." She raised her brows, her expression otherwise blank.

"I assure you, I—" I frowned as she flickered between transparent and solid. "Natalie? Are you okay?"

She didn't reply. She just kept staring off to the side towards the room door.

I looked at the door and then her. Was she seeing or hearing something I wasn't? She flickered in and out of focus again, and I grimaced as blood began to run from her ear. "Natalie, you're bleeding! Seriously, what's going on?" I felt panicked. I didn't think she was supposed to be bleeding like this while projecting herself to me, even if we were technically just in a dream state. What if something was wrong with her?

She turned to look at me as blood poured from her eyes. She wasn't moving, she wasn't blinking, and her face still remained as blank as a canvas.

My eyes widened as I stepped forward, my hands shaking as all the blood running from her ears and eyes began to soak through the white top she wore. "Natalie, you're freaking me out! What the fuck is happening?" My mouth clamped shut in shock.

A deep wound appeared at her neck and then her wrist. Blood now pooled around her feet.

I started pinching myself, trying to see if that would work to wake me up. If she was in my dream, she must be defenseless in reality. "Wake up!" I started yelling at both her and myself. "Wake..." I swallowed my words as a shadowy head peeked out from behind her. My heart was hammering in my chest, as shadowy claws slowly appeared and wrapped around her arm. "Who are you?" I stepped back. "What are you doing to her? How did you get in my dream?"

I dug my nails into my palm with enough force to break the skin, but I still wasn't waking up. I felt intense dread, as if a blast of evil had brushed across my soul. A scream was torn from my lips as the shadow suddenly lunged for me.

Xavier

I was fifteen when I went on my first hunt with my dad. An Echidna, a half-woman half serpent creature, was preying on humans and leaving a string of bodies in her wake.

She had struck my father with her tail, sending him flying through a window. I realized fighting her in wolf form would not stop her easily, so I changed. I waited until the other wolves created an opening, and then I buried a wooden spike through her heart.

Being a wolf and a protector means being strong. It means being smart. It means being able to protect people, especially the ones you love. I clenched my fists as I growled. Ruby almost died because I wasn't able to protect her. I hadn't been strong enough.

Full moon or not, that would never happen again.

I'd been conscious while Ruby screamed for help. With my blood rapidly leaving my body as if it was being vacuumed, I couldn't move to help her.

I'd never felt so helpless in my life. It had been agonizing to watch as the vampire attacked her. I didn't know how, but whoever saved us had also healed my broken spine. That's what that vampire had targeted. He had quickly placed himself behind me, wrapped his arms around me, and snapped my spine. No doubt, it was their way of stopping wolves from shifting.

I tapped my finger against my chest. Despite the darkness surrounding me in the room, my vision was just fine. I clenched and unclenched my hand, testing my strength. Although there'd be no way in hell we'd travel while it was still dark, I needed to be at full strength when we traveled back to the pack tomorrow.

Also, there wouldn't be a full moon tomorrow night. At least I'd be able to shift if needed.

The sooner we got back to the pack, the faster Axel could retrieve the book to help us defeat those bloodsuckers.

I noticed Ruby and Axel had seemed unusually chatty with each other. Yes, I'm bothered by that. I obviously know he is her mate. I also know there must be a part of her that cared about him, even if she didn't show it. She proved that the night we were attacked.

Now that I knew he was on our side, I didn't want to rip his throat out as much. Doing so would hurt her emotionally more than before. I held my hand to my forehead and wished desperately for some pain meds. I didn't get headaches often, but this shit show was getting to me. Not only did we have the Council and vampires to contend with on top of an unexplainable three-way mate bond, but we still didn't know what might lurk behind that barrier in Ruby's mind.

A bloodcurdling scream echoed through the house—Ruby's scream. I bolted out of bed. Her bedroom was right across from mine, so I kicked the door open and rushed in. My eyes scanned the room quickly, but I saw no one.

Ruby was still in bed, her arms and legs thrashing around as she screamed.

I realized she must be dreaming, so I immediately rushed to her. "Ruby, wake up. Wake up, baby. It's just a dream."

She kept screaming, tears flowing from her closed eyes.

Axel rushed into the room. "What's going on?" His eyes were that of his wolf, black pits, while his claws were out and ready to strike.

"She's having a nightmare," I told him. I moved back as one of her legs came close to hitting me. Each time I attempted to touch her, she started to howl louder and push me away.

"What the fuck kind of nightmare is she having?" Axel hissed as he retracted his claws and rushed over to the bed. "Ruby." He cupped her cheek gently.

I couldn't help sinking my teeth into my tongue as he touched her.

"Ruby, wake up! Can you hear me?"

More tears began to flow from her eyes.

He held her arm to stop her flailing, but staggered back when her other hand thrust outward and punched him right in the face.

She bolted upright, her eyes wide as she looked around the room frantically. Finally, she looked at me and then at Axel, who held his busted nose. She began wiping at her eyes.

"Ruby?" I prompted.

She climbed out of bed and walked away, her shoulders rising and falling rapidly with her heavy breathing. "I'm okay," she reassured us, her back still turned. "I-I was talking to Natalie. Olcan left because vampires attacked a pack and killed everyone."

"Fuck!" Axel exclaimed as he stepped up beside me. "When? What pack?"

"I don't know," she replied. "We were talking when—when something happened." She turned around to face us, her eyes red-rimmed and puffy from crying. "She started bleeding out of her ears and eyes, and then her neck and wrist. It was like she was being attacked."

I closed my eyes for a second before reopening them, my thoughts already running rampant with negativity. I took a deep breath and reminded myself that I needed to think positively. After all, Natalie could have appeared like that to Ruby for any reason. Then again, this had never happened before to my knowledge, and Natalie had done plenty of mind links in the past.

"If Olcan's not there, we can call," Axel suggested. "We can check if something actually happened."

I nodded.

Ruby just hung her head as she pinched the bridge of her nose. "Something was behind her, a shadow, or something." She looked up at us, her eyes full of tears. "It attacked me."

"I'm going for the house phone. We'll call and check on them," Axel declared.

He turned to leave the room when Ruby stopped him. "There's something I didn't tell you," she disclosed to me before glancing over at Axel. "Something I saw in the mind link with Natalie and Reika." She swallowed. "The shadows I saw."

Axel squinted his eyes in confusion. "Shadows? What kind of shadows?"

Heading over to the bed, she sat down. "During the mind link, I saw a vision or maybe a memory. I was in a town or city. People were running and screaming and these shadows were chasing after them. The mind link started to break when one of the shadows attacked a woman." She closed her eyes and combed her hair out of her face. "I saw those same shadows again in the pack house, the night we left. At first, I just thought I was just seeing things. However, this is now the third time I've seen them, both in my mind and in reality.

"Why didn't you tell me about this sooner?" I asked her. "Is that why I caught you running that night?"

Ruby nodded. "Yes. I didn't say anything, Xavier, because with everything else going on and our lives in jeopardy, it didn't seem very important. I'm telling you both now. So, what do you think it means?"

Axel shrugged. "Ghosts are really the only possibility for what you saw in the house because werewolves can't smell them. Any other supernatural would have been detectable by their scent."

"Do you think it's all in my head?" she asked tentatively and paused before shaking her head definitively. "No. No, I know something's wrong. Something's not right, Axel." She placed her face in her hands. "I can feel it. Something's not right. Why is all of this happening?"

I looked over at Axel.

He stared at Ruby with concern.

I sank down to my knees in front of her and attempted to gently pry her hands away from her face. I wasn't surprised she felt panicked. She'd been through so much already and there seemed to be no end in sight.

On top of everything, now she had to live with the memory of what that vampire had done to her. She'd become a part of this world now, with so much going on around her, so many things she wasn't used to. There were creatures in my world that would scare anyone to death, and she had already come face to face with one. She was a strong woman, incredibly strong, but too much was being dumped into her lap far too quickly.

I was used to the chaos of my world. She wasn't...not yet anyway.

"Hey, look at me, hey." She finally did and I gently held her chin. "Axel is going to call the house to check on Natalie and the others. As for the shadows, we'll figure it all out when we get back to the pack. Okay?"

Ruby kept breathing rapidly. "We need to find a witch. I want to know what's inside my head. I want to know what was done to me." She placed her hand against her chest, "Something is wrong, Xavier. I can feel it."

Axel frowned deeply, his forehead furrowed to the point that his brows were almost touching.

As he stepped forward, Ruby looked up at him and sniffled.

To my surprise, his hard expression softened as he gazed down at her.

"Once we get you back to Xavier's pack," he explained in a soft voice. " I'll contact the witch that made the scent dampening potions for me. I'll see if she can help. If she can't, I'll have her find someone who can. The warlock here isn't strong enough when it comes to mind links. It's not his specialty. Asking him to help might hurt you both." I didn't miss the way his hand twitched before he stepped back. The indifferent mask he typically wore returned. "Try and get some sleep. We're leaving at daybreak."

CHAPTER FOUR

RUBY

We headed out at daybreak in accordance with the plan and drove throughout the day.

Xavier and Axel repeatedly tried calling Natalie, but the call kept going to voicemail. It didn't fill me with confidence that she was all right. I was terrified that we might return to find a house filled with dead wolves.

We barely spoke to each other. I assumed Xavier and Axel were lost in their own thoughts, just like I was.

At around 5 pm, we started looking for a motel to avoid traveling through the night. Axel took his own room, while Xavier and I shared one.

We might have wished we could continue to travel at night, but that shit wasn't going to happen. Not while we still knew so little about the bloodsuckers. At least Xavier and Axel now knew their scent, but what good would that do if we were attacked again? Thankfully, it wasn't a full moon, so the guys were at full strength, but we were taking nothing for granted. What if there were more than two vampires? Xavier and Axel would be outnumbered, and I wouldn't stand a chance.

Xavier and my room contained twin beds, a television so small, even I could've picked it up and thrown it without effort, and a mini-fridge. I could see Xavier in my peripheral vision on the next bed over as I laid on my back on the incredibly uncomfortable bed, a bedspring digging into me, causing me to shift every three seconds.

He had his hands behind his head as he stared up at the ceiling. I sighed and scooted closer to the edge of the bed to get some relief.

"Are you okay?" he asked as he turned onto his side to face me.

I nodded.

"The shadow that you saw behind Natalie–was it more like a person that was blurry or a plain black shadow?"

"A plain black shadow," I replied as I turned onto my side to face him. "Why?"

"I'm just curious. You saw that first during the mind link and you've been seeing shadows ever since. That has to mean something."

I rolled onto my back. "I know. I feel like it does too. It has to." I rested my arm on my forehead. "There is so much going on, so much to think about. I don't have a headache, but this tension in my head's driving me nuts."

"I know what you mean. We'll get the answers we need soon enough. It won't do you any good trying to speculate or try to find answers where there are none."

I snorted. "That's easier said than done." I rolled back onto my side, the lamp sitting between our beds illuminating his face and making his eyes shine. "Do you think they're okay?"

He nodded, knowing whom I was speaking of. "She's fine. They're okay. We'll leave early in the morning again, and it'll be just a few more hours before we get there." He propped himself up on his elbow. "They're all right."

I could hear it in his voice—he was trying to convince himself of that as well. I bit down on my lip. I hadn't considered the fact that although Natalie was my friend, she was also his cousin—his family. They were all his family. Of course, he would be worried since none of their calls had been returned. "I'm hungry," I muttered softly to myself.

Sitting up, he swung his legs off the bed.

"Where are you going?"

He bent down to put his shoes on before getting up. "I'm hungry as well. I'll go get some snacks from the vending machine in the lobby, okay?"

I nodded and watched him leave before I turned the lamp off. Sometimes lying in the dark offered some comfort. With a bit of light coming in through the window by the door, I could tell if anyone walked by the door.

I was becoming paranoid, but after everything that had happened, I thought I had a right to be. Hence, the knife hidden safely under my pillow.

I wasn't sure when I dozed off, but a rattling sound in the room woke me up. Trapped in the state between awake and asleep, I rolled onto my side to face the door as I rubbed at my eyes. "Xavier?"

When I got no response, I opened my sleep-crusted eyes and spotted someone standing in the corner of the room. I blinked rapidly, my heart skipping a beat as I realized it wasn't Xavier. I jumped up and turned the lamp on before reaching under the pillow for the knife.

When I looked back, I could just make out the form of a man. It did not look like a solid person but instead, it appeared smoky and indistinct. It was seeping into the walls. My eyes bulged as a scream rose to my mouth. I jumped out of bed, tripped, and fell, my eyes still on the smoky form that was almost gone. I got up and rushed to the door. When I opened the door, I almost ran directly into a tall form with a pair of bright eyes staring down at me. Blinded by fear and pumped up on adrenaline, my fist acted on its own.

Luckily, Axel was quick to grab my hand. "Ruby, what the

hell? Why are you screaming?" He focused on the room and moved past me to get into the room.

I pushed him out and slammed the door behind me. "There's someone in the room, *was* someone in the room. It was a shadow." I squeezed my eyes shut. "No, not a shadow. There was someone there, but he turned into smoke." I opened my eyes. I didn't like the way he was looking at me. "He turned into fucking smoke! You have to believe me!"

He reached out to me and held my shoulder. "Hey, I believe you. Come on." He took my hand.

As we walked, I couldn't stop looking around. "Someone is watching me, Axel. Something's wrong here."

"Nothing is wrong with you," he said as he opened his room door and let me in. "Where is Xavier?"

"He went to get food. Do you think he's okay?"

He didn't answer as he went to his window and peeked outside. "He's fine, see?" Since the lobby was a straight shot across from his room, he could see Xavier through the glass door standing at the counter.

I leaned forward to confirm Xavier's wellbeing then breathed a sigh of relief that only calmed me for a second. I hadn't imagined it —I was sure of it. Someone had been watching me sleep.

"There wasn't a scent in the room other than yours and Xavier's," he said as he sat down on the bed. "I guess they could have masked their scent, though."

I plopped down beside him and looked over at him, his statement not helping to calm me down at all. "The person is still here, Axel. All he did was fade into the wall. He's still here. We can't stay here." I sighed as I glanced down at my feet. In my panic, I had run out of my room without putting shoes on.

I didn't know how he could be so calm. If he believed me, there was no way he'd be this calm.

"We can't leave. If someone was watching you, they had a lot of time to hurt you, if that was their intention." He walked over to his backpack where it sat on a chair across the room. He returned with a pair of socks in hand and handed them to me. "They're clean. Put them on."

I stared at the socks but made no move to take them. I just kept seeing the image of black smoke in the shape of a man.

He sighed and bent down. "We can't leave tonight. It's not wise for us to travel at night."

I broke out of my trance when his warm hand lifted my leg. I watched as he slid the socks onto my feet one at a time and slowly, very slowly. My cheeks began to heat, and I rubbed my hands against them. I dropped my hands as he looked up at me. My heart skipped a beat as his hazel eyes bored into mine.

His hand was still on my foot, but the moment lasted for just a second as he looked away and stood up. "No one will get to you," he declared confidently as he walked back over to his bag. "I'll make sure of it." He zipped the bag closed and turned to face me, his long hair hanging over his back and shoulders. "I'll protect you, Ruby. You know that, don't you?"

The promise in his voice was somehow enough to make me calm down. "Yes," I answered slowly. "You know, you're not a complete dick."

The lip arched. "You caught me in a good mood. Give me some time."

I rolled my eyes.

He chuckled as he moved to sit beside me once more.

"Sorry about punching you in the face last night."

Axel touched his nose before leaning his head back on his hands. "No worries. You pack a punch, but your hands are still too small to do too much damage."

I punched him in the side as hard as I could.

He yelped and sat up.

"You were saying?" I stated.

"Damn, did you really have to do that?" He chuckled. "This is abuse."

I couldn't help but giggle as I leaned a little closer to him. "I'm learning from the best." I pulled away as I continued to laugh.

Suddenly, his laughter died away. His expression changed.

My laughter halted. "What?"

His jaws clenched. "I'm sorry for what I did to you." He rubbed his cheek as he looked away. "The dungeon. All of it."

I raised a brow in shock.

Before I could say anything, the room door opened and Xavier walked in. "What's going on?"

Axel got up and headed for the bathroom. "Someone was in her room."

"What?" Xavier asked as he dropped the bag in his hand. "Who? Where are they?"

"They seeped into the wall," Axel yelled from the bathroom before reappearing, his hair now in a bun. "Whoever or whatever it was had been watching her sleep."

Xavier looked towards the door and then back at me. "Shit. I had heard a scream but that moron in the lobby was watching a horror movie. It was so loud, I thought the scream came from it."

Axel picked up his bag and placed it on the floor before sitting down. "There was no scent in the room. None other than the usual nasties you pick up at a motel, anyways. It must have been masked, and we can't exactly knock on every door to check if there is a supernatural inside."

Xavier sighed and picked up the bag he had dropped. He removed two Twinkies and threw one to Axel before giving the bag to me. "You should eat something now. Axel and I will stay up. We'll take turns to watch if this shadow person returns."

I looked from one man to the other. Right now, at this moment, the curse of being mated to both of them felt like a blessing. I took the bag from Xavier and scooted up to the headboard. "I don't think I can sleep now," I admitted as I ripped into a Doritos bag.

"That's fine. You'll fall asleep eventually," Axel replied as he slid down in the chair somewhat and glanced at Xavier. "You're on the first watch."

Xavier threw him a nasty look and sat on the bed beside me. I offered him some of my Doritos but he declined. "Eat. You need it more than I do. Was this one of the shadows like before?"

I shook my head. "No. Those shadows were exactly that, solid shadows. This one was more smoke-like."

He said nothing after that but remained by my side.

Even though I'd said I wouldn't be able to sleep, knowing they were both watching over me had me drifting off pretty soon.

———

Axel

Since I'd taken the last watch until early this morning, Xavier drove us back to the pack. The moment we arrived, I could tell something was off. I noticed Xavier looked wary as well.

Ruby took off running towards the house as soon as the car came to a stop. She ignored me telling her to slow down as she started screaming Natalie's name.

Footsteps approaching us rapidly caught my ear and Natalie appeared, her white hair piled high on her head.

Ruby pulled her into a hug. "Where the fuck is your phone? We've been calling you and Mathieu. Neither of you answered."

"Um, I have no idea where it is, to be honest," Natalie replied. "So much has been happening around here."

"Like what?" Xavier asked as he pulled her into a hug.

"What happened the other night when you mind-linked me?" Ruby added.

Natalie held her hands up. "Okay seriously, what's going on? Come on, I'll fix you guys something to eat. You all look like shit."

Ruby sighed as she followed Natalie into the kitchen.

I lingered in the back while I leaned on the edge of the door. The house seemed quiet, more than usual.

"You started flickering between looking transparent and normal. Then you started bleeding..." Ruby waved her hand over Natalie's body. "...Out of everywhere." She slid onto a stool around the island. "There was a shadow behind you. It appeared after you started bleeding, and then it attacked me. I thought maybe you were hurt, that you were being attacked here."

Natalie looked thoughtful for a moment. She moved a few strands of stray hair away from her face. "No. Our connection broke. I figured you were waking up or something. Nothing like that happened here last night."

"Where is everyone?" I asked. "It's quiet here, more than usual."

"Yeah, I noticed that too. Where's dad?" Xavier asked.

Natalie didn't give an answer as she walked over to the fridge and began removing eggs, bacon, and everything she needed to make a meal.

Of course, I wasn't planning on sticking around to have a feast, I had my pack to check on. All I wanted was to make sure Ruby made it back safe.

"He took the pack to a secret location," Natalie replied as she braced herself on the island.

Xavier frowned.

"He's been moving the pack slowly. After that entire pack was killed, vampires tried to kill the Council member from Europe." She poured three glasses of orange juice for Xavier and Ruby but I declined. "All the Council members are on lockdown right now. They're targeting wolves first, and it's a smart move on their part. However, other supernaturals are being attacked as well."

"So, it's getting out there that they're real then?" Ruby asked.

Natalie nodded. "Yes. Everyone is on high alert."

I scratched my chin and walked further into the kitchen. "Why are they attacking now? They've been living in secret for longer than anyone remembers. Now all of a sudden, they're attacking Council members. Where have they been all this time?"

Natalie sipped from the glass she offered me and shrugged. "I have no idea and right now, we can't worry about that. What about your pack?"

"I sent a message to my beta before we left to head back here," I told her.

Nodding as she listened, she cracked eggs to whisk together.

I went on, "It's only a matter of time before the humans start to connect the dots. They are draining people like they're Gatorades at half-time. Worse yet, they're being sloppy about it. They're not even bothering to hide their kills anymore."

Natalie snorted. "Well, at least now, there is something else on the news other than humans murdering each other. This world is already shit for us, and now we have vampires to worry about."

"They're like any other paranormal that plagues humans and risks the exposure of the entire supernatural community. They'll be dealt with accordingly," Xavier said in a low voice before slamming his fist down on the island. "But for all the training we've done over the years, nothing has prepared us for this. It snapped my spine like a toothpick."

Natalie's face dropped. "What?"

"One of the vampires that attacked us," he told her. "It broke my back. I think if you do some research on how that pack was all murdered, there'll be a lot of dead wolves with snapped spines. Fighting them in wolf form will mean we'll be at full strength, strong enough to rip them to shreds, but at higher risk of one climbing onto our back."

I frowned, as he hadn't told me this. "The one that attacked me didn't do that. It went straight for my chest. My heart maybe?"

Xavier nodded. "They try to not prolong a fight with a wolf. They try to make their first strike...the last. Their scent is their greatest disadvantage. If they learn to mask that, we'll be screwed. I think if they haven't figured out how to over the years they've been in hiding, they can't."

"That's a start then, right?" Ruby asked. "Having an idea of how they'll attack. At least we know that much and can pass it on to other packs. What about sunlight and being staked through the heart? Do you guys think all of that will actually kill them?"

"Sunlight, yes," I replied. "Being staked, no, that's bullshit. They're already dead, so they don't have a beating heart. Go for the head. They also heal quickly, so decapitating them has to be done quickly. You can also completely dismember them. At least that's what I think I saw in that book. It's been years." I rubbed my hands together as I tried to picture the book and everything I had seen within it. "Wolves and a handful of other supernaturals are strong and fast enough to fight them and win. Plus, we smell them so easily." I looked at Xavier. "Thinking about vampire-fighting style now, I think my pack has been incorporating techniques in our training to fight them." I gave him a smug grin. Although I knew now wasn't the time to be petty, there was no way I could let the opportunity pass.

His eyes lowered as his jaws clenched.

I turned away. "I'm going back to my pack. I'll secure their safety and return with the book."

I glanced at Ruby over my shoulder, her green eyes pierced into mine. I looked away without saying anything. It was becoming increasingly difficult for me to look her in the eyes without feeling things I didn't want to. I figured being away from her for a few hours might do me some good.

"Hey," Xavier called behind me.

I got to the front door and turned around to face him. "Yeah?" The time we'd spent together had left us less hostile towards each other, but I still didn't like the guy. As much as I'd never admit it to anyone, that's partly because of how close he was to Ruby. They deserved each other, as they were true mates. She and I were just an accident made by the Goddess.

Even so, I still cared for her...I still dreamt about her.

"Why are you doing this?" Xavier asked. "Helping Ruby and I and willing to pass on useful information so easily."

I inhaled as I buried my hands in my pockets. I looked past him to the direction of the kitchen as Ruby's laughter met my ears. I rarely heard her laugh, but when I did, I tried to imprint it to my memory. "What's going on right now is bigger than land and power. Some things are more important." I cleared my throat as my eyes drifted back to him while Ruby and Natalie began to whisper. "Besides, if we don't work together and these leeches take over, everything will be theirs. That's all there is to it."

I turned away without another word and closed the door silently behind me.

CHAPTER FIVE
RUBY

It felt weird being back in this house. I sat up in bed staring before rising and heading to the window. There has always been something calming about watching the world outside one's window. Whether it is night or day, I can sit at a window and feel a heavy weight lifted off my shoulders.

After Axel left, I chatted with Natalie for a while before relaxing in a luxuriously long shower and going to sleep. I felt exhausted and frankly still on edge after seeing that shadow person watching me. I was trying not to think about the fact that it might have followed us here. I had slept during the day to be awake during the night.

I woke up after 5 pm and found the house empty. I'd been in my room since. Knowing only a few wolves were patrolling the forest, I just wanted to be in my room where I felt at least somewhat safe.

The towering trees outside my window weren't offering me the calm I had hoped for. The forest here was thicker than where Axel's safe house was. I was becoming more uneasy the longer I stared out the window. I felt like within those trees...something was staring back at me.

I drew the curtain and turned away.

Natalie walked into the room at that moment. "Hey," she said as she plopped down on my bed.

"Hey." I sat beside her. "I wish we didn't have to stay here for the night. I know Mathieu will be back in the morning to take us to where everyone else is, but couldn't we have gone into the city, rented somewhere for the night?" I turned to face her. "I mean, there's no one here. If we're attacked, we'll surely die."

She placed her hand over mine and gave me a reassuring smile. "There are several warrior wolves in the forest. We aren't alone. I slept here last night alone and I was perfectly fine."

I'd been trying hard not to panic as she tried to reassure me. I sighed. "It's not just the vampires I'm afraid of. Someone is watching me, Natalie. That shadow guy or whatever that thing was in my room the other night at the motel freaked me out."

"I'd be freaked out too, so I understand."

"I feel uncomfortable being here with everything that occurred before I left. I saw the shadows here as well, so staying right now doesn't exactly make me feel safe."

Frowning, she asked, "You saw shadows here in the house?"

I nodded and told her about what I'd seen during our mind link.

She looked confused the more I spoke. Eventually, she stood up and started pacing.

"I didn't say anything because there wasn't any time to," I added.

She nodded, looking perplexed. "No, no, I get it. I understand why you said nothing. I'm wondering why I didn't see that during the mind link. I doubt Reika saw it either. I think she would have told me if she had."

"You trust her?" I asked her.

Again, she nodded. "I do. She helped me out that night when you guys left, and she's been filling me in on what's been going on with the Council since. She can be trusted. Xavier was telling me earlier about everything that happened with the vampires that attacked you guys." She sat down again.

I let out a sigh. I closed my eyes and bit down on my lip for a second as the vivid memory of terrifying red eyes entered my mind unbidden. "I thought I was going to die," I said in a low voice. "He was tearing into me, Natalie. Have you ever seen a dog bite down on something and shake it? That's what..." I closed my eyes for a moment as my body tensed up. The memory was too painful. "It was the most horrible thing I've ever experienced in my life. I could feel my blood rushing to my neck."

She moved my hair over my shoulder. "I'm sorry you had to go through that. Now you know what these creatures are like, the monsters that they are. All three of you do. As for whoever saved you guys..." She puckered her lips. "I don't know. Either that person was following you guys, following the vampires, or was just at the right place at the right time."

"How did he know where to take us, though?"

"I don't know." She shrugged. "Xavier told me you were all in pretty bad shape. If he or she healed all three of you, they must have been strong. If I had to guess, I would say the person had to be a powerful witch or warlock, or possibly even a demon. Whomever it was, they're an ally if they saved you all. All-powerful allies like that will be needed in the fight to come." Grasping my shoulders, she turned me to face her.

"What are you doing?" I asked.

Moving my hair back on my other shoulder, she hovered her hand over the area where I had been bitten. She closed her eyes for a moment. When they reopened, they were as white as clouds. "There are traces of magic on you. It definitely was a witch or something, but it's fading."

"I didn't say this to the guys," I whispered. "But I think that shadow in my room was the person who saved us. I hadn't realized that might be the case until I woke up the next morning."

Pulling her hand away, she pursed her lips as her white eyes faded back to blue. "That could be true, yes."

"Fight to come?" I repeated. I felt like Natalie knew more than she was letting on. "You said there is a fight to come. How do you know that? Have you had a vision?"

"No, it's just clear if the vampires aren't stopped soon, things will get out of hand."

"Who's going to stop them? The Council members are focusing on their own safety right now."

Despite how crappy the human government could be, I was certain that when, not if, they found out about vampires, they'd use everything in their power to fight back and protect their people. The werewolf Council wanted to hide the existence of vampires even as the bloodsuckers were slaughtering packs one by one.

Natalie smoothed my brows down with a finger. "Our pack and the ones that are willing to fight will have to come together. We have to start hunting the vampires. We will need everyone's help."

"No," I said. "I've faced one of those monsters already, Natalie. I saw his eyes, and now I can't stop seeing them. I can't face another one of them. I don't have the strength you and the other wolves have, so count me out. When that fight starts, I'll be locked in a room surrounded by a circle of guns. That's all I can do to protect myself."

She didn't say anything for a while.

I didn't care how selfish it sounded. Unlike the Council members, who had the power to help and refused, I couldn't help even if I wanted to. If Axel and Xavier had to watch over me at all times, it distracted them and put them at greater risk. Axel had his pack to look after and Xavier needed to help his father to protect their people.

"I saw the way Axel looked at you before he left," she whispered. "Are you two becoming closer?"

I folded my lips in contemplation. I thought of Axel's apology for how he had treated me in the beginning and shrugged. "We're not close, but at least we're civil. He left with us, putting himself in danger and leaving his pack without a real leader. He...um, he apologized for everything."

A smile spread across her lips

I rolled my eyes. "Stop smiling like that. All he did was apologize to me. I would say he owed me at least that much." Despite the truth of my words, I couldn't stop the flutter of butterfly wings in my belly. Axel had seemed different, kinder. It was only a sprinkle of kindness in an otherwise hostile personality made up of 95% asshole. But because of this fact, whenever he said something sweet or did something kind, I knew it was real.

Natalie stayed with me for a while as we talked about some of her past relationships and my failed ones. I cherished the momentary distraction from what was happening around us. Even if it was only for a little while, it was almost like we were just two normal college girls gossiping about boys and our experiences. Not vampires and a war neither of us can fight.

Natalie

I had experienced the vision of Ruby being attacked as if I had been Ruby herself. While I hadn't experienced her pain, I had felt her intense fear as she looked into the petrifying blood-red eyes of that vampire.

As I laid in bed unable to sleep, it felt like I could see those spine-chilling red eyes looking down at me from the ceiling. I closed my eyes as they began to tear up. I'd turned into a liar ever since I got my new powers. While I was doing this for good reasons...it didn't stop how horrible I felt. I couldn't tell Ruby I had seen her attack long before it had happened. How would I explain to her that it had been my job to lead her to it? I wasn't told why, but I could only assume there were things I didn't know, things I couldn't explain.

I was merely a servant.

What good could come from her being attacked by a vampire? I wasn't sure of the answer. The only thing I did feel sure of was that her being bitten was completely unavoidable. If it hadn't happened that night, it would have happened another night and the outcome could have been even worse. Either way, she had to see what vampires were like for herself—they all needed to see it.

The role Xavier, Axel, and Ruby were going to play in the future depended on their hatred for vampires. What better way of solidifying that hatred than by having a true score to settle? That's why I thought she needed to be bitten. The vampires that attacked them had been killed—that part I didn't see. I hadn't known how they would be saved, just that they would be. Even though those vampires were killed, Axel, Xavier, and Ruby would hold this newfound hatred close to them.

Vampires were fueled by hunger and rage. To beat them...it had to be matched.

I said nothing to Ruby when she admitted to being scared because I was terrified too. As for the shadows she was seeing and whoever was following her, I knew nothing about those. I wasn't sure how I felt about being kept in the dark about some of this.

Sensing something, I frowned as I looked over at my door. I swallowed as a metallic taste suddenly filled in my mouth. I bolted upright out of bed and ran to the bathroom where I flipped on my light. I stuck my tongue out in front of the mirror, and crimson droplets rolled off my tongue into the white basin of the sink below. My tongue was dripping with blood.

"Something's very wrong."

I rushed out of the room in my nightclothes, leaving my shoes behind. I wasn't sure exactly what was happening, but death was coming, I could feel it. I rushed to Ruby's room and found her fast asleep. I breathed a sigh of relief, but the foreboding feeling did not fade or even lessen.

I closed her room door and headed back to my own room, unsure of what to do next. All of a sudden, a piercing howl from outside pierced the air. It sounded like a wolf in pain, and the metallic taste of blood permeated my mouth again. My gut twisted as I turned and headed for the stairs.

As I sprinted down the stairs, the front door flew open wildly.

Axel rushed in. He dropped a bulky bag and rubbed his arm as if it were sore from the weight.

I looked behind me to the second floor where Xavier appeared. Without hesitation, he threw himself over the railing and fell to the first floor, righting himself quickly. I took the rest of the stairs two at a time.

"What's going on?" he asked Axel, who was still panting.

Axel turned away to hastily close the door behind himself. "Where is Ruby?"

"Sleeping," I answered. "What's going on? I heard a wolf's howl, and we didn't expect you back tonight," I added. "Did something hap—" I coughed as blood began to pour from my lips. Another penetrating howl rang through the night. I could smell it then, a rancid smell.

Xavier grabbed my shoulder and our eyes met as we heard another wolf's cry.

"No," I said as I wiped at my mouth.

"What the fuck is going on right now?" Xavier asked.

I swallowed as I turned to him slowly and shook my head. "Can't you smell that?"

"I can't smell it. They're too far away. How can you?" Axel asked me.

"I'm an Enchanted, remember?" I turned to Xavier, whose confusion was slowly fading from his face as he realized what was happening. I nodded as he released my shoulder. "They're coming. The vampires are coming, Xavier. We have to get Ruby—now!"

"Are you hearing me?"

It took a moment for me to realize Natalie was speaking to me. I looked down at the backpack she was handing to me and nodded before taking it. "I'm hearing you."

She looked at me strangely for a moment. "We need to move quickly Ruby. I was saying there are tunnels under the house for situations like this. We'll be using them." She bent down to zip up her backpack.

"Yeah, I heard you," I replied.

Axel knelt next to the hefty bag filled with weapons that he arrived with. The book he had told us about laid beside it.

The chocolate brown leather covered book with its aged brown pages appeared much bigger than I'd originally expected. If I were to hold it up, it would cover almost my entire chest. It was titled "The History of the Damned", and I wondered what other paranormal creatures I might find in there.

"We need to move," Axel said as he placed three guns and several clips in his backpack while Xavier did the same. "My beta relocated the majority of the pack, and I sent the rest packing. I was almost out the door when they attacked. I made it to my car and bolted as fast as I could. I figured they'd either be coming here next or another group was already on their way." He stood up and swung his bag over his shoulder. He held his hand up for silence and tilted his head somewhat. His eyes turned black as he called on his wolf, and I watched as the tip of his ears began to elongate.

His brows twitched for a moment and then stopped. "I can't tell how many of them there are, but they're getting closer. They're moving quietly but swiftly. The branches and twigs they don't miss are giving them away." He glanced over at Xavier. "You can smell them now, right?" Axel's ears returned to normal as his black eyes reverted to hazel.

Xavier nodded.

I swallowed despite how dry my mouth was. *They're coming.* Those monsters are coming here. I inhaled deeply but couldn't smell anything.

I threw my bag onto my back and remained to the side while they did their thing. I knew I would only get in the way.

Xavier picked up a dagger and turned it over in his hand before putting it back in the bag and picking up a larger knife instead. "I can't leave my men out there. They're being picked off one by one."

"If you go out there now, you'll just die with them," Natalie said. "We warned the men when you got here about what to expect. You don't know that they won't survive."

Xavier's jaw clenched.

"Those wolves are all dead," Axel suddenly said.

Xavier growled now.

Leave it up to Axel to make a bad situation worse. "Three of my best trained men were killed when they broke into my house, and as I said, my pack has already been incorporating some techniques that are *supposed* to work on them. Maybe some of your men will survive, but you going out there right now in a vain attempt to protect them is foolish."

Xavier's face was twisted with rage, but he recognized the wisdom in Axel's words.

I was thankful that Xavier saw reason since I feared what would happen to him if he went out there with his men. I also hated the idea that the tunnels we would have to take would eventually lead us outside.

Why the fuck do we have to go outside?

I closed my eyes and inhaled deeply. I called on my anger as I tried to push my terror deep down within myself. One of those leeches almost sucked me dry like a Slurpee. We might be running for our lives, but I damn sure wouldn't be running while pissing myself with fear. I had no intention of becoming some blood-sucking asshole's midnight snack.

I opened my eyes and stepped forward. Bending down, I searched through the weapons bag for anything that I could use to protect myself. I found two silver daggers that were long and pointy. They looked almost like ice picks. I secured one dagger up the long sleeve top I wore under my jacket, comforted by the feeling of the cool steel against my skin. I shoved the other into my waist. I grabbed the knife-like dagger Xavier had discarded and shoved it into the side of my boot.

"Someone is ready for war, I see," Axel remarked.

I gazed up at him.

He stared at me with a smirk on his lips.

I narrowed my eyes at him, and he snorted and turned away.

I looked over at Xavier as he approached me and cupped my cheeks. "I want you to stay by my side. Do you understand? When I say run, Ruby, I want you to run."

An agonized howl that sounded like it was just outside the house chilled the blood in my veins.

Xavier's eyes turned black.

My heart started pounding against my rib cage.

Xavier and Axel looked to the ceiling at the same time, and Natalie soon did the same.

I wondered what the hell they were all doing. "What's wrong?"

"Shh," Axel hissed.

I looked at Xavier, and he placed a finger to his lips. I swallowed, the sound of my heartbeat hammering in my ears as he held his hand out to me.

They're in the house!

Swiftly, I placed my hand in his.

Natalie picked up the book on the ground.

I frowned with puzzlement as Xavier removed his bag from his back. He put it on in his front to cover his chest.

He turned his back to me while bending down somewhat. He looked at me over his shoulder and patted his back softly.

After I climbed onto his back, Natalie led us out of the kitchen and past the lobby down a hallway to the right. I couldn't hear their footsteps despite how quickly they were walking. I knew if I'd been walking alongside them, the squeak of my shoes would've given us away.

Natalie led the way in front. Xavier and I were the middle while Axel pulled up the rear. I tightened my hold around Xavier's neck, and he reached up to run a hand down the side of my face.

All three of them came to an abrupt stop.

I thought maybe we had come to a secret door in the wall or something, but then an odd odor had my nose crinkling with disgust.

My eyes widened with realization as I looked behind us.

Xavier and Axel turned around at the same time.

A vampire stood behind us, a woman with the sides of her head shaved and the rest of her hair in a ponytail. She hissed at us, baring her long fangs as her clawed fingers wiggled.

With the lights above us, I could clearly see the black veins running up her throat to stop just under her bottom lip. I hadn't noticed those veins on the vampire that attacked me, but it had been really dark at the time.

Her eyes were as red as the vampire's that attacked me. She smiled, her mouth stretching wide.

My heart began to beat even faster, as Xavier bent down for me to slide off his back. I held onto his shirt as he stepped forward, but he quickly freed himself from my grasp. He touched Axel's shoulder and nodded his head toward my direction.

Axel stepped to my side.

My eyes widened as Xavier's shoulder suddenly snapped.

"No," I said under my breath as I stepped forward.

Axel grabbed my arm.

"No!" I said lower.

Xavier's back hunched and his shirt began to rip as he started to shift.

I removed the dagger from under my sleeve, and Axel began pulling on my arm.

We can't leave him behind. There's no way in hell I'll leave him behind. Human or not, I won't run!

The vampire hissed and Xavier's deep gravelly growl echoed through the house. "Remember what I said, Ruby." His voice was contorted, a blend of the human Xavier and his wolf. He groaned as his right knee snapped. "Run!"

Axel's hold on me tightened, and I had no choice but to run as he pulled me. Xavier charged forward, and I saw a glimpse of dark brown fur appear through the torn skin on his back. We rounded a corner, our legs pumping to propel us forward.

Tears were streaming down my face as I listened to Xavier's deep howls and growls. Axel released my hand so I could wipe my tears as Natalie kicked the library door open. I ran inside after her. Then I stepped away from both of them, my hands on my head as they barricaded the door. "We can't leave him," I said under my voice before turning to face them. "We can't leave him! He can't fight them alone!"

Natalie shoved the book over to Axel as she walked over to a wall with a large painting of a ship being wrecked at sea.

I felt like this house was that ship.

She ran her hand against the side of the painting and then pulled. The painting swung away from the wall like a door. The wall behind it appeared flat and plain. Natalie pressed her hand against the surface. A small square sank in to release a previously invisible door.

I turned to Axel. "We can't leave him, Axel. You said it yourself, we don't know how many of them are out there. He can't fight them all!" It sounded like the house was being ripped apart. Each time I heard Xavier's thundering howls, the blood chilled in my veins.

"Please, Axel!"

He walked over to me and held my face gently as I held onto his hand. "I know," he replied and then released my face to hold my elbow. He pulled me to the open door where Natalie was waiting. I looked behind her at the dark passage before turning back to him. "Axel?"

He handed the book back to Natalie. "Go, both of you. I'll go back and help Xavier, but I need the two of you to leave. Understood? Don't wait for us."

Despite being petrified of leaving Xavier to fight alone, deserting Axel as well only made me feel worse. I didn't want to lose either of them, and I doubted whoever saved us before was hanging out somewhere around the house just waiting to help us again. I had to hold onto what tiny comfort I was getting from knowing at least they'd be fighting together. They'd both stand a chance as long as they had each other.

Natalie said, "Okay."

To my surprise, Axel reached out and gently touched a strand of my hair. Time around us stood still as I watched him wrap it around his finger. "I'll get him back to you." He released my hair, watching as it quickly unraveled from around his finger. His eyes drifted to mine. "We'll see you soon."

My lips parted, but I didn't know what to say. Why did it feel like he was actually saying goodbye? Why did it hurt so much? I raised my hand as if to touch him when he pushed me into the passage and quickly closed the door behind us.

I stood there, scared and confused. With the door closed, I could no longer hear the battle within the house. I could only hear my heavy breathing.

Natalie placed her hand on my shoulder. "We have to go."

I nodded and turned away as we both started running. The only source of light we had was the flashlight in Natalie's hand. I didn't even care about the rats and whatever various insects we ran by...I was too busy trying not to imagine what was happening inside the house.

The ceiling above us shook and dirt and dust fluttered down to us as we paused to brace ourselves in case the ceiling caved in. Natalie looked back at me, her eyes wide. We started running again, faster this time.

We must have been running for at least ten minutes when Natalie's flashlight revealed a door up ahead. We came to a stop, and Natalie held her finger to her lips. She tapped her ear before turning the flashlight off.

I figured she was listening if anything could be heard from the other side, but I couldn't even see my hands in front of my face. I listened as she started shuffling around, and then I heard a latch pull. Natalie groaned as she started pushing on the door. I lent her what little strength I had left, and we managed to shove the door open.

We emerged in the middle of the forest, the darkness around us only made only a little less so from the moon's light above.

Natalie adjusted her backpack and wrapped her arms around the book in her hand.

We both moved quietly through the trees until we were clear to run again.

Despite not being able to shift like a normal werewolf, Natalie still had amazing speed. I knew she was matching my slower pace to stay by my side, so I pushed all my energy and strength into my legs to drive my body forward.

The same noxious odor from before began to tickle my nostrils. Natalie looked over at me as I met her eyes.

Fuck.

She slowed to a jog, and so did I. "Keep running," she said to me as she shoved the book into my arms and pulled two knives from her waist. I stopped jogging as she did. She hissed, "I said to keep running! I may not be able to transform, but I'm still a were-wolf. I can buy you some time to get away. Two of them are coming. Go! Now!"

My body started shaking. I couldn't lose her, too. If she stayed and fought these things, there was no doubt they would murder her. "Come on, Natalie! Axel said we should keep running. Don't do this! You can't fight them."

She turned to me, her eyes turning milky white as her claws began to elongate. "I said go!"

Without warning, a vampire rushed out from the woods behind Natalie while she was facing me.

As I screamed her name, a wolf appeared from out of nowhere, jumping into the air and colliding with the vampire. They fell to the ground in a bundle of claws, fangs, growls, and hisses.

I gripped the book in my hand and started backing away.

Natalie stepped in front of me, as yet another vampire appeared, a woman. Her hair was dark and tussled. She smiled as she looked at me and sniffed the air. She rushed towards us and Natalie charged to intercept her. The vamp swiped her claws at Natalie, who didn't dodge quickly enough. The sharp claws ripped into Natalie's upper arm with ease causing massive gashes, and Natalie slapped the vampire across the face with a deep growl. When the vamp rushed at Natalie again, Natalie drove one of her knives into the bloodsucker's throat before digging her nails into the woman's shoulder. Natalie used the rest of her forward momentum to throw the wailing vampire, sending her skidding along the forest floor.

"For fuck's sake, Ruby! Run!" The unknown wolf that had been fighting the other vampire yelped in pain. The vampire zeroed in on me and flashed his fangs. He rushed forward, but the wolf bit down on his shoulder from behind and flipped him over his back. "Run! Now!"

I turned and ran.

My tongue felt like old sandpaper and my eyes seemed glued shut by dried tears. I felt sure whatever foul stench I was smelling was coming from me.

I rolled onto my back and winced as a rock poked me. Turning back onto my side, I rubbed at my eyes, the sound of singing birds telling me morning had come.

I'd fallen asleep out of pure exhaustion. I tried to stay awake to keep watch, but sleep won the battle. My hand still gripped one of my daggers, and Axel's book was still pressed to my chest. The events of the night before surfaced in my mind. I sighed and closed my eyes as they stung with tears yet again.

I squeezed the book somewhat before sitting up and wiping at my eyes with the small area of my top not covered in dirt. I looked to the side to find my jacket lying beside me. I must've taken it off to cover myself while I slept.

After I finally did what Natalie said and took off, I ran until I felt like my feet were ready to fall off. I slowed some when I could no longer hear Natalie's fight or smell the vampires because I was a wheezing mess.

Still panicked and knowing vampires might follow me, I found a puddle of mud and muck, stopping to lather myself in it before moving on. I figured it might hide my scent. When I eventually came across a small cave so hidden I had almost missed it, I crawled inside and pulled some broken tree limbs and bush over its opening. It was big enough for me to crouch down in and curl my body into a ball.

As uncomfortable as it had been, I figured I would be as good as dead if I kept moving through the forest. If the gunk on me had done its job to hide my scent, the only thing the vampires would have to do was listen and they would hear me stomping through the forest.

I pushed the branches and bush away from the cave's entrance, pushed the book and my backpack out in front of me and crawled out. Thank god, this wasn't a little critter's home. I would have had more problems than just hiding from vampires.

I shielded my eyes against the brightness of the sun and sat on the ground. My stomach was twisted in knots, and I had a headache the size of Asia.

Are they all dead?

The tears burning my eyes that had been fighting to be free—finally escaped. I'd survived the night, and I was both surprised and exceedingly grateful. Had the others survived as well? I closed my eyes for a moment but opened them quickly as unwelcome images from the night before began to flash before my eyes.

I swallowed whatever drops of saliva had been produced in my mouth, my only source of water I had since I had finished my bottle of water last night. I pulled myself up off the ground and groaned because my body ached all over. I had to get back to the pack. I needed to know if the others were okay. I started to walk slowly through the forest.

After I had been walking for a while, I stopped when I spotted a tiny pool of water that had settled in one of the curved leaves of a plant. I dipped my pinkie finger in first and tapped it on my tongue. I shrugged. It tasted like plain old water. I drank it, hoping it was just water from the light rain of last night.

I rocked back on my heels somewhat. It felt like I hadn't tasted water in decades. I was about to keep walking straight when my eyes caught sight of something brownish red splashed on some bushes to my left. I frowned and went in that direction. As I followed the little colored trail, I realized what I was looking at: blood.

My heart started pounding as I came upon a spot drenched in ruddy brown. The metallic smell of blood had me pressing my tongue to the roof of my mouth to stop myself from gagging. I looked around me and my knees grew weak. This was where I had left Natalie, I was certain of it.

I turned in a circle, growing lightheaded at the sight of the blood-soaked ground. I didn't want to wonder if this was all her blood. I took off running, pushing myself despite my pain and exhaustion. Soon I spotted the house through the trees.

"Finally," I panted, and I continued running towards the front of the house.

I eyed the broken front door, hanging at an odd angle. I set Axel's book and my bag down to prepare myself to enter. I had no idea what I might find. Just in case a vampire was lingering around, I pulled out both my daggers. I quickly slammed the damaged front door and held my daggers out in a fighting stance, ready to defend myself against any remaining bloodsuckers. But I heard nothing, and nothing moved. The house was in shambles with blood on the floor and walls. Even with my normal human hearing, if a pin had dropped, I would have been able to hear it in the echoing silence.

After I was satisfied that no monsters were there to jump out and attack me, I relaxed my stance and checked out my surroundings. I walked down the hall we had run down last night, but I didn't get far. The walls and floors were saturated in blood. I closed my eyes and stepped back. *I need to find them! I have to find them!*

What if the vampires took them?

I returned to the lobby and turned in the direction of the kitchen when I came face to face with Mathieu.

He looked me up and down.

"Where are they?" I asked instantly. I knew I looked like a wreck and smelled like the sewer, but I'd never been so happy to see someone. "Where are they, Mathieu? Please tell me they're okay." I stepped forward, my hands now shaking. Somehow, seeing him made me even more emotional. Maybe it was the regretful look in his eyes. I didn't want to start thinking the worst, but if he didn't start talking soon, I would lose my shit.

His dark eyes, so much like Xavier's, drifted away from me.

"Mathieu?" I asked.

"Come with me."

He'd been a man of few words since the moment I had met him, but his silence right now was too much to bear. If Xavier were badly hurt or dead, wouldn't he be losing his mind right now? He'd lost his wife and barely survived that. I didn't want to think about what would happen to Mathieu if he lost Xavier too.

I exhaled a breath I hadn't known I was holding. Xavier must be okay.

I hoped.

"Can you just tell me what happened, please?"

"Xavier was badly wounded. So was Axel, but they are both healing quickly," He explained as we arrived on the second floor. He turned to face me.

I waited for him to say something about Natalie, but he added nothing else. "And Natalie?" I asked as I bent my head back to look up at him.

He combed his midnight hair back and turned away. He looked exhausted and his thick beard seemed to now have more grey hairs than black. "I'll take you to her."

I didn't like the sound of that. We walked in silence until we got to her bedroom. He held onto the door handle before looking back at me. "Don't try to wake her, okay?"

I frowned but nodded.

"You can go in." He opened the door.

I stepped around him to enter. When I saw her, my hand flew to my mouth. A very pale Natalie was lying completely still on her back in the bed dressed in a clean white nightgown. As I stepped further into the room, I could see multiple teeth marks on her ankle, wrist, and arms.

I had to look closely to see that her chest was rising and falling slowly. She looked dead. I started crying. I couldn't stop the tears this time as they flowed down my cheeks.

Mathieu entered the room and placed his hand on my shoulder.

I hunched forward as I covered my mouth to silence my sobs. "Is s-she—dying?" I whispered to him.

"No," he replied. Although he whispered, his voice was still loud enough to hear clearly. "But she's in a coma. They almost killed her."

I held both my daggers in my left hand as I used the back of my right hand to wipe at my tears. My hand fell to my side as I stepped away from him. I placed my daggers on the ground unceremoniously and carried a chair next to Natalie's bed. I sat down heavily, my eyes roaming over her motionless body as my fists clenched in anger.

Mathieu left, closing the door soundlessly behind him.

I reached out and held her hand gently, my eyes tearing up once more at the bite marks at her wrist. The wounds were closed and almost healed, but the bruised skin around the punctures still appeared bright, especially with how white she looked.

"Natalie, it's Ruby. I hope you can hear me. I'm right here with you," I reassured her. I wasn't sure if she could hear me while in a coma, but I figured it couldn't hurt for her to know she wasn't alone.

Her long hair looked as white as the pillow beneath her head. Despite the evidence of injuries, she looked utterly angelic. She was the first true friend I'd ever had. After my traumatic introduction into the supernatural world, Natalie had been someone I knew I could trust, no matter what.

I should have forced her to run with me or stayed to fight with her. I shook my head in helpless resignation as fresh tears fell from my eyes. No, I couldn't have fought with her. I would have been more of a liability than an asset. Nevertheless, I felt sick of always being the one who had to run and leave everyone else behind to fight and die!

I wiped at my tears. "I'm right here. I'm okay, and you will be, too." I rubbed my thumb against her hand. "Wake up soon, please."

Ruby

I woke up with horrible pain in my neck. I had fallen asleep sitting down beside Natalie with my head resting on the edge of the bed.

I stared at her for a moment before getting up and stretching. My clothes felt stiff and I didn't even want to think about how horrible I smelled. Mathieu had said Xavier and Axel were okay, and I doubted they would mind if I took a shower before looking for them.

It must have taken an hour for me to scrub my body and hair fully clean. The floor of the shower was black by the time I finished. Once I finally made it out of the shower, I felt refreshed. I dried my hair with a towel and braided my hair into a single plait down my back before searching the house for Xavier.

He wasn't on the second floor. As I carefully made my way

around ripped paintings and shattered décor in the ravaged halls of the third floor, I soon heard talking. I sped up and stopped at a door left slightly ajar, revealing Mathieu and Xavier inside. I watched as they skimmed through the pages of the book I had carried back with me.

Xavier was shirtless with a large bandage wrapped around his abdomen along with other bandages on his left arm and right shoulder. I smiled as I observed him, and my smile widened when he looked up and saw me.

His long legs carried him to me within seconds as I entered the room. He pulled me into a tight hug that lifted me completely off the ground. If he had squeezed any tighter, he would have crushed me, but I didn't care as I squeezed him back with all my strength. I felt like crying again but managed to hold it in. I'd done more than my share of crying lately, enough to last a lifetime. I hated how I was becoming a crybaby, but this shit was getting to me.

Maybe it was because I never had people I cared about this much. I never had to fear losing anyone. I never had to stress and wonder if someone I cared about was okay.

"I came to look for you but you were sleeping," he said to me as he placed me back onto the floor. "You looked like shit."

I laughed and shrugged. "I figured if I covered myself in mud, all the vampires wouldn't smell me."

He nodded. "I guess that makes sense. One might have come after you except they were all taken care of." He looked down at his abdomen. "It wasn't easy."

I ran a finger gently over the bandage on his shoulder, arm, and then his face. He didn't look like he was in pain as he looked down at me with a smile on his lips, but I couldn't help feeling bad seeing him injured like this.

"I'm all right." He leaned forward and kissed my forehead. "I'm glad you're safe. Natalie said you had gotten away before she fell unconscious. I was out cold after her." He walked back over to

Mathieu. "Axel patched us up as much as he could until Dad got here."

I followed him. "What are you guys doing?" I asked as I gazed down at the book. "Did you find anything useful?"

Xavier placed his hand on the table as he leaned over the book next to me. Its pages were a yellow shade with gold designs around its edges. "Axel was right. Stakes don't work on vampires. Beheading and burning them works, so yes to sunlight and UV lights."

"Vampires were around in my great, great, great, great, great grandfather's time," Mathieu said as he turned one of the pages. Both left and right pages together made up a large picture of a battle between vampires and werewolves. "I never believed the stories about vampires. Some supernaturals have traits like a vampire. I always assumed someone simply mistook one of those other supernaturals for a vampire." He ran his hand gently over the page. "I didn't know Axel's family had this book." He sighed. "Either way, it makes sense vampires would become stories if they've been gone...well, in hiding for all these years."

"The Council must have records on them. They could have told us all the stories were true," Xavier pointed out as he crossed his arms in front of his chest.

Mathieu nodded. "Yes, but they wouldn't have felt the need to come out and say yes, vampires were once real. They were thought to be extinct. The Council doesn't care if wolves believe they existed or not. It's not like having the flu and taking shots to prevent it from happening again. The species was thought to be wiped out, gone...no longer a threat."

Xavier exhaled heavily through his nose and turned away.

I understood what Xavier was trying to say, but Mathieu was also right. Why protect oneself against something you thought could never happen? The thought wouldn't even cross your mind.

"It sucks that countless packs are defenseless now," Xavier

muttered. "They're going to be picked off one by one. How can we get this info to everyone in time?"

"Make a video," I offered. The words were out my mouth before I even thought about what I was really saying. I cleared my throat as Xavier turned around. "I mean, if the Council won't release any information, you have to share what you know. You've fought them and survived. Explain everything you know in the video and show them the book as well."

His eyes turned to slits as he held his chin and appeared to seriously consider my words. He looked over at his father.

Mathieu stared back at him and nodded.

"That's not a bad idea," Xavier said. "Sometimes, the simplest approach is the best. I'll have it sent to all the alphas I know and they can then help with distributing it."

"I suggest doing it while you still have those bandages on," I added.

Xavier frowned. "No. I am the Alpha-to-be for the Blackmoon Pack. I can't show weakness, not even now."

I shook my head. "It's not a weakness. It'll help bring across the message that these creatures should not be underestimated. And since you've already fought them and only came away with these wounds, you shouldn't be underestimated either. You're not an Alpha yet, but you are strong. Once this is all over and you do become the alpha, everyone will look up to you. You would have given everyone the vital information they needed to survive when the Council didn't."

"She's right," Mathieu recognized as he placed his hand on Xavier's shoulder. "It's about time the leadership transfer was done anyways, but with everything happening, it'll have to wait. I've served as Alpha long enough and have made my mark. It's time you secure your future. You know many packs don't like us because we still protect humans. Respect will be earned once we step forward and help them to survive this."

"Okay, I'll do it," Xavier agreed as he closed the book. He sent a proud smile my way. "I'll make the video now before we leave."

I smiled as my cheeks heated up. *Maybe I wouldn't make such a bad Luna after all.* "Where is Axel?" I asked. I wanted to see him as well. According to what Xavier had said, Axel was the one who took care of both him and Natalie in the end.

Xavier frowned somewhat but said nothing as Mathieu replied, "He's helping Randoll with burying the bodies of the wolves that were killed last night. The vampire bodies are being burned."

"Did any wolves survive?" I asked.

Mathieu nodded. "Two others survived. They are helping Randoll and Axel." His face twisted with anger. "Those things destroyed my home. This house has been in the Blackwood family for years, and now all I smell is vampire filth."

"None of them escaped," Xavier told him.

I jumped for joy on the inside. I wished I could learn to fight so I could be of some help, but there was no time to spare to train me to take on a vampire. Most of the wolves outside of Axel's pack were only just learning how to combat vampires themselves.

"How did you kill them?" I questioned Xavier. What if I was ever attacked again and there was no one around to help me? I really needed to be ready, just in case. I understood vampires' weaknesses, so at least that was a start for me.

"In wolf form, I aimed for the head. Ripped it clean off. Once they've been fully decapitated, they are done for."

I nodded. "I need a gun."

Xavier raised a brow as the side of his mouth curved into a look of amusement.

I knew what that look meant. I was just a girl, so why would anyone trust me with a gun? "Yes, I do know how to use a gun, Xavier, so don't be so sexist. I had to stay with a lot of different types of families growing up thanks to the foster care system. Most of the time it wasn't pretty, but some of the foster parents were nicer than others. In one of the better homes, I had a foster Dad named Dave that worked for the FBI. He took me to the gun range and taught me how to shoot. I wasn't half bad at it either."

The smile on his face transformed into a look of surprise.

"I may not be able to bite a vampire's head off, but I sure as hell can shoot one."

His mouth turned upside down as he made a face. "Hmm, all right then, fair enough."

Dave's home had been just about the only one I had stayed in that I didn't hate. I had only stayed with them for a few months, but it hadn't been too bad. Unfortunately, right when I was just starting to have a little hope that maybe I could really stay with them for a while and be happy, the foster mom—Alicia—got cancer. They couldn't take care of me anymore, so it was on to the next placement for me. Other than the men that stood here with me, Natalie and yes, Axel as well, Dave and Alicia were the only ones I'd ever given a shit about in my life. It was strange—I'd only know the wolves for a relatively short time, yet they were already like the family I'd never had. "Is Natalie going to be okay?" I asked suddenly.

Xavier's eyes darkened. "I don't know," he replied as he pressed his fingers into his eyes. "Axel had gotten to her just in time before she could be drained."

None of us spoke and for me, I couldn't because I was too pissed to speak. Natalie didn't deserve this. No one deserved anything like this. A growl made me jump, and I realized it was Mathieu.

His eyes turned black and he looked away.

I stared at him. She was his niece, almost like a daughter to him, and he'd already lost so much. My heart went out to him, but I dared not say anything to comfort him. I feared he might interpret it as pity. It didn't seem like Alphas were big on displaying emotions, not ones that made them appear vulnerable anyways.

He looked down at his watch. "It's 8 am. It'll take a few hours for us to drive to the location where the others are, so I suggest we leave within the next hour."

"Can Natalie travel in her current state?" I asked him.

He sighed and walked away. "She has to," he answered and left the room.

I turned to Xavier and he called me to him softly. My body moved to him instantly as if he had stuck a hook inside me and was reeling me in. He wrapped his arms around me and I sagged against him. His body felt like a warm heating pad. I closed my eyes, relaxing into his touch.

He kissed the top of my head. "Do you want to help me with making the video? We have to do it quickly."

I nodded. "Sure," I replied in a low voice.

He leaned away slightly and brought a long finger up under my chin, gently moving it upward until my eyes met his. "I'm glad you're okay, Ruby. I don't know what I'd have done if those things had gotten to you."

"Oh, it would only be a matter of time before you got another girlfriend." I chuckled.

His face fell.

Mine did too, as I stared back at him.

Suddenly, a wide grin appeared on his lips.

"What?"

"So, you're my girlfriend?"

My eyes widened. *Did I just say that?* I tried to step away from him, but he tightened his hands around me. His lips swiftly claimed mine, and I immediately stopped trying to move away from him. All of sudden, it felt as if I could never get close enough. I moaned softly into his mouth as his large hands found their way under my shirt at my waistline. I reveled in the feel of his soft warmth as he smoothly caressed the sensitive skin of the curves of my abdomen.

He pulled away unexpectedly, and I screamed on the inside for more. When I gazed up at him, his eyes were black and his fangs had appeared. My heartbeat sped up even faster.

"Don't be frightened. My wolf just wanted to taste you too." He lightly kissed my cheek and then my shoulder.

I shivered as his tongue swiped against my skin.

"We should make the video before I lose focus entirely."

I swallowed and nodded.

He pinched my chin suddenly. "And never joke about me replacing you, or you dying for that matter. Understood?"

I nodded yet again, my tongue too heavy to answer all of a sudden.

Xavier smiled. "Good girl."

After I finished helping Xavier with the video, I went back to Natalie's room to check on her. Her backpack from the night before was sitting by the door, covered in blood. I unpacked her things and placed them all in a new clean bag.

I got her dressed before returning to my room to collect my bag. I took Natalie's and my bags down to the car before I headed back inside. All the while, I was lost in thought.

Watching Xavier make that video had been a proud moment for me. He had looked so strong, so confident. He wore his scars like a warrior. I knew everyone who saw the video would heed his warnings and be thankful for his pointers on how to survive.

It wasn't a big deal in the grand scheme of things, but it was rewarding to know that I had given him the idea to do the video. I had contributed something essential to the survival of other were-wolves. I was more than just the helpless human mate, needing protection, and serving no purpose. Fuck that! I was useful, and I had proved it.

I sighed as I plopped down on my bed, a blush making its way up my neck to my cheeks. I had called myself his girlfriend. Even though the moment had already passed, I covered my face in embarrassment just thinking about it. I couldn't believe I'd made that slip.

He seemed more than pleased about it, though. And that kiss... oh man, that kiss...I could still taste him on my lips.

I was his mate, but we had never talked about me being his Luna or even his girlfriend, for that matter. I smiled. Well, it looked like I was officially off the market. I chuckled to myself as I inhaled deeply and then exhaled. I got up and turned in a circle. I had a feeling I wouldn't be coming back to this house for a while or maybe ever.

When this all ended, the house would need a lot of renovation to return to its former glory. The stench of blood inside the house would fade over time, but the walls and floor would be permanently stained with blood. There was no time to clean it all up before we left. No wonder Mathieu was so pissed—the house had been his family for generations. I frowned. I shouldn't have given a damn about this house right now. The house would be fine. I needed to focus on getting out of here and safely indoors again before nightfall.

"See you," I said to my room as I walked out and closed the door. I went to Natalie's room, but she was no longer there. I figured Xavier must have taken her down to the car, so they must have been waiting on me.

As I headed to the first floor, I stepped around a corner and came face to face with Axel.

His hair hung loosely around his shoulders, damp with sweat. He was also shirtless, red scars covering his body, probably from the battle the night before. A bandage wrapped around his side as well, but for the most part, he looked fine. His chest glistening with sweat rose as he inhaled. "How are you?"

I shrugged. "Not great, but I'm alive." I pointed at his side. " How are you?"

He peered down at his side. "Yeah, I'm good. I've been worse.

That bite was just a little deeper than the others. I heard what you did to stay safe out there last night. I wish I could have seen you, covered in mud and all."

I rolled my eyes. "Of course, you would."

He chuckled. "That was smart thinking."

I looked away, not wanting him to see that I was blushing. A compliment or praise from Axel was rare. "Uh, thanks," I replied simply. Neither of us spoke after that as I looked back at him. I soon looked away again, unable to handle the awkwardness and his piercing stare. Seeing him well had caused me to feel happier, though. "So..." I drawled. "Your pack is safe, right?"

He moved his hair behind his ears. "Yeah, they're all safe. My pack isn't as large as the Blackmoon Pack, so it wasn't hard to move them all. They're at another safe house like the one we were at. A warlock's warding protects them."

I crossed my arms over my chest as I narrowed my eyes at him. "You seem to have a lot of warlocks on your payroll. What's up with that?"

He smirked down at me. "You don't need to worry your pretty little red head about that, Ruby." He crossed his arms over his broad chest and leaned on the wall. "I will be checking on that witch to see if she can help you, though. I keep my promises."

I held his stare this time. "So, I guess you're not coming with us then?" Since he wasn't dressed, it was clear he wasn't prepared to go anywhere, but I still asked.

He'd done a lot for Xavier and me as it was. Despite the feud between them and the tension between all three of us, his recent actions spoke volumes about his character. Xavier had said Axel had saved both him and Natalie in the end. I wouldn't tell him this, but having him travel with us would have made me feel just a little safer. "You have to stay with them to keep them safe, even behind a warlock's warding," I added quickly, so I didn't sound like a child about to cry when their mother leaves for work.

He narrowed his eyes at me and stepped forward rapidly, leaving but a small gap between us.

I held my breath.

"Why? Will you miss me, Ruby?"

I blinked, then blinked again while still holding my breath. Why did Axel sound like that just now? I frowned. Why was he looking at me like this? Why was I being affected? Butterflies began to flap their wings furiously inside me, and I stood up straight to hold my composure. "No," I answered and managed to keep a straight face.

His eyes roamed over my face, but he made no move to step away from me. He leaned in further, his nose almost touching mine. "I can tell when you're lying. Your voice becomes too low." He tilted his head to the side.

I stared into the depths of his hazel eyes.

He didn't look away, but I did as he raised a hand to hold a strand of hair by my face. I looked back at him as his jaws clenched, and he slowly released the strand. "Don't worry, I'll miss you too."

I wanted to snort or laugh or say something witty, but I couldn't. He was too close to me. I feared if I spoke, my lips might accidentally touch his. What a disaster that would be! My eyes flicked down to his lips as he licked them, and my heart skipped a beat.

His gaze stayed locked on my face. "I meant what I said earlier. You did well with hiding yourself. You should keep those daggers on you at all times. Xavier will protect you with his life, I know," he said that with a little venom in his voice. "But like last night, you might have to fend for yourself at some point. You have to be able to protect yourself. Do you understand?"

What was with these men and asking me if I understand? I wasn't incompetent. I reached behind me and removed the dagger I'd shoved into my waistband. I brandished it and pressed the tip under his chin. "Don't worry about me, Axel. I'll be just fine. I'm stronger than I look."

The corner of his mouth curved until it turned into a full-blown smile.

I was surprised to see a dimple appear on his left cheek. For someone always so serious, seeing him smile was like seeing the sun after months of rain. I would tell him to smile more, except I didn't want it to go to his head.

He moved to the side to whisper in my ear, "I know. A weak woman would never be my mate."

My heart stopped as he moved to stare at me once more. His eyes drifted down to my lips, and a ringing started in my ear as I began to panic. Was he going to kiss me? What would I do if he did? Was it cheating if he was my mate as well?

Someone cleared their throat, and I stepped away from Axel as if he had burned me.

Axel sighed and looked behind him to find Xavier standing a few steps away from us.

I couldn't tell what the look in Xavier's eyes meant—if he was angry or not. He merely looked at Axel and then back at me.

"Are you ready? We need to get going," Axel said.

I nodded, unable to speak from embarrassment. What had I just almost allowed to happen?

Axel looked back at me.

I gave him a tight-lipped smile. "Be safe."

"I will," he replied. "I'll come and find you after I've checked on my people, and I have information from that witch."

I nodded and stepped around him to join Xavier.

Xavier nodded at Axel.

Axel slowly returned the nod.

We moved away. Though I wanted to look back behind me, I didn't. I could feel Axel's eyes on me, though.

Xavier and I headed down to the car in silence. I felt uncomfortable. What was he thinking about? How much of Axel's and my conversation had he heard?

I shook my head mentally as we walked through the front

door. It wasn't like we had been talking about anything secret. I needed to get my shit together and stop being awkward. Being awkward might cause Xavier to think more had transpired than what actually had.

Natalie's head was resting in the seat of the car I was to sit in.

Xavier opened the car door for me and then gently held Natalie's head up for me so I could sit down. I then placed a small pillow on my lap to rest her head on. I felt uncomfortable having her traveling like this, but I knew there was no other choice.

Xavier closed the door softly and got into the front.

Mathieu maneuvered the car away from the house.

Randoll had left long ago with the two wolves that had survived, so it was just us three.

As we drove down the long driveway to get to the main road, I moved Natalie's hair out of her face and placed my hand on her cheek to keep her head from moving around. An IV drip with fluids was attached to her arm and anchored to the seat that I was keeping an eye on as well.

"Is there anyone in the pack that might be able to help her?" I asked Mathieu.

He shook his head. "Right now, all we can do is keep her comfortable."

A sound echoed in the car, and I assumed Xavier had hit something with his hand. "Reika, we should have called her! She should know how to help Natalie."

"I hadn't thought about her either," Mathieu said as he dug into his pants pocket and pulled out his phone. "Call her, see what she knows." He glanced behind him at Natalie and me before looking back at the road. He turned left as we got to the highway. "Maybe she can mind-link Natalie. See how she's doing mentally."

I cracked my window a little then drifted off into my own world as he drove. My head lulled back against the seat, and I closed my eyes. Even though I had slept last night, I still felt drained.

I just prayed Reika could help. I couldn't do any of this without Natalie. Not only that, but I also knew she did so much for this pack. Losing her would most definitely send everyone into despair. Considering how powerful she had become of late, I wouldn't be surprised if things would get much darker for the pack in this conflict with the vampires if we lost her.

I didn't know exactly how things worked with their goddess, like if wolves prayed to her the same way humans pray to their god. Nevertheless, I sent a prayer to their goddess to protect Natalie anyway. I just hoped she accepted prayers from humans too.

Xavier

I rested my elbow heavily on the window as Dad stepped on the gas. I could tell he was starting to become uneasy because it was already almost 4 pm. I checked on Ruby in the mirror on the door, only to see her gazing out her window.

I had heard what Axel had said to her—only a strong woman could be his mate. I didn't disagree with him because I believed the same for myself. I still wanted to rip his spine out, though. He'd stood far too close to her when he'd whispered it. For so long, Axel had denied his feelings for her, but I could hear them loud and clear in his voice back there.

He wanted her, and there was no hiding it anymore.

I closed my eyes as the breeze tickled my face. Over time, I'd slowly become less pissed whenever I saw them talking. At first, the mere mention of the fact that I was not Ruby's only mate would enrage me. Since I couldn't allow this thing between the three of us to drive me insane, all I could do was accept the way things were. It still pained me to see her with him, but at the end of the day, she was more mine than his—for now anyways.

However, I was no fool. I knew what the wolf bond was like,

and I knew she must have had some lingering feelings for him. I trusted that our bond was stronger than the two of theirs. I wasn't sure what I would do if I ever saw Axel kiss Ruby. It would cut me to my core, but I knew I wouldn't be able to kick his ass or be angry with her.

The bond pulls mates together, and that couldn't be helped. I could only imagine how he felt seeing her with me.

The moment I was about to dial Reika's number, she called on Dad's phone. She instantly asked for Natalie and said she had gotten a bad feeling about her. I shouldn't have been surprised. Reika was a powerful Enchanted, much like Natalie. I filled her in on what had happened. As soon as I told her vampires had attacked the house, she asked me if Ruby was safe. I paused for a moment, finding it strange that she seemed so concerned for Ruby, specifically.

Catching my sudden hesitation, Reika clarified that keeping Ruby safe was extremely important, despite what was going on around us. She was the first human to be mated to a wolf. She and I—and Axel—were making history.

Reika advised us not to force Natalie out of her coma. It could be done, but it wasn't something she recommended. If she dove into Natalie's psyche now, it would be dangerous for them both. Unfortunately, Natalie would have to wake up on her own terms. Reika offered to hop on a plane to aid us since Natalie was out of commission. I refused her offer.

Natalie trusted her, but I didn't. I knew Reika still worked for Olcan. She was too close to the Council for my comfort. Natalie had told me all about how she had played a part in helping Ruby and me to escape, but I refused to trust her completely. Reika recognized that I was wary, yet she didn't seem to hold it against us.

"Thank you, Reika, but I think you remaining there would be wise. We'll be able to keep track of what the Council is doing. If you leave to come to our aid, the Council will turn their attention to you, assuming that you've betrayed them."

Reika saw the wisdom of my words and told me she would keep me updated. For now, all she knew was that Olcan didn't seem too shaken up about vampires still being alive. She told me to keep her updated on Natalie, and our call ended.

I hadn't said this to her, but I wouldn't be surprised if Olcan had known all along about vampires still being alive. The rumor was that the vampires hadn't tried to kill him and instead only attacked other Council members.

"Reika helped Natalie the night you left. She placed Olcan and me under a sleeping spell," Dad guessed after my call with Reika ended.

"If you weren't asleep, would you have stopped Ruby and me from leaving?" I asked him.

He didn't answer right away.

I turned to look at him.

"No," he finally answered. "I wouldn't have stopped the two of you. I didn't need to hear it from Olcan to know he wanted Ruby dead."

"Then why were you so relaxed about the whole thing? You were willing to let us go with him knowing what the outcome would be."

He looked over at me, a deep crease between his brows. "You think I would let Olcan hurt my only son? Acting outright against Olcan would be foolish, but I had no intention of letting him kill you or Ruby."

I felt bad for asking him a question like that. The thump of an erratic heartbeat pulled me from my thoughts, and I frowned. A pained moaning sound met my ears from the backseat, and I hastily glanced behind me to see Natalie trying to move her hand.

Ruby looked at me with wide eyes before placing her hand lightly on Natalie's chest. "Natalie?" she whispered to her. "Natalie? Can you hear me?"

Natalie's head moved from side to side as her heartbeat increased rapidly.

"Dad, slow down!" I called to him.

He slowed the car down to a snail's pace.

Ruby caressed Natalie's hair. "Natalie?"

Her heartbeat started to slow down again, and she stopped moving soon after. I released a breath I hadn't realized I had been holding.

"What was that?" Ruby asked.

I shrugged. "I don't know. Maybe she's slowly waking up," I answered before facing forward again. "Maybe I should have told Reika to come after all."

Dad sped up a little as he checked his watch. "We're running out of time."

"I know that, but..." I froze, my ears twitching as Natalie started to mumble. I turned my head around swiftly to look at her again.

Sweat formed on her forehead as she continued to mumble under her breath.

"Xavier?" Ruby called—her face twisted with worry. "What's wrong with her?" She placed her hand on Natalie's cheek. "Natalie, can you hear me? It's Ruby." She reached down to hold Natalie's hand. "Squeeze my hand if you can hear me."

Nothing happened, but Natalie continued to mumble. Soon she started to shake. Under her lids, I could see her eyes darting from left to right frantically.

Ruby released her hand as Natalie started to twist and turn. "She's going to rip the needle out of her arm if she keeps doing this!" Ruby cautioned hurriedly.

I leaned over just as Natalie's eyes popped open. I paused as I felt a burst of relief to see her awake. Sadly, that relief was short-lived. Before I had time to say anything to her, she started screaming. The scream was so high pitched, I felt my blood immediately rush to my ears. I covered them hastily and fell back into my seat.

Ruby covered her ears. Thanks to the fact that she didn't have the heightened senses of a werewolf, Ruby didn't seem to be as affected as my father and I were.

The car started to sway as blood poured from my dad's ears. My vision started to blur as the scream continued to flow from her lips like something from a horror movie. I could feel a burst of power in the car, and my dad hunched forward with a pained growl as blood dripped from the side of my mouth.

I felt like I was being crushed from the inside out. *What kind of power is this?* I swung around to her again. "Natalie! Stop! Natalie!"

Natalie stopped screaming abruptly. Her hand flew to Ruby's face to hold her forehead. Blood instantly began to roll down Ruby's face where Natalie's nails were digging into her.

Ruby's eyes widened, and so did mine. I grabbed at Natalie to release her hold on Ruby. "Natalie, what the fuck are you doing? You're hurting her."

Ruby's mouth fell open, and her eyes turned white as she started to scream.

Natalie groaned as her head swayed from side to side, and she started screaming once again.

I held my head. It felt like my brain was about to explode. I turned back around to face forward. As dad lost control of the swaying car, I was thrown forward, my head slamming against the dashboard.

"The-they're—going to—kill us," my dad said as he coughed, and blood splashed onto the steering wheel.

This couldn't be happening! What the fuck was happening?!

I reached around my seat and grabbed onto Natalie. I didn't want to do this, but I had no choice. I held her throat and pressed down—she instantly fell unconscious. I just hoped I didn't send her back into a coma.

Was she even really awake, or was she doing this in her sleep?

Natalie's hand fell away from Ruby's face, and her head lulled to the side as her eyes rolled back.

The car skidded to a halt in the middle of the road, and I pressed my fingers into my temples. My heart felt like it was trying to beat its way right out of my chest.

Dad panted loudly beside me as he touched his ear and nose, his finger coming away with blood. He shook his head a little, no doubt feeling disoriented like me. He glanced behind him at Ruby and Natalie before looking at me.

We could both hear them breathing just fine, but when I looked at Ruby, blood started to run from her nose.

Dad started the car again and pulled over to the side of the road.

Ruby's eyes opened, showing her normal green eyes before they changed back to white once more. She started to mutter, her eyes twitching. She began feeling around the car door and pulled the door open, forcing Dad to stop the vehicle suddenly as she stumbled out.

I jumped out as well and rushed to her, scooping her up in my arms. "Ruby?" I moved her hair back from her face and patted her cheek gently as her eyes started to close. "Stay with me. Stay with me, baby."

Dad hopped out of the car to check on Natalie.

I was close to losing my shit as Ruby kept muttering incoherent words, and blood started running from her eyes as they closed. "Fuck! Dad! What's wrong with her?"

He rushed over to me.

Gasping for air abruptly, Ruby bolted upright and out of my arms. She was wheezing with her heavy breathing as she started looking around frantically.

"Ruby! Ruby, calm down, I'm here!"

Her eyes looked as if she widened them any further, they would pop from her face. She began wiping her face, seeming confused as to why she was covered in blood. Her eyes teared up.

I felt like howling because I didn't know what to do to help her. *What had Natalie done to her?*

My dad's piercing howl suddenly rang out around us.

Ruby jumped, her eyes streaming with tears, but she stopped panicking and looked at me. "The-they're all—going t-to die," she stammered, her eyes still as white as the clouds above us.

What the hell is she talking about?

"Who? Who is going to die?" Dad asked as he stooped down.

Whimpering, Ruby closed her eyes and held her head as she moaned. More tears flooded her eyes. "They're all going to die."

CHAPTER NINE

RUBY

It took a while for me to start breathing normally again. I desperately wanted to calm down, I just couldn't.

Xavier sat with me while all the adrenaline inside me took it's time to return to normal.

Then I was speechless. It's not that I didn't want to talk, but...I just couldn't form the words necessary to answer any of Xavier's or Mathieu's questions. I was still in shock.

After twenty minutes, Mathieu told us we needed to get back on the road because it would be nightfall soon, and we had a good bit of traveling left. So, we all piled back into the car. We drove with a horrible silence hanging over our heads.

Natalie was still out cold. Mathieu and Xavier were busy cleaning the blood off themselves with wet wipes.

I just sat in the back, staring out the window. I knew Xavier kept glancing at me through his mirror since it was positioned to see the back window. I pretended not to see him, though. I wasn't ready to talk yet.

I peered down at Natalie on my lap as she slept soundly before looking away once more. Pinching the bridge of my nose, I groaned. My stomach felt weird, and I felt a tingling vibration under my skin.

"Ruby?"

I glanced up to see Xavier staring at me.

His neck twisted oddly since he was looking at me through the small space between his seat and the door. "You okay?"

My lips curved with a weak smile as I nodded, and I could see the relief in his eyes. I started to feel bad.

He had no idea what just happened. He turned around in his seat as much as he could to poke his head around to the backseat. "What happened?"

I sighed as I gazed down at Natalie, noticing a little more color appearing on her pale skin.

"I'm not sure, but I had a vision," I replied in a low voice. "She held me. Then this world, the car, and everything else washed away and was replaced."

"Replaced by what?" Mathieu probed.

I looked up and blinked several times. "A town or city, I don't know, but it was night time. There was smoke, a lot of smoke." I swallowed. "There were vampires killing people."

Xavier's brows instantly knitted at the mention of vampires.

I went on to describe it, "They were ripped to pieces…all those people. There was blood everywhere."

Xavier looked at his father as Mathieu returned the glance.

"I could a-almost feel their pain and fear—i-it was horrible," I added.

Xavier stared at me with such pity.

I shook my head and sat up straight. Seeing those people killed like that, like animals being slaughtered, had made me feel sick to my stomach. Maybe this was why I couldn't get rid of this odd feeling, this tingling all over my body. I decided not to mention the feeling. I was really okay, and Xavier and Mathieu didn't need anything else to worry about.

Xavier looked like he was ready to lock me in a room for the rest of my life. "I'm sorry," he said.

I smiled at him. I hoped it showed him I was fine. "It's okay. I don't know if it was something that already happened or is going to happen, but it felt like I was there."

Mathieu unexpectedly sped the car up, and I quickly placed my hand on Natalie's shoulder to keep her steady.

"It's almost dark," he told us. "We need to get off the road as soon as possible. We have only an hour left to get to the location, and it's almost dark. With Natalie unconscious, if we're attacked, they'll go for her first."

"Okay," Xavier replied. "Not too fast though. We really can't have her doing what she just did a second time. None of us will survive it."

"What happened to you two anyway?" I asked. "You started bleeding from just her screaming. I mean, it was loud, but—"

"It was louder for us," Xavier interjected. "Humans can't hear dog whistles, but it drives dogs nuts and wolves too. That's what it was like. There was a high-pitched ringing in my ear." He looked down at Natalie. "She's never done that before."

"She's getting stronger," Mathieu stated. "She gained a lot of power in a short space of time. It's not like she's been nurturing these gifts to this level gradually. It'll take some time for her to get the hang of it. What happened just now was quite strange, I admit."

Xavier faced forward again and placed his elbow on the window. "That was a lot of power. I've never heard of an Enchanted doing anything like what she just did. No one knows what she's capable of, but Enchanteds usually don't have offensive powers." He snorted. "Well, that was one hell of a mental attack. It felt like my brain was going to be liquefied."

Mathieu removed one hand from the steering wheel to press his fingers into the corner of his eyes. It seemed apparent he was still feeling some lingering effects of Natalie's attack. "If she saw what Ruby just explained, and Ruby reacted the way she did, it makes sense Natalie panicked like that." He placed his hand back onto the steering wheel, and the car accelerated a little more. "I've seen her have visions only to wake up and find cuts on her body as if she actually experienced what she'd seen. Sometimes while in a vision, what she sees will be real enough for her to feel the need to protect herself. Although Enchanteds never experience the pain of shifting, they still go through more than their fair share of suffering."

I again gazed down at Natalie. It seemed too hard to be an Enchanted. I couldn't imagine being plagued with visions of horrible things while knowing there was nothing I could do about them. Right now, I felt sick to my stomach and uncomfortable. If that vision showed the future, all those people were going to be slaughtered.

I wanted to stop it. I wanted to help them. How had Natalie ever managed to live with seeing something so depressing yet still managed to keep even a part of her cheerful demeanor?

I missed the old Natalie. I missed that joyful, perky girl I had met not so long ago. She'd been so quiet and distant in comparison ever since the transfer. I guess with everything happening, it was enough to change anyone. I felt like I was watching her being stripped of her happiness.

"She lashed out because it was too real," Xavier affirmed. "But she shared her vision with Ruby. I know an Enchanted can show someone the memory of a vision, but I thought they couldn't share their visions while they were happening. Apparently, we have much to learn about Enchanteds who have received power transfers."

"I could feel them dying, that's why I lashed out," Natalie suddenly spoke.

I jumped as I looked down and saw her blue eyes staring up at me.

Xavier swung around in his seat to stare down at her.

I glanced his way as I laughed. "Natalie?" I said in disbelief as I held her face. "You're awake!"

It looks like their goddess answers human prayers after all.

She nodded slowly—her eyes half-open. "Water," she croaked hoarsely.

Xavier immediately grabbed a water bottle out of his bag and gave it to me.

I pushed my knee up to elevate Natalie's head somewhat for her to drink slowly.

"I'm so fucking glad you're awake," Xavier beamed with a face splitting smile.

Natalie raised her hand to pull the bottle away from her lips, and I screwed the lid back on it before helping her to sit up. She groaned and held her head. I kept holding her arm just in case she fainted.

"I'm sorry," she whispered as she gave me a side glance.

"It's okay. I lived," I replied.

She smiled weakly at me.

"Welcome back," Mathieu interjected.

Natalie held her head up to peer at him in the rear-view mirror. "It's good to be back, Uncle. I'm hungry."

Mathieu frowned. "We didn't pack any food. It'll be dark in another half an hour, and we're already running late."

She sighed. "Please. I feel like there is a crater in my gut. There's a root I must get. It'll help replenish the blood I lost and speed up healing."

"We're in the middle of nowhere right now, Nat," Xavier said. "There is nowhere to get any kind of root."

Natalie looked out the window to find towering trees on either side of the car. "There is," she stated. "Turn left half a mile from here. There's a town. I'll be able to get it there."

Mathieu sighed. "That's going to take us even more off course. But if you really need it...okay, sure. We'll just have to be on high alert, okay?"

Xavier nodded gravely.

Mathieu studied her through the mirror. "So, do you mind telling me what happened back there? What was that scream?"

"I didn't know I could do that either," she replied. She pulled her nightgown away from her body and then gave Xavier a look. "You changed me? It had better not have been Axel."

He rolled his eyes. "I changed you. You were covered in blood."

She swallowed. The look in her eyes was one I knew all too well. It was the same look I had when I'd woken up after being attacked, the memory—the lingering phantom feelings.

She peered down at her wrist. Although only a red mark was visible, her eyes fluttered closed as she pressed a finger against the bruises.

I placed my hand gently over hers.

Pausing, she looked at me, and her eyes welled with tears. I squeezed her hand in support and understanding as she nodded and leaned back. She turned away from me to stare out the window, and I knew it was just to hide her tears. Nevertheless, she continued to hold tightly to my hand. She cautiously asked, "Is Axel—"

"He's alive," I reassured her before she even finished the question. "He went back to his pack."

"And the book?" she questioned.

"It's with us." Mathieu nodded. "Ruby suggested we make a video. Xavier made one that'll be sent to other alphas that might not have come into contact with any vampires yet. Those packs might not have any information on how to deal with the vampires."

She finally turned my way again briefly. "That's a good idea."

"Yeah," I acknowledged as I blushed. "We made it just before we left the house."

Mathieu made the left turn.

I frowned as the tingling sensation I'd been feeling unexpectedly started to make its way up my arm. My body suddenly felt warm, almost like I was getting a fever.

Natalie's head whipped toward me.

I pulled my hand away from Natalie and pretended to scratch at my chin to distract from the fact that I was purposely trying to move away. I wasn't sure if it was an after effect of what she'd done to me, but I knew I didn't want to ask or say anything about it.

Natalie was already sick. I didn't want to be more of a burden to Xavier and Mathieu, especially right now. The night was fast approaching, and we were about to be caught in it.

"Are you okay?" Natalie asked with concern.

I nodded.

"Are you sure? Are you feeling dizzy or nauseous? I've never done what I just did to you. I don't know what effect it'll have on you or if it'll have any at all."

I gave her my best reassuring smile. "Trust me. I feel okay. My head was hurting earlier, but that's gone now. Honestly, I'm just pretty hungry as well." I placed my hand on my stomach. "I'm starving actually," I told her truthfully.

"We'll stop and grab something to eat. Then we'll get the root you need, Natalie, and find a motel quickly," Mathieu interjected.

"Sure. Trust me. I understand the danger," Natalie said in a low voice as she once again held her wrist.

I was having trouble moving past what had happened to me. I didn't know if I ever would. I wanted to know if only one vampire had bitten Natalie so many times or if there was more to what happened to her. I held my tongue, as I didn't want to make her uncomfortable by bringing up her trauma.

We drove on in silence.

Natalie dozed off eventually, her eyes damp with tears.

———

Natalie

The vampire sank his fangs into my shoulder and immediately went into a frenzy. His blood lust increased a thousandfold as he started to attack me, only to bite me. After that, he no longer wanted to kill me quickly.

He had won the fight. I'll never forget how he declared, "I've never tasted blood like yours," with such disturbing excitement, as my blood dripped from his sharp white fangs. I lost my strength swiftly after he got the upper hand. That was when he started biting me all over. His mouth was like a vacuum, sucking almost all the blood from my body within minutes.

I guess I had my lineage to blame for that. No doubt, he'd never tasted the blood of a demi-god.

On the brink of death, as my eyes slowly closed, I saw Axel appear behind the vampire and rip his head off with his bare hands.

I owed Axel my life.

Many animals lick their wounds because their saliva has antibacterial and antimicrobial properties. Fortunately for me, the same goes for werewolves. In fact, the effect is even stronger in werewolves than other animals due to their size. Axel acted promptly to find all my wounds and stop the bleeding, then rushed me back to the house. I fell unconscious before we got there, but I did remember whispering Ruby's name to him before that.

He had told me he would find her, and then I lost consciousness.

I felt like I was falling down a bottomless black pit. I could hear everyone talking around me, but my lips wouldn't move as I attempted to scream to them. I eventually stopped screaming and just kept falling. It wasn't a bottomless hole after all, and I ultimately fell into a black sea. There I remained, floating, until I had that vision.

Suddenly, I opened my eyes. I was standing in a small town. I looked around confused before concluding what happened with the vampire and the sea of black must've been just an unusually vivid dream. While enjoying the cold night air, I stopped at a stoplight, waiting for the light to change so I could walk across the crosswalk. Without warning, a man ran up and attacked a woman, ripping her throat out with his hand before pressing his face into the wound.

Vampires started pouring into the busy street—the blood, the screams, the fear, and horror that followed triggered my powers. I wanted to help, I wanted to stop the bloodshed around me, and when I was attacked as well, I just reacted.

I screamed with anger and pain on a level like I'd never done before. The vampire was thrown off me, and I got to my knees as I continued to scream. My eyes closed as I focused on targeting all the vampire minds that I could find.

I wasn't sure how I was doing it, but I tried to kill as many of them as I could before whatever was happening to me faded. Enchanteds didn't have abilities we could use to fight. We performed spells that took time and a lot of preparation. We saw the future, past, and present. We were dream-walkers and, apparently, telepaths from what Reika had taught me.

This was when I felt a warm hand on my cheek and without thinking...I reached out.

Ruby had been pulled into my vision. It had been then when I realized I had a vision, and it wasn't real. Sometimes, I could tell it was a vision not long after it started, and other times it took a while.

Since I'd woken up, moving even a hand required more energy than it should. Beetroot was what I needed. The IV drip Axel started had worked well, but now I needed more. I couldn't afford to be this weak when we were at risk of being attacked at any moment.

We arrived in the town just as darkness settled and immediately found a diner.

While Xavier and Mathieu ordered our food, Ruby helped me to the bathroom to get changed.

Somewhere, somehow, all those people were going to die.

I kept trying to put a brave face on, but I felt exhausted and petrified. Feeling that vampire sink his fangs into me, again and again, was the second-worst pain I've ever felt. I couldn't escape the memory of it. I sat in the bathroom stall with my hand over my mouth as I cried, and the worst part was—I knew the worst was yet to come.

———

Ruby

I finished my two sandwiches in record time, and Natalie finished three.

Even though he had eaten four of them himself, Xavier stared at us in disbelief. He told us the waitress inside the diner recommended a motel and had given them directions.

However, Natalie couldn't wait to eat, so we were still parked in the diner's parking lot.

Mathieu remained outside, a beer in hand.

I knew he was upset that we didn't make it back to the others.

It couldn't be helped, unfortunately. Xavier agreed that we had to stop here. It was better to rest in this town for the night, rather than risk driving for who knows how long to get to the next town and then to the pack. A lot could happen quickly and without warning. Xavier didn't want a repeat of what had happened to Axel, him, and me on that highway.

I wasn't interested in being bitten ever again either.

"I'm really sorry about what happened earlier. You weren't supposed to see all of that," Natalie apologized sadly to me.

I shrugged. Of course, I wasn't angry with her. It wasn't her fault. She was unconscious while it was all happening.

"That goes for you and Mathieu, too," she remarked to Xavier. He waved his hand dismissively.

"You don't need to be sorry," I told her. "We were all there. We know what happened and that it was unintentional."

"Yeah, I still feel bad, though, you know? Why couldn't I have discovered these powers the other night?" She sighed. "Everything happens in its own time, I suppose."

"Doesn't it bother you?" I questioned her. "Seeing visions like that, and you're unable to help, unable to warn anyone."

She nodded and stared out her window at the darkness on the left side of the parking lot. "It's incredibly depressing, but when it's about someone I know, I always tell them or warn them if it's something bad. I don't get visions like...that one often." She glanced back at me and then at Xavier with a small smile on her lips. "If I got visions like that on the regular, I'd lose my mind for sure."

"Sooooo," I drawled. "It was the future then? Or has it already happened? Can you tell?"

"It's the future. Sometimes I can tell by what's in the vision."

"Can you try and remember anything?" I asked. "I've been trying to, but the memory is blurry."

"That's because you weren't meant to see what you saw. You were pulled into it. That's why I was asking you if you were okay. I don't know what effect it'll have on you mentally." Her voice was low as she eyed me up and down with concern.

I felt like wrapping my hands around myself to stop her from seeing through me. "I told you, I feel fine."

Xavier was now eyeing me from the front seat, and that was something I definitely didn't want. I could still feel an odd warmth throughout my body, but other than that, I felt perfectly fine. There was no need for me to mention anything and cause panic. Natalie would only blame herself more. "So, do you remember anything? A sign, the name on a building, anything?"

She bit at her lip and shook her head as a distant look appeared with her eyes. "There's nothing familiar about the town, to be honest. Things like that miss me during visions. Sometimes, I'll be somewhere in the vision I've never been or seen before, but it feels normal to me."

I felt useless and could only imagine how messed up Natalie must have felt. "So, there is no way to prevent it. All those people are going to die?"

"Even if Natalie could pick out something, we can't save an entire town," Xavier interjected.

I stared at him with disbelief. How could he say something like that, and so casually? Innocent lives were going to be taken, and we knew about it.

He stared back at me defiantly. "I'm still healing, and Natalie can barely walk on her own. It's just you, me, and Dad. He's the only one out of all of us that's at full strength. We can't go looking for trouble right now based on a glimpse of a future that might change."

I bit down on my lip. As much as I wanted to argue with him, I knew he had a point.

Natalie bumped me with her elbow. "He's right, you know. Sometimes, I get glimpses of the future, but it's only one possible outcome. Anything or everything might change."

I supposed I would have to live with that. I'd always been a loner, and frankly, most humans annoy me. However, I was still a human, so I couldn't stand by and watch my race get turned into snack food for vampires or any other supernatural. Now that I knew about werewolves and the supernatural world, I was completely ready and willing to be a part of it.

Of course, I couldn't exactly be on the front lines, but I would find my place. I looked over at Xavier. For now, just being a Luna would have to do. As Luna, I guess I would at least have a say in decisions about the pack.

"Xavier, what do you think we'd all be doing right now if we were all still just normal college students?" Natalie asked.

I laughed.

"She said *normal*," I teased.

Xavier laughed while she elbowed me.

I sobered up. "I'd be doing overtime at the diner right now."

"I'd be working out right now," Xavier said almost yearningly.

I rolled my eyes. Of course, he'd say something like that. I shook my head and rolled my eyes.

He glanced at me. "What? I'm losing my abs."

"There are more important things in life than your abs, Xavier." I scoffed.

He lifted his shirt.

I tried not to react. *What the fuck does he mean by he's losing his abs?* Even sitting down, I could clearly make out his perfectly chiseled six-pack.

Natalie leaned over to me. "He just wanted to lift his shirt."

He flashed me a wide grin.

Natalie chuckled as she held her chin thoughtfully. "I'd be hooking up with someone."

My mouth fell open at this.

Xavier's face twisted with disgust. "Jesus, Natalie, I really didn't need to hear that."

Natalie laughed.

Xavier and I glanced at each other for a second because it was the first time we had heard a genuine laugh from her in a long time. She'd always been the one to set the mood and make everyone happy. Without her, this bleak world just seemed much more so.

"What?" She chuckled. "It's the truth." She started coughing really loudly.

I quickly gave her the rest of my water.

"I'm okay," she said once she stopped coughing. "I'm fine." She gave the water bottle back to me and paused as she stared at me.

I took it from her. *There is that look again—why does she keep staring at me like that?* "Um, what?" I asked.

She shook her head. "It's nothing. Sorry. I just thought I saw something."

I raised a brow. "Uh, okay, then."

Mathieu opened the driver's door and was about to climb into the car when we heard a scream. People started pouring out of the diner.

My heart began hammering in my chest.

Natalie grabbed my arm, her nails digging into my skin. She held her head up and began inhaling deeply. Her hold on me soon relaxed. "There aren't any vampires. I don't smell anything."

"Me neither," Xavier added as he got out of the car.

Despite the lack of vampire scent, people were continuing to rush out of the diner. My interest was piqued. I hopped out of the car as well, and Natalie followed behind me as we all stood by the car to watch people leave one right after the other.

They all seemed to be in a panic. A horrible feeling settled on my chest.

"What's got their panties in a twist?" Natalie asked with confusion.

I shrugged.

"I'll go check it out," Xavier volunteered as he moved away.

I quickly followed him.

"You should stay in the car."

I snorted and kept walking. "Not a chance."

A man rushed out the door and hopped into his car before speeding off.

"Seriously, what's going on?" I wondered aloud.

We entered the diner to see a few people bundled up at the counter with their heads back as they stared up at the television. I looked around the rest of the restaurant. Sure enough, all the seats were empty.

A woman hurried by me, and I gently tapped her shoulder.

Her wide brown and teary eyes met mine, and I frowned. "Um, what's going on?"

She pointed to the television and rushed out the door, pulling her daughter unceremoniously behind her. I watched her through the transparent door as she picked up the little girl and started running.

The fuck?

"Ruby," Xavier called to me.

I turned to look at him.

He too was now staring at the television. "Look."

The reporter on the news show was a woman with short black hair to her shoulders. "I must warn you, the video that is about to be shown is quite graphic."

My eyes widened as I read the headline.

Vampire sighting caught on camera.

Fuck! I looked over at Xavier.

He stared back at me, and his jaw clenched.

Heavy breathing could be heard coming from the television, and I peered up to see a shaky recording of what appeared to be a man hunched over another person.

The video was being shot through what looked like an iron fence. Judging from all the flowers and trees, I guessed this must have been made in a park.

It was night time, and coupled with the clearly nervous and shaky hand, it was a little hard to see what was happening. The person suddenly stopped shaking as the man that was hunched over sat up.

My eyes widened as blood dripped from the man's abnormally wide mouth, the lamp above them offering some light to see him by. The people around us started to gasp, and more of them began to leave as the man's tongue darted out to lick his lips.

His fangs could not be missed as he stretched his mouth wide once more and fell forward onto the body beneath him, continuing with his meal.

"This can't be real!" a man suddenly yelled. "This has to be some kind of prank!"

The person holding the phone sobbed, and my heart fell as the vampire looked up. His red eyes caught the woman instantly, and within seconds, he was rushing towards her.

I closed my eyes as the woman screams mixed with inhuman growls and hissing, then the video ended.

The reporter returned to the screen, clearly shaken up as well. "The victim's body was found in the park two days after this video was taken, along with the first victim's mutilated body. Both bodies were completely drained of blood. This grisly finding matches several other murders that have been taking place all over the country in the past couple of days."

I stopped listening. My fear—our fear of the humans finding out about the vampires was actually materializing before our eyes. As I looked around at the terrified faces, I started to panic as well but for an entirely different reason. If vampires were now confirmed to be real, they would have no further reason to hide.

The reporter continued speaking, warning people to take this threat seriously, stay indoors during the night, and not to travel alone.

"This is bad. This is really bad," Xavier muttered under his breath. "I knew this shit was going to happen."

The rest of the people in the diner started to leave, even the man who'd been skeptical.

"Hey, I'm sorry, but we're closing," a waitress said to us. She laughed nervously. "Just in case this isn't some prank, you know?"

Xavier smiled at her, but the smile didn't reach his eyes. "I understand." He turned to face me. "Let's go."

As he placed his hand on my shoulder, I winced and bent forward.

He paused. "Hey, are you okay?"

I paused and let out a breath as I tried not to show how afraid I felt. The pain had shot through my arm when Xavier touched me.

Then it faded as quickly as it had come. "A cramp," I lied. "Must be those sandwiches I had."

"Come on, the sooner we find a motel, the better. I think Natalie's going to have to go without that root tonight."

We were almost at the door when a loud explosion rattled the glass windows. We hunched down as we started looking around. Then Xavier rushed outside. I was right on his heels as we ran back to the car. When we turned around, black smoke was bubbling to the sky in the distance.

"It came from the town," Mathieu informed us. "What's going on?"

"Someone took a video of a vampire feeding," I told him. "It's all over the news."

He clenched his fists, his eyes turning black as he rounded the car and pulled the door open. "We need to go. Now!"

Natalie started coughing, harder than before, and as she pulled her hand away from her mouth, her palm was coated with blood. "I can't leave without that root," she said shakily as she fell onto the car.

Xavier started sniffling loudly beside me.

I didn't have to ask what he smelled. I could smell it too, the pungent scent that followed vampires like the rain clouds that appear before a storm.

He grabbed my arm as Natalie climbed into the car. "We have to get the root for her and get the hell out of here," he insisted as he looked at his father.

Mathieu's eyes were still as black as the sky above us.

Natalie started coughing again, and more blood began to spill from her mouth. She was beginning to look pale all over again.

"We have to get it, Dad. She needs it."

"Natalie, why is this happening?" I asked her, my hands shaking by my side. Not from the sight of her blood or the fact I could smell those disgusting vampires, but because of the pulsating heat under my skin.

"The power I used," she said breathlessly. "My body isn't reacting well to it, that's all."

Xavier hissed. "That's all? You're coughing up blood. You look like you're about to pass out!" He closed her car door with more force than he needed. "Tell me where to get that root, so we can get the hell out of here."

CHAPTER TEN

XAVIER

My worst fears were becoming a reality before my very eyes. I believed it would only be a matter of time before the humans found out vampires were the ones committing the recent murders. I had just hoped it wouldn't come to that.

If they found out vampires were real, which they now had, they would start to wonder what other supernatural creatures might be real. This was a total fucking disaster. For decades, these bloodsuckers remained in hiding, no doubt feeding just the same. Now suddenly, one slipped up.

If he realized he was being recorded, why had the vampire left the phone behind for someone to find?

I'd hoped this war they'd started would remain in the shadows of our dark world, but I had been foolish to think so.

In a matter of days, they'd sent the wolf community into a panic. Now they revealed the existence of supernaturals to humans. I might be mated to a human, but that didn't stop me from admitting the truth about them—some humans were too fragile to deal with the existence of supernaturals. Or should I say the majority of them?

Despite how we'd met, Ruby hadn't completely lost her shit at the discovery of werewolves. What she experienced at the hand of that vampire had been another horrible experience for her. And of course, her life was still in danger from the Council. She was being hit on all sides, but she was still standing. In fact, she wanted to go looking for vampires. She wanted to fight. Many wolves wouldn't want to help the way she did, and I felt proud to call her my mate.

Humans were many things, but one thing was certain—they were resilient. History had proven that they could be dangerous enemies, even for supernaturals. The humans would react to this vampire threat quickly. Whether or not they succeeded in containing the vampire threat, the world around us was in for a deadly roller coaster ride while they tried.

"Did you find anything?" Dad asked Natalie, who was scrolling through the internet on her phone.

She nodded and held the phone up to show me a picture of a witch's shop. "She's the real deal. She'll have what I need."

The faster we left, the better, but I didn't want Natalie to suffer any more than she already had. She was still healing from the attack. Then she placed even more pressure on her body by using powers she'd never used before and didn't know how to control. I committed the picture to memory and was about to walk off.

Then Dad spoke, "Are you sure this root will help you, and it's all you need? Can't we find it once we get to the pack?"

Her shoulders rose and fell slowly as she shrugged. "Maybe, but once we leave this town and get to the pack...no one will be allowed to leave. I feel like I'm dying, Uncle. I need that root now while I'm sure I can get it."

"Dad, I'll be quick, okay." I understood his need to get the hell out of this place, but putting Natalie at risk of getting worse overnight wasn't something I was prepared to do. "I can smell it too, but the scent isn't so strong yet. There must not be a lot of them here."

"I doubt there needs to be a lot of them to create chaos," he pointed out.

Just then, another thundering boom echoed around us. The street lamps and the lights in the diner went out.

Ruby's heartbeat increased, and I took her hand to reassure her. She looked up at me, and despite the darkness around us, I could see her just fine. Her pupils were dilated to allow her to see a little better in the dark. I could hear frantic running and a chorus of voices coming from the town, and the lights came back on. "I'll find the witch's shop and be right back."

Ruby held onto my wrist. "I'm coming with you."

I shook my head no. "It's best if you stay here, Ruby."

"I'm coming with you, Xavier. I might not be much backup, but you can't go alone." She inhaled through her nose. "Besides, I don't smell vampires anymore. Can you still smell them?"

I took in the air, and sure enough, the scent was gone. According to what Axel had said, humans couldn't smell the stench emanating from vampires. So how could Ruby smell them? Maybe that bit of detail was wrong?

Those were questions for another time. With whatever vampires in town now gone, I felt a little more at ease. "I can hear what's happening in town right now, and you being there is a bad idea. The humans are looting. They're panicking, and I can't say I blame them."

"Guys," Natalie called to us weakly.

Ruby walked away, clearly determined. "We're going."

I sighed and hurried to catch up to her.

She nodded. "It's only humans running around right now, and I have a werewolf with me. I think I'll be fine. Let's find this shop so that we can get out of here. Things are going to get really bad really fast."

"I know. We're going to have to leave before dawn to avoid the traffic. Trust me, there will be traffic."

Ruby sighed as she shoved her hands into the pockets of her

jacket. "If only these people understood there's nowhere they can hide."

———

Ruby

News of the existence of vampires had sent the world into chaos in a matter of minutes. People were looting shops and supermarkets before rushing home to hide.

Xavier kept me close to his side as we walked through the noisy street. People were running with things they'd looted falling out of their hands. Sirens were blazing as cops tried to gain control over the madness, and fire trucks were already on site to put out the already numerous fires.

I wonder if this is what it's like all over the world right now?

"Hey, what happened with the lights just now?" Xavier asked a man who was about to run past us.

His dark hair tousled, and his glasses rested on the tip of his nose. "Someone tried to blow up the power station transformer. Look, you two need to get inside!" A car's tires screeched, startling the man. He jumped a mile and scurried off.

Xavier held my hand as we raced through the crowds. The stench of smoke hung thick in the air, making my nose burn a little as I watched two women fight for a television. I shook my head in dismay.

Instead of trying to get food, people were breaking into stores for expensive clothes and appliances. They wouldn't have any use for any of that if the vampires attacked. What would they do when they were trapped inside their homes with no food, but they still had a brand-new television or a Gucci outfit? I'd rather have food and a gun over what these people were rolling on the ground and fighting for.

I frowned and squeezed Xavier's hand as I was hit with a wave of nausea. Maybe I needed some of that beetroot that Natalie wanted us to get. Whatever was happening to me started after she showed me her vision. Maybe it was an after effect.

No, if I was honest, I'd been feeling different ever since that vampire attacked me. For a while, I'd worried I was changing into one. I'd felt horrible on the inside, but the feeling had faded, only to return the night they attacked the Blackmoon house.

Being exposed to Natalie's magic made me feel so much worse. *Why the fuck am I sweating so much?*

"Hey." Xavier paused to cup my cheek. "Are you okay, Ruby?"

I nodded more confidently than I felt. "Yeah, yeah, I'm just wondering where the hell this shop is." Someone threw a bottle into a window across the street. "Xavier." I tapped his shoulder rapidly with a smile before pointing to the shop next to the store that was being broken into. "There it is. That's it, right?"

Looking relieved to finally find the shop, he took my hand again as we ran across the street. Twice already, we'd seen people almost get hit by cars. The world around us was starting to look more and more like a war zone.

"You'd think all these people would head straight home," I noted. "None of them seem to realize they're all in the open to be picked off if vamps attack now."

Xavier went up the steps of the tiny store, his hand still holding mine. He was so cute. If I wasn't pressed to his side or if he wasn't holding my hand, he'd lose his shit. He tapped a finger against the open sign and looked back at me. "I guess it's business as usual here, huh?" He opened the door and stepped in.

As I followed him in, my nostrils filled with the heady scent of incense. The shelves upon shelves of books reminded me of the library at my college. I'd expected a shop filled with strange objects and artifacts, not a book shop. My eyes fell on a woman at the back of the room behind and counter.

She didn't look up at us and continued to skim through a magazine casually.

"Hello, aren't you worried about what's going on outside? Someone might break-in," I said to her.

Looking up at us, she smiled. She placed her elbow on the counter beside the magazine and rested her cheek in her hand, "I see no point in panicking. There's a spell on the door to repel anyone with bad intentions. You two made it in, so I guess I'm safe."

"So, you're the witch then?" Xavier asked.

She stood up straight. She looked like a normal woman with slightly greying hair and warm eyes with glasses resting on her nose. "That's me," she replied with a smile.

"What if a vampire tries to break in? Is your spell strong enough to keep them out?" I asked.

She shook her head. "No, but I do have my own ways of getting out of a sticky situation." She closed the magazine. "So, how may I help you?"

"Do you have beetroot? An Enchanted was attacked by vampires."

She raised a brow as she looked from Xavier to me and paused.

I stared at her in confusion as to why she was suddenly staring at me.

She looked me up and down and then tilted her head to the side.

Considering how bad I was feeling after sharing Natalie's vision and the terrible after effects, if that's what they were, I wasn't in the mood to be scrutinized by some strange witch. I lost it and snapped, "Excuse me, is there a problem?"

She narrowed her eyes at me. "What are you?"

I knew this woman wasn't blind. Considering she was a witch, she should be able to tell what I was, shouldn't she? "I'm human," I answered in a low voice.

She made clicking sounds with her tongue as she held her chin.

I looked over at Xavier, who glanced at me before turning his watchful eyes back at the witch.

"Yes, I can see that you're human..." She wagged her finger at me. "But there is something more inside you. Perhaps you are just ill. Your aura is not stable. It's changing colors quite rapidly."

Whatever that means! I suppose that explains why Natalie kept looking at me strangely. "Well," I drawled. "I'm only human. I'm just not feeling well."

Xavier turned to face me, his anger evident by the look on his face.

I braced myself for a cussing.

"What?" he demanded. "Since when? Why haven't you said anything, Ruby?"

"Since the incident with Nat in the car. I didn't say anything because, um..." I pointed to the door. "You have enough to worry about along with Natalie. She's worse than I am. I just feel a little hot and uncomfortable sometimes."

"Ruby, Natalie asked you if you were okay. We don't know how you might have been affected by what happened." He glared. "Are you sure that's all you're feeling?"

"Yes, just a little hot sometimes." I turned to the witch. "Do you have beetroot or not?"

"Sure, I do, but she'll need a little lime juice extract as well. Give me a minute." She disappeared into the back.

I looked over at Xavier to find him staring daggers at me. "I am fine, Xavier. I'll have some of the beetroots as well, okay?" He said nothing but continued to stare at me, and I sighed. "Relax. Natalie is the priority right now."

The witch returned with a brown paper bag and handed it to Xavier. "She has to crush the beetroot with the skin and all, then add the lime juice."

Xavier took the bag from her and pulled out his wallet to pay.

She held up her hand. "It's on the house."

"Um, thank you," he replied.

She shrugged then nodded her head towards the door. "Hard

times are coming," she cautioned as she sighed heavily. "I can hop to another world, but for you folks, you all..."

"I'm sorry, what?" I asked. *Did she just say she could hop to another world?* I knew I shouldn't have been surprised, but I couldn't help it.

She smiled at me like a person would at a child who'd said something adorable. She probably figured out I was new to this world. "It comes with a price, of course. There is always a price to be paid. Your Enchanted friend is now paying the price from using magic she shouldn't be able to." She pursed her lips. "To have done it to begin with, she must be strong, whatever she did." While speaking, she focused on me, a strange expression on her face again. This time, her eyes slowly began to turn violet.

"Okay, thanks for everything," Xavier told her and turned to leave.

"Wait." She held her hand out to me. "Let me see your palm."

I made a face. "Um, why?" I felt unnerved. Willow hadn't been this creepy.

"I don't bite. Let me see your palm."

I looked at Xavier to gauge his reaction. He didn't seem too bothered by her request, so I gave her my hand.

She closed her eyes as her hand hovered over mine. A few seconds passed with me growing more and more impatient before her eyes popped open. "You're mated to him," she suddenly declared, and her violet eyes widened with shock as she looked at Xavier.

He grew tense, and I pulled my hand away from her.

"How is that even possible?" Her eyes began to glow even brighter. "How are you mated to two wolves? You're human."

Xavier grabbed my hand, "Thanks for your help, but that's none of your business. Ruby, let's go."

Her shocked and curious eyes returned to me.

Xavier started pulling me to the door when he halted.

I looked him up and down, wondering why he stopped, when suddenly—I smelled it.

"Vampires," he said under his breath.

I hunched forward as white-hot pain began to roll through my body. The scent of vampires started to grow stronger, making me feel as if I was about to throw up. I staggered away from Xavier.

He held onto me to stop me from falling over. "Ruby? Ruby, what's wrong?"

"I can smell them. I feel sick," I replied as the pain started to subside, but now there was a heaviness on my chest. I stood up straight. My eyes closed as I breathed in and out through my mouth. "It's like I keep getting hot flashes."

"What's wrong with her?" Xavier demanded as he turned to the witch. He called her forward, "What can you see?"

"Something is wrong with her, but I can't tell what. The way her aura is shifting colors like that means her entire being is off balance. That's why I thought she was sick." The witch explained in a low voice as she drew closer to us. She placed her hand firmly on my forehead. "I can't tell why this is happening. Maybe it has to do with her being mated to you and whoever else, but she's reacting to something." The pain dulled to the point where it was at least bearable. "I've never seen anything like this before," she whispered in awe. "No wonder you seemed more than human."

"How can I seem more than human? Yes, I'm mated to wolves, but I'm not a wolf myself. What else is there to make me seem not one hundred percent human?" I was getting angry. How could she say something like that? Reika or Natalie would have sensed if I had any other form of supernatural blood, right?

"I don't know," she replied with uncertainty.

I sighed with frustration as I pinched the bridge of my nose.

She went on, "I've never seen this before. And how can you smell vampires? I thought humans couldn't." She turned to Xavier angrily. "Just who are you people anyway?"

First, it was the barrier in my mind, and now I'm...sick? Chang-ing? I don't even know!

She sighed. "Nevermind. Just keep an eye on her, or you will lose her. If she doesn't die from whatever is happening to her, she will still be at risk from others, wolves especially, if they learn about this."

Too late, I wanted to scream.

Xavier nodded, took my hand, and we left hastily.

With the scent of the vampires growing stronger, we knew we needed to move quickly. The first time we scented them, it might have been only one, but the odor was much stronger now. There had to be a lot of them. "Call Mathieu and see if they're okay. Tell them we're on our way back so they know we're coming," I suggested.

Xavier nodded and pulled out the extra phone Mathieu had given us. I'd lost mine and hadn't had a chance to replace it yet. No one called me anyways, but maybe it was time for us to get new ones for situations like these.

"Dad, we're coming back. We got the beetroot." He paused as he listened. "Yeah, we smell them. We're coming." He ended the call just as a piercing scream rang through the night.

My heart skipped a beat with fright as I spun around. My hand started to shake because I knew that was a woman being attacked by a vampire. I felt it in my bones. With all the looting and chaos, no one would give a second thought to someone screaming.

Another scream rang out—then another.

I didn't think about it, and I didn't give my legs the command to move. Yet before I knew it, I was running in the direction of the scream. It was as if my body was moving of its own accord or I was being pulled by something.

All I knew was I needed to get to this woman. I had no idea what I'd do when I got there, but I pulled my dagger out and kept moving.

At first, Xavier yelled for me to come back, but he soon ran after me after he realized I had no intention of stopping. Of course, with his long legs and powerful legs, he caught up to me fairly quickly. As he wrapped his hands around my waist, another blood-curdling scream resonated through the night air, and frightened people started running past us. He lowered me to the ground and moved to stand before me. "I can't shift. There are too many people here."

I stepped out from behind him and walked forward as if in a trance. I turned in a circle as screaming men and women ran past me. The vision I had seen so long ago during the mind link with Reika and Natalie resurfaced.

My blood chilled in my veins, and I started running against the crowd. Xavier's hands wrapped around my wrist to pull me back, but I yanked my hand away. "This is it, Xavier!" I screamed in panic.

He stared at me as if I had grown three heads.

I knew I must look crazy to him. At this moment, I felt crazy, but this was what I had seen. "This is the vision I saw with Reika and Natalie." I pointed behind me. "I ran that way in the vision, so I need to do the same now. Those shadows were vampires. Why would *I* get a vision about vampires from so long ago?"

His brows pulled together. "I don't know. Are you sure this is the same place?"

"Xavier, I swear it. This is the town I saw in my vision."

He gazed past me, and his eyes narrowed. I looked behind me, but he quickly grabbed my shoulder and turned me back to him. "We need to go now." The words had barely left his lips when a woman behind me started screaming.

I spun around on my heels, startled by the sudden scream, only to see a vampire tackle a blonde woman to the ground. With all the lights, I could easily see his sharp fangs sink into her shoulder and my face twisted as he easily broke her neck.

I fell forward, a scream almost leaving my lips as the ground rushed up to meet me. I held my hands out so I wouldn't fall on my face, and my dagger fell to the side. Growls and hisses reached my ears as I flipped onto my back to see Xavier and a vampire tumbling on the ground in an intense battle.

Despite the street now being deserted by all humans, Xavier couldn't shift in the middle of town. The risk was just too high, especially at a time like this. Confirmation of the existence of werewolves on the same night as vampires would be too much for the human world to handle. Look at how badly they'd behaved already. There were cameras everywhere these days, and the werewolf community being exposed by Xavier was something neither of us wanted. Olcan was already out to get the Blackmoon Pack after what we had done.

Xavier had shifted only his claws as his sole form of defense available against the vampire. He kicked the vampire off him and jumped onto his feet. He stood in a fighting stance and remained still.

The vampire hissed at him and then lunged forward. He recoiled as Xavier swiped at his chest, ripping the black T-shirt he was wearing to shreds.

A young woman ran out from behind a car. The vampire immediately attacked.

My stomach turned as the vampire grabbed her. He turned her to face me and bit rapidly into her throat, before pulling away and ripping her throat wide open. My lips started to quiver as he released her, and she fell to the ground with her hand outstretched to me.

Her hazel eyes fluttered closed within seconds, and the soulless vampire kneeled to finish his meal.

Monsters! Fucking monsters!

I knew the bloodsucking bastard could see me clear as day. He just didn't care. He obviously saw us as nothing more than food. I knew I would be his next meal after he drained that young woman. He didn't even seem to care about his fellow vampire enough to bother to help him out in the fight with Xavier. I could be grateful for that, at least.

The heaviness on my chest grew worse, but I ignored it as I got to my feet. I took a step forward and then another as a tingling sensation took over my body. I was so angry. The world around me started to fade away. Only the vampire remained.

Until today, the young woman beneath him had her whole life ahead of her. Maybe she had a family, kids, a job she loved. Now she was nothing but vampire food, a lifeless corpse being drained in the street. I remembered vividly how deeply violating it felt to be fed on like this. I'd almost died, just like this girl. My body began to shake with a rage I'd never felt before. I wanted to kill this vampire with my bare hands, and the desire to do so was only growing by the second.

The vamp abruptly stopped feeding and pulled back from the woman before glancing to the side. He looked as if he was smelling the air for something. All of a sudden, he turned his head my way and smiled widely with anticipation.

I stared at his red-stained fangs in disgust as blood oozed from his lips.

He wiped his hand across his mouth and patted the woman beneath him. "Thanks, love," he chuckled as he slowly stood to his feet.

Behind us, the growls and hisses from Xavier and the other vampire continued. However, my complete focus was directed on this guy, this creature, this blood-sucking parasite!

The vamp tilted his head to the side.

I did the same.

He smiled in amusement, and it soon turned into thundering laughter. "You're either incredibly brave or very stupid. Since you're human, I'll assume stupid." He looked closer at me. "I must say, you have a rather odd scent. I can't tell if it's your natural body odor or perfume."

I didn't respond, and he stood there waiting to see if I'd reply.

He then shrugged uncaringly, "Whatever it is...has anyone ever told you that you smell deliciously edible?"

I'll just ignore that and the disgusting wink he just sent my way. "Why are you here?" I asked.

His amused expression fell away as if he was caught off guard by my question. He waved his hand to the woman's body by his feet before combing his bloody fingers through his dark hair. "I was eating. What does it look like?"

"Why. Are. You. Here?" I demanded again and this time, stressing each word. "You people haven't been around for forever, so where have you all been?"

He raised a brow and appeared somewhat surprised. Of course, he wouldn't expect an average human to know something like this. "Well, you're an interesting one. What's your name?"

Is this man serious? "Why are you doing this? Why now?" I persisted.

He sighed. "I'm doing this because I can and because *we can.* We're taking back this world. My kind, we're apex predators, and we always have been. We've hidden and lived like rats long enough." He held his arms out wide. "We've waited and waited and waited some more. Now, finally, we can step into the light." His arms fell, and he made a face. "Well, into the light figuratively, of course."

"You're not a predator." I held my right arm and tried not to grimace from the pain. Xavier and the other vampire had moved from where they were before, but I could still hear them fighting. I needed to keep this vampire occupied. If he decided to attack while Xavier was fighting another vamp, I would be as good as dead.

Whatever was happening to me couldn't have picked a worse time. I rarely got sick, but I hadn't felt like myself since that vampire bit me. Like Natalie, I'd received a vision that could have helped to prevent all of this. If I had known the shadows were vampires, I would have told Mathieu. He would have informed the rest of the alphas, and they would've hunted the vampires before they had time to cause all of this trouble. Maybe we could have prevented this from ever happening.

Thinking about that now wouldn't help anything. I hadn't known the shadows were vampires, and I hadn't told Mathieu. Thinking of the past and what-ifs wouldn't stop this vampire from attacking and killing now.

"All of you are pests," I muttered under my breath. I knew he could hear me clearly; his furrowed brows made that clear enough. "You're just monsters and savages. Look at what you've caused in a matter of days. If you plan to take over the world, why are you setting out to destroy it? That's what will happen. That leaves your people with more shit to clean up in the end, but hey, you all won't have to worry about that because it'll never get to that."

"And who is going to stop us?" he bit back. "You?" he asked through clenched teeth. "I admire how brave you are, but it'll only make me enjoy killing you more. Don't act like you humans haven't been destroying this world for decades!" He shoved his hands into his pockets and stepped over the woman's body. "You kill animals to eat them for sustenance, and we vampires do the same. It's how we survive, and we can't help that. Like every living thing, don't we deserve the right to live?"

Well, I guess that settled the argument of whether vampires were capable of rational thought.

"You all should have stayed in hiding," I told him.

His expression filled with fury.

"You're only able to feed on blood to survive. I understand that, but there is a right and wrong way to do that. You know doing all of this is the wrong way, but the thing is, you and your kind like it. Don't you? You do. That woman just now didn't have to die like that. You speak to me as if you are in control of your hunger." I touched my neck. "You don't have to attack humans as if we can't feel it!"

"Ohhhhh," he drawled. "I get it. You were bitten, huh? I can see it." He then tilted his head to the side. "Now I'm curious how you survived." He looked me up and down as he eyed me with suspicion. "Who are you? What makes you think you can stand here and talk to me like this?"

I shrugged. "I thought we were having a peaceful chat."

He started laughing, all the while nodding his head. "I like you. I do. We do have pets, so maybe I'll make you mine." He sighed. "You know, our bite isn't always painful. Whoever attacked you was a fool. He or she should have turned you. Maybe they were just too weak since you're here and I assume they are no longer living." He held a finger up. "But I digress. Anyways, I can be gentle. You don't have to be on the losing side of this, human. Humans, werewolves, or any other creature on this planet won't be able to beat us this time. I promise you that. If you have no problem hanging out with a werewolf, why can't you join us? Werewolves are just as savage as we are. Maybe even more so."

"You've got to be kidding, right? You hunt humans for food. Werewolves protect the humans."

He snorted and shook his head.

"Maybe not all wolves," I acknowledged. "But you vamps can't compare to wolves, so don't even try." I realized I could no longer hear Xavier and the vampire fighting, and my heart skipped a beat.

The corner of his mouth lifted into a smile as he looked at my chest. "You just realized your little friend went silent, huh?" He clapped his hands. "Well, it was truly nice speaking with you, human girl. I love the red hair, by the way. Did I tell you red is my favorite color? I'll ask you once more...join me. Humans are the real pests and parasites of this world. I won't hold it against you that you were born one, but be smarter and accept my proposal. You'll be treated well. You will only be fed on by me, and I'm gentle." He looked at the woman he'd killed and smiled awkwardly. "Well, most of the time, I'm gentle. You'll survive, child. Be smart about—"

"Fuck you!" I screamed. "One of your kind already showed me what your kind is when he ripped into my throat! Take your proposal and shove it up your walking dead ass!" I saw red. His stench and his sick reasoning finally pushed me to the edge. My body started visibly shaking as if I'd been stuck in the cold for days. An ache I couldn't explain began to build inside me.

"Rafael? Where is Malik?" A man's voice asked from behind me.

I spun around.

It was another vampire. His green eyes drifted to me, and he pointed his thumb in my direction. "What are you waiting for? Kill her, so we can go looking for Navia."

Rafael pointed to his right. "He went that way with the wolf. I'm not in a rush. I like this one."

The man looked at me, and his brows knitted. "What's to like other than her scent? Don't forget we have orders, Rafael. If you won't kill her, I will."

It all happened so quickly. His green eyes turned blood red, and he ran at me, his white fangs elongating as he drew closer.

I just reacted. I opened the door to all the pain, anger, and frustration I've been subjected to and screamed as I raised my hand in an attempt to shield myself.

The vampire halted abruptly, frozen mid-attack. With my heart pounding in my ears, I lowered my hand somewhat.

He stared down at his hand.

I did the same as I frowned when red bumps started to appear on his skin.

I jumped as he started to scream agonizingly, and before my very eyes, his skin began to bubble like boiling water. His pale skin began to turn red, and my eyes widened. I stepped back as he appeared to be burning from the inside out.

What the fuck? D-did I just do that?

His skin began to blacken and char, and he fell to his knees. I winced as I heard his bones break, and he turned his head to the side. "Rafael!" he screamed as he fell forward and smoke began to rise from his body.

I swallowed and looked down at my hand uncertainly. My palm was bright red and shaking. My lips parted as I began to breathe slowly.

What is happening to me? I-I killed him. Did I just kill him?

"How did you do that?" Rafael asked, shock evident in his voice.

My head snapped towards him.

"How the fuck did you do that?" he yelled.

Black lines were now making their way from his neck to the base of his mouth. He looked both pissed and confused as he gazed from me to the dead vampire. He crouched down low and hissed at me.

I started to step back.

A loud crash echoed around us, drawing our attention, and I came face to face with Xavier.

He had thrown the vampire he had been fighting into a car's windshield. His eyes were black, and his claws were dripping with blood. He paused as he quickly looked from me to Rafael then to the dead vampire on the ground.

"Pay attention!" Rafael roared.

I spun around to find him inches away from me, causing me to fall backward on my ass. I closed my eyes as Xavier yelled, "No!" I held my hands up to shield my face. This time, I could feel heat coursing through my hands down to my palm, and then there was silence.

A gurgling sound made me open my eyes. I gasped and crawled back on my hands.

Rafael's face was turning from pale to red to a dark burnt shade. He wasn't screaming like the other one did, but his eyes were wide with shock. He then fell to the ground.

I looked away as one of his crisp charred arms broke off his body. I sat up and stared at my hands as the redness from my palms traveled further up my arms. Tears began to sting my eyes.

Xavier rushed over to me.

Behind him, the vampire he'd been fighting fell off the car and gaped at me as if I was the monster. In the blink of an eye, he was gone.

"Ruby! Ruby?"

I could hear Xavier clearly, but I couldn't speak, not with the burning in my hands.

"What the fuck just happened? Ruby?"

Tears began to roll down my cheeks, but they felt hot on my skin. I held my shaky hands out to him, my breathing now shallow, as I started to feel weak. I didn't know what just happened or how it happened, but whatever it was—it was backfiring on me.

"Hot, I'm hot," I forced out as my head rolled to the side.

Xavier quickly grabbed me. "No, no, no. Fuck! Stay awake, okay?"

Though my eyes were mere slits by now, I could still see the panic in his eyes. More tears ran like little rivers down my cheeks.

"Fuck!" He howled loud, long, and hard before looking back down at me. "Come on, baby, don't do this to me. Stay awake!"

"Something's inside me, Xavier." I started sobbing feebly. I felt so weak, I could barely move. The fire burning under my skin raged on. "It's burning me. It's burning me alive!"

The world around me went black.

Luna Darkness

Book Four

CHAPTER ONE
XAVIER

A wolf's first shift was the most painful. Some wolves took hours to complete their first shift and then a few more years before they could transform into their final form. Contrary to the way we were portrayed in movies, most werewolves could actually shift into two different forms. In the first and easier form, we appeared like normal wolves and walked on four legs, except we're about three times larger than your average wolf. In our final form, our pure werewolf form, we shifted to wolf appearance but walked upright on two legs.

We don't shift to our pure werewolf form often because it would be better for a human to accidentally see an overgrown wolf than a hairy wolf-like creature on two legs.

As I stepped forward, my paw print sank into the earth. I kept my head close to the ground as I tracked the scent of my quarry. I looked over at my dad, his dusty brown coat lighter than mine.

He snorted and shook his head.

I stopped walking and called on The Change. I sank my front claws into the earth and winced as my bones snapped and realigned into my final form. Since we were hunting deep in the forest, the chances of running into a human here were slim.

I rose to my feet in my pure werewolf form, my long arms hanging at my sides. Shifting to our final form put a mental strain on the human part of our minds. Fighting in this form might leave a wolf more at risk, if they weren't one with the change. It took years to master, and not all wolves could achieve it. Once mastered, shifting into one's final form was more freeing than turning into our wolves.

Spreading my arms wide, I closed my eyes to take a moment to enjoy it. This final form was the form that made us real werewolves.

I turned to follow the scent again, leaving my dad behind as he changed as well. The further I walked, the stronger the smell became. My head snapped to the side, my ears twitching, and I turned left.

Closer...I was getting closer.

Even with my massive body, I moved silently through the underbrush. When I finally caught up to my target, I crouched low, the claws on my feet sinking into the earth, as I prepared to strike.

My prey looked up warily while sensing my presence, as her innocent eyes cautiously studied the forest around her.

I concealed myself in the dark shadow of a large tree.

Before she could meander away, I attacked, rushing forward rapidly to sink my claws into her massive body. My canine fangs sank deeply into flesh, the taste of blood coating my lips as I snapped the doe's neck with ease.

I sat back, blood dripping from my claws as I removed them from the now dead deer. I stared down at the animal, her lifeless brown eyes still open. I remembered the look of raw fear in her eyes as I had attacked. Being a werewolf could sometimes be a taxing fight between the human and the wolf. It was easier for me to kill a supernatural that had been hurting others rather than an innocent animal like this doe. Something bothered me about hunting like this—not that I'd ever tell anyone. All wolves must learn to hunt, but killing was something I'd never enjoyed. The animals looked at us the same way a human would, with fear and confusion about what we were. Whether they were animals or humans, to our prey, we looked like twisted, horrible versions of the wolves they knew.

I guess some humans might be able to relate to how I felt. I'd noticed some of them seemed to like their animals more than their fellow human beings.

I picked up the lifeless deer to carry under one arm and headed back. Extra werewolf strength did come in handy when it came time to bring dinner home with you. I met up with my dad, who was carrying another deer. Together, we returned to the pack, maintaining our pure werewolf forms for as long as possible.

Before long, we arrived at a small clearing in the forest filled with countless spacious green tents. At the center of the clearing sat a three-story house. This small clearing area and the house within it represented our pack's temporary living arrangements since the vampires launched their attack on the living world three weeks ago. Humans, werewolves, witches, and every living creature with blood flowing through its veins were now prey to these bloodsuckers.

When we arrived, Dad and I gave the deer to Randoll, our pack's beta. He would arrange for the animals to be cleaned and cooked. In one of the outdoor showers we created for the camp, I shifted back into human form and got dressed. The men slept outside in the tents while our women and children slept inside the protection of the house. All we knew of the chaos happening outside our little forest sanctuary came from whatever Axel and Reika could tell us.

My legs froze mid-walk as the rhythmic sound of a helicopter drew close.

More and more wolves stopped what they're doing to look up at the sky.

Suddenly, the fearful cry of a small child pulled my attention. I turned around.

Little Jasmine was clinging to her mother, her little arms wrapped around Amera's neck tightly. Her cherry blonde hair matching her mother's, messy and tangled. Her mother tried to soothe her, but the child only kept crying.

Around us, other children were running to their fathers' tents or clinging to their mothers.

I ambled over to the wailing girl and tapped her arm gently as the noise of the helicopter drew closer and closer, louder and louder. "Hey," I greeted her.

She peeked at me with one cheek on her mother's shoulder.

"Don't be scared. You're safe here," I assured her.

She shook her head and sniffled as she hid her face again.

"Hey, look, I'll prove it."

She peeked at me again, her petite body now shaking.

I pointed at the helicopter as it finally flew over us. "See."

She leaned up and wiped her nose with the back of her hand. Her tiny brows knitted as she searched the sky for the helicopter.

"It's gone. They can't see us down here," I whispered to the child.

She raised a brow. "How?" she asked, her voice a delicate squeak.

"My friend had a witch cast a spell on this place. All that they can see from up there..." I pointed to the sky. "...are trees."

"The humans won't see the camp?" she asked in disbelief.

I shook my head with a smile as I used my thumb to wipe away a fat teardrop on her cheek.

She glanced at her mother for confirmation, still doubting the veracity of my words.

Her mother nodded.

The girl started smiling, "Okay."

"Okay, dry your tears," I urged. "Do you like eating deer? I'll make sure you get as much as you like for dinner. Okay?"

Her smile grew as color returned to her pale face. "Thank you."

"Thank you, Xavier, thank your father—" the child's mother started to say, but her face fell as she looked past me.

The silence among the pack that had been present when the helicopter passed overhead returned, and I wondered why. I turned around to see Ruby standing behind me.

She smiled at Jasmine, who then hid her face again.

I frowned, my anger bubbling to the surface as I looked around me to see everyone staring at Ruby. "Ruby," I called.

She sighed and turned away, but she didn't stop.

I watched her hurry back to the house, and I clenched my fists to stop myself from losing my cool. "She's not a threat," I stated as calmly as I could to Amera.

Jasmine now clung to Amera tightly in fear. She placed the child on the ground, but Jasmine still attached herself to her leg. "We know she's your mate, Xavier. We all also know you don't really know if she's a threat or not. She killed vampires with her bare hands."

"Yes, *vampires*," I said, emphasizing the vampires. Three weeks ago, Ruby had burned two vampires to a crisp without even touching them. After that and perhaps because of that, she was in a coma for three days. By the time she awoke, there wasn't a man, woman, or child in the Blackmoon Pack who didn't know exactly who Ruby was and what she had done to those vampires. The rumor somehow spread to other packs before we could contain it.

Of course, the story managed to make it all the way to the Council. Once the Council learned of what she had done, they predictably wanted her for themselves. In their infinite wisdom, the Council put out a contract for her capture and delivery, endangering all of us.

Our entire pack had to move to a different location to protect her. Axel was able to provide this more secure site. I wasn't happy about the fact that Ruby was his mate as well, but I couldn't deny that he'd been helpful. The man was well-prepared, I'd give him that.

Amera merely gave me a look filled with pity. "Her scent has changed, Xavier. She's not human, and we're not sure what she is. Yes, she killed vampires, but she did so by accident. She didn't know what she was doing. No one here wants to *accidentally* end up as her next victim."

There wasn't much I could say back to her, so I turned on my heels and stormed away.

Ruby had already vanished back inside the house.

The wolves in my pack were my people, my family, but Ruby was my mate. I couldn't stand by and watch them treat her like this. She was my mate, which also meant she was the Luna to be for our pack. Human or not, I had and always would accept her for who she was, whatever she was.

Ruby accepted me being a werewolf. Now, when the tables were turned, I couldn't turn my back on her.

Even so, Ruby had been keeping to herself as of late. She hardly spoke anymore, and I could see that she was clearly losing weight. I felt her putting up a wall between us, and I'd had enough of it.

———

Ruby

I shouldn't have gone outside.

I heard the helicopter and wanted to see what was happening, even though I knew we were hidden under the masking spell over our pack's area. I recognized that I'd been isolating myself lately. It was the price I had to pay, to avoid the scared or judgmental looks like the ones I'd just received.

With many women and kids staying inside the house, my room was usually my only available escape. As I walked by the living room on the way to my room, I realized that for once, it was empty. I went in and closed the sliding double doors. I would probably have it to myself for a while now. Once they smelled me in here, no one else would want to come in.

This led to another question. *Why has my scent changed?*

I'd grown sick of the tests Natalie performed without a witch's help. So far, none of her tests revealed what my supernatural lineage was. There had to be some kind of a supernatural explanation for me to have done what I did.

Magic was there, flowing through my body, but it wasn't the kind of magic Natalie had ever seen. Reika and Willow had been unable to come to us since the world had fallen into chaos. During the first week, vampires and humans fought hard against each other. This battle was just the beginning of this nightmare. The situation only worsened the second week when humans discovered werewolves existed. Then the humans turned on us as well, just as the wolves always feared.

I snorted as I crossed my arms and stared out the window. I had finally accepted I was a part of the supernatural world, the werewolf community specifically, by way of my mates. Then, just that fast, the world went to hell, and I was back to square one. After I burned those vamps from the inside out, it seemed like I wasn't even an accepted part of the werewolf community anymore, either.

The door opened, but I didn't bother looking. I knew it was either Natalie, Xavier, or Mathieu. They were the only people who would speak to me anymore.

"Ruby?" Xavier called softly.

I sighed and glanced his way.

"Talk to me," he said.

"They're all terrified of me."

He joined me at the window and leaned against it as he watched me.

I avoided looking at him. I was barely holding it together as it was, and gazing into his eyes would just make me fall apart. "I don't blame them." I looked down at my hands. "I'm terrified of me."

He reached out and held my hands as he guided me to stand before him. "We'll find out what's going on, and we'll do it together. I'll always be there for you, no matter what. Please don't forget that."

I reached out and cupped his cheek. I knew I had been misbehaving towards him, but I'd needed space. "I'm sorry for shutting you out too. I've just been so tired, Xavier." My hand fell away from his cheek to pinch the bridge of my nose. "What's happening to me?" My hand fell to my side limply, and I hung my head.

His hands slid around my waist. I sighed as I stepped forward to press my body to his. He reached up to gently caress my hair as I lost myself in the warmth emitting from his body.

"Everyone is just confused and scared and not just because of you," he spoke softly. "So much is happening right now. Wolves are dying by the thousands. Not to mention the humans are being picked off one by one by the vampires. These vampires are adding more and more to their ranks nightly. Soon, there will be too many of them, and a battle with them will be futile." He turned his head to the side. "While wolves that can help to save this world are trapped in hiding because humans think we're the same as those things."

I leaned back to look up at him. "But why is the Council refusing to reach out to the humans?" I questioned. "Why not try to come together to defeat a common enemy? Right now, humans are basically helping vampires." I shook my head at the sheer stupidity. "They're so fucking stupid, stretching their resources to kill werewolves that aren't attacking them when they are being murdered in the streets by vampires." I stepped away from him. "Will they do the same when they find out about witches, or demons, not to mention everything else supernatural? This war will never end!"

Xavier held my arm and guided me to the sofa to sit down.

"Right now, it's every species for themselves. It's fucked up, but I think right now, everyone is in shock and is just trying to survive. The wolves out there are scared – terrified even – because no one knows what's coming next."

Something has to be done.

Xavier had said it himself that the vampires were turning more and more humans and supernaturals. With everyone selfishly caring for only themselves, people were being picked off by the vamps more easily. There was strength in numbers, so the humans and supernatural community were divided. Humans didn't even know about the existence of some of the other supernatural creatures yet.

It was just like in a horror movie when every person went their own separate way. Inevitably, they would just be picked off one by one by the evil entity.

"After this..." He rolled his eyes. "...if there is even an *after*, the Council will have no hold on the wolf community. Not after they've left us without help," he stated with a bitter edge in his voice. "The Council has ways and means of protecting the community. Many packs were thankful for the information we sent them about the vampires. Some didn't even know about the vampires."

Natalie came into the room quietly as he finished.

I sighed when I saw her.

"I know, but we need to get back to testing," Natalie insisted as she walked over to us and sat on the arm of the sofa.

"I'm not ready. Just give me a minute," I replied.

"I know this is exhausting," she said. "But we have to do what we have to do. Let's be real here. You don't know what powers you have. We know next to nothing about your magic. All we do know is the shitty situation we're in is only going to get worse."

I heard her implication loud and clear. Every day it took for us to get answers, the risk rose that someone in the pack would hand me over to the humans or the Council. The pack had been uprooted and moved because of me. Men were sleeping outside because there was no space. There was precious little food and water for everyone. In their view, I was just a ticking time bomb, a safety risk for all involved.

I'd been trying not to think about that night. I think the searing white-hot pain I felt before falling unconscious might have been a tiny pinch of what those incinerated vampires felt. While they deserved it, it was excruciating. I couldn't let that happen here. "Okay," I replied

Xavier got up to give Natalie his seat.

I sighed. "I really hate this."

Natalie smiled with empathy, "I know, so do I."

I gazed over at Xavier.

He watched us, his shirt pulling taut over his chest as he crossed his arms.

I looked back at Natalie and nodded.

She placed her hands on my head, preparing to try and break through the barrier in my mind as she had been attempting repeatedly for the past three weeks.

It was exhausting for both of us, and so we were only able to do it twice a week. So far, she had only been able to see quick glimpses of my past that offered no kind of assistance or understanding. Sometimes, I saw what she did. Other times, I saw nothing at all.

"Wait." I suddenly pulled away.

Natalie's hands fell onto her lap.

My eyes darted from her to Xavier and back. "I can't, not right now."

She exhaled heavily through her mouth and pressed a finger at the crease between her brows. "Okay. If Reika were here, this wouldn't be as bad. Unfortunately, she can't leave Romania right now, with everything that has been happening." She gave me a sad smile before she addressed Xavier. "Have you spoken to Axel? He had a witch he was going to contact. I don't know how much more of this Ruby or I can take. It's pointless putting each other under this strain when it's barely working."

"I know," Xavier agreed softly. "I spoke to him and his pack is finally secure. The Council tried to get him to turn Ruby over. He hasn't been able to contact her, and he's not sure when he'll be able to come here."

"We can try again tomorrow, Natalie," my voice was a whisper as I stood up. Axel's pack had to move as well because of me, and I hadn't even been there. My existence was becoming a burden to everyone around me.

It was hard not to feel bad for myself when the world was falling apart and I was just adding fuel to the fire. For now, I just wanted to sleep. Sleeping was an escape from this place, being the only time I felt at peace. Well, as long as I didn't dream about those vampires I incinerated, anyways. "I'm feeling tired, guys. I'm going to go to bed early. Okay?" I gave Xavier a half-smile that was barely even a facial tick.

Natalie stood up, caressed my cheek tenderly, and then nodded.

I turned away quickly, my eyes stinging with tears even as I made my way to my room.

CHAPTER TWO

RUBY

A few days after we moved to this location, I wandered off into the forest seeking a little peace away from the chaos of our living situation. Eventually, I stumbled upon the most peaceful and surreal view.

I found a hill that overlooked a part of the forest covered with flowers along with trees scattered about them. Woodland animals would wander by me, uncaring that I was there. To me, this felt as close as I'd ever get to finding the Garden of Eden.

The large rock that sat perfectly atop the hill served as my not-so-cushioned spot to sit for hours on end.

Since I hadn't been up to it last night, Natalie and I had mind-linked this morning. Of course, yet again, we learned nothing new. All I saw was a glimpse of myself when I was about fifteen years old. I was getting into a cab, a broad smile on my face as I waved goodbye to someone. Then the vision abruptly ended.

Despite the short duration of the vision, I did manage to pick out a few important clues. For one thing, I noticed my hair was shorter, to my shoulder, whereas now it was at my waist. It was also a much darker dyed red as opposed to my lighter natural shade now. Considering I've never dyed my hair before, the change in hair color really stood out. Also, who would I wave to with such a beaming smile? People annoyed me—they always had. My dislike for people in general combined with the lack of a filter between my mind and my mouth meant not many people ended up really getting who I was. This was the main reason I'd felt shocked when I clicked with Natalie so quickly. It was rarer still to earn a genuine smile from me, and such smiles were generally reserved for only the people I cared most about. To earn a smile of that caliber from me, whomever I was waving at must have been important to me. Whomever this mystery person was, I clearly cared about them.

Since I avoided eating in the kitchen or dining room with everyone else, I ate the last of my sandwich in my special spot. Even with my bleak childhood as a foster kid, I've never felt more like an outcast. Feeling alone in a crowd was indeed worse than feeling that way by oneself.

The wind picked up, causing my crimson hair to dance around me as I closed the container on my lap and placed it on the ground beside me. I bent my legs to wrap my hands around my knees and inhaled the sweet smell of flowers drifting in the breeze.

A twig snapped behind me, and it startled me. I swung around and almost fell off the rock in the process. My eyes widened as I came face to face with a jet-black wolf.

He stood a few steps away from me, his mouth ajar as he panted rapidly.

I swallowed nervously as my heart began to hammer in my chest.

Xavier's coat was brown, and I had never noticed a black wolf within the pack. Then again, I hadn't seen all the wolves in their shifted form. Was this a pack member about to kill me? Was this an outsider that had come to turn me over to the Council?

I didn't move and kept my gaze straight into the eyes of the wolf. "Who are you?" I asked, surprised at how steady my voice sounded.

The wolf closed its mouth and stopped panting as his black eyes changed to hazel.

I narrowed my eyes and scrunched my face as my brows furrowed tightly. "Axel?"

The wolf snorted and stepped forward confidently.

I exhaled through my mouth, relieved. "You seriously scared me there for a minute."

He padded over to me.

In my seated position, he towered over me like a mountain. I remained motionless as his cold nose brushed against my warm cheek. I reached up to softly touch the side of his face. I smiled shyly as my finger sank into his silky fur.

He tilted his head softly towards my touch.

His obsidian coat was indescribably beautiful. I wouldn't tell him this, but I was happy he was here. We could be outsiders together.

He pulled away suddenly, walked away, and vanished in the trees. He shifted and returned a few minutes later.

I quickly averted my eyes when I caught a glimpse of his abs as he pulled his shirt down. The last thing I wanted was for him to catch me checking him out. He'd never let me forget it.

His dark curly hair hung loose around his shoulders and messy. The corner of his mouth arched knowingly as he walked over to me and crouched down. "My wolf looks great, right? I know," he joked.

This earned him an exaggerated eye roll from me.

He chuckled as he stared at the forest and stood. He then carefully sat down on the rock beside me.

"You're so full of yourself," I teased him. "You shouldn't have come," I told him seriously.

He shrugged nonchalantly then turned to look at me. "Yeah, I missed you too."

"That's not what I said," I replied quickly.

He used a hand to comb his hair backward casually and stared at me for a moment, his hazel eyes somehow appearing lighter than I remembered them. "You don't need to say it."

Like always, his intense gaze made my heart flutter. I averted my eyes, unable to look at him any longer. In my peripheral vision, I could see he was still focused intently on me, his eyes roaming all over my body.

Stop fucking looking at me like that, dammit!

Neither of us spoke for a moment, and my mind started to wander.

Then, with concern evident in his voice, he whispered to me, "What happened?"

I deliberately avoided his eyes and directed my gaze to the forest floor before the rock. He was asking about the one thing I didn't want to talk about, the one thing I didn't have an answer for. I bit down on my lip as I watched a small insect fly from one flower to another. I recalled the witch from the shop Xavier and I had gone to who had told us she could go to another world. Right now, I fervently wished I could do the same. "I don't know," I finally answered. "I just reacted."

I glanced up at him to gauge his reaction. I feared he might regard me with the same fear and suspicion as the rest of the pack. To my relief, all I saw on his face was concern for me. My lips formed a thin line as I looked away from him, looking to my left to avoid him seeing the pain and sadness in my eyes. I welcomed his kindness. I didn't get much of it from anyone else other than Xavier, Mathieu and Natalie, but Axel would see more than I wanted him to.

"Did you speak to the witch who made the scent-masking potions?" I inquired, "Can she help me?" The sound of him brushing his hand down his pants made me look his way once more.

"I did. She can't help, but she recommended someone that can."

I sensed a 'but' coming, and there was no room for that. If

there was someone who could get through the barrier in my mind, I wanted it done. "But?"

"He's a warlock that practices dark magic."

"Is that really as bad as you're making it seem? If he can help, I want to go to him," I stated.

His chest rose and fell as he inhaled and exhaled deeply.

I arched a brow as he took his sweet time to respond. "Axel?"

"Yes, it's as bad as it sounds. Black magic shouldn't be taken lightly. There is a price to pay for using it. Maybe we'll get lucky and the warlock will be willing to bear the cost of the black magic in exchange for some other form of compensation. However, if you must pay, then that's a problem."

My mouth turned downward as I shrugged. "What's the price?"

"I don't know what the price will be for doing this, but when you think of black magic, think of necromancy. Necromancy is strong magic but comes with a price only a few are willing to pay. You lose a piece of your soul with each life you bring back. Black magic is the same but with countless prices, from taking a life down to losing a hand."

"Okay, then," I drawled.

Axel narrowed his eyes. "Okay. Would you still want the warlock's help if the price is never to have children?"

I grimaced. "Okay, I get it. But we don't know the price. Maybe it won't be anything that drastic. I want to do it. Natalie alone can't help me. The sooner we know what I am and what's in my past, the better."

"I can't say I know how you feel," he said thoughtfully, his voice deep and gravelly. "I was born a wolf. I've known what I am since birth."

I shot him a look that told him just how little he was helping my mood.

He smiled and held a hand up. "What I can tell you is this... whatever you are, Ruby, own it. Nothing good will come from trying to suppress who you really are. Denying or suppressing your powers will only throw you off balance. A wolf who fights the change during their first shift only ends up suffering unnecessarily." He gently reached out and held a strand of my hair the way as is becoming his habit.

To my surprise, I found his sage words to be comforting. I understood what he was saying entirely, but it was easier said than done.

"Trust me," he added.

Do I? Do I trust him?

He stared at me and released my hair. "There's a full moon tomorrow night. That's why I came. If there is an attack, my people are safe. Even with the cloaking spell, you guys are still at risk. You need all the protection you can get."

I tried not to overthink how he had risked himself and his pack by coming here just for me. "How are you so sure your pack is safe without you? How is your father doing, by the way?"

He began rubbing his finger back and forth on his chin as he stared up at a bird soaring in the sky above us. "He's doing better, thanks. I know my pack is safe because there are three witches there, plus the warlock you met. With all their warding and cloaking spells, my people have the best protection possible."

I turned completely to face him.

He looked me up and down as if wondering what I was doing.

I leaned forward, and my eyes lowered into slits. "What's up with you and all these witch friends, huh? I thought werewolves and witches didn't mix."

He shrugged nonchalantly. "I was in love with a witch, once."

I pulled back, my eyes widening somewhat. That was not at all what I'd expected to hear. The fact that he said it so casually seemed to be a testament to how far he and I had come in our relationship. When we first met, if I asked a single question, he'd bite my head off. Now, we were sitting outside together, companionably sharing sensitive information about ourselves.

I smiled inwardly. To be honest, it was nice talking to him. "Oh, I'm going to need a little more than that." I grinned.

He chuckled softly. "Of course, you wouldn't be you if you didn't."

I smacked his arm. "Are you calling me nosy? Because I am." I giggled.

He laughed along with me, but his laughter was short-lived. "Obviously, I wasn't mated to her, but we loved each other." His jaws clenched. "I loved her. My pack couldn't know about us, but her coven was aware of our relationship. Her people didn't approve, of course. I think my dad knew about her, but he never said anything. Believe it or not, when I was younger, I didn't want to be Alpha."

"That's shocking," I grumbled.

He laughed as he nodded. "Yeah, but it's true. My mother was alive then, and I was hoping she'd have another son who would want to take the title of Alpha. Although, I'm the firstborn...but that's another story." He combed his hair back lazily and closed his eyes as he scratched at his scalp.

I found myself wondering what his hair would feel like if I reached out and touched it. He was always feeling mine.

He went on, "When a demon killed the witch I loved, I helped her coven to avenge her death. They welcomed me after that." He snorted and lowered his hand. He stared off in the distance, a crease between his brows. "Funny, how it was her death that made us allies. We later found out the demon that killed her was working for a human."

My heart sank. This explained a lot about Axel's hatred towards humans. One of them was responsible for the death of the woman he'd loved. "I'm really sorry, Axel."

He accepted my words with a brief nod. "So, the witches I know that I can call on for help are all from her coven."

I bit down on my lips and heaved a sigh. I wasn't sure what to think now. A human killed his first love, and now he ended up mated to one. I scrunched my face. *Then again, I might not be human.*

"What?" he asked.

I shook my head slowly. "Nothing. I guess I understand now why you hate humans so much and why you were so upset to be mated to one."

He held my gaze for a moment. "Yes, that's why I hate humans and why I never fell in love with anyone after her."

Well, this is awkward.

"But I don't hate you, Ruby," he added quickly, "Plus, you're not human." His eyes roamed over my face and hair, as if he saw something no one else could. "You weren't from the start. We just need to find out what you actually are."

I folded my lips. "What if I'm some lab rat, some human experiment gone wrong? Or some messed up hybrid? I don't want to hurt any of you. You guys are all I have." The words were out of my mouth before I could stop myself.

Axel didn't hide his surprise either. His face smoothed out as he smiled at me and he reached up to give my chin a quick pinch. "Don't worry about that, Red. We're in this together. You're my mate, remember? We'll figure it out together. I don't abandon my family, so like it or not, you're stuck with me."

CHAPTER THREE

My eyes started to twitch, causing me to press my fingers against them. The twitching stopped, but my eyes slowly started to become blurry until I no longer saw the forest before me.

A white wolf growled at me, its mouth cavernous and its fluffy tail swished from side to side. I watched as the wolf was engulfed by black smoke and a distorted monstrous growl pierced the air. A giant cobra appeared out of the smoke, slithering from side to side. It flicked its tongue at the sky before rising, hood now showing as it hissed.

I stared at long fangs painted red as my head fell back to properly look up at the snake.

The cobra swayed, his movements almost hypnotizing, then it whipped its head forward in the blink of an eye to strike me.

I jumped and grabbed onto the rock beneath me before I almost fell off. I blinked my eyes rapidly as I looked around me. I was back in the forest at my spot.

I sighed as I pressed my fingers into my eyes. This was the sixth time I'd had that vision since the incident when I burned the vampire. No matter how many times I saw it...it always got me.

Tonight would be the full moon and all the wolves were on edge. I'd been out here in the woods since daybreak in an attempt to avoid the other pack members.

Tensions were running high, and I'd rather not have someone finally decide to take their frustrations out on me. Sighing, I gulped down the rest of my orange juice and placed it into the paper bag along with the container that held my sandwich.

Placing my hands behind me on the rock, I leaned my head back towards the sky as I closed my eyes. I attempted to relax and focus on the sounds of the forest – the birds, insects, the wind in the trees – anything to take my mind off the images from the vision. It seemed like someone had pressed the repeat button. Each time I got the vision again, it remained stubbornly stuck in my mind to the point where I couldn't concentrate on anything else all day.

I opened my eyes calmly, expecting to see a peaceful blue sky above me. Instead, I found myself looking directly into a pair of emerald green eyes. I let out a scream so high pitched, probably only dogs—or wolves—could hear it and jumped up frantically, ready to bolt. I belatedly realized it was Randoll.

He placed his hands on his knees and started to laugh. "Oh my god, your face!"

I rolled my eyes and clutched at my chest, a smile tugging at the corners of my mouth. Randoll was one of few werewolves who had been nice to me from the start, back when I was just the human in the packhouse. "You're a dick, Randoll."

He walked forward and flicked his hand at me for me to scoot over. "I know. What are you doing out here?"

I sighed heavily. "I think you know what."

He looked over at me and pursed his lips as he nodded. "Yeah." His red hair was much like mine, but now too long as it covered his forehead.

"You need a haircut," I stated.

He looked up at the strands of hair just above his eyes. "I kind of like it."

"Of course you would," I replied.

He chuckled. "This is cool," he remarked after we sat in silence for a moment. "Nice view."

I nodded in agreement. "It is. Is Xavier looking for me or something?"

He shook his head. "Nah, I...um, was on patrol and smelled you out here."

"Oh," I drawled. I'd have to remember to ask Axel to procure more of the potion to mask my scent. Xavier had tried to reassure me that my new scent wasn't bad. He'd characterized it as 'kind of indescribably sweet.' I still found it very disturbing because there was no way to ignore it like a normal human scent. It was like the constantly delicious smell of fresh bread being made, as Natalie described it.

"How are you doing, Ruby?" Randoll asked as he turned to look at me. "I know the pack is being pretty hard on you right now."

"I'm not doing great, obviously. But as I've said, I can't blame them," I looked down at my hands, at the lines in my palm. "I'm scared of myself too."

"Why?" he asked gently.

I laughed, but it sounded humorless. "I don't know what I am, Randoll. *I do not know what I am.* I don't even know if my real name is Ruby. You have no idea how it feels not to know who you are."

"So, you really don't have any memories from your past?" He probed, his voice low as he leaned over somewhat. "I heard one of the wolves talking. They said Natalie is trying to help you to get them back."

I nodded. "I have memories of my past. Certain memories were just locked away. I can't feel like I've forgotten something if I don't recognize that memory to begin with. Shouldn't you already know this? You're the beta for the pack."

His mouth turned down as he made a face. "Yes, but I'm not told everything. I enforce the alpha's rules and keep the pack in check. Right now, though, everyone is..." He paused and sighed. "Everyone is getting on my nerves."

I could certainly understand that sentiment. While I understood everyone's fear of me, they were treating me as if I had the plague. It got old fast.

"What did it feel like?" he suddenly asked.

"What?" I asked, confused.

He pointed to my hands. "What did it feel like when you killed them?"

I used my tongue to poke my cheek out as I gazed up at the blue sky. "I was having odd pains in my body before it happened. With the first vampire, I didn't really feel anything. He just—he just started to burn to death, and then I realized it was because of me." I was seeing the vampire in my head as I spoke. I could see the confusion and pain in his eyes as he died slowly and agonizingly. "When the second vampire attacked me, I only reacted." I threw my hands up to block myself as I had back then. "He was going to kill me. I was in shock. I didn't know what the fuck was happening other than my hands were burning from the inside out. After that vampire died, my power turned on me." I glanced back over at him.

A deep crease had formed between his brows. "That's what happened?"

I frowned. "Yeah, my powers turned on me after I used them."

He combed his hair back, but the wild curls only sprang forward to cover his forehead again. "That's crazy," he murmured under his breath. "You're a walking, talking vampire flame thrower without the flame." His eyes widened as he grinned. "Maybe it's not fire, but more like a kind of radiation."

"I don't get it," I replied.

"Too much radiation burns, doesn't it?"

"I don't know. Trust me, it was like a volcano was bubbling inside me." I clenched and unclenched my fist as I remembered the pain. "I've never felt anything so painful. It was worse than the vampire bite."

"So, you can't tell when it's coming on to like, move away to protect others? It can just...happen?"

I stared at him for a moment.

He stared back at me expectantly.

I realized he wasn't asking me all of these questions because he was concerned. He was only talking to me to find out how unstable I was, to find out if I could be trusted or if I was a threat.

He made a face as the silence stretched on between us. He started to look uncomfortable because of the way I was just staring at him.

"No, Randoll, I can tell. Why are you asking me all of this?"

He laughed sheepishly. "What do you mean, Ruby?"

I got up and stepped away from him. "I'm a fucking moron to think you're any different from the others. Did they send you? Huh? I bet they sent you to talk to me to see what you can learn because Xavier and Mathieu aren't telling you guys anything."

Randoll stood up slowly. "Ruby, I was only trying to understand what's going on. When Axel turned up yesterday, the others started to get angry. We aren't being told anything other than what happened with the vampires and you and that we all need to hide."

I started shaking my head. I could hear the blame in his voice. "They all had to hide because of me, right? Not like they weren't, *we weren't*, all already in hiding or about to be, right? From...I don't know... the vampires? God, you're all fucking full of it. You're all making it seem as if I'm the vampire threat that has started this mess. My life is fucked too, you know! Have any of you thought about that! No one is safe, whether I'm here or not, Randoll! It's only a matter of time before the humans or the vampires find us and that doesn't have to be solely because of me!"

As I turned away, an unfamiliar sensation started to pulsate within my body. My heartbeat was hammering in my ears. I closed my eyes as I prayed not to go nuclear, not now.

"Please, Randoll, leave me alone." I could hear his footsteps as he drew closer to me. The closer he got, the more I started to shake, and I realized I felt him there. I felt his energy. I felt the energy in the air, earth, and trees around us. It was like a low hum in my ear, a surprisingly soothing sound.

It wasn't the heat like before. While I felt relieved about that, I was also scared. I didn't know what this new sensation meant. I didn't know what any of this meant. "Go, now, please," I whispered urgently.

"Ruby, I'm sorry, I didn't mean to upset you. Everyone just wants to know what's really going on. No one knows what you are. No one knows what you're capable of. If you're powerful enough to kill a vampire, imagine what you could do to us."

"I would never!" I screamed as I spun around.

Randoll was thrown backward by an unseen force.

I gasped and covered my mouth as he tried to catch his balance but fell backward.

His eyes were wide in shock that certainly matched my surprised ones.

My eyes stung with tears as I looked around us at the flowers, bushes, and twigs that had been blown back. I swallowed hard. My hand shook as it fell from my mouth to hang limply at my side. I could have killed him. I could have done precisely what he and the others were afraid of me doing. "I'm sorry," I whispered as a tear escaped an eye. I backed away from him. "I'm so sorry."

Randoll sat up. "Ruby, don't," he said.

I still turned and ran.

Xavier

It wasn't hard to find her. I followed her scent through the forest until I found her sitting under a tree, a curious squirrel sitting in front of her.

Ruby held her hand out and the little critter moved forward instead of away from her. She cocked her finger, her soothing voice vibrating as she tried to lure the small animal in.

It came closer and closer until it could smell the tips of her finger before running away and then back to her.

I smiled as she giggled.

The squirrel ran off when he noticed my arrival.

She sighed as she noticed me, too. She got to her feet quickly and turned, walking away.

It only took me a few long strides to catch up to her. "So," I drawled. "Are you leaving then?"

She stopped and turned to look at me, her brows furrowed with rage.

I sobered up. "I was kidding."

"Of course you were, because you know there is nowhere I can actually go. I'm stuck in a place where no one wants me, and I'm putting everyone in danger."

"That's not true," I replied.

She gave me a flat look.

"It's not true that *no one* wants you here," I corrected myself. "And you know that."

She continued walking.

I strolled by her side silently. A contrite Randoll had found me and sheepishly told me what happened with her. She was getting more powerful, that much was clear. I had noticed it from the moment I caught her trail. Her scent was even more potent than before.

Whatever was awakening inside her became stronger each time she used her powers. She had an episode triggered by an argument. It was a risk to have her around everyone, but what other choice was there?

Axel and I had already discussed the possibility of using black magic, and he knew I was completely against it. Black magic was tricky and risky. It was a chance I didn't want to take. Of course, Ruby was ready to do it, but she was still new to this world and did not truly understand the cost.

"Do you sometimes wonder what's happening out there?" she asked. "What's happening with the war while we hide in these woods?"

"Everyone is hiding, I think," I guessed as I nodded. "I want to be out there fighting, helping to save this world, but we're being hunted by humans, werewolves, and those leeching vampires. Going out there means certain death, Ruby, but..."

Pausing, she raised a brow at me.

"I know what's happening to you right now is hard to deal with," I went on. "We will find out what's hidden in your mind and what your powers mean. Once we know all of that and once you can control your gifts, we can get out of here and bring the fight to the vamps."

A small smile curved her lips as she kept walking. "I'd like that."

My heart warmed to see her smiling, but it vanished as soon as it appeared.

"If things turn out that way, that is," she added. "We don't even know enough about what's happening out there to know what we're really up against."

"I spoke to Axel yesterday when he arrived," I replied. "The vampires are slaughtering everyone and everything that has blood and a beating heart. They have an actual society, complete with ranks. On the bottom, you have the Bleeders... they're ravenous and bloodthirsty. Blood is like a drug to them. They are more crea-ture-like, incredibly pale and hairless and feast on anything. Then you have the higher-ups."

She stopped walking and turned to me. "What do you mean?"

"You have the Bleeders and the Skins. The Skins are human-like in terms of their reasoning and can control their thirst. Among them, you have generals, no doubt very powerful. Then you have the queen." This was just about all the information Reika had been able to gather from the Council. It wasn't much, but it was enough. "That's why so many people were killed in the first wave. They released the Bleeders to wreak havoc."

"Is there any info on their queen?" she asked.

I shook my head. "Not yet, but Reika said she's working on it. She had also heard some whispers about something but would rather confirm it before saying anything."

Ruby sighed. "Okay, then."

I knew what Ruby was thinking—we still knew very little. However, what I hadn't told Ruby and didn't plan to tell her, was that the Council had doubled its efforts to have her found and captured.

They'd dispatched the Council Guards to hunt her down. It would only be a matter of time before we were located. The Council Guards were an elite group of werewolves, which was why Reika had contacted me through my dreams and not a phone. Even then, she had to limit her contact with us.

Mathieu, Axel, Natalie, and I had been thinking about a way to go about moving Ruby, but so far, all ideas we had come up with had a high probability of failing.

The Council werewolves weren't the only ones that wanted her. The humans did as well, and since we didn't have a human source to give us details on that front, we had no idea what they were planning.

"Xavier?"

I blinked and peered down at her. "Yes?"

"I was asking you if Randoll told you what happened."

I intended to walk off, but she held my wrist. "Yes, he did. Don't worry, he didn't tell anyone else but me. He told me he pushed you too far and you got angry. It's not surprising your rage triggered your powers." I frowned as a thought occurred to me.

Ruby's green eyes roamed my face with worry. "What is it?"

"I think maybe that's what we need to do," I replied as a smile slowly started to stretch my lips. "Why didn't I think of this sooner?"

"I'm not following," she grumbled.

I cupped her chin gently. "We need to push you to use your powers."

She narrowed her eyes at me. "That won't work. I have no idea how to even—I don't know how to make it work, okay? I was scared the first time and angry the second time."

As the wheels in my mind turned, my smile grew wider. "Trust me, what I have in mind will work."

CHAPTER FOUR

A drop of sweat dripped into my eye, causing my sight to blur, but I kept running. My heartbeat was pounding in my ears as I ran through the woods, the muscles in my legs now sore and aching. I could hear them behind me, chasing after me as I ran. I forced all my energy into my legs to keep pushing me forward.

A howl echoed through the forest.

I wiped a hand over my forehead as I ran behind a tree and stopped. Pressing my back to its trunk, I tried not to breathe too loudly, but I was exhausted.

I looked down at my right elbow and grimaced at the scratch there from where I had tripped earlier. It wasn't bad, but it was bleeding. As more howls echoed through the forest, I pushed away from the tree and started running again.

I tried to mask my scent as I had done with the vampires. But since my scent had become more robust ever since it changed, I doubted that anything could cover up my smell now. All I'd done was cover myself unnecessarily in dirt and mud.

With it being late afternoon to evening, the sun still shone through the canopy of trees above, something I felt thankful for since I could see where I was running. It hadn't stopped me from tripping earlier. Nor did it prevent me from tripping again, as I stubbed my toe and fell forward.

I bit down on my lip to hold back my scream as I fell, my arms outstretched to cushion my fall. Groaning, I remained on the ground for a few seconds to catch my breath. A twig snapped behind me, and I spun around onto my back.

I swiftly rolled to the side as a dark brown wolf jumped at me, its massive paws coming down hard where I had just been. I got to my feet quickly, my tangled dirty hair covering my face somewhat. I had to duck to the side again, as the wolf charged forward while slashing its claws at me.

I rolled away swiftly and rose to one knee as the animal growled, its black eyes watching me closely. I gripped a stone firmly behind my back as I slowly rose onto my legs.

The wolf stopped pacing a circle around me to snap its jaws in my direction.

I threw the stone suddenly, but the wolf easily dodged it and charged at me. I raised my hand as I tried to use my powers, and the wolf skidded to a halt. I looked at my hand and then the wolf.

Nothing happened. I sighed heavily, and my hand fell limply to my side. "It's not working," I stated the obvious to Xavier.

He made a snorting sound and sat down.

I smiled. "Maybe it's because I know you won't hurt me. Good chase, though."

The enormous paws of a black wolf appeared from behind a tree. It belonged to Axel, the other wolf that had been chasing me. When he fully emerged from behind the trunk, I frowned.

His head was still dipped aggressively and his sharp canine fangs were still on full display.

I glanced at Xavier, who had gotten up, and I threw a look Axel's way when he growled. "It didn't work, Axel. You can stop now."

He snapped his jaws at me with a growl.

My eyes widened as Xavier growled and moved closer to me. "Axel, what are you doing? I told you it didn't work. Stop!"

It didn't seem to matter what I said—he wasn't listening to me. His eyes were still black pits of rage as he snarled.

Xavier answered with a loud growl.

Xavier thought it would be a good idea for Axel and him to chase me as if to hurt me to see if it would trigger my powers. When I first used my powers, I was scared. The second time I was angry. Maybe if they re-created those feelings, I'd be able to access and eventually learn to control my powers. Yet, nothing had happened. No matter how they had howled, growled, and looked as if they might attack me, I knew deep down I wasn't in any real danger.

However, my heart was beating rapidly as I looked at Axel now, and not from the exertion of running either.

He didn't look like he was faking, and it didn't feel like he was either. He looked angry, furious even as he shook his head, his ears flattened to his head.

"Listen," I tried to deflect what was happening. "I'm exhausted, and we should probably head back to the camp. It's getting late. There is a full moon tonight, remember?"

Axel kept circling Xavier and me.

Xavier lowered his head as he sent a warning growl Axel's way.

Axel raised his head and snarled louder while he bucked forward as if to attack us.

"Axel?" I entreated in a soft voice but jumped when he snapped his jaws at me.

Xavier moved to stand in front of me and then stepped back, using his body to push me backward.

I knew he was telling me to run. I couldn't, though. I was too confused as to why Axel was still pretending he wanted to hurt me. At first, this seemed like a good idea, even a little fun, but Axel was really starting to scare me.

"Shift back, now! Do you hear me, Axel? You're freaking me out. Shift!"

Maybe that had been the wrong thing to say because he quickly lunged at me.

Xavier reacted swiftly, slamming into Axel.

They both fell to the ground.

I watched with wide eyes as they bit and clawed at each other, my skin tingling as my slight fear turned to panic.

This wasn't fake anymore. Watching two wolves big enough to swallow me whole fight, was something I'd never seen before. I felt like this fight had been building up between them from the very start, and I feared it would only end with the death of one of them.

I gasped as Axel bit viciously into Xavier's side, and Xavier howled in pain. My body started to shake as blood sprayed from the wound in Xavier's side.

That's when I turned and ran. I ran past them to head back to the pack, but this time I didn't care about the ache in my legs or the branches grabbing and poking at my skin. I needed to get to Mathieu or Randoll. I had no idea what had gotten into Axel, but if he caught up to me, I felt it in my soul that I would be a dead woman.

Maybe shifting so close to a full moon had been a bad idea. If it hadn't been safe for them to shift, why would they do this, knowing the risk?

Like before with Randoll, I started to feel pulsing energy within and around me. I tried to hold onto the feeling, but it kept fading only to return and then disappear again. I groaned as I pushed forward when something barreled into me, throwing me to the ground.

I landed with an oomph sound and rolled to my back as I heard a contorted growl. I held my head back as I looked up Axel's towering pure werewolf form. Being jet black, unlike the other wolves—he was truly something to look at.

His long-clawed fingers twitched at his side as I pulled myself back on my hands to get away from him. A deep resounding growl met my ears, and I stopped moving.

"Axel, it's Ruby. You need to calm down, okay. You're not hunting me for real, remember?"

He bared his white teeth and took a step towards me.

A chill went through my body. "I swear, Axel, knock it off right now! What the hell do you think you're doing? Are you going to kill me? Huh? Don't force me to hurt you, Axel. I have no control!"

He took another step forward.

Now, a buzzing sound rang in my ears as my fear grew stronger. I could see blood on the tips of Axel's teeth, no doubt from biting Xavier. My heart grew heavy as I remembered Xavier and wondered if he was all right. Had Axel killed Xavier?

This wolf couldn't be Axel. It couldn't be. Why would Axel turn on us like this? Why would he turn on me like this? We weren't best friends, but I thought we were becoming closer.

"Axel!" I screamed. His name left my lips before I had the chance to stop it.

He howled loudly as he dove at me.

I screamed as I threw my hand up, and a tingling sensation ran down my arm to my palm.

Axel was thrown back. He slammed into a tree and fell unconscious on the ground.

I held my hand to my heaving chest as I heard his bones crack.

I got to my feet while trembling. I felt weak but not faint, thankfully. I walked over to him slowly. I stared with my heart in my throat as he changed into his human form, his body breaking as he shifted.

I bent down and placed my hand behind his head only to take my hand away to see blood coating my fingers. I had done it. I had used my powers. Yet, in the process, I had hurt someone. I had hurt my mate. A sick feeling settled in my chest as I placed my hand on his cheek. "I'm so sorry," I whispered to him as my eyes teared up. "Can you hear me, Axel? Please, wake up."

The rustling of bushes caught my attention, as Xavier appeared in his human form.

I paid no attention to the fact that he was naked. All I could focus on was my panic, regret, and worry that I might have killed Axel.

"Let me carry him. He's fine. I can hear his heartbeat."

I moved away instantly.

Xavier picked Axel up and took off running.

I did my best to keep up with him. Despite my effort, Xavier was soon so far ahead of me, all I could see was his perfect backside. I slowed my pace until I started walking, the tears I'd been trying to hold back running like little rivers from my eyes.

The feeling of the sun's rays on my skin shining down through the little openings in the canopy of tree leaves above wasn't filling me with happiness like it typically did. I leaned my head back and screamed as loud as I could, and like before, an unseen force left my body to blow the canopy of trees above me back.

I placed my hands on my head as I now stared at the sky above. I looked back down to see Natalie watching me and I rapidly wiped at my tears.

She walked over to me, a look of pity on her face.

We said nothing as we stared at each other for a moment.

"Come on," she urged after a while.

We ambled back to the house in silence.

Axel

I had no idea Ruby was capable of being this annoying. For an hour, she hadn't left my side since I'd woken up. I was only out for about thirty minutes. Since it was 4:45 pm and no wolf would be able to shift after 6 pm, I was able to heal most of my broken bones on my own.

However, I did need little help from Natalie for my cracked skull.

Ruby kept checking on me and asking if I was okay every few minutes. While it was refreshing that she cared so much, it was starting to get on my nerves. She might have gotten a good one in on me, but I'm much harder to kill than she thinks.

"Ruby, I'm fine, okay? Can you stop?" I wasn't a weakling, and I didn't need to be protected or coddled. Not by her, or anyone else for that matter.

Her beautiful face fell.

Seeing the sadness in her eyes was like a punch to my gut. I knew she felt guilty for what happened, but it hadn't been her fault. I reached out and pinched her chin gently as I grinned at her.

The edges of her mouth twitched with a little smile. "Okay, I hear you," she conceded with both hands up in mock surrender.

I knew she'd still be keeping an eye on me though.

"There was a charge in the air," Natalie declared.

I turned to look at her.

She sat perched on the arm of the chair Xavier was sitting on. "The moment Ruby used her power, I could feel it." She shook her head as she pinched the bridge of her nose. "If I hadn't known it was her, I wouldn't have been able to track it. It was like feeling an earthquake. You can feel it, but you can't pinpoint its origin."

"Do you think other creatures will be able to sense her powers?" Mathieu asked.

Natalie shrugged. "I don't know. All of them can sense magic. That includes Enchanteds, witches, and demons. I'm only guessing here, but it would make sense if others can sense her powers since I can now feel it without trying to. It wasn't like that before."

I pressed a finger to my temple, where my previously pounding headache was slowly fading. I glanced over at Ruby.

She'd been observing me before looking away. "It wasn't heat, like it was before," she explained. "With the vampire, it was fire. This time, like with Randoll, it was this..." She looked around as she searched for the right words. "It was energy. I could feel it flowing through my body and in the things around me, the earth, and trees. When I used it on Axel, I felt it coalescing throughout my body and pushing outwards through my arm to attack him."

"So, you can harness the energy in living things then?" Xavier asked. "If you could feel the energy within yourself and use it defensively."

Ruby shrugged. "Maybe, I don't know." She turned to me, her brows furrowing.

I sighed, as I knew what was coming.

"What the hell were you even thinking?" Ruby asked. "I could have killed you!"

"But you didn't, and it worked, didn't it?" I pointed out.

"You could have died," she articulated slowly. "I believed you. I thought something was wrong with you. Never do that again!"

I shrugged as I sighed and placed my elbows on my knees. "I had to make it believable. Your scent is stronger now as well," I added. "We need to do something about that. At this point, even with the barrier around us, vampires and werewolves *will* be able to smell her."

"We don't have a witch that can create a masking potion," Mathieu pointed out.

"Right," I acknowledged as I leaned back. "I'll have to make a call then. Tomorrow I'll have to go get it, but I won't be able to return right away. In the meantime, Ruby, there is an underground room built on this house, a bunker. You'll have to stay there in order to minimize your scent getting out."

Frowning, she mumbled under her breath, "Great... Sure."

"Less than ideal, I know, but it's just until I get back," I added.

She nodded. "There is something else," Ruby revealed as she faced the others. "I had a vision."

Xavier leaned forward. "When?"

"Today... this morning, that is. There was a white wolf, black smoke, and a giant cobra, and I saw little else. Every time I have this vision, it always ends with the cobra eating me."

"How long have you been having this vision?" Mathieu inquired, concern evident in his voice.

"A while," she replied as she glanced back and forth between Xavier and me.

I noticed we were both shooting her the same angry look.

"I didn't want to say anything. Plus, as weird as it is, massive cobras like that don't even exist for me to be scared of, right?" No one answered, and her face fell. "Wait, they do?"

"Was the wolf a normal wolf or a werewolf?" Mathieu probed further.

"Ahh, I think it was a werewolf. It looked too big to be a regular wolf."

Mathieu hummed thoughtfully. "There are no white werewolves in existence. According to myth, the first of our kind, the purest of all werewolves, was white. No one has ever actually seen a white werewolf, though. "

Ruby made a face. "Well, I think a white werewolf would be pretty awesome-looking and probably less frightening. I'm not trying to call you guys scary, but in all honesty, you are."

Mathieu nodded in agreement. "Our final form is meant to be scary. The first of our kind was said to be white, angelically beautiful because he had our goddess's affection. He was her first creation. The stories say he became tainted by darkness, corrupted. He lost his white fur and transformed yet again into a hideous beast that walked on two feet."

Ruby listened attentively with an obvious fascination.

Her interest made me remember when I had first heard this story. "That's why we have two forms. The first is of a normal, albeit unusually large wolf and the last, that of a bipedal beast, a hybrid of both man and animal. It also explains why changing to our final form is difficult to achieve for most wolves. You're at risk of losing yourself to the animal and remaining in that form."

"Okay, I see," Ruby replied. "Well, that is both tragic and fascinating. Tragic in that you all have to suffer through it but fascinating that it's even possible."

I snorted. "You wouldn't think it's fascinating in the least, if you'd experienced it," I told her.

"Until you get used to it," Xavier added.

Without warning, Natalie rose to her feet abruptly.

So did Xavier and I as soon as we noticed how the color of her eyes had already shifted to white.

Natalie's head kept moving from side to side as if she was watching something.

Xavier and I shared a look before glancing over at Ruby to make sure she was all right.

Ruby appeared fine, though clearly, she shared our concern for Natalie as she and Mathieu stood as well.

We all knew by now that Natalie's visions rarely brought good news.

"No, no, no," Natalie repeated while swaying a little. She lost her balance and rocked backward as if to fall but caught herself. She reached up to hold her forehead. When she looked up at us after a moment, her eyes had once again resumed their normal shade of blue.

"What's coming?" Mathieu questioned her.

I clenched my jaw. I'd been right to take the risk and come here after all. I had hoped this wouldn't happen, that an attack wouldn't come, but I wasn't surprised something was going to happen.

"They're coming," she whispered to him as her glossy eyes drifted to Ruby. "The humans are coming for her."

CHAPTER FIVE

RUBY

I wished I could vanish. I wished one of my powers, or even my only power, was the ability to teleport to anywhere I wanted. Better yet, I just wished I were normal.

I didn't want to wish I had never known about werewolves because then I would never have met Xavier, Natalie, and Axel. Not knowing about werewolves would've meant I wouldn't have known about vampires and their plans of world domination. Alone in life with no one to help me, no doubt I would have lost my life the first night the vampires attacked.

I'd been badass enough to look after myself in general, but not when fighting a supernatural being—a vampire. I still had nightmares about the vampire that fed on me. I sighed as I closed my eyes.

Who was I even kidding? If I were being honest, I wasn't quite as much of a badass as I liked to think. I hadn't been able to protect myself against those sick bastards the night I found out Xavier wasn't human. *Xavier* had saved me from whatever sick plans those motherfuckers had in mind for me that night. The world I'd fallen into had its good and bad bits, so taking away one bad thing might result in taking away something I didn't want to lose.

Natalie's words echoed in my head for a moment before I sat down stiffly. *The humans are coming for me.* "There is a full moon," I whispered. I gazed up at the others with wide eyes. "There's a full moon tonight. You guys will be defenseless. We have to leave. We all have to leave now, before nightfall!"

"Ruby," Axel spoke.

Without further hesitation, I jumped to my feet. I wouldn't have the annihilation of this pack or any pack on my hands. "Then I'll leave! I can't let this happen because of me! If I'm not here, the humans will move on," I added.

"Even though we won't be able to shift," Xavier attempted to reason with me. "We're still stronger than any human. Remember that, Ruby. No one can leave right now. It's a full moon tonight, yes. So we know we'll be more at risk out there than being here on the grounds."

I turned my back to them and walked away. I had all this power. Yet, instead of solving my problems, it was only creating more pain and worry. If only we'd been able to find out who I truly was from the start, then maybe I would have learned about my powers and how to control them. Then I'd be an asset in this fight against the vampires, instead being seen as a threat by every side. The vampires hunted me out of fear now, instead of just food, while werewolves and humans alike were just trying to capture me.

Olcan probably wanted to dissect me at this point, and it was highly likely what the humans wanted to do to me too.

"She's not wrong," Axel unexpectedly acknowledged.

I turned around to look at him.

"I have the number for the warlock," he went on. "I can call him and ask him for help. We can't let them get their hands on Ruby, and you all know that. She does need to leave," Axel affirmed.

"Are we seriously back to this right now, Axel?" Xavier asked him in disgust. "We talked about this. It's a no to using black magic."

I frowned unhappily. This wasn't Xavier's decision to make.

"We're not asking that warlock for help, Axel," Xavier argued. "We can handle some humans on our own, whether there is a full moon or not."

Axel shook his head. "You're being naïve, Xavier, and you're underestimating humans. Something that I'm expected to do, not you."

Xavier said nothing as his face hardened.

"Right now, we have no choice," Axel continued. "They're coming for her. We can't let them get to her before we know what she is, or before we know why a barrier was placed in her mind and what's behind it. If you have another idea of how to save her right now, let me hear it."

"And what if you take her to the warlock and the price is too high?" Xavier retorted. "Won't we have to find another way then? So, we can think of another way together now."

Axel rubbed at his forehead with evident frustration. "Xavier, we can't bypass something that might work because we're stuck on what-ifs. If we go to the warlock and the price is too high, we will leave and find another way. If we go to the warlock and it can be done, we would have saved ourselves a lot of time and trouble."

Xavier shook his head. "Axel, I don't think—"

"We're running out of time!" Axel interjected. "She is growing stronger. Her powers are growing stronger. Eventually, the slightest thing might trigger her. She might kill herself and us."

"This is my choice to make!" I yelled.

All eyes turned to me.

"This is my choice to make." I lowered my voice as I sighed. "I understand that there might be a price, Xavier. However, ignoring a viable option simply because we don't know what that price is, or if it can be paid or not, is foolish." I pointed to Natalie. "Nat said they're coming, and we're here bickering. I want to go to the warlock."

Axel nodded.

I continued, "But I'm not leaving now, not if everyone is staying."

Axel frowned. "What?"

"I ran once before, and I won't do it again. It's because of me that the humans are coming for us. My powers might be unstable right now, but if they attack us, I can help. I know I can, and I need you all to trust me on that. I'm the one person who can protect us all... sure, I could kill us all too, but that's not the point." I exhaled heavily through my nostrils. "Just put me in front of everyone, and I'll protect us."

Axel scratched at his jaw as he scrunched his face. "That plan might work, Ruby, but that's not enough. Plus, you can't guarantee you won't lose control. Okay, we need to think about this without arguing. We're going in circles, and we're wasting time."

"Okay," Xavier replied. "If you're not here, Ruby, they will attack anyways. So it's better if you leave, I agree with that. You're the one they want, so all we can do is defend ourselves the way we would if you were here to be protected. Hopefully, when they realize you aren't here, they'll leave to find you. You staying and hoping your powers make an appearance isn't a plan at all. It's a gamble. If that fails to pay off, we're all in trouble in addition to them getting you."

"The entire pack can't leave," Mathieu finally spoke up. "It's almost nightfall, and the vampires will be hunting. We can fight humans but not vampires. The pack has to stay, but you, Ruby, you have to leave."

With his input, the decision was made.

"How long before they arrive?" Axel asked Natalie, who had been quiet this whole time.

I felt surprised when she didn't have anything to say.

"I saw them arriving at night." She nodded. "And we only have two hours tops of sunlight. I would say they are coming soon."

"I wonder how they found us?" Mathieu mumbled to himself before turning to me. "Our pack doesn't have another safe house, none with warding as strong as here that is."

Axel snapped his fingers suddenly. "Speaking of warding, I need to check on ours." He removed his phone from his pocket, dialed a number, and held it to his ear. The longer the phone rang, the more his brows knitted. The call went unanswered and he hissed as he redialed. "Something is wrong. She's not answering." He peered down at the phone. "The witch that did the warding spells isn't answering." He turned to Natalie. "Can you check if the warding is still strong? Her magic is tied into it. If she's okay, the warding should hold, but if not..."

Natalie stepped forward. "Wardings aren't my thing. I can check if I still feel its energy, but that's all. If it's down, we'll lose one of the greatest advantages we have."

"Check if it's stable." Axel turned to Xavier. "Whether it's stable or not, we have a fight to prepare for."

———

Ruby

Xavier entered the room with a backpack I had grown sick of seeing. Seeing it make an appearance meant I'd be running for my own protection once more.

He placed it on the ground by the door and walked over to me. "Are you ready?"

I shook my head. "No. I don't like the idea of leaving you behind, Xavier."

"I don't like it either, but you have to. Dad and I need to stay

here to help the others, so you have to go with Axel and Natalie."
He held my cheeks in his hands.

I bent my head to snuggle further into his hands.

He continued, "Since Natalie said the warding is still there but
weak, something must have happened to the witch."

Knowing now what that witch and her coven meant to Axel, I
could only imagine how angry he must have been. "Yeah, I know.
Is Axel still unable to get through to her?"

Xavier shook his head.

I sighed. "Okay." I listened to the commotion outside the
room's door. Some of the wolves that had been sleeping outside
were moved inside the house. Warrior wolves would stay outside
to be positioned around the house and within the woods.
Mathieu had given the pack a choice—stay and fight or leave and
fend for themselves. Anyone that left would be allowed to return
in the future. A few wolves chose to go, and I didn't blame them.
Something was wrong with the warding. Even without the
humans attacking, it would only be a matter of time before
vampires sniffed us out, especially with my scent mixed in with the
cocktail.

With all that was happening, I knew the pack would only hate
me more. "I'm so sorry for all of this," I whispered.

Xavier pinched my chin. He tipped my face back for me to
look at him.

I closed my eyes and shook my head. "Don't try to tell me I
shouldn't be sorry. You and I both know we were found because
of me."

"We were found because someone betrayed us and told the
humans. That's not on you," he replied. "We have nowhere else to
go from here, so this is where we have to make a stand and fight.
The warding is down, but we should fight here tonight rather than
run and end up defenseless against vampires on a full moon. If
your powers can indeed be helpful, Ruby, and I think they can,
you have to learn to control them." He shook his head. "The

warlock will help, and whatever happens here tonight, you'll be able to avenge it."

I stepped away from him. "Stop talking as if you're going to die tonight."

He sighed. "Ruby—"

"Shut up, Xavier!"

"Okay," he said softly and held his hand out to me. "Come here."

I went back to him without hesitation.

He kissed the top of my head. "I wish I could come with you, but as much as I hate to admit this, I know Axel will look out for you. And Natalie as well."

I looked up at him. I knew Axel would protect me, but I chose not to say anything. I doubted Xavier wanted to hear my thoughts about Axel and his ability to protect me. Both men had been civil for the most part, and their hatred for each other wasn't so stifling anymore. Axel and Xavier weren't on the road to becoming best friends, but I loved that they were getting along for the most part.

We all had no room to think about what would become of our three-way mate bond right now. Once this was all over, we'd have to figure it out. I didn't want to think about whom I would have to reject or who would reject me.

At first, I had thought Axel would be the one to reject me. Now... I wasn't so sure.

I reached up and ran my hand through Xavier's hair. "Be careful, okay?" I tipped up on my toes and kissed him.

He instantly snaked his hands around me and crushed me to his body.

"Or I'm going to be pissed," I whispered against his lips when I pulled away. "And you don't want me to get pissed."

He smirked down at me. "So you think you can take me now, huh? Is that it?"

I poked a finger against his chest. "I know I can."

He looked thoughtful for a moment. "Yeah, I think you

could." He kissed my forehead. "I'll come and find you soon, okay?"

We pulled away from each other.

Xavier went over to the door and grabbed my bag.

We made our way downstairs together and I tried not to seem cowardly by keeping my gaze down to avoid looking anyone in the eyes. I stared ahead with my spine straight, and my head held high. I knew what they all thought of me, but I wouldn't allow them to think I was a sucker.

The nasty looks were like hot metal on my skin, but I endured it and kept walking. The moment we stepped outside, Xavier quickly grabbed my hand, and the wolves positioned outside stopped what they were doing. It took a moment for me to realize what was happening when I heard the speeding car, and then it appeared.

It skidded to a halt. Three men from the pack that had chosen to leave the pack, jumped out.

"They've blocked us in!" one of them yelled.

Xavier released my arm as Axel moved up to my other side.

"Who?" Xavier asked as he stepped forward. "What happened?"

Another car returned as well with three other men. "The humans created a blockade at our exit. We're trapped," the man that had first spoken replied.

"The vision changed," Natalie stated from behind me.

I turned to look at her.

Her brows furrowed. "The vision I saw was during the night..." She stared at me. "It's changed."

Randoll walked up to Xavier, his shirtless chest glistening with sweat. "I'll take two others and check the woods. Maybe there is a path we can take out of here to avoid them."

Xavier clenched his jaw. "The women and children can't leave tonight. They'll be picked off first if vamps attack us. Plus, a large pack of wolves traveling together will be like a buffet that vamps will smell from miles away." He then looked over at me. "Find a pathway quickly."

Randoll nodded, pointed at two men, and they all took off into the woods.

Xavier turned to me and led me back inside the house. "If there is a path, you guys need to take it and get out of here," Xavier glanced at Axel. "Don't leave her side." He turned and walked away.

"Xavier!" I called.

He kept moving away as he called back to me, "I'll be right back."

I turned to look at Natalie.

Her face was still scrunched up, no doubt annoyed that her vision had changed. "We only have an hour left before sundown. If we're to leave, it has to be now," she said.

Axel nodded. "It's best if Randoll checks the forest first before we make a run for it. If they've blocked our exit, they might have men in the woods right now, because the only option we have now is to escape through the woods."

I took a deep breath and then another. "Okay, maybe I should go down to that bunker you were talking about earlier. Is it well hidden? Humans can't smell me, right? Everyone can tell them I'm not here, and we will see if they'll leave."

Natalie puckered her mouth in thought. "We could do that, yes, unless they whip out dogs to track your scent."

I sighed. For every solution, I was met with a "try again." I'd really like to get my hands on whoever informed on us. I looked around at the people all gathered around, some still staring at me while others were busy having their own conversations.

A loud boom echoed through the woods, and the house fell silent.

Axel, Natalie, and I exchanged a look.

I dashed towards the door as another boom sounded, this time closer.

Once outside, we ran into Xavier and four other men. "What is that?" I asked.

"Bomb," Xavier replied as his eyes changed to black. "It's after six. We can't shift."

Axel grabbed my hand to tug me back.

I pulled away. The time for escaping had passed… the only remaining option seemed to be that we face these people. I hoped a fight didn't have to happen. I closed my eyes and listened to my heartbeat.

I tried to focus on the fear and panic I was feeling and decided to use them to call on the power within me.

"Ruby, don't," Natalie warned.

My eyes popped open. "I have to try," I replied through clenched teeth.

Just then, a loud voice boomed through the trees, *"We don't want to fight! We're only here for the girl!"*

I clenched my fists.

Randoll stepped out of the woods while carrying an unconscious wolf. Two humans in black army gear had guns aimed at Randoll, who had blood running down his face from a wound on his forehead.

"Your friend isn't dead! He tried to attack us and was shot with a tranquilizer. We don't want to fight. We only wish to talk!"

Behind Randoll, two more humans appeared, their guns pointed at the other wolf Randoll had taken with him.

Then from behind them, a man stepped out with a loud-speaker in hand. His chestnut blonde hair was cut low, and unlike the other men that were dressed for war, he was wearing a black skin-tight t-shirt. He stopped walking, and so did the others as his dark blue eyes fell on me instantly. He looked me up and down.

I returned the gesture to him.

Clearly, he was the one in charge here. He looked at Xavier and motioned with his hand to the man in Randoll's arms. "Your friend will be fine. He just needs to sleep off the drugs." His hand fell to his side. "We apologize for—"

"Cut the shit and get to the point," Axel cut him off. "What do you want?"

The man's eyes fell on me once more, and the corner of his mouth arched with a smile. "We want to talk to the alpha." His lips stretched into a genuine smile, one mixed with almost excitement. "Hello, Ruby, our little vampire slayer. It's nice to finally meet you."

CHAPTER SIX

RUBY

"We're an elite fighting group created to hunt vampires," General Presley explained. "After the first week, the first vampire wave, the government created the P.E.A, the Paranormal Eradication Agency. Every member has been selected from multiple government agencies based on their skill sets. We all possess skills that will put us at an advantage above the average human."

"So, you're a vampire hunter, basically?" Natalie asked.

Presley nodded. His eyes wandered to me.

I stared back at him with a blank expression.

Mathieu had invited him in. So here we were, a happy bunch just sitting in the living room, having a chat. The fight that we had expected to happen... didn't. While I was pleased that lives would not be lost tonight, this man—General Presley—was here for me.

Over my dead body would I be leaving with General Presley, no matter how much he insisted he was on our side.

Axel remained close to me. Xavier stood by his father's side, but he kept looking my way. He looked just as unhappy as I was about the entire situation.

The way that I saw it, all of this talking was wasting time.

General Presley would eventually get to the part where he needed me to go with him. Maybe the fight was only being delayed until then because there was no way in hell I was leaving—not with him, anyways.

"So, you see, my people aren't the ones targeting wolves," Presley directed this comment to Axel, who was making no effort to hide his animosity towards the General and his men. "We're on your side. It's clear for anyone to see...well, obviously only some people know that werewolves have been living alongside us peacefully for who knows how long." He looked back at Mathieu, "If you guys had been killing and targeting humans, someone would have noticed. You don't... you know... eat hu—"

"No," Axel interjected. "We do not eat humans. However, if werewolves were hunting humans, there is absolutely no guarantee you guys would have noticed." Axel smirked. "Vampires aren't the only supernaturals humans need to fear. They are just the only ones on a murdering-slash-world-domination rampage."

As much as I already disliked Presley, Axel's tactic to scare him was a double-edged sword. He was telling Presley that there were more supernaturals out there to scare him, but this had essentially put other supernaturals onto his radar. Something he would no doubt report. Especially after what they'd experienced with the vampires, if and when humans discovered other powerful supernaturals, they would kill them purely out of fear, just as they had done with the werewolves.

"Fair enough," Presley acknowledged quietly as he sent a look to two of his men standing by the door. "My point is, werewolves aren't the threat. Vampires are."

"If only the rest of your people would realize that," Mathieu replied. "You're killing the one species that can truly help with fighting the vampires... the only ones willing to fight, actually. Humans aren't generally well-liked by the supernatural community."

Presley frowned. "I know. Humans can be difficult, stubborn, and untrustworthy at times. We can also be kind, helpful, and persistent. We have our good and bad sides, just like anyone else. You invited a human into your pack, so you must have seen..." He smiled at me as he paused. "...we're not all bad."

"What are you doing here, General Presley?" Mathieu asked bluntly.

"There are no vampires to be hunted here," Axel added defensively.

Axel's protectiveness for me was clear, and it made me blush. We'd come a long way from where things were before. Natalie and Xavier were no longer the only ones that genuinely cared for me.

Presley got to his feet and walked to the window beside the bookshelves, his hands clasped behind his back. He turned to face us after a moment. A new emotion appeared in his eyes, a seriousness that hadn't been there before. He stood straight, his chest and head high. "We need your help." He then turned to me. "We need *your* help, Ruby."

"She can't help you," Xavier replied before I could.

Presley sent a puzzled look Xavier's way in response to his territorial behavior.

I'm certain he was wondering whether Xavier was my boyfriend. What he didn't know – and probably never could've guessed – was that the other one standing by my side was mine as well. My eyes widened at my thoughts. Why was I thinking of Axel as if he was my man? He's my mate, not my man. There was a difference. I rolled my eyes at myself. Now wasn't the time to muddle over my feelings for Axel. I wondered what Presley would think when he found out I wasn't just Xavier's girl but his mate. How would he react to that? Would he freak out at the thought that humans could be mated to wolves?

"What happened to her was an accident. She can't help you when she has no control over her gifts," Xavier added quickly.

"I can't help you," I told him.

He shook his head. "You can. You killed two vampires," Presley insisted.

I clenched my jaws.

"This is true, right?" he asked. "You burned them to death without even touching them."

I shifted my weight from one leg to the other nervously.

Presley stepped forward.

Axel pinned him with a glare.

He stopped abruptly. "What are you?" Presley asked. "Tell me that, at least. If you don't want to help, maybe there might be others in your species that will be willing to. To be honest, we are losing to the vampires. More of them pop up every night. We need help. We need to help each other."

"How would I help?" I asked. "Xavier's right. I can't control my gifts, but even if I wanted to help, how would I?" I swallowed hard before I continued, "There aren't others like me. I'm the only one of my kind. How would I help to stop a global attack by myself?"

Presley didn't seem surprised by what I said.

I had to wonder if he already knew. Did he know everything already about Xavier, Axel, and me as well? No, he couldn't. The only rumor that had gone around about me was that I killed two vampires, not how I did it nor the fact I'm mated to two wolves.

"We have a private facility," he replied. "You'd be taken there, and we'd be able to examine your gifts."

"Examine?" I asked.

Beside me, Axel shook his head vehemently. "He means you'll become a lab rat," Axel seethed.

My arm twitched as I picked up a burst of energy coming from him.

"Why do you need to test her abilities in a lab?" Axel took a step forward. "If you want her help, she'd join your team. She'd use her powers in the field to offer help. How will running tests on her solve anything?"

Presley's brows furrowed.

"There is a better and faster solution," Axel went on. "Get your people to stop hunting werewolves! Here's a history lesson for you. Werewolves were the ones to eradicate vampires before. If you morons let up, we'd be able to do it again. What do you think will happen if you kill the vampires' main rival, huh?"

Presley inhaled deeply, irritation evident in his features as he too, stepped forward. "Thanks for the history lesson, but you said it yourself. She can't control her powers. She'd be taken to a private facility to train. Being on the field with us means she'd have to know *how* to work alongside us. We'd need to know how her gifts work and understand how they can be incorporated with our plans and resources in order to maximize her impact." He unclasped his hands from behind his back. "As for making demands to cease killing werewolves, I can't do that."

The sensation in my arm grew as Axel clenched his fists. "And why is that?"

"I don't have the authority. I'm in charge of the P.E.A, and that's all. I'm not in a position to make demands. I don't get a say in matters being handled by other departments."

"And we're not in a position to give up one of our own," Axel rejoined with a deep growl in his voice.

"Axel," I warned.

He kept his sharp eyes trained on Presley.

The two men by the door stepped forward.

Natalie stood up from where she had been seated.

They stared at her with narrowed eyes as she blocked their way to Presley before turning to watch Xavier as well, who stepped forward, no doubt in case they attacked Natalie.

"We only need her help and that's all," Presley explained. "I get that you're angry about your people being killed and that you don't trust us, but we're all dying out there. Vampires are killing everyone, and my job is to work on killing them." He raised his hand to point his finger at me. "Behind you stands the only solution I currently have. You say there is only one of her, but are you sure of that? If we're able to test her blood, her genes, maybe we can locate others. We'd stand a chance in this fight with powers like hers on our side. Testing Ruby to see if her powers might be useful shouldn't be a problem. She'll be helping to save lives."

"It shouldn't be a problem?" Axel enunciated slowly, his voice low.

I closed my eyes and grimaced as the tingling in my arm started to change. I raised my hand to wipe away sweat from my forehead and my heartbeat spiked as I realized what was happening. I looked at Mathieu as he stared at me. Then I winced as I heard Axel's deep growl.

His claws had pierced through his fingers.

Presley's eyes widened as Axel's fangs elongated.

Axel's energy, his anger, was affecting me. I stepped back and away from everyone as I gritted my teeth to try and hold back what was building up inside me. Why had Axel's anger affected me? Whatever was happening to me right now wouldn't be a shock wave, and I sent a petrified look Mathieu's way.

"Axel! That's enough! Calm down!" Mathieu thundered.

I jumped as his baritone voice echoed throughout the room.

Axel stepped back and retracted his claws.

The level of dominance Mathieu had used was only making me feel worse. I gazed down at my hands and whimpered as I saw how red they looked. The blue veins at my wrist turned red, and my eyes widened. I was sure that hadn't happened the last time.

"Ruby?" Natalie whispered, "Are you okay?" She took a step towards me.

I looked up quickly and stepped back as I held both my hands on my chest. "Don't!" I cried.

Natalie froze.

I looked directly at Axel. "Stay back, all of you."

His fangs vanished and his rage died as his face twisted with concern. He and Xavier shared a look.

I turned to Presley.

He stared at me with shock, fear, and fascination all rolled into one. "What's happening to her?" He hesitated. "Is she losing control?"

"Trust me," I answered through clenched teeth, "you better pray I'm not. I suggest you all stop the fucking arguing. Going or staying is my decision!"

The temperature in the room spiked.

Axel stepped towards me cautiously. "Come with me, Ruby." He held his hand out towards the door.

I swallowed, suddenly feeling parched. I moved towards Axel, maintaining a safe distance from him as I went by him to go through the door. Now would be the worst possible time for me to have a meltdown. I sent an apologetic look to Xavier.

Axel closed the door behind us. "Let's take a breather, okay?"

We made our way up through the house.

It took a few minutes, but I managed to get my powers back under control.

Axel remained by my side in silence as we stood on the second floor's balcony. The full moon hanging low above us, coupled with the cool night's wind, created the perfect environment for me to calm down.

Ever since I met Xavier and started to become comfortable with his pack, I realized I had a deep love for nature. Now that one of my powers was the ability to detect and maybe use the energy in things around me, my bond with the earth had only grown stronger.

As Axel and I headed back downstairs, I wondered if this ability was evolving. At first, I had been able to sense the energy within the earth, trees, and another person, like I had while Axel was chasing me. However, it didn't affect me directly. Yet, just now, Axel's energy caused a physical reaction in me. It was as if my powers had been awakened by his energy.

I was able to use my own energy as a weapon when I forced it from my body. What if I was able to absorb and use energy from the earth, trees, flowers, animals...even people?

The house was alive with whispers and hushed conversations. No doubt, everyone was on edge since there were human men with guns casually hanging around.

Axel and I walked into the living room, and everyone fell silent. They glared at me, and I ground my teeth as I stood my ground.

A few people finally looked away as they continued with their conversations.

"I'm truly loved around here," I mumbled sarcastically to Axel.

When he didn't reply, I looked at him to find him staring daggers at a group of men whispering among themselves.

I frowned as I bumped his arm with mine. "Hey, is everything o..."

He walked off before I was able to finish my sentence. "Say it again!" he thundered to the men.

The room fell silent again.

The men stood up straight as Axel stood in front of them.

I looked around, confused about what was happening until I realized what Axel had said. Those men must have been talking about me.

"You heard what we said, so we don't need to repeat ourselves," one man said as he crossed his arms over his chest.

Axel stepped forward and this time when he spoke, his voice was low and somehow more intimidating than when he had yelled, "Say it again."

Another man snorted, as he looked Axel up and down. "You don't belong here. Stop walking around here like you're the alpha for us. You should leave and take that *thing* with you too."

"What the fuck did you just call me?" I yelled. A hand came down on my shoulder. I whipped around, ready to tear the person a new asshole for touching me and found Xavier looking down at me. I calmed instantly.

His eyes darted away from mine, as they turned black. He stepped around me and into the room.

Several people stepped out of his way.

I wasn't feeling his energy, but I didn't need to with the clear dominance within his walk. "A thing...is that what she is?" he asked slowly and calmly, his voice dangerously low.

The wolves that had been whispering didn't answer.

"I asked a question... is that what Ruby is? A thing? Aren't we all considered 'things' to humans and some other supernaturals? Hmm? No one here has the right to judge Ruby for being different. A werewolf born alone without a pack or knowledge of what they were would be exactly like she is now. Be thankful that you have a pack around you and show some compassion for the fact that she doesn't." His shoulders rose and fell as he inhaled deeply. "Apologize to your Luna," he ordered. "Apologize!"

The men glared at me, their jaws tightly clenched. All mumbled an apology.

Xavier turned around to face me as Natalie, Mathieu and General Presley entered the room.

"Someone here betrayed us," Natalie announced.

Now, the room was overtaken with whispers.

Axel and Xavier walked back over to stand beside me.

Natalie went on, "The humans found us because they were told about our location."

"A mind link will be done tonight to find who this traitor is," Mathieu added. "These are dark, confusing times, but we're the Blackmoon Pack. We remain strong through our reliance on each other and our loyalty to the pack. We have to be able to count on one another and trust each other. If we can't stand together as one, we will fall." He glanced over at General Presley. "Our pack might have been attacked tonight on a full moon because someone here betrayed our location and put everyone at risk." Now he gazed at the men in the room. "I know some of you recently started to question whether I have been acting in the best interest of the pack. Rest assured, the pack's safety is my number one priority, and every decision I have made has been with the pack's security in mind. Yes, Ruby has the power to kill vampires, which means she has a power that none of the rest of us do. Her power will help to save us all. I know tensions are high right now, but Ruby is one of us. She deserves our support and respect. Whoever was angry enough to reveal our location, step forward now, and you will not be punished."

I'd never been lucky enough to hear Mathieu speak to his people, but the sincerity, respect, and love in his voice explained why he was so loved and had one of the largest packs. I felt a tug on my heart as I stared at Mathieu, but then I caught Presley staring at me. I narrowed my eyes at him.

Presley looked away.

No one stepped forward.

Mathieu nodded to Natalie to proceed with the mind link.

Presley stepped back. No doubt, he wanted to see what was about to happen but from a safer distance.

I was surprised Mathieu was allowing him to see this. Even so, I dismissed him from my mind because I was too curious about what was about to happen. I'd never seen Natalie do a mind link on the entire pack.

She rolled her shoulders and exhaled as she closed her eyes.

Everyone in the room did the same. The house, crammed top to bottom with wolves, was silent enough to hear a pin drop.

When Natalie reopened her eyes, they were as white as snow. Everyone else's eyes opened, but they remained still as Natalie's eyes started blinking rapidly. It went on like that for a few minutes. Suddenly, she took a deep breath and staggered slightly.

In a blink, Xavier was there to support her.

Around the room, many people began groaning and pressing their fingers into their temples.

I knew how they felt. Mind links could be draining and even

painful at times. Having someone rummage around your thoughts and memory was as unpleasant as it sounded.

"Where is she?" Natalie yelled, the tips of her ears turning red, as she grew angry. "Where is she?"

A deep growl echoed through the room and several people from the center of the crowd were backing away.

Suddenly, from out of nowhere, a wolf flew through the air, knocking others over in the process. It charged me at full speed with sharp white canines bared.

Everything happened so quickly I could barely process it. As Mathieu grabbed me and pulled me behind him, a loud pop echoed through the room.

The wolf fell to the ground, motionless.

All eyes turned to Presley, who had his handgun raised. "It is only a tranquilizer," he reassured us as he placed the gun back into his holster.

I stepped around Mathieu to see the wolf. I watched as the unconscious wolf began to shift into Anna. Although there were plenty of people in the pack that I knew would love to see me disappear for good, I wasn't surprised that Xavier's ex-girlfriend was the one who ultimately revealed our location to the humans. She hated me from the very start, and everything that had happened since had done nothing to improve the situation or our relationship.

"Amazing," Presley remarked, clearly fascinated.

Randoll stepped forward and covered Anna's naked body with his jacket.

"Lock her up," Xavier told him.

Randoll picked up Anna none too gently and left the room.

I watched Randoll carry her away, and my shoulders fell dejectedly. Even though she was a world-class asshole, I felt terrible. To be clear, I didn't feel bad because she was a traitorous bitch. I felt bad because I knew she placed the entire pack at risk as a result of her hatred towards me. Once again, my presence had a negative impact on the pack. I sighed. Logically, I knew it wasn't my fault, but I couldn't help but feel responsible.

Mathieu placed his hand on my shoulder. "You need to come with me."

I leaned my head back somewhat to look up at him. I looked at Xavier and Axel, who were watching me.

Axel looked as concerned as I was about Mathieu randomly wanting to speak to me, while Xavier looked almost apologetic.

"Why?" I asked.

Mathieu removed his hand from my shoulder and gave me a stern look before walking away.

I felt like I was in trouble. I also knew whatever Mathieu had to say to me wouldn't be to my liking.

If I was truly a part of the Blackmoon Pack now, he was my alpha too. I followed behind him obediently as my heart hammered in my chest.

CHAPTER SEVEN
MATHIEU

I took Ruby to the small office I'd created for myself. She walked in ahead of me and I closed the door behind before crossing the room to my makeshift bar.

Ruby paced as she quickly pulled her hair into a ponytail.

I poured her a glass of brandy.

She hesitated as I handed the glass to her, her green eyes looking up at me with more pain than any woman her age should have. Her fingers wrapped around the glass slowly as she stared into the glass almost thoughtfully before putting it to her lips. She took a sip and then downed it all in one gulp. She shook her head and gave the glass back to me before sitting down.

I smiled at her as I took the glass back. From the moment I met her, Ruby had impressed me with her courage. She had a level of bravery uncommon not only among humans, but supernaturals as well. Despite the non-stop pressure and stress she'd been under since the fateful day she'd discovered who Xavier *really* was, she still held her ground. Of course, she had her understandable moments of fear and doubt, but she never let it get the better of her. Most people would have folded by now.

Ruby was going through a strange transformation without any

information as to why it was happening or how it would progress. I need only imagine being a young transitioning werewolf all alone and without a pack to get a bitter taste of the pain she must be feeling. Xavier had been spot on with that reference.

Xavier cared for her deeply, and I could tell by watching them when they were together, the feelings were mutual for her. I didn't know how strong the physical feelings of the mate bond were for her, but the chemistry and affection between them was obvious. They might have gotten started on the wrong foot, but they were headed in the right direction now.

What Xavier didn't know was that his mother and I hadn't gotten along in the beginning either. Our mate bond had triggered upon seeing each other, but we had to learn to live with one another. Little flaws we both initially found annoying about one another eventually became unimportant as our love grew, and two years after the day we met, Xavier was born.

Xavier and Ruby reminded me of his mother and myself. Despite all that had happened and was happening, I'd been happy Ruby was mated to Xavier. Putting all the strangeness of a three-way interspecies mating bond aside, she was more than a human. She would strengthen us—this pack would be the first to evolve. I had skeptical thoughts about her in the beginning, but by now I knew Xavier had found himself a worthy mate.

Now, if we could just deal with the vampire threat, then we finally could get back to our lives. Yet, even if we did manage to vanquish the vamps for good, I knew the world wouldn't be the same after this. It would take time for the world to recover.

"How are you feeling?" I asked her.

She sighed deeply. "My powers weren't triggered by what just happened, if that's what you're worried about."

"But they activated when Axel was arguing with General Presley?" She nodded.

I'd noticed how close she'd been getting to Axel, and Xavier had too. What was surprising to me was that both Xavier and Axel didn't appear to have that burning flame of hatred between them anymore. It had happened so gradually, I doubt either of them had noticed. Had Ruby ended years of bad blood between our packs by being with them both?

At first, I thought Axel would surely reject her. Now, I knew he wouldn't. How a relationship would play out between all three of them, I couldn't begin to guess.

Ruby pinched the bridge of her nose. "Anna hates me so much that she risked everyone else's life."

"Anna hates everyone," I replied as I leaned on the edge of my desk. "She's always been a bitter girl. I think the only person she's ever cared about was Xavier."

Her hand fell away from her face as she stared at me. "He has that effect on people. It's impossible to dislike him for long. I should know. I certainly tried." She gave me a wry smile.

"The Xavier Effect seems to be working on Axel as well. He's another person that doesn't tend to play nice with others."

A blush crept onto her cheeks. "Going on the run together and being forced to work together in order to survive has caused them to look past the issues they had in the past."

"Or it's your doing?" I postulated.

She frowned.

"Axel could only fight the mate bond for so long," I added. "And so could you. Xavier and Axel are mated to you and not each other, but their shared love for you has changed them... and for the better."

She looked away, but her blush deepened. "Thank you for what you said back there," she replied after a moment, changing the subject.

My lips parted and then closed once more. She wouldn't feel so positively towards me when I told her the reason I wanted to talk to her. "You're my son's mate, the future Luna for this pack. You don't need to thank me. But..." I crossed my arms over my chest. "I need you to go with General Presley."

She got up instantly, her eyes wide with surprise. "What?"

"Ruby..."

She shook her head vehemently. "No, Mathieu. How could you say that? I don't care if he claims to be on our side. They will do to me what Olcan wanted to do."

"Olcan wanted to kill you, Ruby," I replied calmly. "Presley needs you. There is a difference."

"You're too trusting," she muttered.

I chuckled. "I trusted you, didn't I?" I asked pointedly.

She sighed as she moved away. She placed her palms flat against the wall and began pushing herself back and forth as if she was doing push-ups. Her hands fell to her side after a moment. She turned to look directly at me, her eyes glossy and filled with panic, though she kept a straight face otherwise.

"There is no other way, Ruby," I explained. "I would not say this to you if I felt like General Presley would hurt you. Besides..." I glanced over to the open window and the moon shining bright in the sky. "He's desperate. We've been protected here and have no idea how bad things have gotten out there." I looked back at her and stood up. "He came here for you. While things are calm now, it might not stay that way for much longer because he won't leave without you. In the end, if they can help you with honing your powers, maybe you'll be able to break through that barrier in your mind yourself."

"Plus, if I lose control, it's better I hurt them than you guys," she said jokingly. The sadness returned to her eyes as she hung her head. "I don't want to go with him, Mathieu. You might not have a bad feeling about this, but I do."

"Let me put it this way. He has the firepower to kill us all right now. His men are out there in the forest waiting. We'd still kill many of his men if it came to a fight, but the grim reality is there is a full moon. You know what that means. I'm not saying to trust him. I'm saying to trust me. You are indeed changing and changing into something strong... dangerous. Eventually, no one will be able to hurt you. Not vampires, not Olcan and the Council, nor even General Presley."

"What if I'm changing into something that will hurt you guys too?"

I walked over to her and placed both hands on her shoulder. "You're mated to one of us. We're your people. Focus on finding out what your powers are and how to control them. We can find out what you are later on down the line, and the same goes for your memories. We have to work with what we have at the moment. Okay?"

She swallowed hard and nodded. "Ok. I'll go."

Of course, it would be useful to understand how she knew Lovette and had access to the rest of her memories. Yet, if those memories didn't somehow show her what she was and how to control her powers, we would have just wasted a lot of time.

Her powers were growing stronger by the day, and that was what we need to focus on right now. If humans were coming to us for help, the situation out there must be dire. We would work with General Presley. By cooperating, hopefully we would build trust with the humans. In time, perhaps they would allow us to help them hunt our common enemy.

"I'll come with you," Ruby announced as we entered the room.

Presley released a sigh as if he had been holding his breath. "Good," he replied. "Thank you."

"Don't thank me yet. I'll leave with you, but I'm not leaving without Axel and Xavier."

I smiled and shook my head. I should have known she'd have her own terms.

Presley shook his head. "I'm afraid that won't be possible. My orders are to take you back and only you. My team doesn't hunt werewolves, but the people that hired me don't like anything supernatural right now. Except for you, of course," he added the last bit quickly.

Ruby stepped forward to stand inches away from him. "The people that hired you are killing the wrong supernaturals. They're idiots. They are killing the ones that can help them. This world belongs to us, too. The Blackmoon Pack has been protecting humans for generations." She pointed to Axel and Xavier. "I leave with them, or I don't leave at all." Her hands fell to her sides, and her voice was low when she next spoke, "Since you said you won't be leaving here without me, I will defend my family if you attack us. Understand this: I'm not affected by the full moon. Do you really want to risk pissing me off, General Presley?" She leaned forward and whispered, "I don't have any control, remember?" She stepped back and smiled widely, practically daring General Presley to cross her.

I glanced over at Xavier and Axel, unsurprised to see them gazing at Ruby with proud expressions on their faces. Several wolves were looking on with shocked expressions. I smiled.

"Okay," Presley replied after a moment. "Let's go." He paused to look at me.

I nodded as he walked out of the room.

Ruby glanced over at me as if asking if she had done well.

I nodded approvingly and winked at her.

"When did you become such a badass?" Xavier teased as he walked up behind her. He kissed the top of her head before placing his hand on my shoulder. "We'll be back soon."

I placed my hand on his shoulder and squeezed. "You have no other choice but to come back." I pulled him in for a hug, a rare action, but I needed to hold my son. While remaining positive was important, I knew there was no guarantee this would end well for all of us.

Ruby glanced at Axel and smiled before winking at me.

He smirked and left the room.

"Take care of each other," I advised as I released Xavier.

He took Ruby's hand into his.

"We will," the couple replied in unison.

————

Ruby

It took an hour for us to get to a town. I wasn't ready for what we saw.

I'd always been a fan of apocalyptic movies. There had always been something about a city in ruin with the heroes and heroines fighting to survive that seemed entertaining to me. Now, I was a part of something like that, and it wasn't entertaining at all. It was terrifying.

As we drove through the small town slowly, I looked from side to side in shock at the destroyed buildings, burnt cars and rubbish scattered everywhere. We were driving through what was now a ghost town with not a soul in sight. Then it hit me—a whiff of the repulsive stench I'd come to associate with vampires.

I looked over at Xavier on my right and then at Axel on my left.

Axel was busy staring out his window, his fists clenched.

The world was being destroyed piece by piece. Our car had to drive up onto the sidewalk because three abandoned vehicles were poorly parked in the middle of the road. I gazed around, a little frantic at the loud sound of tires screeching echoed outside.

I caught sight of a dog bolting across the road as the car behind us regained control. I sighed heavily and turned back around. "This is depressing," I said sadly.

"How do you think they feel?" Axel asked as he pointed through his window.

Sure enough, a man and a woman were sprinting, machetes in their hands. Their clothes were shredded. The car's light from behind ours illuminated them. I frowned at the dirt and blood caked to the woman's face as she watched us drive by.

"I can smell them," Axel observed. "It's faint, but I can smell them."

"I've recently come to understand," Presley shared from the front seat. "That vampires have a distinct odor that can be detected by supernaturals. I'm sure it won't surprise you when I tell you we humans have never observed a scent."

"No, humans wouldn't notice anything out of the ordinary. Vampires hunt everything with a bloodstream, yes, but humans are their primary source of nutrients. Mostly because they lack the ability to detect them. The average human wouldn't know a vampire stood right behind them until their fangs pierced the human's neck."

"You speak about us as if we're useless," the driver snapped.

My brows rose as Xavier and I shared a look. Clearly, Axel had hit a nerve.

"I didn't say your kind is useless." Axel exhaled and turned back to his window. "I'm simply stating a fact. I also said the *average* human. Smelling them comes in handy when trying to find them."

"They are everywhere now," Presley explained.

I sat up.

"I don't know what those two were doing out, but they took a big risk," he continued. "You look at this town, and you'd think everyone is just hunkered down indoors for safety, but most of the people are actually either turned or dead. "

Axel spoke again, "I don't think the vampires have thought this through. Yes, humans aren't their only source of food, but it would be stupid to wipe humans off the face of the planet. That's what will happen if they are all dead or turned."

"As plentiful as these vampires are," Presley replied. "It'll be years before they can completely wipe out the human race. Even so, a few days ago, we raided a coven and found sixty humans being kept as a food source."

"Oh," I whispered. "That makes sense then." I kept trying not to imagine the things those people must have gone through. They were being kept as food like cattle. The General's comment triggered a memory from the day I had burned the vampires. I remembered the vampire Rafael had offered to keep me as a pet. According to him, I'd be cared for, and I'd be his food source in exchange. I shuddered. "Those humans you guys found, were they being treated well, or were they in cages and such?" I inquired hesitantly.

"Cages, others were chained up in rooms. Why would you ask if they were being cared for?" Presley responded as he turned to look at me.

"A vampire I met said he'd take me as a pet. Were there any other humans there, ones that didn't seem like they were being treated too badly?"

Presley shook his head. "No. I doubt vampires know how to care for anything. They're savages."

"Not all of them," Xavier replied.

Presley scoffed. "They are all monsters." He turned around once more to say something else, but as he did so, the car in front of ours exploded.

Our vehicle stopped abruptly, sending me flying forward, but Axel quickly grabbed me.

"What the fuck was that?" Presley yelled.

As I looked up, a cloud of black smoke rose out of the fire.

"What the hell?" Presley said as he too, stared at the smoke as it swirled into the sky and vanished.

A shadow dashed by Axel's door. "That wasn't a vampire," he said.

I spun around, almost falling off the seat as the car behind us exploded as well.

"We need backup now! We have the asset, but we're under attack!" Presley yelled into his phone.

Our driver stepped on the gas. He swung around the burning car and sped up as Presley continued to yell into his phone. "What the hell was that? That wasn't a vampire?"

"I don't know, it was like smoke," Axel replied. "It could have been a demon."

"Just fucking great, now there are demons. Why would it attack us?"

Our car swung violently from left to right, and I hung onto the back of Presley headrest. "It could have been hired by someone to attack your team, or it's doing it on its own accord. Either way, demons aren't to be messed with, so I suggest driving faster."

"I'm going as fast as I can!" the driver yelled as he glanced back at us.

My eyes widened as the smoke appeared before the car. "Watch out!" I shouted.

The driver swung around and stepped on the brakes.

Again, I was thrown forward and was grabbed by Xavier this time.

"Fuck this," the driver hissed as he got out of the car.

"No!" I yelled.

It was too late. He was already outside shooting at the smoke. Of course, the bullets did nothing, as the smoke engulfed him and his body fell to the ground like a sack of potatoes.

Presley growled with rage, like he too, was a werewolf. "All my men are dead, all of them!"

I paused, however, because I could've sworn I glimpsed a face within the smoke.

Xavier reached over and grabbed Presley, who was trying to get out of the car. "Werewolves can't fight smoke, and we're not at full strength yet. You're human, so what can you do? We need to go!"

Presley ignored Xavier as he got out of the car.

Xavier followed and exited the car.

I slid out of the vehicle behind Xavier, and Axel followed.

It had become painfully obvious that we couldn't outrun this thing by driving, so our only option was to make a stand and fight.

I sank my nails into the palms of my hand as I tried to dig deep into myself and harness my power.

"Who are you? What are you?" Presley yelled as he raised his gun. "You just killed innocent men!"

The swirling smoke stilled for a moment.

I frowned.

We all watched as it began to coalesce somewhat.

I suddenly realized something as it charged at Presley. I ran forward and pushed Presley out of the way. "No!" I screamed.

The smoke heading to attack him on the ground—suddenly halted.

Xavier and Axel ran up to me, and I was yanked back by one of them. I shook them off, however, and pointed. "Look."

A man's body was starting to appear as the smoke came together to create a shadow.

My heart was beating so loudly, it hammered in my ears. I looked at the shadow up and down. "It's you," I blurted.

The shadow's head tilted to the side.

"What's going on, Ruby?" Xavier asked.

"It's him—the warlock Axel's witch friend recommended. Axel called him before we left."

The shadow stepped closer to us.

I narrowed my eyes. "You didn't have to kill them." For some reason, I felt like I'd seen this shadow before. I grabbed Axel's arm. "You!"

Xavier stepped in front of me.

I peeped around him as the shadow began to shimmer, and a man, a real man, appeared. He had black eyes, much like a werewolf, and red hair. We watched as he brushed his hands down the sleeve of his long black coat. "Hello, Ruby," he said pleasantly. "Nice to see you again."

I stepped out from behind Xavier.

The warlock's black eyes remained glued to me as I backed away from Axel and Xavier to move further away from him.

Axel held his hand up to the warlock as he took a step forward. "Stop. What's wrong with you? I'm Axel, the one that called you. You didn't need to kill those men."

A gunshot echoed, and the warlock staggered backward as Presley shot him and then again and again. Almost as if someone had pressed a slow motion rewind button, I watched as the bullets pushed themselves back out of his body and the holes in his chest healed. His hand shot out, and smoke engulfed Presley.

"No!" I yelled.

It was too late. Presley fell backward, and his gun fell from his hand.

"Don't worry," the warlock reassured me. "He's only unconscious. After all, you told me not to kill him."

"You bastard!" I screamed.

"Do you know this guy?" Xavier asked.

I turned to him to explain, "This is the guy who was inside my dungeon. The same one who was inside my motel room." My eyes narrowed at the warlock. "Were you the one that saved us when vampires attacked us? I know you've been following us."

The warlock smiled. "As I said, it's nice to see you again, Ruby. Shall we get going?"

CHAPTER EIGHT

RUBY

The awkward silence in the car was unbearable, for me at least. I kept my eyes glued to the warlock as he drove. Although he was busy driving, I knew he could feel my eyes on him. How could he not with the bad vibes I kept sending his way?

As soon as I heard his voice, I realized who he was. The deep tones of his voice contrasted with his somewhat soft features.

His hair appeared to be almost the same shade as mine, just slightly paler. Now that the darkness in his eyes had receded, his irises were chocolate brown. Though he must have been in his late forties, I saw no evidence of wrinkles, no doubt a result of using black magic to retain his youthful appearance. He might be handsome for an old guy, but I still didn't trust his ass.

"I'm not a threat, Ruby," he suddenly declared.

I rolled my eyes. "Well, we both know that's bullshit, since you actually threatened to kill me," I contended. I didn't understand his intentions at all. This man had threatened to kill me when he visited me in Axel's dungeon, so why had he bothered to save me when that vampire had almost drained me dry? Nothing made sense in this supernatural world.

The only reason I had gotten into this damn car in the first place was because Axel asked me to. Presley and his men were out of commission, and it wouldn't have been wise for us to stay out in the open. Xavier was already uneasy with asking a black magic user for help, so he shared my discomfort with the situation. He rode in the backseat with me while Axel sat in front with the warlock.

"What?" Xavier questioned, clearly puzzled. "How do you two know each other?"

"When Axel kidnapped me, this guy showed up in the dungeon where I was being kept. He knew about our mate bond and that it could never be discovered. His dislike for me was clear then, so I'm not sure what game he's playing now."

Axel looked over at the warlock angrily.

"I have no intentions of hurting Ruby now—you can trust me on that," the warlock quickly told him.

"How did you know about the mate bond?" Axel probed.

The warlock smiled. "I have my ways," he answered with a smirk.

I huffed in disgust. "Ways of being a creep, you mean," I muttered. "What's your angle? First, you wanted me dead. Now you're helping me... helping us. Why?"

He inhaled deeply and exhaled heavily. "Personal reasons drove me to say those things to you in that dungeon. At first, I thought a werewolf being mated to a human would only bring about heartache and pain. Now, however, I see that it's necessary."

"How so?" Xavier prodded him.

"Humans and werewolves will need to come together in order to defeat the vampires. What better way to prove werewolves and humans can work together successfully than a mate bond between the two species?" He shrugged his shoulders. "Besides, other supernaturals are staying out of this fight. Fighting the vampires separately won't do anyone any good. The vampires are turning more and more humans and supernaturals. If all supernaturals and humans stand together, we'll outnumber the vamps. It's a simple solution."

"Uniting all the species won't be an easy task," Xavier pointed out.

The warlock nodded in agreement.

The bastard hadn't even told us his name yet. I wouldn't be asking him though. I wouldn't want him to operate under the impression I was actually interested. Besides, Axel had been the one to call him, so he must know what this monster called himself.

I tilted my head to the side. On the other hand, maybe I should consider toning down my attitude. If he was a black magic user capable of helping me with the wall in my mind, he probably also had the power to make things easier on me in terms of paying the price for the dark magic. It was probably smarter to avoid giving him a reason to make it any harder on me than it needed to be. "It's not a bad idea, though," I interjected helpfully.

The warlock turned his head to the side, no doubt surprised I was agreeing.

Xavier looked over at me quizzically.

I shrugged. "What? You know it's not a bad idea, even though it came from him."

Well, I tried to be friendly, and that's what counts, right?

The warlock chuckled. "I like your spunk, Ruby. I always have. You have a backbone."

"Can you read minds?" I asked him.

"No, why?"

Fuck you, you motherfucking, red-headed, black magic using cocksucker!

I smiled innocently. "No reason."

"How did you know about our mate bond?" Xavier asked, refusing to let him get away with his previous vague non-answer.

Even though I sat in the back, the way his cheeks puffed out told me he was smirking yet again.

"Well," he drawled. "I used black magic, of course. Look, I

know everyone has questions, and I can answer a few of them. I can't do that right now, though. We need to get to my place as soon as possible. I need to focus on driving, if you all don't mind."

"I mind," I replied as he ran a red light. I would have been shocked if he had stopped, but I was even more surprised the stop lights were working.

"I know you do," he quickly countered as if he had been expecting me to say that. "But there is a full moon tonight, so you two gentlemen won't be much help if we're attacked. Fending off a vampire attack right now, especially if it came from more than one vamp… well, let's just say that wouldn't be ideal. Not even my magic is that strong." He glanced over his shoulder quickly before looking back at the road. "Unless you decided to help out, Ruby."

"Her powers don't work like that, Malcolm. You know that," Axel grumbled.

So, his name is Malcolm. Huh, he doesn't look like a Malcolm to me.

"Well, maybe she would feel inclined to help if a vampire attacked her, wouldn't you, Ruby?" he asked.

I didn't say anything because I was lost in thought. Something just seemed so familiar about Malcolm. It wasn't just the times we'd met in the past. It was in the way he spoke, his hand gestures, and the way he smirked as if he always knew something you didn't.

"You seem familiar," I murmured to Malcolm.

He nodded. "Yes, we just talked about that."

"That wasn't what I meant." I narrowed my eyes at him. "There's something about you that's familiar. It's like deja vu, but with just your face." I leaned forward somewhat. "I met you before, didn't I?"

"Before?" he repeated.

I slapped my hand on my thigh. I felt like something was just within my reach, but I couldn't grab it. It was the same feeling I always got when I tried to think past the last memory I had. The feeling I got whenever Natalie tried to access my past. "I met you before I met Xavier, didn't I?"

He didn't reply.

Axel looked over at him. "Did you?"

"Maybe," Malcolm answered vaguely.

Axel turned to face him now.

I wrung my hands with worry. If I had met Malcolm before our meeting in the dungeon, he must have known who I was before. "Tell me," I ordered through clenched teeth. "You met me before. Tell me who I was then. Who are you? Do you know what's happening to me?" My eyes widened. "Was it you that blocked my memories?"

"It wasn't me. I don't know what's happening to you, Ruby, but I'm not surprised something is," he declared.

I frowned.

Xavier voiced my thoughts before I could. "What's that supposed to mean?"

Malcolm sighed and pinched the bridge of his nose. He then combed his hand through his hair.

I watched him with growing anxiety. "Can you please tell me who you are? I *know* you."

"Trust me, you'll want to talk about this once we get to my place," he answered after a moment.

My heart skipped a beat. I clenched my fists as my vision inexplicably changed. Suddenly, I could see Xavier and Axel's energy, a bright wavy white color. Yet Malcolm's energy was black mixed with white. I blinked, and it was gone. I could still feel it though. Whenever my emotions became more intense, it appeared to trigger one of my abilities. It seemed safe to conclude my powers were closely tied to my emotional state.

Right now, I was feeling pretty anxious. The longer Malcolm took to answer, the more nervous I became. My hand began to twitch, and the lights on the dashboard started to flicker.

Xavier reached over to hold my hand, but I pulled away.

Malcolm looked down at the blinking lights on the dashboard.

Axel looked around at me. "Are you doing this?" he asked me.

My attention was still focused on Malcolm. "Tell me," I demanded again, my voice low. "I need to know."

Malcolm sighed heavily. "Fine. I should seem familiar to you, Ruby, but I had nothing to do with your memories being locked away. I didn't even know your memories were taken until I saw you much later after our first meeting, and you had no idea who I was. When we met originally, it was brief."

"None of that answers my questions!"

The car made a horrible sound.

Malcolm gripped the steering wheel tightly as the car swayed. "If I'm to tell you anything, you need to calm down!"

This man had some fucking nerve. First, he wanted to kill me. Then he saved my life—more than once, in fact. Next he admitted he possessed information about my past that Natalie and I'd been frying our brains in mind links for weeks trying to find.

Now he wants to hold out until we get to his house and has the balls to demand that I calm the fuck down until we get there? What the hell?

"Don't tell me to calm down! You have no idea what I'm going through right now! I want to know what you know—everything you know!"

The car bucked forward and stopped.

Malcolm slammed on the brakes. He turned around to face me. "You know me because I'm your father!"

Xavier

I wasn't the 'I told you so' type, but I so wanted to rub those words into Axel's face right about now. Malcolm hadn't told us the price for helping Ruby, but he had revealed something that might be worse than any payment he might have asked for.

Malcolm drove off again after dropping the 'I'm your father' bomb as if he hadn't just rocked Ruby's world. No one spoke as he drove.

Axel threw a look my way before looking at Ruby.

Her wide eyes hadn't left Malcolm since he'd revealed that he was her father.

Malcolm was a warlock who used black magic, but Natalie hadn't sensed magic like that within Ruby. What had he meant when he said he wasn't surprised she had powers? What had he done? Was his black magic the reason why Ruby was now developing powers?

"Stop," Ruby said softly. "Please stop," she said again, this time a little louder.

Seemingly ignoring her, Malcolm kept driving. His red hair, much like hers, swayed as he shook his head. "We can't keep stopping, Ruby. We can't be out here much longer. It's too dangerous," he warned.

This man couldn't be serious. How could he be so oblivious right now? Then again, I had sensed it from the moment I'd met him—an emptiness about him. After all, he had threatened to kill her—his very own daughter.

"Stop the fucking car!" she screamed at the top of her lungs.

Again, the lights on the dashboard began to flicker.

I reached out and gently placed a hand on her thigh as she hunched forward and held her head with a moan. "Ruby, listen to me..." I whispered to her.

She only smacked my hand away. When she looked up at me, a tear fell from her eye. "Stay away from me," she directed through clenched teeth. Her eyes then drifted to Malcolm. Her face twisted with pain as she stared at him. "Stop! Stop! Let me out! Stop! STOP!"

Suddenly, we all rushed to cover our faces as the glass in

Malcolm's window shattered to pieces. The car swayed and then skidded to a halt.

Ruby jumped out of the car quicker than I was able to grab her. "Ruby!" I yelled after her.

Axel jumped out of the car to follow her.

I opened my door and Malcolm did the same.

As Ruby ran towards the forest, a cloud of smoke pulled her back.

I grabbed Malcolm's arm and pushed him back against the car. "Let her go!"

After a brief moment of hesitation, he retracted his magic.

Ruby spun around to face us.

"We don't have time to go chasing after her in the woods!" Malcolm exclaimed.

"You piece of shit!" Ruby shouted.

When I looked back at her—I deliberately did a double-take. I blinked my eyes rapidly as I wondered if something was affecting my vision.

Her eyes were flashing from black to green. It was the same black as her father's or mine, the black of supernatural power. It represented yet another new manifestation of her growing abilities.

When Axel stepped forward, she pinned him with a glare that could freeze water. "Stay away from me," she whispered. Although she spoke at a quiet volume, the threat and anger in her voice were unmistakable. She looked over at Malcolm. "You're my father. If you've changed your mind about wanting to kill me, why not reveal yourself and tell me what I am? Tell me who I am! You've been lurking around while my life was being ruined!" Her eyes changed to black and remained that way. As her voice rose in volume, her scent grew stronger. That sweet aroma would draw vampires to us very soon. Her head twitched, and she winced as she held her head. "It hurts," she groaned.

Axel took another step towards her.

Malcolm stopped him.

"What's happening to her?" Axel demanded.

Malcolm moved towards her slowly. "I shouldn't have told her I'm her father. She was getting worked up already but..." He sighed, as he looked her up and down. "It was time to tell her the truth."

Ruby snorted as the wind began to pick up around us. "It was time to tell me the truth, huh? You've had many chances to tell me the truth—countless maybe! You might have saved me from this entire fucked up situation if only I had known the truth. You could have answered so many questions I needed answered. I didn't need to have Natalie hammering inside my head! No, you weren't interested in telling me anything! You preferred to resort to killing me—your own daughter! What did I ever do to you, huh?" She pressed her finger into her temple. "Who blocked my memories? What's my real name?"

"Your real name *is* Ruby. I know you're angry, and you have every right to be. But listen to me... we can't stay here much longer. Just come with me, come with us, and I'll—"

"Fuck you!" She screamed as her gorgeous red hair swirled around her, though no wind blew to whip it up.

I looked closer and realized her hair was actually floating, almost as if she was submerged in water.

"You're lying, and I'm not getting into that car! You're not my father. You can't be."

Malcolm took another step closer to her. "I am your father, Ruby. It's the truth. I can prove it, and I can help you get your memories back. I'll tell you everything you want to know. I just need you to calm down!" He held his hands up. "I won't hurt you. Do you honestly think Axel and Xavier would let me? I can feel your magic, Ruby. It's unstable, and you're losing control. Just breathe for me."

Axel leaned his head back and inhaled deeply before looking my way. "They're coming. I can smell them."

I turned to Ruby and held my hands up.

When she turned to me, her features softened somewhat and her pitch black eyes glossed over with unshed tears. "Xavier," she pleaded in a wounded voice.

I nodded my head to her. "I know, babe, I know you're angry. You can smell them, can't you? Vampires are coming, and we don't know how many. We can't stay here. The stronger you get, the stronger your scent becomes."

She opened her mouth to say something, but hunched forward instead as she held her head. She began groaning in pain, and her body began to shake. When she stood up, her face was covered in sweat, and her eyes were squeezed shut. "Make them stop. It's too much!"

"What's too much?" I asked.

Her eyes opened a little and squinted, as if it was too painful for her to open them all the way. "Pictures, flashing pictures—I can see it all. I can see me." She held her head with both hands. "Xavier, make them stop!"

"Help her," I growled to Malcolm. This was his fault. After all, he could have told her something else, anything else, just to get her off his back until we had reached his house.

Malcolm, however, said nothing, as he looked her up and down. "I didn't know her powers were growing so rapidly," he whispered to himself. He kept staring at her as if she was an animal at a zoo. "How has she gotten this strong this quickly?"

I grew irritated. We didn't have time for this. She was in pain, and the more power she used, the harder it would be for her to calm down.

Axel yelled impatiently, "How about you keep your curiosity to yourself and fucking help her? We need to go!"

We stepped back swiftly as the ground around Ruby cracked.

"Shut up!" she shrieked, as the ground cracked further. "Stop talking about me as if I'm not standing right here." She raised her hand.

Malcolm was sent flying back against the car, enough to push the car away. He fell to the ground.

Ruby stepped forward as the ground beneath her feet continued cracking. "You abandoned me," she accused through clenched teeth, "Do you know how hard my life has been? I've had no one since the day I was born. I have no idea where I come from, nothing!"

Malcolm then got to his feet.

I watched as red lines began to spread up her arms, and Axel and I stepped back.

Not Malcolm—he stepped forward.

Crowding her wasn't helping. If we could've shifted, Axel and I might have been capable of subduing her. Unfortunately, that wasn't an option tonight. If she lashed out now, we wouldn't heal as quickly under this full moon. Trying to physically control her now—when she could burn us from the inside out—would be foolish.

"I didn't know about you, Ruby... not until it was too late. I didn't know I had a daughter. I didn't know you existed."

Ruby froze, and the air temperature around us started to rise precipitously. Suddenly, Ruby raised her hand toward Malcolm again.

This time, Malcolm's head quickly whipped to the side as if he'd just received a slap from an invisible hand.

I internally noted the odor of vampire stench growing ever stronger, and I prayed we could somehow get Ruby under control before we had a group of bloodthirsty vampires surrounding us.

I felt useless watching Ruby like this. I wished I could do something to help her, to calm her down. Ultimately, I understood this was something between a father and daughter. He was far more capable of helping her than me.

Malcolm faced Ruby, as his hand fell limply away from his cheek to reveal a long gash now visible across his face. After dripping blood that looked black instead of red, it began to heal quickly.

I'd always avoided black magic users in the past because I didn't trust them, so I guess it wasn't so surprising that I had no idea their blood was black.

When he'd been shot earlier, Malcolm had healed before he had even started to bleed.

I hadn't given much thought to it then, but it was just more evidence of what he was.

His eyes turned black, and his features hardened. The darkness I'd suspected lurking beneath his skin and hidden behind his soft-spoken voice revealed itself as he hissed at Ruby. "Fuck it."

Axel rushed forward to attack him.

I charged forward as well. I wasn't sure what he was about to do, but I felt like it wouldn't be anything good. His entire body turned to smoke as he passed through Axel and me. A cold chill surged through my body as he went through me. I glanced down at my hands to find that black smoke was making its way up my body from my feet.

I tried to turn but doing so took more effort than it should. The same was happening to Axel. When I finally managed to look Ruby's way, Malcolm held his arms wide, and she was covered in smoke.

"Ruby!" I shouted as the smoke began to vanish along with her. I couldn't believe what I was seeing. "Ruby!" My nostrils began to burn with the vampire's scent, but as I looked down at my body, the smoke now to my chest, I too was vanishing. A metallic taste sprang to my mouth as the smoke reached Axel's and my throat. Then I heard the loud hisses of vampires.

A male vampire ran out of the woods, his eyes blood red with his mouth open wide as he growled. The smoke engulfed my head, and the vampire passed right through me, as did another one that charged at Axel.

My vision started to blur, but I counted four other vampires before my vision went completely black. My sense of touch and sight was gone entirely, and I was surrounded by an impenetrable darkness. I strained my ears to listen for a sound, but I heard nothing. I also couldn't move my body with the exception of my hands. All I could do was clench my fists as my body started to move as if I was floating.

My heart hammered in my chest, but panicking wouldn't help me out of this place—wherever this was. The moment we made it out of this nothingness, I would be punching Axel in the balls for creating this mess by calling Black Magic Malcolm in the first place. At this point, I felt like we'd have been better off with the humans.

I landed suddenly with a loud oomph, and I heard Axel touch down with a satisfying thump somewhere nearby. I rolled to my side and got up quickly while shaking my head, the darkness in front of my eyes fading slowly. The first thing I noticed was the soft crackle of a fireplace.

When my eyes cleared, I turned to my left to find a healthy fire roaring in a massive fireplace. I quickly surveyed the rest of my surroundings—luxe black leather sofas, thick grey carpet, and three swords hanging above the fireplace.

Axel was scanning our new environment as well.

"Where are we?" I asked.

Axel shrugged. "I don't know, but we need to get out of here and find Ruby. I should never have trusted that fucker. Did we just teleport?"

The sound of boots approaching caught our attention, and we both moved into a fighting stance.

"Yes, you both just teleported," Malcolm explained as he rounded a corner, a glass of water in hand. He took a sip, waved his hand, and two other glasses of water appeared on the coffee table between Axel and me. "You both should drink something. You won't notice it until I say this, but you're both very thirsty."

I suddenly felt parched, as if I hadn't tasted water in a century.

If I had planned to reject his offer of water, there was no way I would now.

Axel and I dove towards the glasses. We finished our drinks in one long gulp, and the glasses magically refilled.

We finished them again.

"This water better not be poisoned," Axel grumbled as he downed his third glass of water before turning to Malcolm.

"Where is Ruby?" I asked as I stepped forward, the glass in my hand cracking as I squeezed it.

Malcolm raised his right hand. The glass in his hand fell and vanished before it could hit the ground. Our glasses vanished as well. "Ruby is fine, I assure you. No, Axel, the water wasn't poisoned. We couldn't stay out there much longer, so I had no choice but to ask for help."

I narrowed my eyes at him. "Ask for help? From whom?"

That smirk I so hated returned to his lips. "You'll find out soon enough." He held his arms out as his smile widened. "Welcome to my home. Come on, I'll take you to Ruby. She's still unconscious."

CHAPTER NINE

RUBY

I opened my eyes, and all I could see was white. I got up off the floor unsteadily, my body feeling as if all my energy had been drained away.

"What the hell?" I wondered aloud as I turned in a circle. I was in a white padded cell with no door. "Hello!" I shouted, but it sounded like my voice was only bouncing around the room.

"Hello!" I yelled again, as I started to panic.

The last thing I remembered was Malcolm coming at me and engulfing me in his black smoke. I stopped pacing as I remembered the vision I'd been having, the one with the wolves engulfed by black smoke and the cobra.

Maybe the black smoke in my vision was Malcolm. If so, what did the wolf and the cobra mean?

I pressed my fingers to my temples, massaging them as I felt a headache coming on. "Hello!" I shouted a little louder as I placed my hands on my knees. "Malcolm? I know you can hear me."

The sound of a door opening met my ears, and I spun around to find Malcolm staring at me with his hands in his pockets. "Have you calmed down?"

This man has some serious issues.

"You locked me in a padded cell. Let's see how much longer I'm going to remain calm if you keep me in here."

"Are you calm?" he asked once again.

I sighed deeply. "Yes. Where are we?" I questioned. "Where are Xavier and Axel?"

Malcolm stepped to the side and held his hand out as if gesturing towards an open door. "You're free to leave. You'll be able to see them."

I narrowed my eyes at him, but trying to read him was a waste of time. I stepped forward and walked past him indignantly. He was so high on my shit list right now I doubted he could ever work his way off of it, and I wasn't about to let him forget it.

In the blink of an eye, my surroundings changed completely. I suddenly found myself lying down on a comfortable bed in a spacious and brightly lit bedroom.

Axel and Xavier were both standing over me while Malcolm sat in a nearby chair with his legs crossed.

I sat up abruptly.

So I was sleeping the whole time?

I filed that away in my mind as I swung my legs off the bed. "You're a real piece of work, you know that?" I informed Malcolm.

He nodded. "So I've been told several times," he admitted with a chuckle. "You might have a headache for a while."

"Here," Xavier directed as he handed me a glass of water. "You don't feel thirsty, do you?"

The moment he said that to me, I instantly felt parched. I grabbed the glass of water from him and began chugging it down. I didn't think I'd ever been this thirsty in my whole life. I was about to ask for some more water when the glass filled up on its own. I narrowed my eyes at it and then looked at Malcolm. I wanted to reject the new glass of water, but I couldn't. "Why am I so thirsty?"

"The magic I used to teleport us here had its price. Let's just leave it at that," Malcolm responded.

I sent a confused look Xavier's way.

"The same happened to us," he informed me as he pointed at Axel and then himself. "How are you feeling?"

"My powers are under control." I smiled at him with a hint of embarrassment. "Sorry about it taking—wait, how long have I been out?"

"About an hour is all," Malcolm answered.

I handed the glass back to Xavier, but my face twisted at the pulsating pain in my head. "Why is my head hurting so much?" I questioned.

Malcolm got up and left the room.

As I watched him leave, I had a brief vision of the shadowy snake's beady eyes. I felt a sudden chill and it was gone as Malcolm closed the door.

I hate snakes.

I still can't believe he's my father. How could he be? Why would he lie about something like that? Other than his red hair, there wasn't anything else that showed any kind of family resemblance. I looked around the room at the black and dark red theme while narrowing my eyes. I eyed a painting beside the door that looked like blood running down a window and puckered my lips thoughtfully.

Okay, we had the same taste in terms of décor color, but that didn't mean anything.

Did it?

I wasn't sure how to feel. He was my father, but I felt nothing towards him. Well, nothing *good* towards him. I did feel something though... anger and confusion. He had explained why he changed his mind about wanting to kill me, but why had he wanted me dead to begin with? How could he, especially knowing that I was his flesh and blood?

Had I done something so horrible even my own father hated me, and I just couldn't remember doing it?

"Ruby?" Xavier said, his dark eyes watching me with concern.

I looked up at him.

"Did you guys get headaches too?" I inquired.

Xavier shook his head.

"No," Axel responded. "I'm not surprised you did, though. You certainly put on a show earlier, Red."

I gave him a tight-lipped smile. "Yeah, I guess so." When my powers were triggered earlier, it seemed the angrier I got, the more I felt the energy. The more I felt the magic, the more I wanted it. I felt powerful, more powerful than I ever had in my life. It actually felt amazing.

Something about it was also scary, though. What if my power controlled me, instead of me controlling it? What if I gave into that euphoric feeling and became addicted? After how good I had felt when I used it last time, a part of me couldn't wait until I used my magic again. Becoming addicted seemed possible. "I've never felt anything like that," I whispered. "I felt in control. I felt unbeatable —right up until Malcolm engulfed me in smoke and I couldn't see anything anymore, that is."

"Your eyes changed to black," Axel informed me. "They were black like Malcolm's and ours. I've never seen you do that before."

I frowned, as I looked his way.

"Same with the red veins running up your arms," Xavier added.

"I don't know about my eyes, but when my powers triggered during Axel and Presley's argument back at the house, I noticed the veins on my wrists were bright red," I told them.

"Here," Malcolm offered as he entered the room.

I stared at the brown liquid in the glass he was handing to me.

"It'll help with the headache," he said.

I arched a brow at him and hesitated.

He sighed and took a sip. "See, it's not poison. I don't want to hurt you, Ruby."

I took the glass from him. "So you keep saying." I pinched my nose before swiftly gulping down the unpleasant smelling concoction.

Malcolm returned to his seat across the room and explained calmly, "You were losing it and calling vampires to us in the process. Arguing with you was wasting time, so I acted. Now here we are. On the plus side, we were able to avoid two hours of driving. We can fight all you want here, but not out there, where we could be attacked at any moment."

I watched as a snake appeared from behind his chair to slither down his arm. I shot a meaningful look at Xavier and Axel before cocking my head in the direction of the snake. I was hoping they'd remember the vision I'd told them about, although the cobra in my vision had been significantly bigger. "Interesting pet choice," I mumbled before looking Malcolm's way. "Why do you have a pet cobra?"

"He's not a pet," he replied.

Axel stepped over to the bed and sat down beside me. "Why didn't Natalie sense magic like yours within Ruby?" he asked Malcolm. "If you're her father, it would explain her powers. I've never seen a warlock or witch with her abilities, though."

"That's because she doesn't have witch magic." Malcolm got up and moved away to turn his back to us. "You see... I wasn't born a warlock." He turned around to face us once more. "I was born human, like Ruby."

"I'm sorry, what?" Axel sputtered as he crossed his arms over his chest. "How did a human manage to acquire magic, especially strong black magic like yours?"

"Easy," Malcolm replied with a shrug of his shoulders. "I tied my soul to a shadow demon."

My brows dipped as I frowned. "The cobra?" I guessed.

Malcolm nodded. "Yes, it's a shadow demon, not a pet cobra."

"Why would you do that?" I asked, bemused.

Malcolm smiled sadly.

I suspected it was the most genuine expression he'd shown since we'd met, or should I say... met again.

He returned to his chair and reclined in it, his finger pressed against his temple and a distant look in his eyes. "Your mother and I were in love."

My face dropped as I stared blankly at the mention of my mother. While I felt no connection to Malcolm, even hearing a mere reference to my mother had my heart beating a mile a minute. I didn't know who she was, but knowing I was about to find out sent my anxiety sky high.

"One day, she vanished." Malcolm's unfocused eyes were glued to the floor as if he was seeing something else entirely. "She left without a warning or note. She simply disappeared. It was years later when I got a lead on her location. By the time I got there, it was already too late. I found out she had been pregnant when she left me, and..." he paused as he stared at me. "...she died while giving birth to a baby girl."

I was shocked at the pain within his eyes. I placed my hand over my heart as it skipped a beat. Growing up, I had thought of so many possible reasons for how I had ended up an orphan. At one point, I even convinced myself that my parents must have been murdered. Eventually, I came to accept the idea that most likely, my parents just didn't want me.

Yet, in all those years of imagining plausible scenarios, I never once thought of the possibility I had killed my own mother. I swallowed har. While I could see in my peripheral vision that Xavier and Axel had turned to gauge my reaction, I couldn't look at either of them right now. I would burst into tears.

I had killed my own mother.

I kept my eyes on Malcolm and our gazes locked. "Is that why you wanted to kill me? Because I killed the woman you loved?" I couldn't find it in me to say 'my mother.' I was a child, a baby, but because of me, my own mother lost her life.

"No," he told me as he shook his head. "That's not why I

wanted to kill you." He placed his elbows on his knees as he leaned forward. "I wanted to kill you to prevent another human from falling in love with a wolf."

I was dumbfounded. "What?"

"Are you saying Ruby's mother was a werewolf?" Xavier asked, shock and disbelief evident in his voice.

It finally clicked.

I looked from Malcolm to Xavier and then back at Malcolm. "Is this true?"

"Yes," Malcolm affirmed.

I got up and walked away. I ran my hands down my head and hair, overwhelmed and confused by Malcolm's revelation.

Natalie had been sure I didn't have werewolf blood. According to her, my magic or blood was unlike any other supernatural creature she knew of. She probably had never come into contact with a hybrid werewolf-human child before, so that must be why she'd been wrong in her assessment.

"Yet, your mother was not an ordinary werewolf. She was an Enchanted," Malcolm stated.

I spun around to look him in the eye. I knew Enchanteds were descendants of the goddesses so did that mean...?

No... was I part human, part werewolf, and part demigod?

I held up my hands. "Hold on, just hold on, I..." I exhaled heavily. "...just slow down for a minute, okay? You said my mother was an Enchanted? What does that make me?"

Malcolm stood to his feet. "Yes, your mother was an Enchanted. She was a powerful one at that...an Elder, as I came to understand later. As for what that makes you, I can't—"

"Wait," Axel interjected as he pointed at Malcolm. "An Elder? You were in a relationship with an Enchanted Elder?"

Malcolm nodded, and from the look on his face, he knew what Axel was getting at.

This time, however, it didn't take me long to realize what was being said. I froze where I stood, praying Malcolm wouldn't say the name of the Elder I was thinking of.

"You're talking about Elder Lovette," Xavier concluded.

While it wasn't a question, Malcolm nodded.

I released the breath I'd been holding.

Malcolm looked my way.

I shook my head, telling him not to say it.

"Your mother was Elder Lovette."

I exhaled through my mouth slowly. In and out, I breathed, but my hands wouldn't stop shaking, and the tears wouldn't stop flowing. I clenched my fists and then my jaw as I held my head up. "Lovette is my mother, huh?" I pinched the bridge of my nose while nodding. "Okay," I swallowed and looked back at Malcolm. "How? I want to know everything from the start."

Malcolm rubbed at his eye uncomfortably.

I didn't care how this made him feel. "I need to know, and you said you'd tell me everything. I want to know about her—"

"I didn't know her as Lovette," he replied, suddenly cutting me off. "When I met her, she went by a different name. When she vanished, I searched everywhere for her, but it was pointless because the woman I knew didn't exist." He chuckled, but there was no humor in it. "Do you know how I found her? I was walking by what appeared to be a shady fortune teller's shop one day during the course of my search for your mother. The fortune teller opened the door the moment I walked by. She stopped me and announced she could help me find what I was searching for. Of course, I thought she was just messing with me. After all, how could she know I was looking for something? How would she have known to exit her shop the exact moment I was walking by?" He rubbed his hands together before placing them palms down on the handles of his black wingback chair. "It turned out that the shady fortune teller was actually a real witch. She helped me to find what happened to Lovette. Unfortunately, by then it was too late. You had already been born, and she was dead. I was in a three year long relationship with the Grand Elder of a species I didn't even know existed. She died, and I realized I never really knew her at all."

For the first time since meeting this man, this warlock... my father, I felt sorry for him. I looked at Xavier and didn't even want to imagine the pain I'd feel if I lost him.

Things had changed so much in our relationship that now... I even felt the same about Axel. He'd more than proven himself to me. Although I was closer to Xavier than I was with him, losing Axel would be just as painful.

Malcolm was feeling the pain of knowing Lovette and losing her, even if he had only known the version of her that she'd been able to show him at the time. I didn't know her at all, but knowing she had died because of me and that I wouldn't meet her the way I'd met Malcolm was like suddenly having a wound that might not ever fully heal. The pain would always be there, dull and aching.

"The witch couldn't locate you, Ruby," Malcolm went on. "So I took matters into my own hands. The witch told me progeny resulting from a human and Enchanted relationship was unheard of, especially one from an Elder. She believed it must have been why Lovette died and that you couldn't have survived either, but I couldn't give up there. I needed to know if you were alive or not. Desperate and out of options, I finally asked a demon for help. Tying myself to the demon was the price to find you, and I paid it. You were all I had left of Lovette."

"Then why did you want to kill me?" I asked, still confused. I felt I'd asked this question too many times already. "Why? You don't hate me because Lovette died giving birth to me, so what? What did I do?"

"I watched over you for years. Then everything changed for me when you met Xavier." Malcolm looked at Xavier and shook his head. "I couldn't let what happened to Lovette and me happen to you too. Humans and werewolves don't mix. I thought if your bond were ever discovered, some other werewolves might think being with a human would work out. They'd look for their mates not only just among wolves, but also among humans too." He stared at Axel and then me. "What would happen when more and more humans learned about werewolves? It'd be only a matter of time before they discovered witches, warlocks, demons, and all other manner of supernaturals out there." He held his hands up and dropped them back down on the arms of his chair. "I knew it would mean chaos and death, and I wasn't wrong. It ended up happening anyways, it just had nothing to do with your mate bond, Ruby. I..." He sighed deeply. "As selfish as it might sound, I thought you'd be better dead than to be the cause of a war between humans and supernaturals."

"I don't know," Axel replied as he shrugged. "Maybe this is just me, but I feel like there were plenty of other options you could have thought of other than killing her." His condescending tone came out crystal clear as he dug his hands into his pockets.

Xavier's head bobbed in agreement.

I didn't know what to say. I stood there quietly, Malcolm's words still repeating in my mind about Lovette, the demon, and his reason for wanting to kill me. He had tried to protect me, but his means of doing so were twisted. I took a deep breath and walked back to the bed to sit down. I sat there as the silence within the room stretched on.

"Natalie checked Ruby," Axel suddenly announced. "And she has no traces of werewolf or Enchanted magic. Lovette couldn't have been her mother."

I looked away from the spot on the floor that had held my attention as my mind wandered.

"Trust me, she is," Malcolm insisted. "There are puzzle pieces still missing, but Ruby is most definitely my daughter. This means her mother can't be anyone else other than Lovette. Yet, the powers Ruby has didn't come from Lovette or me. That means I need to know what's hidden in her mind as much as you three do."

Natalie and Reika had insisted they had seen Lovette within my memories, and she had been crying. *Maybe I had indeed met*

Lovette, but how? How could I have a memory of a woman who died when I was born?

"I can do the spell now, if you're ready," Malcolm offered.

While they spoke, I kept staring at the locked door.

"What's the price?" Xavier questioned cautiously.

"Just blood—her blood. I'll be doing blood magic, so that'll be all," Malcolm explained.

"I'm ready," I said softly. I was already overloaded with information, but I couldn't wait any longer to know what happened in my past. I had to know.

Malcolm got up. "I just need to gather a few things. I think it would be best if we do this in the living room." He left us alone.

No one spoke.

Neither Axel nor Xavier said anything to me.

I felt grateful for the silence. The last thing I wanted to be asked right now was if I was okay. I didn't want their sympathy or their pity.

We walked to the massive living room in silence.

The cobra locked in an enormous glass cage caught my attention immediately. I studiously avoided looking into its eyes, particularly now that I knew it was a demon.

Within the middle of the room was a large circle drawn with white chalk. There were symbols and writing I didn't recognize within it. At its center sat a small black bowl.

"Please step inside the circle," Malcolm instructed me politely.

I looked at Xavier and then Axel, like a child being told to do something but needing approval from their parents.

Axel moved a strand of my hair behind my ears, and Xavier nodded reassuringly.

I inhaled deeply and held my breath as I stepped into the circle.

"Stand at the center, Ruby," Malcolm directed.

I released the breath I was holding and did as he told me.

He stepped into the circle as well.

I did a 360 turn as the red candles outside the circle lit on their own. I turned back around to face Malcolm.

Without warning, he grabbed my hand and sliced my palm with a knife.

I screamed and tried pulling away, but his hold on my hand tightened.

Axel and Xavier stepped forward as Malcolm held my clenched fist over the black bowl.

I grimaced as I watched my blood drain into the container.

After a moment, he forced me to open my palm, and he waved his hand over mine.

I marveled at how the wound had completely vanished as if it had never been there at all. I still pinned Malcolm with a glare as he twirled my blood around in the bowl. "You could have warned me," I snapped at him.

He didn't seem to care as he merely kept gazing into the bowl. "My way worked better," he replied calmly.

I took the time to observe him more closely. When he looked at me, I realized his pupils weren't round but instead had a slight elliptical shape—similar to a cat or snake, but more subtle.

He released his grip on the bowl.

My hands shot out to catch it before it fell. However, it remained effortlessly suspended in the air, and I gave Malcolm a dead stare. I opted for saying and doing nothing while I watched as he pressed the knife into his palm and cut himself.

I frowned as his black blood poured in and the contents of the bowl began to bubble.

He rubbed his fingers against his palm, and the wound vanished just as mine had. He plucked the floating bowl out of thin air.

I tried to keep a straight face as he drank the bubbling liquid. I swallowed hard. My mouth turned downward in disgust as he closed his eyes as if he enjoyed the taste.

When his eyes reopened, they were as black as a starless night sky.

This time when he dropped the bowl, I only watched as it fell instead of trying to catch it.

Again, without warning, Malcolm grabbed my head roughly with both hands.

When I gazed into his eyes, I gasped as the world around us fell away, replaced by a hospital room.

His hands dropped from my head, and I surveyed my surroundings.

Frantic nurses were running around like headless chickens.

A woman's piercing scream rang through the room, as Malcolm stepped forward, his black eyes wide. "Lovette," he mumbled under his breath.

I looked at the crying woman on the table.

Her pure white hair looked matted in some areas and tangled in others, her face covered in sweat. Her cheeks were bright red from exertion as she bit down and groaned in pain.

"Mom," I whispered under my breath as I stepped towards her.

"Just one more push, one more big push!" the doctor between her legs yelled.

As Lovette screamed, the lights and equipment started to flicker.

"She's doing it again!" the nurse to my right shouted.

"Focus!" the doctor admonished. "If this baby doesn't come out soon, they will both die. She's lost too much blood!"

My heart kept hammering in my chest, my palms sweaty and my knees growing weak. I never in a million years imagined I'd watch my own birth. Here I was though, staring at my beautiful mother and the pain she suffered to give birth to me.

I looked away when Lovette pushed and screamed. Looking back again, I saw the top of a baby's head crowning.

However, Lovette stopped pushing and fell back onto the bed, panting. "I can't," she moaned as she shook her head from side to side.

"I love you so much," Malcolm said.

When I looked back, he was trying to hold Lovette's hand, but his hand only passed through hers like smoke.

"The baby's heartbeat is dropping fast!" a nurse yelled.

The doctor cursed loudly. "We have no choice, Ms. Lovette, we have to do a C-section."

A loud alarm blared in the room, and the nurses went into a frenzy.

"We're losing them! Both of them!"

I felt panicked. The urge to jump in and help caused my fingers to tingle. I looked over at Malcolm, surprised to see a black tear rolling down his cheek.

He was breathing hard, his shoulders rising and falling rapidly.

I wasn't sure if time had jumped forward, but the room went quiet, as all the nurses and the doctor were just staring at Lovette and a bundle wrapped in her arms.

The baby was still.

When Lovette moved the blanket away and picked up the baby's hand, it looked pale, deathly pale. Lovette sobbed weakly.

I swiftly walked around to the side where the baby was and felt shocked to my core at what I saw.

I was dead.

"How? I-I don't understand," I said as I looked to Malcolm for answers.

He looked back at me with the same confusion.

"I died?"

"You will live," Lovette said weakly.

Her sweet singsong voice sounded like music to my ears.

One of Lovette's tears fell onto my little forehead. "Save her, save her, and not me."

My eyes stung as I suddenly started to cry.

"Oh my god, the baby's alive!"

I stepped closer to see myself as a baby, face red as I cried.

Lovette smiled weakly, her eyes now barely open. "I'm sorry. Your life will—will be hard, my beautiful girl. But—you'll save— so many lives." Lovette's head fell back and she flatlined.

I felt sick as this all unfolded in front of me.

"Lovette!" Malcolm yelled, but his multiple attempts to grab her were futile. None of this was real. There was a time many years ago when it had been, but right now, it was all a memory.

Tears rolled down my cheeks as the doctors tried to save Lovette, but she was dead.

I started bawling as I held my head. "Enough! Enough! I've seen enough."

Malcolm wasn't listening to me. He was lost in the memory, his eyes wide with his cheeks black from his tears.

"Malcolm!" I screamed. "I can't watch her die! Stop this, stop!" I pressed a nail into my wrist and winced as blood sprang to the surface.

We both woke up abruptly, and I looked around the room frantically before rushing out of the circle.

"No!" Malcolm roared, and the cobra in the cage began to hiss loudly. "No! I need to go back!" He rushed at me.

I waved my hand, sending him flying back. "I hate you!" I ran from the room, ignoring Axel's and Xavier's call.

All I could think about was how it felt to watch the life leaving my mother's eyes.

CHAPTER TEN
AXEL

I found Ruby sniffling and wiping her tears away in a room filled with animal wall hangings. I flinched as I saw the taxidermied wolf heads and furs, but at least they belonged to normal wolves and not werewolves.

Malcolm is one sick fuck.

While I could sympathize with him and his pain of losing Lovette, that was as far as it went. He had wanted to kill Ruby because he didn't want her to experience what he had, but that wasn't his decision to make. Everyone's life was filled with mistakes, poor choices, small victories, and everything in between. It was all theirs and theirs alone to face.

We all get help on our life's journey, but killing someone to avoid something we *thought* might happen to them was ridiculous. I understood the chain reaction he had spoken of, but there were so many ways to prevent that.

The epic interspecies war he wanted to kill Ruby in order to avoid happened anyways and was much worse than he had imagined. The girl he had wanted to kill now actually had the power to destroy the ones who started this war.

"Ruby?" I said as I approached her.

Her sniffling stopped and she stiffened, as if she'd just now heard me come into the room.

"Talk to me, Red." I walked around the sofa to face her, and my heart dropped at the sight of her bloodshot eyes.

Her face was soaked with tears. Her expression twisted with pain as more tears rolled down her cheeks.

My heart went out to her, and I dropped onto the sofa beside her to pull her into my arms.

As she sobbed, she clutched at my shirt as if her life depended on it.

The wall protecting my heart against her suddenly crumbled. I closed my eyes and kissed the top of her head as she cried. She felt so small in my arms, but I knew her small frame belied the size of her kind heart and luminous spirit.

Malcolm had vanished into the wall in a cloud of smoke after Ruby ran off, leaving Xavier and me to wonder what the fuck was happening. Xavier had wanted to look for Ruby, but I told him I'd find her and he needed to find Malcolm.

Finding her wasn't hard. Her scent was now hard to miss. Before leaving this place, Malcolm needed to make a potion to block her scent, or we wouldn't get a mile at night without being attacked by vampires.

I didn't have any idea where our next destination would be after this. Whatever alliance was created with Presley and his people was now nullified. I wasn't sure where to go from here.

Ruby pulled away from me and sighed as she wiped at her eyes.

I moved her hair back from her face. In the beginning, I judged her to be a weak human, unworthy of being my mate. Even though she cried in my arms now, I'd seen her strength and determination time and time again throughout this whole ordeal. "What did you see?" I asked her.

She closed her eyes for a moment. When she reopened them, they were glossy with fresh unshed tears, but she composed herself. "Lovette—I saw Lovette—she-she was giving birth."

She looked at me with such raw sadness my heart constricted as if I could feel her pain, and I reached out to caress her cheek.

"S-she was giving birth to me," Ruby went on. "She's really my mother."

I felt like there was more, so I said nothing.

Ruby swallowed and looked away, a distant look in her eyes as if she remembered something.

"I died," she stated.

I frowned. "What?"

She sighed. "I died. The delivery was a difficult one, and I—died." She turned to gaze my way again as her brows dipped with confusion. "She said, 'Save her, save her and not me,' and I—I came back to life."

I narrowed my eyes. "So, the doctors helped to bring you back or—"

"I just came back to life," she interjected.

My frown deepened.

A person coming back to life wasn't unheard of in the supernatural world. Still, it was extremely rare. Essentially it was giving life, something only gods and Necromancers did, and Necromancers paid a high cost for the privilege.

"That's strange, yes," I replied.

Ruby gave me a look that said 'no shit.' "She said something else. She said my life is going to be hard, but I'm going to save many lives. What do you think she meant by that?"

I shrugged. Maybe Lovette had known about the powers Ruby would develop. Perhaps, she had even known about the vampire invasion, but how? I knew Enchanteds had the ability to see the future, but I'd never heard of any who could see it so far in advance.

Enchanteds also didn't have the power to bring anyone or anything back to life. If Lovette wasn't able to save Ruby herself, then who had?

"I don't know," I replied. "But considering what's happening now with your vampire frying powers, I would say she wasn't wrong."

"She died right after she said that," Ruby murmured as she palmed her face. "I watched her die. She died because of me." She sniffled loudly.

I moved her hair over her shoulder. "No, she didn't," I told her and I acted without thinking as I kissed her shoulder.

She startled, her eyes wide as she stared at me.

I stared back at her, a little surprised at myself, but I didn't regret it. She was my mate and she always would be. So of course, I was attracted to her. Of course, I wanted to feel her skin on mine and her lips against mine, but she was Xavier's more than she was mine. Of course, that was also my fault.

I had mistreated her in the beginning. "We both don't have the full story, but it's clear she saved your life. You didn't kill her, Ruby. From what you've said, like a good mother, she gave up her life for yours."

I placed my hand on her cheek, and swallowed hard as my wolf awakened. Being close to her and not being able to touch her was sometimes painful. My wolf yearned for her, but because of the way I treated her before, I kept denying him the chance to ever get close to her. "I know you're hurting and not much I say will make you feel better. But tell me this: did your mother seem angry about saving you and not herself?"

Ruby stiffened and shook her head. "No."

"Did she not seem relieved when you came back to life?"

She nodded, her green eyes not looking away from my black ones. "Yes, she did."

"Then she didn't die in pain. She died happy, knowing she had saved her only child. You're the daughter of Lovette, the most beloved Enchanted Elder. Ruby, that's an honor you and only you hold."

She smiled.

Even if it was only a slight smile, I felt proud that I had been able to help put it there. Ruby had witnessed a horrible thing, one that would haunt her for a while, but maybe she'd hold onto the good in the situation. "You also know where you come from. That's one puzzle piece found."

"Thanks," she murmured.

I rubbed my hand against her cheek. "Anytime, Ruby."

"Are you okay? Why are your eyes black?" she asked as she reached a hand out to my face.

The moment her fingers touched my face, I kissed her. The restraint—I'd been holding back for so long—just broke. My wolf howled with joy the moment she didn't pull away or slap me but instead leaned into the kiss. Her lips tasted better than I'd ever imagined, and I snaked my hand around her to pull her closer to me. It wasn't a gentle kiss—I'd never been good at being kind—but she matched my urgency and vigor, my need to taste as much of her as I could. Her lips were so incredibly soft.

When I felt my fangs descending, I feared I'd hurt her. I broke our liplock to kiss her cheek, chin, and then neck. She moaned softly, and I captured her lips once more for her to moan into my mouth.

She pulled away, her breathing now labored as she stared at me.

Perfect, she's perfect.

I swallowed hard and removed my hand from around her waist. "Sorry, I..."

She stared behind me, however.

When I turned around, Xavier stood at the door watching us.

Fuck. Wait, why should I care? She's my mate as well. He must have known that eventually Ruby and I would grow close. The mate bond wouldn't allow us to stay apart for too long.

She got up with a look on her face that I couldn't quite understand.

She walked over to him, stood on her tippy toes, and kissed Xavier as well.

It wasn't as heated as our kiss, and while I felt a stab of jealousy, it wasn't as strong as I had expected it to be.

When she pulled away, Xavier cupped her cheeks, the love in his eyes evident as he pulled her in for a hug.

This scenario was never what I expected when I found my mate, but here we were. I was watching my mate kiss another man, and unbelievably, my wolf didn't want to shred him to pieces.

Ruby pulled away and turned to face me. She looked a little happier. Her cheeks stained red with a bright blush. "Is this as weird for you guys as it is for me?"

I nodded. "It's weird."

Xavier looked at me. "It is, but something we knew would happen sooner or later."

I didn't detect any hate or anger in his voice. Maybe a pinch of jealousy, but I felt the same, so I couldn't fault him for that.

"Are you okay?" he asked Ruby.

She nodded.

"What did you see?"

I listened as she told Xavier the same thing she'd told me.

Her eyes became glossy as she explained how her mother died.

Xavier consoled her. "Do you think you can continue?" he asked her. "I doubt that was the only memory locked away."

Ruby shrugged. "I don't know. I-if that was the first memory, I-I don't feel eager to see the others. Maybe my past was locked away for a reason... to protect me."

"True." I nodded. "But there might be things in your past that might be able to help you and us. Lovette is your mother, so Olcan won't be able to touch you now."

We all stared at Malcolm as he walked in.

Ruby smiled. "I'm really going to enjoy seeing the look on Olcan's face when he finds out." She crossed her arms over her chest.

Malcolm moved further into the room. His hair appeared tussled, and he still had black stains under his eyes.

During the ritual with Ruby, Xavier and I had watched as he'd cried in black blood.

"I understand you're angry, Ruby, but we have to continue," he said.

Ruby shook her head in disbelief.

I also felt shocked that after what he had just seen, after what Ruby had just been forced to witness, he'd want to continue so soon.

He sighed. "What we saw was only the tip of the iceberg. There is more to see. You died... something happened, or Lovette did something to bring you back. I need to know what. You were born human, but maybe coming back to life did something to you, and that's why you have the powers you do."

"How?" Ruby asked.

Malcolm shrugged. "I don't know. That's why we need to continue with the ritual."

Xavier crossed his arms, much like Ruby.

Ruby looked over at me.

I understood the uncertainty in her eyes. "Xavier and I will be there. Whatever you see, we'll be there."

She gazed at Xavier next.

He cupped her cheek. "We do need to know what else is hidden."

I didn't miss the curious look on Malcolm's face at the bond between Ruby and us.

He frowned for a moment before the expression disappeared.

Xavier looked his way and uncrossed his arms to bury his hands in his pockets. "We'll continue with the ritual, but not tonight. We can do it in the morning."

"Ruby is tired," I added.

Malcolm looked my way as the side of his mouth arched somewhat with a smirk.

I narrowed my eyes at him.

Malcolm bowed his head. "No problem. We'll continue at

dawn. Pick whatever rooms you like." He turned to leave the room but not before pausing to look at each of us with a curious gaze. He then left the room.

Ruby turned away, her face in her hands. "That soulless man can't be my dad," she mumbled.

Xavier placed his hand on her back.

"He's your father Ruby, not your dad," I said.

She turned around and puckered her bottom lip.

I couldn't help smiling at how adorable she looked as I stated, "The title of Dad is earned."

"Yeah," she drawled. Her lips parted as if she intended to say something, but she changed her mind. "I do need to get some rest," she acknowledged with a slight yawn.

I stood up. "Well, goodnight," I said, knowing Xavier and her would be sleeping together. I'd just pick a room close to theirs in case I needed to get to Ruby quickly.

"Wait," she called.

I'd pulled my hair from its ponytail as I turned around. A long shower was definitely in order.

"Can you..." she paused and looked at Xavier.

He stared back at her in confusion.

Looking at me again, her cheeks were pink.

I frowned.

"Can you stay with me as well?" she asked in a small voice.

I raised a brow as Xavier and I eyed each other. I think watching her kiss Xavier was enough for me for one night. "Um, I don't know, Ruby."

She stepped forward. "Please?"

How could I say no to that?

———

Unknown

I listened to the humans screams echoing from multiple rooms throughout the castle. Little did they know, no one would ever hear their cries. Their pitiful wailing was like sweet music to the ones who could actually hear them.

I stopped by an open door and looked inside, watching as a Bleeder stabbed a woman in her throat before latching onto her neck. It stuck his claws into the woman's gut and ripped her throat open with its fangs, its head leaning back as it licked its blood-coated lips.

The woman's teary eyes were on me, and she merely winced, almost dead, as a second Bleeder ripped her left leg clean off. A third Bleeder then attacked the second Bleeder, and a fight ensued between the hairless rats.

The room was soaked in blood, with dismembered bodies scattered into pieces all over the floor.

I shook my head and slammed the door shut. Bleeders were necessary but a complete nuisance.

The further I walked, the darker the castle got, until I had to rely completely on my vampiric ability to see in the dark in order to avoid tripping over the bodies on the ground.

A Bleeder stepped out of a room as I walked by. Upon seeing me, it bowed and covered its bald head as if I was going to hit it. It cowered back into the room.

I continued down the hall of death, the stench of blood causing my fangs to ache.

I entered the elevator and was happy to be leaving the lower castle. Not many humans and supernaturals could handle the transition to vampirism well. They often became mindless, blood-thirsty creatures that disgusted even Skins like me.

The elevator dinged and the strong smell of blood from four stories below disappeared. I stepped out of the elevator and into the red-lit room. Sensual music was playing from hidden speakers while naked Skins mingled among themselves on the floor. Sheer material hung from the ceiling, something I'd always hated. Our queen chose the décor, and she was quite proud of it.

A human woman appeared before me, a thick collar around her neck. She placed her hand on my cheek, her eyes hazy with lust. My gaze followed the chain attached to her collar to the Skin holding it, a woman with pale blonde hair.

I sighed.

The blonde got up and yanked on the chain, causing the human to fall to the ground. "Don't you know never to touch a General?" She hissed at the human.

The woman curled herself around the vampire's leg.

She kicked the human away. The human only returned to latch onto her leg once more, and the vampire smiled.

I walked away.

The blonde placed her hand on my chest. "Are you going to see the queen?"

I turned to her.

She leaned her head back as she stared up at me. "Tell her we miss her. She hasn't joined us in weeks."

A few other vampires nearby mumbled in agreement.

Without warning, I grabbed her hand swiftly and broke it. Her hiss and scream silenced those around us. I turned away without saying a word. The only thing I hate more than Bleeders were these worthless horny Skins.

I finally made it to my destination.

One of the guards standing by the door opened it to give me entrance.

Once inside with the door closed, all sounds from outside vanished. As a vampire with heightened hearing, not being bombarded with the smallest noise was a blessing.

The room was the same as it had always been except for the male and female humans lounging together to the corner.

A young human woman smiled at me, fresh fang marks on her neck.

"General," a soft voice met my ears.

I lowered my eyes to the floor as my queen stepped out from within her closet. "Do you come with good news, my child?"

"She was located by a scouting team but vanished before she could be captured."

She said nothing in response.

Even as I gave no outward sign of my fear... on the inside, I was panicked. This fear only worsened as she walked over to me.

"How?"

I swallowed hard. "Magic—she was with two wolves and a warlock."

She hissed loudly, and the humans began to whimper fearfully.

"But," I added quickly. "Her scent has gotten stronger. She's being tracked as we speak."

She reached a hand out to me and held my face, her long nails scraping my skin.

Despite being 6'3 in height, I had to lean my head back to look up at her.

My vision filled with red as she fixed me in a dead stare. It wasn't just her irises that were crimson. The color engulfed her entire eyeball—pupil, sclera, and iris alike. "That girl holds power that should no longer exist," she said softly. "I shouldn't have to tell you how important it is that she be found before she learns what she is." She leaned closer, her black hair that hung down to her thighs moving forward. "Before she learns to control her power and undo all the hard work we've done to reclaim this earth. Do you understand?"

"Yes, my Queen," I replied and flinched as she released my face but not before one of her nails sliced the skin under my left eye.

I stared at her back as she walked away and swallowed hard as I watched her skin move with her stride. She began removing her silky white dress one thin strap at a time, her skin almost as white as the dress.

The humans started to cry softly, terror in their eyes as her left shoulder suddenly dislocated, and she hunched forward. "Leave me, and don't return without that girl."

I turned and opened the door, as the sound of breaking bones, ripping flesh, and the human's piercing shrieks flooded my senses before the door closed behind me.

***

Ruby

I was burning up. I wasn't sure why, but I felt like I had been placed inside a furnace as someone was turning up the heat. I slowly opened my eyes, reluctant to be pulled from my slumber. I relaxed again when I understood the reason why I felt so hot.

Xavier's massive leg was draped over my lower body while Axel's arm was over my stomach. Both of them were breathing heavily and emitting more heat than an electric blanket.

Maybe sleeping with both of them had been a bad idea... and yes, we only slept. Still, it was the best sleep I'd had in a very long time. I drifted off to sleep knowing no one on this planet was more protected.

Despite the current state of the world, I was a lucky woman to have these two strong men by my side. Although maybe not so much right now, because if I laid here any longer between them, I might burn to death.

Before getting up, I took a moment to admire them both. On my right laid Axel, my dark knight, with his fire and attitude. Strands of his long hair were covering the side of his face, and I smiled as I remembered our first kiss. Where Xavier and I always shared soft, sweet, slow kisses, kissing Axel had been the complete opposite. Our kiss was deep, passionate, and raw, yet it held the same love I felt with Xavier.

I studied Xavier on my left and sighed. All of this began because he tried to protect me, and I was happy I had met him.

We'd started out disliking each other a little, and then our relationship had grown into something I didn't know was possible. I didn't think a man like him would ever be...my man.

I'd never had someone in my life who always had my back, and I knew I would have that forever in Xavier.

Okay, enough of this, I'm starting to melt.

I untangled myself, which took a lot of effort and patience in order to avoid waking them both.

Eventually, I was on my way downstairs in search of the kitchen.

Once I made it to the first floor, I walked by the spacious living room. When I looked inside, I saw Malcolm's cobra—his shadow demon—pressed against the glass of his cage.

The cobra/shadow demon stopped moving as it caught sight of me and started to turn to smoke.

My eyes widened nervously. "No, fuck no." I started speed walking away from the living room as fast as I could. After a few minutes, I finally made it to the kitchen.

I quickly discovered I had escaped from one demon only to run right into another.

Malcolm sat at the kitchen island with a cup in hand, steam slowly rising from it. "Good morning," he said in a husky morning voice. With the bags under his eyes, it was obvious he hadn't gotten much sleep.

"Good morning," I mumbled under my breath as I walked to the fridge and removed a bottle of water.

"If you wish, I can make you some coffee or tea," Malcolm offered.

I opened my bottled water. "No, thanks. This will do for now."

He nodded and went back to staring into his cup.

I had hoped I'd be alone for a while before I'd have to deal with Malcolm and his ritual. He had said at dawn, and clearly he had meant it.

"How did you sleep?" he asked.

I squinted my eyes at him. "Good. You didn't, I'm guessing?"

He peered up at me before looking back down at his cup. "I want to say I'm sorry about last night. I was insensitive and blind to your pain. You had just watched your mother die and yourself as well," he murmured.

I sucked in a breath, caught off-guard by his apology.

He pushed his cup away, but instead of looking at me, he stared straight ahead. "What I have done—tying myself to that demon, using black magic—has had its negative effects on me. I feel fewer human emotions, and it's only gotten worse over the years."

I closed my water bottle as I listened intently.

He went on, "That's the true price I had to pay. Every day, that shadow demon feeds on my grief from losing Lovette as well as the sadness of losing my only daughter." He looked up at me as he said this.

I gritted my teeth. I wasn't about to say I forgave him. Everything still felt a little too fresh, so I said nothing.

He continued to speak, "It's a price I thought I was willing to pay. The anguish I felt every day at having lost you both threatened to overwhelm me. I was barely hanging on. Having my suffering taken away seemed like a gift at the time, but now, I feel nothing in moments when I should."

"Okay," I said as I pressed a finger against the crease in my forehead. "What was she like?"

Malcolm inhaled and exhaled deeply through his mouth. "Level-headed. Sometimes, annoyingly so." He smiled. "For a woman who possessed her own kind of magic, she was very logical in her thinking and was a lover of science. I guess for her, science and magic were like fraternal twin brothers—similar but not identical. That was the way she looked at it, at least." He gazed at me and his smile grew wider.

I had no idea how to react. Suddenly, Malcolm was this warm, authentic man. Not the one I'd been growing to dislike.

"You have her eyes, gorgeous emerald eyes," he said tenderly.

"And I got your hair," I added.

He chuckled as he ruffled his own hair. "Yeah..." He pulled his cup back to him and looked upward. "We made a beautiful kid, Lovette."

I frowned because I felt sure he'd just said that as if he was speaking to Lovette.

"Sometimes I pretend she's here with me, watching me, hearing me." He took a sip of the contents in his cup. "It helps." He placed the cup back down and sighed. "Loving someone with everything you have can sometimes break you. Do you love them?"

I looked away with a blush. "Um, why?"

"Because they love you, both of them. They feel the mate bond more than you do, I'm guessing."

I nodded. "They do, and I-I do too. Love them, I mean."

He nodded and reached into his pocket.

My heart stopped for a second as he handed me a photo of Lovette. It was a picture of her at the beach with her dark hair blowing in the wind as she held her beach hat down on her head, her smile wide and radiating joy. I recognized hints of my own smile in hers. My chin began to quiver. It seemed like she'd been an amazing woman, loved by so many. Right now, I could count the people who actually liked me on one hand, and the rest were pursuing me from every direction. How would I ever live up to being her daughter?

"You can keep that. The image from the picture is burned into my brain," he said to me.

I whispered, "Thank you," as I held it to my chest. "I'm ready," I announced.

He frowned.

"I'm ready to continue with the ritual. I want to know everything."

"Okay. This time, whenever you're ready to leave, just say so and I'll end it."

I nodded.

We made our way to the living room, encountering Xavier and Axel on the way.

They stepped back to allow us to proceed.

Now standing inside this circle again, knowing I might see something horrible, my hands shook with fear. "Will you have to cut me again?" I asked.

Malcolm shook his head. "No, that won't be necessary. Just give me your hand."

I looked over at Axel and Xavier just to see their faces before inhaling and giving my hands to Malcolm.

His eyes turned black instantly, and the candles around the circle lit just like before.

The world around us faded away to be replaced by a small bathroom.

My eyes widened as I observed myself at fifteen years old, lying in a bathtub with my wrist slit open. I glanced over at Malcolm.

He looked at me before turning to stare at the pale Ruby of the past, submerged in water up to her chin.

I touched the scar on my wrist. This wasn't how I remembered ever getting it. I thought I had gone through a depressed stage in high school and had cut myself then. This version of events felt foreign.

The past Ruby's eyes were half-open and dazed as she bled out.

Malcolm and I watched as a small floating ball of light appeared in the room.

It drifted to the bathtub and landed on her arm. Ruby gasped and sat up as if she'd been jolted.

All three of us watched as the soft light began to grow until it morphed into Lovette.

The past Ruby began to cry. "It's you, isn't it?"

"Yes, my beautiful girl," Lovette replied, her voice soft but sounding like an echo. "Why did you hurt yourself?"

"I-I did something terrible. I—a girl was bullying me, and I reacted. I-I didn't mean to hurt her, but I reacted and—and..." Ruby looked down at her open wrist and started to cry harder.

I sucked in a breath as I stared at this memory. "This is..."

"...trippy?" Malcolm asked as he finished my sentence.

I nodded. I was looking at my younger self and my dead mother. This was more than trippy.

"I burned her. She just started to burn!" Past Ruby sobbed.

Lovette kneeled beside the tub.

Past Ruby went on as she wept, "I met him. I met my dad right before I saw the girl. He said he was my father, and—I-I was so angry. He left me, all alone, all these years. You left me!"

I was surprised as much as Malcolm when Lovette reached out and was able to touch my past self's cheek.

Lovette took past Ruby's hand and healed the wound on her wrist. "I didn't leave you, sweet girl. I'm always here, always watching, but I can't always appear to you like this. I can't interfere with your life." Lovette tilted her head to the side as she gazed at the past me.

A thought occurred to me as I stared at my mother in this memory. If what she had just said were true, what would it take for me to see her now, in the present?

Lovette spoke to past Ruby, "You're a special girl, Ruby, more than you'll ever know. It's not time for you to die. There is too much left to be done, and you haven't even gotten started."

The past Ruby frowned as she looked from Lovette to her healed wrist and back. "I don't understand?"

Lovette sighed and stood up as she turned to face Malcolm and me. She seemed to be staring right at me.

I made a face and glanced at Malcolm as he peered back at me.

"I'll take your memories of this day. Never spill your blood again, my child, not yet, for your blood is that of the Goddess."

"Mom?" I said tentatively as I stepped forward.

Lovette smiled at me—she smiled at *me*—and reached out her hand.

Her image then started to fall away.

Abruptly, Malcolm and I returned to the real world.

"No! No! Send me back!" I screamed.

Xavier and Axel approached me.

I stepped back. *Lovette was speaking to me. She was there!*

Malcolm staggered out of the circle, his eyes wide as he stared at me as if I had just grown a second head.

"Send me back, Malcolm! She was there!" I pleaded.

"How?" he whispered to himself, "How is it even possible?"

I frowned at him. "What is wrong with you? Who cares how? She was right there, *really* there! Let's go back!" I shouted as I stepped closer to him.

He stepped back.

I froze then looked over at Xavier and Axel, who were now watching him with concern as well.

"What's wrong, Malcolm?" Axel asked.

Malcolm stared at him, his eyes still wide with shock. "It—it can't be possible," he stammered.

I stepped back as the cobra appeared out of a cloud of smoke to wrap around Malcolm's neck.

"Malcolm, what the hell is going on?" Xavier asked as he stepped forward to stand protectively in front of me.

The cobra sank its fangs into Malcolm's neck as he went pale, his eyes still black pits. "I think—I think she was saved, b-but how?" Malcolm stated in a weak voice as he pointed at me. "She was saved by the Goddess, *your* goddess. She gave Ruby divinity."

Alpha Chosen

Book Five

CHAPTER ONE

RUBY

Not too long ago, I began my new life as a college student. But that was the beginning of the end of normalcy for me. Now, those college days seemed like a lifetime ago. Before then, I was a normal girl, an orphan. I was nobody. The only thing unique about me was the red hair that hung down to my ass.

At this moment, however, I was staring at Malcolm, my father and a black magic user, as he told me I'd been given divinity by a goddess—whatever the fuck that meant. On either side of me stood my two werewolf mates, Xavier and Axel, who looked just as confused as I did.

Thrust abruptly into the supernatural world after I saw Xavier transform when he saved me from being raped, it felt like I'd been continuously taking blow after blow ever since then. I had questions stacked upon questions with barely any answers.

I blinked rapidly. "I'm sorry, what? What do you mean I was given divinity?" I suddenly eyed the snake wrapped around Malcolm's neck, its fangs buried into his skin. My eye twitched. "Why is that thing biting you?"

Malcolm turned his head somewhat to look at the snake. "The deal I made with him was that he could feed on my emotions, and in return, he lends me his power."

The snake removed its fangs and then vanished into a smoke cloud, the same way it had appeared.

I couldn't imagine living like that, tying myself to a demon for power.

"As for you having divinity, I mean exactly that," Malcolm stated. "I'm only guessing this from the memory we just saw of your mother. What she said about your blood being that of the Goddess and never to spill it. It's a damn good guess, however, because it explains so much. The Goddess..." He glanced at Xavier and Axel. "...Your goddess saved Ruby at birth. She gave Ruby her powers, her divinity."

I rubbed at my temples.

"That can't be possible. A god just decided to give a mortal their divine power? Why?" Axel wondered aloud as his eyes drifted to me. "How?" he asked before turning Malcolm's way once more.

Malcolm shook his head, a frown on his face. "I don't know." He pinched his chin as he turned away. "But it would explain why Ruby has the power to kill vampires so easily. Now, we know why she has no ties to any other supernatural creatures," he added. His eyes narrowed as he looked me up and down as if he were trying to see the power lying within me. "You have power none of us has ever seen. If you learn to control these powers, Ruby, you'll be... you'll be able to do what you did to those vampires to any supernatural."

"Okay, no, I don't want to do that... to anyone." I held my hand up and took a step back. "This is more than I signed up for. As a matter of fact, I didn't sign up for any of this."

"Aren't you curious, Ruby?" Malcolm prodded. "Why would a goddess give you divinity? Why not a pureblood werewolf? Why save you?"

Malcolm appeared more excited than I did, and for the life of me, I couldn't understand why. He was getting so worked up, I was surprised his little snake demon didn't return to siphon off some of his extra emotion. I don't think he intended for it to sound as if I wasn't worth being saved, but that was all I could think of when I heard his comment. I said nothing as I walked away. I closed my eyes for a moment and could see my mother staring at me. The memory Malcolm had just helped me to see wasn't only a memory. I could feel it in my bones.

My mom had really been there. She had appeared to me as a ghost when I was a teen, but she had indeed been there in the mind link between Malcolm and me.

"I want to go back," I whispered under my breath as I opened my eyes. I turned around to tell Malcolm this.

He snapped his fingers. "Lovette; you were saved because of her. In the vision we saw of her giving birth to you, she asked someone to save you, not her. She wasn't talking to one of the nurses or a doctor. She was talking to the Goddess herself."

"So, are you saying the Goddess was going to save my mother, but she told the Goddess to save me instead?" I pondered.

Xavier combed his hand through his thick black hair as he sighed loudly. "This is insane," he muttered.

I agreed with him. "Who is this goddess, anyways?" I asked as I looked from one man to the next. "No one ever refers to her by name, and I've been too occupied to ask why. Since the Goddess is clearly real." I held my hand up. "Not that I doubted this, but if what Malcolm is saying it is true, who is she? What's her name?"

"She has no name," Axel explained, his hazel eyes twinkling for a moment as they reflected the light from above us.

"She's eternal and she's everything; she has no name," Xavier added, a certain reverence vibrating in his voice as he spoke, "She's just *The* Goddess."

I nodded and turned away. Looking down at my hands, I

quickly folded them into fists. I closed my eyes as I inhaled deeply, my powers buzzing under my skin. *So this is what I am?*

What am I? I was a human and an Enchanted, and I had a god's divinity, so what did that make me? It became obvious there was no name for what I was. There had never been another like me, and while many might have felt special in my shoes, I felt angry and confused.

A god would not give up their power for no reason, not without payment of some sort. What price would I have to pay for the privilege of living?

My heartbeat slowly started to increase the more my thoughts ricocheted off the walls in my mind. I heard footsteps come close and I pulled in the energy around me and released it.

Whomever it was stepped back, and I hung my head. I wasn't feeling happy my powers had just done what I wanted them to. Instead, I was angry that I'd just used the same powers I wanted to reject.

"Ruby?" Xavier called.

I shook my head, my back still turned.

"We don't know everything yet," he continued.

"That's what I'm tired of!" I snapped back as I spun around. "Every answer leads to more questions, and I'm sick of it. I've lived all this time without knowing who I am. If your goddess, the same goddess that caused me to be mated to the both of you, is the one that saved me, what is the cost, huh? Don't you see it? Everything, all of this has been planned. All of this."

Thinking about it only made me angrier. My life had been shit. Now, I'd discovered my mother, an Enchanted, put me in this position to begin with. I looked around the room. "If you're here, I fucking hate you."

"Ruby!" Malcolm yelled.

I turned to him. "Don't say my name! You don't get to say my name. You wanted to kill me, remember? No matter how you try to justify it, you wanted to kill me. So, honestly, *Malcolm*, you don't get to act like you give a shit!"

"Ruby, I get that you're confused right now and rightfully upset, but..." Axel's words trailed off.

I stared at him, my gut twisting further with anger.

His eyes flashed black at me. "Baby, listen to me."

My anger dissipated. Maybe it was the way he was looking at me or the endearment he had conveyed. Our relationship had only recently improved. Considering we started from a place where he hated the idea of me being his mate, affection coming from him was enough to soothe my swirling emotions.

His eyes returned to hazel.

I found Xavier looking at me with concern.

"I didn't stand a chance," I whispered, but I knew they could hear me clearly. "She knew all of this would happen to me." I shook my head at Malcolm.

As always, his face was a blank canvas, but his eyes glimmered with pity for me.

I went on, "Lovette knew from the start, from the moment the Goddess saved me, that this would be my life. She knew vampires still existed and would try to reclaim the earth." I shook my head. "My father wanted to kill me, and my mother was okay with me living the way I have, the way my life has been up until now. I don't know which is worse."

I didn't want to freak out, but I couldn't stop the rage coursing through me.

How much worse will this all get?

My body grew tense as I remembered the memory Malcolm and I had just seen of me when I was fifteen.

I rubbed a thumb against the scar on my wrist. The hardships of my life's hardships finally pushed me over the edge after Malcolm had approached me and told me he was my father. He had told me my mother died after giving birth to me, and I had just lost it.

That was when I first used my powers. When I burned a girl... that was it for me. I was already seen as a freak and outcast, so burning someone without even touching them just made things worse.

As the memory was revealed to Malcolm and me, my old feeling resurfaced—the utter defeat—the agony of my memory on replay in my mind.

I wished I'd never met my father.

I wished I hadn't known that I had killed my mother.

"It's starting to get hot in here," Malcolm observed, sounding a bit nervous.

"It's her," Axel murmured under his breath. "Ruby, maybe we should take a walk?"

"Let me be angry, dammit!" I shouted loudly.

The furniture around me was pushed away by an unseen force emitting from me. I wanted to be angry; I wanted to scream and cry. I wished I hadn't been saved. "Why does this all have to be so complicated? Huh?" The room's lights started to flicker as well, but I couldn't contain my powers, and I didn't want to. "Maybe the vampires won't destroy this earth. Maybe it'll be me—an out of control...thing!"

Xavier spun me around to face him. "That isn't going to happen. I don't know what exactly you saw, but with the powers you have, and maybe some you haven't even discovered yet, you're in a position to do more than Axel, Malcolm, and me combined. I'm not mad that the Goddess saved you. I'm not angry that you're my mate. I understand you feel used, but I—"

I shook my head and stepped back. "I can't..." I watched as the sadness in his eyes grew. I looked away, unable to bear it. Nevertheless, the pain within my own chest was growing rapidly, and I was not sure I could control it. "I need some space."

I walked out of the room, my hand covering my mouth to stop my sob as I walked briskly down the hall.

Axel

I discovered Ruby in a well-furnished sitting room gazing thoughtfully at a life-sized painting of Lovette.

I found myself staring at the portrait alongside Ruby, mesmerized by the ethereal woman depicted there. "She was beautiful," I mumbled with admiration.

Ruby looked over her shoulder at me. "She was, yeah," she replied softly.

I took that as an opening that it was safe to join her. It was funny to think of me being wary of Ruby, but I now knew she could throw me across the room onto the bed with just a thought. I swallowed hard at the prospect and buried the images that appeared in my mind.

Once I was at her side, she held her hand out in front of her.

I stared at the scar on her wrist, the same one I first noticed a while ago. At the time, I had decided it was best not to ask.

"I thought I got this scar when I tried to kill myself when I was depressed," she explained. "I experienced depression after bouncing from foster home to foster home as a teenager, but it wasn't the precipitating factor for the suicide attempt." She swallowed hard, and her hand fell to her side as she looked up at the painting again. "Malcolm found me when I was fifteen. He told me who he was and who my mother was, and I lost it. The stress and pain from feeling responsible for my mother's death triggered my powers, and I hurt someone." She exhaled heavily and turned her back to her mother's portrait. "I went home and did this afterward. My mother appeared to me as I was dying."

I looked up at the portrait before looking at her once more. "She saved you?"

Ruby nodded. "She did, but she stole my memories as well. She placed the block in my mind." She turned to face me, tears in her eyes. "In the vision, while Malcolm and I were there, she was too... I don't know, but she was really there. She was there *in* the memory, with Malcolm and me. I don't know how to explain it, but she looked right at me."

"Maybe she was," I told her. "Lovette was powerful, very powerful. If she and the Goddess are responsible for all of this, she was more powerful than we ever knew."

Ruby sighed as she lowered her head and placed her palm on her forehead. "My head is killing me."

"Maybe you need to lie down," I suggested as I held her shoulders.

She stepped forward into my arms.

Surprised by this, I happily wrapped my arms around her and held her soft, warm body to mine. She felt so small in my arms, so vulnerable. "I hate seeing you like this," I whispered as I kissed the top of her head.

She gazed up at me. Her green eyes appeared brighter than they usually were. Without thinking about it too much, I dipped my head and kissed her passionately. She responded instantly, her lips meeting mine hungrily as her arms lifted to wrap around my neck. I snaked my arms tightly around her waist and lifted her off the ground somewhat.

All I wanted at this moment was for her to feel at peace, to feel some kind of happiness amid the mess that had become our lives.

She stiffened after a moment.

I placed her back onto the ground. Our lips parted. My eyes roamed over her face as I grew concerned at the cloudy look in her eyes. "Ruby?" I pinched her chin and tilted her head back.

She kept gazing blankly up at me as if she were seeing through me.

"Ruby?" I called again.

Her body started to shake.

The lights flickered above us.

I peered into the hall to see if it was happening there as well. I could hear Xavier and Malcolm rushing through the house to get to us with my heightened senses.

"Blood," she mumbled, her bottom lip quivering. "There's blood everywhere."

"Blood. What are you seeing, Ruby?" I urged her to tell me.

Her eyes rolled back, and she fell unconscious in my arms.

My heart skipped a beat as fear rushed through me.

CHAPTER TWO

RUBY

I saw a woman smiling up at a rather tall man. Her black hair hung in loose curls down her back. The man slid his hand around her waist and pulled her to him. I could tell he was a vampire from his pale skin—I could feel it in my bones. She held her head back, and he dipped his head to her throat. He looked my way, his eyes as red as blood.

Suddenly I stood amid a battle between werewolves, vampires, and humans, my heart hammering in my chest with fright. It didn't take long for me to realize it was a battle from long ago because of how everyone was dressed. Some were in armor wielding swords and wooden shields. The vampire Bleeders I got a glimpse of were pale, hideous creatures, wearing mostly torn, dirty pieces of clothing. Calling them 'rags' would be a generous description.

Even though I knew it was a vision, it felt all too real. I had to keep ducking and dodging to avoid the swords. I dove out of the way and fell onto my back as a werewolf pounced on me. He loomed above me, his giant claws poised to rip my body to shreds.

———

Ruby

It was the wind on my face that woke me, followed by the sound of singing birds.

I moved my arms and realized I was lying in the grass. I opened my eyes quickly, a headache throbbing at my temples. The twirling pale blue and white sky above caught my attention. It looked like paint being slowly stirred.

I sat up and looked around the never-ending garden as it stretched on further than my eyes could see.

"Where the hell is this?"

Before the vision, I was in Malcolm's home and talking to Axel, so why did I wake up in a garden?

"Axel?" I yelled as I got up off the ground, my eyes still taking in the garden, but I soon realized it was more of a meadow than a garden. "Xavier?" I called out again, but my voice just echoed around me.

There were countless kinds of flowers surrounding me, but the meadow was completely devoid of trees. I was utterly alone, and images from the vision I had before waking up in this place flashed in my mind. I closed my eyes and pressed my fingers into my tear duct.

So much blood, I had seen so much blood. *What the hell was that vision?*

The wind picked up around me, blowing the scent of the flowers up to my nostrils.

Is teleportation one of my gifts? I hope to God—or the Goddess— it's not.

"Malcolm!" I screamed. I figured if anyone could come and find me, it would be him. He'd been tracking me for years, keeping his eye on me, so wherever this place was, he'd better be able to find me.

I turned in a circle and froze as I spotted a large white tree I hadn't noticed before. I narrowed my eyes as I stared at it; even its trunk looked paperwhite.

"Maybe this isn't real," I whispered to myself as I started walking towards the tree. The tree looked as if it had been painted white—leaves, branches, trunk, and all—resulting in a stunning visual effect that literally took my breath away.

Standing alone in the meadow among the countless colorful blooms, and with such a peculiar look, the white tree's sight mesmerized me. As I drew closer, a white paw appeared from behind the tree, and an alabaster wolf stepped out from behind it.

I stopped moving, my heart skipping a beat as the massive animal, as large as a werewolf, pinned me with her gaze. She bared her teeth and growled low.

Fuck!

The wolf held her head up and began sniffing the air before sitting down, her eyes still on me.

Though she had stopped growling, I remained motionless where I stood. I wasn't sure if movements would spook her, and I had no intention of becoming dinner.

Long ago, Mathieu had told me white werewolves were a myth and that only the very first werewolf was white. Did that mean the wolf in front of me was the first wolf? Did this have something to do with the Goddess?

After a few minutes, the wolf got up, ruffled her tail, and turned around.

I watched with confusion, my heart hammering against my chest as the massive beast walked back behind the tree. I started looking around me once more, my need to get away from this place growing.

"Ruby?" a voice called my name.

I spun around to see a woman emerge from the opposite side from where the wolf had walked. My breath hitched in my throat as I looked right at my mother.

Lovette stared at me, a loving smile slowly grew on her lips.

"You're so much more beautiful in person," she said as she stepped closer to me. She held her arms out to me for me to come forward.

As much as my body wanted to run into her arms, I remained still. My features hardened as I stared at her. "You didn't have to take my memories."

Her smile fell away, immediately replaced by a saddened expression. Her white hair appeared to be as white as the dress she wore and the tree at her back. She looked angelic, and even though her luminous smile had dimmed, she was still so beautiful.

Since I had my father's red hair, I was trying to see what features besides her green emerald eyes I had. I could find none.

Is this woman really my mother?

"I didn't have a choice, Ruby," she explained as she moved forward.

I stepped back.

She sighed and moved her hair behind her left ear. "You might not believe me, but it was for your own good."

"My own good," I repeated. "Everyone seems to know what's good for me. That includes my father, who wanted to kill me *for my own good.*"

She looked away, her green eyes darting back and forth as the wind began blowing the flowers around us. "Your father went down a dark path."

"Because he loved you," I stated almost instantaneously.

The wounded look on her face hurt me more than I had expected. "I mean, he did what he thought was right to be able to find you. He was willing to do anything to get you back."

"As would Axel and Xavier," Lovette added with a knowing smile.

I started blushing. "Right," I drawled as I looked away. "Where is this? Where are we?"

Lovette stepped forward again.

This time, I didn't move away. The way she lowered and tilted her head to the side made me smile internally because I finally found something similar between us. I did that a lot.

"That's not important right now," she told me as she stopped in front of me. "What's important is that the block I placed on your mind and powers is now completely gone. Your memories will all come back over time, but your powers... those will be coming a lot faster." She lifted a hand, but it fell quickly back to her side.

My body had gone stiff the moment she'd moved her hand. I thought she intended to touch me. I tried my best to hold myself together, considering I was talking to my *'dead'* mother.

She explained, "I didn't only block your memories, but your powers too. Ruby, if I hadn't done that, your already-difficult life would have been far worse. I made it so your powers would start to be awakened once you met Xavier and Axel. Then you would have people around you who would be able to help you, supernaturals who would accept you, and not humans that would fear you, try to kill you, or try to study you."

"Why me?" I asked after taking a deep breath. "Why did it have to be me? Why did the Goddess give me her power?"

Lovette turned and walked away for a few steps, her palms open and brushed against a few tall flowers that stood high enough for her to touch without bending. Her shoulders rose and fell slowly as she inhaled deeply.

Where my red hair was almost to my bottom, hers fell past hers. "Only someone like you can bridge the decades of separation between werewolves and humans. You're the only one who will be strong enough to do what's needed in the end," she stated with conviction.

I shook my head. She was wrong about that. The Council actively wanted me dead, and even in the pack I was to be Luna for, I was liked by very few and trusted by even fewer. How would I possibly unite werewolves and humans? "You're wrong. I can't possibly unite werewolves and humans, and you know it. Werewolves fear me right now, and the Council wants me dead. The only people they trust even less than me are humans and vampires. What did you mean when you said I'm the only one who will be strong enough? What will I have to do in the end?"

"You saw it before you came here," she said as she pointed at me. "You saw a battle between the species, didn't you? The vampires are succeeding in this invasion because the creatures of the world are more divided than ever. Ruby, you're special. You have the blood of a god running through your veins, a power that you can control instead of it overwhelming and killing you. That's what I meant."

I pressed a finger to the crease between my brows. The headache from earlier had stopped the moment I saw Lovette, but now it was coming back.

Lovette continued. "You could be mated to Xavier and Axel because you've never been *only* human from the start. You have Enchanted blood, but the divinity inside you overpowers that gene. That's why Natalie wasn't able to detect your Enchanted gene while testing you."

"But aren't Enchanteds descendants of the Goddess anyways? Don't all Enchanteds have the Goddess's divinity?"

She shook her head. "No. A long time ago, Enchanteds had more of her power, but it's become diluted over the years. She *gave* you her divinity. Her pure power was passed onto you, so it's much different from what you were already born with."

"Oh," I drawled. "What will I have to do in the end, then?" I doubted I'd be able to speak to her after this, so I wanted to know everything.

She merely looked at me without answering, an apologetic expression on her face.

I arched a brow questioningly, showing her that I was waiting for her response.

Still, she said nothing.

I rolled my eyes before looking away from her to stare at the tree. What was the significance of that thing, anyway? I glanced back at her.

She was still watching me. "How are things between you and the boys... Axel, especially?"

Was she serious? Were we going to have a cute mother-daughter chat about the two men my life had been intertwined with? "I, um..." I started to say but trailed off. I cleared my throat. My eyes still cast to the flowers below my feet. "It's going as expected. Xavier has been supportive of me and us from the start. Axel, not so much." I looked up at her.

She moved closer as she nodded.

I got the feeling she already knew how things were going with Axel and me, like everything else, but she wanted to change the subject. While I did want to know what was going to happen to me, it was clear she didn't intend to tell me. Maybe she couldn't, for some reason. Even though I wanted to hate her for making a choice that had turned my life into a freakish supernatural movie, I just couldn't find it in me to be angry at her any longer. I was seeing and speaking to my mother, the woman who gave her life to save me. I figured I'd better take the chance to have a mother-daughter conversation with her while I had it. This could be the last time I'd ever get to talk with her for all I knew.

"I um, I love them both, but..." I swallowed hard. "I feel angry at myself sometimes for caring about Axel."

"Why?" she asked.

I shrugged. "In the beginning, things were rough between us. He hated the idea of being tied to a weak human, and I hated him for the way he treated me initially. He abducted me, and... I should still hate him, but I don't. I can't. A part of me will always be angry about it, and I feel like I'll always be a little angry at myself for falling for him after what he did. Yet, I can't help my feelings. I care about him. He's done so much to help me. He left his pack behind just to be by my side. He's proven himself, and we've been growing closer. I just..." I sighed. "I know our mate bond brings us together no matter what, but am I a fool to love him after what he did?"

"I can't give you the answer to that. The men in Axel's bloodline have always been strong but very stubborn. He had his own pain that he'd been carrying with him for years. If your father is any example, pain makes people do stupid things sometimes. I can't tell you to forgive him. You have to decide if he's worth forgiving. However, what I can tell you is that you need both Axel and Xavier by your side. A new era is coming, but you will need them by your side in the war to come before that."

"I don't want to be a part of a war!" I exclaimed, my voice growing louder.

She gave me a pitiful look. "No one, not you nor anyone else, gets a choice. Fight or die. Those are the available options. Accept who you are, Ruby, or everyone dies. *Everyone.*" She came closer and placed her hand on my shoulder.

Whatever momentary anger I had been feeling towards her faded, and I caved. My eyes began to tear up as I reached out and touched her as well. My hand didn't pass through her like I thought it would.

A tear fell from her eye as she yanked me to her.

We squeezed each other so tight I thought I would break her and she'd break me. I tried to hold back my tears, but they came rolling down my cheeks anyway.

"I'm sorry, Ruby," she whispered to me. "I'm sorry I allowed all of this to happen to you, about taking your memories and leaving you in the dark for so long, but I saw what was coming. The Goddess showed me who you'd become—a greater woman than I ever was."

I placed my forehead on her shoulder while shaking my head, and she pulled away. "I won't be. I'm a mess."

She chuckled as she cupped my cheeks, her eyes roaming all over my face. "You don't know what I do, and no, I can't tell you.

Too much is at stake. Sometimes we have to let the future unfold as it was meant to."

I rolled my eyes.

She laughed again.

My heart tightened because her laugh sounded precisely like mine.

"You're strong; that's why the Goddess picked you," she imparted softly. "Now you just have to believe that you are." She placed her hands on my shoulders and squeezed. "Trust yourself and your powers. Stop fighting them. Stop fearing them."

"I don't want it," I answered firmly. "I don't want the Goddess's power."

She pouted somewhat as she placed a hand on my cheek. "It's too late for that." Her hand fell away from my cheek and she grew serious. "You need to find General Presley. You will need his help."

I frowned at the mention of the human general who wanted me to help him, to help the humans. "Um, why? After the way we left him out in the open like that, he's probably dead."

She shook her head. "He's not dead. Find him." She stepped away from me, her eyes tearing up again. "You will figure it out. Trust your powers." She reached a hand out to me but kept stepping away from me. "I love you."

When I moved to go after her, my legs were rooted where I stood.

I sat up with a gasp, my eyes wide as I looked around the room frantically. I placed a hand over my pounding heart and gripped my shirt. When I inhaled, I could still smell the flowers from that meadow. I could still smell my mother.

My hand flew to my mouth, tears escaping my eyes as I turned onto my stomach and pressed my face into the pillow behind my closed lids. I could still see her. I could still feel her warm hand on my cheek. I laid there, my face in the pillow, as I cried for her to come back.

CHAPTER THREE

The night just seemed so silent, not even the insects were calling to each other. Ever since the vampires attacked, it was as if the animals had all gone into hiding. Vampires were indiscriminate feeders. They targeted animals like cows, dogs, goats, and horses as well. All warm-blooded animals were fair game for vamps.

I crossed my arms over my chest and inhaled, smelling oncoming rain in the air. I could feel the cold wind on my skin, but it didn't bother me. Werewolves had higher temperatures than humans, so I remained outside to enjoy the quiet night's peacefulness. Nights or moments like this didn't come around often, especially not when you were constantly on the run.

Axel had gone looking for Ruby after she stormed out of the room, and I allowed him. She said she wanted space, so I'd given it to her, but we couldn't leave her to be alone. I no longer felt bothered by them getting closer to each other. He was her mate just like I was, and I knew the pull she had. Therefore, I expected Axel was experiencing the same. Many might call me crazy or call him crazy for being okay with this, but this was how things had to be.

Fate, the Goddess, or destiny had thrown us together and it was clear now—we were stronger together than apart.

I would never reject Ruby; the thought alone made me ache inside, and I knew Axel wouldn't either. He loved her, and so did I. Her happiness and safety were all that mattered, and I knew I spoke for him as well. Despite this, I had to admit, the way we were currently living wasn't how I saw my life turning out before Ruby came along.

I saw myself finding my Luna and becoming the Alpha for my pack. I never expected to share my Luna with anyone, let alone another Alpha. The Goddess must be responsible for whatever allowed Axel and me to co-exist respectfully. Werewolves (and Alphas in particular) aren't exactly known for being good at sharing anything, much less a mate.

I uncrossed my arms and buried my hands in my pockets as I stared at the pitch-black forest ahead of me. It was a good thing Axel had gone looking for Ruby. After he'd found her, she got a vision and fainted. She'd been out for six hours now and counting.

I couldn't help worrying about her. The more we went down this path of finding out who she was, the more I felt it was best we let sleeping dogs lie... for now, at least.

Her powers were growing. Now that we knew where her ability came from, I couldn't help but think the divinity inside her might eventually be too much for her to handle. She was under an immense amount of pressure. She'd been living all this time with an essential part of who she was locked away. I wished she hadn't learned the truth about what happened when she was born before she truly understood how to control her powers. The more she learned about herself now, the more unstable she became.

Honestly, learning something like that would mess me up too. I would also be enraged to find out that I was just a pawn in the Goddess's chess game. I frowned as a thought occurred to me... *I am a pawn, actually. I'm Ruby's mate, and that makes me as much of a pawn as she is; so is Axel, for that matter.*

I clenched my fists as I shook my head and looked up to the sky. "You're playing with lives," I muttered and hoped the Goddess could hear me.

Malcolm had checked on Ruby multiple times already since she'd been asleep to see if she was okay. She was fine, but somehow she refused to wake up. Nothing he'd tried so far had worked, and so he decided to leave her be. Whatever was happening to her, maybe it was best not to interrupt it. Unfortunately, this was a poor time for her to fall into a coma. Malcolm's warding around his home was durable but could still be breached. Vampires were actively pursuing us, along with the Werewolf Council. By now, maybe the humans were as well.

The light to the patio switched on and a cloud of black smoke appeared beside me.

I sighed as Malcolm appeared from within it.

"Where did you get this?" he asked curiously as he held up Axel's book.

I had forgotten Axel had taken the book with him. I stared at the thick writing on its cover, *The History of the Damned*, and shrugged. "It belongs to Axel. It has a lot of info on vampires and how to fight them."

"You say that so lightly. You don't know the importance of this book, do you?"

I shrugged again.

His green eyes narrowed at me. "I'm not from the supernatural world and I know what this book is, while you and Axel don't? This is the only book in existence known to contain complete and accurate information on the vampire species for your information. I'm shocked something so valuable is not in the werewolf Council's possession under lock and key. How did Axel's family manage to keep it hidden from them?" He opened the book while shaking his head. "Unbelievable."

"Listen, up until the vampires crawled out of whatever hole they were hiding in, we thought they were extinct or even a myth. I wasn't exactly puzzling over where the vampire information was. The fact that they were gone was good enough for me," I said indignantly. "As for how Axel's family kept the book out of the Council's hands, you'd have to direct that question to Axel himself." I didn't care that this man was Ruby's father. He had threatened to kill her. Even though he felt like that was the only way to *save her* from the same fate as her mother, I'd never trust him around her.

I'd never trust him, period.

"Besides, you're a black-magic user. I don't doubt you know many things you probably shouldn't," I replied with distaste.

Malcolm shook his head. "Well, thanks to being a black-magic user, I found something no one else would," he retorted as he skimmed through the book's pages.

"What are you talking about?"

He looked my way, his eyes turning black. He then peered back down at the book, waved his hand over it, and the pages started to flip on their own. "There is demon magic emanating from this book," he replied as he watched the pages turn until the book was open at its center.

I grew curious.

"No one other than a demon or a black-magic user would have been able to sense it." He held his hand over the book, and a black mist began to flow from his hand to cover the book's pages.

We both watched as the pages began to change.

I moved closer as the writing on the pages morphed into pictures.

Once the mist cleared, Malcolm and I sported the same shocked expression as we stared down at the book.

"I—what? What is this?" I asked rhetorically.

Malcolm said nothing. His eyes were still wide in shock while glued to the book. "As I said, this is the only book that has accurate intelligence on the vampires."

I shook my head. "In all the stories I've heard of vampires,

vampires and werewolves have been at it since the beginning of time. The two species hate each other, so what the hell does this mean?" I couldn't look away from the picture of a female werewolf and a male vampire holding hands. The picture captured so much that I could clearly see the love in their eyes. A vampire and a werewolf together didn't seem possible to me.

The woman on the left page wore a deep green dress with a large green emerald around her neck, the color matching her eyes. The man on the right page wore a loose-fitting white silk shirt, its first two buttons undone with his black hair cascading down his shoulders. His eyes were a striking blue against his pale skin. Below them on the rest of the page was a war being fought between vampires and werewolves, a complete divergence from the love depicted between the woman and man at the top of the page.

I tapped a finger on the page. "Since you know so much, do you know what this means? Why would a vampire and a werewolf be holding hands like this?"

He shook his head. "I don't know. I knew *of* the book. I didn't know what was inside it. How did Axel even get his hands on this?" He turned to me with a questioning look on his face, as if he was the owner of the book and had just discovered who had stolen it.

"It's been in his family for generations, I think. Why?"

He kept staring at me as if he was trying to judge if I was telling the truth. "Okay." He looked back down at the book and turned a few pages before returning to the center. "I'll have to go through it thoroughly. There might be more hidden pages."

Suddenly, Ruby's scent engulfed my senses. I turned around as she stepped onto the patio.

"Hey," she greeted me, an apologetic look in her eyes.

I held my hand out to her. She took it, and I pulled her to me then kissed the top of her head. "Hey, how are you feeling? You've been out for a few hours."

"I, um... I feel okay." She gave me a weak smile, her eyes

looking a bit swollen. She looked Malcolm's way and cocked her head towards the book in his hand.

"What was your vision about?" Malcolm queried.

Ruby eyed the book in his hand as she answered, "I, ah, I saw a vampire, a man, and I don't know, it looked like he was about to feed on a woman, but she looked willing." She rubbed at her eyes and sighed. "Then I saw this battle from many years ago. People had swords and shit. Vampires and werewolves were fighting. It was... horrible." She looked from Malcolm and then up to me. "I could almost smell the blood."

"A battle, huh?" Malcolm repeated.

I knew what he was getting at.

Ruby nodded at him and combed her hair back from her face as the wind blew it forward. "Yeah..." She bit down on her lip. "I saw Mom."

Malcolm closed the book in his hand slowly. "During the battle?"

"No. After the vision ended, I was... somewhere else. It was a meadow. I don't know where exactly. First I saw a white wolf, and then I saw *her*. I saw Lovette. She was truly there."

"How?" I asked.

She shrugged. "I don't know. She told me she was sorry for taking my memories and that we need to find General Presley."

Considering she had been out for hours, I doubted that was all they had talked about, but I understood her not wanting to go into details. She had been given an opportunity most people never received—a second chance to speak to someone they loved and lost.

I shifted my weight from one foot to the other. "Why do we need to find Presley?"

She shook her head. "I... she didn't say, exactly, but I think it's for us to work together with the humans."

"Are you talking about the humans I saved you guys from?" Malcolm asked as he glanced at Ruby and then me.

Ruby nodded. "Yes. He wanted my help to fight the vampires. Mom said this isn't the first time vampires have tried to take over, but this time, they are succeeding because the creatures of the world are divided. We have to work with humans to have a chance at defeating the vampires."

Malcolm gave me a look the moment Ruby had said this wasn't the first time vampires had tried to take over.

I knew he was having the same thought as I was, about the werewolf that had sacrificed herself to end the war. Sometimes, I think about what life was like for supernaturals back then, being able to live openly and not in hiding as we did now. What had that freedom felt like?

Once this was all over, I guessed the supernatural community at large would have to come forward. Many would try to remain in hiding, and those who'd already been outed, like werewolves, would be discriminated against. However, I had hope that I'd live long enough to see this world the way it should be, with everyone being allowed to live openly and peacefully on the earth they were born on.

Supernaturals deserved that.

"What were you two doing, anyway?" Ruby suddenly questioned.

Malcolm opened the book once more and showed her the pictures we had found. "This book was emanating demon magic. I picked up on it, and then found this..." He opened the book at its center to show her the picture there.

Ruby reached out a hand to touch the woman and man. She pulled her hand away quickly, as if the page had stung her.

Malcolm quickly closed the book. "What is it?" he asked her. "Did you feel something?"

"It's them," she whispered. "It's the woman and man from my vision."

———

Axel

I stared down at the page Malcolm had found in my book. I wanted to know how a book coated in demon magic had been passed down in my family for generations.

Werewolves could sense demons, smell them, but we couldn't detect their magic if it had already been used.

"Where did you really get that book?" Malcolm asked suspiciously.

I looked up at him and closed the book. "I told you, it's been in my family for years."

"It's coated with demon magic. A demon wouldn't have done that for free. They do nothing for free," he rebutted.

"I don't know," I told him for the second time. "I don't know why demon magic was used to hide pages of this book, okay? Or how a werewolf got herself involved with a vampire centuries ago. It doesn't take a genius to realize they were a couple, and that's without Ruby's vision confirming it. All I know is this book..." I tapped it with a finger, "...has been in my family for a long time. If you want more answers, I suggest going back in time, Malcolm. That's not even what's important here. What is really curious is the man and woman in the picture." I tilted my head to look at Ruby. "Did you see anything else? Anything you feel might be important?"

She shook her head. "It all happened pretty quickly. Nothing else is standing out in my mind right now, but I'll give it some thought."

"I don't get it," I muttered, more to myself than the others. "In all the stories I've heard, vampires and werewolves have always hated each other."

"That's what I said," Xavier added. "I don't think we have time to focus on this right now. Okay, a werewolf and a vampire were together years ago. Things were different then. I doubt it has anything to do with the mess the world is in right now."

"You're probably right," Malcolm agreed. "I'll keep checking the book. If there are any more pages, I'll find them. Maybe I'll find something that can help us now."

I gave the book to him.

Malcolm nodded. "You three can go look for Presley. If he's alive, I doubt he'll want to see me after I killed his men. If I discover anything else, I know how to find you." He said nothing else as he walked from the room, his snake appearing on his shoulders out of a black mist.

I looked at Ruby and her eyes met mine. I could almost feel her lips on mine from the brief kiss we had shared earlier. "Are you okay?" I whispered to her.

She nodded. "I'm okay, yeah."

"So, you saw your mom, huh?"

She gave me a tight-lipped smile and nodded.

I knew what it felt like to see someone you thought you'd never see again until the day you died. After the love of my life, Lilith, died years ago, I changed. I became quiet, distant, broken. I yearned to see her face, to hear her voice. Finally, she appeared to me again one night, and I got a chance to say my final goodbye. After she vanished again, it felt like I was losing her a second time. I grieved all over again, and a small part of me wished I had never seen her again.

Xavier and Ruby started to talk about the white wolf she saw, but I was busy just watching her, imagining what I'd do if I lost her too. Losing Lilith had been hard, painful, and the worst part was since she was a witch and our relationship had been a secret, I hadn't been able to speak to anyone about what was happening.

I didn't want to speak to anyone, anyways. Talking about it had been much too difficult.

Ruby, however, what I felt for Ruby, the completion she'd brought to my life, without her I'd...

I killed my negative thoughts.

A human had killed Lilith, and finding out my mate was

human sent me spiraling, causing me to make decisions I'd hate myself for until the day I died. I had hurt Ruby, insulted her, I had locked her away in—

I clenched and unclenched my hands as my self-loathing grew to a crescendo. Her even speaking to me was a blessing I'd never take for granted. Even back then, as much as I had wanted to hate her, I couldn't, and I couldn't reject her. Lilith told me not to harden my heart, but it happened anyway, and I wasn't able to accept Ruby the way I should have when she came into my life. Lilith had told me to keep *The History of the Damned* safe. For a while, I kept it close, but there didn't seem to be a reason to keep doing it as the years passed. I *wanted* to forget about the damn book. It had become a reminder of Lilith.

"Sorry, what? I didn't hear that." I turned to Ruby as I realized she was calling my name.

She sat down, her long red hair hanging over her shoulders. "Presley... Mom said I should find him, but I have no idea how. Apparently, I just need to trust my powers and they will help me."

"Then I guess that's what you do need to do," I told her. "Decide where we need to start. Wherever you go, we'll follow."

She rolled her eyes. She looked from Xavier to me and then back before smiling.

It did feel good to see a genuine smile on her lips.

"Yeah, okay." Sighing, she got up and ran her hand down the front of her black blouse. "I guess we can start where we last saw him."

CHAPTER FOUR

RUBY

I impatiently waited as Axel came to a stop on the road where we left Presley. That night, Malcolm killed all Presley's men to get to us, and then I discovered Malcolm was my father. It was just one of many eventful nights since. I'd lost count of how many there had been.

I kept tapping my finger on my thigh, my nerves getting the better of me as I tried to figure out how the hell I would locate Presley. We hopped out of the car together, the mid-morning sun warming the earth. Traveling by day was the safer bet... to an extent, at least. While we could avoid the vampires during the day, we still had to watch out for the humans hunting werewolves.

"Do you guys have his scent?" I asked them both.

"No," Xavier mumbled back as his nostrils flared.

"Too much time has passed," Axel added.

I sighed.

The road looked completely bare. It was as if the multiple exploded cars from that night that left the road littered with glass and dead bodies had simply vanished into thin air, spirited away by a supernatural janitorial crew Perhaps vampires had gotten to the bodies, but why were all the wrecked cars gone too? I doubted vamps had use for those.

We all walked away from each other in separate directions, our eyes on the ground looking for any clues.

I sighed. "Well, this is a dead end."

"There might be something here." Xavier kept looking around us as if he'd seen something, but the place was empty.

Axel kicked at a rock, sending it rolling off the road and towards the tree line at the side of the road. "This place was cleaned. If I had to guess, I'd say humans did the cleaning. Vamps wouldn't have bothered. There's nothing left to find now." He turned, walking back to the car.

I narrowed my eyes at the spot the rock had been. I headed over to the spot while snapping my finger to get the guys' attention, my eyes glued to the ground. "I found something." I closed my eyes for a moment and tried to remember everything from that night. I then opened my eyes and began turning in a circle, visually reconstructing everything in my mind as it had been that night. "When Malcolm attacked Presley, this is where he fell." I pointed to the drop of dried blood on the ground.

Axel and Xavier drew closer.

Xavier bent down and scratched at the small red spot on the ground. "Yup." He stood up. "That's blood, but it could be anyone's, Ruby."

I looked up at him. "But what if it's his? Maybe I can... use this." I stared back down at the blood and got on my knees. Inhaling deeply, I placed my hands on my thighs and sat back on my heels. "Okay, Mom, let's see if I can do this."

"What are you going to do?" Xavier asked.

I honestly didn't know. "Not be afraid, like Mom said. I guess?" I shrugged, with no confidence at all that I even could do this. I exhaled and held a hand out to hover over the blood on the ground. I closed my eyes and shuffled forward a little. I waited and waited, but nothing happened. My shoulders slumped as I made a face. "So much happened just now," I mumbled sarcastically. "Trust my powers, my ass."

"Hey," Axel interjected. "You can't just wait for something to happen. Relax, open yourself up. Your power belongs to you. You don't belong to it. Stop waiting for it to do something, okay? Trusting yourself means opening up to whatever needs to happen."

"You know, you're not just as dumb as they say you are," I teased with a grin.

He smirked. "No one says that. Not unless they want to die," he whispered as he stood.

"Try again," Xavier urged.

I nodded, a little more confidence seeping into me.

I stared down at the blood for a moment. I breathed slow and even as I stretched my hand out again, and closed my eyes. I reached out to the power within me. As I did, that buzz of energy seemed to be there. Instead of waiting for it to act, I grabbed it and began telling it what to do.

The darkness behind my lids began to fade. An image appeared far away, gradually coming closer and becoming larger as it did. I rocked back as I was thrust into an image of the night we had left Presley.

Vampires had appeared shortly after we left. Since I'd met the vampires being referred to as Skins, the ones that looked human, I figured the creatures I was looking at were Bleeders, with their pale, hairless skin. They started feasting on the bodies on the ground when Presley woke up. He killed one of the vampires and was about to be attacked by another one when his backup arrived. Cars carrying more men appeared, killed the vampires, and collected the bodies on the side of the road. Presley was helped into the back of a vehicle while the wrecked cars were placed on truck transport.

Presley watched while six additional bodies were placed alongside the bodies of the men Malcolm had killed in the back of a van. The vampires had been killed, but those men lost their lives in the process of retrieving Presley. I could almost feel the anger and regret emanating from him.

A tall man—his brown eyes as dark as his skin—approached Presley. "What happened here?" he asked.

Presley didn't look away from the van with the dead bodies as he replied, "We retrieved the girl, but she was taken from us before we made it back to base."

The man continued to stare at Presley.

After a while, Presley finally looked at him. "Okay," he said with a nod. "We'll head back to base."

The vision cleared. I opened my eyes and got to my feet shakily. I rocked back on my heels to fall.

Xavier reached out and grabbed my arm.

"You okay?" Axel asked.

"What did you see?" Xavier added.

I released his arm after balancing myself. I tried to calm down, but I could still feel my power humming in my veins. I swallowed as I squeezed my eyes shut, then opened them.

Xavier frowned. "Your eyes are black."

"I know," I replied strenuously. "I-I'm trying to stay in control, but it's—not working. I, um, I saw what happened after we left Presley. Vampires found him, but so did his people. They headed back to their base, wherever that is. When we find that, we'll find Presley."

I walked around and away from them, my fingers pressed to my temples. The last thing I wanted to do was to hurt them. My powers had done what I had wanted. Now I had to learn how to come down from the high of using them. "We should head back to Malcolm's and figure out how to locate—" a hand wrapped around my elbow and yanked me to the side. I looked up at Axel in time to see a bullet pierce his shoulder.

Confused and in shock, I couldn't get the words out to ask what the hell was happening before Axel pulled me behind his back. I stared wide-eyed at Xavier.

His eyes had turned black as he hunched forward, his eyes on something behind us, and he growled while his fangs elongated. He fell to a knee and began to shift when a wolf appeared out of nowhere and sprang at him.

Axel released me and rammed his shoulder into the wolf, stopping it from attacking Xavier, who was still shifting.

I looked behind me to find a man with a scar under his left eye, his gun aimed at me. Everything was happening so quickly that when he pulled the trigger, I stood frozen.

Axel appeared in front of me and he shot hit him in the back. His hands resting on my shoulders dug into my skin, but I couldn't say or do anything as he began to lower to the ground. His hold on me tightened as he coughed up blood.

"Axel?" I softly said as I fell to the ground with him, my eyes wide and stinging with tears. "Axel!" I screamed as the fight between the unknown wolf and Xavier rang in my ears.

Shaking with my chest hurting as if a hand was wrapped around my heart, I looked up to see that three more men joined the first that had shot Axel.

They were all dressed in full black, along with another transformed wolf— then it hit me. These had to be the men from the Werewolf Council. They had to be.

I looked down at Axel on the ground, blood soaking through his shirt at the shoulder as his hand gripped at his chest.

I felt a rush of energy from within the earth rise and engulf me. As I stared down at Axel's black eyes and he peered into mine, black veins began to make their way up to his neck from the wound in his shoulder. Embers of my anger ignited into a roaring fire as my rage consumed me.

I got to my feet slowly, an electrifying sensation coursing through my body. I felt better than I ever had before. I could feel the power within me, filling me up completely. I felt invincible. I felt like I couldn't be touched.

I channeled my anger from Axel was now lying on the ground,

his skin turning pale, all because he took bullets intended for me. "You shot him," I accused through clenched teeth, my eyes on the man with the scar under his eyes.

He had just made the biggest mistake of his short life.

"I was aiming for you," he replied with a smirk.

I lost it. I stopped thinking of everything except my rage as my power erupted inside me like a volcano. All I could see was the man with the gun still in his hand.

The sickening smile on his face faded as his hand holding the gun began to rise.

The men around him backed away nervously.

"What the hell are you doing?" one of them shouted.

"What the hell, man? Lower the gun!" another added as they kept backing away.

"It's—it's—her," the man I was targeting choked out.

I forced him to throw the gun to the ground as I held my head up, my fists clenched at my sides.

He fell to the ground, his back arched as his clothes began to rip. His shoulder snapped and he howled in pain as his left leg followed. "Stop—her!" he yelled.

The other men looked my way.

I didn't care what they did. There was nothing they could do to stop me, and this man was going to pay for what he had just done to Axel. I could no longer hear Xavier and the other werewolf fighting. There was nothing except my rage and my power coursing through me.

The man's transformation continued, his bones breaking and rearranging as fur began to burst from his skin.

"Stop! Stop!" He cried out, his face now shifting as a snout began to appear where his nose and mouth were.

I flicked my wrist and his head snapped to the side, the sound of breaking bone echoing in my ear, but my rage didn't die as I had expected it to. If anything, it was fueled even further when the other men aimed their guns at me.

I held my hand out, warmth rolling from my core to the tips of my fingers.

One of the men dropped his gun. He flashed his fingers as the now-hot gun burned him. His eyes widened as he watched the weapon on the ground begin to melt.

Before the other men could do the same, their guns started to melt as well.

No one else would be shot today. "Axel won't die alone today." I held my other hand up, causing their bodies to go stiff until the first bone snapped in each of them as I controlled their change.

As I called on the wolf inside them to come forth, someone yelled my name. "Ruby! That's enough!"

My hands fell to my side, my palms still warm as I looked into Olcan's strange central heterochromatic eyes, the blue outer rim of his eyes fading into brown in the middle. I said nothing as he stepped past his men.

I narrowed my eyes at him.

He stopped, his arms held up in surrender. "I only want to talk." He lowered his hands, his eyes roaming my face and body.

I saw the excitement within his eyes, and it made me sick. First, he wanted to kill me, and now he was fascinated by me? I looked down at Axel, the veins now covering his left cheek. I pointed at him as I looked at Olcan.

His face twisted with confusion.

Then Axel groaned as if in pain, grimacing as he rolled to his side.

I opened my palm as the bullet that had been in his back flew into my hand. I stared down at the bullet in my palm and watched as it turned to dust.

"Heal him." I brushed my hands on my jeans. "Or everyone here that I don't care about... dies."

———

Ruby

While driving to Olcan's house with Axel lying in my lap in pain, I was distracted enough to get my powers under control. I had been trying not to panic at the black lines spreading across his face or the way his lips were getting darker while his skin got paler.

He looked like he was dying.

Now, at Olcan's house with the sick bastard himself sitting across from me, I wanted nothing more than to wring his neck with my own hands.

"So," Olcan drawled as he crossed one leg over the other. "You're Lovette's daughter, huh?"

"Yes. What do you want, Olcan? You wanted to talk, so talk," I countered.

He chuckled.

There had just been something about this man that had bothered me from the moment I met him. Maybe it was his odd eyes and bald head that created a bizarre combo for me. "Where is Axel?"

He uncrossed his legs and looked towards the door. "He's safe. He was shot with a bullet that's poisonous to werewolves, but he's being treated as we speak. He'll live."

"That's good news for us both," I remarked.

He smirked. "There is something different about you, Ms. Saunders. I wonder what it is. The impressive amount of power you have, maybe?"

"Is that what you want, Olcan? You always seem to want something from me. The last time we met, you wanted to kill me, so what do you want now?" I did not intend to waste time chit-chatting with this man.

The mischievous look he'd been wearing vanished and a serious expression took its place. He looked every bit of the no-nonsense Council member you'd expect him to be. "The first time we met, I didn't know about your significance, your power, or your lineage. You being Lovette's daughter changes a lot." He gestured to me.

I shook my head. "Drop the act, Olcan. You would have killed me anyway and buried the truth about me being Lovette's daughter. You would have done anything to hide the fact that Lovette had a child with a human." I spat the words at him.

The angered look in his eyes at the mention of Lovette being with a human brought me more satisfaction than I'd expected.

"You can help the werewolves," he declared after a moment of utter silence. He was changing the topic. "You have the power to fight with us, to protect us from the vampires and humans. You're one of us."

"I'm not one of you," I told him bluntly. "I'm mated to werewolves, but I'm half human and half Enchanted; that is what I am. I will fight for all creatures against the vampires, and that includes humans." I flicked a finger. "Humans shouldn't have attacked werewolves while vampires ran free as the real enemy, but they were scared and confused. Besides, no matter how powerful you think I am, I am not powerful enough to save werewolves from both human and vampire enemies at the same time. The vampires alone are barely being held at bay." I stood from my chair. "We need allies. I don't know about you, but I'd much rather make allies of the humans than the vampires. Humans and werewolves need to work together to defeat the vampires. It's the only way any of us stand a chance."

He laughed loudly at this before settling once he realized I wasn't joking.

"I'm not kidding, and you know it. You also know fighting the vampires alone will get us all killed. They outnumber us, and those numbers grow every night."

"An alliance? With humans?" His eyes rounded. "Listen, Ruby, you're new to this, new to this world. Something like that will not happen easily," he said condescendingly.

I opted to ignore him. "You're new to this world as well,

Olcan, or have you lived in a world overrun by vampires before?" I arched a brow questioningly.

He rolled his eyes at me.

I didn't care how he felt. I had a point to make, and I was making it. "You say an alliance can't happen, but the same was once said about a human being mated to a werewolf, right?"

"Okay, Ruby." He held his hand up. "Tell me, how did you find out you are Lovette's daughter?"

I clasped my hands behind my back as I answered, "The block in my mind was removed."

"And what else was revealed? How did you get these powers? It's because you're a hybrid, yes?"

I shrugged. "Does that even matter right now, Olcan? Listen, I'm going to be honest with you. You're asking questions that I refuse to answer right now because I frankly don't trust you. You could easily try to use any information I share with you against me. Since we both know you wanted to kill me, how about proving you are trustworthy before expecting me to share sensitive information with you? Help with the alliance between werewolves and humans, and I'll share what I learned about myself with you." No way would I spill everything to him. For all I knew, he was just waiting to know where my powers came from so he could kill me where I stood, or worse—and I did believe he was capable of worse.

"Fair enough, Ms. Saunders." He held his hand out to me.

I squinted as I peered down at it. That had been easier than I thought. "What's the catch?" I asked him.

Olcan shook his head. "No catch. You said you'll tell me all you know, and that's all I need. Do we have a deal or not?" He tilted his head to the side as he held his hand out.

"We have a deal." Still feeling suspicious, I shook it firmly before quickly pulling away.

CHAPTER FIVE
THE VAMPIRE GENERAL

The sound of humans screaming in pain and agony never got tiring.

The smell of fresh blood was abundant in the air as the Bleeders maimed and tortured the terrified humans they found hiding in the basement. The pitiful people were smart enough to avoid hiding in the upper rooms where we would've found them immediately. Yet their foolish plan merely delayed the inevitable, especially since there was only one way in or out of the basement.

It hadn't taken long for the Bleeders to sniff them out and find them, but I gave them an A for effort.

I had already sorted out the humans to be killed from the humans to be turned. Now all I had to do was wait for the Bleeders to feed before we could move on. I released the young woman in my arms, her body hitting the ground with a thud. The beautiful pale blue eyes that had drawn me to her were now pale and lifeless.

Running my tongue over my fangs, I swallowed the last of her blood.

One of my soldiers walked towards me. "General," he greeted me, his eyes briefly drifting to the blonde-haired beauty at my feet.

I could have turned her, but though she was beautiful, I found her high-pitched voice annoying. I certainly wasn't interested in listening to *that* for centuries to come.

"We've picked up on the girl's scent, though it is faint. They must have been out during the day. We do know she's traveling with wolves, and they are on the move."

This news piqued my interest. The wheels in my mind began to turn as I stared down at the girl at my feet.

The growls and hisses of two nearby Bleeders penetrated the air as they fought over what appeared to be a man's arm.

"Enough!" I yelled.

They both dropped the arm and held their heads down in shame as they backed away.

I knew the hunger inside them, their insatiable taste for blood. The difference between Bleeders like them and Skins like me was that I could control my thirst. "Find her location by tomorrow night," I commanded before looking at the man still standing by my side, his red eyes on me. I walked off towards the building's exit. "I'd like to meet Ms. Saunders in person."

I exited the building and stepped out into the night that had been my beginning and end for more years than I cared to count. I didn't remember what it was like being human. I couldn't even remember what the sun felt like on my skin.

Nevertheless, I could remember the very moment the Queen herself turned me and made me her son as if it was only yesterday.

We'd waited so long for this, to feel the cool night air on our skin again, to live openly and not cramped together like ants. Decades... it'd taken decades for us to get to where we were now. We'd waited for the right moment for so long, and I'd be damned if I let one little girl ruin it all.

———

Ruby

Maybe making a deal with Olcan hadn't been the wisest decision, but what other choice did I have? It felt like I was running out of time, like something loomed on the horizon and I wasn't prepared for it. The world was reverting to the Dark Ages, and I felt like the walls were closing in on all of us.

The power inside me—the Goddess's power—was strong; it was intoxicating and like nothing I'd ever felt before. Yet, it was also scary. I lost control when that man shot Axel. All I had wanted was to see him suffer.

I killed a man in cold blood. Each time I thought about it, a chill ran down my spine. Even worse, I felt nothing at all when I did it. Killing him—taking his life—hadn't fazed me at all. This was what Mom should have warned me about—the superiority and emptiness that came with having the power of a god. I had no idea how I had controlled his shift. I just looked within him to the animal at his core and called it forward without really thinking about it.

I think it made sense, though. The Goddess created werewolves, so no doubt she had control over them as well. I had her power, so I had that control as well.

"This is so fucked up," I whispered to myself as I walked down the quiet hall to Axel's room.

Olcan wanted to know everything I knew. He wanted to know where my power was from and what I was capable of. He'd seen what I could do, and I didn't want to even think about what would happen if he ever got the kind of power residing within me.

I hadn't been able to sleep last night after arriving here. Between worrying about Axel, finding Presley, and wondering if the Goddess had made me a monster, I couldn't fall asleep for even a minute. My thoughts kept repeating on an endless loop. Before I knew it, it was dawn and another day of living this hell.

For the entire day, I locked myself in a room to practice using my powers. What other chance would I get other than when I was in danger and had no choice but to react? If I did not learn to control my abilities, I feared I might be consumed by them.

I might have almost burned the building down once or twice, but in the end, I was able to control the heat within my body. Calming down wasn't as hard as it had been before. The first time I had killed vampires, my powers had backfired on me, burning me as well. It wasn't an experience I cared to repeat.

Lovette had said my powers would start to grow quickly, and I could see that happening.

"Xavier!" I called as I spotted him at the end of the hall. I hadn't seen him all day.

He held his hand out to me.

I drew closer and slid my hand into his.

He kissed the back of my hand before kissing my forehead, and the tension between us from when I had told him I needed space at Malcolm's dissipated.

"I heard you practicing today." He pulled back but kept holding my hand.

I nodded. "I was trying to."

"How was it?" He moved my hair behind my ear, his eyes darting back and forth over my face.

"Hard, but I'm getting there, I guess... I, um, I don't know who that person was that killed..."

"Hey, hey," he interjected as he pinched my chin. "You were protecting yourself and us. It was either them or us. Olcan's loss is on him. He attacked us."

I tried to find comfort in his words, but I could still hear the sound of the bones breaking in that man's neck as I had killed him. "Yeah," I drawled, "You're right. What have you been doing all day? I didn't see you even once."

"I went out for a bit. I've been working with Olcan's men to try and track down Presley's base." He released my hand to comb his hair back.

I noticed the bags under his eyes. *It looks like he didn't get much sleep, either.* "And?" I probed. "Any luck?"

He shook his head. "Not yet, but we're still working on it. We found one working computer in this dump, but as expected, there is no internet connection to check if there are any army bases close by. One could have been created after the invasion."

"Okay," I mumbled as I stepped to the side to lean against the door to Axel's room. "I hope Presley doesn't hate us now after what happened. He might have been the only human willing to work with us."

"Well, if his mind has changed about an alliance, we'll just have to change it back again," Xavier said with a casual shrug.

I hoped it'd be as easy as he was making it seem.

"I'm surprised Olcan agreed to the alliance," Xavier stated.

I didn't intend to tell Xavier, or Axel for that matter, about the deal I'd made with Olcan. They would object to it, of course. "I don't trust Olcan, but at least he sees that we can't win this war against the vampires by standing alone. Fighting together is vital for our survival."

"Yes, and I don't trust Olcan either. He's a snake. I doubt he'd try anything after seeing what you're capable of," he added. "He just can't be trusted. If he agreed to this, something must be in it for him, and it can't be good."

Xavier was right about that. Something was indeed in it for him.

"I heard the other wolves talking about you," he went on. "News about you being Lovette's daughter is spreading fast. Olcan would have killed you to keep it a secret, but now he can't touch you. The backlash would ruin him."

After Olcan saw what I was capable of, I was sure he wanted to cut me open and dissect me even more than he did before. I frowned. "They're talking about me?"

He nodded. "You're Lovette's daughter; you're royalty. Now

that you're clearly a major asset in winning back our world, don't be surprised if you start getting treated differently."

I said nothing. I wasn't sure what to expect, but I'd never been one to love the spotlight. I knew almost nothing about my mother other than she was loved and respected. Many looked up to her, and now they might look up to me. What if I let them all down? What if the Goddess picked the wrong girl? "Oh, okay," I whispered.

Xavier chuckled, no doubt noticing the terrified look on my face. "Relax, Ruby. All I'm saying is everyone else will now see what I've always seen—that you're special."

He leaned down and I closed my eyes as his soft lips pressed to mine in sublime union. He held my waist firmly and pulled me close to his hard body, and I reached up to wrap my arms around his neck. He broke our kiss to trail light, soft kisses down my neck, and my body shivered. It was so easy to get lost in the moment anytime this man touched me. "Breathe," he whispered in my ear.

I did as he commanded, inhaling deeply and exhaling through my mouth.

He held me tight. "Don't think about what anyone has to say about you or what they are expecting from you. Okay?"

I nodded. "Ok."

He placed a final kiss on my shoulder. "Has Natalie contacted you?"

I shook my head.

He looked away, his brows furrowed. "She hasn't mind-linked with me either. I'm worried about them. I don't know if the pack is safe or not." He ran his hand down his face, pulling his cheeks down. "Natalie should have contacted us by now."

"I'm sure they're okay," I told him with a smile. "But I can try doing a mind link myself. That should be easy compared to the things I've done so far. Right?"

He placed his hands on my shoulders. "You're getting stronger, but mind links aren't as easy as they seem. You could really hurt yourself and the person you try to make the connection with. Let's not push your powers too far."

I moaned at the feeling of his hands running up my shoulders and neck to cup my cheeks. I knew he was only worried about me, but I wanted to help. I had only started training myself during the day when I had gotten tired of sitting around, doing nothing. Axel was still out of commission, and Xavier was busy with Olcan. Sitting on the sidelines was driving me crazy.

For the most powerful person here, it seemed like I wasn't needed for shit unless there was killing to be done.

Becoming a weapon was not how I saw my life turning out. You didn't need a college degree for it, that was for sure. Not that I had a college to return to anyways. My scholarship was toast by now.

"I'm not pushing myself. In the beginning, I could only feel my power when I lost control and it was triggered. Now, I can constantly feel it buzzing just beneath my skin. Lovette said I should trust my powers, and I'm starting to. I can contact Natalie."

His hands fell away from my face. "I know you're getting stronger. I just want you to be careful, that's all. As you said, they're probably okay. If Dad wasn't okay, I'd feel it. Let's focus on one thing at a time. Right now, we need to focus on Presley."

I wanted to fight him on the matter, but I knew he was right. "Okay."

Smiling, he kissed my forehead and backed away. "I'm going to find Olcan. I hadn't asked him before, but he must know something about the vampire queen. Maybe I'll tell him about what Malcolm found."

"Okay," I murmured, wishing we didn't have to rely on Olcan of all people for help.

He turned away and left.

I watched him as he walked away. When I could no longer see his towering muscular figure, I groaned and palmed my face. After a moment, I turned and knocked on the door to Axel's room.

"Come in!" he greeted from the other side of the door. When I entered the room, Axel was sitting on the side of the bed. He looked up at me.

As I closed the door behind me, my eyes roamed over his shirt-less body. The black veins had completely disappeared, and he looked much better since color had returned to his skin. "You heard Xavier and me talking, didn't you?" I asked as I sat down beside him and scooted further up on the bed, so my legs dangled just above the ground.

"I can't say I could help it," he replied with a smirk.

I bobbed my head. "Werewolf hearing, right?'

"Right," he answered with a grin.

I chuckled. "How are you feeling?"

He looked away, the smirk on his face slowly fading. "Better," he answered after a while.

I had a feeling this wasn't entirely true. I placed my hand on his that rested on his thigh. "You saved my life," I said softly.

He shook his head as he flipped his hand over to hold mine. His thumb caressed my hand. "You saved mine, actually," he whis-pered as he leaned over and kissed my temple.

Axel being affectionate always caught me off guard.

He squeezed my hand before releasing it and turning to face me. "How are *you* feeling?"

I gazed back at him in confusion. I wasn't the one who'd been shot. "Ah, I'm fine."

He kept staring at me expectantly.

I smiled. "I'm fine, really. I'm keeping it together."

"What you did was—"

"I know," I said sharply, cutting his words short. I knew what he wanted to say. "I know it was crazy, and no, I don't know how I did it. I just reacted. But even so, I still feel—horrible inside."

"He tried to kill us, Ruby. He doesn't deserve your sympathy. I'm sorry you had to do what you did. However, Olcan is respon-sible for that man losing his life. His approach for 'just wanting to talk' was foolish. Ruby, if anyone attacks you—be it werewolf, vampire, or human—I want you to defend yourself."

"Yeah, Xavier said the same thing about Olcan being responsible," I told him as I stared down at the glass of water on the bedside table.

"And he was right." His baritone voice vibrated with the strength of his conviction.

My eyes slid to his.

He reached out and picked up my hand. "Now, tell me where Olcan is, so I can rip his fucking heart out."

The fact that he said it so calmly and casually made me believe he truly intended to kill the man. "He agreed to the alliance with the humans. I'm sorry, but you can't kill him."

Axel released my hand and stood. "That just means I can't kill him *yet*."

With him being shirtless, I couldn't look away from his rippling abs. Shaking my head, I swung my legs onto the bed and laid down to get comfortable. Closing my eyes, I sighed as Axel's scent from the pillow engulfed me. "I wonder where Reika is right now. I'm surprised she's not here with him," I commented, my eyes still closed.

The bed dipped at my feet as Axel sat down. "Probably with the Enchanteds; it's every species for themselves right now."

"Sad world," I mumbled. The lack of sleep was finally catching up with me. "It feels like it's been a week since I last slept."

Axel picked up my legs and removed my shoes. "You need to rest, Ruby. You need to keep your strength up."

The door flew open, and I sat up quickly, my heart in my throat.

Axel was already on his feet, ready to defend.

One of Olcan's men stepped into the room. "Vampires were spotted a mile out, and they are approaching us quickly. Get ready. We're going to be attacked." He walked swiftly out of the room before either of us could respond.

Axel turned to look at me, his body suddenly tense.

I stared at him. "Are you well enough to…"

He nodded. "Yes. I can shift. How the hell did they find us so quickly?"

The stronger I grow, the stronger my scent becomes. "They must've followed my scent. We need to find Xavier and Olcan," I answered hastily as I headed for the door.

Axel grabbed his shirt before rushing out the door behind me.

As we dashed through the hall and down the stairs to find the others, my heartbeat started to pound in my chest. I didn't think I could ever get used to this life. I'd never get used to being hunted, and I'd never get used to all the near-death experiences.

What had changed, however, was my confidence. We might be the ones under attack, but I knew the vampires wouldn't be leaving this place alive.

Axel and I entered the room.

"We need to get Ruby out of here," one of Olcan's men announced.

"Forget it. I'm not going anywhere," I stated firmly.

All eyes turned to look my way.

"I don't need to run, and neither does anyone else." I called on my power, allowing its enticing hum to fill me. "If we stand together, these bloodsuckers won't stand a chance." I knew my eyes had just turned to black, and I grinned widely. "Let's show these asshats why they should be afraid of the Big Bad Wolves!"

"You heard the lady," Olcan announced, his voice echoing through the room as his multi-colored eyes turned to obsidian as well. "Let's remind these vampires who we are! We've hidden in fear long enough!"

CHAPTER SIX

We placed werewolf fighters at each window and exit on the first floor. Every entrance a vampire could possibly enter was being guarded. Some wolves shifted, while others maintained their human form. We all waited impatiently for the impending battle.

Axel and Xavier stood on either side of me, while Olcan and one of his men chose to position themselves next to Xavier. Given Axel's current sentiment toward Olcan, this was probably a wise choice on his part.

While I heard nothing but silence, I knew with their heightened hearing, the werewolves could hear everything outside. Each time I started to speak, Xavier or Axel would hold their hand up to stop me... I needed to remain quiet. Vampires had heightened hearing just like werewolves, and the ones outside were no doubt listening for us.

We all had our backs to the wall beside the front door, the werewolves fangs and claws at the ready as I tried to hold onto the bravado I had felt earlier.

I hadn't caught a whiff of the rancid scent that followed vampires like fleas, so I guessed they weren't close enough to us yet.

Axel nodded at me.

I leaned forward and waved a hand to gain Olcan's attention. "Did you manage to find Presley?" I whispered as softly as possible, my lips barely moving, but I knew he could hear me clearly.

He shook his head. "Not exactly." He leaned forward and whispered back but loud enough for me to hear, "We did find car tracks, so the base can't be far from here. I'd say 15 miles, maybe, or perhaps more, since we weren't able to sniff them out while searching today. I sent two men ahead to see if they could locate the base, but they should have returned by now."

"We have to go," I whispered to Xavier.

Olcan shook his head vigorously. "Not now, when vampires are on our heels."

"I know, Olcan. I meant we have to go as soon as this is over. I just... I'm just worried about losing control and hurting one of you. I don't have control the way you might think I do."

"That doesn't matter, Ruby. In war, control isn't the most important thing. In war, we have to break ourselves free from the restrictions of doubt that could hold us back. We have to do what needs to be done because our opponents will do anything to win. Those Bleeders who are coming won't have control over their bloodlust. I hope you know that. They intend to kill us all, and we need to think the same. You need to focus on doing maximum damage to them in order to ensure we all make it out of here alive."

"Okay, I get..." my words trailed off as the vampire's scent clogged my nostrils.

The sound of breaking glass echoed through the house.

Axel and Xavier both placed their hands across my body as the sound of wolves in battle traveled to our ears.

"Get to the second floor!" Axel yelled.

I shoved his hand away from me. "I'm not running!"

Xavier grabbed me around my waist before the words had completely left my lips and threw me over his shoulder.

"Put me down!" I yelled. "You assholes!"

Xavier was already halfway up the stairs as he ignored my screams.

While upside down, I watched as the front door was kicked open and three vampires rushed inside, one being tackled by Axel.

Xavier and I got to the second floor just as a window to our left shattered. He lowered me to the ground quickly, and I had to catch my balance as a vampire barreled into him.

This was the first time I'd seen a Bleeder in person, and my skin felt itchy at the sight of the ghastly thing.

It looked hairless and pale with jagged, sharp, bloody teeth. Its wide red eyes were frantic and unfocused, while its animalistic growls and hisses were chilling.

Xavier slammed the creature into the wall and sliced its throat open with his claws. He then stuck his arm into the creature's chest and ripped its heart out.

We watched as its lifeless body fell. In my peripheral vision, I noticed a Bleeder rushing up at me from the stairs.

My powers reared inside me as I spun around to face it. I held a hand up as it dove at me, and the vampire froze, suspended in mid-air.

Its eyes were watching me as drool fell from its mouth.

"Burn, bitch," I said through clenched teeth.

Its skin began to bubble.

I released it, causing it to fall to the ground where it began to shriek and bend in all angles, its thin skin melting off its body. The smell was disgusting, but the angered hiss of another vampire down the stairs had me backing away.

The moment it lunged to charge up the stairs, a massive wolf tackled it to the floor. I turned and ran with Xavier behind me as two more vampires appeared. There were more of them than I had imagined. From the sounds of howls and growing banshee-like screams, I knew they were pouring into the house still.

Ringing pinged in my ear, and I spun around when I heard breaking bones.

Xavier was shifting, and the vampires were right behind him. They obviously weren't going to wait until he'd completely shifted to attack.

I held both hands out, squeezing my eyes shut as I dug deep into that pit of intoxicating power inside me. When I opened my eyes again, I could see the white energy around us and the black aura surrounding the vampires. I opened myself up to the energy as I stepped around Xavier, calling it forward as Xavier continued to shift behind me. As I released the buildup of energy pulsating through my body, a scream rolled up my chest to burst forth from my lips.

The vampires were knocked back, their bodies breaking from the force. They fell like broken dolls, their pained cries hurting my ears.

Xavier ran around me, his claws scratching against the floor as he charged towards the vampires. I watched as he ripped into them and smiled at their weak attempts to stop him. He grabbed the last one by its thin ankle and began dragging it away.

Shaking my arms from the tingling sensation within them, I moved back the way we had come, following Xavier and the vampire. I could still feel the earth's energy around me, almost begging for me to consume it, to use it.

I started running, my legs pumping hard when a window to my left shattered and something slammed me into the wall. My hand shot out, my intentions to send the vampire snapping its jaws at my neck flying back through the window, but it bit down on my arm and wrapped its arms around me.

We went falling through the window together, its revolting odor burning my eyes as we fell. I grabbed the creature's face as we fell and forced all the heat inside my body into my arms. I turned us so the vamp was on the bottom to take the brunt of the fall, but even so, the impact rattled me.

I rolled away from the hissing and shrieking creature, trying to ignore the sharp pains in my back and ankle.

Looking down, I realized my ankle was broken. I bared my teeth as it suddenly snapped back into place. I sat up to stare down at my feet in shock.

Okay, that's new.

Looking around me, I stood up and winced as I heard a crack in my back as if a bone had reset itself. I hadn't figured self-healing would be so painful. I'd seen the guys do it so many times without even flinching.

I looked down at my arm while the vampire's cry grew quieter and quieter, the bite on my hand starting to burn. I watched as my blood dripped onto the ground and loud hissing filled the night. The vampires were no doubt being drawn to me, but I didn't move. I didn't run. I didn't feel fear.

My face twisted with rage as they started to circle me, their red eyes like headlights in the night.

I kept turning in a circle, looking from one to the other before holding my bloody arm up. "Hungry?"

Some of them held their heads back, veins protruding from their necks as they inhaled deeply, while others bared their fangs at me.

"None of you deserve my pity," I whispered to myself. I exhaled as I let go of my emotions and inhaled as much energy from the earth as I could take.

One rushed at me and I slapped it across the face, sending it rolling on the ground.

Now realizing I wouldn't be easy prey, the others took a step back.

I could see their aura, the darkness surrounding them, and I tilted my head to the side thoughtfully.

I looked down at my bleeding hand and clenched my fist. As adrenaline coursed through my body, my heart pounded in my chest, and my breathing was labored. I looked up as one of the vampires rushed forward, and I just *reacted*.

The vamp came to an abrupt halt just in front of me, its

clawed hand inches away from my face. I stepped closer until its face was inches away from mine. I envisioned all the corrupt energy inside the vampire flowing into me. When the corrupt energy obeyed and flowed into me like I wanted it to, it wasn't unexpected. Yet, the pain that came with it took me by complete surprise and left me breathless. Nevertheless, I gritted my teeth and kept going. After the first vampire lay dead at my feet, the intense energy draw became a like chain reaction, jumping to the next closest vampire.

One by one, they crumbled to the ground, their hands over their ears or clawing at their own chest as I took their lives. I started to tremble the more I took from them as I caught glimpses in my mind of grisly scenes of torture and horror that would've made crime scenes from serial killers look positively friendly.

Arms grabbed me around my waist and pulled me back from the vampires, and like the others, it fell to the ground.

I pulled away from the person holding me without even looking. I could taste blood on my tongue as I kept hearing the screams of so many dying humans.

I fell to the ground and began forcing the energy I had taken from the vampires into the earth. I couldn't hold it. I knew if I did, I'd die.

I fell back on my ass once all the evil was all expelled from my body, and I looked behind me.

Xavier stood there, naked. "Ruby?"

"I'm fine," I answered hoarsely as I got up.

I swayed as if to fall.

Xavier grabbed my arm quickly.

Although my eyes were blurry, I blinked rapidly at what looked like a man standing in the distance. My vision cleared, and I narrowed my eyes as I realized it was indeed a man.

His red eyes told me he was a vampire. With the semi-darkness around us, I could barely see his face, but his eyes were bright enough to be seen from the distance between us.

"We're being watched," I mumbled under my breath to Xavier.

He raised his head to look as well. He released my arm and stepped forward, a growl rumbling in his chest.

I was too busy finding it odd that I could almost feel fingers inside my mind. My face twisted with discomfort as I looked away from the man to hold my head.

Axel and Olcan appeared by our side, the sounds of battle inside the house now growing faint.

The moment Xavier rushed forward, no doubt to chase the man in the distance, Olcan grabbed him and pulled him back. "Don't!" he yelled.

Xavier yanked his arm for him to release him.

"That's a General, you idiot! Look at the uniform. Does that look like a Bleeder to you?" Olcan added.

We all looked in the direction of the man in the distance. I couldn't see his clothes, and I didn't care to. All I cared about was getting rid of the feeling like he was inside my head. *How is the bastard doing it?*

I created a block in my mind, a metal wall if you will, and the prying fingers started to slip away.

I frowned as the General turned around and headed away.

Axel stepped forward. "Why isn't he attacking us?"

"I don't know," Olcan replied in a hushed and confused voice. "But we should count ourselves lucky."

"If he's a General, shouldn't we try to capture him? He could lead us to the Queen!" Xavier exclaimed.

Axel nodded, sharing his frustration that the vampire was now gone.

"No matter how strong she is," Olcan began as he pointed at me, then frowned at my disheveled state, "Which doesn't look like much, right now, Ruby's not ready to fight a General. Generals are turned by the Queen herself. If we kill one, we'll lead the Queen right to us. That's a fight we can't win right now." He looked towards the forest. "However, if a General came here after she already lost one, she must really want Ruby."

"Well, he just walked away without even trying to take her," Axel pointed out.

"Maybe he wanted to see what she's capable of first," Olcan guessed with a shrug. "Or maybe it was a message that they can take you whenever they wish."

"I felt him inside my mind," I revealed.

Everyone stared at me in silence.

I shrugged. "It was as if he was trying to read or see into my mind."

Wiping blood from his hands, Olcan stepped around us to head back to the house. "You better hope he didn't actually see anything, because if he did and tells the Queen, whatever chance we had at winning was just lost."

———

Olcan

We left at dawn after burying all the men I lost. Being raided by those vampires last night had ruined my plans. All I had to do now was help Ruby with finding this Presley person, and my part in this mess would be over.

Good men... I had lost good men.

I clenched my fists as, even now, her scent licked at my nostrils. When night fell, we'd be attacked again, no doubt. There was no hiding for her anymore, not while she smelled like a walking candy.

"When you guys escaped from Xavier's pack, you masked your scents somehow. Can't you do that now with Ruby?" I asked Xavier and Axel.

Ruby turned around to look at me. "It doesn't work on me anymore. We tried."

"Of course it doesn't," I mumbled to myself as they turned around to continue walking.

"Pick up the pace, Olcan. We need to find the base before sundown," Xavier urged impatiently over his shoulder.

Do these kids really think I'm a machine like they are?

Ruby stopped walking. "Can we rest for a little?"

Xavier nodded. "Okay, five minutes, but we really need to keep moving."

She sat down immediately with an exhausted sigh.

The road looked deserted, the forest on either side of us quiet except for the sound of a few birds and the wind in the trees.

I removed my bag and took a bottle of water out of it. Gulping it down, I watched Axel and Xavier chat among themselves.

I'd noticed Axel had changed. He wasn't the same brooding asshole he had been when I first met him. Xavier had changed as well. He didn't seem to be the naïve, immature kid he used to be. He seemed more like the Alpha he was born to be, ready to lead. The person that interested me the most, though, was Ruby herself.

It was laughable how those three thought they were successfully hiding where Ruby's power originally came from. I already knew she possessed divinity given to her by the Goddess. All I needed to know to successfully set my plans in motion was how she survived for so long with so much power.

Last night, she had killed those vampires by absorbing their life energy—their soul, one might say. It had almost killed her, but she had done it. I know this group didn't hold a lot of love for me; few people did if I was honest. I didn't care what anyone thought of me. All I cared about was learning the information I needed to know. Unfortunately, for that to happen, I needed to gain Ruby's trust. I felt up for the challenge, though. *I'll do whatever it takes to get what I want from these assholes.* "What did it feel like?" I asked suddenly. "What did it feel like when you killed those vampires last night?"

All three of them turned to look at me.

Ruby looked away, her brows slowly pulling together.

I assumed she was recalling what had happened.

"It was like a living death," she answered in a low voice. "I could see death, smell it, and taste it. That's all these creatures are—death and hunger."

"The Bleeders, at least," I clarified.

She gave me a confused look. "Bleeders or the Queen... it doesn't matter. That's what they all are. Look around you; they are killing the world. What happens after humans (and maybe even other supernaturals) cease to exist? What happens then?"

I didn't say anything, and neither did the others. "I'm going to take a piss," I announced as I threw my bag over my shoulder. "Don't think about leaving me behind."

"Make it quick because we just might," Axel shot back. He might not be brooding anymore, but the asshole part of him was still alive and well.

I continued walking in silence until I knew I was out of their hearing range. Then I quickly removed my bag and the small solar phone inside. I held it up to the sun, my eyes darting around the forest as the screen flashed, the sun's rays powering the device.

It finally came on, and I dialed the only number saved. "What the fuck were you thinking?" I whispered as soon as the person answered. "This was not what we talked about."

"Hello, Olcan," the vampire General's deep voice replied calmly on the other line. His words were said slowly and nonchalantly.

His tone pissed me off even more. "I lost all my men! All of them! I told you to wait and I'd give you the girl." I clenched my fist, my rage increasing. "Why didn't you just take her? The Bleeders weren't necessary!"

He sighed. "Plans change, Olcan. The Queen gave her orders, and I obeyed them. Or do you no longer want to be a part of an alliance with her? It was your idea, after all."

I released my fist and exhaled as I pinched the bridge of my nose. "The deal with the Queen was that she'd allow me to find the girl and hand her over. In return, I'd be given Ruby's powers, or did the Queen lie about knowing how to do that?"

I pulled the phone away from my ear as the General hissed.

"Be careful of your words, wolf."

"Why didn't you just take her? You saw what she did. She's growing stronger. The Queen won't be able to—"

"To what?" he interjected, his voice coming out as a low hiss once more. "To kill her? Keep traveling with the girl, Olcan. Follow her to where the humans are, and report the location to me." He hung up.

I had to hold myself back from crushing the phone. I turned it off and threw it into my bag before covering my face with my hands. For years, I'd served as a Council member, and what did I have to show for it?

The other Council members, the self-righteous pricks, were too damn stuck up and trapped in the past to think long term. For years, I'd been telling them we needed to find a way to harness the Enchanteds' power and transfer it to other wolves that could transform. This would bring all werewolves closer to the Goddess, benefitting the entire werewolf society instead of just a few werewolf hybrids. Just thinking about how much stronger werewolves could become if our warriors had Enchanted powers sent chills down my spine.

Even though werewolves aged slower than humans, Enchanteds aged even more slowly, much like witches. In fact, before the truth of the Enchanteds' relationship to the Goddess was revealed, we actually thought Enchanteds descended from a werewolf bloodline tainted by witches.

If I had known from the beginning who Ruby was, the power she had...

My thoughts trailed off as a twig snapped within the forest, and I froze. I picked up my bag slowly as I listened for a heartbeat.

The moment I heard it, I looked up and was engulfed by a cloud of black smoke.

Xavier

"Hey!" Ruby called. "What's wrong?"

I turned my back on the forest as I faced her. "Nothing," I responded. "I thought I heard something."

"Why is Olcan taking so long?" She groaned as she got up off the ground, brushing her hand down the back of her pants.

My eyes drifted to Axel.

He was staring at her ass, then his hazel eyes wandered to me as he arched a brow.

I shook my head as I turned back to the forest. I couldn't fault him for enjoying the view.

"How far does he need to go to take a piss? I can't even hear his heartbeat," Axel said with annoyance. "I'm going to go find..." His words trailed off.

I turned to look at him. "Oh, I hear his—wait, there are two heartbeats."

Suddenly, a man fell from above and all three of us stepped back. It didn't take long before I realized it was Olcan crawling away on his arms to get away from the black smoke above him.

"Malcolm? What the hell are you doing?" Ruby yelled in shock.

Malcolm materialized out of the smoke. His red hair looked tousled and messy, his face red with anger. He pointed at Olcan on the ground. "You should ask him what he's doing, or what he's already done, for that matter."

"What are you talking about?" I asked.

Olcan got to his feet, his backpack falling off his shoulder. "Who the hell is this? Do you know who I am, boy?"

Malcolm's eyes narrowed. "Boy?"

"Olcan, meet my father." Ruby waved her hand from one man to the other. "Malcolm, meet Olcan, a member of the Werewolf Council. Now you both know each other, so what the hell is going on?"

"Your father's a demon?" Olcan inquired with his eyes wide. "How is that possible?"

"He was human. He made a deal with a demon," Axel told him as he stepped forward, his arms crossed over his chest. "That's not important right now. Malcolm, why did you do that?"

"He was speaking to someone in the forest." Malcolm pinned Olcan with a glare.

Now, all the color drained from Olcan's face.

"He was talking about Ruby, that they should have taken her, and that losing his men wasn't a part of their deal." Malcolm turned to Olcan, his jaws clenched. "This Council member is working with the vampires."

Axel was the first to act. He immediately charged at Olcan.

Olcan was quick, grabbing him by the shoulder and throwing him on the ground.

I barreled into Olcan with all the strength in my body. I climbed onto him quickly, my claws piercing into the sides of his neck while Malcolm trapped his left arm above his head and his legs.

"Move and I fucking kill you!" I barked in his face.

He stopped moving, but his right hand remained holding my wrist.

"You backstabbing little parasite! You betrayed us... betrayed your own kind!" I added, my face inches away from his.

"My own kind resents me!" he yelled back, his voice strained from my grip on his throat.

"Whose fault do you think that is, Olcan? What did you think would happen over time when you kept fucking everyone over like this?" Ruby asked him. "Your men getting killed last night is on you. Those men thought they could trust you... How could you?"

I tightened my hold on him. "What have you told the vampires? It was you, wasn't it? You gave them pack locations! You've been helping them with slaughtering the people you're meant to protect!"

He groaned. "You know nothing! You can't help someone that doesn't want to be helped!" he bit back. "I've tried for years to help our species, but you fools are just so stuck in your ways. Secluding ourselves from other species, not evolving, not becoming more powerful will be the end of us. We could all be like her. Don't you get it?"

"You'll never be like her," I yelled.

He clenched his jaws, his lips forming a thin line.

I could see the hatred in his eyes, and I knew he could see the same in mine. "Where is the Queen? What did she promise you?"

"You want the truth, young Alpha? I don't know where she is, but your pack was to be next," he whispered as he tried to ease himself up off the ground.

I pushed him back down.

Olcan winced as blood began to pour from the hole in his neck created by my claw. "Your father has always stood against me," he choked out. "The vampires were helping me to rid myself of anyone who stands against me and my plans. In the vampire's new world, the wolves that stand with me will be more powerful than ever! That's the deal I made with them."

How had this man remained on the Council for all these years?

"Natalie and my father, where are they?"

He smirked.

I punched the ground beside his head, my fangs elongating. "Where are they?" I yelled, my saliva spraying onto his face. "If you found us, you must have found them. I swear to the Goddess, if you've hurt them..." I picked him up by his throat and slammed him back down to the ground, the sound of breaking bones filling my ears. "Where are they?"

He closed his eyes as he started coughing. "They weren't there. When we got there, they were long gone. All of them—the entire pack was gone."

My hand loosened around his neck, but that was what he had been waiting for. Quickly, his hand holding my wrist transformed. He clawed me across my face, and I howled in pain as I fell back.

The rest of his transformation came quick, but so did Axel's as Olcan overpowered Malcolm's mist and broke free. Axel's black wolf tackled him back to the ground, both of them still mid-shift.

"Take Ruby!" I barked at Malcolm.

He nodded to me.

"The fuck he will!" she yelled in response.

With the cut on my face burning and my anger igniting my insides, I wasn't interested in dealing with Ruby's stubbornness. I waited for an opening and ran forward. I fell on the ground to slide between both Axel and Olcan. I ignored the stones cutting into my skin as I reached out and embedded my claws in Olcan's underbelly.

He recoiled in pain, his brown wolf limping as he tried to remain standing. He snarled at us, and since I was still on the ground, I could see his underbelly already healing.

Axel's black wolf growled in response, blood dripping from a deep bite on his front right leg. Olcan was experienced, so even with the two of us, taking him down would be difficult. I got to my feet quickly and ripped my shirt off my body.

Realizing I was about to shift, Olcan targeted me, foam at the sides of his mouth. As he came at me, his eyes shifted from black to their original color.

I knew he did it so I could see the hatred within them, his intent to kill.

Since it was too late to stop the shift, my right shoulder dislocated. A wolf is most vulnerable mid-shift, so Axel rushed forward to protect me.

What we didn't expect was a tree limb from above reaching down to wrap around Olcan's body. It yanked him back, and his body slammed against the tree's trunk. More branches began to wrap around him, pinning him where he was.

Now, I looked Ruby's way.

Her hands were outstretched in front of her and shaking, her eyes as black as tar. She closed her eyes, her face turning red with strain as black veins began to crawl up her arms and Olcan's bones started to break.

His gut-wrenching howls of pain were cutting through the silence around us, and all we could do was stand and watch.

She was controlling his wolf as she had done before, forcing him to change back to his human form. When he had changed enough to speak, he began screaming her name.

I walked forward as I slowly commanded my shift to revert.

Axel started changing back as well.

"You were going to kill my father," I accused as I stopped in front of Olcan, droplets of blood rolling down his body from where the branches cut into his skin. "You almost got us killed—Ruby killed. Even worse, you betrayed your oath as a Council member."

He opened his mouth to speak, a smirk on his lips.

I reacted. My hand pierced through his chest easier than I had thought it would. Inside his body was burning hot. I closed my eyes as I ripped his heart from his chest.

I'd been soft for too long. Maybe Olcan hadn't lied about my father and Natalie having left before he arrived. Even so, if I let him go—if we let him go—he would only try to kill us another day.

He would only try to kill Ruby another day, and that I wouldn't stand for.

CHAPTER SEVEN

RUBY

We walked until almost sunset when we made our way off the road and into the forest. First, we had planned to camp outside with the guys taking turns keeping watch. Then we found an abandoned house and decided to sleep there for the night, instead.

The dilapidated house didn't offer much cover from a vampire attack with broken windows and rotting doors, but it was better than sleeping outside.

Since Malcolm was with us, he agreed to set wards around the house for the night to hide our location and mask my scent.

So far, Malcolm's wards seemed to be the only thing capable of blocking my scent. I couldn't walk around with a ward in my pocket, and yes... I had asked if I could. Sadly, wards could only be set if I was inside a structure.

The guys locked me inside the house while they did a quick sweep of the forest before nightfall. It took me a while to find a spot in the dirty house to lie down comfortably while I waited for them to return. There was an old mattress at the other end of the room, but the odors coming from it were beyond questionable.

To be honest, the entire little house gave me the creeps. Who the hell decided to live all the way out in the middle of nowhere?

The soft squeak of a mouse met my ears. The little critter ran by me and headed for the door. I watched as his tiny body slipped through a hole in the door, and I smiled. He had no idea what was going on in the world. This house and the surrounding forest was his entire little universe.

I closed my tired eyes and immediately saw Olcan's face in my mind. What happened to a person to make them become so selfish? Or was he just born that way? I'd never understood how some people could ruin others' lives just to make themselves feel better or improve their own lives. Olcan was fine with his people being massacred and turned into monsters just as long as he got what he wanted.

I understand Olcan thought what he did was right. He thought making a deal with the devil was better than watching his species be slaughtered, and he believed werewolves would be made stronger in the process. The problem came when he decided to double-cross and sacrifice everyone else who didn't agree. Countless wolves must've lost their lives thanks to his betrayal.

In the beginning, I wanted to run away from all of this. I didn't know what I was or where I came from. Yet, knowing now that I could help save the lives of so many people, how could I not do my part?

It did feel scary, and I didn't know what might happen at any given moment. Yet, if I could save a single life, it'd be worth it. I opened my eyes and held my hand up in front of my face. I had to become stronger. I had to find out what my limits were. It seemed as if I was capable of anything, everything, but I knew I must have had limits. I wasn't a god, and I wasn't immortal. However, I felt this wave of invincibility whenever I called on my power, and it scared me. I'd realized that the more I used my powers, the easier it was becoming to control them.

Olcan said something to me that I hadn't been able to stop

thinking about. He'd said, *"In war, control isn't the most important thing. In war, we have to break ourselves free from the restrictions of doubt that could hold us back. We have to do what needs to be done because our opponents will do anything to win."*

Too bad Olcan took that a bit too far. I thought werewolves were big on honor, but Olcan had none at all.

Despite everything Olcan had done, I hadn't expected Xavier to kill him. If anything, I had expected Axel to do it. If Axel had been the one to kill him, it wouldn't have been so shocking. Xavier... Xavier was someone else a few hours ago. At that moment, when he stuck his hand into Olcan's chest, my own heart had stopped beating. I'd only seen Xavier kill one other werewolf. He had killed a suicidal werewolf months ago when we just met. Last night was the first time since then that I'd seen him in such a dark place.

We had walked in silence for hours afterward. I think both Axel and Malcolm were shocked as well.

I believe everything happening to all of us would hit a breaking point sooner or later. As Xavier walked away from Olcan's lifeless body still strapped to the tree, his face was utterly devoid of emotion. I didn't see regret or even anger.

An old, discolored glass sitting on the tiny kitchen counter across the room fell to the ground and shattered. My hand flew to my mouth to stop the scream that rolled up my throat. I got up quickly and looked through one of the windows. The world was growing dark outside, and still, the guys hadn't returned.

"Where are you guys?" I whispered to myself as I glanced back at the broken glass on the floor. There were no lights inside the house, so as night drew closer, the place got darker. I couldn't see in the dark like Axel and Xavier. I walked to the door but decided against going outside. I'd rather be stuck in here with a ghost than attacked by a vampire out there. "Hurry back," I whispered. "This place is really starting to creep me out."

———

Axel

"We should head back now," Xavier told me.

I turned around as Malcolm appeared by our side.

I fanned at the black mist in front of my face and shot him an annoyed look.

He merely shrugged and fell in stride with Xavier and me.

We walked in silence, but I was keeping an eye on Xavier. He had surprised me earlier. I hadn't thought he had it in him to kill Olcan. I couldn't believe he killed a Council member without blinking an eye. The bastard had it coming, that's for sure, though I did feel a little angry that I didn't get to end his pathetic life myself.

In the beginning, I didn't see Xavier as capable of becoming a strong Alpha, an Alpha who could make the tough decisions without showing remorse or regret. We were raised to be strong, resilient, and fearless—Alphas more so than other wolves. I saw him as weak because he fell for Ruby so quickly. Xavier hadn't questioned or fought against the mate bond and had left himself open to being used. Back then, I'd believed Ruby and our mate bond had to be some kind of trick or witchery.

Today I saw Xavier act as a true Alpha, not a young Alpha-to-be. I saw a brave and decisive Alpha who took the initiative and did a thing few would've had the courage to do. If allowed to live, Olcan would have stopped at nothing to kill Ruby and see his evil plan of vampire/werewolf alliance to fruition, and Xavier knew it.

"Do you think Olcan told the vampires about Presley, then?" I pondered.

"He did," Malcolm replied with a shrug. "He was told to report back once he'd found the base."

"That General will be following us," Xavier commented as he

stepped over a broken tree limb. "We're going to end up leading them straight to the humans."

"We don't have a choice," I shot back. "We have to go there, and it's too late to turn back now."

"I wasn't suggesting turning back, but once we get there, we need to let them know the vampires aren't far behind."

The forest around us got so quiet. It was unnerving. With nightfall upon us, I was used to hearing the insects as they came out for the night, but all I could hear was our footsteps. It was as if we were utterly alone in the world.

"I found something else in the book," Malcolm suddenly announced as he stopped walking. "It's why I came looking for you."

I frowned at the look of worry on his face. "What is it? What did you find?"

"This isn't the first time the vampires had done this," he announced. "That's what the war was that we saw in the book. They tried taking over a long time ago and were stopped."

"How?" Xavier asked the question I was thinking of.

Malcolm shook his head as he pinched the bridge of his nose.

"Malcolm?" I called to him.

He looked up at me, his hand falling to his side. "A werewolf sacrificed herself. She accepted the Goddess's power. While she ultimately defeated the vampires... it killed her," he finally answered.

My heart fell. "Are you saying Ruby will..."

He nodded. "Yes. That's what Ruby will have to do. She won't only use the power given to her by the Goddess, she'll become the Goddess."

Xavier walked away as he combed his hand through his hair roughly.

"Her body is what the Goddess wants." My voice dropped low with disbelief. "She gave Ruby her power from birth to groom her for this, for when she will have to take over her body."

The loud sound of a tree falling echoed through the forest.

I looked around.

Xavier's claws were retracting, a large claw mark across the tree's trunk. "No," he growled, his shoulder tense. He turned to face us, his eyes black as coal. "The Goddess can possess someone else. Not her."

"There has to be another way," I told Malcolm, my heartbeat pounding in my ears at the thought of losing Ruby. "Not her, I can't lose her too."

"I'm telling you what I know!" Malcolm tossed his hands up in frustration. "That's all. Dammit, I don't want this either! She's my only daughter. Yet Ruby is also the perfect candidate. She was born an Enchanted with a part of the Goddess already inside her. All the Goddess had to do was give her more—a higher dose of her divinity, if you will." He walked away, his head down. "There's a tiny possibility she might not die... maybe the Goddess did this to avoid killing her. The werewolf who died before wasn't an Enchanted."

"This is fucking bullshit!" I yelled. "Isn't the vampire Queen just another supernatural being like us? Why does it take a god to kill her, huh? Even though Ruby was born half Enchanted, you know hosts possessed by gods never last long. Mortals aren't built to host or wield the powers of divine beings. Ruby won't survive this!" I looked at Xavier, my eyes wide with panic. "She won't survive it, no matter how strong she is now. Ruby's been lucky to have survived this long. You saw what happened when she killed those vampires the other night. She almost died! Just like before, her powers almost burned her to death!"

"We can't tell her about this," Malcolm stated resolutely as he turned around. "This fight isn't hers alone, so killing the Queen isn't her job or duty alone. She won't have to accept the Goddess if she doesn't even know it's possible to do so."

"Okay." Xavier sighed as he walked forward. There was no color in his face. "She doesn't learn of this. We'll find Presley, work with the humans, and stop this from ever coming to pass. The first time this happened, the world wasn't as advanced as it is now. We'll find another way."

I knew he was feeling the panic I was. "And what if there is no other way?" I asked as I clenched my fists so hard I felt my nails pierce into my skin. "What if Ruby has to accept the Goddess in the end?"

"Then she'll just have to, and we'll lose her. It means we have failed to protect her as we should have." Malcolm replied softly.

Releasing a frustrated breath, I stalked away.

"She can't do that!" Xavier yelled from somewhere behind me. "She can't!"

"If it gets to that point and she doesn't," Malcolm replied coolly, "We all die."

We walked back to the house in silence. Why did it take a goddess to kill the vampire Queen? How could she possibly be that powerful?

We found Ruby asleep in the corner of the shack, her legs curled up to her chest. She looked so small, so fragile, and perfect. Her pink rosebud lips were parted somewhat, her breathing slow.

I inhaled her scent and lost it. I couldn't take it. I couldn't handle looking at her while knowing I might lose her. I stormed out of the house, shifting as I ran.

"Axel!" Malcolm called.

I ran back into the forest, the black fur of my wolf bursting through my skin.

"Axel!"

Ruby

I'm not sure what happened with the guys while they were in the forest last night, but they returned as new men. They were all so quiet, so distant and tense. I knew I was missing something, but what?

"What's going on?" I asked Xavier as I pulled up at his side, the midday sun causing sweat to break out on my upper lip.

He looked down at me and smiled, but it didn't quite meet his eyes. "What are you talking about?"

"I'm talking about why you're all so quiet and tense," I said loud enough for the others to hear, although I knew they could hear me just fine before. "You've all been acting strange since last night. What did I miss?"

"Nothing, Ruby," Xavier replied. "I think everyone just has a lot on their minds is all. I certainly do," he added quietly.

I realized I was being insensitive. I had hoped Natalie would finally appear to me while I slept last night, but there was still no word from her. "The warding around the camp was getting weak before we left. Maybe that's what drove them to leave."

"Yeah, maybe," he replied. "I hope so."

"You don't have an Enchanted in your pack, do you, Axel?" I stopped and waited for him and Malcolm to catch up.

Xavier kept walking, apparently lost in his thoughts.

"I don't." Axel shook his head. "But the witches have their ways to contact me if they need me," he confirmed, a few strands of curly hair in his face.

"Do you miss them?" I wondered as Malcolm walked ahead of us.

Axel nodded. "I do."

"Your father, how is he?" I questioned him.

His face fell. He sucked his bottom lip in and released it, as his teeth grazed the skin. His lip seemed so much plumper afterward. I looked away quickly as he stared down at me, no doubt hearing the way my heartbeat increased.

My stomach did a backflip as he held my hand.

"He was up and about when I left, but that feels like so long ago. The witches there have been helping him, so he's doing okay, I guess."

I nodded, his thumb caressing the back of my hand a sudden distraction. Axel and I didn't speak about his pack or past very often. With the way things had been, no one had the time to sit and chat.

I was mated to these two men, and sometimes it didn't feel like that. Although I was mated to Axel, we never talked about being officially together. Finding your mate meant finding the one you would spend the rest of your life with, but things got complicated when you were mated to two wolves instead of one. Xavier and I grew close from the start and made our relationship official, while Axel and I were still just finding our footing.

Although things were civil between both men, it still got awkward from time to time. There were more important things to think about right now, though, like... oh, I don't know—the world ending and the pressure of trying to save it.

I'd deal with this mess of a relationship when this was all over. For now, I'd enjoy their embrace, their words of encouragement, and the delectable kisses we stole from time to time. Yes, for now, I'd enjoy having two men by my side that I knew would do anything for me. I glanced up at Axel before looking at Xavier walking ahead. I'd do anything for them as well—anything.

Suddenly, Malcolm removed his coat and threw it in the air. The garment turned to smoke and vanished. If it came to it, I might make Malcolm suffer a little before helping him. He was an asshole sometimes, but I had to admit, his skills frequently came in handy. I hadn't fully forgiven him for wanting to kill me, but I certainly didn't want anything bad to happen to him. So yes, I'd save his sorry ass, too.

I smiled.

Look at me, talking about saving other people's asses. What is the world coming to?

"Wait," Axel suddenly commanded as his hold on my hand grew tighter.

Ahead of us, Xavier spun around and started pointing towards the forest for us to get off the road.

"What's going on?" I whispered to Axel as we ran quickly to the forest.

"Humans, we hear humans," Axel whispered as his eyes scanned the forest.

"Maybe it's Presley's men?" I whispered back.

Malcolm shifted into smoke and vanished.

Xavier pulled up at my side. "Or hunters," he countered and then nodded at Axel.

They both started removing their shirts. I chuckled at them speaking to each other without words. It was kind of hot, if you thought about it—my men having a private language centered around protecting me.

My wandering naughty thoughts were washed away as men rushed forward with guns aimed at us.

"Don't move!"

Commands kept flying at us from all angles.

"Hands up! Get your hands up now!"

"Don't even think about it, wolf!"

I held my hands up.

Xavier and Axel started to wolf out, their eyes changing as they snarled at the men, but they remained in human form.

"Stop! If you shift, we'll shoot!" one man yelled.

I placed my arm on Xavier's as he leaned forward somewhat, his ears elongating as a loud growl emitted from him. "Don't," I whispered to him. "Don't be the animal they think we are."

A burst of black smoke suddenly confused the men.

Axel, Xavier, and I stepped back to avoid being engulfed by it.

"Malcolm, no!" I shouted. Within the black cloud, we could hear men screaming while gunshots echoed around us. "I said stop, Malcolm! Stop it!"

The smoke disappeared and Malcolm materialized before us. Without warning, another gunshot echoed through the forest, and Malcolm staggered backward.

Presley stepped forward, his gun raised.

I ran forward and stood in front of Malcolm. "General Presley, don't shoot. Please listen!" I pleaded. "Please!"

He lowered his gun ever so slightly but then looked at Malcolm and raised it again. "You killed my men."

"They aren't dead. Check for yourself," Malcolm replied nonchalantly.

"Not these men, you motherfucker!" Presley yelled.

I turned around to face Malcolm. "Leave," I murmured to him. "You killed his men. Please, you need to leave. You can find us easily, can't you?"

Malcolm stared at me in shock, then he sighed. He burst into a cloud of smoke without another word.

I quickly turned back around to face Presley, who looked ready to murder someone. "Look, I support you wanting to shoot him again. Sometimes I feel the same way about him. In fact, I'll even cheer for you when you two finally get to fight it out, but not right now. I didn't know he would kill your men, okay? He was just trying to protect me. I'm sorry, I really am. I'm on your side, Presley." I lowered my raised hands as he lowered his gun.

More men appeared, their guns aimed at us.

"Stand down!" Presley yelled at them before turning to me.

"I need your help, and you need mine," I told him calmly.

He arched a brow at me. "What makes you think I still want your help?" he shot back.

I pinned him with a look. "You do, and you know it. The vampires are heading here. They're looking for you," I told him.

All the men started to exchange worried glances.

"We have a lot to talk about." I stepped forward. "I got my memories back," I revealed.

This news had his brows touching his hairline in surprise.

"Shall we go then?" I prompted.

———

Ruby

It took half an hour for us to get to Presley's base. The looks we received as we walked through the base's halls were a mixture of curiosity and outright disdain.

"I need to show you something," Presley announced as he pushed two double doors open and led us into a massive hall.

"Ruby!" Natalie screamed from across the room. Within seconds, she crossed the room to pull me into a hug.

"Natalie," I said softly as I squeezed her to me.

Behind her, the rest of the pack turned to see what was going on. Mathieu stood up, a wide smile making its way to his face.

"Dad?" Xavier called out in disbelief as he stepped away to greet his father.

Natalie pulled away, and we stared at each other for a moment before hugging each other again.

"I'm so glad you're okay," I confessed with a sigh as we released each other once more.

"I missed you, too," she replied before looking at Axel. "Even you."

Axel chuckled. "I can't say the same."

Natalie flipped him off as he walked away.

"Come on." She took my hand. "They've been asking for you."

"Who?" I asked.

She stared at me as if I was crazy. "The pack, of course. We've all been worried sick about you guys," she replied as if it should've been obvious to me.

I frowned.

In the beginning, the pack blamed me for being on the run, and the animosity was palpable. However, by the time I left the pack with Presley, the dislike had started to fade as they realized there was a war being fought on all fronts. I was being hunted by The Council and vampires, not to mention the human hunters. "That's, um, good... I think. I'll be right there."

Natalie looked at Presley, who stood by the door, and nodded to him before turning away. Then she jumped onto Xavier's back and they hugged as Mathieu patted his son's shoulder.

A little girl waved at me with a small, timid smile on her lips.

I smiled wide as I waved back at her.

"The strangest thing happened to me," Presley began as he moved to stand next to me. "Natalie appeared to me in a dream, saying she needed my help." He turned to face me, his hands clasped behind his back. His chestnut-blonde hair seemed longer than it was the last time I saw him, and his blue eyes seemed paler. His eyes still seemed just as unreadable as ever. "She told me you'd come to find me soon."

I puckered my lips as I looked Natalie's way. "She saw a vision of this happening, I guess." I continued watching her as she spoke animatedly to Xavier. Xavier wore a large grin, and his shoulders appeared more relaxed. I smiled broadly.

"She told me the warding around her camp was weakening. She knew they'd be attacked soon, so she needed my help until you came to find me," Presley stated.

I swung my gaze over to him. "And you helped them, just like that? Aren't the people you report to mad that you have an entire werewolf pack here when you should be hunting werewolves?"

"Like I had told you before, my team doesn't hunt werewolves. I'm on your side, Ruby. Never forget that. So, yes, I helped her." He glanced Natalie's way.

I narrowed my eyes as his eyes lingered on her a little too long. I tried to hide my smile.

He turned back to me. "The sooner we get started, the better."

I nodded as I inhaled deeply and sighed. "I know. Just give me a few minutes, okay?"

"Sure, I'll let you catch up with your family. I'll be back soon." He strode away, closing the doors behind him.

I turned around to find Mathieu calling me over. *My family*, I thought to myself as I joined them. It was nice to hear someone say that.

Mathieu patted me on the shoulder as the little girl from before handed me a glass of water.

"Thank you," I replied to her.

She beamed at me before running back to her mother.

The other wolves were all looking at me strangely. I bumped Natalie with my elbow, "Am I missing something? Why is everyone looking at me like that?"

"I had a vision of you killing more vampires. I told them all about it," she whispered back. "That actually happened, right?"

I nodded. "Oh, so much happened, so much." I sat down, as did everyone else.

Axel, Xavier, and I told them about everything that had happened, from the beginning.

Everyone looked particularly shocked to hear that Xavier was the one who killed Olcan.

"That backstabbing prick," Natalie snarled through clenched teeth. "I haven't been able to contact Reika. He must have killed her. Maybe he found out she was on our side or that she had helped you guys escape from the pack when he wanted to take you guys to Romania."

"Maybe," Mathieu replied, his dark hair like Xavier's but longer while brushing against his shoulder. "Did he say anything about the other council members?"

Xavier shook his head. "He didn't."

Axel excused himself, saying he was going to get something to eat.

Mathieu offered to show both Axel and Xavier where the cafeteria was.

"So," I drawled as I turned to face Natalie. "You mind-linked Presley, huh?"

The smile appearing on her lips was the one I'd hoped to see. So I hadn't been wrong about the chemistry I'd been sensing between those two. Presley had looked at Natalie in the same way I'd seen Xavier and Axel look at me.

"I did. He was the only person I could think about to help us," she admitted. "We were going to be killed. I wish I had seen that Olcan was behind it all, though."

"I'm just glad you guys are okay. Xavier was starting to worry," I told her.

The door to the hall opened again.

I sighed.

Presley made his way over to us, his eyes on Natalie for a moment before he looked at me. He finally came to a stop at our table. "Ruby, it's time. We need to get started."

"Alright." I pushed my chair back.

Natalie got up with me and pulled me into a hug.

So much tension that I'd been holding in for days finally faded away. "We'll talk when I get finished, okay?"

She nodded before pulling away.

I then followed Presley out the door and down the hall. "Where are we going?"

"You're about to meet 'the people I report to,' as you called them."

"This isn't going to be fun?" I asked dryly.

Presley shook his head without looking behind him. "I doubt it."

CHAPTER EIGHT

I walked behind Presley in silence, observing and absorbing everything I saw.

People were walking quickly back and forth, all seeming to be in a rush, while we walked casually. Three times we were stopped as Presley was asked to sign a document and god knows what else.

People kept giving me odd looks.

I tried to ignore them, but it was starting to bother me. I'd never enjoyed being the center of attention.

"They've all heard what you're capable of," Presley voiced as he kept walking ahead of me. "We're happy you've decided to help us."

"Whatever it takes to get these vampires," I responded.

He remained silent.

After several minutes, we came to large white double doors.

Presley placed his hand on a scanner and the door unlocked for him.

We stepped inside the room and I immediately had to take a step back as a woman walked in front of me, a stack of files in her hand.

The sizable room seemed filled with computers and so many soldiers. At the other end of the room, a wall stood covered in large screens, all showing something different.

I understood none of it.

"This is where the magic happens," Presley said loudly as he marched forward.

While he stepped straight forward freely and confidently, I had to dodge and weave to avoid bumping into people.

He stopped at a desk with a woman typing away quickly at her keyboard, her eyes darting back and forth between the three computer monitors before her. "We think we've found the Queen."

My jaw dropped with shock. "What? How? Are you sure?"

"We've been able to hunt these vampires—finding their covens and all—because we've modified one of our satellites to pick up on areas devoid of heat signatures. Vampires don't have a heat signature. We think it's their skin that causes it, much as if a human put on an insulated jacket. We discovered this when a diplomat had to be located by satellite. We noticed the dense dark zones around his house and realized it was surrounded by vampires. So, wherever you see a large dark spot..." He pointed to a screen across the room of what indeed looked like a map of America but with multiple black spots. "...that's where the vampires are."

"That's a lot," I murmured more to myself than him.

"It is," he agreed.

The map was almost completely covered. While some black areas were larger than others, it was discouraging to see a visual representation of how quickly and completely the vampires were taking over the United States. If America looked this bad, I didn't want to think about what the rest of the world looked like.

"Show her," Presley stated while pointing to one of the monitors on the lady's desk. "There, that large black area... it's one of the larger ones we've located. There are a few human heat signatures." He turned to me. "We sent in a team to do recon on the area, and we got footage of what looked like a female vampire surrounded by guards being led inside an old building."

"How do you know it's her from just getting a glimpse of a female vampire?" I inquired. "We have no idea what the Queen looks like, or if she even looks human."

"That's true," Presley agreed with a nod, his arms clasped behind him as usual. "But whoever that woman was, the fact that she was so heavily guarded suggests she has to be important."

"Okay, what do you want me to do, then? I assume you want me to do something."

He nodded. "I do. I want you to join the team I'll be leading. Come with us to that location. We don't know if it's the Queen, but if it is, we'll need you there."

At this point, several soldiers had stopped what they were doing to listen to our conversation. Actually, they were all just staring at me.

The noise in the room decreased as Presley waited for my response—as they all waited.

"Yes, sure," I agreed, sounding a lot more confident than I actually felt.

Everyone resumed work with great haste.

There were still others staring at me, but they didn't bother me much. I'd decided if this was where I needed to be from now on, I had to get used to being in the spotlight for a little while. Eventually, they would all just get used to seeing me around, and hopefully the extra attention would fade.

Presley cocked his head to the side. "Come with me." He moved away. "Time to meet the others. They want to see your power for themselves, if you're truly capable of killing vampires."

I hurried to catch up with him.

He placed his hand on another scanner, this time for an elevator.

We stepped inside, and I wondered if the guys could hear my

pounding heart wherever they were. Yup, I was freaking out. I had no idea what I would even say to these people or do.

We rode the elevator in silence to Floor D3. I exhaled as the doors opened.

Presley walked out.

I followed him.

A long hall loomed ahead of us with a door at the other end, and once more his hand was the key to opening the door.

The moment the door opened, I heard it—the unmistakable hiss of a vampire. My body grew tense as I stepped into the room. Sure enough, there was a vampire—a Bleeder to be exact—chained in a glass box.

The room was all white, with three televisions to my right. Two men that looked like doctors were in what looked like an observation room to my left. The Bleeder's red eyes landed on me and it rushed towards me at full speed until its chain yanked it back. Bright UV lights switched on inside the box and the creature began to scream in pain, something like steam rising off its skin.

The UV lights turned off once more, and the Bleeder cowered in a corner, its crimson eyes still trained on me.

"Hello, Ms. Saunders," a woman's voice echoed in the room.

I looked towards the televisions that had been off when we came in.

They were now on, with the silhouette of a man on the first and third television screen. A woman with chocolate brown skin and black eyes appeared on the one in the middle.

"Hi," I drawled.

The woman smiled. "It's nice to finally meet you, Ruby. May I call you Ruby?"

"Sure," I replied. "And you are?"

"I'm Rebecca," she told me. "My associates would rather remain anonymous. You understand."

I looked at the other two screens, then glanced at Presley as I shook my head. "Not really, but okay."

She gave me a little nod and clasped her hands on the glass desk before her. "We've heard many things about you over these past few months. You have a gift that General Presley says is vital to our efforts to destroy these creatures." She gestured with her hand towards the vampire in the cage.

It hissed back at her in response.

She didn't even flinch, and her eyes drifted back to me. "What General Presley hasn't been able to confirm for us, however, is exactly what you are," she added as she smiled.

Though her smile was quite beautiful, I knew it was fake. It looked like something she'd practiced and forced for so long that now, maybe to her, it even felt real.

"I'm half-human," I replied, "And half-Enchanted."

"Enchanted?" one of the men repeated.

I could not tell which one spoke as I answered, "Yes." I stared at both men.

Rebecca was nodding her head. "Yes, that's right. Within the werewolf species, they have Enchanteds, female wolves that can't transform. Yes?" She leaned forward, her eyes narrowing. "So any hybrid children of an Enchanted and human would have the gifts you do, then?"

"No," I told her. "They wouldn't. My gifts are unique in the supernatural community as well."

"Ruby," Presley spoke as he turned to face me, "we would like you to kill that Bleeder. Show us what you're capable of."

The Bleeder seemed to understand everything being said as he stood up. He hunched forward somewhat, his eyes now darting back and forth frantically. He hissed at us, saliva draining from his mouth. The pale creature ran forward, but once more the chain around his thin left ankle yanked him back, and the UV lights switched on. He fell to the ground in agony again, his hands covering his bald head as steam rose from its body. The light switched off, and the creature continued to whimper like a dog on the ground. The way he was curled up, looking so fragile and helpless, I felt a pang of pity for him.

Whoever this man once was, he didn't ask to be turned into this creature.

"That's not a being deserving of pity, Ruby," Presley whispered to me. "Not anymore."

The vampire held his head up then, his eyes on Presley.

I tilted my head to the side as I watched him get onto his knees.

The Bleeder held its head back as if smelling the air. "F-fil-ty," he stuttered hesitantly, the word coming out in pieces.

Presley's eyes grew wide for a moment.

"F-fil-ty hu-man," the Bleeder finally managed to utter.

"It's never spoken before," Presley noted.

The vampire smiled wide, his eyes drifting to me.

I hadn't known Bleeders were still capable of speech. The Skins, like the General I had seen, were the vampires who carried on conversations, exhibited logical thought, and could still pass for human.

"Y-ou... die," the vampire hissed at me as his black tongue darted out to lick his lips. "Queen w-w-will..." He shook his head. "Kill... y-y-you. Make... o-one of of... us."

"It's saying the Queen wants to make you one of them," Presley clarified as he unclasped his hands from behind him and crossed them over his chest.

"I know," I told him and stepped closer to the cage. "Where have you all been?" I asked the vampire.

He started laughing, a contorted sound as if he was also coughing.

"If your Queen wants me, tell me where she is, so I can go to her."

His laughter grew louder.

I clenched my jaw as I felt my power awake within me. "Tell me!"

"Blo-blood," he replied in a low hiss. "B-lood, blood, blood."

His face began to twist as if he were in pain, and he tried to crawl closer to the glass. He started to chant the word, and he grew clearer each time he said it.

"Tell me where your Queen is, and I'll give you blood."

"Ruby." Presley's voice vibrated with concern.

I ignored him and pressed my wrist against the glass.

"Tell me where your Queen is, and I'll give you blood. Tell me."

He started shaking his head wildly and suddenly lashed out with so much force, a link on the chain opened and snapped.

Presley stepped back, and a blazing alarm went off inside the room.

The vampire started banging on the glass wall, and the UV light within the box came on.

"Turn it off!" I yelled to the people within the observation room. "I said turn it off!" I shouted again, my eyes turning black, and the light switched off.

The moment the light switched off, the vampire attacked himself, biting out a chunk of flesh from his arm.

I held my hand out, imagining myself holding the vampire by the throat and within the cage.

He lifted off the ground. He started clawing at his throat.

I raised my other hand, restricting his movement further. "Tell me where she is or die," I demanded.

The Bleeder's red eyes bulged as if they'd pop from his head. "Die," he screeched out.

I ground my teeth. "So be it," I stated and allowed it to fall to the ground. I imagined a flame being lit inside his body.

He instantly began to wither and twist on the ground. His body folded backward, his head almost touching his waist as the surface of his skin began to burn.

Presley stepped forward as the vampire slowly started to writhe less, and then stopped moving altogether, his body turning to ash.

The alarm in the room went silent.

I turned to Rebecca and the men, who'd been watching the entire thing. I stepped closer to the televisions, my eyes still as black as obsidian. "You have your proof, but I will only help you if you stop hunting werewolves." I straightened my spine and channeled the dominance I'd seen Xavier and Axel display. "Then, and only then, will I help you. Werewolves must be able to come out of hiding safely so they can help us in this fight. What you all don't understand is that this isn't the first time vampires have tried to take this world, and a werewolf was ultimately responsible for defeating the vampires in the previous fight. We can't win this war divided, and you're all fools if you think you can."

Rebecca's chest rose as she inhaled deeply.

I went on, "This world doesn't belong to humans alone. It never has, and it never will. This is *our* home—every creature, human and otherwise. Humans don't have the skill or strength to hunt these vampires the way werewolves do. It doesn't matter how many guns or bombs you have in your arsenal. So..." I crossed my arms over my chest. "That's my condition. Do we have a deal or not?"

Rebecca stared at me.

I held her stare. I would not back down or show weakness. I knew my eyes were still black, and I wasn't about to change them back to make the humans comfortable. I might be human, but I was an Enchanted as well. My mother was an incredibly gifted Enchanted who helped the werewolf community and made her mark in the supernatural world. I was my mother's daughter after all, and I would make my mark as well.

"Okay, Ruby," Rebecca agreed as she leaned forward. This time when she smiled, it met her eyes. "We have a deal."

———

Ruby

"I'm proud of you." Natalie threw her arm around my shoulder. "It definitely sounds like you handled it like a boss. I taught you well."

"*You* taught me well?" I told her with a laugh.

She nodded. "Of course I did. It sure as hell wasn't those two knuckleheads!" She pointed at Xavier and Axel walking ahead of us. "Are you really sure they're going to stop the hunting were-wolves, though?"

I nodded. "I'm sure."

"And the Queen?"

Xavier and Axel halted their steps at the same time to look around at me.

"Don't even say it," I told them. "Presley wants me there, so I'm going. Neither of you can burn vampires alive with your mind, can you?"

Neither of them answered me.

I shrugged. "Then I have to go. You're both acting like you won't be there anyway."

"I just hope it was really the Queen," Natalie said. "It'd be good to get this nightmare over with. To be frank, I'm not the slightest bit upset that I won't be able to come. I'll leave this fight up to the pros." She patted my shoulder. "Just make sure you all come back in one piece."

"I'm not a pro." I stepped towards the door leading to the training room. "All I have is some power. I don't know the first thing about actual combat, like the hand-to-hand type stuff."

"I'd suggest you not worry about that," Axel stated. "With your power, a vampire shouldn't be able to get close enough. Leave the rest to us." He stepped forward, pinched my chin, and pushed the door to the training room open.

Xavier moved close, kissed the top of my head, and entered behind Axel.

The door closed softly, and I looked over at Natalie.

She was staring at me with puppy dog eyes. "That was so cute.

They are so cute. I'm liking this two-mates thing." She raised her head up to the ceiling. "Goddess, I've seen what you've done for others and—"

I yanked her hand. "Shut up and come on."

We entered the training room and found everyone staring in our direction. The room fell completely silent. All the soldiers stopped what they were doing. The tension and animosity in the room was stifling.

Axel and Xavier walked over to a barbell set like they owned the place.

Everyone, including Natalie and me, watched as Axel stacked all the weights onto a bar and lifted it with ease.

He made a face as he placed it back onto the ground with one hand. "Maybe we should just spar," he suggested to Xavier as he removed his shirt.

Xavier smirked. "It's been a long time coming."

A loud clunk echoed through the room.

All eyes turned to a man who'd dropped a dumbbell, his eyes on Xavier and Axel.

"Hmm, the love in this room is strong," Natalie said sarcastically. "Oh, here we go," she added as the man started making his way over to Xavier and Axel, his bare chest glistening with sweat.

Natalie and I joined them.

"Hey, guys, look what we have here. It's our new best friends, the werewolves," the soldier began. "So, I heard you guys can't transform on a full moon. That sucks."

"Jack, don't," another man cautioned him.

Jack smiled and shrugged his shoulders. "Hey, I'm only making conversation." He then turned back to Xavier and Axel.

This man was looking for trouble. For sure, he intended to piss Axel or Xavier off, and then shit was going to hit the fan. I could see it happening already.

"Literally every story about werewolves says they transform on a full moon."

"Do you believe every story you've ever heard?" Natalie questioned him with a sweet smile, but I could hear the distaste in her voice. She leaned forward.

Jack arched a brow at her. From the way he looked her up and down, I guessed the fact that she was gorgeous hadn't escaped him.

"So, I guess you believe in Santa Claus, too?" she asked him.

"Are you about to tell me he's real?" he asked her.

She shrugged. "He might be. Who knows?"

Jack turned back to Axel. "That was pretty impressive with the barbell and all. So..." He stepped closer as he narrowed his eyes at Axel. "Our team doesn't hunt werewolves, so I've never seen one of you guys wolf out. I hear it's pretty amazing."

A few men chuckled behind him.

This seemed to fuel his ego as he started laughing. "How about you show us those black eyes, freak?"

The corner of Axel's mouth arched with a smirk.

I stepped forward. "How about I show you mine?" I offered as I stepped in front of Axel, my eyes having changed from green to black. "*Pretty amazing, right*?" I said it the same sarcastic way he had.

He made a face. "Yeah, but I wasn't talking to you, sweetheart. I was talking to your little boyfriend behind you, or can he not speak for himself?" He peered behind me at Axel. "So, can you speak?" He looked at Xavier as well. "Either of you?"

"Hey!" I snapped my finger at him. "Back off."

He peered back down at me, then chuckled and held his hand up as he looked back at his friends. "Just having some fun, honey. Calm down."

"Don't... call me 'honey', asshat," I told him through clenched teeth.

He frowned as it started to get hot in the room. He looked me up and down, the smartass look on his face vanishing.

I could see him attempting to hide his fear.

Typical bully.

I stepped forward.

Xavier, Natalie, and Axel stepped back.

Sweat started to drip from Jack's face.

"So, I see no one has told you bullying isn't nice, no matter the age. I don't like bullies."

He kept stepping back when another taller soldier appeared behind him. He placed his hand on Jack's shoulders and tugged him further back. "Leave them alone."

Jack sent us a look of utter repulsion. "Gladly," he snapped as he walked away.

I rolled my eyes which turned back to my regular emerald green.

"Sorry about him. He's not the brightest bulb we have here." The tall soldier held his hand out to me. "I'm Alonzo. You're Ruby, right?"

I shook his hand. "I am. How'd you know?"

"Come on... redhead that can burn vampires with a look... of course I know who you are! We all do." He released my hand. "Plus, I think everyone just felt how hot it got in here." He looked at the guys behind me. "I don't think the equipment we have in here will work for you guys, but we'll work something out."

"Work it out how?" Xavier questioned.

Alonzo pinched his chin. "How about a fair fight between one of you and one of us? Of course, you'd have to go easy on us but—"

"No thanks," Axel answered quickly.

Alonzo frowned. "Why not? Trust me, I'm not like those guys. I just think it would be cool."

"No, we get what you mean, but us going easy wouldn't make the fight fair, now would it?" Xavier tilted his head at him and glanced at the other men in the room. "We'd have to hold back. If it's to be a fair fight, we can't do that. We won't make ourselves lesser to please anyone here. Look, we're on the same side here, but we're not here to kiss ass and make friends. There are more important things to deal with right now than stroking egos. We don't need to fight to know who the winner is, and that's just how things are. It's no disrespect to any of you. Werewolves have spent decades hiding who they are so they can blend in, and we won't anymore. We might not be human, but we're people, too. We feel love and hate like all of you. Good and bad exist in our race just like yours. We might have our differences, but a lot is also the same." Xavier glared at Jack. "We aren't monsters, and none of you can force us to be something we're not. What we are is different, and the last time I checked, that's fine." Xavier exhaled heavily as his eyes wandered back to Alonzo.

Surprisingly, he grinned. "I agree. The vampires are the monsters here." He held his hand out to Xavier. "I'd rather have a wolf fighting beside me any day."

Xavier shook his hand.

Jack sucked his teeth as he walked past us. "You're a fucking sellout," he told Alonzo.

Alonzo didn't look fazed in the least.

A few other soldiers left with Jack, but many stayed behind. A few continued with their workout, while some walked over to us, introducing themselves.

I stepped away from the group as Natalie's eyes turned white.

She told them her eyes were white because she was an Enchanted, and the soldiers appeared interested in learning more.

I smiled. If this was what the world would become after this ended, it was a world I couldn't wait to see.

CHAPTER NINE
NATALIE

The vision I'd just had faded, and I swallowed the lump forming in my throat. I blinked rapidly, the fog before my eyes clearing, but they immediately started to burn with impending tears. I squeezed them shut to hold the tears back as I reached out and placed my hand on the cool wall for support. Sometimes, being able to see into the future was more of a burden than a gift.

I opened my eyes and inhaled deeply before continuing down the hall. For two days, I'd enjoyed having Ruby and Xavier back. While everyone had been busy, it'd been nice just being able to see each other. My vision made it clear that would be ending soon.

"Natalie?" I turned around.

General Presley was just stepping out of a room. He closed the door softly and walked over to me. "It's pretty late. Are you okay?"

"Ah, yeah, I was just going to Ruby's room," I told him, my nails digging into my palm behind my back.

I was not sure when it happened or how, but there had been this connection between Presley and me ever since I got here. He wasn't my mate, but I definitely felt attracted to him. I'd never been crazy about finding a mate. While I'd found human men attractive before, I'd never dated any seriously or had strong feelings for any of them. I've never had strong feelings for any man, wolf or human; relationships had never been my thing.

However, something about Presley always made me smile when I saw him. The first time we met, after he had discovered our camp and wanted to take Ruby, there had been no time to find him attractive. Then I mind linked with him asking for his help, and he came through. I guess something about being in each others' minds built a greater level of intimacy between us. I'd noticed our eyes locking with each other quite a bit since then. When he was around, it felt like the chemistry between us was palpable.

He carried himself so well, and while he was intense at times, I liked it.

"Oh," he drawled as he looked down for a second. "And here I thought you were looking for me."

I arched a brow at this.

He closed his eyes. "Sorry." He chuckled. "That sounded so much better in my head."

"Less cheesy?" I asked with a chuckle.

"Way less."

I turned to walk away. "So, do you ever sleep, or are you always working?"

He stepped in stride next to me. "Always working," he replied with a smile. "Wanna know what my secret is?"

I nodded.

He exhaled heavily as if he was about to drop a bomb on me. "I'm a robot." He continued walking, his face showing no signs of him joking.

"You're not serious, are you?"

He stopped and turned to me slowly.

I looked him up and down, my eyes narrowing somewhat.

Suddenly, he started laughing. "I'm not a robot, Natalie. Seriously, relax."

To my surprise, a dimple on his left cheek popped out. Shaking my head, I stalked off. "Ha-ha-ha, laugh it up."

"I can't believe you actually fell for that," he chuckled as he caught up to me.

I shrugged. "I'm a werewolf, remember? I bet most people would believe you were a robot before they'd believe I was a werewolf. As a government operative, I am sure I don't have to tell you that Artificial Intelligence has come a long way. Hell, who knows what government technology is really capable of?"

He puckered his mouth, a look of contemplation on his face. "You're right. My outlook on many things needs to change now that I know there are people like you in the world. There is so much we humans don't know."

"You have no idea," I muttered under my breath as I exhaled.

"Hey..." He touched my elbow lightly. "Are you okay? You look a little pale."

I halted to look up at him and gave him a tight-lipped smile. "I'm okay, I'm just... I feel like I'm barely needed around here. I mean, when this all started, I was helping to protect Ruby. Now, she's the one who'll protect us all. Xavier, Axel, and Mathieu have been busy training with your men, and me..." I shrugged. "I'm just here, the girl with the visions. I wish..." I stopped talking as two soldiers, a man and woman, walked by us.

They both looked at us as if we were committing a crime.

Presley turned to them, his lips parting to say something.

I placed my hand on his arm. "Don't," I stopped him. "It's not worth it."

"I'm sorry. A lot of the people here are..." He sighed. "Not everyone has graciously accepted the revelation that supernaturals are real. You guys are stronger, faster, more powerful beings, and they feel threatened. To be completely honest, with vampires murdering everyone, they are terrified of all supernaturals."

I shook my head as I bit my lip. "I know they are, but you don't need to be sorry, Presley. You're not them, and I can never thank you enough for what you did for my pack. I'm going to check on Ruby, okay? I need to speak with her."

He stepped back with a nod. "Of course."

I smiled at him and moved away.

"Natalie?"

I looked back at him.

He buried his hands in his pockets. "There is no one else like you in the world, and you are needed. Please always remember that. You saved your pack when you contacted me."

The look in his blue eyes had my chest tightening, and I swallowed hard.

A few seconds passed with us just standing there and staring at each other. Sharing this moment with him was making me sad, because I knew nothing could ever or would ever happen between us.

"Thanks." I smiled and turned away, the burning behind my eyes returning. There were things I needed to tell the others before they left. I just had to figure out how to explain that I could have stopped so many things from happening.

——————

Ruby

The room I was given was more like a broom closet, but nothing I wasn't used to. For the past few months, I'd been dealing with worse, anyway. The tiny bed against the wall was surprisingly comfortable, but still, I couldn't sleep.

One of Presley's teams in the field was killed by vampires, so the Queen's attack was delayed. Fortunately, it gave Xavier and Axel time to work with Presley's men, so they could become familiar with working alongside humans and vice versa. Tensions weren't as high as they were when we initially arrived. Even though

I still got the odd curious or hateful stare, I felt less bothered by them.

Anyone who didn't like me could just kiss my ass for all I cared. Whether they liked me or not, I had a job to do here. I was going to kill the vampire Queen and make sure the rest of the world survived, no matter what anyone else thought of me.

I groaned and rolled to my side. That was partly why I couldn't sleep. I saw the way the humans who actually wanted to work with us looked at me, as if I was a celebrity or some kind of savior. I'd never experienced any of this before, especially being looked at with love and admiration.

I turned onto my stomach and stared at my door. When did I start referring to humans as such, as if I wasn't one of them? I closed my eyes and sighed, but I opened them a second later as my door opened.

"Why aren't you sleeping?" Natalie asked me as she walked in and closed the door behind her.

Sitting up and folding my legs lotus-style, I made space for her to sit beside me. "I could ask you the same thing."

She held her head back against the wall and sighed. "I can't sleep."

"Same," I grumbled. "What's on your mind?"

She quirked her mouth a bit before turning her head to look at me. She exhaled heavily. "I've just been thinking about when you guys leave to kill the Queen."

"If it *is* the Queen," I interjected.

She shrugged. "If it's her or not, I've just been thinking about when you guys leave."

"Are you worried that we won't come back?" I asked her.

Looking away, Natalie blinked slowly. I noticed her eyes looked puffy as if she'd been crying.

I nudged her with my elbow. "Whether it's the Queen or not, we're all coming back."

She turned her gaze to me. "I know you all will," she said softly before smiling. "Are you scared?"

I combed my hair back and out of my face. "I'm terrified. I feel like everything is just beginning and ending at the same time. What if it is the Queen?"

"Then you kill her," she answered matter-of-factly.

I snorted. "I don't even know how," I mumbled.

She placed her hand over mine. "When the time comes, you will."

My eyes roamed her face for a moment. "How do you know that?"

She shrugged. "I just do. The Goddess wouldn't have picked you if she didn't believe you could do what needs to be done. Plus..." She tilted her head towards me as she looked at me from under her lashes. "You aren't fighting this alone. Hell, you've got two hot Alphas out there backing you up, not to mention the best soldiers the U.S. government has to offer."

I smiled and nodded.

We both sat in silence for a moment.

"So, you and Presley," I broke the quiet.

Her head snapped towards me in surprise.

I chuckled. "Come on, it's obvious. So, what's going on with you two?"

She smiled and shook her head. "Nothing right now. I think he likes me, though."

"Do you like him?"

She nodded, and the smile on her lips faded.

I could see something was bothering her.

"I do like him, but nothing will ever happen between us."

"You don't know that, Natalie. I mean, I know you're not big on finding your mate anyways. Just remember, with the way things are going right now, it's important to tell people how you feel."

Staring down at her hands, she turned a bead ring around and around her finger. "Yeah, you're right." She turned to face me and pulled me into a hug. "I'm so glad we became friends. You are the sister I never had."

I was frozen for a moment, a bit confused, but then I hugged her back. I pouted as I became emotional and squeezed her closer. "I'm glad too. And I feel the same way about you. In fact, I hate everyone but you."

Chuckling, she pulled away. "I think there might be at least two more people you don't hate around here. You should take your own advice, you know. Talk to the guys about how you feel about them."

I bit at my lip to hide the smile growing on my lips.

She narrowed her eyes at me as she looked me up and down. "What? Ruby, you better tell me."

"I kissed them," I whispered.

Her eyes widened.

"Yup, I kissed them both, and we kind of all slept together."

Her mouth dropped as her eyes widened further.

"Hey, get your mind out of the gutter! Nothing happened!" I exclaimed.

She pinned me with a look that said she didn't believe me.

"I swear, nothing happened. We just slept together in the same bed. It was after I found out Malcolm was my dad and everything about Lovette being my mom. I... needed them. I needed them both."

"Wow," she exclaimed in astonishment. "So, things are better between you and Axel?"

I nodded. "Things are better. I think we'll both always remember what happened, but I've learned so much about him, and him about me. With becoming..." I gestured down my body. "...this, and all the emotions and everything happening, Xavier and I have had our moments when we've felt far from each other, but... I know I can count on them both."

"So you guys are legit going to go along with this crazy throuple?" she asked with a wide grin.

My face started to burn with a blush as I nodded. "I mean, I don't want either of them to reject me, and I don't think either of them wants to reject me, either. So..." I inhaled and exhaled deeply, the heat in my cheeks transferring to the rest of my body. "I guess this is how things will be between us."

"I've missed out on a lot." She sighed, despite the pleased look on her face. "Today, I saw them both laughing together. It was like watching a unicorn peeing."

I made a face. "I don't even know what—wait." I squinted at her. "Are unicorns real?"

Natalie busted out laughing. "Hell, no."

"Oh," I said with a laugh. "Well, Xavier and Axel have their moments." I rubbed my eyes. "And in other news, I... um, I spoke to her. My mom, I mean."

"I know. Xavier told me," she replied softly, a look of concern growing in her eyes. "He told me she's the one who took your memories and power."

Her expression made me want to cry. I nodded, my throat suddenly becoming dry. "I wish I could see her again."

"You won't see her again, not like before."

I frowned. "What do you mean?"

"The Goddess won't allow it. You'll see her again after you die, but you can't let that happen."

"Damn," I drawled as I unfolded my legs for them to dangle off the bed. "Harsh."

"Sorry."

"How do you know what the Goddess will or will not do?"

A knock came at the door, then it opened, revealing Presley on the other side. "I sent another team in. You need to see this."

Ruby

The room filled with soldiers remained quiet. No one was typing away at the many keyboards or walking around in a rush. Everyone seemed focused on the large television on the wall, showing a somewhat shaky body cam video of humans being removed from two trucks and being led into the same building the vampire Queen was observed entering.

My stomach clenched as children were led out of the truck as well.

Being that it was nighttime and in the forest, the only light came from the moon and two large lights above the building's front door.

"That's a General." Xavier pointed to the screen as another car pulled up to the house, and a man headed over to it.

"How do you know?" Presley asked.

Axel stepped forward, his arms crossed over his broad chest. "We encountered one before. It looks like this vampire is wearing a full red uniform with black lines down his arms—the same uniform as the one we saw earlier. "

My blind ass hadn't been able to make that out with the General we had met. Now, however, I could see it with the subtle lighting. We watched the man on the screen walk towards the car to open the passenger's door. A woman stepped out of the car. All that could be seen was the top of her head a second before she was immediately flanked by the guards, who appeared to be wearing black uniforms with red lines. They walked closely by her as they led her into the building, and the door closed behind them.

"We can't tell if it's even the same woman as before," I told the others as I looked away from the screen.

Everyone in the command room filed out, heading back to their assigned tasks.

"The humans... all those humans are also our priority," Presley replied. "We leave in an hour."

"What?" I asked as I spun around to face him. "An hour?"

"Yes, Ruby." Presley's brows knitted. "If we wait any longer, all those humans will be killed."

I looked back at the now-frozen screen and swallowed the lump that had lodged in my throat. Yes, we needed to save all those humans, but I hoped I'd have more time before facing the Queen. "You said you had ways to help me with my power. Yet I've been here for two full days, and I've only been training with the guys," I told him as I turned to face him.

"We had a way of helping you—a person, to be exact—but our asset was lost. Now that I know what you are and what you're capable of, my help wouldn't have been much help at all. Are you ready for this, Ruby? We have to act now, or all those—"

"I know," I interjected, cutting him off. I clenched my fists at my sides as I pictured the children I had seen in the video. "I'm ready."

Presley nodded his head sternly, his eyes drifting to Natalie briefly. "We move out in an hour." He then turned to a soldier. "Get them ready."

The soldier saluted him. "Yes, General."

Presley moved away.

I immediately turned to Natalie. I shook my head at her as my heart hammered in my chest as if it was trying to break free. "I'm not ready."

"We'll be there with you," Axel tried to comfort me.

I looked his way.

His hazel eyes drifted to Xavier.

Xavier nodded in agreement. "If that was the Queen, we might not get another chance like this," he added. "We've got this."

I chewed on my bottom lip and released my clenched fists. "Okay," I exhaled. "It's now or never, I guess."

I stepped closer to the television as the video started playing again.

———

The Vampire General

I closed my eyes and inhaled, and it was as if I could still smell her. I finally understood why Bleeders who had come into contact with her became so bloodthirsty.

I saw why the Queen was so interested in her. Ruby Saunders was not of this earth; I could smell it in her blood. The memory of her killing those Bleeders jumped to the forefront of my mind, and I opened my eyes. I was staring up at the ceiling with my head held back on the sofa, but what I was actually seeing was her sucking the life from those Bleeders.

The Queen had said there hadn't been someone like her in a long time, but I suspected there had never been anyone like her. We decided to enact our plans now because the earth's creatures—both human and otherwise—had grown so far away from the Gods. The fewer who worshipped the gods, the further they fell out of the gods' favor. Creatures of the earth had more power centuries ago. The poor fools had no idea how far they had fallen. Not only that, species no longer allied with each other. They were too busy keeping to themselves and hiding from humans.

Sadly, we had miscalculated the weakness of our greatest enemies. As divided as the werewolves had been, they still held their Goddess close—much closer than we knew. The bitch even left one of her children to thwart our efforts.

I wanted to see what the whelp was capable of. I wanted to see who this girl was that my Queen both feared and desired to have as her own. I saw now that she had reason to. I smiled as I looked to the ground at the two humans lying there, their eyes lifeless and dull. I could also see how much more powerful we'd become if she became one of us.

A supernatural who was turned became full vampire, not a hybrid. They became as bloodthirsty as the rest of us and turned into a Bleeder or a Skin. Yet, this Ruby had the blood of a goddess running through her, so what would happen if she turned? When

I asked the Queen, she merely grinned like a Cheshire cat and assured me Ruby would become "a very powerful ally" for us.

A knock came at the door.

"Come in," I said softly.

The door opened as a female vampire with a severely humped back and sagging, wrinkled skin slowly walked in. She was one of the Queen's Seers, and one of three Enchanteds the Queen had turned over the years. All three women were extremely powerful and very old vampires who had retained their ability to see into the future.

It finally clicked, and I couldn't believe I hadn't seen it before.

That was why the Queen wanted Ruby. If an Enchanted with diluted divinity could become so powerful from the turn, what would happen with someone like Ruby, with her raw divinity?

"The Queen would like to speak with you," the woman said in an eerie voice, her completely black eyes unreadable for even me.

I said nothing as I sat forward.

The Seer closed her eyes. She inhaled deeply like someone about to dive into water and she slowly started to stand straight. A bone in her back cracked, and as she stood upright, her black eyes turned red. "General Carden," the Seer greeted me. I could hear the queen's voice mingled with her voice. She looked at the bodies on the floor. "Relaxing, I see."

"No, my Queen, I'm planning for the upcoming attack," I confirmed.

The Seer walked over to the bodies and bent down. She moved the hair out of the woman's face before standing once more. "Where is she?"

I stood from the sofa. "I have my eyes on her. She's with the humans, my Queen."

"Then why haven't you taken her, Carden? I'm running out of patience," she asked through clenched teeth. "Olcan gave you her location before she found the humans. Why didn't you take her then?"

"I wanted to see what she was capable of, and I also wanted to see into her mind," I replied.

Even though I wasn't literally in the Queen's presence, the Seer's eyes were now her eyes. They instilled the same fear as if I were looking at the Queen herself.

After a moment, she rolled her hands in a circle, as if telling me to hurry up. "Okay, and what? What did you see?"

"Not much before she felt me inside her mind and blocked me, but I did see a memory. I saw William."

Her hand shot out and grabbed me around my throat.

I could feel blood running down my neck from where her nails had pierced my skin.

Stepping closer, she pulled me down to stare into her eyes. "Never say that name," she hissed before looking down at my throat. She released me slowly and sighed. "That better not be all you have to tell me." She arched a brow as she licked my blood from one of her fingers as she turned away.

"No, my Queen," I replied promptly. "The werewolf confirmed they were on their way to a human army base."

She turned her head but didn't look around. "Mm... well, you know what to do then, don't you?"

"Yes, my Queen," I replied obediently.

Now, the Seer's shoulders began to slump as she bent forward into her position before.

"Wait," I said.

The Seer turned to look at me, the red eyes of the Queen fading.

"My brother... has his body been retrieved?"

"Yes," she replied. "Those vermin killed your brother; they killed my son. Humans are the pests of this earth, never forget that. I want that base destroyed, do you understand?" She turned back around and stepped from the room slowly.

I clenched my teeth at the annoying tingling sensation of the wounds on my neck healing.

Axel and Xavier were given earpieces to speak with everyone else if needed, along with the other werewolves that volunteered to come with us. There was no point in giving them guns or any of the other gadgets the humans had strapped to their bodies. They'd just be ripped to pieces when they transformed. Of course, with their heightened hearing, they really only needed the earpieces for the teams that would be too far away from us.

I was given one as well, along with a gun. I stared down at it in my palm and moved my hand up and down as I felt its weight. It seemed kind of silly for me to have a gun when my powers were more potent than any bullet, but Presley thought I should have one just in case.

"It has UV bullets," Alonzo clarified as he secured his bullet-proof vest.

"Okay," I replied. "Why the vests, though?"

"The vampires obviously won't be using guns, but our gear gives us a little cushion when they attack us. You have your powers to rely on, Ruby, but keeping that gun on you won't hurt. It works great against the Bleeders."

"What about the Skins?"

"It works on them too, but while one bullet can kill a Bleeder, it takes a bit more than one for the Skins," he explained. "When this all happened, it took a while for the military to make a weapon that could kill them. The Bleeders can be killed easily, but the others..."

"Yeah, I know. Do you know if anyone has ever faced a General?" I asked him.

He sat down on top of a trunk filled with guns. "Well..." He looked around us before leaning forward. "I heard some of the higher-ranking officers talking. A General was killed in Paris."

I stepped closer to him. "Really? How?"

He shrugged. "I'm not sure how, but he killed sixty people before they could kill him."

My eyes widened for a second. "Jesus."

"Mmhmm, and get this: apparently, the Generals have special abilities. The one they killed in Paris could move things with his mind." He shook his head. "As if they weren't hard enough to kill as it was."

I realized that back at Olcan's place when we had been attacked, Olcan had said the Queen had already lost one of her Generals. None of us had even bothered to ask him how he knew that. But this explained why I could feel the General we had met in my mind.

Another soldier called Alonzo, and he walked away.

However, I remained there as I wondered what power the General we had seen in the video had. I placed a hand on the gun strapped to my side when Natalie appeared beside me.

"We need to talk," she told me, her face pale as she grabbed my hand and pulled me away from the others. "Now."

I allowed her to drag me to the corner of the room. "Um, yeah, sure, what's wrong?"

"I'm not going to beat around the bush, so I'm just going to rip the Band-Aid off," she whispered. "This is harder than you think."

My brows dipped at her now-panicked state. I placed my hand on her shoulder and shook her gently for her to look at me and stop looking at the others so wide-eyed. "Natalie, you're freaking me out. What's going on?"

"I knew you were going to be attacked," she said, her words coming out in a rush.

My nose wrinkled as I smelled blood. I looked down to see that she was sinking one of her claws into the palm of her hand. My hand fell from her shoulder as I stepped back.

Sighing, she released her hand. She looked relieved as she clenched her fist.

"What?" I asked, my voice low. "Which time?"

She stared at me from under her lashes, a look of regret in her eyes. "The first time you were bitten by a vampire, when you, Xavier, and Axel ran from Olcan."

I started blinking rapidly, not sure if I was hearing her correctly. "I'm sorry." I held my hand up. "What are you talking about?"

Sighing, she combed her white hair backward. "I saw a vision of you being attacked before you left."

My stomach twisted with anger and confusion.

Natalie stepped forward, her words coming out rushed, "I couldn't say anything. I swear. I wish I had been able to, but the Goddess wouldn't let me."

I stared at her for a moment, unable to speak.

She visibly swallowed as she waited for me to say something.

I couldn't formulate the words. I was upset she had allowed that to happen to me, she had been the one to encourage Xavier and me to leave, and all along, she had known we would be attacked and almost killed. "Did you know Malcolm would be there?" I asked softly.

"What?"

"The person that saved us that night, it turns out it was Malcolm. Did you know he would be there to save me?"

She looked away.

I shook my head as I clenched my fists at my sides. "You didn't know if I was going to live or die, and yet, you helped it to happen by offering to facilitate our escape from Olcan?"

"The Goddess wouldn't have let you die." She moved closer to me.

I raised my head. I knew in my agitated state that my eyes were shifting from black to green and back.

With a gasp, Natalie stepped back.

"You've been working with her all this time?" I demanded. "How much have you known, Natalie? What other secrets are you hiding? You could have warned us all about the vampires. You could have given us all a head start on defeating them. We could have stopped all of this."

"Nothing could have stopped them at that point, Ruby. I wanted to tell you, I swear I did, but I literally *couldn't* say anything. The Goddess forbade it."

"Well, how are you telling me now? Huh?" I asked her.

She sighed heavily.

I couldn't believe her. I felt like I didn't know her at all. The Natalie I knew, or I *thought* I knew, wouldn't have kept something like this a secret. I turned away from her.

Sure enough, Xavier and Axel were looking our way. From the angry look on their faces, they heard our conversation.

"Ruby, please, you have to believe me. I wanted to tell you, but I couldn't... I'm sorry," Natalie pleaded.

I kept moving away from her. She was the very first person I learned to trust after falling into this world, and now she was telling me she knew all along about The Goddess's plans for me. "Did you know everything? Did you know about my mom and Malcolm?"

"No, she didn't tell me anything other than war was coming

and you'd play a major part in it. She wanted me to stay by you and help guide you, but that's all I knew. I swear."

"Guide me, huh?" I glanced at Xavier and Axel. "Is no one in my life there without a purpose to serve for the Goddess?"

"Let's go, everyone, time to move out!" Presley yelled as he entered the room. He looked at Xavier and Axel, and then followed their stares to Natalie and me. He frowned as he stared at Natalie and then at me. Remaining silent, he walked off purposefully.

"Why are you telling me this now?" I asked her.

She stared at me, the rim of her eyes red with tears. "It's time you knew. I know you're angry at me. You have every right to be, but no matter how hard or painful some things that happen are, they can't be stopped. If something is meant to happen, it will."

I had no doubt my eyes were rimmed with tears too, as I snorted and turned away.

"Ruby?"

I stopped but didn't turn around.

"I'm truly sorry," she apologized.

I clenched my fists as I walked past the guys, then stopped at the door.

Natalie told Xavier and Axel goodbye.

Xavier replied, "We'll talk when I get back."

"I love you, and I am sorry," she apologized as she embraced him.

I closed my eyes at the pain in her voice, but I felt too angry to look at her.

That night, I had been so terrified and confused. I thought I was going to die, and she knew it would happen. I thought Natalie was my friend, the only true friend I've ever had. Apparently I'd been very wrong. Did she approach me that day in the library because the Goddess told her to? Or did the Goddess make her do it without her even knowing?

I pulled my hair into a high ponytail and then made a bun.

Fuck the Goddess.

I was so goddamn sick of her intervention in every aspect of my life, from my birth to my mates, and now even my friends. My life had been nothing but heartache and pain thanks to her. Now I was off to kill a vampire Queen with no clue how I would even do it. The Goddess had used everyone in my life to shepard me to this point. Could I even rightfully call it *my* life?

I stepped outside.

Presley, who had been waiting, led me to one of six helicopters.

My rage was only continuing to steadily grow as I got into the helicopter.

Presley helped to strap me in and kept sending odd looks my way. When Axel and Xavier joined us, they both sent me looks of concern.

I avoided looking at them all and closed my eyes as the helicopter lifted off the ground.

The sooner this all ended, the sooner I could vanish and have nothing to do with Gods, or anyone who expected something from me for that matter. I'd grown tired of everyone looking to me to bring an end to this war.

I felt so tired of all of this.

My eyes were stinging with tears, but I kept them closed as I squeezed the straps around my body. If I looked at Xavier or Axel, I would break down, and right now, I needed the anger coursing through my veins.

I needed my rage to do what had to be done.

———

Ruby

I wasn't sure how much time had passed since we left the base. This was my first time flying in a helicopter, but my mind was too crammed with thoughts to focus on the experience. My gaze remained glued outside at the blue sky and white clouds.

Natalie's words had been replaying in my mind since we'd left. She had known what would happen to me, and even if she hadn't known everything about who or what I was, she knew enough that we could've gotten in front of this mess earlier. I didn't buy her crap about The Goddess not allowing her to tell. She just told me now with no apparent objections from the Goddess.

How had she been able to look me in the face all this time? That night had been one of the worst experiences of my life.

Sighing, I looked towards the guys and found them speaking to each other, but since I wasn't wearing a headset, I couldn't hear them. Axel's hazel eyes drifted to me, and the knowing look he gave me, one of pity, made me look away. I didn't want anyone's pity.

Both he and Xavier were a part of the Goddess's plans too. She did this. She made it so I would be a mate to them both. I still didn't understand the reason for that, but everyone in my life had been placed there by her like little chess pieces on a lifesize gameboard.

I grew up an orphan. I had no one to love or love me back, no responsibility but to survive and care for myself. Suddenly, I was supposed to put that all aside and save the world. I could think of a lot of better ways I could have been groomed for this.

Presley tapped my leg.

I looked to the side.

He pointed downwards that we were about to land.

I nodded. Holding onto the straps across my chest, I clenched my jaw as the helicopter started to descend.

Once on the ground, Presley helped me to make my way out of the helicopter, and I realized we had landed alone.

"Where are the others?" I asked as I glanced at the other seven men who had flown with us.

"Circling the perimeter; we can't afford for the Queen to escape. There are werewolves with each team, so hopefully, that'll give us an advantage. Our team will be going in through the front door."

"Oh." I turned in a circle. The forest seemed so quiet, unnaturally so. "There's something wrong with this place. I can feel it."

"Are you okay?" Axel whispered to my ear.

I looked his way. I knew he wasn't asking me about what I was feeling right now. He was asking about what had happened with Natalie.

I nodded. "I'm fine, I'm just nervous. You're all putting too much faith in a novice."

"We're putting our faith in someone that has proven she can do what no one else can," Presley replied. "We're all new to this threat, Ruby; we're all just novices trying to survive."

"Team three in location," a voice reported over the earpiece we all had.

Presley replied that they would wait for all the teams to get into position. "We need to use up the sun while we have it, guys. The vampires can't and won't try to escape while the sun's out. We need to act now," he announced. "Even with the sun on our side and the element of surprise, stay on guard. We could all still be slaughtered."

Five minutes passed before all teams reported that they had landed and were in position. Presley quietly led us through the forest with Axel by his side up front to lend a listening ear to the forest while Xavier stayed at our rear. I walked in the middle with the other soldiers.

The closer we got to the vampires' hideout, the more I feared they might hear my hammering heartbeat and know we were coming.

This is it.

I felt like throwing up. At the same time, I was eager to see this war come to an end.

The smell of vampires hit me like a ton of bricks, and I had to hold back from coughing.

Ahead of us, Axel held his hand up for everyone to stop. He then whispered to Presley, who then gave hand signals to his men.

I watched as they all grabbed their guns and began fanning out somewhat.

Xavier came up beside me and held my hand. He squeezed it gently before raising it to his lips. I sighed as some of the tension in my body left as he mouthed to me, "*I'm here.*"

I needed to remember I wasn't doing this entirely alone.

Presley called us forward to the tree line where we bent down to stare at the house a few yards away. The three-story building was run-down with blacked-out windows. The massive parking lot in front of it made for the perfect ground for what we planned. We heard no sounds, no birds or insects, and the wind around us went still. The vampires' scent was so strong, my eyes began to water. There was most definitely a lot of them here.

I think the Bleeders were the ones with a more pungent scent. When I killed that vampire so long ago, a Skin, he had a vampire's scent, but it wasn't as horrible as the Bleeders.

"Move in," Presley directed through his mic, and all guns were aimed as his men started moving stealthily forward, breaking through the tree line. He looked at me. "Are you ready?"

I nodded as I called on my power, allowing all of it to flow through me like a river. "It's now or never," I replied.

He tilted his head towards the house, and we moved forward as well.

Xavier walked in front of me, with Axel at my back alongside General Presley.

I looked past Xavier to see another team breaking through the tree line as well on the other side of the parking lot. I noted the three werewolves along them were already in their wolf form.

"Wait," Axel suddenly commanded, and we stopped.

"What?" Presley whispered back, a look of annoyance on his face.

Axel's eyes changed to black as he looked around us. "Something's wrong," he said ominously.

Yeah, no shit. This place is beyond creepy.

"We can't hear anything," Axel stated the obvious.

"Yeah, so?" Xavier asked.

Axel shook his head. "It shouldn't be this quiet, even in the daytime. You and I should be able to hear them, at least one of them. There's nothing," Axel replied, his fangs and nails elongating as he spoke. "It's daytime, but not all of them would be sleeping. Wouldn't they have guards awake?"

I spun around to look at Presley, who was now looking around us as well. My body jolted as thunder clapped above us, and we all looked up as the beautiful blue sky started to change. Black storm clouds rolled in.

I looked over at Xavier with panicked eyes. "Does that seem unnatural to anyone else, or is it just me?"

Xavier started to remove his shirt, and so did Axel.

A lightning bolt struck the ground in the parking lot, the world around us dark as if it was evening, going on to nighttime.

The front door to the house opened and a man stepped out. The red uniform with black was unmistakable.

Axel's wolf by my side looked at me.

I clenched my fists as I looked back at the General.

The vamps knew we were coming.

"He's doing this," Xavier said in a strained voice as he fell to the ground, the brown fur of his wolf bursting through his skin. "Look at his... eyes."

Sure enough, the vampire's eyes were a pure white instead of the typical crimson. His hair which stopped just above his ears was a matching shade of white. With his pale skin, his overall features combined to form an exotic look I would've never associated with a vampire. That was, until he looked directly at me and smiled, revealing razor-sharp fangs. Those were familiar, at least.

The sound of the breaking ground came from behind us, and

we spun around to see a Bleeder digging its way from out of the ground.

Presley fired at it straightaway. The bullet lodged itself between the creature's eyes, and it fell dead.

Lightning struck the ground again. With each flash, more Bleeders began to appear from beneath us.

With the sun blocked out, we'd lost one of our biggest advantages.

Presley yelled out orders and gunshots started to echo all around us.

Axel jumped into the air and tackled a vampire making its way towards us.

Xavier remained by my side, his head low and his legs wide apart as he readied himself for an attack.

I reached out and placed my hand on Xavier's side. I closed my eyes as I inhaled deeply. The sound of wolves growling and snarling mixed with resounding gunshots, and the chilling hisses of the vampires filled my head. I tried to clear my mind as I gathered as much energy from the earth as I could pull.

Without opening my eyes, I sensed a Bleeder making its way towards Xavier. I held my hand out, releasing the energy I had absorbed.

I opened my eyes in time to see the Bleeder flying backward as if he'd been thrown, along with another two behind it.

The werewolves ripped into two of them while Presley shot the other. Thunder rumbled over us. Lightning struck just in front of Xavier and me, sending us flying backward.

I looked up in time to see the sky open as another lightning bolt started to descend to the earth. Using my mind, I pushed Xavier's wolf out of the way just in time, and the bolt struck the ground where he had been lying just moments before.

He got to his feet and shook his head but was tackled by a Bleeder.

"Hello, Ruby," a voice said from behind me.

I turned around.

The General slapped me across the face, sending me skidding across the ground. "Oh, I'm sorry. The Queen wants you alive. I forgot for a second there."

Easing myself up on my hands, I got up slowly, a cut on my arm already healing. "She's not here, is she?"

He chuckled. "Of course not. Did you all really think we wouldn't know men were watching us? Oh, I'm Alaris, by the way."

I don't give a shit what this monster's name is! As I got to my feet, I clenched my teeth as my body started to grow hot. I focused on channeling it all into my hands.

The vampire vanished from my sight. One moment he was standing there, a sinister smile on his pale face, and then he was gone.

This asshole is mocking me. He's toying with me, but if I can't even handle him, how will I ever face the Queen?

"Now, I'd prefer it if you didn't try to burn me," Alaris whispered from behind me.

I spun around, releasing the built-up heat in my hands, but it caught a Bleeder instead of my intended target.

"Wow," he said from my left as he watched the Bleeder turn to ash on the ground. "I'm impressed, but also very disappointed. Are you really the girl my mother fears?"

His mother?

A soldier ran up beside me and began emptying his clip into Alaris. I watched as he yelped in pain as his body was knocked backward with each bullet that entered him. He vanished before our eyes. Suddenly, the soldier by my side was yanked away.

I watched Alaris break the soldier's neck and decapitate him with ease, as if he were nothing but a toy soldier instead of actual flesh and blood. My knees grew weak, and I felt utterly sick to my stomach.

I screamed, my body shaking with emotion, and the ground

beneath us started to crack. Tree roots appeared from beneath us, lashing out at Alaris and striking anyone close enough.

All of this death and killing; none of this is right!

Lightning hit the ground beside me, sending me flying and falling onto a Bleeder who instantly tried to bite me. I grabbed its face and threw it off me with more force than I knew I was capable of.

"Well, well, now you're showing your true colors, Ms. Saunders," Alaris teased.

I got to my feet as he approached me slowly. I watched as the holes in his chest started to heal.

He dove as roots from the earth lashed out at him, but he stood in front of me within the next second.

"Where is she?" I yelled at him.

He smiled. "Come with me, and I'll take you to her. There won't be anything or anyone left alive here or back at your base, anyway."

My face fell. "What did you say?"

A werewolf suddenly tackled him to the ground, and a Skin attacked me. I hadn't even realized there were a few of them among the Bleeders.

"You smell amazing," the man hissed as we struggled on the ground.

Kicking him in the side, I flipped us over and grabbed his throat. "You don't!" Black veins appeared on my arms, and he physically caught fire beneath me. I got off him, my heart now pounding with panic at what Alaris had said. I looked around at the bodies on the ground and those still fighting before I spotted Alaris with his fangs in a werewolf's throat.

The smell of blood was strong in the air, mixed with the pungent odor of the vampires. I walked forward slowly, my eyes trained on the General.

He looked my way and stood up, wiping his hand across his mouth.

"What have you done?" I demanded. Despite the distance between us, I knew he could hear me just fine.

He held his palm out as a lightning bolt began to dance within his palm. "While all your forces are here, many of ours are at your army base. There will be no one left alive."

For a second, I couldn't breathe as Natalie's blue eyes flashed within my mind. It felt as if a hand were holding my lungs and squeezing them. "No," I said under my breath.

The roots still protruding from the ground started to move erratically as I lost control of my powers. Natalie, Mathieu, and all the others were in danger. This wasn't just a trap for us.

The sadness in Natalie's eyes before we had left was all I could see. As angry as I was with her, I had every intention of going back and talking things over. *What if she's—*

I didn't finish the thought as my face burned with rage.

Alaris held his hand up to the sky. A bolt of lightning fell into his palm, and he threw it at me.

I couldn't move, and I didn't blink as it came to me. I merely closed my eyes.

The impact rocked my body, but I remained standing as I absorbed the bolt. It was pure, raw energy, and I could feel the hairs on my body standing on end. As I opened my eyes, I sent the bolt rolling back towards him.

It burned through his chest, its power tripled by mine. He rolled onto his side as he gripped at his chest and reached up to the sky with his other hand.

Thunder rumbled above us as three bolts broke through the clouds.

I bit down on my lip until I tasted blood and reached out with both hands. Energy—it was all energy. I drank it into my body as if it was water and I hadn't had a drop in years.

The bolts changed their position, all three bolts hitting me at once. I felt like an empty battery being charged as I consumed it all. I smiled as my body started to emit small bolts of lightning.

Bleeders and Skins alike were being killed, fried to a crisp, when suddenly someone barreled into me.

"You fucking bitch!" Alaris yelled as he climbed on top of me on the ground. He put his hand around my throat to cut my air off as he reached up to the sky with his other hand. "The Queen wants you alive, but she never said you had to be in one piece."

The cloud above us opened. A ray of sunlight broke through, killing a Skin as it ran into the light. Lightning struck, the bolt coming down onto Alaris and me.

I closed my eyes.

I thought of my mother's words, to stop fearing my power, to open myself. My hand holding Alaris's wrist reached out, and instead of the bolt falling into his hands, it hit him full force. The smell of his burning skin had my nose burning, and he released me to get away. Before he could get anywhere, I grabbed his face, pouring all the heat I could muster into his body before kicking him off me.

I held my hands up to the sky, commanding the clouds to move away, and they complied. Sunlight broke through the darkness around us, as did lightning. The screams and shrieks of vampires filled my ears, and I laughed maniacally as those screams grew louder.

Alaris himself turned to ash beneath my feet.

I heard someone yell my name, and I spun around. Presley was stooped down over a soldier on the ground, and I could see the large burn mark on the soldier's shoulder and neck.

My hands fell to my sides, and the lightning storm stopped.

All around, werewolves and soldiers were staring at me, some in awe, others in fear, and some visibly trembled.

I walked over to Presley slowly.

The soldier on the ground stared up at me with watery eyes.

"I'm so sorry." I fell to my knees beside him.

His chest, shoulders, and neck were badly burned.

I leaned over him, saddened to see the hurt and pain I had

caused him from using my powers. This was precisely what I had feared, inadvertently hurting someone when I used my powers. Tears started rolling down my cheeks. Then something unexpected happened. As a tear from my eye landed on the soldier's shoulder, he started to heal. I placed my hand over him because I knew somehow, I could stop his pain. I tried to visualize absorbing all the injury and inflammation in his body into myself. His face went from a grimace of discomfort to one of relaxation.

"Thank you, Ruby," he whispered.

I squeezed his hand to acknowledge. I stood and walked to another wounded soldier on the ground, a deep burn on his chest.

He was gasping for breath, and I took the hand he weakly held out to me. I healed him as well, sadness welling up inside me. It seemed like for every good thing I'd done so far, I'd hurt someone in the process.

"We need to get back to the base right away," I told Presley as he appeared to my left. "They're attacking the base. We have to save Natalie and the others."

We spotted a cloud of black smoke a mile out from the base.

Xavier couldn't sit still, and before the helicopter even landed, he opened the door and jumped out.

Axel followed behind him.

I waited until the helicopter was at least on the ground before getting out and rushing towards the building.

Around us, there were dead bodies scattered on the ground, both humans and vampires.

"How did they attack during the day?" I asked out loud as I looked around me.

"Natalie! Dad!" Xavier yelled as he entered the building as Axel and I followed close behind.

Soldiers rushed in behind us, and the werewolves that had gone with us killed the vampires that still appeared to be alive but wounded.

"Fuck," Presley mumbled.

When I looked around, he was staring down at a female soldier on the ground who was writhing in pain, her arms and legs bent in odd directions.

"What's wrong with her?" I asked.

He pointed to the bite mark on her neck. "She's turning," he answered through clenched teeth and pulled out his gun.

I looked away.

Gunshots began to echo around us, and I tried to block out the fact that these soldiers were being forced to kill their colleagues and friends. How had the vampires done this? How had they attacked during the day? The dead vampires scattered around us couldn't have been the only ones who attacked the base, so where were the others?

I pushed those thoughts away for the meantime as I rushed around like everyone else, trying to spot a familiar head of white hair.

"Have you seen Natalie? She's the werewolf with white hair," I asked two men who passed by me carrying a dead vampire in their arms.

They shook their heads, and I kept moving. I felt so fatigued, my body spent from all the power I had used, but I needed to find her. I was running by the cafeteria when I looked inside and saw her. My heart dropped and shattered into a million pieces as I rushed inside. I fell to the ground beside her, ignoring the pain in my knees from the impact. "Natalie? Natalie, it's me, we're—oh, my god," I didn't know what to do, I didn't know where to look or where to heal first.

Her body was covered in bite marks, her blood creating a pool around her. I screamed for Xavier and Axel as I started to heal her wounds. She looked so pale, her blue eyes so dull. I tried to avoid looking at her face, or I'd lose concentration. Everything that I had been angry at her for was now irrelevant.

"Ruby?" she asked weakly.

I wiped my tears away, smearing her blood on my face in the process. "It's me, it's me. It's okay, I-I can help you. I can stop the bleeding." I wiped my face again and got up to move to her other side.

Axel rushed into the room.

I looked his way, his wide hazel eyes causing more tears to roll down my cheeks. "Help me," I choked out. "Help me, please! She's dying." Her hand wrapped around my wrist, and I looked down at her, a hot tear sliding down my cheek. "It's okay, just hang on, okay. Where the fuck is Xavier?"

"He found his dad. Mathieu's wounded," Axel replied.

"Ruby, stop," Natalie whispered.

I moved on from the bite on her wrist and placed my hand over the one on her shoulder.

"I said stop."

"I have to heal you!" I yelled at her, my frustration causing my hands to start shaking.

"I can feel it happening, Ruby." She closed her eyes for a second before opening them again. "I can feel the change happening. They didn't just drink from me this time."

I started crying as my hand fell away from her neck.

"I'm sorry I didn't tell you everything. I-I wanted to but—"

"None of that matters anymore, Natalie, there has to be something I can do. You can't become one of them!"

"This was meant to happen, Ruby. I told you before; what's meant to happen will." She started coughing.

Presley rushed into the room behind Axel. The color drained from his face as he rushed forward, but he stopped at where Natalie's blood had pooled on the ground.

"Listen," Natalie whispered.

I wiped her blood away from the corner of her mouth. Never before had I felt so utterly useless.

"You might feel as if your life is being played with, but it's not. You've been given a gift and the chance for your legacy to live on forever, Ruby. You'll never be forgotten, and everyone will know who you are, the woman that saved us all. I-I won't be here, but I'll die happy that I had the privilege of being your friend."

"Jesus, Natalie, stop, please, just stop!" I tried once more to heal the bite on her neck but she moved my hand away. "I can't do any of this without you, dammit! I don't know what I'm doing! Every time I think I have everything handled, I turn around and see that I've hurt someone. If—if I'm so powerful, why can't I save you? What good are my powers if they can't save you!"

"Not everyone can be saved, Ruby..." Her face twisted in pain. "Trust your powers," she added after a moment, "and a door will open for you."

She closed her eyes.

I panicked for a moment thinking she was gone, but her lips parted as she started chanting under her breath. I leaned forward, but it was a language I didn't understand. A wooden box suddenly appeared by my side, and she fell silent.

"Take it," she choked out, her hand slowly rising to grip at her throat. "Take it."

"What's in it?" I asked.

Her eyes widened as she growled at me, the sound contorted and deep.

Axel suddenly grabbed my arm and pulled me away from her.

She started crying loudly. I covered my mouth to silence my sob as her back arched off the ground.

"No!" I cried. "Please, don't let this happen to her."

But the Goddess didn't reply; she did nothing as we watched Natalie begin to transform, her eyes shifting from blue to red and then back. "Don't let me—die one as—one of them," she begged. "Let me die... as an Enchanted."

I pulled away from Axel.

Axel stepped forward, his claws at the ready to kill her.

I pushed him out of the way. "Don't touch her! Don't... don't touch her. I'll do it." I looked down at her, my eyes blurry with tears. "I'll do it." I held her stare for a moment, my hands shaking at my sides.

She slowly stopped crying. Her eyes stopped changing color and remained blue as her body stopped bending in all angles.

Xavier rushed into the room, his eyes darting around before landing on Natalie, and he raised his hands to sink his fingers into his hair. "Natalie?" he called in shock, his eyes instantly tearing up.

She turned her head to him, a weak smile appearing on her lips before she looked my way once more.

"Don't burn her, Ruby," he called to me.

"I won't," I replied, my voice cracking and barely audible. "I'm so sorry. I love you, Natalie."

Her eyes slowly closed, the smile still on her lips as she took her last breath.

We all stood there in silence for what felt like forever.

I couldn't cry, I couldn't move, and I couldn't look away from her.

She was gone. Natalie, my best friend—was gone.

"What did you do to her?" Presley asked, his voice heavy with emotion.

I closed my eyes. "I put her to sleep and then stopped her heart," I answered before opening my eyes and picking up the box, her blood on the bottom dripping on the ground as I headed away from the room.

When I stepped out of the room, Mathieu, along with a few other soldiers and werewolves, was being carried to the infirmary on a stretcher. I stopped them, and moving from one person to the next, I healed them all, Natalie's box still in one hand.

I felt numb, as if I was just going through the motions without any conscious thought or intention.

Everyone stayed silent, their watchful eyes filled with sadness and pity.

It became too much for me. After everyone was healed, I walked to Natalie's room, her sweet scent filling my nostrils as I stepped through the door.

Clutching her box to my chest, I sank to the floor by her bed and started screaming until my throat felt sore and could no longer make any sounds. Then I just laid on the floor and sobbed until I had no tears left.

———

Axel

No one was talking.

We had won a major victory against the vampires by killing another General, but it didn't feel like we had won. It felt like we had lost.

Ruby hadn't left Natalie's room since yesterday when it all happened, and Xavier hadn't said a word to anyone. The entire Blackmoon Pack had been silent, their eyes reflecting the grief within them. I only recently became acquainted with Natalie, but I recognized right away that she was a good woman who cared deeply for her family and her pack. So many other lives were lost as well, both human and werewolf.

I made my way to the command room.

Xavier, Mathieu, and General Presley were there.

"If we're attacked again, we'll be wiped out," Presley remarked to me as I joined them. "We don't have enough men, and it's going to take some time before reinforcements get here. More than half of my men are..." He sighed as the muscles in his jaws clenched. "We've both lost too many people," he said sadly to Mathieu.

Xavier turned away. "And we still don't know where the Queen is."

"Right now," I finally spoke, "we need to get the manpower before even thinking about the Queen. Presley's right. If we're attacked right now, we're all dead, and the Queen wins." I sat down and crossed my legs.

No one spoke for a moment until Xavier turned back around, his hand on his chin. "One werewolf pack isn't enough."

I sat up as he said this, my eyes narrowed with interest. "What are you saying?"

"We need to ask the other packs for help," he explained.

It was a good idea, but also one that had a very small chance of working. "My pack will help. Getting the other packs to come out of hiding and do the same—let alone work alongside humans—won't be easy."

Mathieu began drumming his fingers on the table. "It might be easier than you think."

I frowned. "How so? Right now, werewolves hate humans more than ever. No offense," I gestured to Presley.

He shrugged. "None taken. I get it. What are you thinking, Mathieu? Do you have a way to get them to help us?"

"Not me," Mathieu replied as he looked from Presley, to Xavier, and then to me. "Ruby."

Xavier stepped forward, his arms crossed over his chest.

I know he was feeling protective of her right now because I felt the same way. What she did in that parking lot—controlling the weather like that—I'd never seen anything like it. On the one hand, it seemed as if there was nothing she couldn't do. However, we had both seen the lost look in her eyes the moment she had to end Natalie's life. She needed time to heal from something like that.

I could feel the emptiness within her.

"I don't think we should bother her right now. She needs some time to herself. What could she possibly do to get all the packs here anyways?" Xavier asked.

"We tell them who she is," Mathieu mumbled more to himself before nodding, as if his own idea suddenly made sense. "We need to let the other packs know who she is, who her mother was, and that she has divinity. She's the one chosen by our goddess for this; they *will* follow her. We have no reason to keep hiding who she is."

"He's right," I agreed. "And I think it would be best to keep her distracted right now."

Xavier clenched his jaws as he looked my way. He bit down on his lip, his eyes darting back and forth thoughtfully. "Okay, but why not take another step forward and ask the other supernaturals for help. Werewolves and humans can't win this war alone when there are vampires that can manipulate the weather, even with Ruby on our side. Her job is to kill the Queen, but there are still tons of vampires to get through to *get* to the Queen. We need more power on our side."

"I can do it."

We looked around and found Ruby standing behind us.

I hadn't even smelled her. "Your scent... I didn't smell you." I looked her up and down.

Stepping forward, her face looked pale, and her eyes were a little swollen. Her expression showed no emotions of sadness or anger; her eyes looked appeared dull and devoid of emotion.

I hated it.

"I masked it." She sighed. "It's as if each time I'm forced to use a large amount of my powers, something else gets unlocked. I, um, I can do it. I can try to contact the other werewolves and ask for help."

"There is one problem," Presley said. "We won't be able to spread the information fast enough. Cell phone towers are down or barely working."

"That won't be needed," Ruby replied. She opened the box in her hand and then closed it.

"Is that something that can help?" Xavier asked.

She shrugged. "Natalie told me to trust my powers and a door will be opened for me. I've been thinking about it, and maybe she meant a literal door. I, um..." She swallowed hard as she looked away. "I think she knew she was going to die." She glanced at Xavier. "The way she knew we were going to be attacked that night."

"Then the Goddess allowed her to die," Xavier replied, his eyes changing to black.

Ruby only sighed. "Yes, she did, but now we have to make sure

Natalie didn't die in vain. Wherever this door is, when I find it, maybe I'll get some straight answers about how to end this."

Xavier and I shared a look because we both already knew how this had ended the first time. What if Ruby learned about the werewolf that had died after becoming The Goddess's vessel? I would not survive watching Ruby die.

"Yeah." I stood up. "Let's just start with how to get the other packs here."

Presley took us all to a room much like the one the Bleeder was kept in. The room was smaller than the Bleeder's had been, and didn't have a cage. While I entered, the guys stayed in the observation room.

I felt so numb inside and so tired. I hadn't been able to leave Natalie's room after I had closed her door behind me; therefore, I hadn't eaten anything in hours. I couldn't even think about food—not when she was gone, especially not when I'd ultimately been the one to take her life.

I wanted it to be me who fulfilled her request to ensure she felt as little pain as possible as she passed. I wanted to be the one to grant her final wish of dying as herself, as an Enchanted, but it killed me inside that it had to happen. I believe now that Natalie had known it would happen, and that hurt even worse. I wanted to be angry that she had kept something like that from us—something that could have been prevented had we only known—but I didn't have the strength to be angry.

I just missed her—I missed her so much.

"Ruby, did you hear me?" Presley's voice echoed in the room.

I turned to the clear glass separating me from the guys and shook my head. "No, sorry. What did you say?"

"I said we'll be right here if you need any help," he repeated.

I nodded as I pulled the chair out from behind the desk, the only furniture in the room, and sat down. Placing the box on the table gently, I stared at it for a moment as I exhaled through my mouth before opening it.

Inside laid a silver dagger, its handle encrusted in dazzling crystals. The first time I opened the box, I immediately closed it. The energy it emitted called to me, but what was scary to me was how it somehow felt familiar.

I could see myself in the shiny, double-bladed steel. The longer I looked, the more the urge to pick it up grew. As I grabbed the dagger, the blade instantly started to glow. As a peaceful feeling of security washed over me, my hold on it grew tighter.

"We're right here, okay? Just call out if you need us."

Xavier's voice over the intercom broke the trance-like state I was in. I didn't bother looking. I just nodded and placed my other hand on the handle as I closed my eyes.

"I know," I finally answered after a moment.

I placed the tip of the blade onto the table and remained in that position, my hands wrapped around the pleasantly warm crystals. After a few minutes, I cracked an eye open.

"Nothing is happening." My other eye opened, and I looked down at the dagger, its blade still glowing. "Maybe this thing is just a knife that glows."

"Remember what I told you when you were trying to locate Presley?" Axel asked. "Don't force something to happen, Ruby. Let it happen."

I rolled my shoulders as I adjusted myself on the chair. "Okay," I replied as I exhaled through my mouth. "I can do this."

I closed my eyes and relaxed my grip on the knife. I focused on the way my power was reacting to the energy coming from the knife—on the feeling of peace within my heart, the weightlessness of it. My chest had been feeling tight yet hollow ever since Natalie, and what I felt now had my eyes stinging with tears.

I wasn't ready to feel peace, not yet; not until I avenged Natalie's death and all of this was over. I opened my eyes, ready to give up on the dagger, but the room I sat in slowly faded away around me. I looked to the guys and found them standing there, their watchful eyes on me. Then they faded away like the rest of my surroundings, and I found myself seated at a table in the meadow. I recognized it as the same meadow where I saw Lovette.

I got up quickly, turning in a circle as I looked for her. "Lovette?" I called. "Mom?"

"She's not here," a voice informed me.

I spun around to find a woman standing behind me.

The large white cloak she wore covered her body entirely. I bent down somewhat to see the face hidden by the large hood over her head, but all I could make out was darkness in the space a face should be.

My hold on the knife tightened. "Who are you?"

"I have many names," she answered, her voice echoing softly around me. "And no name."

My eyes widened. "You're—you're the Goddess, aren't you?"

"It's nice to finally meet you, Ruby," she responded.

I sighed. *So this is the Goddess, the woman who fucked up my life completely.*

"That wasn't my intention," she contended.

I froze. "Don't do that. Don't read my mind."

She tilted her head to the side, her face still in darkness. "As you wish," she replied.

"Is this yours?" I waved the knife.

She nodded. "It is. It was given to Natalie as a means for her to contact me."

My jaw clenched as she said Natalie's name. She didn't deserve to talk about Natalie after what she allowed to happen to her.

"She's dead," I responded through clenched teeth. "But you must know that."

"I know. She's at peace now," she replied calmly.

I shook my head. I know I should probably show more reverence or whatever, standing in the presence of a goddess, but honestly, I was too pissed to be submissive. "You could have saved her," I pointed out, my voice cracking as I got emotional.

The front of her cloak moved away as her hands moved to her shoulder to push the garment over her shoulder.

I couldn't stop staring at her arms. Her skin looked black with bright dazzling stars, and I felt like I was staring at the night sky. She was wearing white armor that covered her breasts, knee-high silver boots, and a white shirt and shorts with silver chains on them. Her legs were covered in stars like her arms, and her stomach was bare. I frowned at an odd marking like the moon where her navel should be that appeared to be actually moving on her skin.

She was beautiful. I couldn't help wondering what her face looked like. "Are there other gods like you?" I questioned her as I looked away from her stomach to her hooded face.

"Yes," she answered. "Many. I was appointed to handle the situation on your earth."

"My earth?" I repeated, and then I remembered the witch who had said there were other worlds. "Oh, right, okay then. Why did you save me?"

"Out of all my descendants, Lovette was my favorite. She... valued all life, and she understood many things on a higher level. She asked for my help, I presented her with the terms, and she agreed."

"Okay. Why am I mated to both Xavier and Axel? What does that have to do with all of this?"

She inhaled as a meteor shower flashed across her chest.

I couldn't stop my eyes from widening in astonishment, but her chuckle caused me to look away quickly.

"I apologize. I know my skin can be quite distracting." She moved her cloak so it covered her again.

I had to admit I felt disappointed by this; her skin was just so mesmerizing.

"You were destined to be mated to Xavier at birth," she explained. "It was after Axel lost his first love that I mated you to him. His family played a part in the previous war, and he has his role to play in this one. The Bluewater and Blackmoon packs needed to come together once more, and both humans and were-wolves needed to see that a union between both species is possible and allowed."

"So our bond is meant to bring the packs back together, and also, what... um, start a new era between humans and super-naturals?"

"Precisely. As you've all now realized, Amythia can't be killed without the species of Earth uniting," she replied.

I held my hand up for her to stop. "Wait, hold on just a minute, the vampire Queen's name is Amythia? Why does it take someone like me to kill her, anyway? Is she that powerful?" I questioned.

"She's a demigod."

I blinked and said nothing while I tried to process this new information. After a moment I nodded. "Yeah okay, that makes sense. So why can't one of you just kill her, then?"

"Gods can walk among you, but not for long periods. We can enter your minds, but to use a vessel, it has to be strong enough to contain our divinity. Otherwise it dies rather quickly. Amythia's lineage began from a goddess and the father of demons in a rather... gruesome and barbaric manner we don't need to discuss."

I made a face. "That's fine."

"Therefore, her kind is particularly hard to kill. The first of her kind was banned from both her father's realm and ours," she added.

I snorted. "So, we're stuck with her. Wonderful, that's great," I said sarcastically as I looked down at the knife in my hand. "How do I kill her, and how do I contact all the other werewolves?"

"You can mind link all of them. You have my power, Ruby, an abundance of it, so you're capable of many great things if you trust yourself. Nevertheless, when the time comes to take Amythia's life, you will accept me. You'll become my vessel, and then I will kill her."

I took a breath, the sound of this not sitting well with me. "So, I'll have to do the same thing that has probably killed a ton of other vessels? That's great; so will I survive, then? Since I'm different?"

"No," she replied bluntly. "You were born of a powerful Enchanted and a human and were given divinity at birth. You're strong, Ruby, the strongest supernatural I've seen in a long time, and I am proud of you for all you have done and survived so far. Yet, no matter how strong you are, you cannot survive having all my divinity. There are some positives, though. You will reunite with your mother and Natalie when this is all over."

My brows knitted tightly. I had nothing to say, so I walked away.

"You were saved for this purpose," she went on. "To be my earthly vessel."

"I wasn't given a choice," I muttered under my breath.

"When the time comes, you will have to pierce your heart with that dagger. This is the only way to end Amythia, Ruby."

I shook my head, no longer finding the warmth from the dagger comforting. "I won't do it," I said softly before turning around. "I won't do it. I can't give you my body. Don't you get it? My life has never been mine, never! Now, I'm expected to give my body and my life away too?"

"Your body will die, but your spirit will live on with the gods," she added.

I laughed humorlessly as I looked around the meadow. My face fell as the flowers around us started to die.

"Or would you prefer I take back my divinity and you die now?" she asked. "Mind you, if you choose death now, your soul will be erased. You will not pass on, you will simply cease to exist."

The sky above us grew dark.

I clenched my fists. If she was trying to scare me, it was working, but I refused to be used any longer. She gave me this power, and I would use it to kill Amythia. I would do it my way with the help of the werewolves and every other supernatural.

I can't give my body up, I just can't do it!

"Choose!" The Goddess yelled, her voice like a clap of thunder rumbling from the sky. "Make a choice, child, and I will find someone else to save your world!"

My lips parted as I watched the Goddess approach me. As much as I wanted to run for my life, where would I run to? Also, why was she bothering to give me a choice and not simply taking her power back?

"Take it, then!" I blurted out.

She stopped in front of me.

"Take your divinity back, and let me die here. I'll cease to exist, and you'll still have the vampires to deal with," I yelled as thunder echoed loudly above us. I nodded as I exhaled heavily. "You can't do it. You can't take back what you've given me. I have to give it back willingly. Right? You can't possess my body without me permitting you."

"You're either incredibly brave or incredibly stupid, girl," the Goddess grumbled, her voice now deep and dark.

Goosebumps dotted my flesh just from her voice. "I pick brave," I said softly.

She turned on her heel, her cloak billowing around her, and she vanished.

The ground beneath me started to crack. As I ran towards the table and chair still sitting in the meadow, the ground opened up, and I fell in.

Have you ever had a dream where you're suddenly falling and you startle awake? That's how it felt as I fell into darkness.

My back hit cold, hard ground. I opened my eyes to see I was back at the army base.

The door flew open and the guys rushed in.

"Ruby? Ruby? Are you okay?" Xavier yelled in my face, his eyes wide and frantic as he looked me over.

"Can you hear us, Red? What happened?" Axel questioned from my other side.

I slowly pushed myself up into a sitting position, both of them helping me. My mouth felt dry, and my tongue felt like sandpaper. I cleared my throat as I rubbed at my aching head. "I saw the Goddess."

They all grew silent.

I looked up to see Presley looking down at me with eager blue eyes. "To kill the Queen, I'll have to become her vessel—"

"No!" Xavier announced before I even finished speaking. "You can't do it."

"We'll find another way," Axel added, but he suddenly stood. He staggered backward as he placed his hand over his chest, his hazel eyes turning black.

I looked him up and down with concern. "Axel? What is it?"

"Something's wrong," He looked towards the door. "Something's wrong with my father, I can feel it. I have to go." He headed out.

I hurried to my feet.

"Wait," Presley called out to him. "I'll have a helicopter take you, it'll be faster."

"Okay," Axel replied as he walked back over to me, pulled me into his arms, and kissed me hard. He released me after a moment. "I have to check on my pack, but I'll be back. Just please don't do anything foolish until then, okay?"

I stared into his hazel orbs. "I make no promises." I breathed the words out.

He kissed my forehead then nodded to Xavier, who did the same in response, and left with Presley.

Xavier and I stood in silence for a moment.

I turned to him, my lips parting to say something.

He shook his head. "No," he said decisively.

I frowned. "You have no idea what I was going to say," I countered.

Xavier bent forward and kissed my cheek. "We can't go with him. He can handle his pack on his own. Right now, I want to know everything that happened with the Goddess, and don't leave anything out."

Even though it was midday, my skin tingled with goosebumps as a chill ran through me. I got to my knees slowly. My legs felt weak as I stared at Natalie's grave.

A quick ceremony was held yesterday. I surprisingly managed to make it through the service without having a mental breakdown. What I think allowed that to happen was my rage. The vampires had taken so much from everyone, both human and nonhuman. People had lost their family and friends to those monsters, and it had to come to an end.

I closed my eyes for a moment as the wind picked up around me, and I couldn't help wondering if it was Natalie's spirit.

"I miss you," I whispered as I listened to the wind in the oak tree above her grave. "I did what you told me. I opened a door, and I spoke to her—the Goddess. I can't do what she wants, Nat. I just can't do it." I opened my eyes. "I don't want to die," I finally admitted to even myself. "I want to see this all through and be alive to see the world that comes next. I want to be a part of this world, to make it better. She gave me the power to help, but we're the ones down here fighting, winning and losing ourselves and the ones we love, only for her to jump in at the end to claim Amythia's life? Hell no. I want to take Amythia down, and I want to be alive to celebrate when this is all over. Haven't I earned that after everything I've survived and sacrificed? If I only get control over one thing in life, it should be my own body!"

I sighed as some of my anger dissipated. I sat there for a moment as I reflected on the conversation I had with the Goddess. For now, I had to keep fighting the fight. To win, or even begin to have enough strength on our side to stand a chance, I had to mind link with the other wolves.

"I wish you were here right now. I really could've used your help with this." I sat down on the ground and bent my legs lotus-style.

My shoulders rose as I inhaled deeply and then dropped as I exhaled. Closing my eyes, I tried to remember how I felt the first time Natalie had mind linked with me.

I stepped into that pool of power within me, sinking slowly at the deep end until I felt full. My body felt electrified, and I focused on that feeling as I thought of Xavier as well. I thought of my intentions, what I needed my power to do. I inhaled sharply as I was thrust into his mind. Images began to flash in my mind, even some of myself but seen through his eyes, and I grimaced as I felt a strain on my mind.

I clenched and unclenched my fists as I tried to gain control of myself, to not push myself too far into his mind. I didn't want to spy on his thoughts and feelings. I just wanted to communicate with him.

I soon noticed that his thoughts were all cocooned in some kind of pale blue light.

"His aura," I whispered to myself as I opened my eyes. Similar blue lights like Xavier's started appearing within my mind, and with it, I could feel each wolf.

I smiled widely as I located more and more wolves. My hands

still clenched and unclenched to help keep me balanced. I tried not to get carried away by the exhilarating feeling.

"Natalie, I did..." I started to say, but when my eyes landed on her grave, my face fell. Right, she wasn't really here with me.

The feeling of elation I experienced vanished as I tried to not lose focus. I exhaled as I released my clenched fists and continued mind linking with each werewolf, their bright lights filling my mind. It was as if I stood in a white room, surrounded by floating blue lights, each representing a person.

"Hello," I greeted them. "My name is Ruby, and maybe some of you have heard of me. For those who haven't, let me introduce myself. I'm Ruby Saunders, the daughter of the late and beloved Grand Elder, Lovette."

Soft whispers came from each light.

I continued speaking, "I will make this short because time is of the essence. I'm half-human, half-Enchanted, and my mother hid me from the world so that one day, I could help to save it. Yes, I'm a half-breed, but one blessed by the Goddess herself, blessed with her divinity to help with the destruction of the vampire threat."

The whispers grew louder.

I felt rushed but I kept speaking, "I know this is confusing and you're all scared, but the vampires are growing stronger while we cower and hide. Soon, we won't stand a chance against them. Why should we wait until that happens before we band together and take back our world? The humans were wrong for hunting us. They have now seen the error of their ways. I will never overlook or forget the bloodshed they lent a hand in. I can feel your pain, all of you, and I'm sorry, I'm so very sorry about what you've all had to endure. Long ago, werewolves and humans came together to battle these creatures, and they won. We can do that again, but only if we come together. Humans and werewolves can unite, and I'm proof of that. Lovette proved that the moment she fell in love with a human, the moment she gave birth to me." I exhaled heavily. "I wasn't looked down on by the Goddess for not being a pure-blood. Instead, she blessed me. Despite the power I possess from the divinity she gave me, I can't do this alone. None of us can do this alone. I'm tired of watching the ones I love die! Aren't you? If we do nothing, more lives will be lost, and our pain will only grow worse! We have to stand together, and not just survive this, but end it. You must recognize that this *is* an invasion of vampires bent on the dominion over and obliteration of all other species, and if we do nothing, we will all die!" I turned in a circle, blue auras all around me to the towering ceiling in the room glowing brighter than before. "Werewolves have always been protectors because of their strength and power," I said more softly. "I'm asking you all to be those guardians again. You all now know my location and that I'm the mate to both Xavier of the Blackmoon Pack and Axel of the Bluewater Pack. Join us, and let us put an end to this. Let's remind these bloodsuckers of our true power, and that they are nothing compared to us!"

Cheers were coming from each light, the room coming alive with their howls and roars.

"Their power is nothing compared to ours! This is our world, and we're ready to take it back!" I took a sharp intake of breath as my eyes opened, and I was once more sitting at Natalie's grave. My breathing was labored as I wiped away a tear from my cheek. I hadn't even realized I was crying, but I had been able to feel the emotions of all those werewolves. Their pain and sorrow flowed through me as if their emotions were my own.

I hugged myself as I leaned forward, fresh tears streaming down my cheeks. Was this what the Goddess had to endure, so many emotions from so many wolves?

A blue light flashed within my mind, and I instantly knew it was Xavier. I looked behind me to find him standing there with the pack, their eyes all on me. I got up quickly while wiping at my tears, but there was no point in trying to hide it.

"We all heard you," a woman informed me, her eyes red with unshed tears.

"We're proud to have you as a part of our pack, Ruby," a man added as he stepped forward.

"Luna," another man said, followed by another, and soon, they were all calling me their Luna as I was pulled into one hug after another.

I didn't know what to do or say.

Xavier stood off to the side, a smile on his lips.

I awkwardly hugged everyone. Never had I felt so much love aimed at me. I guessed this was what it must feel like to have a family.

They all surrounded me, some thanking me for healing them from when the vampires had attacked.

After a while, it was just Xavier and me.

We stood in silence as we both stared at Natalie's grave.

"Do you think she's watching us?" He broke the quiet.

I smiled. "I know she is, and I know she's at peace. The Goddess said Natalie and my mom are both with her."

He hummed his response as he took my hand.

We walked back to the base slowly.

I pressed myself to his side.

Throwing his hand over my shoulder, he pulled me closer and kissed the top of my head. "How are you feeling after doing that? You really pulled it off."

I grinned at the pride in his voice. "I feel okay, good actually. I could feel them; I could feel all of you." I stopped walking.

So did he.

I turned to look up at him. "They were all so petrified."

"You just changed that," he told me as he moved my hair behind my ear. "You reminded them that they aren't weaklings and gave them hope. I'm proud of you."

I hugged him, and he crushed me to his hard chest as he kissed the top of my head. I melted in his arms as I listened to his steady heartbeat. "What if I have to do what—"

"No," he shot back before I had even finished speaking.

I looked up at him, resting my chin on his chest.

"No," he repeated.

"But what if I have to do what she wants? What if I can't kill the Queen on my own, and I have to become the Goddess's vessel?" As much as the thought of giving up my body made me feel nauseous, I needed to consider the chance that I might have to do it.

I was just welcomed by the Blackmoon pack as their Luna. They were all my responsibility now, and if other packs turned up, they would also be here because of me. They would have all come out of hiding because I asked them to, so what would happen if I couldn't kill the Queen? We'd lose this war, and the lives lost would be my fault.

I couldn't live with that.

"I just asked thousands of werewolves to put their faith in me, to fight with me. There is no room for failure, Xavier. We failed in our raid of that coven, thinking the Queen was there, and we lost so many because of it, including Natalie. I can't let them down. If I have to die to keep my word, I will."

He held my shoulders firmly, his head shaking wildly. "Never say that, Ruby, never! You aren't going to die, and you won't have to sacrifice yourself. Do you understand me? I won't let that happen, ever. Demigod or not, we can and will kill her together. Okay?"

I couldn't look away from the emotions within his eyes, his fear of losing me so raw I could almost feel it within me.

"Okay? Promise me you won't use that dagger," he pleaded.

"Okay," I agreed as I looked down.

Desperate, he grabbed my chin.

"Okay, I promise, I won't use it."

"I cannot lose you, Ruby. I can't—not you, too," he rambled out a little. "I won't." He kissed me, long, hard, and passionately, his love and emotions transferring to me in waves.

I wasn't sure what came over me, but I pulled away and the

words left my lips before I could stop them. "I love you." My eyes widened as I heard what I had said, and I tried to step out of his arms.

Xavier tightened his hold on me, his eyes turning black. He kissed me again, his elongated fangs grazing my lips somewhat.

I didn't care. I wanted to feel him, taste him, and I had meant what I had just said. Natalie had told me to be honest about my feelings, tell the people I love that I loved them. I couldn't stand that she had died thinking I was angry at her.

From the start, Xavier had been looking out for me; he'd been saving my life from the moment we met. The Goddess had said I was mated to him at birth, so he'd always been the one for me. I knew I loved him, body and soul.

"I love you, too," he whispered against my lips as he pulled away. "My Luna."

I grinned. "I like the sound of that."

Xavier

Two wolves walked by me and nodded their greeting, but their brows were furrowed in curiosity. No doubt, they were wondering why I was grinning like a damn idiot.

From the moment those three words had left Ruby's lips yesterday, I hadn't been able to stop smiling. However, that wasn't the only thing I had to be happy about. Everyone was in high spirits, the air thick with the smell of hope. A few hours after Ruby had mind linked with all the wolves, some of them had found us. By dusk more arrived, and now, at midday the following day, another pack of forty-five wolves arrived.

Presley had also confirmed that military reinforcements were being sent and would arrive within a day. Being unable to travel through the night was a bother, but it was better to be late than dead.

The way I saw it, the people joining us now weren't late. On the contrary, they were right on time. Ruby had been trying her best to be sociable with everyone, but she didn't exactly enjoy being treated as if she were royalty. Unfortunately, extra attention was to be expected when you were the daughter of Grand Elder Lovette and blessed by our goddess. I couldn't be prouder to be her mate, but she was clearly uncomfortable being in the spotlight.

Despite the mask of sociability she wore, I could tell that she was anxious about Axel. He hadn't returned, and we had no way of contacting him. She tried mind linking with him last night, but after doing it on such a large scale, she wasn't able to connect with him.

"Xavier, more werewolves have arrived. They traveled through the night to get here," a soldier said as he approached me, a pile of towels in hand.

"What's with the towels? Are they hurt? They shouldn't have traveled through the night," I wondered.

He shook his head. "No, they are fine. Just raining outside," he answered with a smile. "There are kids in the group, so they need these."

"Oh, okay." I nodded and he carried on. "Hey," I called after him. "Thanks for the help."

"Don't mention it!" he replied before leaving.

The tension between my pack and the humans when we first arrived was now all but gone. For the wolves that had arrived recently, it would take some time for them to be as comfortable, but I trusted that we'd get there.

I kept walking slowly as I headed to Ruby's room, my hands buried in my pockets. No way in hell would I allow her to use the dagger to accept the Goddess. She promised to not do it, but I needed to keep an eye on her.

I stopped walking, my brows pulling together, as I came upon an odd scent. It was there one second and then gone another. I started walking fast, as a sense of dread filled my chest. Once I got to Ruby's room, I opened the door without knocking.

My heart skipped a beat at the sight of her floating above her bed, her long red hair dancing around her body. A vampire's scent immediately filled my nostrils as I turned to the window, and sure enough, the General we saw before, the one who had walked away from us, was suspended in the air outside her window.

I rushed forward as he moved his hand, calling Ruby forward, and she started drifting to the window. I dove at her to knock her out of the air, but her body floated higher and I missed. I collided into the wall, cracks appearing from the impact.

I hurried to my feet as her body slipped through the window. Without thinking, without hesitating, I dove through the window, my hand outstretched to her. Alas, my claws merely scratched her ankle as I fell.

I started shifting midair, howling to issue a warning to the others. By the time I landed on the ground, I had completely shifted. Though I registered the pain of the impact, I rose quickly even as I felt some cracked bones begin to heal. I started running through the forest, my head up as I tried to follow them. I howled to her, praying she would hear me and wake up from whatever sleep the vampire had put her in.

After two minutes of following them, they vanished from my sight. I swiped my claws at a tree trunk in rage, shredding it as three other transformed wolves joined me. I started shifting back, and the pain of my bones re-breaking was nothing compared to the pain in my chest.

I was reminded of the agony I had to endure when Axel had taken her, a pain I never wanted to feel again. Turning to face my father's wolf, I closed my eyes for a moment as my rage started to get out of control, my wolf in a panic. "We have to find her," I growled as I opened my eyes.

My father released a growl before turning to run back to the base. The others followed him.

I peered up at the sky, my clenched fists shaking at my sides before I took off in a run.

———

Xavier

My fist came down hard on the table, breaking it in half. The room went silent, and I turned away. Combing my hand through my hair, I tried to get my wolf under control. When I turned back around to face the others, my eyes were back to their normal steel gray.

"We can find her," Presley stated confidently.

I pinned him with a glare. I wasn't angry at him (and he knew it), but right now, I wanted to rip the world and everyone in it apart until I found her.

"How?" Randoll, our pack's Beta, asked as he combed his curly red hair out of his face. His scarlet locks just flopped right back down, no matter what he did to try to control them.

"I had her ingest a tracker when she arrived," Presley replied.

"You did *what*?" I saw red and rushed forward, but my father stepped in front of Presley. A deep resounding growl emitted from him as his dominance filled the room.

Randoll and the three other wolves within the room lowered their heads submissively.

I fought against it for a moment before doing the same. The difference between the other wolves and me was that I did it out of respect, as I could easily defy him now. My strength had grown immensely over these last few months. "Why?" I asked through clenched teeth.

"For a scenario exactly like this one. I knew we weren't the only people who were interested in her, and her safety was mission-critical. She's also not the only person with a tracking device, Xavier. I wouldn't do that to her. I have one, as do many of our higher-ranking officers."

"Does she know?" I asked as I held my head up.

My dad stepped to the side, revealing Presley once more.

"No, I thought it would be best to not say anything in case she got the wrong idea and refused, but our eyes have to be on an asset like Ruby at all times," he responded. The facial tic I experienced at hearing him call her 'an asset' had him clearing his throat. "She's special to us all. I understand to you and Axel more so, but her safety means everything to me as well. We can stand here and argue about this, or you can let me help with finding her."

"Your men that went with Axel, have they reported anything back yet?"

He shook his head. "No, we lost contact with them." He then stepped over a leg of the broken table on the ground.

We all walked to the command room quickly, and I tried to contain my anxiety as I allowed Presley and his people to do their work. However, I couldn't stop myself from stepping forward the moment a red dot appeared on one of the screens with a map and began beeping. "Is that her?" I narrowed my eyes at the screen.

"Yes," Presley replied. "It looks like they are going north."

"We have to go get her, now." The sooner we got moving to go get her, the sooner I could get her back where I could protect her.

How could I have let this happen?

My dad placed his hand on my shoulder. "We can't go after her half-cocked, Xavier, and you know that. No doubt she's being taken to Amythia, and if that's the case, we need to be prepared. We need to gather everyone before we can go there. We have no idea what we'll be walking into."

I could understand the reasoning behind his words and that they rang with truth, but I needed to get her back. The more time we wasted, the more her chances of being killed by the Queen increased. "I hear you, I do, but we can't wait any longer. The

Queen is going to kill her, Dad. We promised... I promised Ruby that I'd be there with her—I'd fight this war with her; all of us. If she's forced to fight the Queen alone, the Queen will kill her, or the Goddess will."

"I'm not giving my men the order to leave, Xavier," Presley replied. "I'm sorry, but rushing in will get her and us killed."

I stared at him, my face no doubt turning red. My wolf was clawing at my insides, panicked that even right now she might be suffering.

If Axel were here, he would share my feelings that we needed to act now. I shook my head. "It's like you all don't understand that she's going to die."

"Xavier, we understand that. I know how you feel, son, I do, but listen to—"

"The only way Ruby can kill the Queen is by killing herself!" I yelled.

The command room grew silent.

My dad frowned. "What are you talking about?"

Axel and I never told anyone about what Malcolm had found in the book, that Ruby would have to become the Goddess's vessel. Ruby didn't know I already knew that detail before she spoke to the Goddess.

There was no more room for secrets, however.

"When Ruby becomes the Goddess's vessel, it'll kill her. She won't survive it," I answered. "If she's forced to fight the Queen alone, she'll have no choice but to do it, and we'll lose her." I ran my hand down my face. "Either the Goddess kills her or Amythia does, but the only chance we have of her surviving this is if we're there with her, if we fight with her!"

"But she's been living with the Goddess's divinity. She's capable of killing vampires. We've all seen it," Presley argued.

I shook my head. "Amythia isn't just a vampire. She's a demigod, and the power Ruby has now will be nothing compared to how powerful she'll be once the Goddess enters her body.

That's the kind of power that will be necessary to defeat Amythia without our help." I nodded to Randoll as I walked to the door.

He and the other wolves in the room followed me.

I wasn't going to lose her, not to the Goddess or this damn war. "The price for the Goddess' power is Ruby's life, and she shouldn't have to pay that price to save us all. I'm leaving, Presley. You and your men can stay, but Ruby is one of us. She's our Luna. More than that, she's my mate. I'm going to go get her, and there's not a thing anyone can do to stop me."

CHAPTER FOURTEEN
RUBY

I stretched and rolled to my side before I realized my bed felt different. My eyes cracked open, and I instantly sat up, becoming a little dizzy from the sudden movement.

I couldn't look away from the woman and man staring at me, my eyes looking from one to the other.

The man wore a vampire General's uniform and I had a strong feeling he was the one who'd been trying to see into my mind. His hair was a dusty blonde skimmed his ears and his red eyes narrowed the more I stared at him. He looked to be over six feet.

My eyes drifted to the woman. Surprisingly, she was even taller than he was. I was stunned by her beauty.

Her black hair was bone straight and fell below her bottom. Her skin looked milky white, almost as white as the dress she wore, but it was her red eyes that did it for me. They were completely red —pupils, irises, and sclera. A chill went down my spine as she smiled at me and flashed her pointy fangs.

"It's so lovely to finally meet you, Ruby," she greeted me, her voice so sweet and soft.

Despite her pleasant voice and appearance, instinctively I knew that there was nothing sweet or soft about this woman.

What I saw before me was the perfect predator—stunning, with an allure that would draw anyone to her. That is, until they found themselves hopelessly tangled in her web of lies and deceit.

"I'm Queen Amythia." She then waved her hand towards the General at her side. "This is General Carden, my firstborn son. I think you've already met, haven't you?" she asked him, and he nodded. "Good. Now that we've all been introduced, let's get down to business, as you humans say."

"I didn't know vampires could have kids," I retorted, deciding to ignore what she had said about getting down to business. It was taking all my strength to keep my heartbeat steady. I didn't want her to have the satisfaction of knowing I was afraid of her.

Her red-painted lips stretched with a wide smile. "There is a lot that's not known about vampires."

"Aren't you all dead? So how can you give birth?" I questioned.

She laughed. The sound was soft and beautiful, sensual even, as she walked to a chair at the other end of the room.

My eyes slid to Carden for a moment and caught his eyes roaming my body. I pinned him with a glare, and the corner of his mouth twitched with a smirk.

"I didn't give birth to him the way humans do." She sat down and crossed her legs at the ankle. "I turned him personally. He's one of three sons that I've turned over the years." Her face suddenly fell. "One of which you killed."

"He tried to kill me," I told her.

She glanced at Carden before looking down at her feet poking out from beneath her dress. "I see. He was given orders not to," she whispered more to herself.

Is this really the vampire Queen? I was expecting a ghastly creature, not this—not someone that appeared to be so angelic. It was her eyes that gave away her true demonic nature.

"I know what you're thinking, Ruby. My eyes bother even

some of my own." She turned to face me again. "We're not monsters or savages, you know."

I snorted.

She arched a perfect brow at me. "How things have happened is unfortunate, but we're only trying to survive. We just want a home like you and every other creature on this earth."

"You're doing that by killing every other creature. I can think of a few other ways you could have done this," I said bluntly as I shrugged.

She shook her head. "Humans never would have accepted us, and we have no intention of living like the supernaturals of this time." She took a deep breath.

I found myself wondering if she was actually breathing. I looked at Carden, and sure enough, his chest wasn't moving.

"We tried that once before, and it didn't end well, as I'm sure you now know." She leaned forward, her eyes narrowing at me. "Your scent is quite distracting."

"Let me go, and it won't be a bother to you anymore," I told her.

She chuckled. "I don't mind it that much." She glanced at Carden. "Leave us," she commanded.

He turned away after taking another long look at me.

She waited until he closed the door behind him before turning to face me. "Now, we girls can chat."

I said nothing as I stared back at her.

How am I going to get out of this one?

It had taken so much out of me to kill that other General, I ended up losing control. Here I would have to go through Carden and other skilled vampires who might be outside—not to mention Amythia herself. I knew I didn't have the power to handle all of them on my own—not without the Goddess. And I wasn't exactly eager to bring her into this if I could help it.

Carden's scent woke me from my sleep back at the base, but the moment I opened my eyes and saw him, he plunged into my mind, forcing me back to sleep. I hadn't stood a chance. How would Xavier and the others ever find me? This wasn't how I saw this going. This wasn't how this was supposed to happen. *I'm not prepared!*

"Ruby?" Amythia called. "Are you feeling okay? You look a little pale."

"Enough of this nice girl act, Amythia. Stop acting like you actually care, *Your Majesty*. What is it that you want from me?"

She reclined in her chair and ran her hand down her dress. Her nails were at least six inches long and all pointy.

I didn't want to think about all the lives those things must have taken over the years.

"Vampires and your kind didn't always hate each other, you know. There was a time when supernatural creatures and humans co-existed peacefully." She looked nostalgic as she spoke. "Those were better times."

"I know, but I also saw the war that happened," I replied.

She frowned. "You had a vision of the past?" she asked.

I nodded.

"Well, there are rules among the supernatural community, Ruby, rules that can't be broken. They were broken back then, and the world broke too. But enough about all that. What I would like right now is to see your power."

"I'd rather not do that, if you don't mind," I replied politely but firmly. I didn't like the way she was looking me up and down. I felt like an animal at a circus being told to do a trick.

Her face fell, a crease appearing between her brows as she stood up.

I quickly did the same.

"Do as I ask," she said with an edge in her voice.

I clenched my teeth as I stood my ground. I called on my power, allowing it to rest at the tips of my fingers.

I opened my mouth to speak when she suddenly blurred from

my vision. When she reappeared much closer, I jumped back in fear, and I held my hands up to defend myself.

Her mouth dislocated like that of a snake getting ready to eat a large animal, and my stomach clenched.

Amythia was no longer the beautiful queen. Now the real creature stood in front of me. Her eyes grew larger and more cat-like as black veins appeared from her neck up to her mouth. Her slick, bone-straight hair blew behind her like a black curtain, which only made her pale skin appear even whiter. She calmed down as quickly as she had become angry, and her mouth slowly went back to its normal state, the bones in her jaw snapping back into place.

"Beautiful eyes," she murmured.

I looked her up and down, my hands still up defensively. The room started to grow hot as I released my power.

She wagged a long finger at me. "There is no need for that. I merely wanted to see if you truly have the Goddess's divinity." She reached a hand out as if to touch my face and then stopped. "So much power you wield; I haven't felt divinity in a millennium. You have no idea how special you are, child." Her hand fell to her side, and the black veins on her face vanished as well. "You don't understand how much stronger you'll be if you join us."

I frowned as my hands dropped somewhat. "That's what you want... for me to become a vampire?"

She shook her head. "No, you'd be more than just a vampire. One thing that isn't widely known about vampirism is that it doesn't affect those with divinity the same way as it does other supernatural creatures. Ruby, you would retain your current abilities while gaining those that come with vampirism. You'll be the strongest creature on the earth... next to me, of course. You'd be able to topple the gods themselves."

"I don't want to become the most powerful creature on this earth!" I yelled, my obsidian eyes reflecting in her scarlet ones. "What I want is for this bloodshed to be over!"

"It never will be unless you become one of us! My Seers didn't see you before our invasion, your Goddess made sure of that, but you've changed things for the better. Join us, and all of this comes to an end. The lives of everyone you care about are in your hands, Ruby. You only have one option: join me, or die. If you choose death, I get to watch as this hellhole finally burns."

"I'd rather die than become like you!" I ran at her, the temperature inside the room instantly becoming warmer.

I didn't make it anywhere close to her before she hunched forward and a wing appeared from her back. The skin-like wing, like that of a bat, slapped me, and my entire body went flying. The sound of my shoulder blade breaking echoed in my ear as I slammed into the wall over the bed.

The side of my face hit the concrete wall so hard it cracked as I fell onto the bed, out cold.

———

Ruby

I was all too familiar with the hard ground of a dungeon and the chill that comes with it. I didn't even have to open my eyes to know. It brought back memories from a confusing time at the beginning of my whole journey, but it also made me wonder if Axel was okay.

How crazy is that?

I opened my eyes and sat up slowly, happy to see that there were no chains on me. With no windows in sight and only torches outside my cell to provide light, I realized I was alone.

I sighed.

Well, that didn't go well.

As I got up, I checked my shoulder. Thankfully, it had already healed. I touched the side of my head to feel a part of my hair that felt matted. I'm sure being thrown across the room by that bitch had caused a pretty nasty wound, which fortunately appeared to have mended while I was out. I felt particularly grateful for my supernatural healing abilities right now. That head injury would've been tough to survive otherwise.

What made Amythia think I would ever become a vampire? Did she really think I'd believe her bullshit about everything coming to an end if I agreed? Who knows what would really happen to me if I turned.

"Help!" I yelled as I held onto the rusty old iron bars. "Help! Can anyone hear me?"

I knew I was doing the dumb thing everyone did in the movies, but what else was I supposed to do? I knew I had to be miles away from any human or supernatural capable of helping me.

My hands fell away from the bars as I frowned. *Why am I sitting in this cage? I'm Ruby Saunders, daughter of Lovette and vessel to a freaking goddess! I need to remember who and what I am. Why am I yelling for help?* I acted without thinking earlier and without knowing my opponent. I just couldn't believe after everything this woman had caused, all the lives lost because of her and her vampires, she'd think I'd want to join her.

I closed my eyes and listened to my breathing for a moment. I then focused on the soft crackling fire of the torches and began calling the heat from them into my palm. I reached out to touch the iron, intending to melt it and hopefully walk right through. I opened my eyes and immediately froze as red eyes stared right back at me.

A man stood outside the bars, his head tilted to the side as he watched me.

The torches had dimmed somewhat, but I could still make out his burning red eyes and blonde hair. I bared my teeth at him and reached out to grab the bars when he spoke.

"I wouldn't do that if I were you. You'd alert all of them that you're trying to escape."

"I am trying to escape, and you can go tell your Queen that. Just try to stop me, and I swear I'll fucking turn you to ash!"

He tilted his head to the other side like a curious puppy.

I frowned.

"My Queen is in purgatory," he replied.

My frown deepened. I realized he didn't smell like a vampire. "Who are you?" I kept my powers at the ready but folded my hands into fists. Unfortunately, I didn't seem to possess the same heightened senses as the rest of the werewolves. So far, I'd only been able to smell vampires and not the distinct scents of other supernaturals. Being an Enchanted, that ability could pop up sooner or later. "You're not a vampire."

"Who I am doesn't matter. I was sent by your father," he responded cryptically.

I stepped back as his body burst into a cloud of smoke. I watched as he slipped through the bars without touching them and then materialized inside the cell with me. "My presence will only go undetected for a few minutes, so we need to get moving." He held his hand out to me. "Take my hand, and don't burn me."

I hesitated as I looked from his hand to his eyes.

He made a face. "Now, Ruby. We need to go *now*." He reached out and grabbed my wrist, and before I could speak, we both turned into smoke. We floated through the bars and materialized on the other side.

"We need to hurry." He started walking quickly ahead of me. "Whenever I say take my hand, do it."

"Okay," I drawled as I walked closely behind him.

Thank you, Malcolm! How did he find me so quickly?

"My hand," the demon commanded.

I quickly grabbed his hand when I realized we were at the door to exit the dungeon. We once more turned to smoke and passed through as I eyed the two dead vampire guards by the door. "How did you find me? How did Malcolm find me?" I inquired as we ran through a dark hall. No doubt we'd be heard soon, so the sooner we got out of this place, the better.

"Do you two need directions?" Carden appeared in front of us.

We skidded to a halt.

He looked the demon up and down before looking away dismissively. His eyes then fell on me. "Did you really think you could get away that easily?" He looked me up and down as well, but the lust within his eyes was unmistakable as he inhaled deeply. "The Queen promised me your hand once you've become one of us, and you *will* become one of us. Then I will enjoy making you mine *in every way*."

I clenched my jaws tightly and tried not to think about how nauseous his comment made me.

"I might be wrong, but I think she's already taken, two times over. You're a little too late!" The demon interjected as he laughed.

Carden hissed at him as he rushed forward.

Instead of attacking him, The demon turned around and grabbed my arm. As he threw me towards the wall, I turned into smoke, and Carden slammed into him. My scream lodged itself in my throat as I came out on the other side of the wall. The freezing-cold air felt like a thousand needles poking every part of my body.

My power flared inside me as I flipped over, causing heat to flow throughout my body so I could no longer feel the cold. I realized I was falling down along a snow-covered mountain. The sounds of a battle met my ears, and I could make out transformed werewolves and vampires fighting below. The bright flash of guns being fired lit up the ground, and I knew they had to be from Presley's men.

It was daytime, but the sky was so heavily clouded, barely any sunlight was breaking through.

My quick descent slowed as I used my powers to levitate. Directly below me, three Bleeders looked up, their fangs dripping with blood. The heat I had absorbed from those torches blasted from my hands as I landed on the ground, killing them.

A wolf's thundering howl echoed, and more wolves began to

howl in response. I could feel it within me, their calls to the others of my arrival. I watched as a large brown wolf came running towards me. He rose on his hind legs and trampled a Bleeder on his way to me.

He was suddenly thrown to the side as a Skin attacked him, and I winced as the Skin bit him on the shoulder. I'd never felt Xavier's pain before, or Axel's, for that matter. A gunshot echoed so close to my body, I ducked instinctually. I felt so disoriented with everything happening around me.

Presley came running towards me, a gun in each hand. "Stay alert, Ruby. Oh, and welcome back!" He turned his back to me and raised his guns, killing two Bleeders, before looking at me over his shoulder. "I gave you a tracker! That's how we found you!" He pointed to our right.

I stared open-mouthed at an opening in the mountain, where countless Bleeders and Skins were pouring out onto the field. I looked around us at the humans and werewolves being slaughtered, and a feeling of dread rested on my chest, the scent of blood and death filling my nostrils. "We're losing!" I yelled.

I turned to our left as a Bleeder came charging at us.

Presley fired three shots into its chest.

I used my powers to send the creature flying towards the sharp rocks on the mountainside.

Xavier ran up to us, completely and unabashedly naked, with blood and cuts covering his entire body.

"Are you okay? Where is Axel?" I asked.

"I'm fine," he answered, his chest rising and falling rapidly. His eyes darted around quickly as he remained on guard. "He's not here. We lost contact with him after he left." He cupped my cheek. "If he returns to the base, he'll know to come here."

I didn't care that he'd smeared blood on me. "I felt your pain," I told him as I pointed to the bite on his shoulder. Gunshots echoed in our ears as another soldier and wolf joined us, creating somewhat of a circle around us. "If he was hurt, I think I'd know. The Queen is inside the mountain, Xavier. I saw her."

"Good. This is where this ends." His eyes were on something behind me before he quickly moved me to the side.

A chill went through my body that had nothing to do with the snow around us as I stared at the opening in the mountain. More Bleeders were pouring out as if there were no end to them, their stench overpowering even the smell of blood and bodies littering the ground.

"Well, now we know where they've been all this time," Presley said under his breath. His arms lowered. "We have to fall back."

I glimpsed defeat in his gaze. I narrowed my eyes at the gaping hole in the mountain and started walking forward. I exhaled, releasing the fear holding me captive. As I inhaled, I called on the earth's energy and held my hands out on either side of me. A prickling sensation coursed through my body, and I closed my eyes briefly as it filled me.

I opened my eyes the moment a Bleeder came rushing my way, but Xavier, once more in wolf form, tackled it before it reached me. I kept my eyes on the mountain, my focus unwavering as the hell-spawned creatures got closer. The sound of their feet trampling on the ground and their loud hisses filling the air was enough to drive fear into any warrior. I didn't focus on that, however, or the fact that I stood against an army.

I got down onto one knee and dug my fingers into the earth, sending all the energy I had collected back into it, but aimed at the vampires. Spikes made of earth shot upwards, piercing through the Bleeders' bodies and limbs. I watched as the spikes rolled forward like an ocean wave, impaling and dismembering the Bleeders and Skins, their cries of pain causing the humans and wolves behind me to erupt into cheers.

The feeling of accomplishment, of victory, was short-lived because only a moment passed before more came rushing out of the mountain. "Are you fucking kidding me?" I yelled as I stood up. I spun around to look at Presley.

He paled and raised his guns. "Fall back! Fall back, now!" He started yelling, but then jumped back as black smoke appeared beside him.

Malcolm's face materialized within it. "Am I too late?" Malcolm grinned.

Now, all around us, more demons started to appear. Some looked like normal humans, while others had tails, horns, and wings that dragged behind them. The demons with wings took to the sky and unleashed their power on the vampires. Black crystal-like daggers rained down on the Bleeders and Skins like rain.

Howls rolled up to the sky from within the forest behind us. I closed my eyes and sighed as a feeling of relief washed over me. I turned around to see Axel's wolf, his fur a midnight black against the snow.

Behind him were more wolves than I could count. Among them were other women and men, their cries of anger as loud as the wolves' howling. They kept pouring from the forest, the entire length of the tree line.

This is it. Presley and Xavier appeared at my side. However, my face fell as Axel ran past us along with everyone else. He dove into the Bleeders like a wrecking ball. I swallowed hard, my brows knitted as I felt his rage, his pain.

I placed my hand over my chest as I looked at Xavier's wolf, and he looked at me before rushing forward into the fray.

"Hello, Ruby," a woman said as she appeared by my side. "My name is Ms. Clayton, but you can call me Cassandra."

"Hi. Nice to meet you."

She smiled, her hair a midnight black with a lone streak of white hair that she moved behind her ear. "Axel dated my daughter long ago. Maybe now isn't the time for that story, but I wanted you to know I'm an ally."

My brows touched my hairline as I realized who this woman was.

Axel told me long ago he dated a witch who was killed by a demon possessing a jealous human. This was her mother. "Hi." I shook the hand she held out to me. "Thank you for coming."

She smiled, her eyes a bright violet. She placed her hand on my shoulder. "Axel has told me a lot about you. He is so proud of you, and I am pleased to see how being with you has made him whole again."

"Axel, he seems..." My voice faded away.

She frowned, a pained expression appearing on her face. "We were attacked... half of his pack... his father... they didn't make it." She squeezed my shoulder and walked away as a sword materialized in her hand. She moved expertly among the Bleeders.

I ran forward, my fists clenched. This was our time. The time to teach these creatures what it meant to feel fear.

***

Ruby

I screamed as a Bleeder turned to ash beneath my hands. I wasn't sure how much time had passed, and I didn't care. All of them—I wanted to kill all of them. The more blood that soaked the snow beneath my feet, the angrier I got, and the more powerful I became.

A foot connected with my side, sending me toppling over. I got back onto my feet quickly, barely feeling the impact. A pulse emitted from my body, sending the Skins, who were rushing towards me, backwards.

I held my hand out and envisioned holding them all by their throats as I pulled them forward once more. Spikes appeared from the earth to impale their bodies. I turned away, moving onto the next Bleeder or Skin I knew had taken the life of an innocent human or supernatural. They had all killed mercilessly, and they would all suffer for it.

Panting, I turned in a circle, taking note of the supernaturals fighting along with us that I'd never seen before. A large black snake shot upward from within the earth, killing two Skins, and I watched as it then turned into a woman. Her forked tongue flicked out of her mouth and she nodded to me before transforming once more and burrowing back into the ground.

I felt it then, a probing within my mind, and I turned around.

Carden backhanded me across my face. I staggered backward, my eyes blurry for a moment, but I caught myself before I fell. When I looked up as my eyes finally cleared, he was already gone.

Suddenly, he appeared in front of me and embedded his sharp nails into my shoulder. I screamed in agony as red-hot pain sped through my body like a bullet train. His red eyes pierced into mine as he quickly pulled his hand out of my shoulder and vanished again when I reached out for him. He appeared once more, his nails piercing into my lower back and thigh at the same time.

Using his vampiric speed, he disappeared yet again, but not before I felt his nail slice down my forearm to my wrist. I fell to my knees as I pressed my right hand to my chest. I couldn't feel my left hand anymore, as if he had damaged the nerve. I could feel the prickling feeling of my body trying to heal itself, but my blood was still oozing from the wound on my arm.

"Accept the Queen's offer, and this ends..." He appeared before me and started walking around me in a circle. "Look around you, Ruby, look at those that are dying. You can stop this with a single action." He came to a stop right in front of me, his uniform stained with blood.

I looked up at him from under my lashes, my leg now going numb, as well.

He went on, "Your power will be equal to our Queen. She has plans for this world, plans that'll be better for everyone if you're on our side. Look at you now—weak and beaten. That will change."

"You know," I gritted out. "I didn't think you'd be the chatty type."

He raised his hand to slap me again, and I fell backward onto the ground.

Just then, a spike appeared from beneath the earth. He stepped back, but not quick enough, and it sliced him across his chest.

"I'll tell you what I told her!" I yelled as it lowered back into the earth, and I pulled myself onto a knee. "I'd rather die than become one of you. I'd rather die than be some kind of pet to you! Freak!" I spat on the ground.

The black veins under his mouth stretched even further up along his face.

I felt him burrowing into my mind, and I groaned as he started to force thoughts and images into my mind. I pressed a finger to my temple, my jaws clenched tightly as I tried to stop seeing the years he'd spent as a vampire. I couldn't push away the images of the decades spent inside the mountain, of the parties and human carnage, of humans being turned as they grew their army for this day.

"Do you think you or anyone here stands a chance against all of us? If you won't come willingly, I'll make you, but I won't fail my Queen!"

"You've already failed her!" I shot back.

He came at me, the intent to kill in his eyes causing them to burn brighter. "Fool!" His nails elongated even further, and he became as pale as I had seen the Queen become.

I tried to stand but couldn't; my leg was still healing.

A wolf appeared out of nowhere and tackled Carden to the ground.

I fell forward as I exhaled with relief when I realized it was Axel in his final form.

The towering black werewolf with the body of a man and beast grabbed Carden by his throat, his nails ripping his flesh.

I looked away as I moved my left shoulder, feeling finally

returning to it as they continued to fight each other while rolling on the ground. Soon they stopped moving.

Axel was over Carden on the ground, their legs tangling together.

I frowned as neither of them moved, but my frown quickly turned to utter gut-wrenching dread as Axel fell off Carden. My hand flew to my chest, Axel's pain hitting my body like a ton of bricks.

Carden removed his arm up to his elbow from Axel's chest.

Axel looked at me, his black eyes fading to hazel as he started to return to his human form, his bones breaking and re-joining.

The sight of the gaping hole in his chest had bile rising to my throat. I fell forward onto my hands, tears instantly springing to my eyes. "No!"

He started gasping for breath, his fingers digging into the earth at his side.

I shook my head, my heartbeat hammering in my head. "No!" I looked at Carden, at the smug grin on his lips, and at Axel's blood dripping from his hand. I fisted my hands on the ground as I released my rage. A shock wave emitted from me, knocking everyone backward, vampire and otherwise. I got to my feet.

Carden's face fell when I moved as quickly as he had been. I appeared before him and grabbed his face. I focused on the black aura around him and began consuming it.

He raised his hand to hit me, the one coated in Axel's blood, but it remained suspended in the air as I used my powers to hold it there. His eyes started to bulge as I pushed him to the ground and climbed onto him. The darkness in him flowed into me, my eyes now black, bottomless pits. I didn't stop as his hunger flowed into me, his memories, and the carnage he'd taken part in. I let it all fuel my rage, my hate, my pain. Soon, he laid beneath me as nothing but a dried-up carcass.

I fell off him, ignoring those that had been watching the entire thing. My focus was on Axel as I crawled to him quickly. My eyes darting over his body frantically as I watched his blood soaking the snow beneath him. "I-it's okay, I-I can heal this." I held my hand over his chest, my eyes burning with tears. I could see inside his body, and he wasn't healing on his own like he should. He started healing, but it stopped. My hand started shaking. "Come on!"

"He punctured my heart, Ruby," he told me, his voice weak. He coughed, blood spluttering from his mouth, dripping down along his chin and neck.

I shook my head as I turned my attention back to his chest. "I can help you! Let me help you, please!"

This can't be happening! Not him, please not him!

My chest was on fire, my insides boiling, as I could feel him slipping away. He closed his eyes, and I screamed his name.

Ms. Clayton ran towards us, her sword falling from her hand.

"Help him! Help him, please!"

"I-I can't—I," she stuttered.

More tears streamed down my cheeks.

"Ruby," Axel called, his sweet voice a mere whisper.

My heart caved. I never told him, I never told him how I felt. We had a rough start, and I held onto it even when he proved to me he deserved my love.

He moved his hand to touch my hair, and as it fell once more, I grabbed it and held it to my chest. "Finish—this..." His Adam's apple bobbed as he swallowed, and his hand slipped out of mine. "I love you." His eyes closed.

My world shattered.

I peered up at Ms. Clayton, who now had tears rolling down her cheeks. I looked around us, at the battle still raging on, at Presley, who had a deep wound running down his leg, but still, he kept reloading his gun. Across the field, my eyes landed on Xavier in his final form. He killed a Skin, ripping its head from its body before turning to me, his large hands folding into fists.

"I love you, too," I whispered to Axel as I called on my power.

Xavier howled as he fell onto all fours and began running towards me.

I called on my power, and the knife the Goddess had given me appeared in my hand. I looked away from Xavier gaining on me. He wouldn't make it in time—he wouldn't stop me. I bent over Axel's body and kissed his already-cold lips, the ache in my chest growing worse.

No one else would die for me, not today.

I plunged the knife into my heart, and the earth around me cracked.

Ms. Clayton, werewolves, demons, and vampires were thrown back roughly, and then pulled forward, only to be thrown again as another wave emitted from my body.

"Thank you," I heard the Goddess say in my mind as my eyes closed. All I could hear was Xavier howling in pain.

When I reopened my eyes, I could feel every living thing around me as if I were directly connected to it all. I looked down at my hands as the black veins there began to crawl up my arm. Soon, my entire body was engulfed in it, even my face. It was as if I were now a passenger in my own body, but I didn't care. I gave everything to the Goddess as I sat in a corner, the feel of Axel's cold lips still on mine.

I touched Axel's body.

He turned to dust and vanished.

As I stood up, thunder rumbled above us. A Bleeder rushed at me, and its thin pale body disintegrated to ash. I turned to face the mountain.

CHAPTER FIFTEEN
PRESLEY

I got to my feet after being knocked over by Ruby's power. I watched as her hair began to change from red to black, the vibrant color changing from the roots downward. Xavier, who was in his wolf form, got up, and when she turned to glance our way, she looked almost unrecognizable.

Her body was covered with black veins. With her midnight-black hair and eyes, she looked every bit of a goddess to me. I knew the person I was looking at was no longer Ruby Saunders. I was stunned with wonder. Right now, the rest of the world literally stood still. No one knew what to expect next. Even the Bleeders had stopped attacking. It appeared they weren't mindless enough to think they'd stand a chance against her.

I was wrong. All at once, as if following some silent command, all the Bleeders went running for her, bypassing us as if we weren't even standing there.

She merely turned to the mountain, and as she waved her hand, the earth beneath us moaned.

I watched as the hole in the mountain cracked further and started breaking, crashing onto the vampires still coming up from within.

She took a step forward, the snow beneath her feet melting. As the Bleeders and Skins got close enough to her, they started bursting into clouds of ash.

Malcolm appeared at my side as Xavier rushed forward, cutting down as many Bleeders and Skins as he could while they focused on attacking Ruby.

She didn't need the help, that was clear. I watched in stunned astonishment as she kept casually walking towards the entrance of the mountain, vampires dying at her feet without her even lifting a hand.

Even I could feel the shift in the atmosphere as heat suddenly surrounded us.

"Shit," Malcolm swore.

I looked in the direction he stared at. He was looking at a demon and a Skin who were battling each other in Ruby's path.

As she drew close, the Skin began to shriek in pain, its skin burning. The demon cried in pain as well, his skin turning red.

Xavier knocked him out of her way.

She kept walking. She didn't even look.

"What the hell," I mumbled under my breath.

Beside me, Malcolm hissed. "That's not Ruby anymore. Anyone in her way will die." He looked around him and placed his finger at his throat. "Stay away from her! Don't get too close! Kill the ones she doesn't!"

"What if she turns on us?" a demon yelled back.

"She won't if you stay the fuck away from her! Let's go!" His voice thundered as if he was using a microphone.

The demons nodded their heads in response.

He ran forward with them but then stopped to look back at me. "Are you coming?"

I looked at the mountain, at the way Ruby had expanded its opening and exhaled. "I'll handle things out here."

I wasn't retreating. The Bleeders around us were few enough

for my men and a number of other witches, demons, and were-wolves to handle. Fewer and fewer of them were getting by her.

I looked at the blood-soaked ground where Axel's body had been and reloaded my gun.

I turned away, firing five bullets into a Skin before she fell, her body convulsing as the UV bullets burned her from the inside out. Xavier had said if Ruby ever became the Goddess's vessel—she would die.

I glanced over my shoulder at the mountain as Ruby vanished inside. If she didn't die, what would she become?

Ruby

The inside of the mountain didn't look the way I expected it to. It looked as if I had stepped into a hotel that had been raided. I assumed it only looked a mess now because of all the Bleeders and Skins crawling out of a large opening in the ground. I paid no attention to Xavier and the others still locked in battle.

My eyes were on the six guards standing in front of a large elevator. How was there even electricity in here?

"Where is she?" I asked. Inwardly, I frowned because my voice was no longer mine, but that of the Goddess.

The guards in red that we had seen on the video all looked at each other before turning back to me.

I realized they all looked identical. They all had a brown complexion and the same white streak of hair in their black hair.

None of them responded.

I gazed upward. Above me, the ceiling was painted with the same battle we had seen in *The Book of The Damned*, and I wondered if they thought I really needed to use an elevator to get to her. One of them vanished, but I could now track their movements easily, their vampiric speed no longer an issue. The moment he appeared in front of me, his red eyes burning like a flame, my hand darted outward, and the elongated nail on my index finger pierced through his forehead.

His eyes rolled back as black veins appeared from the wound in his forehead, and he fell to the side, his body hitting the ground loudly. It was my turn to act. My lips curved with a smile as I stepped forward and then vanished. I reappeared at the same spot I had been a second later, and a line of blood began to ooze from puncture wounds between all other five vampires.

It felt as if I was doing all of this, and at the same time, I wasn't. I felt the moment my nail pierced their skulls, but my actions were being guided by something else... or someone else, I should say.

"I need you to give me full control, Ruby. Your conflicted thoughts are restricting me." The Goddess's voice echoed in my mind, and without me doing it, my body bounded off the ground towards the ceiling.

"You almost killed a demon out there," I replied as she kept breaking through the ceiling, floor after floor.

"I don't have time to argue with you, Ruby," the Goddess replied impatiently.

Then, within my mind, where I was already partly restricted, I was thrown onto a chair and bound with chains. "Goddess!" I screamed as I tried to break free, but it was futile. She didn't reply. I felt nothing and had no control over anything anymore, and I felt like I was now a bystander in my own body.

All I could do was watch as the Goddess slaughtered every vampire she laid her eyes on before moving onto another floor. I stopped struggling for a moment, my attempts to get free a waste of time. I made the choice to give my body to her, and now I had to live with that choice.

I was here for the time being, but I would die the moment the Goddess left my body. I sighed as she arrived at a room flooded with red lights. At least I'd be able to see Axel, my mother, and Natalie again, but what of Xavier?

I know I'd broken his heart; I had felt it.

Countless humans were cowering in the corners, either naked or barely clothed, some wearing nothing but collars around their necks.

The Goddess only glanced at them before walking towards the door at the end of the hall.

The moment she got close enough, it was thrown open, and Amythia walked out, her wings emerging from her back. She smiled widely. Her fangs descended as her face began to morph into something hideous, and her skin turned an ugly shade of grey. Her eyes grew large as her ears became long and pointy. "You're foolish to stand against me, Ruby," she smirked. "I gave you the chance to willingly join me. Now that option is no longer available to you."

The Goddess shook her head. "Is that so?" The Goddess replied as they began walking in a circle. "Can you repeat what that offer was? I'm afraid I'm not Ruby."

Amythia stopped walking as she narrowed her eyes. "Yes, you're right. You're the Goddess bitch now, aren't you?"

The Goddess's lips parted to speak—*my* lips parted.

Then without warning, Amythia charged at us—at the Goddess—ice dagger in hand. The Goddess moved quickly, appearing beside Amythia and grabbing her by one of her wings. She released Amythia swiftly as Amythia's other wing bent at an odd angle, the claw-like spike at the tip of her wing missing The Goddess's face by an inch.

I winced as I watched. After all, this body was still mine for now. If the Goddess lost a hand or a finger, it was my body being dismembered, not hers.

Both women fought viciously, the Goddess taking blow after blow while delivering some of her own. I tried to escape from the chains, but each time I tried—they grew tighter. I gave up as the

Goddess threw Amythia into the wall, the impact causing the wall to shatter as Amythia fell through.

She got to her feet, her already-deformed face twisted with fury that one of her wings was broken. She exhaled, and fog drifted from her mouth as frost began to crawl up the walls. As quickly as it formed, it began to melt, a clash of fire and ice within the room.

To my surprise, Amythia reached behind her and ripped her broken wing from her back. "I bet when you talked to Ruby, you failed to mention that the Goddess who was raped by the Demon King and gave birth to my kind was your sister."

"That's not information any mortal needs to know," the Goddess retorted.

My eyes widened in shock.

"I think they'd find it interesting to know that you are only helping in this fight because of your own need for vengeance, your obsession with eradicating my kind," Amythia replied silkily, and she stepped back as the heat coming from the Goddess grew intense. She smiled.

I found it odd that the Goddess didn't seem to realize Amythia was only taunting her. While Amythia's revelation was surprising to me, it explained a lot. I didn't see any other deities intervening the way the Goddess had.

"Make no mistake, Amythia, this is where your bloodline ends. You don't have any offspring, and your Generals are dead. You have no one to pass your power or throne to. When you die, the creatures you have plaguing this world will die, too." The Goddess laughed mockingly. "You're not welcome in the demon realm, and nor that of the Gods. You're nothing, and you'll die as the queen of nothing."

Amythia's crimson eyes seemed to burn even brighter as the Goddess's laughter and harsh words appeared to have their intended effect. "We'll see who dies today!"

Both women ran forward, their bodies colliding in a clash of power and years of built-up animosity.

Behind them, Xavier rushed into the room in his human form, along with Malcolm and a few others. They ran forward, but even with the Goddess's cry that they shouldn't... it was too late.

Ice daggers shot towards them from Amythia's back.

The Goddess held her hand out, a flame burst from her fingers to melt the daggers, but not before some of the daggers had met their targets.

Amythia backhanded the Goddess across her face and then sank her fangs into the Goddess' arm.

The chains around me loosened, and I quickly unbound myself as the Goddess grabbed Amythia's face with her other hand. Steam began to rise from beneath the Goddess's hand.

Amythia released the Goddess' arm, tearing the flesh. Two wolves bravely tackled her, but she killed them with ease. One of her eyes was burned shut and swollen, but she smiled widely before bursting into laughter.

For a moment, I could feel what the Goddess was feeling again as she looked down at her arm—*my* arm—with the flesh hanging loosely. I could feel the Queen's venom making its way up my arm.

To my surprise, the Goddess raised her other hand and sliced the arm off.

Amythia's face fell.

The Goddess smiled haughtily. "Did you think turning me would be that easy?"

Pain wracked me as my body started to break, and I wished I hadn't gotten up from that chair. The Goddess started to shift into a wolf, and I felt the entire transformation. My body was torn apart, only to be mended back together into a brand new form. Soon, a large white wolf stood where the Goddess had been. She growled threateningly at Amythia.

I laid on the ground in my mind as the Goddess continued to do what she wished with my body. I was awash with cold sweat, my eyes wide at the traumatizing pain I had just felt. I hadn't been ready for it.

"Ruby?" The Goddess called to me.

I looked up weakly.

"I'm sorry, my child," she said apologetically as she bent down to move my hair from my face. "I'm sorry for this pain, but I'm proud of you. We don't have much time left. Your body can't take much more of this."

I started crying because I'd truly had enough. The life I was given wasn't mine, and because of that, I'd suffered my entire life. There were moments that were good, but how many of those moments were good compared to the ones that were bad?

"I hate you for making him mine, and then taking him from me!" I started crying. "Axel... Axel died saving me because of you!"

She sighed, then cocked her head to something behind me. "You'll be free of this suffering soon. You'll be able to join them."

I looked over my shoulder.

My mother, Axel, and Natalie stood there. They looked like they were glowing, their smiles wide as they waved at me.

I sat up as I wiped at my tears, my heart filling with joy from seeing them, but I shook my head. "I can't leave Xavier." I turned back around to face her. "Please, I can't do this to him. I just—I used the knife—I just wanted this to end, but I can't leave him to suffer from losing his mate. The pain might kill him. I would have killed him!"

"The pain might make him stronger," the Goddess replied as she stood up. She pointed behind me.

I looked around.

Axel was directly behind me in his wolf form. His eyes were hazel instead of black.

"Go to him, Ruby," the Goddess advised calmly. "I want you to trust me, okay? Trust me, I won't let this be the way your life ends."

I reached out, and as I plunged my paws into Axel's black fur, a feeling of being at home took over. The Goddess vanished, and I was once again cut off from her emotions and feelings.

Back inside the room, Amythia's other wing was broken. The Goddess was limping due to a deep gash down one of her front legs, and Xavier was now lying on the floor with an ice dagger in his thigh and shoulder. The bodies of other demons and were-wolves littered the ground around them.

Although there was blood running down his face and he looked a little worse for wear, Malcolm was still standing.

The Goddess's hind legs suddenly snapped backward.

Amythia's eyes widened with fear. She rushed forward but was swiftly engulfed by Malcolm's black smoke.

He gritted his teeth as he tried to hold her as the Goddess shifted into her final form.

I smiled. Even though it wasn't truly me, I felt proud at the majestic creature my body became. The Goddess's white wolf, now on two legs, howled so loud the earth trembled.

Amythia broke free of Malcolm's hold, but as she tried to attack him, the Goddess attacked her. She grabbed Amythia's face and hand. Before Amythia had a second to counter-attack, the Goddess' wolf bit down hard on Amythia's neck, piercing skin and flesh to the bone.

The Goddess shook her like a rag doll.

Malcolm hurried to help Xavier up before pulling the daggers from his body.

"We can't leave Ruby," Xavier told Malcolm.

I looked over at Axel by my side as tears began to stream down my face.

Black veins began to appear on The Goddess's body, and it slowly started to enter Amythia, who was stabbing the Goddess with her nails, trying and failing to break free from her hold.

"Ruby is at peace. Leave!" The Goddess shouted.

I knew she was speaking into the minds of Xavier and Malcolm.

"Now!" she yelled insistently.

Xavier started to protest. I looked away as it took the four remaining werewolves and Malcolm to drag him from the room.

The mountain began to moan, almost as if it were in pain, as pieces of the ceiling began to fall around us.

It started to burn where the Goddess had bitten Amythia's body, and she became covered with black veins. Her pale skin started turning red and bubbling. It was like she was being burned from the inside out.

The Goddess simply ignored the numerous cuts and wounds Amythia's claws inflicted as she fought for her life. It was clear at this point that Amythia's fighting was futile.

I could hear the shrieks and cries of the other vampires as they sensed their Queen dying and felt her pain.

"I want to speak to him! Please, Goddess, let me say goodbye!"

"Speak!" she yelled back.

I closed my eyes as I envisioned Xavier's face. I thought back to the first moment I saw him so long ago in that library. I re-lived our first kiss.

"I love you so much!" I choked out, and I heard his cries of pain in my mind in response.

The Goddess crushed Amythia's body to her as they—we—exploded, taking the mountain along with us.

———

Xavier

I could feel her dying.

As I was dragged from the room, my cries and protests were ignored as I felt Ruby slipping away. As she went—my heart broke piece by piece.

Amythia was destroying her body, ripping into her flesh to break free, but still, Ruby held onto her.

She promised me—swore to me—she wouldn't do this!

I was dragged outside and held by my own men to stop me from rushing back inside as the mountain began to crumble. All around us, vampires were withering on the ground in pain, their bodies burning. All I could focus on was Ruby leaving me. As she had grown stronger, so did our bond. She could feel me, and she could feel Axel, the way it was for pureblood wolves. I felt like our bond was finally complete, and now she was leaving me!

I stopped fighting, my body going numb as I heard her voice echo in my mind.

"I love you so much."

"No! No! Ruby!"

The mountain exploded, knocking everyone close backward with debris flying everywhere.

A large rock knocked me over, and I groaned as I moved it off of me. As the dust started to clear, I stared at the mountain. The last piece of my heart, the piece that had held on after hearing Ruby's voice, broke into tiny pieces and disintegrated.

I could no longer feel her. In the spot where she had been, I felt hollow, as if my heart had been carved out of my body and removed.

Half of the mountain was destroyed. I fell forward, my fists beating the ground until my hands were bloody. My fangs and nails elongated. Hot tears streamed down my face, and I didn't care if I wasn't upholding the werewolf way of not showing emotion.

I placed my hands on my head.

Malcolm fell to his knees beside me, his face slick with tears.

I howled to the clearing sky above us until I lost my voice, and a dead silence settled around us.

For others, the war had been won, but for me—I'd lost everything.

CHAPTER SIXTEEN
XAVIER

SIX MONTHS LATER

"It's been six months since the vampire invasion turned the world upside down. Cities are being rebuilt, but for many citizens of the world, life will never be the same. A bill to outlaw the killing of werewolves and all other supernatural creatures has finally been approved after months of debate. However, many humans are still scared and skeptical of the supernaturals walking among them."

I switched the TV off and reclined in my chair. Still, the black market sales of captured supernaturals wasn't being reported in the news. I understood the fear the humans felt of the unknown right outside their door, of the beings more powerful than them. When they looked at us, they didn't see us as individuals capable of both good and bad. They grouped us all together and decided we should be feared. Supernaturals were capable of feeling fear, as well. We were still being hunted and exploited for our powers and abilities.

I looked down at the numerous files on my desk. Werewolves were once more falling into the protector role, just as we had so long ago. With Presley's help, a task force of supernaturals and humans had been created to keep the world in balance, or attempt to, as we all tried to adjust to this new normal.

I looked at Ruby's picture on my desk and swallowed as an ache rippled within my chest. The pain of losing her hadn't faded. The loss was still raw after so many months. I knew it would remain that way until the moment I saw her again on the other side. Thankfully, assuming the role of the new Alpha of the Blackmoon pack kept me busy and helped me to remain grounded enough not to lose myself in the grief. Yet, on nights like this, the pain of not having her by my side as Luna was almost unbearable.

Leaving my office, I made my way outside, where torches were erected as we feasted under a new full moon.

Randoll patted me on the shoulder as he walked by me, his arm over his mate's shoulder.

I watched them with a smile as they gazed at each other with love.

"Alpha Xavier," a small voice called from behind me.

I turned around to see little Accalia running towards me. I bent down to her level, and she ran into my arms.

I faked falling over from the force. "How many times have I told you not to run around like that, miss? I would hate to see you fall and hurt yourself, but most of all, hurt someone else. Don't you know how strong you are?"

Her smile widened. "I fell yesterday, and I didn't cry. Mommy says I'm going to be the strongest one in the pack when I grow up." She moved her black, curly hair from her eyes.

I nodded. "Your mom is right. Do you know why you'll be the strongest?"

She nodded.

"Why?" I asked.

She glanced at her mother, who was watching us. "Because I'm an Enchanted," she grinned as she looked at me, her brown doe eyes bright with pride.

"That's right. You're special. There was a girl in our pack that was special, just like you. Did you know that? Two of them, actually."

She bobbed her head vigorously. "Natalie and Ruby!" she exclaimed enthusiastically, catching the attention of a few other wolves nearby.

"That's right. Natalie and Ruby were Enchanteds just like you, and two of the most powerful." I poked her chin and her giggle washed away some of the sadness that had settled on my heart. "You will follow in their footsteps and be the third most powerful. Okay?"

"Why did they have to die?" she suddenly asked.

My brows knitted. My arms twitched as my wolf awoke at the mention of their deaths.

Her mother quickly took her from me.

I clenched my fists, knowing my eyes had changed to black. "Forgive me." I looked away before glancing back at her, ashamed as Accalia looked at me with uncertainty.

Her mother smiled sadly at me. "There is no need for that," she told me and ushered Accalia away.

I stood there for a moment as I closed my eyes to focus on my breathing, to focus on the sounds and smells around me. I needed to ground myself to avoid getting lost in my grief.

"Are you okay?" my father asked with concern.

I nodded without turning to face him. After a moment, I opened my eyes and exhaled through my mouth, my racing heartbeat slowing. "I'm fine," I told him as I turned around. "I'm getting better at controlling the bursts of anger." Laughter met my ears, and we both looked Randoll's way as he and his mate and a few other wolves chatted among themselves. "The loneliness is what's most painful."

"I wish I could say you'll get used to it, but you never really will. At least, I haven't," he said sadly.

I looked his way.

"You'll always feel like half of your soul is gone, but it'll get easier to work around as the years go by. You'll find new ways to cope with it."

Right now, it felt like that might never happen.

"Presley's team found werewolf remains in a warehouse yesterday." Since he'd stepped down as Alpha but still needed to keep himself busy, he'd joined the P.I.A., the Paranormal Investigation Agency. Now he worked with General Presley. "The whole thing is being covered up, though."

"We sacrificed everything to save the world, but as we expected, the humans are being humans."

"Yes, but I mean we got orders to cover it up," he clarified.

I pulled a face, my interest piqued.

He nodded. "We found out the warehouse was purchased a few months back by a shell company."

His words rolled around in my mind. "Again, I'm not surprised. I knew it would only be a matter of time before someone decided to round us up and turn us into test subjects, with or without our consent." I shook my head as I looked away, my eyes moving from one wolf to the next, and my fists clenched. "I understand the hatred Axel had for them."

Dad didn't respond, but from my peripheral vision, I could see he was studying me closely. "Not all of them are bad, Xavier. Please remember that. She was one of them."

"She was never one of them!" I bit back.

Above us, a clap of thunder echoed through the night, followed by lightning.

Two bolts struck the ground, and the night returned to silence.

Dad looked me up and down strangely.

I shook my head. "That wasn't me."

"Well, that can't be anything good," he replied.

Suddenly, an echo of gasps erupted through the pack.

Dad and I walked forward as a crowd started to form. My

Alpha instincts kicked in and had me walking forward quickly, ready to defend my home and my people. However, I didn't make it very far before I froze in my tracks.

A scent I didn't think I'd ever smell again washed over me.

Beside me, my dad gasped, "This isn't possible."

I rushed forward in an instant, and the crowd parted for me, my anxiety rising. As I came to a stop in front of the crowd, I watched as everyone else stood with their mouths open in shock as two wolves walked from out of the darkness of the forest.

My heart grew heavy as I stared at the black and white wolves. I reached up and combed my hair back with both hands, praying to the Goddess my eyes weren't playing tricks on me.

There stood Axel and Ruby.

A short laugh of bewilderment escaped my lips. "Ruby?" I asked in disbelief.

The white wolf walked forward, her head low as she smelled the ground, but her eyes were on me.

"Is it really you, Ruby?" I stared into her black eyes, and I got my answer as they began to change to the stunning emerald eyes that had haunted my dreams for months.

She whimpered as her shoulder dislocated.

Both of them began to shift, fur turning to skin and paws turning into hands and feet.

Laying on the ground, naked, was Axel and Ruby.

Axel rose quickly, brushing the dirt and leaves off.

Ruby remained lying on her side, her knees pulled up to her chest.

I quickly took my jacket off and covered her, my eyes roaming her face. I reached out, my hand shaking as I moved her red hair from her face.

"Xavier?" she whispered.

I felt as if my heart would explode with joy. I picked her up slowly and crushed her to my body. I kept taking deep breaths, inhaling as much of her scent as I could just in case she suddenly vanished. "How?" I asked as I placed her gently onto her feet.

My dad joined us to give Axel pants.

"How is this even possible? You died." I looked at Axel as he pulled his zipper up, his curly hair now down his back. "You both died."

"The Goddess sent us back," Ruby responded softly.

Behind us, whispers erupted among the pack.

"I-I don't remember what happened after I died," she went on to explain. "I just woke up in the forest, but..." she placed her hand over her heart as she frowned. Her eyes became teary. "I do know that's the last time I'll ever shift." Her hand fell away from her chest as she smiled sadly. "I'm only a half-breed now."

I stepped closer to her and shook my head as I took her hand into mine. I couldn't believe I was touching her, seeing her, hearing her. "You've never *only* been half anything, Ruby. You're so much more than just a half-breed. You're the woman who gave her life to save us all. You're our pack's Luna, and most importantly, you're my whole world." I wiped away a tear that escaped her eye. "You're home now."

Turning to Axel, I exhaled heavily. "You gave your life to save her. For that and more, you're welcome to join our pack. I'm sorry about your father and the wolves you lost. The ones that survived are already among our ranks."

He nodded as he looked around us, a smile growing on his lips. "Thanks, Xavier, and thank you for keeping my pack members safe when I was gone. As for myself, like Ruby, I don't remember where we were or what happened after I died, but I do remember there are plans I need to see through."

"Okay," I said.

Suddenly, we were bombarded by pack members who greeted Axel, and then Ruby was dragged away from us. Questions of how she was alive and where she'd been were thrown at her from all directions.

"I'm still mated to her," Axel told me.

I took a deep intake of breath. "Yeah, I figured," I muttered low.

"How are we going to do this, then?" He tilted his head to the side to look at me. "Neither of us is going to reject her."

"The world has changed, Axel. I doubt anyone will care anymore if she's mated to the two of us." I watched her as her voice drifted to me on the cool night's wind while she clutched at the front of my jacket to cover herself up.

Spending months without her had been the worst time of my life. I had prayed to the Goddess to send her back to me, and she had answered. I had begged night after night for this. I swore to the Goddess I'd be fine with her being mated to Axel as long as I got to be with her again, as long as I got to see her smile. Our relationship might be taboo, but her loving him didn't mean she loved me any less, or vice versa. "We both love her. We'd both die for her, and I think that's enough common ground for us. That's all that's needed to make this work."

He watched her as well, his arms crossing over his chest. Along with the longer hair, he looked considerably more muscular than when he had died.

Ruby looked a little different too. She had a glow to her skin that hadn't been there before. They must've been with the gods for a while.

What had it been like? What happened to them? "Can you tell me if you guys saw Natalie?" I inquired hopefully.

Axel sighed. "No, I can't remember anything. I think that's maybe for the best."

I nodded.

He uncrossed his arms as he turned to face me.

My eyes drifted to him, curious as to why he was watching me so intently.

"But I don't doubt that she's happy. Something in me tells me Ruby and I were too. Tell me, Xavier, are you sure this is something we can do, this relationship, while you two lead this pack?"

"Do you love her?" I asked him.

He frowned. "Yes, of course I do. She's my whole world—my everything."

I nodded as I held my hand out to him.

He hesitated only briefly before shaking my hand.

An unspoken truce formed between us.

"And you'll always be a part of this pack, whether you live here with us or not." I nodded at him. "So as far as I can see, that's all we need to make this work."

———

Axel
Two Years Later

I leaned against the window as I stared up at the full moon hanging low in the sky.

Behind me, Xavier kept pacing back and forth.

I closed my eyes as I finally had enough. "Would you stop doing that? You're not helping my anxiety," I growled.

He stopped pacing. "Anxiety? You look perfectly calm to me," he shot back in a loud tone.

I turned to face him. I shrugged my jacket off and sighed as I threw it over the back of a chair. I then removed my tie and unbuttoned my shirt. I had flown 16 hours straight to get here. I was dying for a bath and something to eat, but none of that was more important than what was currently happening. "I'm not calm at all. When I took Olcan's place as Council member, I had to master the art of appearing impassive to everything. Apparently, it's starting to become second nature." I sighed. "How's the pack been?"

Xavier sat down, his leg tapping the ground nervously, then he made a face. "Really? You want to talk about the pack right now?"

I shrugged as I turned back to the window. "Just making conversation. It's better than panicking."

"Are they here yet?" Malcolm inquired impatiently as he entered the room.

I looked over my shoulder to see him carrying a black stuffed bear that was almost as big as he was. "What the hell is that?" I asked with a chuckle.

He placed the hideous thing down on a chair. "It's a teddy bear. What does it look like?" He patted its large head. "It's for my grandkids. I'm going to be a granddad now."

"Yes, we know. You tell that to literally everyone who will listen to you," Mathieu chimed in with a laugh as he sat down, the wooden chair squeaking under his weight. "So, how is she?"

"Still in labor," Xavier groaned with an exhausted sigh, as if he were the one in labor. "We can't even hear what's going on in there. Turning the office into our bedroom was a bad idea."

"Ruby wanted privacy." I shrugged. The office had those special sound-proof walls, which had seemed ideal for a bedroom in a house full of werewolves, but right now, I just wanted to know what the hell was going on in there.

Xavier snorted.

Mathieu chuckled. "I was like this when your mother went into labor, but of course, she wasn't like Ruby. We've never had a half-human, half-Enchanted give birth in our pack."

"Well, there is a first time for everything," Malcolm added, his green eyes—so like his daughter's—bright with excitement.

It was nice to see him looking so cheerful. I know how important it was to Ruby that the deal he had made with that demon was broken. It had taken some time, but it had finally happened. With the two years that passed, the war that took my life and Ruby's already seemed like a lifetime ago.

The world had transformed as supernaturals grew more

accepted day by day. There were those who still remained hidden because there were humans that still preyed upon and exploited them. Yet, for the most part, a new dawn had begun.

The pack nurse walked in, blood smeared on her scrubs.

Xavier jumped to his feet.

I stepped forward. "Where is she?" I questioned, my words coming out more forceful than I intended.

"Are the babies okay?" Xavier added.

She smiled at us, amused at our obviously panicked state.

I didn't find it amusing at all.

After one of the babies turned the wrong way, Xavier and I had been pushed from the room and locked out. The pack nurse was on my shit list for that one.

"She's fine, and the babies are healthy. You can see them now." The nurse stepped to the side.

Xavier rushed by her, a quick thanks leaving his lips.

"Thank you," I told her as I rushed from the room as well, hot on Xavier's heels.

I was right behind him as he opened the door. My eyes immediately landed on the love of our lives with our kids in her arms. She looked at us standing at the door, and the nervousness I had been feeling for hours faded away.

She smiled at us.

As if commanded, we both moved forward at the same time.

In her arms were both babies. One was wrapped in a pink blanket while the other was swaddled in blue.

We stood on either side of her.

I leaned down and kissed her forehead.

Xavier did the same.

Malcolm and Mathieu finally joined us, Malcolm carrying in his massive teddy bear.

I became completely focused on the tiny little bundles of love in Ruby's arms.

She looked exhausted, her hair damp and knotted, with her eyes puffy from crying.

"You did great, babe." I ran a finger down her cheek.

"We're so proud of you," Xavier added.

She closed her eyes for a moment as she smiled and laid her head back against her pillow. "I'm so tired," she said weakly. "Let's not do this again."

We all chuckled.

The nurse joined us to do some final checks on Ruby.

I took the time to admire my kids—our kids—as the nurse checked them out as well.

The girl—our daughter—had red curly hair, my hazel eyes and Xavier's full lips, while our son had Xavier's dark hair, Ruby's emerald eyes, and my brown complexion. Both kids were the perfect blend of Xavier, Ruby, and me.

A feeling of accomplishment I'd never felt before filled me. The amount of love I already had within me for these kids felt overwhelming and scary.

"You guys can hold them, you know. You don't have to stand there staring like that," Ruby told us softly.

Xavier paled.

I reached down and took the little girl from her, my heart swelling so much it felt like it would explode within me.

After a moment, Xavier reached down and took the boy into his arms.

We both looked at each other, a message that *this is real, we're fathers* passing between us.

It was as if in a matter of hours, the world had changed. It would never be the same for us again.

"Have you all decided on names?" Malcolm stepped forward.

"The girl will be named Natalie," Ruby announced, her eyes becoming a little teary.

"Perfect," Xavier mumbled as he began to bounce somewhat.

"And we decided on Caleb for the boy," he added as he looked to me for confirmation.

"After weeks of fighting about it," I shot back.

He rolled his eyes.

Sometimes I could not figure out how Ruby managed to put up with this man on a regular basis.

She was incredibly stubborn, though—even worse than me.

Xavier and I had come a long way from where we started, when I had wanted to rip his throat out each time I saw him close to Ruby. Now we shared a three-way mating bond, a pack, and two babies with her.

Being a Council member meant being away from the pack for long periods, but knowing Xavier was here with her made it easier for me. I knew he was the only other person that would do whatever it took to protect her. Taking on the responsibility I had meant I'd been able to make sure werewolves finally had the rights and freedom they deserved. Yet I never would've been able to do that if I didn't have Xavier at home protecting all that was important to me in this life.

It pained me sometimes to be away from my family and my pack, but now, looking down at this precious little girl in my arms, I knew I would do anything to make sure she and her brother grew up in a world that was safe for them.

Ruby

"Okay, that's enough, we want to hold our grandkids." Mathieu reached out and took his grandson from Xavier.

Malcolm took Natalie from Axel.

They all looked so happy as they bickered among themselves about who would be teaching which of the kids what. I didn't want to tell them all I was dying to rest.

My body felt broken, and I felt like I was staying awake from sheer will to see the guys with the kids. The complications started when we discovered Caleb had turned the wrong way during my labor. Thankfully, the nurse was able to coax the breech baby into the right position, but there was no time to call the guys back into the room before the twins were born. Babies have a mind of their own sometimes, and these two just couldn't wait to join the world. They might have inherited a hint of Xavier's impatience as well.

"Oh, no," I interjected as I wagged my finger at Axel. "My daughter will not be groomed to become a Council member, and Caleb will make his own choices, Xavier. My kids will have control over their own lives, over their own destiny, so kindly do not make plans for them. They're only a few hours old, after all."

"Well, the Luna has spoken." Xavier chuckled as he winked at me.

Axel started laughing. "Suckup," he mumbled under his breath.

"Prick," Xavier shot back.

I pressed a finger to my temple. Caleb and Natalie weren't the only kids I had to deal with around here, and it showed. "Can you both please stop it?" I groaned.

Axel sat down beside my bed. "How are you feeling?" he asked.

I looked over at Xavier, Mathieu, and Malcolm as they continued to gush over the babies. "Like I finally have the family I always wanted," I told him.

He picked up my hand and kissed the back of it. "How do they both have features from all three of us? I don't think that's normal."

I shrugged at his question, as I had no idea. That had been my first thought when I saw them, but given how our story had gone so far, why should anything surprise me? "Normal isn't a word that should be in our vocabulary at this point. I'm a human and Enchanted, I was also a deity for a short time, and I'm mated to two werewolves. Normal doesn't exist for us."

He nodded in agreement before rolling the sleeves of his shirt up to reveal his muscular arms, covered heavily in tattoos.

"I've missed you." I pouted. The way he smiled back at me made me feel like all he saw was the most beautiful woman in the world, no matter how I looked after pushing out two babies. "Will you be able to stay a while before going back to Albania?"

"They'll have to drag me away kicking and screaming because I'm not planning on leaving here for a while," he answered.

Xavier suddenly turned to us. "What? You're staying?"

Axel grinned at him.

Xavier's face twisted with a little disappointment in response.

I closed my eyes as they started to bicker again, but it was cut short as Natalie made a sound and once more had their attention.

I smiled, as it reminded me of how Natalie had been. She knew how to gain the attention of everyone in an instant. I sighed as I remembered her gorgeous blue eyes. I hoped she would watch over my kids from the gods' realm.

My chest tightened because more than anything, I wished she was here with us. I gasped and pulled my hand up to my chest as a chill ran down my arms.

The guys turned to me, concern written on their faces.

"Are you okay, Ruby?" Malcolm moved forward.

I held my hand up and nodded. "I'm okay, I'm just tired."

He nodded. "You should get some rest."

I turned my head to the side to stare out the window across the room as the chill that had run down my arm traveled down my cheek as well. I bit my lip to hold back my tears because I knew, deep within me, it was Natalie. "Hey, old friend," I muttered under my breath as my eyes grew heavy, my lids lowering a little. As the moon's light shone through the window, I swore I saw a brief glimpse of glowing blonde hair and bright blue eyes peeking in.

I recalled a conversation I had with her so long ago. She jokingly said she might never have kids, but she promised I'd get the family I deserved, and that would be her family, too. Back then,

I hadn't thought much of it. Yet she had known so much, she might have known this was how everything would end. I could not imagine carrying the burden of being aware of your own death, yet continuing on with life with a positive outlook, as if there would be no end. Natalie was my hero, a daily inspiration to trust and accept my fate while living life to its fullest.

I hoped my daughter grew up to be as brave and strong as Natalie was.

"Guess what," I whispered as my eyes finally closed. "I finally have the family you promised. I finally have *our* family."

CONTINUE THE WORLD

Want to know what happened before Luna Rising?

Read Bloodmoon Wars Series!

Bloodmoon Wars Series

The Awakening

The Enlightenment

The Revolution

The Renaissance

The New Age

Ever wonder what happens after a wolf dies?

Read Wolf Reborn series to find out!

Wolf Reborn Series

Wolf Reborn

Wolf Burdened

Wolf Scorned

Wolf Fallen

Wolf Embraced